THE UNDEAD. THE FIRST SEVEN DAYS

SEASON ONE

COMPILATION EDITION OF BOOKS ONE TO SEVEN

RR HAYWOOD

Copyright © R. R. Haywood 2012

R. R. Haywood asserts his moral right under the Copyright, Designs and Patents Act, 1988, to be identified as the author of this work.
All Rights reserved.
"The Undead" ™ and "The Living Army" ™ are Trademarks.

Disclaimer: This is a work of fiction. All characters and events, unless those clearly in the public domain, are fictitious, and any resemblance to actual persons, living, dead (or undead), is purely coincidental.

No part of this publication may be reproduced, copied, stored in a retrieval system, or transmitted, in any form or by any means, without the prior written consent of the copyright holder, nor be otherwise circulated in any form of binding or cover other than that in which it is published and without a similar condition being imposed on the subsequent purchaser.

Design, Cover and Illustration by Mark Swan

FOREWORD

Dear Reader,

Thank you for either buying or downloading this book, The Undead, The First Seven Days.

The Undead was started in May 2012. I was then a serving police officer and had been for a long time. I was good at my job and enjoyed it immensely, but my first love was always literature. I loved to read and often wrote short stories as a child.

Sadly, my house suffered a catastrophic fire when I was sixteen, which destroyed all of those early stories.

I didn't write creatively for many years, until, in 2012, I read a book called Three Feet of Sky which I thought was brilliantly unique. On researching the author to seek more work I discovered the book had been self-published - which blew my mind.

I can still recall that exact feeling. That suddenly there was a whole new world starting which was not dominated or controlled by middle class graduates acting as agents or publishers. That ordinary people, like me, who never got past High School, could have a voice and give our stories to the world.

I also recall being very frustrated with the books I was reading. They were all so samey and bland. I later learnt, after being traditionally published, that most editors working in mainstream fiction are London or New York centric and are all trained to the same standard. Which means they apply the same rules to every book, which in turn strips out the individuality and the often unique voice of the author.

In turn, that means we, as readers, are picking up books in book shops which somehow feel like they've all been written by the same group of small writers.

That's not what I ever wanted from reading. I wanted bold creativity and unique stories told how the writer felt like telling them.

And so I set forth and duly started The Undead. I was only ever going to write seven books and use them as a way of teaching myself to write. I'd never intended to go past Day Seven.

The first editions were very rough. My grammar was, and still is poor. But I didn't care. I was in love with writing and was soon dedicating every spare minute I had to writing more Undead episodes.

Nobody read the first books. But later, when I'd finished Day Seven, I put them into The First Seven Days and released that as a book, and that was my turning point. The First Seven Days starting gaining an audience and ten years later the series is now over thirty books and is still growing.

I've just yesterday released The Undead 31. Winchester. That book charted inside the top 30 for the whole of the UK charts, and is number one in multiple Amazon charts in three different countries.

I've now sold over 4 million books and become a Washington Post, Wall Street Journal, Audible and Amazon Allstar bestselling author with over thirty Kindle Bestsellers. I left the police in 2017 and now write full time, and I make regular videos on TikTok and YouTube giving advice to other new writers who, like me, are from a working class background.

All of this is to say that what you are about to read might be a tad rough in parts. It has been fixed up from the original edition. Typos and formatting mainly, and some rework where it was needed, but largely, this is the first thing I wrote, so do forgive the somewhat often clunky nature. But readers often remark that it is a delight to see the progression of my own skill from book to book.

I do hope you like it and please do leave a review. I am still (mostly) an indie author and mean a great deal.

Much love

RR Haywood

June 2024

THE UNDEAD
The First Seven Days
Season One

"Ready, Dave?"

DAY ONE

CHAPTER ONE

**My name is Howie. I was named after my father Howard, but it became too confusing to have two Howards, so I became Howie.
I am twenty-seven years old, and I work as a night manager in a supermarket.
This is my account.**

Day One
Friday
Mid-July

'The unseasonably hot weather has caught us all out. Not just our store but stores right across the region. Head Office is working round the clock to get the summer seasonal stock out to us. In the meantime, if we get customer enquiries, please remind them they can still purchase online and collect in store...'

My god, this is boring. I'm hot and uncomfortable. Being the night manager means most of this doesn't apply to me. I can't see our usual quota of taxi drivers, drunks, and whatever other poor sods coming into the store at night, asking why we don't have Bermuda shorts on offer yet, or why have we only got ten different sun creams instead of over bloody thirty of them.

'Onto other news...' the general manager drones on. 'The morning managers have reported a definite improvement on the readiness of the store for the daily trade. That, in my opinion, is down to the appointment of the new night manager...'

Shit, that's me. This is like being in school when the teacher stops and looks at you; then everyone else looks at you, and you get that fluttery, panicked feeling of missing the question.

'Er...' I sit up properly to see the other managers are all smiling at me. Apart from Paul, that is.

'We have seen an increase in trade during the hours of darkness too,' the general manager continues, 'and a drop in staff sickness and absence.' He peers down at a sheet of paper in front of him. 'Wastage has been reduced by over twenty percent and,' he looks up at me with that genial smile, 'unbelievably, we have seen an actual increase in sales of our promotional offers, which, ladies and gentlemen...' He casts his eyes around the room, '...Is unheard of for a twenty-four-seven store...'

I hate that fucking phrase. Twenty-four seven. It's just so, so...

'So, Howie, the floor is yours,' the general manager looks to me. 'Please impart how you have achieved this within three months of being appointed.'

Paul is glaring. Can't blame him, really. He was the night manager for twelve months and sat in these meetings every two weeks, moaning about how *"it was all so different at night"* and *"you don't understand the pressures we're under."*

Different? Pressure? The only difference is that it's dark outside, and as for pressure, the bloody store hardly has any sodding customers cluttering the place up and making a mess.

'Ha!' I start off with a blurt of laughter, then inwardly curse at myself for doing it. *Yeah, great start, Howie, really great.* 'Um, well, we kind of, er... Just worked a bit harder?' I offer while feeling a blush creeping up my cheeks.

'Specifics, Howie,' the manager says, urging me to share my excellent managerial skills. 'Head Office is interested and wants to know what is being done differently.'

Ooh, that causes a ripple through the shark pool. These career-hungry bastards have just heard the words *Head Office* and *interested* in the same sentence. To have Head Office interested is either the precursor to a death sentence or something glittery and gold.

Paul isn't glaring now. The poor sod has dropped his head and looks beat, completely beat, like he's ready to start making a noose.

'Specifics,' I say slowly while rubbing my jaw to try and look all clever and serious. 'Well, er...staff absence is down because, er...'

What do I say? The night staff have been the night staff since time began. A collection of misfits and slightly odd folk, who, for many reasons, just don't like working in the day. Be that because they have a general hatred of humanity or an almost vampire-like existence, where the sight of the sun would burn them to death. No one knows. I can't tell the general manager it's down to the quick poker session we have during the lunch break either. That's really not allowed, like really not allowed.

'I think it's only too easy to see the staff simply as resources and not as humans with feelings and emotions.' *Oh shit, stop, Howie.* 'So in order to maximise the efficiency of the night staff, I simply make the working environment a nice place to be.' *Howie, stop, really stop now.* 'We all get on with each other and er...well, I may have bent the odd rule, not broken, I hasten to add.' Jesus, Tesco rules are carved in stone and carry a sentence of death by firing squad.

'What rules?' the general manager barks, losing his enthusiastic persona.

'Er, well, the spreading of breaks is the main one, really. I know during the day you have to make sure the break times are staggered, but on nights, we go down to a skeleton crew, which is rotated, and we take our breaks together, which helps build a feeling of camaraderie.'

'Right,' the general manager says slowly, as though he's just been told the secret to immortality, 'wastage?'

'Wastage?' I shift again. The reduction in wastage is down to getting barred from the poker game if you break anything. 'Er, just being like really careful...'

'The increase in promotional sales?' the general manager prompts.

Everyone is staring at me now, apart from Paul almost weeping into his hands.

Yeah, the promotional sales. Whoever sells the most gets the first hand for free in the following nights poker game. 'Promotional sales? Well, that's just down to, er, an increase in promotional awareness and outlining the benefits of maximising sales, and how those benefits cascade down to everyone.'

'Good,' the general manager nods with interest, 'very good. A rising star in our midst, ladies and gentlemen, and someone to watch out for.' He beams round the room, happy again.

Cheers for that, I'll be testing my tea for poison now and watching out for trip wires next to the big waste crushing machines.

'Keep it up, Howie, and you'll be back on days before you know it,' he adds before finally turning his attention to the produce manager for an update on why sales of turnips have gone down. Thank fuck that's over.

I hate these meetings, but the good thing is that they earn me an extra night off. I'll stick around until my lot start at 9 p.m., then be off home for junk food, sofa, and maybe even a couple of beers.

Eventually, the meeting ends, and suddenly, I've got a whole bunch of new friends. Even the gorgeous cashier manager gives me a smile, which just makes me blush and walk into the back of a chair.

'Well done, Howie,' Steve, the home deliveries manager, pats me on the back.

'Head Office, eh?' someone else nods meaningfully at me. Duty managers, shift managers, staff managers, more managers than you can shake a stick at, but Tesco work to a formula, and as much as we all moan about corporate greed, they are bloody good at it.

The other problem with the big meeting is that all the managers are required to be at work at the same time, which translates to no spare office space, no free computers to work from, and not even a spare desk to sit at while the rest of them polish their name badges and slick their hair down.

Instead, I stroll about the store and smile at people while carrying some bits of paper. Always works, that does.

Five o'clock soon comes, sparking a mass exodus of office people running out the store to start doing whatever normal people do on Friday nights.

I get some office space and a computer and get my shit together as the evening rolls on while listening to my small FM radio broken out of my drawer now the other tie-wearing bastards have all gone home.

By nine o'clock, I'm pretty much finished and stretching back, looking forward to my pizza and beer.

'*Reports from Reuters suggest the riot was sparked by one assailant biting into several members of the public within the shopping centre...*'

Did he just say biting? Bloody hell. I grab the radio and twist the volume knob up.

'*Details are still coming in, but we do know the area is being flooded with police in an effort to bring order...*'

'Evening, Howie.' Glancing up, I miss the rest of the report as Bert, the night shift security guard, walks into the office, prompting me to roll my sleeves up properly.

'Bert, how are you?'

'Smartness makes the man,' he smiles, giving me a smile that suggests he saw my scruffy half folded sleeves.

He's a grey-haired chap in his sixties, but Bert screams ex-army. His shoes gleam from being relentlessly bulled, and his trousers have razor sharp creases running down the front. His sleeves are either down and fastened properly or rolled up above the elbow with exact precision – something he likes to remind me about when he sees me looking scruffy.

'Meeting okay, was it?' he asks, taking a radio from the charging unit.

'Fine. Profits up, wastage and sickness down. They're very happy.'

'Didn't mention the poker games, then?'

'Funny that, no, I didn't,' I laugh as he adjusts his black tie. He holds the coveted position of CCTV controller, staying within the secure room to watch the millions of live feeds from the millions of cameras dotted about the store. Unless he's popping out to play poker, that is.

'Oh well, what they don't know won't hurt them. You're off tonight, aren't you?'

'Oh yes,' I grin, locking my fingers together behind my head as I stretch out. 'Pizza, beer, and my sofa.'

'Young man like you,' he tuts, 'should be out, finding yourself a nice woman. Or a bad one,' he adds with a wink.

'Yeah, one day... I'm still holding out for the cashier manager. She actually smiled at me today.'

'Did she now?' he chuckles. 'You'd best go buy a ring, then.'

'Yeah, alright,' I laugh. 'Here, have you heard the news? Something about a riot and someone biting...'

'Caught the tail end of it as I was leaving home. Er, somewhere in Europe, I think...'

'Oh, not here, then?'

'God, no,' he shakes his head, 'storm in a teacup somewhere.'

'Oh.' Losing interest, I put my radio down and start getting ready to go while listening to the night staff gradually filing in, and I smile at the difference in them now.

Three months ago, they were sullen, withdrawn, and stayed in horrible, little cliques. Now I can hear them laughing and sharing jokes while avoiding mentioning the poker game for fear of the late shift staff hearing them.

That's all it is really. We have something the others don't. A secret thing that we can all enjoy with a sense of doing it together. The poker games are only ever for a couple of quid, and the biggest pot ever won was only a fiver.

'Evening!' stepping out the office, I call down to the men and women gathered by the lockers, getting a chorus of replies in return. Happy people smiling and joking, and it almost makes me want to stay at work. Almost.

'Mr Howie.' Turning around to see Dave, one of the night shelf stackers standing there.

'Dave, how are you?' I don't bother trying to correct him calling me Mr Howie. I've said it to him loads of times, but he still does it.

'Fine, thank you, Mr Howie,' he nods briefly, then walks past towards his locker.

'Dave, we had a meeting today. Performance is up, wastage and everything bad is down, so er...' He stares at me with a completely blank face. 'Well, the offer is still there if you want to move onto working days.'

'No, thank you, Mr Howie,' he replies dully. A hard-working man, exceptionally quiet, and he never joins in with the banter or jokes. His breaks are kept to a minimum, and even during his hour-long meal break, he takes enough time to eat, and then goes back to work. Mind you, no one ever takes the piss out of him either. He might be small, but something about him discourages stupid comments.

'Okay, well, let me know if you change your mind.'

'Okay, Mr Howie.'

'I'm off tonight.' He stares at me without expression. 'So, er...have a good night.' I smile. He walks off.

Wishing them a pleasant evening and getting some mild, well-meaning abuse for having a night off, I make my way out and start the walk home.

It's a beautiful, warm night, sultry even, and it feels more like somewhere in Spain than the south of England.

Boroughfare is a nice enough town, close to the sea but inland enough to avoid being classed as a resort town. Midsize, and it's the same as anywhere else, with lots of houses surrounding a town centre.

My place is just off the centre. Noisy, but cheap. I have the top half of a house, with a young couple living underneath me. A residential side street with brick built houses and slate roofs. Average as average can be.

The quickest route is through the side streets, but it only shaves a minute off the journey, and the night is lovely, so I walk back through the High Street, watching the crowds of people moving from pub to pub.

It's packed, really busy. I guess the hot weather is drawing everyone into the centre. People laughing and singing noisily makes me think of my sister living in London. Sarah is a PA for one of the big investment banks. She moved there a few years ago. I know she loves the weekend "networking parties" as she calls them.

I kind of feel like I want to join in and be out with the crowds, drinking, having fun. It's not really my scene, though. I'm not fashion-conscious or stylish, and I don't go for whatever the latest trends are.

Twenty-seven and still shy as hell round pretty girls, and it's only been the last few years that my hair has started looking even remotely decent. Dark, curly, too long, and permanently messy. I don't work out or do anything other than work and piss about at home.

Pausing at the door of the pizza place, I spot a fat bloke inside. I've never learnt what his name is, but I know he likes drinking. He comes into the supermarket most weekends, tanked up and swaying while he buys loads of junk food, crisps, chocolate, pies, and frozen chips.

I feel bad calling him the fat bloke as he's a nice man, always polite and jovial, willing to share a joke, and he's never aggressive like some of the drunks are. Looks professional too from the nice suit he's always got on.

It's just one of those things. Time rolls on, and you end up meeting people time and again until suddenly it's too late to be asking their name.

'Hello, mate,' I say with a grin, joining him at the counter.

'Hi,' he grins and even holds a hand out, 'supermarket man, yeah, hi! How are you?' He's sober but still really friendly, and this early in the evening, I can see his tie is done up properly, and he looks sharp and switched on.

'Fine,' I nod back amiably, 'night off.'

'Good for you, having a pizza, eh? Don't blame you. They're nice here. Have you tried the meat feast?'

'Oh yes,' I give him a knowing grin.

'You enjoy it, then? Working at Tesco, I mean. I heard they look after their managers quite well.'

'Yeah, it's not bad,' I shrug. 'Lucky to have a job these days.'

'True,' he sighs. 'So you out then or off home?'

'Pizza and home for me.'

'Really? Young bloke like you on a Friday night? Come and have a beer with me if you like.' He means it too. Not a fake, polite offer, but a genuine one.

'Nah, thanks anyway.' As much as I'm sure it would be nice, the town centre at weekends really isn't my scene. Too many pumped up lads wearing t-shirts two sizes too small for them, and women screaming into mobiles phones.

We make small talk until the pizzas are handed over in their lovely, warm cardboard boxes, and after exchanging polite farewells, I make my way through the town to the side street and down to my building, and up to my first-floor flat.

Television on, quick change of clothes, couple of cold ones from the fridge, and within minutes of walking in, I'm sat on the sofa, eating the first slice of thick-crust meat feast while flicking through the channels.

I check the movies out first, but they're all old ones I've seen many times. Next, I check for something funny, but again, it's all repeats, dramas, repeats, documentaries, repeats.

Out of sheer desperation, I flick higher through the numbers until I start hitting the news channels and see footage of the riots they mentioned earlier on the radio.

Some of the footage is awful, and I mean awful. Poor quality, grainy, and obviously snatched by low-resolution cameras in poor light.

Some of it, however, isn't awful. Some is high definition and taken by someone using a modern phone, who at least knows how to hold their hand still. Full colour, full audio, and utterly shocking, filming people with awful injuries, wounds to their faces and necks, bleeding, with noses or ears ripped away. The most shocking thing is seeing police officers and people in uniforms fire handguns into crowds of bystanders; then more police officers using shotguns and assault rifles.

Then more footage is showing SWAT teams and riot police deployed onto streets. Shooting and using huge sticks to batter people writhing on the ground. Gunshots and screams in nearly every segment shown. Injuries too, and so much blood. Blue, flashing lights on cars. Sirens warbling, and people running, and as it goes on, so I start to recognise some of the places they are talking about.

Riga in Latvia. Cities in Lithuania and Estonia. Then Poland and the German border towns. Footage from Moscow in Russia. Budapest. Rome. Zurich. Famous landmarks glimpsed in the backdrop. I've never seen anyone being killed before, but right now, it's been shown without censorship, making me flinch and screw my eyes closed. An Italian cop firing a handgun into a group of people running after him. Except they look weird, like stiff-legged and jerky. He still shoots them, and they still keep running.

The other thing I see are people biting each other. Savagely too.

Like they're high on some kind of drug and just going nuts, biting into necks and arms, into anything they can reach. It's bloody gross, and just the thought of being bitten by a drug addict repulses me.

What sickens me even more, however, is the sight of the news anchors in obvious glee at having something so meaty and awful to report on. You can see it in their faces, and I bet the notes they are making on the bits of paper in front of them are in preparation for whatever awards news agencies give each other while pausing dramatically, with fingers pushed into ears as they take fresh information in.

When the main news channels show disasters, they seize on one or two bits of footage and loop it over and over while going through their lists of experts to either phone up or get them into the studio.

This is different because I don't see the same bit of footage twice.

The funny thing is that I was quite calm at first, thinking all these places were a billion light years away and just weird, crazy European cultures having a squabble that would never, could never affect this country.

England, however, has a long history with rioters, and it isn't long before I'm starting to think maybe all those council estate kids in London might flare up again and starting looting JD Sports and Argos.

Then the footage starts showing the same things happening in Luxembourg, Belgium, and France.

France? Bloody hell. That's only a few hours away from where I live. Yeah, fair enough, you've got to get a ferry or a train under the channel...the Channel Tunnel. The tunnel that connects France to England.

Shit. The realisation seems to hit across the board, and I watch the news anchors loosen ties and unbutton the top buttons of shirts, or roll their sleeves up.

There's no mistaking the next bit of footage. The bloody Eiffel Tower is in the background, with masses of people running and screaming. More gunshots – pistols first, then the sustained firing of automatic weapons.

Suddenly, the reasons given for it change.

The anchors start talking about pandemics, contagions, and a fast-acting virus spread by airborne particles or transferred by bodily fluids. Time and again, witness reports state people were being bitten to death. Only they didn't stay dead; they got back up and started biting other people.

This isn't the Friday night I expected to be having, slouched back, with my feet on the coffee table.

Instead, I'm on the very edge of my sofa, flicking up and down the channels, trying to see the difference between the news reports, but it's all the same, and when the first channel starts to transmit the technical error message, I don't really pay too much attention but flick past it in a hurry to see the developments.

Then Euronews goes down, and Sky News reports, they are losing contact with outside agencies. BBC News loses satellite connections.

Things start breaking, phone calls drop out, and for the first time in what is probably television history, the news anchors start to panic.

With a shock, I realise it's gone one o'clock in the morning. I've been glued to the television for hours; then it dawns on me just how fast this thing is spreading.

'*...still we have received no government updates. This is a live request for any government official with knowledge or advice to be given to the people of the United Kingdom to make contact with either our news department or any of the main broadcast news agencies.*'

Fuck me. They're asking for the government to get in touch, literally asking if anybody is watching to phone them.

Flicking through the channels, the same request is being made live by multiple news anchors as they beg for someone to tell them what to do.

My stomach starts churning, and I feel sick with worry. Sarah, my sister, will be out in some swanky central London wine bar. Paris is only about an hour train ride from London.

I've got to call her and tell her to get home and lock the doors. I grab my phone, but there's no signal. I live right by the town; the coverage here is excellent. I turn it off and back on, hoping it's my phone playing up.

It isn't. Still no signal. Landline, then. I dust the thing off and use my mobile to find Sarah's number, and I'm halfway through before I realise there is no dial tone on the landline. Nothing, just an empty, faint hiss.

I press the clicker down several times, but that makes no difference, and I glance back at the television, with my stomach dropping again at the sight of the blank screen.

Sky News, BBC News, ITV News, all of them gone. Just blank screens from one channel to the next. Even the technical error messages are gone.

What do I do? No mobile, no landline. No contact with anyone. My parents live in the next town along, just a few miles away, but at this time of night, they'll be tucked up in bed. Maybe I should get to them. I bite my bottom lip, trying to think what to do when I hear noise coming from outside. Footsteps. Someone running.

I get to my lounge window and look out to see a guy running from the direction of the town. A big man too by the looks of it, but he's still shifting quickly despite his size. I spot him giving fast, furtive glances behind him like someone is chasing him.

The fat bloke. Definitely him. Running down my street in his smart suit.

Leaning out, I can see several more people running in the same direction; only they are going much faster than he is and gaining quickly, which, in turn, seems to be making him panic more, and even in the streetlights, I can see his face is flushed bright red as he gasps for air. Poor bastard will have a heart attack if he doesn't slow down.

The group's dynamics start screaming out in my head. The way they people chasing him are running stiff-legged and weird, with no clear cohesion to their movements. Just like on the footage, but this is Boroughfare, a small market town in the middle of bloody nowhere. Then I hear the fat bloke whimpering in panic as he snatches a glance behind him.

'HERE,' I yell out, reacting from instinct and start waving my arms to draw his attention as he looks up with an expression of utter terror.

My front door is locked. He won't be able to get through. A couple of quick steps, and I'm out my lounge and into my tiny hallway, opening my flat door. Down the stairs, past the door to the downstairs flat, and I get to the main front door and go out into the street.

I run down the garden path and into the street, waving my arms for him and shouting for him to keep going. They're bloody close to him now. Maybe five or six of them, men and women, and all of them dressed like they've just come from the town.

The next few seconds are a blur as the fat bloke seems to realise he's done for and comes to a sudden stop. A second of nothingness, of near silence, and he turns to see them coming in hard and lashes out with a weak punch, but they dive in as one, ripping him from his feet in the blink of an eye.

The fat bloke screams with a high-pitched wail full of pain that freezes the blood in my veins. I start moving towards him, but even from this distance, I can see the people are tearing at his flesh with their teeth, ripping him apart with their mouths, tearing into his face, neck, and arms. Blood spraying everywhere, soaking their faces.

'WHAT THE HELL IS GOING ON?' an old man in his pyjamas shouts, striding out of his front door. 'I'M BLOODY SICK OF YOU PISSHEADS FIGHTING EVERY NIGHT.'

The speed they move with from the fat bloke to the old man is frightening, like a pack of animals that want the fresh meat instead of the carcass on the ground, and they burst up and into him with the same frenzied manner.

I've got to do something. I feel compelled to help, but there's nothing I can do. I start creeping backwards towards my front door, with the overwhelming instinct to go slowly in case they see me.

Lights come on a few doors away from the group, and a thickset man comes flying out the front door in his boxer shorts while brandishing a baseball bat. He doesn't hesitate but goes straight at them, battering them off the old man, with the sickening thuds of wood beating hard into skulls.

He gets some good shots, really good shots. The sort of shots that would see the average person going to hospital with a fractured skull, but they don't flinch, and within seconds, he's off his feet and on the ground too. I didn't see his wife come out, but there she is, phone in hand while she screams at them to leave him alone. She even tries grabbing one of the attackers to pull him away, but he launches up to bite into her face. She holds her ground, and for a second, the pair of them stagger around while thrashing violently until her legs give out, and she drops as more join in, biting at her legs and arms while screams and howls fill the air, and yet more people rush from their homes, with lights coming on all up and down the street.

I stop at my gate, transfixed at the sight, frozen in utter shock of seeing people running out from houses, clutching phones as they scream and shout before being taken down amidst trashing limbs. Confusion everywhere. Instant chaos, and I spot a blood-soaked man stagger up the path of a house and in through the open front door, followed by awful screams a few seconds later.

Movement to my right, and I snap my head over to see the fat bloke going from prone to upright in what must be his first sit-up in fifteen years. He gets slowly and awkwardly to his feet, then staggers about; his legs heavy and awkward. Blood streaming down his face, and as he turns towards me, I get the creeping realisation of how utterly stupid I am.

I just watched hours of footage of people being bitten to death and getting back up, and here I am, gawping like a bloody fool at the fat bloke's head lolling about in a jerky manner and his arms hanging loosely at his side like he's got no control over his fine motor skills. Then he finally turns to face me, and I see the red, bloodshot eyes in the sodium streetlights as his lips pull back to show his teeth.

That does it, and I leg it away, sprinting for my front door as Simon, my downstairs neighbour, comes out of his flat.

'What's going on?' He looks half asleep, dressed in tracksuit bottoms, with no top on.

'Get back inside,' I whisper urgently.

'What's up with you?' he asks. 'What's going on?'

'Get the door shut and keep your voice down.'

'Don't tell me what to do,' he snaps. I've not had much contact with my neighbours Simon and Laura, but what little I've had has left me thinking the bloke is a bit of a prick.

'Mate, seriously, close the fucking door.' I glance back while Simon keeps a firm grip on the handle of the outer door, refusing to let me shut it.

'Are you drunk?' he asks, scowling at me.

'No! Close the fucking door.'

'Simon, I'm trying to sleep,' Laura appears in the doorway of their flat in her bra and knickers.

'Howie's pissed,' Simon says, as though it explains everything.

'No, I'm bloody not,' I reply, still trying ineffectually to get the door closed. Thing is, being an average English bloke, I don't want to physically push him away, so we end up playing tug of war with the front door.

'Well, I'm telling the landlord tomorrow,' Laura shouts. 'I've had enough of this...'

'Shut up,' I hiss, turning to see the fat bloke staggering through our shared garden gate.

'Don't you fucking tell my bird to shut up.'

'I'm not your bird, Simon!'

'Oh, fuck...please...get this door shut. He's coming...'

'Who?' Simon asks, looking past me to the garden path while we swing the door closed and open. 'What, him? What's he gonna do? Sit on ya?'

'Who's he on about?' Laura asks, stepping out to join Simon looking down the path. 'He's covered in blood. 'Ere, mate, you alright? Simon, ask him if he's alright.'

'You alright, mate?' Simon calls out. 'You been hurt?'

'Oh, god,' I murmur, backing away from the door.

'Fucking pussy,' Simon says with a tut, giving me a filthy look as he goes out the door to stand on the garden path. 'Christ, mate, what happened? You get beaten up?'

'Did he get beaten up?' Laura asks. 'Simon, ask him if he got beaten up.'

'I just did.'

'I'll call an ambulance,' she says, disappearing inside her flat before coming back, with her mobile held in front as she jabs her thumb at the screen.

'Simon, get back inside,' I plead.

'Oh, man up,' Laura snaps while staring in frustration at the phone. 'Bloody network's down again...'

'SIMON,' I scream in warning, but it's too late as the fat bloke speeds up and charges with incredible speed for the last couple of metres, giving Simon no time to react, slamming in hard, with his teeth biting into Simon's neck as he screams out, taken off his feet from the weight of the impact and hitting the ground with a sickening thud.

No time to think, and I run towards them, grabbing at the fat bloke in an effort to pull him off, but his sheer weight prevents me doing anything. In desperation, I start beating down on the back of his head as he bites deeper into Simon's neck.

'GO BACK,' I shout as Laura comes running out, screaming in panic. She goes straight for the man attacking Simon, grabbing at his arms in a vain effort to pull him away.

Growling behind me like the sound of a dog, and I turn fast to see more of them charging across the street towards us.

'Laura, now! GO NOW!' I try pulling her arm, but she lashes out, striking me in the face, sending me staggering back a step. I try again and grab her arm, but she pulls it free, screaming at me to get off, screaming at Simon to get up. Noise everywhere. Howls and screeches; people in agony. A car screeching past, smashing into other cars further up the street. The sounds of breaking glass. Chaos and bedlam, and everything happening so quickly, but within that utter mayhem, I notice Simon has gone quiet and still, with his eyes closed as the fat bloke slowly lifts his head to stare at me through those red, bloodshot eyes and blood pouring down his chin. The blink of an eye. The beat of a heart. More of them coming in through the gate, and Laura still pulling at the fat bloke. There's nothing I can do, and feeling like an utter coward, I get inside and slam the front door closed, catching a glimpse of the attackers lunging at Laura as the door shuts.

I get up into my own flat, locking and bolting the door before moving into the lounge to stare down out the window.

The sight is incredible and will stay with me forever.

Laura on her back, wearing just bra and knickers, with a huge group of people pushing their heads into her body, biting down into any part of her flesh they can access: legs, arms, neck, torso. One even bites deep into the top of her breast, tearing a chunk of flesh away. If she screams out, I don't hear it, and in shock, I look up and out to see my street looks like a war zone, like a huge movie set.

Bodies all over the place, and people running about, screaming, and being chased. Several get taken down as more of the attackers start charging into front doors. The screams and wails of women and children mix with the deeper, harsher tones of men.

Then another noise comes to the fore, and I look back down to hear the flesh being ripped and torn from Laura's body. Like dogs eating a bone. Gnashing, growling, wet sucks, and tears.

The first heave comes without warning, and the vomit propels from my mouth onto the ground below, hitting with a wet splat. Half-digested pizza, beer, and bile all mixed in, burning my throat and making my eyes water.

I drop to my knees and heave the rest of my guts onto my lounge carpet. Retching and gasping for air, with tears stinging my eyes.

Minutes go by. Long minutes. My throat burns. My head spins, and then finally, I kneel up and peer down to a sea of red, bloodshot eyes staring up at me.

CHAPTER TWO

'Bollocks,' I mutter at the sight. What do I do? Shit. Shit, shit, shit.

Grabbing a coffee mug from the low table behind me, I go back to the window and pull my arm back, which just splashes the cold coffee in my face and makes me yelp in fright while staggering about for a second before I launch the mug hard at the old man in the pyjamas. It hits him straight in the face, knocking him back onto his arse.

I look for something else to throw. The remote control for the television is the closest object, so that gets launched out too and smacks Laura on the shoulder, but she doesn't flinch. I don't even think of how the hell she's back on her feet after being chomped on by so many people.

Instead, I grab anything within reach. Books, DVD cases, even an empty vase gets launched hard and hits a woman on the head, shattering into fragments. She goes down, and I watch in horror as more of them walk over the broken glass, the shards lacerating their feet, but they don't stop moving.

Missiles get launched one after the other, doing nothing whatsoever to stop them as the flimsy, cheap outer front door gives way, and they start pushing into the communal hallway.

'Cock it!' I run back to my flat door to make sure it's locked, but it's cheap and flimsy too. This is southern England. Doors don't need to be fortified. Arse. 'Barricade,' I mutter the word as the idea pops into my mind and look about for something to use, but my hallway is small, with no furniture.

Into my bedroom, and I grab my bedside drawers to carry back, putting them behind the front door before standing back to proudly view my barricade. One small chest of drawers.

Maybe I need more. Howls and screeches from the other side. Thumps as they run up the stairs.

I definitely need more.

Into the lounge, and I sweep the flat-screen television off the solid, wooden cabinet and start to drag it towards the door, but the DVD player and satellite box are still in the cabinet, plugged into the wall. The cabinet refuses to budge, the wires taut and holding. I open the glass doors and yank them out, forcing the leads to break while I swear foully under my breath.

The cabinet is stacked behind the door, and I spend the next few seconds trying to position the chest of drawers on top of it before realising that one cabinet and one chest of drawers won't be stopping anyone.

The coffee table is added, and I keep going, dragging or carrying whatever I can find. I even get my heavy double mattress and stuff that into the pile. It's not great, but it will slow them down, and it's about all I can do.

I head back into the lounge and look out with a gasp of frustration at the huge crowd pushing beneath my windows. All of them pushing forward, trying to get to the front door, groaning, hissing, howling, and screeching.

There must be dozens of them, crowding towards the front of the building, and more coming from across the street.

Nothing else for it, so I go back to missile launching. I look around and see my old DVD player on the floor, pick it up, raise it high, then slam it down into the middle of the crowd as hard as I can. It smashes into the head of one of them. I can't tell if it is a man or a woman, but I see them go down, and the space is quickly filled as they all push forward again.

Then I do the same again with the satellite receiver box, smashing it down into the middle of the crowd.

In the kitchen, I spot the kettle. It is an electric, stainless steel one, nice and heavy. I grab it and start back to the lounge, stopping after a few steps to turn back to the kitchen, where I fill the kettle with water and switch it on, then grab everything I can. Pans, plates, cups, bowls, the sugar and coffee pots, and the bread bin. All of them ferried into the lounge to be dumped by the open window.

Back and forth I go until the kitchen fills with steam, making me realise I'd forgotten to put the lid on when I filled the kettle. Grabbing at it too hard, I splash hot water onto my hands, scalding my skin, which just makes me swear even more.

Back at the window, and I slowly pour the hot water down onto the upturned faces, watching as the water sizzles onto bare skin, sending small clouds of steam up, which has absolutely no effect other than washing some of the blood from them.

In desperation, I raise the kettle above my head and throw it down as hard as I can. It strikes with a loud whack, and another body drops out of sight.

Yeah, that's better, much better. *Blunt trauma beats hot water.*

I take a heavy ceramic pot from the pile and throw it down hard. It strikes a shoulder, and the impact is enough to make the body stumble and fall from view, trampled underfoot as the space is quickly filled.

A frying pan is next, and I launch it down. It hits one on the head with a metallic dong.

It's like shooting fish in a barrel. I've never been in a fight or caused physical injury to another person before in my life, but I am now. I'm slamming down everything I can find and watch as they impact on the heads beneath me.

Some shots are good. The toaster was great, nice and heavy, and straight onto the bald head of a man – he goes straight down, but again, the space is quickly filled.

I keep going, fury and anger driving me to scream abuse at the ragged faces, but within minutes, my pile is diminished, and the front garden is littered with household objects while still more of them stagger in.

I run back to my hallway and stare at the door, listening to the loud bangs and noises coming from the other side. The door rattling in the frame, and the first sounds of wood starting to break are soon heard. They'll be through in minutes, and even my super awesome barricade won't stop them. I have to get out.

My bedroom and lounge both look out over the front. I could probably get down, but there's too many of them outside. I'll be dead within seconds. Maybe the back, then? I run into my kitchen, then the bathroom, shouting in anger at seeing the windows are too small to climb through.

I search for anything left to throw, and my gaze falls onto the gas hobs as I think about the hot water. Then I remember reading books about medieval times when they poured hot oil from castles onto the invaders.

Finding a bottle of vegetable oil in the cupboard gives me a small sense of victory before I realise all my saucepans are now in the front garden. I have nothing left to use to heat the oil. My microwave is still there, but I have no pots or bowls.

I could lob the microwave at them. It's nice and heavy and might drop one, but what good would that do against so many?

A sense of doom comes over me as I head back into the lounge and over to the window. My lighter is still in the corner of the sill, taunting me. I gave up smoking a few weeks ago as I was getting hard looks from the senior managers every time I popped out for a smoke. Jesus, I could do with a smoke right now.

I might not have any cigarettes, but I have got alcohol, and maybe that will lessen the horror of what's to come. I head into the kitchen and reach up for the bottle of brandy on top of the fridge, and give thanks that I didn't think to grab it in my hunt for missiles.

I take the bottle back to the lounge window and look out as I lift the bottle to drink it straight. Taking a big glug, then grimacing from the harsh bite hitting my throat. Jesus, it's like paint stripper.

One thought leads to another, and I stare at the bottle with fresh interest. Brandy is flammable.

I could use it like a Molotov cocktail... It might burn the house down, but I'm pretty much dead already – it's only a matter of time before they get in.

I dash into the bedroom and tear some strips from my pillowcase, stuffing them into the brandy bottle to soak the amber liquid up. I've seen this done in movies and feel confident of how to do it – you light the end and throw the bottle. What could be easier?

At the lounge window, I hold the bottle, with the brandy-soaked strips of material dangling limply from its mouth and light the end, grinning evilly as the flames take hold.

'Have some brandy, fuckers ...'

My cool and witty one-liner becomes a yelp as the wick bursts into flames, making me panic and throw the bottle down into the crowd. It hits one on the head and bounces off to roll about unbroken, cushioned by the stupid fat head that it struck on the way down.

That's it. My last good idea cocked up. But within a few seconds, I see smoke coming up from the crowd, then a whooshing noise, with flames licking up between the bodies, and I watch as the flames keep rising up. Not that they pay any attention or even try to move away. Even when a couple of them set on fire, with the flames climbing up over their clothes.

The stench of burning flesh hits my nose, making me gag and move away from the window as thick, black smoke billows up into the lounge, carrying that smell of cooking meat. I cough and retch again, heaving on my knees once more, puking bile.

A faint noise penetrates the sound of my coughing. A car horn and coming closer by the sound of it. Lurching to the window, I try and look out, but the smoke is too much, so I go into the bedroom and pull the curtains down to see an armoured cash-in-transit security van in the middle of the road.

I open the window as the horn sounds out again, loud and clear in the still night air, and the reaction is swift as the infected people in my garden jerk round and start staggering towards it.

'HERE, OVER HERE,' I lean out the window, screaming and waving at the van in the road as it rolls forward a few feet while sounding the horn on and off, with a line of infected stumbling and jerking after it.

They stream out of my garden, and I hear the thumps as they go down the stairs, then appear, running up the path and out into the street, with more of them staggering from houses and appearing in the night, and within seconds, there's a massive crowd of them.

The van stops and seems to wait for them to get close; then the reverse lights come on, and the van goes backwards at speed, slamming into the dense crowd, causing a backwards ripple effect. Then the van shoots forward again, sounding the horn, leading them on and away like the Pied Piper.

Within minutes, the street has cleared.

CHAPTER THREE

I wait at the window, listening to the noise from the van ebbing away. Stunned and silent, the after-effects of the excitement and adrenaline making my hands tremble as I rub my face.

I can't stay here; it isn't safe. They have gone for now, but they could come back.

No phones. No way of calling for help, and this, whatever this is, is happening everywhere. That makes me realise the police won't be rushing to my rescue any time soon.

My parents have a detached house in a nice, quiet area. They always go to bed early, and I know they lock the doors, so maybe they're okay. I don't stand a chance of getting to London, not right now anyway. Fuck it. I hope to hell my sister is okay, but right now, all I can do is get to my parents' house.

I look at my watch. It's almost 4.30 a.m. Being mid-July, the sun will be up in half an hour or so. I need to get moving while I've got a chance. I don't own a car, so unless I can find something to drive, I will have to walk.

In the hallway, I stand, staring at the barricade. I don't know if any of them are left out there, and I'm too scared to remove the barricade and look.

I go into my bedroom and pull a couple of sheets from the airing cupboard, then tie them together with a duvet cover. I go to the window and look outside to make sure it's still clear, then tie one end onto the leg of my double bed, and drop the sheets down. They reach to a couple of feet above the ground.

Weapon. I need a weapon if I'm going out there. I root through the kitchen drawers to find my biggest carving knife with a nice, sharp, pointed blade.

I put the knife into my belt, with the blade resting against my leg. Then an image of me lying on my back, with the knife sticking in my leg fills my mind. I need a sheath, but kitchen knives don't have sheaths.

I find the small rucksack that I use for work and put the knife into the main compartment, leaving the top open, and I try to wedge the knife into the top zip so that the handle is left out, with the blade in the bag.

I put the bag on my back, but it hangs down too low – I can't reach the handle. I tighten the straps and raise the bag further up my back so I can reach back with my hand and grasp the handle.

An old claw hammer is added to my pathetic arsenal, but at least I have something that I can use. I think back to the man in boxer shorts hitting them with a baseball bat. He hit them hard, and they got knocked away, but they came back. So I know that hitting them won't kill them, but maybe it will buy me a few seconds to run.

I go back to the bedroom window and start to climb over the sill, grasping the bed sheets with both hands. I wait, sitting astride the window ledge, listening, and looking up and down. No noise and no movement. The night's veil is just starting to lift. Only a few minutes until sun is up. I don't know if that is a good thing or not.

I need to go, but I'm bloody terrified, and the final act of leaving the safety of my home is almost too much for me to contemplate.

Staying here isn't an option. They could come back, and my front door won't take another battering, and so, while shaking with fear, I clamber over the ledge and start lowering myself with my hands.

I feel extremely vulnerable, with my legs dangling beneath me, and I keep looking around, imagining that one of them will come out of the door, so I run into the road, with the hammer out of my waistband and in my hand.

The sight is worse at ground level. The micro-detail so very much worse as I get a close-up of the frenzied attack. Blood stains are everywhere, and a white car parked just a few feet away has bloody handprints smeared across the bonnet and a corpse trapped under one of the front wheels.

A crash behind me, and I see one of the things stagger out from my front door. That's enough for me. I'm off, giving it billy big legs, sprinting until I feel my lungs will burst, and my legs are hurting. I slow down and look back, but he is gone from sight.

I keep walking fast, sticking to the middle of the road, looking left and right; my ears straining for any noise. The quickest route is straight through town and down the High Street, then onto the dual carriageway.

A few minutes later, I reach a side street that feeds into the town centre and edge forward slowly until I reach the building line. I pause, listening intently and trying to summon the nerve to keep going. I've never been so terrified. Why is it so silent? Is that good? My mind starts imagining the infected things are all waiting somewhere, ready to jump out and eat me.

At least the sun is almost up now as the night sky gradually ebbs away. Even the birds are singing, and I spot seagulls flying overhead, calling out in the early dawn.

Come on, Howie. I force courage where there is none and move towards the junction of the High Street, cautious and slow. I step out and see the right is clear, and almost breathe a big sigh of relief until I look left and see an enormous crowd of them gathered around the armoured security van that led them away from my house, now stopped in the middle of the road.

Why did it stop? It hasn't crashed from what I can see. Maybe there were just too many bodies to drive through? I think to run back and start easing away when the hatch on the roof of the van opens, and a man climbs out to stand, looking down at the crowd as they swarm around him like fans at a rock concert.

Then the man looks up and spots me staring over while I stand still, unsure of what to do. 'RUN,' he shouts at me.

I take a step forward, and he shakes his head. 'NO, RUN. RUN NOW.'

I don't know what to do. He saved my life, and I can't just leave him to his death. Maybe I could get a vehicle and do the same as he did – lure them away with the sound of a horn.

I look back at the van and can see that there are hundreds of the things surrounding him, spread out in a wide circle, all pushing forward. The man looks safe enough now, but it won't take long for them to either climb up or use each other to trample on and gain height.

I run down the road to the closest car, but it's locked and secure. This is the town centre, and no one in their right mind would leave a car unlocked here. With a jolt, I see the pizza restaurant further up the road and remember the conversation I had with the fat bloke just a few hours ago.

He was right there, chatting like normal as we ordered food. Dressed in his smart suit and getting ready for a few drinks. The images of his torn flesh flood through my mind, of the blood loss, the arteries opened up, of the horrific noises he made. Pain inside. Other feelings too. Too many of them. Confusion. Denial, even. This can't be happening. It *can't* be real. This stuff happens in movies. Not in real life. Yet here I am, as real as anything. I even blink and look back up the road to see the horde of infected things, and the guy still on the van roof, waving at me to keep going. A surreal moment that makes me pause and hold still as my frazzled brain struggles to process it all.

Then in the middle of that slack-jawed, confused moment, I spot the pizza delivery moped lying on its side outside the restaurant. The distinctive white box on the back, and before I know what I'm doing, I'm running over and wrenching the thing upright, wincing at the sticky blood on the handles.

An old thing with a twist and go grip to keep it simple for the students and teenagers who use it to earn a few extra quid. Thank fuck the key is still in the ignition.

I wheel the moped out into the road and wave up to the guy on the roof of the van a few hundred metres away. I point at the moped and gesture that I'll drive away and try to get them to follow me. He shouts back and waves, maybe trying to tell me something, but the distance is too great to hear the words.

I get on the moped and turn the keys to the off position and then back on before pressing the start button as the moped splutters noisily to life. The loud noise so familiar to me from all of the times I have had takeaway delivered and heard the moped coming up the street.

As the sun rises, and daylight fills the street, I look back to the van, expecting the infected people to be already coming for me as my hand readies to twist and go, and lead them away, but something is different.

The outer ring of the crowd has turned and started towards me, but they are moving slower, much slower. Shuffling and dragging their feet. They were fast and wild just a few minutes ago, like predators after prey, relentless and sustained. Now they are stumbling as if they are walking through deep water; each step a struggle.

I look all about, fearing some kind of trap, but they are all the same. Some are turning and heading my way; others remain standing around the van, and whereas before they had a menacing aura, now they are a stumbling mess. The steps they take are thudding, with straight legs and arms hanging limp, and heads lolling about. They keep knocking into each other too, bumping away and going off course, seemingly unable to follow a straight path.

I look to the guy on the van and raise my arms, with the international signal for *what the fuck?*

He raises two arms, palms up, the international signal for *fuck knows*. Then he starts doing something else, waving and gesturing, but I can't get what he means.

I step off the moped and push the stand down with my foot, leaning the bike over to rest in situ, with the engine still running and ready to go.

Taking a couple of tentative steps towards the mass crowd, I watch them move and shuffle. What's happened? Why have they changed?

The crowd is still too thick to attempt a rescue. There are hundreds of them, and only about half are turned in my direction; the rest are still surrounding the van. I need to get them away too.

I go back to the moped and press the horn. A feeble warble sounds out, but I keep my finger pressed down on the button. This appears to focus the direction of their stumbling, and I notice more of the crowd turn away from the van towards my direction.

I keep pressing the horn and twist the accelerator grip, thinking that I will rev the engine, forgetting the bloody thing is twist and go, and the moped shoots forward, pulling me along. In my panic, I twist the grip more, and the moped pulls away faster, with me still hanging on.

The kickstand bangs into the road surface, propelling the moped off to the right. I slip and fall over as the moped veers off and crashes into a parked car with a loud bang before clunking over to the ground; the engine spluttering for a few seconds before it dies out. I scrabble up and twist around to see the horde is still shuffling slowly, and the guy on the van is covering his face with one hand, and even from this distance, I can see him shaking his head.

'I'm okay,' I call out while grinning like a bloody fool, bounding up to my feet as though nothing happened. I run over to the moped and lift it up again. It starts first time, and I wheel it back into the road, pressing the horn and waiting until they get closer. Staring at them and taking in the awful details of the injuries and the blood. At how they are people, but not people.

The closest one is maybe twenty years old and dressed in his designer jeans, with his muscles bulging from his tight top, and his hair all gelled up in the middle in that messy-on-purpose style that I hate. A torn, ragged wound in his cheek flaps open to show rows of teeth, and there is dark red blood all over the front of his once white t-shirt and down his arms. There is also a dark stain across the crotch of his blue jeans, but it doesn't look like blood. He must have pissed himself when they got him, which makes me feel better. I was terrified, but at least I didn't wet myself.

I'm not much older than him, but I've always hated the weekend town centre crowds. Preening, strutting fuckwits. My hair is curly and always messy without the need for gels and sprays.

I think back to the times when I had been out in the town at weekends, getting barged into by idiots like this, who flared up, with their arms puffed out.

I've always worked. Maybe it isn't the best job, but I've held it down and made duty manager, and I know that if I do the hated night shifts, there will be a chance for promotion.

No, there *was* a chance for promotion, but that's gone now. It's all gone ... Everything has gone. Jesus. This is it. I saw it happen on the news. Every country. Everywhere. I saw it happen in my own street, and how fast it can spread. The end of the world. There's no going back from something like this. Not now.

A deep sense of sadness fills me, and I start breathing hard as I think of my workmates being savaged by monstrous, preening pretty boys like this. They were always coming into the supermarket at night, especially after the clubs had kicked them out, throwing stuff about and taking the piss out of the staff.

I think about the fat bloke and the life he must have led. Maybe he was deeply sad at his obesity. A reject from society like the rest of us, but he was polite and friendly, and always willing to stop and exchange a few pleasantries, and he never looked down his nose at us either.

I look up and watch the pretty boy, with a weird anger rising up inside. Anger like I have never known before. I can feel my breathing becoming deeper and harder, my heart hammering in my chest. A feeling I have never had before. Consuming my mind. Something in me snaps, with a feeling of such ferocity it drives my actions without conscious thought, and before I know it, I've drawn the hammer from my waistband, stepped forward, and smashed the hard metal end into the side of his head. He drops instantly, and I go down too, pounding the hammer into his head, shattering his face, and crushing his skull, driving the blunt-ended weapon into his head. Blood and brain matter spray up and coat my arms. My hands become slick and glistening; terror and rage mixing into a deadly cocktail. All reason is gone.

I stop suddenly, becoming alert to my actions. What is left at my feet is not recognisable. The head is pulped, gone, destroyed. I destroyed it. I killed it. I killed one of them, and my chest heaves as I struggle for air and stagger backwards.

A sudden movement to my right; another one lunging at me, and in reflex, I lash the hammer out in a backswing as it leans in with teeth bared. The force drives the thing off to the side, spinning into a woman wearing a nice, blue dress. Full-figured, with a heaving cleavage, and long, brown hair, but her face is slack, and her eyes are filled with blood.

She staggers toward me, leaning forward from the waist. Lips now pulled back and ready for the bite. I feel repulsed and step backwards while thinking it's wholly wrong to hit a woman. That's how I was raised from a child. You never hit a woman.

I blink and move away a step as I look at the woman. She appears uninjured, without a bite mark or blood on her until I look down and see a chunk of muscle in her right thigh has been bitten away.

A groan from my left, and a young man with tribal tattoos all over his arms and neck shuffles in, then lunges as though surging to bite. I lash out and slam the hammer into the side of his face. He goes down hard but keeps moving, and rolls onto his back before sitting up. I strike him again harder, and I see his head snap to one side as he's flung over and feel, and hear the crunch of bone in his cheek breaking. Yet, within seconds, he's back to sitting up.

I spin the hammer round so that the claw end is now the weapon and drive it down into the top of his skull, cleaving through the bone. The force I use pushes the claw into his skull too hard, and it sticks. I try pulling it out, but all I do is pull him towards me.

I put my foot onto his chest and pull harder, and the strength of my pull forces his body into my foot. I stagger backwards and fall down; the hammer left sticking out the top of his head, at which point I become aware of just how close they all are now and still shuffling in. Every one of them staring directly at me, and hundreds of pairs of red, bloodshot eyes watching my every move. Groans sounding out. Feet shuffling. Bodies moving.

Then the sight of the fat bloke snatches my breath away. He's right there, waddling along, with the rest of them as he staggers towards me. Pretty boy is on the ground right in front of him, yet the fat bloke goes straight over him, trudging his big feet over the corpse. Fast, conflicting emotions course through me. Just seconds ago, I felt an overwhelming sense of shame and guilt at the anger, which drove me to kill that thing.

My fingers scrabble for the zip to the bag's main compartment. I get my hand in and feel the plastic handle, and pull the long kitchen knife out.

Still moving backwards, I look at the shiny blade, then at the mass of infected people, then back to the blade.

'Fuck this,' I mutter.

I'm off, running away as I throw the knife off to one side, then regret the action immediately. I go back, grab the knife, and start running again.

Towards the end of the street, I slow down and look back to see the top of the armoured van is empty.

I scan about for a few seconds, but I can't see him. There is just a mass of infected people on a slow march like a zombie protest through the town.

I keep moving, and after a few minutes, I see a mountain bike with no lock propped up against a wall. I grab the bike and start pedalling like crazy down the High Street and onto the main road, leaving the crowd far behind.

CHAPTER FOUR

I know it's still very early in the morning, but there would normally be delivery trucks, milkmen, commuters, all slowly emerging as the day wakes up.

Now there is nothing. It's so quiet. One of the pedals starts to squeak with each rotation of the cog, and it's that single noise that keeps me company on the quiet road.

I haven't cycled in a long time, and it doesn't take long before my thigh muscles are hurting.

My life consisted of working all night, then sleeping in the day, eating crappy food, and drinking too many beers in front of the television. I'm paying for it now as I feel exhausted and drained.

My parents' house is a fifteen-minute drive away from mine. How long will it take to cycle to them?

I try to work it out. A car going at about thirty miles per hour would take fifteen minutes, so if I cycle at fifteen miles per hour, it will take me half an hour.

I have no idea what speed I am doing, but it must be at least fifteen miles per hour; then I try to remember what speed normal walking pace is. I'm sure it was on TV once ... I think it was four or five miles per hour, and I reckon I am going much faster than walking pace.

My arse hurts, and my legs are on fire, feeling weird and pumped up. I think ahead, trying to choose the route I should take. One takes me through the side streets, residential roads with houses, and the other would take me on the motorway. Cycles are not allowed on motorways, so I would be breaking the law, whereas the alternative would take me via the houses and all the things lurking about.

I think I'll risk being arrested. In fact, being arrested would be the best thing in the world right now. A nice, safe cell in a locked police station.

The squeaking pedal and I cycle down the junction and onto the motorway.

It's still early but hot as hell, and the sweat is pouring from my face. I hold the bike steady with one hand while I pull the bottom of my t-shirt up and start wiping the stinging sweat from my eyes and face.

A noise from behind – a car engine, loud and fast. I drop my hand to look back over my shoulder and see a red car coming up behind me; the engine screaming out into the quiet air. I immediately put my hand up and start waving.

I'm in the outside lane, closer to the middle section, which is the same as the car, and it's coming bloody quickly, so I start to move over towards the middle. The car does the same, so I start swerving back to the outside lane, but again, it changes course. For a second, it feels like the car is aiming for me, but at the last second, it swerves to the side and goes stonking past at such a high speed the slipstream causes me to wobble. I catch a glimpse of a woman driving. Then as it pulls ahead, I see someone in the back seat, but it looks weird, like the passenger is lurching forward to speak to the driver.

Then the car veers off and strikes the safety barrier with a loud crash. The speed so great and the angle of impact so hard, it immediately flips the back end up and out, causing the vehicle to roll over and over in the air. The noise is incredible – a thudding, awful boom, followed by near on silence as the vehicle sails for long seconds before crashing back down to earth. Rolling with terrible, wrenching, metallic screams. Glass imploding, and a whole wheel shorn off to go bouncing down the road. Debris flying far and wide, and the vehicle scoring a long, deep gouge in the tarmac before it comes to rest on its roof.

All is instantly quiet again, apart from the squeaking of my pedal as I cycle faster towards the wreck.

The car is utterly destroyed. The front end is crumpled in, and the remaining front wheel looks buckled. The windows have shattered into thousands of tiny pieces glittering on the road, and I catch scent of burning rubber mixed with chemicals in the air, petrol too.

As I give a final burst of speed, I hear a loud crunch and feel a sudden loss of pressure from the pedals. The chain snaps audibly and twangs off to snarl into the rear wheel, which causes me to lose control. I squeeze the brakes and steer to the right to avoid a collision, but the bike hits some of the liquid, and the back tire loses grip, causing me to fall off and slide along the debris-strewn road.

How is that possible? How is it possible that on an empty motorway, I fall off my bike to smash into the only pissing car here?

Noises coming from the car snap me back to reality, and I'm up, scrambling towards the driver's window as a slender arm drops out, the fingers clenching into a fist.

'Fuck!' The movement makes me jump back, fearing one of those things is about to come flying out at me.

'Help!' a female voice, low and weak, and I go lower onto my stomach, crunching over broken glass to see a woman with blonde hair upside down being held in place by the seatbelt as the deployed airbags sag down at her sides and from the steering wheel.

'Hey! Are you hurt?'

She snaps her head over, staring at me with relief through normal, blue eyes filling with tears.

'I'll get you out, okay? My name's Howie. Can you move?'

I try to remember what should be done now. She could have a neck or spinal injury, so should stay still until the emergency services get here. Only there aren't any emergency services now. No firemen to cut the roof off, and no paramedics to get her onto a spinal board.

Fluids are still leaking from the car; the pungent stench of fuel and chemicals. Can it explode like they do in movies?

'I'm going to pull you out,' I say it as gently as I can, but there really isn't any choice. She has to get out of the vehicle.

'Okay,' she replies quietly, obviously shocked. Grasping her hand,

I start applying pressure, but out of fear of hurting her, I don't pull hard enough, then realise the seatbelt is still on.

'The seatbelt, can you undo it?' She looks at me, then slowly turns her head to grope for the clasp. 'Hang on,' I say, fearing she will fall on her head. I lie flat on my back and push my hands up against her shoulders. 'Okay, do it now,' I say and hear the click as she pushes the button down and drops on my head.

'Sorry,' she gasps from somewhere on top of me.

'S'fine,' I say, somewhat muffled as we wriggle and writhe, with poky bits of broken car digging into our bodies. I slide out of the wreck and twist around to start pulling her out by her arms as she seems to revive a bit, with colour and life coming back into her face.

'Just...a bit...further,' I say as she slowly comes out of the mangled window.

'Okay... Keep going...' she replies, her voice a little stronger now.

'Does your back hurt?'

'No. I think I'm okay.'

'Thank god for that. What about the other person?' I ask tentatively, thinking the person in the back might not have survived.

'Gordon!' she gasps as her upper body is pulled free and stares up at me before letting go with an ear-piercing scream. I drop her in panic as she starts thrashing about violently. 'MY LEG! MY LEG!'

'What the...' I blink and swallow, my heart once more going like the clappers as I drop down and edge in closer, thinking there must be a shard of metal stuck in her leg. 'Let me see. Please just...'

'MY LEG! MY FUCKING LEG!'

Wiggling closer, I try and get a view of the inside, then spot the back of a man's head moving in the gap between the seats.

'I think he's alive,' I shout, my words trailing off with sick realisation at the same time as he lifts his head up to show his mouth dripping with blood from the hole he has bitten into the back of her calf muscle. He growls once like a dog, then sinks back down to bite again, causing a fresh burst of agonising screams.

'Fuck!' Pushing myself out of the vehicle, I get free and grab her wrists. 'Hold on,' I say through gritted teeth. She screams in complete agony but slides free from the car. With her leg shifted, the man immediately starts writhing towards the gap left by her exit.

A quick glimpse shows me that one of his arms has been removed at the shoulder joint, shorn clean off, with thick blood pumping out. Even in the midst of such carnage, I can't help but notice the blood flow is nowhere near what I would expect. It falls out in thick globules rather than pulsing out in a stream.

'My leg...fuck! It hurts... Oh...fuck...it hurts...' she screams in agony.

I look down at her leg and the blood pouring out from the wound. The bite must be down to the bone. I need to stop the bleeding, but I don't have any bandages. I take the belt off of my jeans and start to wrap it around her thigh.

'We've got to stop the bleeding,' I say.

'Okay,' she gasps. Glancing up, I figure that the man inside the car is moving slowly enough to give us time.

Wrapping the belt around her thigh, I thread it back through the loop and start cinching it tight as she stares down at the wound. 'I'm bleeding out,' she gasps. 'Pull it.'

I wrench back on the belt, trying to form a tourniquet, but the muscles in her thighs are too hard. She still screams out from the pain and starts clutching her belly too, writhing in agony.

'Shit, I'm so sorry!' Dropping down again, I loosen the belt and push it further up her thigh, feeling very awkward at seeing her smooth expanse of skin and her knickers. 'God, I'm so sorry, so sorry.'

'It's okay...' she says, her voice ragged and harsh. 'Do it, just fucking do it.'

Wrapping the belt round again, I pull on the free end and gradually apply more pressure. I stare down at the pulsing wound, but there is no change.

'Fucking pull it, then,' she growls. I heave with all my strength as she screams out. Her hands reaching up to grab at my arms. I pull the belt harder and harder, and I even get my foot onto her thigh for leverage as I cinch it tighter into her flesh.

'Almost,' I pant and keep going, determined to get enough pressure so the blood stops coming out. If I can stop the blood flow, I can dress the wound and try releasing the tourniquet a bit; maybe it will clot on its own. Fuck it, I should have signed up for the advanced first aid course.

She falls silent as I slowly ease my grip, and the belt holds in place. The bleeding now much less than it was.

'I've done it,' I say hoarsely.

No response. I twist round to see she has gone quiet, like she's asleep. Her hands out to the sides.

'Hey! Hey! Wake up,' I gently move her head but get no response. Tapping the side of her face, I try and wake her. Still no response. I lower my head so that my ear is next to her mouth, and I can feel very soft breath on my cheek.

A groan sounds behind me from the infected man trying to crawl out of the car, stretching his remaining arm out towards us. I rush in and drive my right foot down onto his head, sending a jolt up through my leg, but I keep going, stamping over and over as he gargles and snaps his mouth. I aim for the neck and finally feel a crack under my foot.

Hobbling back to the woman, I drop down to rest my ear against her mouth. There's no breath this time. 'Wake up. Come on. Please wake up,' I plead, feeling for a pulse in her neck, but there is nothing. I try her wrist. No sign of life. I lift her eyelids. I don't know what I am looking for, but they always do this in the movies. It must be the pupils; to see if they dilate. There is no movement, just blank eyes looking a bit bloodshot.

In desperation, I lower the side of my head to her chest, trying to hear a heartbeat. I stay for a few seconds, attempting to calm my breathing so that I can listen properly. Nothing. Just silence. She's dead. I sigh deeply, swallowing and thinking to rise when I hear a single thud, and hold still. Another. Then another. A heartbeat for sure. She's alive.

An explosion of motion, and her arms grab hard, pulling my head into her chest as her heartrate goes nuts, and my world fills with soft breasts squishing into the side of my face, which at any other time would be quite nice.

Not now though, and I try to pull away, but her grip is too strong, and her fingers dig into my scalp, clawing at me. I can't get leverage to move, so I try and prise her fingers from the back of my head, but they are so strong I can't move them.

I can hardly breathe from her boobs going in my mouth and

covering my nose, and I start panicking at hearing the growls coming from her throat. God knows how, but I get a hand up into her hair, fix a grip, and yank hard enough to snap her head back, and manage to slip out from under her vice-like grip.

I fall back, rolling away and catching sight of her eyes now horrifically red and bloodshot. Her lips pulled back, showing me her perfect, white teeth, with drool spilling out, and no sign whatsoever of the person I just tried to save. Nothing. No recognition. Just an animalistic beast snapping its mouth open and shut.

'Fucking bitch! You fucking bitch!'

I get to my feet and kick her in the face, then do it again, pulling back like a footballer, ramming my foot into her nose. I feel the bone crunch, and her head snaps back. Terror grips me. I'm in shock from seeing her die and come back, but what came back wasn't the same as the woman that died. My foot slams into her face again and again, and she takes a remarkable amount of blows before she finally lays still.

I stagger away, with my hands to my head, deeply in shock. My vision blurring, and hot tears stinging my eyes. The shorn-off wheel on the ground, the buckled vehicle upside down amongst the glittering shards of glass, and the pooling liquids mixing with the blood from the two dead bodies. The two bodies I killed.

That woman was alive in my arms, pleading for me to save her life. She spoke to me, and we shared something. Maybe only a few seconds in time, but we shared a connection. Two living people. She was alive and spoke to me, and I failed. I failed to save her.

If I hadn't fallen off that bike, if I had got up quicker and moved faster, and if I had pulled hard enough the first time, I might have saved her, but I didn't do those things, and she died.

It's my fault. She looked at me, spoke to me; we made eye contact, and I told her that I would help her.

The sickening action of kicking her replays in my mind – the image of my foot connecting with her face. This is awful; the most awful thing I have ever done, and nothing will ever be the same again.

I tried to save her, and I failed.

But then she came back and was attacking me. The strength in her hands and arms was incredible. She turned and became infected or whatever those things are, and I had to stop her, didn't I?

My mind whirls as I try to make sense of what's happening, justifying the actions to myself, reasoning, and rationalising. If I didn't kill her, she could have got me or someone else. But we're in the middle of a motorway, with no one else nearby. Who could she have hurt? Did I kill her through defence, or was it murder, with an act of vengeance, carried out through fear and rage?

I have to change this thought process. She was not a *she* when I kicked her; she was infected. One of them.

The woman from earlier on was not a young lady out for the evening, getting excited about wearing her new, low-cut, blue dress. She was not a *she*. *It* was infected, and *it* wanted only to make me the same as them.

The quicker I get that into my head, the safer I will be, and the greater chance for survival I will have.

I lower my hands from my head, resolute, changed, and hardened.

I walk away without looking back.

CHAPTER FIVE

Half an hour, and I'm still on the motorway, with fields on both sides. I haven't seen or heard anyone, and with the adrenalin all gone, I feel totally and utterly drained.

I need to find a vehicle. Walking will take too long, but then there isn't exactly a good supply of cars on the motorway. I see houses in the distance over the fields and clamber over the crash barrier and down a ditch to cross the land.

After the smooth surface of the motorway, the field is uneven and hard going. It looks to be pasture (I think that's what they call it), the type of land that animals graze on. I realise that I have no idea what different types of land there are or what different crops look like, or even if they can be eaten or not. I work in a supermarket, selling produce all day. We get training on certain things so that we can sound convincing to the customers and increase sales, but I can't remember anything useful.

The field borders a lane, which I follow into the village. The first few houses are detached and large, but gradually they get closer together until a pavement starts running down both sides.

I reach the junction into the village and realise I've been here a few times before. Normally when the motorway was closed off, or my dad wanted to take the scenic route. I know there's a garage workshop at the end of the main road. Hopefully, they'll have something I can use.

I keep to the middle of the road, passing open front doors, which look creepy in the silence. Blood on the ground too. Huge, wet stains like someone was brought down here and bled out, but there is too much blood to have just been from one person. Then again, the human body has something like eight pints of blood in it. I try to imagine what eight pints poured onto the floor would look like; probably like that woman back on the motorway.

Then I spot a white UPVC door smeared with blood, and the more I look, the more of it I see. On windows. On doorsteps. Splashed up walls and across kerbs. Sinister and terrible. It stinks too, with a metallic tang hanging in the hot air.

This was a mistake. I should have stayed on the motorway.

I reach the small collection of shops on the right, opposite a small village square, where we used to park to visit the cake shop, and as I get closer, I get a feeling of impending doom just before the small square comes into view crammed full of infected people. The same as they were in my town. All of them shuffling and groaning quietly, and all gathered in one place.

I come to a complete stop. There must be thirty or forty of them, dressed in differing styles of nightwear: pyjamas, nighties, pants, knickers, and bras. Some are naked. All of them are covered in blood.

I can't understand why they are all here. Maybe they're gathering from some remaining spark of intelligence drawing them to the heart of the village. I slowly back away one step at a time, watching for any sign that they've seen me.

Behind me, I hear glass bottles being knocked over and spin round to see an infected male shuffling out of a doorway, kicking milk bottles with his feet, making them spin off to shatter on the road.

If I move quickly, I can get past him, but another one comes out of the house opposite, staggering into the road, heading my way as the village square infected people all react from the noise and shuffle round to see me.

'Shit, shit,' I murmur quietly and start back, thinking that I can still make it through the middle of the two behind me, but more come lurching from houses further down the road, blocking my escape route. I turn back to the road ahead, but the village square horde are spilling into the road, coming at me.

I start running for it, aiming for the newsagents while praying that it's open. As I run past the cake shop and the butchers, a quick thought enters my mind of the massive knives and cleavers they would have, but the door is locked and too solid to force quickly. I run on, towards the newsagents.

The horde is across the road ahead of me, coming from my left, slow moving, and I pass them by a few metres as I reach the shop and bounce off the door. I slam at it again, glancing back to the encroaching horde getting closer by the second, and start whacking at the door, begging it to open.

'Shit, come on! COME ON!'

Looking down, I see the word PULL marked clearly on the door in big letters and yank it open, stumbling through, and pull it shut behind me. Slamming the lock in place, I look for bolts, but there are none. Instead, there are two metal hooks meant to hold a bar, but I can't see the bar anywhere.

I move away from the door as the infected get to the other side, banging into the door with loud groans. Their twisted, gruesome faces smearing blood and saliva over the glass panes, but at least they're not launching themselves at it like last night in my flat.

I back away, with my eyes fixed on them and stumble into a shelf full of chocolate bars, and the sight of them makes me realise just how hungry and thirsty I am. I grab a bottle of Lucozade from the chiller cabinet and start guzzling the sweet liquid down before finishing off with a loud belch, and feeling the instant rush of energy spiking inside. A Mars bar. A Snickers. Another Lucozade, and my sugar levels go nuts as my body starts thrumming, and I stuff more into my bag.

That done, I widen my eyes and think of what to do while my heart beats faster from the energy coursing through me. That's when I see the cigarette display behind the counter.

All of the supermarkets have been fitted with sliding metal doors now in a vain attempt by the government to hide cigarettes away. I thought smaller shops were covered by the same laws too.

I did give up smoking, but hey, I'm surrounded by zombies, and civilisation has fallen. Fuck it, time for a smoke.

I take some tobacco and rolling papers. Tailor-made cigarettes are too expensive, so I switched to tobacco some time ago. There was nearly always someone selling duty-free tobacco from their holidays. After smoking roll-ups for so long, I couldn't go back to normal smokes – the taste is disgusting.

I open the packet and roll a smoke, with my hands shaking a little, but it's quickly done, and I use a lighter from a display pack on the counter.

I inhale deeply and feel the nicotine receptors joining the party held by the sugar dudes in my brain. All of which combines to make me feel somewhat lightheaded. Swaying a little, I lower down until my forehead is resting on the cool countertop while listening to the infected groan and bump into the door and windows.

The dizzy spell eases, leaving me with a pleasant buzz, and as I open my eyes, I spot a baseball bat wedged under the counter. 'Thanks very much,' I say into the quietness of the shop and pull the bat out. These shops open early and could be easy targets, especially in the dark winter mornings.

The smoke from the cigarette in my mouth curls up into my eyes, stinging them. I clench my eyes shut and wait for a few seconds before opening them gently and blinking the tears away.

As I focus again, I see someone standing at the back, behind a bead curtain that separates the shop from the private area. He's a big man too, with a fat gut straining against the material of his short-sleeved shirt now covered in blood from the ragged bite wound on his neck.

He moves slowly forward through the bead curtain, with bloodied drool hanging from his mouth, and his horrible, red eyes staring at me while his head lolls about.

I look about for an avenue of escape, but the only way out is through him. Unless I use the main door, which right now doesn't seem a viable alternative.

The shopkeeper shuffles on; his bulk filling the aisle as he heads towards the counter. I stand still and spit the cigarette away to the side, not taking my eyes off him.

As he gets closer, I watch his head lolling back and forth, and to the sides, but all the time, the red, bloodshot eyes stay fixed on me. Then his head hangs down, with his chin to his chest, and he looks up at me, menacing and very scary.

He walks straight to the counter, and I grasp the baseball bat at the base with two hands and slowly twist my upper body off to the right, raising the bat behind me, ready to strike.

We stare into each other's eyes, fixed, unmoving; neither of us blinking, and long seconds go by. His lips peel back to show yellow, uneven teeth. He can just feel the bite. He can visualise sinking his dirty, yellow teeth into my flesh.

I think to say something cool, but nothing comes to mind, so I just hit him in the head with the bat instead. It's a good hit too, and he goes flying off to the side, colliding with some shelves and sending chocolate bars and tins of beans over the floor.

I put the bat down on the counter and pick the heavy till up, yanking it hard to pull the cable free before I raise it above my head and slam it down on the squirming man as he wrestles with the shelving on the floor. The till smashes into his head, and I move out from the counter to see he's now dead. Like properly dead. Like not-coming-back-to-life-from-some-weird-infection dead. Not with his brains leaking out like that anyway. I've never seen brains outside the head before in real life. They look weird, like little sausages all stuck together.

Stepping through the curtain with my bat raised, I see a small stock room and a flight of stairs going up. To the back of the stock room is a door – barred and bolted. I move over to the door and peer through a grimy window to a small backyard and a wall a few feet away. All empty and quiet.

I pull the bolts back, tug the door open, and peer out into the yard. It has a high brick wall and a wooden gate. I go over to the gate, raise the latch, and lean out to see a small, clear road.

Going left will take me towards the garage I was originally heading for, but an idea forms in my mind, and I turn back.

I close the gate quietly, head into the stock room, and shut the back door, pushing the bolt into place.

With the bat raised and ready, I climb the stairs to the flat above the shop and check the rooms.

Once I'm sure it's all clear, I go back down into the shop and find the cans of lighter fluid on display and some nice, big boxes of matches.

Back upstairs. The windows are old sash and already open in this sultry summer weather, and I look down to about fifty infected all gathered at the front of the shop. I have flashbacks to last night when I was trapped and my ham-fisted attempt at making a Molotov cocktail resulted in me puking up. I don't intend to stick around and watch this time.

I pull the little plastic spout on the first one, up-end the can, and squeeze a jet of liquid out onto the crowd below. It takes quite a long time to empty each can, leaning out and bending over to prevent any spraying on me or the windowsill.

I open the box of matches and pause for a second, hardly believing what I am about to do. Mass murder at any other time. I strike a match and flick it out, but it expires before it falls a few feet. I try another, and the same thing happens. The third time, I lean out and brace my feet, ready to pull back in. I extend my arms, strike a match, and shove it into the open box, pushing it into the dark heads of the little sticks. The box flares instantly – a bright light and stench of sulphur. I drop the box and pull myself in, ducking down below the window just before the whoosh hits, and the flames sear up, with black smoke already billowing up.

I risk a quick look out and gawp at the flames spreading quickly, leaping from body to body. Time to go before I puke from the stench, and I'm off, running down through the shop and out the back door, and into the alley with my new bat in hand.

Reaching the end of the alley, I turn left again, which takes me out onto the main road. I look back down to the shop and see thick, black smoke and flames licking at the side of the building, but the weirdest thing are the bodies on fire just standing there, like they haven't got the sense or intelligence to move away. Even the ones standing on the outside aren't moving away. They just stand and wait, and then catch alight.

I move away and head towards the garage, thinking about how

they seem to follow each other. Last night, I watched as they massed at the front of my house and behind my front door. But I was screaming abuse at them from my window, alerting them to my presence. Then the armoured van went past, sounding the horn repeatedly. Was it the noise of the horn that pulled them away or the already huge stream of other infected in its wake?

The thoughts give me hope. Maybe I can carry something that will distract them with movement or noise – something I can throw if I get cornered or trapped. There are plenty of children's toys that bounce about with loud noises and flashing lights. I should have kept a can of lighter fluid and matches... I could set one of them on fire, which will draw others to it while I get away. The thought process makes me realise how much I need supplies and weapons. The bat is good. It's longer than the hammer and means I can keep them away from me. A gun would be perfect, but I have no idea where to find one. The only guns in Britain are shotguns and farmer rifles. Even a double-barrelled shotgun only gives two shots at a time, but a shotgun is also long and heavy – like a bat.

I think of the movies and news reports of robbers using sawed-off shotguns. That would make them smaller and lighter to carry but reduces their secondary use as a blunt instrument or a ranged weapon.

The police have guns. You see them quite a lot these days – armed police, with pistols on their belts. They keep the bigger guns locked in armoured boxes in their cars. I guess there must be armouries in the police stations.

That gives me another thought... Maybe the police are holed up in their stations? If they have weapons and strong buildings, they could remain safely inside. Boroughfare has a police station in the town centre; maybe I should have gone there first.

Ridiculously, I wonder if they would arrest me if I was armed with a gun.

CHAPTER SIX

Finally, I reach the sprawling collection of buildings, workshops, and lockups at the end of the village.

Big double wooden doors face out onto a hardstand. Oil stains on the ground, and a single fuel pump in the middle, hardly used as the price is always so much cheaper at the supermarkets.

There are, however, two cars parked up. One on a jack, with the driver's side wheel missing, and the other one a tiny, silver Nissan Micra, which, unfortunately, is locked.

I head over to the reception door, which is also locked, and look through the window to see the lights are off and no obvious sign of movement from within. There might be an easier way in at the back, so I trot off, looking for another door while hoping the Micra is just in for a service and isn't broken down or something.

More doors at the back, but they're all strong looking, and the few windows are barred too. Back at the front, I check the double doors, but they are flush together and well secured. The reception door is the best option as the top half is a large glass pane.

I stand listening for a few seconds, knowing I'll have to be quick: smash the glass, get in, find the keys, get out, and go.

I pull the bat back and swing at the glass pane in the door. The glass is toughened and fractures, but stays in place. Another swing, and the bat smashes a hole in the glass, but the pane remains in place. It takes bloody ages and makes a hell of a noise too. I should have bust a door open or, you know, like shouted that I am here to alert every single infected person in a ten-mile radius.

Eventually, and after much sweating, kicking, cursing, some sulking, and some more swearing, I finally bust a hole big enough to climb through.

I slip my bag off and put it through the hole, then climb in, which is harder than I thought it would be as the bottom ledge is too high to step over, and I don't want to enter head-first, so I hop my right leg in and straddle the bottom of the frame, then shift my weight over to draw my remaining leg in. Which is all going swimmingly until the bloody burglar alarm goes off. Screeching merrily away after sneakily waiting for me to smash a massive hole in the door.

'Bastard fucking shitty, cunty, bastard arsing, cock-faced fucking thing!' I fall inside, grab my bat, and smash the alarm box off the wall, which warbles sadly before cutting out. 'Wanker,' I mutter, giving it what for before heading deeper into the place, seeing a counter for fuel payment and stuff for sale. Oils and lubricants, and other stuff. No keys, though. Why would there be keys? It's not like anything is trying to be helpful right now, is it?

I go behind the counter and check drawers and cupboards – again, nothing.

A door leads into the workshop area, and I go through. It's very dark as the grimy windows are not letting much light in, so I flick the lights on and wait for the fluorescent strips to blink on.

Tool drawers and various machinery are positioned around the outside, with shiny, red sets of sliding metal trays, with cool logos on them – everything seems to have a *Snap-on* sticker on it, but there is a small metal key cupboard on the wall. Which is locked. Awesome.

I search and find a large, flat-headed screwdriver. Taking this back, I force the end into the gap between the metal door and the frame, levering hard to prise the door open.

Inside are a few rows of hooks, with various keys hanging down and two sets of car keys on fobs. One of them has the *Nissan* logo on a metal clasp. I take the keys and head back into reception to see an infected woman trying to walk forward while leaning her head and shoulders through the hole in the door.

I use the bat and strike downwards on her head. The impact bends her over the frame, and I swing upwards, smashing her back out of the door, and I gingerly peek out to see her stretched out and motionless, with her head at an unnatural angle. The neck broken from either the force of the blow or the impact from hitting the ground.

I start to clamber through, but my rucksack gets caught, so I go back in and take the rucksack off, throw it out, and try again, tripping as I go and nearly landing face first on the dead woman. I roll off with a yelp, grab my bag and bat, and rush to the car before anything else happens.

At least I got the right keys and gain entry to the Micra without anything exploding or making noise. And while looking about, I turn the key in the ignition and shoot forward with a jolt.

'FUCK,' I scream out in frustration at my own rushed, panicked state and try again, but this time, I keep my foot down on the clutch and make sure the manual gearstick is in neutral.

The car starts, and I pull away from the village, glancing repeatedly at the rearview mirror and the plumes of black smoke billowing up into the sky.

The fire will spread quickly in the warm, dry weather, and I think of all the damage being caused. No fire engines will come racing to the rescue. No police will cordon off the area, and no ambulances will ever arrive to treat the wounded and hurt.

It will just burn and burn until there is nothing left.

CHAPTER SEVEN

'There are survivors. You are not alone.
Do not come to London. We are completely infested.
I repeat, DO NOT COME TO LONDON.
If you are in the south, then we advise you head to the Victorian Forts on the south coast.
Take whatever supplies you can carry: water, food, medicine, and clothing.
Stay out of the cities and towns. Head to the forts on the coast.'

A deep, reassuring voice blasting from the radio on a loop that repeats over and over, with a faint click between each repeat. I found it by turning the radio on and twisting the old-style manual tuning dial until the voice was coming from the speakers, making my heart race again.

I keep listening to it, hoping someone alive will cut in and speak, but it just repeats over and over.

It's still calming, though, and whoever recorded it did so without hint of panic of distress. I try to picture the man recording the message, and my mind creates an image of an older, refined man, groomed and sophisticated, with a beard, definitely a beard.

I think of the forts on the south known as Palmerston's Follies and what I remember from school history lessons. I know they were built during the 1800s to fight off a French invasion that never happened. There's quite a few of them, I think, dotted along the coast.

Some of them have fallen to ruin, but then I'm sure a few have been preserved by historical societies, and I curse myself for not paying more attention to my own local history.

The most famous are the three or four big, round things in The Solent, the stretch of water that separates the mainland from the Isle of Wight. They are amazing feats of engineering, used now as private hotels or left to decay.

If I can get to my parents, I could send them to the forts and then try to find my sister.

The message on the radio says London is infested and not to go there, but I'm not leaving her. If there is a chance that she is holed up at home, then I have to try.

※ ※

THE REST of the drive is, thankfully, uneventful, and I soon reach my parents' small village and slow down on seeing a gathering of people outside their local shop, wincing when I realise they're just more infected, and I tense up, praying that I don't see my dad amongst them. He always goes down for the early paper and could have walked unwittingly into them without realising what was happening.

He's not there, and I let the breath go, offering a quick prayer to any God listening.

Unlike the previous village, this shop is on the main through-road, and it's a modern, large convenience store, more like a mini supermarket, and as I go past, I see movement inside. I think to keep going, then slow down, and realise my dad might be inside. What if he went for his newspaper and managed to run and hide like I did? Maybe I should go home and check first, but if he is inside, I could be too late if I have to come back, and I'd never forgive myself for that.

I slow the car and look back at the infected people. Five of them, three males and two females.

One of them looks like a delivery driver, wearing matching blue trousers and jacket. Another is very old. Even from here, I can see his hunched-over, thin frame and wispy, grey hair, with a white vest tucked into his sleeping shorts pulled up nearly to his chest.

The two women are late middle-aged, and both dressed in sensible trousers and sleeveless jackets with pastel-coloured shirts. They look like the early-to-bed and early-to-rise types, who only drink sherry at the weekends, and who are always perfectly behaved and have expertly trained, small dogs. Fortunately, there's no zombie dogs that I can see anywhere. Can dogs even get infected? I have no idea. The last one is a young male, dressed in jeans and a t-shirt.

I watch them all shuffling outside the shop, pressing their bodies against the door and windows. I can't see any more of them anywhere. Just these five. Shit. I just want to go, but I can't risk my dad being inside.

Right. Decision made, but if I'm going to do this, then I have to be quick. The noise and movement might draw more, and I don't want to end up trapped inside too.

I ease out and leave the engine running for a quick getaway, and take my bat as I head towards the infected. Then I stop and go back to close the car door, with the image of an infected person getting in and waiting for me on the backseat.

Too many movies.

I slam the door on purpose so they hear me and watch as the old man turns around to start shuffling towards me straight away; then within seconds, they're all moving towards me, as though an unspoken message has passed between them.

I need to separate them as they are too close together for me to risk attacking them all in one go. Even with the range of the baseball bat, it would only take one of them to lunge quickly, and I could get bitten.

I look at the area, noting the pavement has obstacles: a bike rack, litter bins, and a post box. There is a high step down from the pavement to the road. These are things which will impede my movements and could cause me to trip or fall, but the road is wide and clear, with no obstructions.

Moving off to my right, I lure them into clear ground. I'm choosing my battleground, selecting where to fight, and it feels strange. There is almost a sense of excitement, a weird feeling, like just before the roller coaster moves off. I am scared yet exhilarated.

The old man is nearest. He saw me first and has the head start. I thought his old age would make him slower, and the others would go past him, but they move at roughly the same speed. It appears the infected are not hampered by age or infirmity.

Watching the old man come towards me makes me uneasy – he looks very old and frail, and I'm getting the same feeling as I had when the girl in the blue dress was in front of me. Attacking a woman or the elderly seems wrong. Then I remember how I felt after the motorway when that woman tried to bite me and suffocate me with her boobs.

They're not people. They are infected.

I raise the bat up, poised and ready, and wait for him to come, watching the saliva hanging down from his mouth, and he pulls his lips back as I snort a dry laugh at the sight of his gummy, toothless mouth. What's he going to do? Suck on me?

He should be carrying a blender or a knife and fork or maybe have a carer to help him make flesh soup. I almost feel sorry for him, and then I see his hands curled up like claws with nasty, jagged fingernails and remember the strength of the woman from the car accident was incredible, and he probably has the same strength too. His fingernails look like they could rip flesh open.

Fuck him. I step forward and swing the bat hard into the side of his head, and he goes spinning off to my left.

I move to the right, going around the side of the small group as they all turn to follow me. I move back to the left, and they all turn again. I move right, and again, they all move as one. Synchronised zombies.

I lead them into the road before I run round the back of them, watching as they do a shuffling about turn and bump into each other; then I see my advantage and dart forward to whack the delivery driver hard on the shoulder, sending him into the two women, knocking them away and creating more space between them all.

The delivery driver goes down with one of the women. Both of them groaning audibly as they start trying to get back up but hamper their own efforts by constantly pushing each other back down. The old man is still down, and the young lad is closest now.

I step out so that I'm facing his left side and smash the bat into his face. His nose explodes, with a sickening crunch of bones that I hear upon the impact of the bat. He stumbles backwards and falls onto his arse, but instantly tries to get back up, so I bunch power and strike the side of his head like a golf-swing and send him flying off to the side.

A growl behind, and I spin round just as the other dog walker woman lunges at me, with her lips pulled back, showing her teeth. I aim an uppercut but miss, and stagger forward into her with the momentum of the swing. A mistake made, and quick as a flash, she's into me, driving forward as I try and go back, and trip over one of the others I knocked down. Sprawling out on the ground, and suddenly, this seems like a very bad idea very poorly executed.

Growls and groans all around me as I lash out with the bat, whacking bodies, but they keep coming in. The old man crawling at my side. I whack him hard with the bat, then roll the other way into the other woman, who tries to lunge in for the bite, and in the panic, I just about get the end of the bat into the side of her head, pushing her away as the other woman staggers in and readies to drop on me. I get a foot up into her belly, holding her off while she dangles down, drooling spit down my leg while I whack small, hard hits into the other one.

'SHIT!' I cry out as the delivery driver comes in from the other side and take a quick swing to keep him away. On my back, with one leg up, holding the woman at bay while hitting left and right, twisting from the torso while my stomach muscles scream in pain, and then, if that wasn't enough, old, gummy grandad joins in and starts crawling back. 'FUCK IT!' A nice, healthy dose of fresh rage detonates, and I start lashing out with hard, brutal hits before wrenching to the side and letting the woman braced against my leg fall down next to me, giving me space to get up and away. But no. That can't happen because the young man, who should be bloody dead, is back on his sodding feet and coming in to join the feast. Wank it, and at the point, I think I am royally screwed, but a young Asian lad appears behind the young man and swings a cricket bat into his head, driving him away.

'Thank fuck!' On my feet, and I start laying about me with the bat, hitting heads and body parts while the Asian boy does the same. Both of us bashing skulls until I stagger back, gasping for air and looking at the mangled corpses littering the ground while the lad carries on, battering down at one of the women, hitting her over and over.

'I think she's finished, mate,' I say as he carries on. 'Mate, she's definitely finished. Or, you know, just carry on...' I add as he unleashes a fresh barrage of blows.

Eventually, he stops and steps backwards, holding the bat with both hands down at his front. Blood all over his shiny, white trainers. He looks young, no more than fifteen years old, dark-skinned with black, gelled hair. Indian or Pakistani, maybe Sri Lankan, but his eyes are blazing from the kill.

Behind him, the shop door opens, and an older woman comes running out, angrily yelling at the boy. 'What did you do that for? I told you to stay inside.'

The boy spins, seeing his mother coming, and swallows while darting a look at me.

'He was trying to help us,' the boy shouts back, squeaky and high-pitched, showing his age.

'No, *you* could have been killed, you foolish boy, and don't talk back to me! Don't you *ever* talk back to me!' she shouts back at him with a mother's fear-loaded anger and switches into a language I can't understand until he finally hangs his head with a look of shame and starts back towards the shop. The woman stays and looks at me, and when she speaks, her tone is forcefully polite.

'Thank you for what you did. I am sorry for my son; he is young and foolish...' she trails off, looking about at the bodies and the woman's brains beaten out of her head. 'I can't believe what's happened...what's happening, this is...just so... Have you seen more of them? We tried calling the police, but we cannot get through – 999 is not working. We cannot get hold of anyone.'

'It's everywhere,' I reply, wiping the sweat from my face as the adrenalin once more wears off. 'I'm from Boroughfare, and the whole town is gone. I went through Littleton on the way here; that's gone too... I, er, I saw it on the news last night. I think it's worldwide...' I take my turn to trail off as the blood drains from her face, and she presses a hand to her cheek.

'I'm, er, looking for my dad, Howard. He comes down every morning for a newspaper. Have you seen him?'

She stays silent for a few seconds.

'I'm sorry, what...what did you say?' She looks back at me with a confused expression.

'My dad...Howard? He comes down every morning for a newspaper. Have you seen him today?'

'Oh, Howard. Yes, we know Howard, always so polite. No, we have not seen him. There is just my family – my son and daughter, and me, of course.'

'Is your husband not with you?'

'No, he is visiting family at home in India...' her voice becomes very soft.

'I'm sure he is okay. Maybe it is just Europe that's affected. Look, why don't you go inside? It's not safe out here in the open.'

'Yes... Do you want to come in?'

'No, thank you. I have to go to my parents' house; they live on the estate. Listen, I heard a broadcast on the radio, and it said that people should go to the forts.'

'What forts?'

'The old ones, the Palmerston Forts. There's quite a few of them all along the coast. The radio said London was infested, and people should head over to the forts and take food, water, and medicine.'

'Oh, I think we should stay here and wait for help. We have enough food, thank you.'

'I don't think it will be safe here; those *things* are everywhere,' I point at the bodies on the ground. 'And other people might want to take your food. Maybe you should take what you can carry and go. Do you have a vehicle?'

'We have a van – my husband uses it for the cash-and-carry.'

'Take your van, load it up with as much as you can take, and then leave,' I urge her.

'What about my husband? What if he comes back and cannot find us?'

'Leave a note for him, and also one that tells other people where you have gone so they can go there too, but do it quickly.' She glances back at the shop, clearly unsure of what to do. I can see her dilemma –

the shop looks strong and secure, a safe place. 'I saw these things last night. They were different. They weren't slow like these were. They were fast. If they change again, they won't stop until they have got you and your family.'

She stares back at me. The suggestion of a threat to her family has sharpened her instincts for survival.

'Where are these forts?'

'Check the Internet if it's still working. If not, look at local maps. Do you sell maps?'

'Yes...yes, we have maps.'

'Check them and find the nearest fort, then load up, and go. Please don't stay here. It's not safe.'

She goes to move away, then hesitates. 'Will you come? We could travel together...'

'I can't. I'm sorry... I have to find my family. I'll try and get my parents to follow you. I'll ask them to come here first and see if you are still here, but don't wait for them, load up, and get going.'

She nods and walks back to the shop, still in shock. I'm worried that she's not taken it in and will try to wait it out. Her son comes out of the door, walking towards his mother. A teenage girl comes out behind him and stands back, holding the door open.

'Hey, thanks for your help again, mate. I just said to your mother that people are going to the forts on the coast. She said you had a van. I really think you should load up with food and water and go there as soon as possible. Take anything you can carry.'

'Are you going there too?'

His mother interrupts before I can answer, 'No, he has to find his family. Go back inside, please.'

I turn and walk to the car, and head into the estate. My parents moved here a few years ago. The old house was the family home. This is their new house, and it feels different, still homely and welcoming, but not the same.

My dad retired two years ago. He was an engineer for a telecoms company and had a good retirement package, but he quickly got bored of playing golf and went back as a part-timer.

My sister and I bought him a new set of clubs for his 60th birthday.

Well, I say *we* bought them, but my sister paid most of it as she earns a fortune. I paid what I could, but still, it's the thought that counts.

Their new house is detached and modern, but the large driveway is empty. Dad bought a new Toyota when he retired and always leaves it on the driveway, proudly cleaning it at every opportunity.

I leave the Micra on the street, with the keys in the ignition, and walk towards the house, seeing the front door and all the windows are closed.

The first bad sign is that the front door has been left unlocked, and I enter, with my bat gripped and ready, pausing for a minute in the hallway, eyeing the stairs ahead of me. The lounge to the left. The dining room to my right. Silence inside, and I close the front door gently behind me.

I want to call out but don't want to risk alerting any infected that I am here. I go into the lounge and then the dining room, and finally the kitchen to see two half-drunk mugs of coffee on the side; both are cold.

I go upstairs, with my bat raised, but find nothing in the two guest rooms. The bathroom is clear.

My parents' bedroom is also vacant. The drawers are empty and thrown around, and the wardrobe is open, with clothes lying about. It looks like they were in a rush. I go back downstairs and check the rooms again, finally spotting the notepad on the dining room table, with a handwritten note in my mother's writing.

HOWIE,

Dad got a phone call last night from an old colleague working in France. They said what was happening, awful things. Dad spoke to your sister. Sarah is safe at home, locked in and secure. The phone line went down when we were talking to her. We kept trying to call you, but all the numbers were engaged. We are going to come and get you, but I suppose if you are reading this, then we have missed each other.

Stay here, Howie. We will try your place and come back here before we get Sarah. We left the front door

unlocked in case you left your key behind. You can lock the door, though. We both have our keys.

Please stay here, Howie. We will be back soon.

Love, Mum and Dad.

I READ the note over a few times. Sarah is safe, thank God. The relief is massive and washes over me, with a great sense of fatigue following close behind. Hunger too. I head into the kitchen and find a Cornish pasty in the fridge that I wolf down in seconds, followed by another, then a mug of hot, sweet tea.

I try the home phone but find it dead – there is not even a dial tone. I check the router. Lights flashing red – no Internet and no phone line.

After locking the front door, I go upstairs into the bathroom, strip off, and have a hot shower, watching as the water runs red and black from the gore and grime while wondering how long it will be before the power goes off.

My clothes are too dirty to put back on. They're covered in blood and need to be thrown away. The blood could be infectious, but then I would have nothing to wear.

I remember that there are some old clothes of mine in bin liners in the loft. I'd left them at the old house, and Mum kept nagging me to go and sort them out, which I never did.

I wrap a towel around my waist and find the long stick to open the loft hatch, and climb into the loft, and turn the light on. The loft is boarded out, and I can see a pile of black bags with white, sticky labels marked 'Howie'.

I find an old pair of jeans I used to live in years ago, then a white t-shirt to go with it until I stop and think that maybe white will stand out a bit. Plus, it shows the dirt and gore a bit too well. I put it back and find an old, black jumper instead.

Finally, with nothing left to do but wait, I go into the lounge and lay down on the sofa, thinking through all that has happened. Thinking of the horror and carnage. Of the death and awful things I have seen, and for a second, my mind buzzes with emotions and weird feelings, and I think I'll never be able to sleep again.

But then within seconds, my eyes grow heavy, and my breathing slows, and eventually, after jerking awake a couple of times, I drift off to sleep.

DAY TWO

CHAPTER EIGHT

Day Two
Saturday

I drift back to consciousness. Stretching with a long, pleasurable groan while thinking how much I love dozing on the sofa in the afternoon on a day off.

Then the events of yesterday come slamming back in one solid stream of images and memories, and emotions, and reactions, making my heart whump in my chest as my eyes snap open.

The things I saw on the news reports, then watching as the fat bloke was taken down outside my house, and the carnage that followed. Throwing missiles at them. Setting them on fire. Puking and screaming, and panicking. Then into the town centre, and the guy on the cash-in-transit van. I fell off the moped and feel a pang of humiliation at that memory; then my mind instantly floods with images of me attacking the infected people, hitting them with the hammer, then the motorway, and the car accident. That woman. I tried saving her. She died. She came back. I stomped her head in. I feel sick.

The village. The newsagents. Throwing the cash register on the head of that infected guy, then setting more on fire. Then the shop near here, the Asian lad that came out to help me.

Memories coming thick and fast, swimming in my head, and I stagger up to my feet, wondering where I am. My parents' house. The note. Are they back? I move too fast from waking so quickly and rush into the hallway, and can instantly tell the house is exactly the same as when I went to sleep. They're not here.

Into the kitchen, and I run the cold tap to wash my face and drink deep, easing my parched throat. My mouth tastes like shit too. Like someone took a dump in it while I slept. What the fuck is happening? Is this real? Am I dreaming?

I splash more water on my face, then lean in to dunk my head under the flow, shivering when it hits the back of my neck.

Too many thoughts flood my head as I remember what happened, then think of the news reports again, and how they said it was everywhere. It was definitely in Europe, and I saw footage from Moscow, and Russia's landmass is attached to China and a ton of other countries too. They'll all be hit. The rate of spread was staggeringly fast. Jesus, I saw it with my own eyes.

One person gets bit, and they attack everyone near them, and every single one of those then becomes infected and does the same. Two minutes at the most. That's it. Two minutes from the point of being bitten to becoming one of them.

There must be *some* safe places. The governments have strategic policies for everything. They would have initiated some lockdown protocol, but then all the movies show the top brass going to underground facilities while the masses suffer, and some handsome underdog hero that everyone said would never make the grade somehow saves the day and gets the girl.

A sudden thought hits me. If, say, a country like China or another nuclear power saw what was happening and how it was coming towards them, wouldn't they try and stop it by any means possible. Shit. Maybe that's happened already. Maybe right now there are major cities being hit with nukes.

Slow down, Howie. I draw a breath and force my mind to slow down by focussing on something mundane like drinking water. Simple. I bend down again and drink more as the image of a rotting corpse floating in a reservoir pops helpfully into my head, causing me to spray the water out all over the window in front of me.

How does the water supply work? I have no idea. You turn the tap on, and water comes out, but where does it come from? The water is treated, so there must be treatment places where they add chemicals. There was something in the news years ago about water companies adding fluoride to the supply, but I don't remember why that was a bad thing.

How easy would it be to infect the water supply?

I stare at the remaining contents of the glass; the water looks normal. It's clear, and there is no noxious smell or odour. I didn't taste anything foul when I first drank it, but the thought is there now.

Maybe if I boiled the water, that would make it safe.

What would Ray Mears do? He would use earwax and moss and make a slingshot from cow turds before building a tree house city and living like a demigod.

I wonder what Ray Mears is doing now? Has he survived? It would be ironic if the television survival experts were all infected, roaming around Welsh valleys, biting sheep.

The water I spat out is dripping down from the window, but at least it's still light outside. I check my watch. It's 9 p.m. I slept for hours. It must have been midday or maybe 1 p.m. when I finally laid down on the sofa. My parents should have been back hours ago.

Where are they?

They said to stay here and wait, but that was hours ago. It would only have taken them an hour, at the most, to get to Boroughfare and back.

I think back to the massive crowd of infected in Boroughfare town centre. If my parents had driven anywhere near that place, they could easily have become overwhelmed. I hope that my dad would have had the sense to avoid going through there.

I should wait here, but if they are not back by now, then something must have happened. I head into the dining room and write a note, telling my parents that I waited until 9 p.m., and that I am going to check Boroughfare; then I will come back here. I tell them to lock up and stay safe.

Heading towards the door, and another thought strikes me. Rushing back, and I add a quick PS to the note.

Don't drink the water! Boil it first. Think like Ray Mears!

My bag is still in the Micra, but I did bring the bat inside with me. The end of which is filthy, with crusted blood and bits of dried gore. I go back to the kitchen and start running it under the tap. What am I doing? Who cares if the bat is dirty? I start towards the front door, then stop, and go back to the kitchen and out into the garden to look for any other weapons I could use. I don't want to use knives as their range is too short. Unless I could find a sword, but swords aren't exactly a household item.

Nothing obvious in the garden apart from a wooden bench and a clothesline, neither of which would make particularly good weapons. Unless you're Ray Mears, of course.

I open the back door to the garage and step in, knowing my dad has loads of tools all hung up in properly marked slots. Everything neat and tidy, and I stand for a minute, eyeing them in turn.

The shears look good, but again, the range is too short. I want something long to keep them away. A garden fork? Ah, but they'd get stuck on the prongs. A metal spade? No, it lacks the striking power. Then I see an axe hanging on the wall, with a plastic cover over the metal end.

I take it from the hook and pull the plastic cover off. It's longer than the bat, and the handle is composite with rubberised, non-slip grippy bits. The blade looks sharp too. Not sharp enough to cut my finger when I press gently, but I can imagine the damage that it could do. The other side of the metal head is squared off – a perfect blunt instrument.

I should ditch the bat, but it has proven to be a very good weapon. Maybe I could use both.

I potter out to the garden and start practising swinging the bat and axe at the same time like a heroic Chuck Norris. Mind you, he's old now. Maybe more like that Paco Maguire from all the action movies. Yeah, that's more like it, all rugged and muscly, and handsome, swinging a bat and axe about while fending off imaginary zombie things. Darting this way and that. An attack from the side. I take them down, then spin to kill the ones trying to bite my bum. A damsel in distress waiting over yonder, all quivering with heaving bosoms. Which just makes me think of the woman from the car accident suffocating me with her breasts, and I lose focus and smash the bat and axe together, jarring my arms so hard I drop both and instantly feel stupid while in my head, the damsel in distress shrugs, calls me a twat, and walks off.

I leave the bat in the hallway by the front door and step outside to see some bastard has taken the Micra. The fucking apocalypse is here, and some shit steals the crappiest car possible.

I do look up and down, in case it rolled away, or I left it further up, but nope, definitely not here. I end up doing that thing that everyone does in these situations and standing there for a few minutes, looking all around in case it should magically reappear.

Walking out of the estate, and I notice that the driveways of the other houses are now all empty. Most of these had cars on them when I got here earlier. That explains why someone stooped so low as to steal a Nissan Micra instead of a nice BMW or Mercedes.

It takes me several minutes to get down onto the main road, where I aim towards the shop, hoping there will be something I can use. It's still light, but that won't last more than an hour or so.

The shop comes into view, and I can see my Micra looking small against BMWs, Mercedes, and Range Rovers from the posh retirement estate.

As I'm trying the handle of the Micra, a man steps out from the shop, which makes me stare guiltily like I'm trying to steal his car while pondering the fact that I stole it in the first place.

'Can I help you?' he asks in a polite but firm voice. An older man in his fifties with dark hair, greying and swept back.

'Hi, this is my car,' I point at the Micra.

'Oh, I see. Well, I'm sure there must be some misunderstanding.'

More men come out from the shop, with a collection of weapons held in their hands: knives, bats, metal poles; then another guy walks out wider, with a double-barrelled shotgun resting across the crook of his arms, with a deliberate act to show me he's armed.

The group try to look menacing, with stern faces, but they're all overweight, retired accountants and bankers with greying hair and wearing a collection of golfing trousers.

'What's going on? Why are you all here?' I keep my tone polite.

'Ah, well, you see,' the man who came out first says, 'there's food here. Food and supplies, and well, we thought we would take care of it and keep it secure, if you like. Until the authorities can get a grip on this, er … situation.' He pauses. 'Of course, you are welcome to join us.'

'Thank you. I appreciate that, but I'm heading to Boroughfare…'

A deep voice from the back rumbles out, 'Boroughfare's gone, mate …'

'Yeah, I know. I was there at the time. May I ask what happened to the family that owns this shop? A woman and her two children?'

'Ah, I see, yes… No sign of them, I'm afraid. We came down from the estate a few hours ago. Well, the ones that are left did anyway. We got together and decided to make our base here because there's plenty of supplies, and it's on the main road…and er…and all that.' He speaks with a clipped, almost military manner, nodding while he talks.

'Okay, they must have gone, then. Did you see a note? They said they would leave a note saying where they were going.'

'Ah, yes, there is a note, but not in English, you see. None of us could, er… Well, we couldn't read it.'

'That makes sense,' I nod back at the group. 'Did any of you hear the radio message about the forts?'

Looks pass between them, a sudden interest, and I can see they are all looking at me keenly. Some of the men from the back move closer.

'The Forts? What forts are those? We haven't heard any radio message. Was it an emergency broadcast? We've been scanning the medium and long wave frequencies but not heard a thing.'

I relay the message I heard on the radio saying that London is gone, and people should head to the Palmerston Forts.

'Ah, I see. Right, well, there we go, eh, chaps? the British Government has a plan. Did they say which fort precisely?'

'No, just that. The Micra had it on the radio earlier. Didn't the person who stole…er…who took it hear the message?'

He starts looking at the men gathered around him. 'Who brought the Micra? Nigel, was it you? No, must have been Malcolm, then. His car was in the garage for a service. Malcolm, where are you?'

Another man pushes through the crowd – thin build, glasses, and floppy, blond hair. He looks sheepish. 'Sorry about your car,' he says. 'I thought it had been abandoned.'

Yeah, from right outside my house. Well, my parents' house. Anyway. 'That's okay, mate. Did you hear the message on the radio?'

'No, but I only drove it here.'

'It might still be on. Have you got the keys?'

'There are survivors. You are not alone. Do not come to London. We are completely infested. I repeat, DO NOT COME TO LONDON. If you are in the south, then we advise you head to the Victorian Forts on the south coast. Take whatever supplies you can carry: water, food, medicine, and clothing. Stay out of the cities and towns.
Head to the forts on the coast.'

I TURN the volume up loud as the men gather closer round the front of the car, and then more come out of the shop, women and children. People shouting for everyone to shush and be quiet. One of the men leans in to look at the front of the radio, at the FM frequency setting and rushes back into the shop as they all start talking and moving about quickly. A sudden need for action, and the hope of a safe place to go.

'Ah, now hang on, chaps, hang on a minute. We need to organise ourselves and gather supplies, plan our route, and travel in a convoy,' the spokesman is shouting as they rush off.

They disperse, heading back into the shop, and I'm instantly forgotten. It's just me, the Micra, and the keys in my hand.

I drop the axe into the passenger side. My bag is gone, but at least I have the car. I start the engine and reverse out onto the main road. Pulling away, I see the spokesman stop and wave an arm briefly as I speed off down the road.

CHAPTER NINE

On the same motorway as earlier, and within a short time, I see the wreck and the two bodies lying by the mangled car. I keep my speed up and get past quickly.

Habit of hand kicks in, and I put the indicator on at the three-hundred-yard sign and take the junction that heads into my town.

I come off the motorway, trying to think of my route. I need to get to my place but avoid the town centre. I hope that Dad would have thought this too and taken the longer route. With any luck, I'll be following in his wake.

I skirt around the town and drive towards my flat through suburban streets, seeing signs of devastation everywhere. Abandoned cars with doors open, glass on the road, front doors hanging open, and windows smashed. What shocks me the most is just how much blood there is. Smeared over car doors, splattered against windows, and in some places, just pooled in puddles. I spot a trail of it leading down a garden path.

Movement ahead of me, and I ease the speed off as a child shuffles into view wearing teddy bear pyjamas, and my blood runs cold at the sight. At the blood on his tiny limbs and smeared over his face. Then he turns to look at me; his head lolling about, and his eyes as red and bloodshot as all the others I've seen. It's just bloody grim, and I swallow the urge to cry right now. To burst into tears at the sight of a kid in teddy bear pyjamas. At the awful fear he must have felt when it was happening. Does he feel anything now? Is there any part of his mind left? Do they even feel pain? I think back to setting the shop on fire yesterday, and how they all stood there and let the flames burn them, showing no reaction as to their plight.

It's too awful to think about, and the kid is too awful to see, so I keep going and drive on by, staring ahead as I pass while clenching my jaw and wishing, with everything I have, that I could do something to help him.

I get to my road and pull up outside my house. The scene looks surreal, like someone has created a movie set and carefully placed all of my household objects near the dead bodies.

My toaster stands out the most, and something about the image upsets me deeply. Memories of making tea and toast when I got home from working nights, tired and looking forward to sleep, and this time, I can't stop the tears streaming down my face. I know in truth that the reaction is really from seeing the little boy, but telling myself I'm crying over the toaster somehow makes it okay.

But then it's not okay. Nothing is okay, and nothing will ever be okay again. The safety and comfort of my home is gone. I think of old news reports of faraway places suffering from war or natural disaster, and refugees giving accounts on losing everything, and how they can never go back.

I felt sad for them but no real empathy. How could I? We live like kings, with everything we could ever need or want. I try to push the thoughts away. This isn't the time to dwell now. I can grieve later when my family is safe.

There's no sign of my parents here, and I don't want to go inside and double check. I know they would have seen this devastation and feared the worse, so I try to work out what they would do next.

Their note said that they would go back to their house, but they never arrived. Either they changed their minds, which is unlikely, or something stopped them. The road ahead leads into the town centre – the same route I took last night. If they didn't go back, then they must have gone that way. I have to go and see.

Driving forward slowly, I realise that it's almost dark, and I speed up. I really don't want to be out when it's night.

I get to the T-junction, with the High Street ahead of me. The right leads down to the roundabout and away from the centre, and the left leads into town and the main shopping area, bars, and cafés. The right is clear, but the moped I crashed into the parked car is still there.

I look to where the massive horde was last night, but there is no sign of them. The armoured van is still in the middle of the road, and again, I wonder what happened to the driver.

I turn left and drive towards the van, stopping next to it, and I can only guess that it was just the size of the crowd that prevented him from moving on. He should have turned the other way and lured them away from town.

I start to drive on, but I get a sudden idea, so I stop and take the axe with me. I head over to the van. It's a big, blue, square-looking thing, with some symbols on the side and big writing on the back saying *Police Follow This Van*. I could never work out if that was an instruction to the police, or if they were telling potential robbers that the police were actually following them.

The front doors are locked, and there's no sign of damage to the front of the vehicle. The man climbed out of a roof hatch last night, but the van is too high, and the sides too smooth to climb up.

I get back in the Micra and park it tight alongside the van, but like a dick, I wedge the driver's side tight in and have to clamber over the passenger seat, then up onto the roof of the car, then up onto the van to peer down through the still open hatch.

'Hello?' I pause for an answer but hear nothing, and lean down to look through before lowering down into the van properly. A black swivel chair at a small desk, and one side given over to numbered shelves and compartments; each filled with cloth money bags bulging with cash.

A door leads to the cabin, currently wedged open with a small fire extinguisher, and I spot the keys are still in the ignition.

'Yes,' I mutter my victory and drop into the driver's seat to twist the ignition on, but the van doesn't start, and I notice the flashing icon on the dashboard that tells me why the van stopped.

He ran out of fuel. Simple, really.

When I clamber out, I notice the daylight has almost gone now, and the last few rays are just peeking down the street as the sun gives way to night, and as I look about, I spot the single infected shuffling towards me.

'Fuck me,' I mouth. The guy's huge. At least six-foot four, with muscles bulging out of his forearms, and biceps the size of melons, and the obligatory shaved head, and no neck. Dressed in black too. Black trousers and shirt. He must be a bouncer from one of the local clubs, and I watch as he shuffles along, with his arms hanging limply at his sides and spot the bite wound to the top of his bald head.

Shit, I wouldn't want to meet him on a normal day, never mind now. Thankfully, he's still some distance off. I turn away, intending to get back in the car, when I notice he's stopped to stand completely motionless, with his head raised, as though he's staring at the sky.

I look up, thinking maybe he's seen something, but only the night sky is above us. No other sounds. No anything.

'You alright?' I call out, with a sudden thought that maybe he's not infected after all. He's not lolling his head or anything now. Just standing there, staring up. 'Mate, you okay?' I take a step towards him, frowning in confusion as he opens his mouth and lets out a huge, guttural roar. And instant later, and I hear more of the same thing. Voices roaring out. Some from the left; then more from somewhere behind me. Others to the right. More further away. Some closer. More and more joining in from all directions, and all emitting that deep, terrifying roar, like wolves signalling each other, and it's quite possibly the single most frightening thing I have heard.

The echo rolling about. The awfulness of it. The animalistic sounds so far from being human. There must be hundreds too.

Then it stops, with an absolute cessation of noise, and the silence that follows is truly deafening as the big bouncer drops his head and stares straight at me, then starts shuffling slowly with that same awkward, stiff gait, but within a few strides, he becomes more cohesive and coordinated.

The streetlamps all ping on as I watch. One after the other going down the street, bathing the world in false light, but enabling me to see the transformation on his face as he goes from that slack-jawed look of sublime stupidity to something altogether very different.

Back to what they were last night. Back to the wild, frenzied things. His head still lolls but nowhere as much, and the fear spikes higher inside me as the adrenalin starts dumping, priming me for flight or fight, and there is no bloody way on god's green earth I am fighting that massive thing.

I leg it for the car, launching myself into the passenger side head-first, which is another monumentally stupid thing to do as the car is too small to twist round in properly, especially seeing as I have a massive axe in my hand. The fear rises, with panic setting in, and I twist onto my back, desperately trying to reach the open door, watching as he runs towards me, all six-foot four of angry, wild, saliva-frothing, steroid-pumped, angry zombie with red eyes.

'SHIT!' I get a hand on the door and try to slam it shut, but I'm too slow, and he's through the open gap, driving his head in at me. With a strangled yelp, I get my knees up as his lips pull back, showing two rows of bloodstained teeth.

I kick out, frantically trying to keep him away, but it's like kicking a tree. My feet keep going, cycling back and forth, and the soles of my trainers strike him repeatedly in the face, smashing his nose and jerking his head back, but he keeps coming at me, gnashing his teeth while snarling like an angry dog. Somehow and more by accident than design, I get both feet into him at the same time and use every ounce of strength to kick out with enough force to knock him back onto his arse.

A frantic split-second decision. I don't have the time to scrabble up and close the door, so I look round in desperation and see the keys in the ignition. Reaching out, I grab and twist them, and the blessed, little Micra engine comes to life. I twist again and stretch down to push the accelerator with my hand, but it's not in gear, and the bloody thing just revs but doesn't go anywhere.

Multitasking has never been my strongest skill, and it certainly isn't now, and it gets decidedly worse when the bouncer lunges back in for round two while I'm on my back, trying to get a car in gear, which won't happen unless the clutch is pushed down. 'Fuck off,' I shout out, battering him away with my feet again while reaching to push the clutch down at the same time as frantically jabbing the stick into first gear. The bouncer's nose breaks with a nasty crunch, and blood spurts out, spraying the inside of the windscreen and sending hot spatters over my face. Grunts and growls, hisses, and muttered, angry curses is all we manage as I kick and kick. My stomach muscles screaming in agony while the poor car grinds the gears as I heave to get the clutch down.

'FUCK IT! JUST FUCK OFF,' I scream in part frustration, part anger, and a whole lot of fear. Cycling my feet again and creating an equal force that just about holds him at bay, but my thighs and stomach are searing in agony. A burst of panic. A rush of fear, and in that second, I get enough cohesion and strength to finally get the clutch down and the car in gear, but that only creates another problem because if I lift the clutch too quickly, then the car will stall.

Another frantic twist as I scream out and wedge myself head down into the footwell, and get my hands to the pedals – one on the accelerator and one on the clutch, revving hard while feeling the bouncer's body weight slowly getting further into the car, crushing my legs as he thrashes to bite, rocking the car on its suspension.

I lift my hand from the clutch, and the engine bites, but there is no motion. The fucking handbrake. The fucking stupid handbrake. 'FUCK!' I bellow out, furious that I will die here like this and start clawing away, trying to find it. Then my hands grip the end, and I push the little button in and feel it drop. The car shoots forward, scraping along the side of the armoured van, but the huge bouncer comes with us, still thrashing and still gnashing. I kick with everything I have, bucking and heaving as the car speeds up. My head in the footwell. Everything a blur. Everything crazed and wild.

Then he's gone. Falling away, and the removal of his weight gives me a second of relief while I hope to hell I don't crash the car.

I try to raise my head, but I can't stretch high enough, so I wait a few seconds and then pull my hand away. The car splutters, and the engine dies; then it stops. I twist round and look out. I am inches away from a bench, aiming straight at the building line on the right.

I pull myself into the driver's seat, dragging the axe from underneath me and pushing it into the passenger side. My stomach muscles are in agony, and my thighs are burning. My chest heaves as I try to suck in air. I twist the key off and back on, putting my foot down on the clutch, and I look in the rear-view mirror to see the bouncer is already up and running at me, and only a few metres away.

I push the gear stick into reverse and thrust the accelerator down as I twist my torso in order to see out of the back. The car gathers speed as the bouncer runs at me, and we collide with a massive bang as he comes headfirst through the back window, showering me in glass, and still he gnashes, snapping his mouth open and closed. I anchor the brakes on so hard he flies back out and thumps bodily down onto the road.

Absolute terror grips me, but something else too – that rage I had yesterday. That searing, burning anger that makes me grab the axe and rush from the car to see him already sitting up. His face all ripped up from grazing along the road. Blood everywhere. One of his legs broken and poking out at an angle, but before I can think, I'm there and swinging the axe down into his head, sending the blade deep into his brain, splitting his cranium open, which bursts the grey matter out like the yolk from a boiled egg.

I pull the axe back, and he slumps over to the side, but the anger is coursing through me. So I chop his bald head off, and in my wild, righteous victory, I kick it hard, sending it rolling away as pain explodes in my big toe.

'Cunt! You fucking cunt! That fucking hurt...' I hop about, cursing and muttering as another infected man comes staggering at me from the left, with another one right behind him. Only a few paces away, and I have just enough time to lift the axe up, step backwards, and strike out. I aim for the head but miss, and strike his neck, splitting it open and sending him away from me; blood pouring out of the wound.

No time to change position. The next one is already charging in, so I swing the axe backwards and use the blunt end to crush his skull. He goes down from the blow, and I hit down at him, pulverising his head.

There are more coming. The noise and action must be drawing them in. I get back into the car and drive on, squinting through the fractured and filthy windscreen.

Ahead of me is the narrow, older part of the High Street now blocked off by a large metal drop barrier used during the evenings to stop vehicles going in, making it pedestrian only.

The barrier is down, giving me no choice but to turn right, and as I gain the view, I finally see where all of the infected from earlier went. Hundreds of them and not that far away either. There's less street lighting down there too, which gives them a massed, dark, shadowy look that sends shivers up my spine.

There's no way I can get through them in the Micra. Maybe a tank would do it, but not this thing.

Twisting round in the street, and there's more behind me running up the street. At least five or six. Fuck it. No way back and no right turn. The only option is through the precinct.

Out of the car, axe in hand, and I start running, keeping to the middle of the road. The shops and cafes are all closed, and doors and windows are barred and bolted, secured against a weekly invasion of drunken youths.

To my right is one of the bars. The outside seating area looks like a riot has taken place – chairs and tables thrown all over the place, and massive stains of blood just about everywhere. Bodies too. Corpses that lie still in all manner of gruesome positions.

The bar has a large, open frontage, and the doors are pushed back, with no way of quickly securing them.

Glancing back, I see that some of the infected chasing me have reached the precinct, and I watch in second of surreal awe as one of them runs into the barrier so hard he somersaults over and lands in a heap. Doesn't stop him though, and he's back up, running with his zombie mates.

Then the massive horde are pouring from the corner. More of them run into the barrier that's now pushed forward by the relentless surge.

I can run faster than them, but for how long? Something tells me this lot will never get tired or have to worry about warming up properly or pulling muscles.

'FUCK!' I scream in frustration at the sight of more coming towards me from ahead, trapping me in the bloody precinct.

Spinning round and round, I search for any way out. Then I see it – a set of old double doors. Huge, Victorian, ornate things, and one of them is open, with warm, orange light spilling out onto the street.

That's my only option, so I take it, charging across the street as I run through, over, and round the metal chairs scattered everywhere.

Heaving for breath, I get inside and slam the door closed behind me. Finding big, sturdy bolts on the inside of the door and even bigger, sturdier metal bar that I ram into place before gasping for air as the infected hit the other side.

CHAPTER TEN

I bend over to get my breath, panting heavily from the exertion of running flat out, and notice I'm in a small hallway at the bottom of a flight of wooden stairs covered in a deep red, luxurious carpet. Red coloured walls too and soft lighting overhead.

Without any idea what this place is, I start heading up the stairs, reaching a small landing with a desk like a reception. A set of double doors to the left, thick ones too like fire doors and painted gloss black.

I try to use my foot to push one open a little, with my axe ready to hit out at anything that appears, but the door is too heavy. I push harder and have to step forward as I do so. The door yields and slowly opens.

The sound of disco music drifts out, getting louder as I push open the door. I pause for a second, trying to peer through as the gap widens, and I slowly get a view of the inside and look about, taking it all in, totally stunned.

A large, dark room filled with chairs and tables, and a bar running down the right side, with discreet back-lighting and glass shelves filled with bottles of spirits – each one with old-fashioned metal pouring spouts stuck in the top. A catwalk in the middle, jutting out from a stage, and two shiny metal poles sparkling in the low light as disco music beats on, like the soundtrack from a retro porn movie. Flashing, red lights on the stage, and spotlights shining down on the catwalk.

The whole thing is amazing. I had no idea this place was here, but the most stunning thing is the woman on the stage wearing just a thong, with some kind of collar fastened round her neck, secured to a chain that stretches out behind her through the curtains. She's one of them, one of the infected things. Right there in front of me. A bloody topless zombie woman leashed to a pole dancing stage.

She's obviously seen me judging from the way she's straining forward, pulling against the collar, with frantic, little lunges, twanging the chain each time she pulls forward, but the weirdest thing are her enormous, fake breasts that remain motionless despite her hard tugs against the collar and chain.

'What the fuck ...?'

I step in and close the door. Stunned to the core and still breathing hard from the fight and running. Sweat dripping down my face as I take it all in. The collar's nearly as thick as her neck, and the chain looks solid too. I've never been to a lap dancing place or a strip club before, so I don't know if this is normal.

It looks expensive, and the seats all look new and very plush. I look about, spotting a DV booth at the back and a man lying on the dance-floor, slumped, with his back against the booth.

He looks dead, like proper dead. A dark suit, with a white shirt underneath, and he looks very smart. Apart from the knife handle poking out of his chest, that is.

I kick one of his feet gently and jump back, ready to react. Nothing. I kick again a bit harder, still nothing.

Using the axe, I nudge his shoulder. He slumps over onto his side, but there's still no signs of life. Grimacing, I lean in and gently touch the side of his neck as I feel for a pulse. Not finding one, I lift one of his eyelids and see the eyes are lifeless and pale, but thankfully not red, and bloodshot. His skin is cold too, like he's been dead for a while.

This is the first real dead body I've seen, and it feels weird. It's not one of those things out there or like that woman on the stage, but a real person. I even chopped a bloke's head off a few minutes ago, but this just feels different. A proper dead body, a murder victim.

How senseless is that? The whole world is collapsing, and someone still has time to commit a murder.

The thought brings me back to my senses. What if the killer is still here? I spin around, half expecting someone to be standing behind me with another knife, but there's just me and stripper lady. Which makes me think someone put her into that neck collar, but then I guess if this is some kind of kinky place, then maybe she had it on already.

I move away from the dead man and walk towards the bar to check behind it. Nothing there. All clear.

There's no sign of disturbance in the club either. All the tables and chairs are tidy, and the bar top is clear and clean.

As I look about, my eyes come back to the stripper lady tracking me as I walk about, straining against her collar and chain, and as I walk down the side of the catwalk, so she follows me. Her breath coming in strained hisses, blasting in and out but barely heard under the retro porn music twanging away.

She's very pretty, but with harsh, garish make-up on her eyes, and peroxide blond hair hanging down to her shoulders. She's very slim too, which just makes those enormous boobs look even bigger. I can't see any injury on her; maybe it's on her back.

I edge closer, watching her. She looks almost normal. The disco lights hide her red eyes. I can't hear the growls or snarls she must be making either, and from all those things I see beyond the beast to the woman inside. Is the woman still inside? Is there any shred of her mind still intact? She looks so normal, and I can't help but reach out to touch her outstretched hand, expecting it to feel cold or like what I'd think a dead person should feel like. But it's not at all. Her skin has warmth and is soft and pliable.

Then two things happen at the same time.

First, she animates a second after I touch her and makes a desperate lunge to get at me as those hands I touched become rigid like talons.

Which is also when a door in the corner of the room slams open, flooding the area with bright, white light and a man walks in, pulling his fly up, which makes me flinch and spin while my hand is still stretched out and I accidentally slap one of her big boobs. Which isn't soft and pliable at all but rock hard. Like a rock.

The man stops and we stare at each other in silence as I slowly drop my arms down to my side while hoping he didn't see me slap the dead stripper's boob.

'Did you just slap her boob?'

Bollocks. 'I. Well. I was seeing if she was okay...' I try to force a natural tone, but I just sound stupid.

'You were seeing if she was okay? Well, is she?' he asks, with a twitch of a smile at the corner of his mouth.

'Nooo... I don't think she is.'

He shakes his head and walks further into the room. 'Relax, mate. But hey, they are fucking great, aren't they?'

'What are?'

'The tits. The big, fake tits you were slapping. I should know. I fucking paid for them.'

He stops at the other side of the catwalk. Dark suit, white shirt, dark tie. He plucks at the shirt cuffs under the jacket sleeves, pulling them straight and giving me a glimpse of gold-coloured cufflinks. He looks like a London gangster from the movies, with dark hair slicked back and designer stubble. He smiles at me, charming and nice, yet there's an aura about him, a threatening undertone. It is in his swagger and the sharp movements of his hands. He looks straight at me, holding eye contact. 'So... What do you think?'

'Er, yeah... They look great, really nice.' I nod like I'm talking about a new car.

A look of anger flashes across his face. 'So you *were* looking at her fucking tits, then?' He stares at me, unblinking.

'No! I was...'

'Take it easy, mate. I'm only messing with you,' he says with a sudden switch. 'She's a fucking stripper. She wants you to look at her.'

Alarm bells are ringing in my head. There is a dead man lying, with a knife buried in his chest just a few yards behind me, an infected stripper tied to a chain on a lap dancing stage, and this bloke is trying to joke around.

I want to ask him about the dead man, but for some reason, the thought of mentioning it scares me. I feel awkward. He is staring straight at me, and I can't think of anything to say.

He moves over to the end of the bar and pours a large shot of something into a glass.

'Do you want a drink, mate?'

'No, I'm fine, thank you.'

'Have a drink with me.' A command, not a request.

'Just a coke then. Please...'

He freezes, holding the bottle a few inches from the bar top. The look of anger flashes briefly across his face again.

'Okay, coke it is.'

He takes a glass bottle of Coca-Cola from a fridge and pops the lid off, then places a small, black napkin on the bar, and finally the bottle on the napkin. 'So, what's it like out there?' he asks, straight back to being calm and natural, like any bartender making conversation.

'Awful, really awful. I got trapped and ran through the precinct, but I got in here and locked the door with that metal bar.'

His mouth turns down at the edges while he nods. 'Good work... Quick thinking under pressure. You've got good nerves and an eye for the ladies too. I could use a man like you here. You working?'

What the fuck? 'Er, yeah. I...I have a job.'

'Oh, shame. Well, have a think about it and let me know. I'm Marcus, by the way.' He extends his hand over the bar.

I don't want to shake his hand. I really don't want to get that close, but I move forward anyway, too worried of the consequences.

I swap the axe to my left hand and lean forward with my right. His grip is very firm, and he squeezes my hand.

'I'm Howie.'

'Nice axe, Howie.'

'Yeah, it's, err...a good axe.' I heft the thing up and down as though we are talking about a tennis racquet.

'You've used it, then?' a casual question, but he looks at the bloodstains on the metal head as a fresh look of anger flashes across his face. 'I hope you ain't dripped blood up my fucking stairs. Do you know how much it fucking costs to get blood out of that carpet? I'll tell you – it costs a bloody arm and a leg. I know cos I have to get it fucking cleaned every week. I keep telling those gorillas not to bleed 'em on the fucking stairs.'

The darkness stays on his face a few seconds more as he lifts the glass and takes a large gulp, and his fingers are white as he grips the glass.

'Anyway, Howie, drink your *coke* before it gets warm. You must be thirsty after all that running about.' Straight back to calm like Jekyll and Hyde.

I take the bottle and drink some of the liquid. Despite the circumstances, the drink feels nice and cold, and I down it all.

'Fucking hell, tiger. Take it easy. Here, have another one.'

Marcus puts another bottle on the napkin, and I take it quickly. Too quickly, and he flashes another dark look at me.

'Sorry, I'm really thirsty.'

He shakes his head, shrugs nonchalantly, and pulls out a bag of white powder from the inside pocket of his jacket, and empties a small amount on the bar top, then takes something black out of his pocket. A long, thin blade shoots out of the black thing, and he uses it to chop at the powder, creating a thin line. He leans down and pushes a finger into the side of his nose, then snorts the line before repeating the action with the other side as I watch on, completely absorbed. Then he stands upright and blinks a few times before smiling at me.

'Do you want some, Howie?'

'No, thanks.'

'Suit yourself, Howie.'

I can't help but wonder how she got into the collar. Who bit her? Why did that man get stabbed? More than anything, though, I know that I should leave. Quickly. The way he keeps saying my name is freaking me out. 'Is there another way out of here?' I ask politely.

He wipes at his nose again with the back of his hand; then his fingertips flick at the nostrils.

'Course there fucking is, Howie. Do you think the health and safety lot would let me open without having another exit? Fucking wankers. They're always in here, getting a free eyeful of the birds in the dressing room.' He pauses for a few seconds, looking at me. 'It's out the back... But you don't want to go yet, do you, Howie?'

Barbed question.

'I'm sorry, but I've really got to go.'

He stands, nodding for a few seconds, staring at me as his mouth slowly purses.

'Well, I think that's fucking rude, Howie. Giselle is on stage, and you've had a grope of her tits and taken advantage of my good nature, with free drinks, and now you want to go? That's not very nice, is it?' He walks slowly towards the gap in the bar, wiping his nose, adjusting his tie and cufflinks all with small, quick movements of his hands. 'You see what happened to the last cunt who tried to take advantage of me, Howie?' He motions to the dead man. 'He tried to take the piss too. Won't do that again, will he, Howie?'

'Look, mate, I don't want any trouble. I'm just trying to find my parents and get out of here. It was very kind of you to give me the drinks.'

'No, no, no, Howie. You don't just take a free drink. There ain't no such thing as *free* in this world, Howie. You always have to pay.' As he steps through the hatch, I start moving backwards, away from him. 'Nothing is free, Howie. Now you've had a look at the girl in my club, which I paid for, had a grope of her fucking tits, which I paid for, and had a drink, which I paid for.'

'Please, Marcus, I just want to leave.'

'You ain't fucking leaving, Howie,' he snorts with laughter. 'Not until you understand that nothing is for free.'

'Okay, what do you want? I don't have any money.'

He walks towards me and casually picks the knife up from the bar, holding it down at his side while he stares directly into my eyes.

'Mate, what are you doing? Please just let me go.'

'Howie, Howie, it's not that I don't want to let you go. It's that I *can't*. If I let you go, everyone will say that Marcus is a soft touch, that he's fucking lost it. Respect, Howie, you got to have respect. You understand that, don't you?'

'Marcus, you don't have to kill me. The whole world has gone mad. I've just been chased by... By those things, for god's sake. Please, just let me go. I won't ...'

'You won't what? What won't you do, Howie? Call the police?' He starts laughing. 'I don't think they'll help you now, Howie. It's just me and you, and our little debt.'

'Debt? What do you want, then?'

He stops, with a slight smile forming on his mouth. 'Well, Howie, seeing as you groped her tits, I think you should say sorry. Giselle was always moaning that the punters were fucking rude, trying to get free gropes.'

'Okay, I'm very sorry. I really didn't mean to cause any offence, and I apologise.'

He shakes his head. 'I don't think that will be enough, Howie. You will have to apologise to *her*,' he motions towards the stage with the knife.

Turning round, I make a point of looking at Giselle, still pulling against the neck collar.

'I'm really sorry, Giselle. I hope I didn't offend you. Please accept my apologies.'

After years of practise of calming down irate and angry customers in the supermarket, I surprise myself, with how sincere I sound.

He looks at Giselle, then back at me. 'Hmmm, good apology, Howie. But you know what will really say sorry and show Giselle that you mean it?' His voice is very low.

'What?' The hairs on the back of my neck are standing up.

'A kiss, Howie. A nice kiss to say sorry always works with women. They fucking love it. Tell you what, Howie. Seeing as its quiet in here tonight, when you're giving her a kiss, you can have another feel of her tits. How about that? A free grope.'

'No, no, I don't think that's right.'

'Oh, you don't think that's right? Who the fuck are you? Trying to stick your fucking dick in her mouth, weren't you? You fucking pervert! Now it's fucking wrong, is it? I say what's fucking right and wrong in my fucking club, not you.'

I lift the axe a little, just a slight raise. More to reassure myself that I'm still holding it, and a maniacal grin spreads on his face as he spots the movement.

'Oh, now, Howie... Howie, there's no need for that. Just go and give Giselle a little kiss and you can go.'

'No, mate. No way.'

'Give Giselle A FUCKING KISS.'

'No.'

He walks towards me, the knife steady in his right hand. The other hand wipes at his nose, then checks his tie, smoothing down the front of his shirt and jacket. He walks around the edge of the catwalk. I start moving backwards but only have a short distance before I'm trapped by the stage, and Giselle straining at her leash.

'Where you gonna go, Howie? The exit is the other side of the stage.'

Giselle tracks his movement as he walks round the edge of the catwalk towards me. Her upper body leaning forward, straining against the collar.

'Look at you backing away like a pussy. Big fucking man a minute ago when you were alone with Giselle, weren't you? Now look at you.'

'What? Mate, please...'

'Please what? You fucking pussy.' The mocking morphs into a snarl as that dark look flashes across his face again.

My right hand brushes against the back of a chair as the images of the last twenty-four hours whirl through my mind. Breathing harder now, heart hammering in my chest, and I look down at the blood and gore on the metal axe head. 'About twelve...' I say, looking back up at him as he blinks, with a glance of confusion.

'Twelve what?'

'First one with a hammer, then two with my feet. I tried saving her but... Then a few with a baseball bat. I also set some on fire and burnt a village down...' I take hold of the back of the chair and start walking towards him, dragging the chair behind me. 'The first one with the axe was huge. I chopped his head off; then some more after that. So I reckon, Marcus, that I have killed about twelve of them since last night, and I run in here to find shelter and meet a fucking psycho instead, so you know what you can do, Marcus? You can FUCK OFF.'

I launch the chair at him, swinging my arm from behind me with all of my strength. It would never really hurt him, but his reaction is to step back and laugh just as Giselle drops down and sinks her teeth into the top of his head; her hands clawing at his cheeks. She bites down hard too, with blood spurting out and pouring down his face.

He screams and lashes out. The knife still in his hand, and he keeps stabbing the blade at her shoulders. She gets cut again and again but keeps going. He sinks down, slashing at her hands on his face, cutting his own skin, with the desperate effort to get her off. His legs buckle, and he drops down as Giselle tears a chunk of scalp with a horrible, wet ripping sound, leaving him writhing in agony, clutching the top of his bloodied head while Giselle strains forward, with a chunk of hairy scalp hanging from her mouth.

Giving them both a wide berth, I run around the side of the catwalk, looking for the exit. The toilet door is there, but nothing else. It must be through the stage.

I climb up and push through the curtain. The back area is dark and dimly lit by red bulbs. Not giving my eyes enough time to adjust to the gloom, I go blundering through and trip over a big box, sprawling onto the stage floor surrounded by feather boas, thongs, chains, whips, and bottles of pressurised whipped cream.

Lifting my hand up, I stare in wonder at the set of glittery handcuffs and look down to see another one of the neck collars, with a chain attached. Moving quickly, I head back out to the front, attaching a leather strap at the end of the chain to one of the shiny metal poles on the stage.

Giselle is still trying to reach down to Marcus writhing about on the floor in front of her; his wails of pain sounding easily above the disco porn music. From this view, I can see where she was bitten – right on her once perfect backside, with a huge chunk of flesh torn away.

Once I am at Marcus' side, I put one end of the handcuffs through the chain and close the loop. I then lean down and grab at Marcus' wrist, attaching the handcuff and locking it securely on him before jumping back as he surges up to attack me.

'YOU CUNT,' he screams; his face covered in blood.

I move backwards away from him as he comes at me. The handcuffs pull the chain, which goes taut from being secured to the pole, and he is jerked back off his feet, screaming as he starts clutching at the manacle on his wrist. 'No! Fuck! NO!'

He keeps pulling, then starts tugging at the chain. He follows the line and sees it is secured to the pole but only with a leather strap. 'I'll cut you up, you little fucking runt,' he growls as he starts towards the edge of the stage, but Giselle lunges at him again, driving him back. With his back turned, I rush forward and grab the fallen knife from the ground.

'Looks like you're stuck, mate.'

He spins round to me. His face immediately changing as the fury ebbs away. 'Please, I was only joking. I wouldn't have done anything to you. Come on, Howie. Please let me go.' He grimaces in pain, rubbing his hand on his stomach.

I lift the hatch and nip behind the bar, and after finding a clean glass, pour a large shot from the bottle he used a few minutes ago. 'Have a drink with me, Marcus? No? Okay, suit yourself.' I gulp it down in one mouthful, but the fiery liquid burns my throat and makes me cough and spit it out over the bar.

Cool, very cool.

'Howie, come on, mate,' he pleads. 'Let me go, eh? Eh, mate? You wouldn't leave me like this, would you? YOU FUCKING CUNT, I'LL SLICE YOU INTO BITS AND FUCKING FEED YOU TO HER!' He switches between sobbing and wild fury as the cocaine and adrenalin pulse through his body. Constantly working at the handcuff, as though he can slip his wrist through, then pulling at the chain. He finally stops pulling and touches the top of his head. His hand comes away bloody, which he stares at, looking confused, and then grimaces again, and bends over from obvious pain in his stomach. 'Jesus, that fucking hurts!' he gasps and pulls the cocaine from his jacket, shaking and trembling as he fumbles to get it open but drops it on the floor; the white powder bursting out over the carpet. He drops down and snorts his nose against the floor, snuffling about like a hungry pig.

'Howie, you can't leave me like this. I'll die,' he begs, on his knees, one arm wrapped around his stomach, and his face covered in white power turning pink from the blood pouring down his face. 'Fucking hell, not like this... NOT LIKE THIS!' he shouts into the air before attacking the handcuff with his free hand, ramming his arm back again and again, which drives the metal edge deep into the flesh on his wrist, cutting him open. More blood pumps out, but he doesn't stop. If anything, it drives him on to tug and yank with all his might.

He stops instantly. Going completely still, he stares at me with wide eyes before grabbing at his stomach and bending double. Edging forward, I watch him sink to the floor, clutching his mid-section as he screams in agony. The pain seems to intensify as he screams louder and then trails off, breathing in hard, shallow pants.

Then he's gone. Dead. Completely still, and there's no doubt about it – he just died. Not breathing, not moving, nothing. Shit, I did that. I caused him to die. Was it from the bite or the cocaine, or too much blood loss?

Rocking back, I cast about in shock until movement catches my eye. He twitches, his limbs spasm, and the twitches increase, as though an electric current is being put through him. He doesn't scream or cry out, but just spasms for a few seconds until he sits up in one smooth movement, turning his head to stare at me through red, bloodshot eyes and drool already coming out of his mouth as he tries to stand up with jerky, spasmodic movements.

Giselle has already lost interest in him and has turned to face me. Both of them drooling and groaning quietly, but thankfully, both of them are chained up.

CHAPTER ELEVEN

The exit is through the back of the stage, a rear door that leads out onto a set of concrete steps going down to the ground floor.

Doors at the bottom of the stairs leading left and right, and what must be the street door ahead of me. A red fire extinguisher is hooked on the wall. The street door is solid wood, and I have no view of what's on the other side.

I've lost my bearings and can't work out if the door opens onto the High Street. It must do. How far up am I from the entrance to the club?

No, it opens out to the rear of the club. I went in the main entrance and turned left into the club, then out the stage door, and turned right down the stairs. It must be the rear.

So these other doors must lead into the shops on the High Street. I can't remember what shops are in this area. There must be windows in the shops. I would be able to see out to the front and maybe the rear and then work out the safest escape route.

If I open the street door and the infected are there, I might not be able to close it again. I try the doors that must lead into the shops, but they're locked. They don't look that formidable, so I try to push against one of them. It yields slightly, so I take a step back and slam my shoulder against the door, just like they do on TV, and bounce straight off, yelping at the pain in my shoulder. Next, I kick at the door, aiming at the middle, where the lock would be. The door holds, but it doesn't feel that strong, and I kick again, harder. The door still holds, but I can feel it starting to buckle. Another two hard kicks, and the door bursts open.

My great plan backfires as I hear a loud and constant beeping sound. The alarm. There's maybe a minute before it starts sounding properly, alerting every one of those things in the area. *Here's Howie. Come and eat him.*

I rush in through a storeroom. Boxes stacked up and clothes rails, with garments hanging off them, but without lights, the place is shadowy and foreboding.

I go through the eerie storeroom to an office area, where I find the alarm panel illuminated on the wall. A standard ten-digit number pad, with buttons marked ENTER and RESET.

Shit. There must be a code. I know most places have them written down somewhere. The high call-out engineer costs for resetting the alarm means they nearly always put it somewhere close so staff that are either half asleep or half drunk from the night before can switch it off.

It's too dark to see anything, and I waste vital seconds looking for the light switch, eventually finding it. I then see a desk with a computer and a yearly planner on the wall, with the staff annual leave marked out. Box files and folders are stacked untidily on shelves, with new till receipt rolls spilling out of them.

I check on the desk, sifting through bits of paper as the constant beeping sound spurs me on, then the desk jotter which is just full of doodles, scribbles, and mobile phone numbers. Opening drawers, I root through calculators, highlighter pens, a stapler, a hole punch, and more crap that all goes flying as I get more frantic.

The countdown is done, and as I reach for the shelves to check along them, the alarm starts wailing properly. A full-on ear-splitting warble that makes me want to shake my head to get the noise away.

In my mind, I can imagine every infected stopping still to slowly turn and listen to the stonking great alarm blaring out.

I stare daggers at the alarm panel, contemplating smashing the fucking thing with my axe. Then I see the six-digit number. Right there on the panel, written in pencil. Shaking my head, I key the numbers in and press ENTER, breathing a sigh of relief when the alarm cuts out.

I go back into the storeroom. A door leads to a toilet, and I find the staff room – just a small kitchen really, with a cheap table and chairs. There is a small worktop, with a sink, a kettle, and an old two-slice toaster. They make these staff rooms unwelcoming to try and put the staff off spending too much time in them. A two-slice toaster so you can only do enough for yourself and not encourage others to loiter.

Something about the kettle and toaster, and the thought of tea and toast sends a pang of sadness through me like being really homesick.

As I turn to leave, a pin-board on the wall catches my eye. The board is full of pictures of young women on nights out. The staff all out for a laugh, pictured in various poses, holding drinks, and pulling faces. They look young and carefree. The images might have been taken just a few days ago. Young people, with their whole lives ahead of them, working together, going out, and drinking, having relationships. Listening to music, discussing what outfits to wear.

Bloody hell, it's all gone now.

That sense of sadness fills me completely, and I suddenly feel very lonely. Maybe it's better to be like Marcus and get smashed out of your face on drugs and alcohol.

Leaving the staff room, I decide to check the rest of the store. If it's safe, I will stay for a little while.

I leave the key in the door in case I need a rapid exit. Finally, I find the door that leads onto the shop floor.

It's very dark. There are rows of clothes hanging from rails against the walls and various standing rails on the floor. The shop looks big, and I can see the brand name *New Look* on every available surface and wall. Of all the shops I could have gone into, I get a ladies' fashion store. Hang on, they do men's clothing as well, don't they?

I move deeper into the store, crouching down to move between the rails until I'm flat on my tummy, poking my head out from under a load of dresses to stare at the large display windows at the front.

Dressed up mannequins adorn the plinth, glittering and looking *just fabulous, darling* under the subdued and expertly fitted lights.

Other than the mannequins, there are shit loads of infected staring in. Nasty, bloodied faces pushing against the glass as they sway and move about. I stay completely still. None of them are actually looking at me or even in my direction.

I decide to wait for a while to see if they will move off, but after a few minutes, the hard floor starts to make me very uncomfortable, and despite the warm summer, it feels quite cold.

Moving backwards on my belly, slithering away out of sight, I stay low until I am sure that the many clothes rails will keep me blocked.

On my way back towards the door of the stock room, I stop at a rail of thick, woollen cardigans. They are women's sizes – size 10 at the front and getting larger as they go back. I have no idea what size I am in women's clothing, so I take one from the back.

I head into the dark staff room and start trying to put the kettle on. The cardigan is so big the sleeves extend well beyond the length of my arms, and the thick collar pretty much swallows my head too. After squabbling about to roll the sleeves up and free my eyes, I get the kettle on and root about until I find a large, chipped mug. Two big teaspoons of sugar, a tea bag, and some milk from the fridge. Opening the fridge, I find a loaf of bread on the middle shelf. Who keeps bread in the fridge? Maybe it's a policy of the store. Rule one of *The New Look Charter*. Section one, subsection two: all bread will be kept in the fridge.

Shaking my head, I finish brewing up and make use of the bread by getting some toast on the go. A couple of minutes later, and I've got a fresh, steaming cup of tea and two slices of lovely toast, which are devoured almost instantly.

It tastes lovely and serves to remind me how hungry I am, so I keep going, toasting more bread, and even finding some marmalade in the fridge.

Sitting back, I feel the first slightest sense of contentment since last night. Bloody hell, this only started last night. It feels like that was weeks ago.

I've already had countless lucky escapes, but I have got to be more careful and think clearly. I have to get back to my parents and see if they have returned, then head for London to find my sister.

Right now though, I can't do anything until the hundreds of infected outside piss off and go somewhere else. I lean forward to rest my head against the thick material of the cardigan.

Better go and check in a few minutes.

Can't stay here too long.

CHAPTER TWELVE

I wake with a start. Wondering where I am. I have that slightly sick feeling that you get when you can't immediately place your surroundings.

I've dribbled on the cardigan as I slept. It looks like a slug has crawled across my sleeve, and I wipe at the wet saliva on my cheek. I really need to pee as the slightly too tight jeans are pressing into my bladder, which is full from all the tea I drank.

Blundering about in the dark, I find the staff toilet and take a long piss, feeling that lovely, relieving sensation as my bladder empties. Even in the gloom, I can see my piss is dark, and I remember the urine colour chart on the wall of the staff toilets in the supermarket. If your urine was too dark, it meant you were dehydrated.

Drink more water and stay healthy.

I need to drink more water. I should prepare my journeys now and plan accordingly. I need another bag to carry water and supplies in, and more weapons – definitely more weapons.

I go back out onto the shop floor and, once again, inch forward until I am in the same spot, peeking out between long dresses. The infected have gone. I can't see any now.

It has just gone 2.30 a.m. I must have dozed off for a couple of hours. I feel better, but my mouth feels furry, and I need to brush my teeth. Again, I chastise myself for not thinking about this before. Washing, eating, and getting water are essential now.

Once satisfied that the front is clear, I move off deeper into the store. The men's section is tiny in comparison to the main area and is sectioned off by high display walls.

I crawl through until I'm completely blocked from view and start looking for something to change into.

I need dark clothing that I can move quickly in. I find some black cargo trousers, with pockets on the sides like combat trousers. These are fashionable, with bits of material hanging off. I find my size and try them on. They have a belt supplied and fit well. I yank off the hanging material strips and loops until they look fairly normal.

My trainers are filthy and covered in dried blood, so next, I head for the shoe section, but they only have thin, plimsoll-type fashion shoes, like those nasty, black things we had to wear for PE at school. There is one pair of boots, but they are high, with big heels and designed to be worn with the sides hanging down. No good.

On to upper garments, and I find a thin, long-sleeved, black top with a hood.

The bags are no good either, just fashionable explorer-type bags with thin straps. Mind you, they'll have to do. I take one and find new boxer shorts and socks, and stuff several pairs of each into the bag. Then I put another top in after pulling off the tags.

Finally, I put a slightly thicker jumper in the bag too before heading back into the staff room to use the small sink to wash my body and change my underwear.

Dressed again, I feel better, cleaner, and more prepared. I'll need sturdier shoes, though. I have had to use my feet several times already to kick and stamp, and these flimsy trainers don't give any protection.

The Tesco supermarket where I work isn't too far away, and I know we sell work boots in our clothes section. Plus, my store is open twenty-four hours, so it would have been open when this started on Friday night, and there's a rear staff door with a keypad entry system. I know the building like the back of my hand, and I should be able to get in and out quickly.

The home delivery vans are parked out the back too, and the keys are in the duty manager's office. It's risky, but it would mean getting decent supplies, a good bag, strong boots, and a big van to drive about in rather than a little Micra.

All I have to do is get out of here and use the side streets to reach it.

The only window facing the rear of the building is in the staff room, and this has frosted glass, with bars on the frame. I go through and open the smaller window first, listening until I am sure there are no sounds. The larger window is sealed shut – probably to prevent staff passing goods to people outside.

I can't hear anything, but the risk is too great. I make my way carefully through the shop floor, moving between the clothes stands until I am a just a few steps away from the front windows.

The streetlights are still on outside, but I can't see any infected in front of the store. There are two lady mannequins on a raised plinth in the window display, and I step up to stand between them.

This gives me a better view of the street. To the left, there is the massive horde milling around the door that I went through some time ago. There must be hundreds of them.

Looking intently at the horde on the left, I fail to see the single male infected staggering past the window from my right until he is inches away, and I stand stock still as he slowly passes by.

The front is out of the question; there are simply too many of them. The second that I exit the store, they will see me, and although I've outrun them so far, I can't take that chance of getting trapped again.

The rear exit is the only choice.

I get to the back and cinch the rucksack straps as tight as they will go, and heft my axe while wondering if I should go slowly or burst out.

I decide on the slower option. I can always try and pull the door shut if one of them comes at me, and it will be a lot quieter as well. I push the metal bar down gently, keeping my movements very slow and controlled. The door is well used and is fairly easy to open. I peer out, alert for the slightest movement.

All clear.

Axe in my left hand, and a firm grip on the door handle with my right, I lean forward.

Still no infected, and I look up and down the small service road running along the back of the shops. Then I take the fire extinguisher and prop the door slightly open. It looks closed, but I know that I can get back in if I need to.

I stay to the side, keeping low and using the cars to cover me. It is much darker here, with no street lighting, and it's not long until I'm away from the shops and back into well-lit suburbia. Rushing along while trying not to make a sound.

After a few minutes, I pass a car in the middle of the road that has crashed into the parked vehicles. The windscreen smashed, and the doors hanging open. I quicken my pace and rush by.

Some of the houses have lights on inside that offer the street a warm, inviting glow, and I want to think of people sitting inside, watching television, and drinking tea instead of having to deal with this horror. I make haste until I reach the end of the junction and stop to stare across the road to the Tesco garage on the other side now all in darkness.

The front door has been smashed in, and I can see packets of items littered on the forecourt. The fuel pumps have an automated system for credit cards at night, and the small shop is closed.

After several minutes of watching for any movement, I go over the road and cross the forecourt, reaching the shadows on the other side without issue.

Over a small wall, and I'm into the supermarket car park – a vast, open space, with plastic-roofed trolley bays dotted about.

There are very few cars here. Just a row of some dozen or so parked in the area that the night staff use.

The main building is ahead of me. Brightly lit like a glowing beacon standing proud in the night, with the massive, red Tesco sign shining on top, but I can't see anyone moving about from this distance.

To the right of the building, there's a very high fence, which runs around the back to the gated entry point for delivery trucks.

I move right and keep to the edge of the car park, skirting round until I reach the high fencing. At the gate, I enter the code, and it buzzes to show that the lock is disengaged.

I push the gate and enter the rear compound, stopping to look about and make sure it is clear before I proceed. The gate has the same keypad on the inside, so there is no need to keep it open for a fast exit.

To my left is the side of the main building, sheer and windowless. There are several home delivery trucks parked to the side in bays, facing towards the gates. A wide, sweeping access road goes around the rear of the building to the delivery bays. There are wooden benches set aside, used by the staff that smoke or those who want to sit outside during their breaks. I can see from here that the staff access door is closed.

Keeping to the far side, I move forward until I get a full view of the back of the store. There is a long Tesco truck backed up to the loading platform and someone moving around in the shadows. Watching quietly, I wait until the figure moves into the moonlit road, and I see that it's an infected male, big built and shuffling along slowly towards the rear staff door.

The lorry in the loading bay means that there will be open doors into the storerooms so the stock can be taken in. I could go that way, but it is a big area. I want to go in the side door so I can get to the security office and use the cameras to look around the store.

There are just as many cameras in the staff and stock rooms as there are on the shop floor. Loss prevention, they call it. But in reality, they just don't trust the staff.

If I want to use that side door, I'll have to deal with him. Keeping low and to the perimeter, I make my way round the side of the building, then start coming back towards the side door from the other direction, sticking to the dark shadows at the side.

I am still at least thirty metres from him when he spins round, suddenly aware of my presence. There is no pause or delay as he starts running at me, gathering speed despite his jerky motion.

I step away from the building so I have space around me, moving left and drawing him out into the open.

He's dressed in blue trousers and a blue polo shirt with the Tesco logo and looks to be in his late forties, with a big gut hanging over the top of his trousers. One half of his face looks torn away. I don't recognise him, but he looks like a truck driver.

I will only get one shot at this before he is on me. I lift the axe and hold it ready just as he gets in range. Then I step to the right and swing at his head. The impact sends him careering off, and he sprawls onto the ground. I move in before he can get up and slam the sharp edge into his brain. There's a sickening crunch and squelch as his skull bursts open, and the soft matter underneath is destroyed.

I pull the axe out and look around me, checking that the noise hasn't drawn anyone else and feeling rather proud of myself. How many is that now? I told Marcus it was about twelve. So including Marcus and this truck driver, I make that about fourteen of the things I've killed. No, hang on. Marcus wasn't one of them; he *turned* into one, but that was after he got killed. Shit, so can I count him or not? Actually, that makes me feel quite bad that I killed a real person. Fair enough, he was waving a knife at me while snorting cocaine, and trying to urge me to shag his zombie stripper girlfriend, but even so.

Shit, get a grip, Howie. Standing here like a fool, adding up your body count. At the staff door, I key the numbered code into the keypad and listen for the buzz and click as the lock releases. Easing the door open, I peer into the gloomy interior, pausing so I can listen for movement.

Inside, I move down the corridor to the security office. The door is closed but not locked. I enter the room and see several monitors on a desk in front of a keyboard and a joystick. Two swivel chairs are in front of the desk.

Bert is sitting in one of the chairs, with his arms hanging down at his sides. Huge pools of blood have formed underneath him, and there is a packing knife in the blood under his right hand, and bizarrely, I notice that even at the point of taking his own life, he still took the time to roll his sleeves smartly above the elbow. I can see old, army-style tattoos on his forearms, faded with time.

He was a very proud man, and in a way, I almost feel glad that he decided to choose his own fate rather than face becoming one of *them*.

The problem now is that in order to get to the monitors, I'm going to have to go through the big pools of blood on the floor.

I walk gently through and go to push the chair out of the way. The chair is not on wheels, though, and pushing it causes my feet to lose grip and slip from under me. I land heavily on my knees in the pool of blood as my head stops inches above Bert's groin. I go to stand up, but the floor is like ice now, and my trainers can't get a grip, so I have to use the chair to lever myself upright, then twist round, and fall into the second seat, by which time my trouser legs are soaked through. I only just put these on too. Idiot.

Shaking my head at my own incompetence, I look toward the monitors.

I know how to move between all of the cameras and have them displayed as a split screen with four, eight, or up to thirty-two very small images. The joystick controls the camera movement and focus.

The company invests heavily in state-of-the-art security. A camera in one corner can be zoomed in to read the packaging from an item on a shelf in the far corner.

Starting with the staff area, I commence flicking through the live feeds, and I'm surprised that there are no infected in the back rooms. I go through the different sections: the canteen, the office areas, and the locker rooms, but they're all clear.

In the dry goods stock room, the largest of the storage areas, I can see a big mound on the floor near the far corner. The dry goods room is very dark, and it's hard to see what it is.

I zoom the camera in and can see that the heap is made from stacked-up bodies. It's too dark to see clearly, but there are at least seven or eight bodies, all on top of each other.

'What the fuck...' muttering to myself, I move the camera about but cannot see anything else, and all the rest of the staff area is clear.

Selecting the shop floor cameras, I start looking at the main store feeds and instantly see another huge pile of bodies in the wide central aisle. Full colour, and with the lights on within the store, I can make out every gory detail.

Bodies, lots of bodies, all piled on top of each other into a big mound. Men, women, and children, and all of them with various injuries, bite marks, ragged flesh hanging open, limbs bitten through, bones exposed. The sheer amount of blood is immense, with large pools spreading out from the big mound.

Several mops and buckets stand nearby, and I can see someone has made an effort to clean up. With shaking hands, I use the joystick to flick through the other camera feeds, spotting slick, bloody drag marks going through the aisles, where the bodies have been dragged along.

Most of them have severed jugulars, necks slashed open with deep wounds. Some of the bodies on the top and outer edges are visible to the camera, and I can see the red, bloodshot eyes staring lifelessly.

There is a single arm on top of the highest pile, as if it has been chucked up there.

This is the last thing I had expected to see. I knew that the place would be crawling with infected, but I wasn't expecting them to be proper dead and certainly not stacked up like this.

The next monitor along has been left focussed on the store entrance. Movement catches my eye, and I see an infected female staggering into the store like she's seen prey. I check the list for the camera numbers and track her through various feeds. I lose her for a second, then find the right feed, and blink in surprise at seeing a man in Tesco uniform standing in front of the customer service desk, facing the oncoming infected female.

For a second I think he must be infected, given that he stands completely still, with his arms hanging by his sides, and I try to zoom in closer to see who it is, but the infected woman blocks my view as she charges at him.

'What's he doing?' I murmur, thinking he'll be taken down, but at the last second, the man lifts his right arm, drops down, and spins off to the side in one fluid motion, coming to stop, with his back to the camera. I can't see who it is, but I do see the orange-handled butcher's knife in his hand and notice the knife is reversed, with the blade upright, resting against his forearm. The blade that just sliced across the throat of the infected woman, who has crashed into the desk and is now on the floor, with blood spurting from the gash in her jugular.

I watch on in stunned silence as the man walks over to stare down at the woman he just killed and bends down to pick one of her legs up by the ankle, then starts dragging her towards the central aisle as I frantically change camera view.

He comes into view in the central aisle, but with his head down and the promotional banners hanging from the ceiling tiles, I still can't see who it is and watch as he carefully avoids walking in the slippery wakes of blood he must have left before.

I hit buttons, changing cameras, cursing when I get the wrong ones, and working through all manner of aisles, nearly all of them covered in blood stains, until I get back to the middle aisle and stop to gawp in utter shock.

Dave.

It's him. The small bloke that never really speaks. What the fuck? I check again, blinking and shaking my head. It's definitely him. The same short, fair hair cut close to his scalp. The small build. The same man. He could be anywhere from late twenties to early forties. There was even a bet running in the canteen on his age. The other night, staff were asking him how old he was, but he never said. In fact, I can't think of a time when he said more than five words in the same sentence.

I watch on as Dave drags the body round to the far side of the heap and pushes it onto the pile. An arm flops out, and he lifts it up and pushes it back in. It flops out again, and he tucks it under another body. Neat and tidy.

He then turns and walks back down to the service desk covered in knives. Small to large, and all laid out neatly.

Dave stops, picks up a thin, metallic sharpening tool, and turns away to watch the door while running his blade up and down. Otherwise motionless. Unblinking. Unflinching and appearing entirely and completely unafraid.

CHAPTER THIRTEEN

I leave the security office and make my way onto the shop floor with my axe, listening to the awful, piped music still playing through the speakers. Sickeningly redolent against the macabre view of the blood smears criss-crossing the once polished floor.

I reach the end of the middle aisle and look up to huge mound of bodies, never thinking that in my life I would ever see such a thing. The smell of it too. A strong tang of metal in the air. The minerals from the blood. Faeces too. Piss and sweat, but that blood, so crimson and stark on the floor, and the mop buckets that have obviously been used to try and clean up.

Then I get very nervous at creeping up on Dave while carrying an axe.

'Dave... It's Howie,' I call out, but my voice breaks, so I cough and try again. 'Dave? You there, mate? Is it okay if I come down?'

Dave appears at the end of the aisle ahead of me, with his knife and sharpener held in his hands. 'Mr Howie,' he says in greeting, as though everything is entirely normal. Then I remember the stack of bodies out the back too and glance again at the mound in the central aisle.

He must have killed at least a hundred of them, and in the glaring light, with that stench hanging in the air, and that fucking awful music playing, my insides react, and I bend double to puke and heave the contents of my stomach over the floor. I pause, thinking it's over; then more comes, and I retch again until nothing but bile comes out, burning my throat and bringing tears to my eyes.

'Some water, Mr Howie.'

I blink up to see him holding a bottle of water out. I didn't hear him move, and for a second, my eyes rest on the blade in his hand before I nod and take the water, unscrewing the cap to take big, soothing gulps to ease the pain in my throat.

'Sorry, Mr Howie.'

I look up again, thinking he's saying sorry before cutting my head off, but he just stands there, with a very slight, pained expression on his face.

'For the bodies,' he continues, and I turn to slowly look back at the mound. 'Every time I try to clear them up, more come in.'

That was a long speech for Dave.

He doesn't look or sound threatening. In fact, he looks the same as he always does. His shirt tucked into his blue trousers, and his fleece zipped up, with the collar down. Then I notice a single spot of blood on the back of his hand, and he blinks at it before walking off back to the service desk. I follow him down and watch as he takes an antibacterial wipe from a pack and starts methodically cleaning the blood from his hand. I don't know what to say or even think but just stand in silence, watching him until he finally glances at me.

'I paid for them, Mr Howie.'

'Eh? Do what?'

'The wipes. I left some money by till number one.'

'Right,' I say, looking over to till number one. 'Er, it's fine, Dave. Don't worry.'

It's all too much, and I sway a little, then flinch as Dave rushes to my side and helps lower me down to the ground to sit, with my head between my knees, the axe at my side.

'Rest, Mr Howie.'

He goes back to sharpening the knife and watching the door but then stops, and walks off towards the chilled drinks cabinet by the front, and returns to hand me a bottle of Lucozade. I take it with a nod and once more start drinking.

'I haven't paid for it,' he says.

'S'fine,' I say after guzzling most of it down. 'How long have you been here, Dave?'

'Eleven months, Mr Howie.'

'No, I know that. I mean how long now?'

'Since Friday.'

'You've been here since Friday? Since this started?' He nods. 'Why are you here, Dave?' He stares at me, expressionless, then looks down at his uniform and back at me. 'No, I don't mean why are you *here*. You work here. I mean why are you still here when this is happening?' He doesn't say anything. 'Don't you have a family?'

'No, Mr Howie.'

'A home even? Where do you live?'

'South Street.'

South Street is in the town centre, right by the High Street. That area would be crawling with infected.

'No family or relatives?'

He shakes his head and continues with the sharpening. I watch him work. His eyes never leave the front of the store. He stops, and although he remains expressionless, there is a change in his eyes. I twist round but can't see anything, so I stand up and look out the front to see several infected coming across the car park.

Dave calmly puts the sharpener back on the desk, then hovers his hand over the handles of the knives, and selects a smaller, straight-bladed, black-handled knife, then reverses both so the blades are upright against his forearms, and starts walking towards the entrance doors.

He stops a few feet back from the doors and stands waiting. I grab my axe, lumber to my feet, and go down to stand beside him. He looks at me, then at the ground between us.

'Too close, Mr Howie,' he states matter-of-factly.

'Sorry.'

I take a few steps to the side.

He turns his head back to the infected. Four of them, three males and one female, and all dressed in formal evening wear. Like they've been to a posh function. The men in dark suits and white shirts, and the woman in a gold-coloured, shimmering gown, and the sight is just another odd thing to see. The four of them staggering in a line all dressed up, with blood on their faces as they lurch across a vast car park.

'What the fuck?' I mouth the words, earning a glance from Dave just before he runs out, going straight towards the female, and as she leans in for the bite, he sidesteps and brushes the straight-bladed knife against her throat, slicing the flesh apart while extending the other knife out front like a sword that he plunges into the neck of the next one, driving it deep into his throat before spinning with incredible dexterity, pulling the knife free, and dropping down to a crouch. A pause. A beat of a heart. A blink of an eye, and he explodes up and into the next one, repeatedly stabbing into the ribcage as he drives it back before pushing the point of one of the knives in through the infected male's eye.

One left, and Dave lets him come on. Waiting until the last second before spinning round the back of the infected man to grip his hair and yank him back, exposing his throat that he saws into with the knife, cutting through an artery that sprays an arc of hot, red blood high into the air.

Then he simply lets the body slump to the ground and turns a slow circle to scan the rest of the car park while I stand by the entrance, still holding my axe, with my mouth hanging open.

He was so clinical. Not savage or violent. Well, it was violent, incredibly violent, but not in a demented sense, like when I swing my axe about and hope for the best. He was precise and exact.

Dave checks the area and then walks back to the one with the knife sticking out of his eye, leans down, puts his foot on the dead infected man's face, and pulls the knife out. He wipes both blades on the guy's suit and starts walking back towards me, but stops at the female, bends down to grasp her ankle, and starts pulling her into the store, nodding as he passes me. 'Mr Howie.'

I go after him as he pulls the body up the aisle. 'Dave, you don't have to stack them up.'

He stops and looks back me, then down at the body, and after a second's worth of thought, he lets go, and the leg splats down in the bloody pool. 'Okay, Mr Howie,' he says before walking back to the desk and the pack of wipes.

'Dave, have you got anywhere else to go?'

'No, Mr Howie.'

'Listen, mate, you can't stay here. They'll just keep coming, and you can't keep stacking them up. They'll decay and rot, and... Fuck me, the electricity won't last that long either.' He doesn't reply but carries on scrubbing his hands and the blades of his knives with the wipes. 'Dave, I heard there's survivors heading to the forts on the coast. You could go there. Just take a delivery truck from the back.'

He pauses to look at me. 'I can't.'

'Why not?'

'I can't drive.'

'I can show you. It's really easy.'

'I don't have a licence.'

'Dave, no one will care. There's no police or authority now; there's no anything. I saw it on the news as it happened. The whole world's gone, mate. Everything. You can do what you want, but staying here is…it's just nuts.'

He seems suddenly unsure, with an expression on his face that I have never seen before, like the notion is too much to grasp, and despite watching what he did, I can't help but see a raw vulnerability laid bare as he just blinks and stares at me.

'Or,' I say slowly, 'you could come with me?' He stays looking at me and doesn't move a muscle, but somehow his focus sharpens. 'I have to find my parents, then my sister. She's in London. Then I'm going to the fort.'

I stop gabbling, not knowing why I'm telling him all this. He could kill me without hesitation, but then he looked so lost and floundering, and he hasn't shown any threat or signs of evil intent towards me. In fact, he has acted the same as always, and he would be very handy to have nearby.

'Okay, Mr Howie,' he says promptly. The worried look now completely gone from his face.

That's it. No hesitation or questions, no wondering about who or where. He makes an instant decision, and he is back to being normal Dave.

'I need to change my clothes. I'm covered in blood,' I say, walking off towards the clothing section on the far side.

'Blood, Mr Howie?'

'Not mine. Bert, the security man, slit his wrists in the security office.'

'Oh.'

'You could get some more clothes if you wanted to, Dave.'

'I don't have enough money.'

'It's okay. You can just take them.'

He seems unsure again.

'Err... I'm a manager, Dave. I can sign for them to be given out.'

'Okay.'

At the clothes section, I drop my bag down and start looking about. Most of the clothing is cheap and brightly coloured. *Cheap and not cheerful* as the clothing manager calls it out of earshot from the higher-ups, of course.

'Take what you need, Dave. Whatever you want. I can sign for it. I've been using dark clothes so far, trying to keep hidden in the shadows. What do you reckon? About right?'

'Camouflage is the art of concealing personnel or equipment from an enemy by making them appear to be part of the natural surroundings.'

I stop and stare at him for a second and process what is probably the biggest speech I have ever heard him give, and he said it parrot-fashion, reeling it off from memory.

'So, were you in the army, Dave?'

'Yes.'

He has already chosen black jeans and a very dark, green top. He takes these and walks to the changing room, closing the door behind him.

The conversation is over.

I choose the same jeans as Dave and start to get changed. My legs are soaked from the blood that has seeped through.

'I'm going to get some wipes to clean my legs.'

No response.

I head into the health and beauty section and find the same wipes that Dave used to clean my legs thoroughly, and then put the new jeans on. I put several packs of the wipes into my bag. My trainers are ruined, and I head back to the clothes section and find a pair of plain, sturdy, black boots. The explorer bag is quickly filling up.

Dave comes out, dressed in the dark clothing, and selects a leather belt from a stand, and hands it to me before getting another and threading it through his belt loops. I do the same and put the belt on.

Dave then tucks his top into his jeans, but I don't bother.

'I need a new bag, mate.'

I indicate the explorer bag, and he nods before setting off to the sports aisle. I follow him and watch as he takes various bags off the shelf and checks them through. He settles on a Berghaus medium-sized rucksack with side pockets and a tight, elastic mesh at the front. He hands me a dark blue one, and he chooses dark green. I transfer my stuff to the new bag.

I watch as he puts the knives into the mesh pocket, blade first. He tests the elasticity and seems satisfied. Leaving the large, orange-handled one in the mesh, he draws the straight-bladed knife back out and carries it in his hand.

'Ready, mate?'

He shakes his head. 'Food and fluids, Mr Howie.'

I follow behind as he selects high-energy protein bars, glucose drinks, bottles of water, and first aid kits. Each time he hands me some first and then puts the same in his own bag.

Eventually, the bags are full, and he stops to look at me. 'We should eat now.'

Then he's off into the aisles, taking cooked chicken from the meat section, then packets of microwavable rice, and finally, tinned vegetables.

I follow behind, taking the same things while figuring he seems to know what he's doing, and I did promise earlier that I would plan and prepare better.

We go through to the staff canteen area, where Dave dumps the contents of his packets and tins onto a plate and starts digging in, eating it all cold.

'We could heat them up in the microwave. There's still power,' I suggest, pointing at the microwaves.

He looks at me, then carries on eating.

'Fair enough. Cold it is.'

CHAPTER FOURTEEN

A few minutes later, and we're in a Tesco home delivery van, pausing as the back gates open from a sensor, and just for a second, I hold my breath, expecting to see hundreds of infected charging in.

There isn't. Just a big, empty car park, and we head across it, leaving the bright lights and giant mounds of human corpses behind, and I glance at the blood red Tesco sign in my mirror and snort a dry laugh. 'If they only knew...'

'Knew what, Mr Howie?' Dave asks.

'Nothing, mate. Talking to myself. So you were in army, then? How long for?'

'Fourteen years.'

'Quite a while, then. Did you go overseas much?'

'I'm not allowed to say.'

'Oh, right, of course. What part of the army were you in?'

'I'm not allowed to say.'

'Sure, yeah, of course, um, right...'

Bloody hell. It feels rude to keep asking questions. He's obviously a private man, but the silence is uncomfortable, and I feel the need to fill it. 'I live in the town too, other side of the High Street.'

Silence.

'I was at home when it happened. Yeah, er...watched it on the news. It's everywhere. Russia and some other countries...'

Silence.

'My parents live the other side of Littleton. I went there, to their place, I mean, not Littleton. Although I did go to Littleton too and then burnt it down. Um...'

Nothing.

'They left me a note. My parents, I mean. Said they're coming to look for me, so that's why I came back, but I can't find them.'

And still more silence.

'My sister lives in London. She called my parents and said that she was locked in her flat. That's where I'm going to try and find her... There was an emergency broadcast that said people should head to those forts on the coast. That's where I thought we would go, you know, after I find my family.'

Silence again, and this time I leave it unfilled.

On the motorway, I slow down as we pass the wreck from Saturday morning. The woman's body is still there, and the male corpse is still half out of the upturned car.

Dave looks at the wreckage as we go through.

'I saw that happen; it flipped over right in front of me. The woman was still alive, but she died while I was helping her.'

Dave looks at me and nods, doesn't say anything, then looks ahead again.

We pass the shop where I met the Indian lady and the estate survivors, but the cars are all gone now, and the shop looks deserted. Even the shelves look empty. I guess those people took everything and got away. I hope they made it.

Then we drive into the estate, and I feel my insides tense up as I navigate the turns, praying my mum and dad will be at home, waiting for me.

'Fuck,' I whisper the word and clench my jaw at seeing Dad's car still isn't back, then try to give myself false hope by thinking they could have ditched the car and walked back.

They haven't. I know they haven't, and I lock the van up and walk into the house to find it is exactly as I left it a few hours ago, and the note still on the table. I come to a stop, not doing anything, not thinking anything, and not really paying attention to Dave rushing off about the house.

'All clear, Mr Howie,' he says, coming back to the dining room.

'What is?' I ask him, my voice dull and lifeless.

'The house, Mr Howie. I checked it.'

I stare at him for a moment then finally nod. 'Yeah. Thanks, Dave.'

Grief and loss surge through me. They must be gone. Their note said they'd come back after checking my place, and they're not here. Something's happened. An image of my mum and dad being infected flashes through my mind, making me turn away and tense up again. Then I think of them running in terror or suffering slow, agonising deaths. Christ, they might have been in one of the hordes that chased me or even killed by Dave in the supermarket.

The thought sickens me, and I slump down at the dining table and wonder if they would try and attack me if they were infected. 'Dave, did any of the other staff from work turn into those things?'

'Yes, Mr Howie.'

'Did they try and come for you?'

'Yes.'

'Did they show any signs that they recognised you?'

'No, Mr Howie.'

That's it, then. My parents would go for me. I already knew the answer, really. The fat bloke knew me, and he still tried to attack. The same with my neighbours.

Bloody hell, that hurts so much. The pain inside at the thought of my mum and dad being killed, and it's getting worse as memories from childhood flood through my mind.

I think of Christmas and the effort my parents always made for our birthdays. Then I think of the retirement party we had for my dad, who then went back to work a few weeks later.

The pain is too much. They're gone, been taken away by those evil things. They tried to come and rescue me, knowing they were going into danger, knowing the risks, but they still tried. The pain crushes my heart, but I can't break down here. This isn't the time. They were good people, decent, loving, and nice, and if I find my sister... No, *when* I find my sister, I will have to tell her that they are gone.

I look about, seeing the things they worked so hard for and rest my eyes on the note Mum left me as that rage starts to build again. I think of Marcus and his fucked-up club. How dare he breathe the same air as my family. He isn't worthy of anything. Not life, not love.

All around me are the things they cherished: photos of my sister and I adorn the walls, the ceramic pot I made in school and gave to them as a present proudly displayed on a shelf, my mother even kept my old clothes in the loft. She was too nice to throw them out.

The rage gets worse. The thought of it. The very suggestion that they are dead, or worse, that they're infected and one of them.

The infected did this. They took them away from me. That's not right. I think of that little kid in the teddy bear pyjamas and the young woman in the blue dress. I think of the woman in the car accident and realise I don't even know her name. I think of Marcus and Giselle, and Bert in his office, and once more, I think of my mum and dad and surge up from the chair, and head into the kitchen. This isn't right. Not right at all, and it can't be left like this. Not like this.

I wrench the knife drawer from the cabinet and slam it down onto the kitchen top, then look up at the rows of knives stuck to the magnetic strip on the wall.

Moulded, high-tensile stainless steel, bevelled grips with small, black rubber inserts. One of them is a huge cleaver. We joked about Mum using it on Dad if she got fed up with him being at home.

The thought of my parents drives me on, and I take the cleaver and head back out to the van with my axe. Staring straight ahead, eyes fixed. Dave gets in next to me without a word said, and I notice he's taken two more of the knives from the same set on the wall.

One of those fucking things took my parents. I don't know which one, but I'll find it. There will be a sign, some kind of aura, an evil presence. Something. I don't know. I don't care, but I'll find it, and I'll hurt it; then I'll purge that town and raze it to the fucking ground.

'Where now?' Dave asks as we pull away.

'Boroughfare.'

'Okay.'

CHAPTER FIFTEEN

The pain consumes me. The need for revenge blots out all thought and reason.

I want to see them suffer, burn, be ripped apart, and die horrible, painful second deaths.

I don't know if they feel pain, but I hope they do. I think of all the bad things I have seen: news reports of families torn apart by violence, offenders getting away free because of a weak legal system – not able to exact revenge because the authorities say that vigilantism is wrong.

But it isn't wrong. It can never be wrong. *They* hurt my family. They can't be arrested or tried in a court. Nobody will come along now and say nice things to calm my rage, but there has to be punishment, and if I can't deliver it, then I will die trying.

I stop the van just before the precinct, not remembering having driven here, not realising I'm back in Boroughfare already.

The metal barrier ahead of me, and I can see the massed infected beyond it. I press the horn down and keep it held. Watching as the infected start toward me, but it's daylight again, and they shuffle along, barely at walking pace.

I push my anger and impatience through that horn; my fist pressing into the middle of the steering wheel. Then I start to punch it, with pure grief taking over my mind, slamming one fist after the other, rhythmic and constant.

Dave is saying something, but I can't hear him from the blood pounding through my skull. 'What?' I snap, glaring at him.

'Keep your space. Don't get drawn in. Strike and move. Keep a firm grip on your weapon, aim for the head or neck.'

I stare at him and nod. 'Right.'

I wait for more of them to get round the barrier and start revving the engine; foot pushed all the way down. The engine screaming out, readying to go for it.

I put my seat belt on and see Dave doing the same. He looks at me, then back at them, and motions forward with the flat of his hand.

'NOW.'

I lift the clutch up, and the engine surges ahead as I work through the gears, building speed, building power, and the last few seconds before impact seem like slow motion.

I see the infected coming forward and take in all the incredible details. The spittle and drool hanging from their mouths. The injuries on them. The dried blood and their red eyes staring at us; then in the weirdness of that second, I notice a picture stuck to the front of the radio. A young boy smiling, blond hair and white teeth, and my mind makes me think it's the same boy I saw in the teddy bear pyjamas, and I feel a fresh surge of utter rage inside me. That poor kid. My family. My mum. My dad. That little boy. Rage. Rage unlike anything I have ever known, and at the last second, time speeds back up.

Then we're impacting, and I see the first infected lean forward, with mouths opening for the bite as the van ploughs into them, pulverising their heads before sending their bodies flying off to the sides. Bumps and bangs sound out, and the wheels jolt as we go over bodies. Everything happening so quickly. The noise of it. The feel of it. Slamming into people, into bodies, into the infected and driving deeper into the crowd.

I keep my foot pressed down until the front of the van slams them against the barrier, and we stop with a massive crash, jolting us both forward against our seat belts.

The impact is immense, setting off the airbags that explode out with more sensations. Pain to my chest from the seatbelt. Pain in my neck from the jolt, and as we come to rest so I look ahead and see bodies of squashed infected between the van and the barrier, pressed like fruit. I had no idea that the human body could be compressed so much.

Dave is out of the door ahead of me, and I rip my seatbelt off and burst out too, with the axe in my hands to see a large, thick, gory wake of blood and bodies behind the van. But there are more on their feet, coming towards me, and I remember Dave's words. *Strike and move. Aim for the head or neck.*

I slam the sharp side of the axe into a face, cleaving the skull, then step away, and strike again, bringing the axe down over my head, bursting them apart, and almost cutting heads in half.

That rage gets worse. Searing and awful. Like a whole new reality inside of me. Like I've stepped into another plateau of existence, where everything I do is sped up and faster. Every detail in microscopic glory, and in my head, in the middle of that utter fury, all I can think is that I am death, and I have come for you. For them. For what they did. For that boy in the teddy bear pyjamas. For my mum. For my dad.

I dart forward, cracking skulls and destroying them. The axe isn't sharp and will not slice into their jugulars, but it has weight, and more than that, it has anger and fury behind it, and a thirst for revenge, and that power compensates for the lack of cutting power. Instead of cutting them, I gouge them open, hacking the flesh apart as the axe is forced through them.

More are coming now. I want them to come. I want all of them to come. There are no thoughts now, no rational thinking. Just strike and move, strike and move.

I keep going, and the rage that I had before is nothing compared to what it's like now. It was cold and seething, murderous, and ready to plot and plan, but this is unleashed, berserk, abandoned fury let loose, encouraged, and allowed to explode.

I twist the axe round and start using the blunt end, swinging out to the left and right, aiming for the side of their heads.

A good impact, and they go straight over with crushed skulls. A lesser impact sends them spinning off. If they are not killed outright, they get up and come back. Good, I want them to come back. I want them to suffer.

I have drawn them on, towards the rear of the van. Dave is nearby, and I get a fleeting glance of him whirling and spinning, with a huge wake of bodies left behind him.

My hands are covered in blood, and my grip is failing. I clench the axe handle and step forward with a massive overhead heave, and miss the head, and hit the shoulder, forcing the axe down into the collarbone, almost severing the shoulder. I pull the weapon back, but the axe-head is loose, rattling on the end of the shaft. I move back and throw the thing at the next one coming at me, smashing it down and away.

'EYES ON,' Dave shouts from my left.

I look over and see that he has taken the massive cleaver from the van and sends it spinning across the ground at me, aiming for a body lying a few feet away. I race forward and pick it up, staring at the shiny, massive blade.

'Grip it with both hands like a sword,' he shouts, then turns, and starts back into his group.

I take his instructions and grip the large handle with both hands while looking at the huge crowd of infected still coming on. Fuck yes. I charge in with wild abandon and start slashing at anything close to me. Cutting through flesh like a hot knife through butter. Bloody hell this thing is sharp as anything, and I drive too hard, biting the blade deep into someone's rib cage.

I pull back and remember Dave going for their throats. I look to the next one and push the blade at the neck. The jugular opens, and hot blood pours out. I keep going, dancing round them, stabbing, and thrusting. I lack the finesse that Dave has, but sheer, blind, psychotic rage spurs me on.

I move backwards towards the building line behind me and glance back, then double take at seeing a DIY shop just a few doors up.

Oh, yes. Fucking yes.

I run up, but the doors are locked.

An infected comes at me. I slash at his neck, and as he bends forward, I go behind him and use his head to propel him forward into the door, smashing the glass pane. Then I pull him back and drive him forward again. The glass explodes, and I pull him away to kick at the frame until the door bursts open. The alarm goes off instantly, but it's a mere distraction to me.

The shop is a Viking wonderland, chock full of heavy, sharp things that make my eyes light up.

I take a sledgehammer and move back towards the door, and wait for the first infected to come through the door, and take a huge, overhead swing, bringing it down hard enough to burst the skull apart, with brains flying off all over the place. I step back as another tries to push in, and again, I heave the hammer overhead and watch as the head explodes like a melon bursting apart.

I leave the bodies in the doorway making a natural barrier and head back inside, perusing weapons. The sledgehammer is good, but it's heavy and will become very hard work. I select two lump hammers – big, solid lumps of metal on the end of short handles.

I go back outside, clambering over the bodies to see more infected coming towards me, and go at them, with a hammer in each hand like clapping the hammers together.

The effect is amazing, and I batter away as the rage builds in me again. I kill men and women, the elderly, and the young. I don't care. I only want them to die.

After a few minutes, I ditch the hammers and get back inside the DIY shop to find something else, and spot a brightly-coloured display stand at the back, with a huge sign over the top, offering a free demonstration in tree cutting this Saturday.

Tree cutting?

I rush over to blink at the massive chainsaw resting on the display top with a long, fierce-looking blade full of big teeth. I pick it up and test it. Very heavy. A switch marked ON/OFF. A long pull cord. I put the switch to ON and pull the cord. The engine roars to life, but the blades remain still.

Two handles, one at front and one at the back. A lever is at the front. I pick the chainsaw up and press the lever. The engine increases in pitch, and the blades spin round. Then I notice a pair of protective glasses nearby and pop them.

Safety first.

The infected are already in the shop, coming for a chomp, so I go into the first one and scream out as the spinning blade tears a rib cage apart. I kick that one aside and keep going, sawing through them one after the other, with chunks of flesh and bone, and blood, and gore spray-coating me from head to toe.

I get outside and keep going, then lift the chainsaw to head height, and start sweeping left and right, cutting through neck after neck, with this magnificent machine ripping through bone, tendons, sinews, and flesh.

I lean my head back and roar, screaming at them to keep coming, and they do, pouring to their deaths, leaning in for the bite only to be torn apart and kicked away.

I can't stop. This is it. This is the destruction I have craved, and I don't see them as people now. They are not men or women, not adults or children, but they are something else. A new species, like an evil entity sent to consume us.

The chainsaw doesn't stop. It keeps hacking and cutting through the crowd, but the weight is heavy, and I'm soon sweating and breathing hard, but the exertion is worth it, and I keep going, ignoring the pain in my arms and shoulders as I twist and attack, and tear them apart.

Then it runs out of fuel and simply stops while wedged halfway through an infected body, who falls away, taking the chainsaw with him while my arms and shoulders scream out in relief.

I move backwards and look about. The mess is an awesome sight. Not awesome like in a cool movie. It's awesome like something you can't otherwise describe, with a long trail of broken and destroyed bodies leading from the DIY shop back to the Tesco van. The other side is even worse, and I realise Dave has easily killed three or four times the amount I took down.

Exhausted, filthy, but somehow satisfied, I walk back into the DIY store and take two new axes, then go over to the Tesco van while ignoring the remaining infected still shuffling about.

I climb into the driver's seat, slam the door closed, and sit slumped, looking down at the gore coating my clothes.

Dave gets into the passenger side, looking remarkably clean, save for some blood splatter on his hands and arms.

'Better?' he asks.

'Much better.'

He doesn't reply but takes a pack of wipes from his bag, and starts the cleaning process I saw him do in Tesco. Hands, arms, face, and then weapons.

I put the van in neutral and switch the keys off, then back on. Surprisingly, the van starts first time, so we sit in silence, working through the pack of antibacterial wipes as I catch glimpse of myself in the side mirror and the two clean eye patches on my face where the glasses were. Everywhere else is covered in gore.

We drive in silence to my parents' house, and this time, I don't even glance at the car accident on the motorway. I use the shower while Dave makes food. Then we swap.

We put our clothes into the washing machine, then into the tumble dryer, and Dave checks the house, securing every door and window, drawing curtains and dropping blinds before coming back into the kitchen.

'Sleep now?'

I nod. 'There's two spare rooms upstairs. Help yourself.'

He disappears, and I hear his footsteps on the ceiling above me.

A few minutes later, I am in the other spare room, collapsing on the bed, drained and exhausted, and the last I remember before sleep pulls me under is the light going off as the electricity cuts out.

DAY THREE

CHAPTER SIXTEEN

DAY THREE
SUNDAY AFTERNOON

I wake quickly, transitioning from sleep to awake in an instant to find I'm bathed in sweat and sitting bolt upright in bed. Fleeting images of torn bodies ease back from my mind as the dream fades and disappears, leaving me momentarily confused.

I'm at home. Not my home in Boroughfare. My parents' house. Why am I here? A few seconds to blink as the memories of the last two days come crashing back. The world is over. Everyone is either dead or infected and one of those things.

One of those things. What are those things? Zombies are from the movies, and it feels weird to even think of them like that. This is real. This is happening.

Too many thoughts too soon from wakening, and I blink at the window, seeing it's light outside.

Anyway, zombies are dead, and dead bodies don't bleed. Those things certainly bleed. Especially when Dave cuts their heads off, and they spray blood all over the place. I cut a few open like that too, but that was more by accident than design. Dave was something else, the way he was killing them. The speed of him, and I think, on reflection, that I am more of a blunt trauma man. The axe was good. Nice and heavy, and easy to split skulls open, and if you get the swing right, you can easily lop arms and legs off.

What else did I use? Oh, yeah, the sledgehammer. That was amazing, but really only a one-trick weapon, great for an overhead smash but too heavy and tiring.

Then there were the two lump hammers. Again, they were effective at one on one or even a couple of them at a time, but again, they lack the range. The chainsaw was bloody amazing, really, truly amazing, and I regret not bringing it with us. A few people armed with chainsaws could destroy tons of infected, but again, they are heavy and too reliant on fuel. If one part breaks or jams, it would be rendered useless. Good point. I'll stick with the axe until we find some guns.

Guns? What the fuck? I'm a supermarket manager, not a soldier. What do I know about combat or fighting techniques? Dave, on the other hand, is not all he seems. He said he was in the army for fourteen years, but he wouldn't say anything else about his time in the service. I've met loads of ex-service people; quite a lot of them had seen action in the Middle East. Some had physical scars. Others had scars that weren't so noticeable. Post-traumatic stress disorder, they called it.

But Dave doesn't betray any feelings or emotions. The only time I have seen him give anything away was last night in the supermarket when I told him he could do what he wanted. He clearly had nowhere to go, no family or friends. The thought of taking away his routine must have scared him. He could have run or even closed the doors. Every staff member is shown how to close and shut off the automatic doors in case of emergency. Dave didn't shut them, though. He stayed on the shop floor. He even killed the rest of the staff as they were turned. I wonder if any of them fought alongside him until they were taken down. If they did, then Dave didn't hesitate but killed them too. Blimey. Would he do that to me if I get bit?

Routine must be important to him, as well as having someone in a position of authority – of *perceived* authority, anyway. Fourteen years of army life must have moulded him. But then other long-serving military people I have known weren't like that.

Anyway. What now? What's next? My parents clearly haven't got back, so from that I can only assume they are not coming back. Shit, that hurts. A pang inside. Deep and raw. The thought of them going out to look for me and getting hurt by those things brings back that rage I had yesterday. That searing, driving energy that made me attack and kill. I've never felt anything like that. Not even close. What I felt was something else, something deeper, a base state of being, an instinct to exact revenge and hurt those that hurt me.

To be honest, I didn't even know people could have such feelings. Other than maybe serial killers.

Am I a serial killer? Crumbs. That's a bit worrying. No, but hang on. Those things aren't people. The bodies are just carriers for the infection inside. An infection that just happens to make them want to eat other people.

Whoa. That's a bit alarming. If they can bleed, and what possesses them is an infection, then maybe they will recover. What if it's just a forty-eight-hour bug? Jesus, they might recover of their own accord, and I've already slain shitloads of them. Plus, I burnt down a village. What will I say if they all go back to normal?

Oops! Sorry about that. I thought you were all zombies. My mistake. Never mind. No harm done.

I banish such thoughts away and finally get off the bed to look out the window at a gorgeous summer day. The air almost looks hazy with the scorching sun. I glance at my watch. It's almost 3 p.m. I've had a few hours of sleep, but my body is hurting like hell from all the physical exertion. My legs hurt, my arms too. Actually, pretty much everything hurts.

I head downstairs, pausing to flick the light switches a few times while remembering the power went off as I fell asleep. I always thought it would last longer if like the world ended or something. Shows you what I know.

I reach the kitchen to see Dave sitting at the counter, drinking what looks like coffee. I cross to the fridge and open the door, but the light doesn't come on.

'Power's gone,' he says in that dull, monotone voice.

'How did you make the coffee, then?' I ask, somewhat gruff and somewhat sleepy while somewhat squinting.

'Gas.'

'Gas?' I look over to the gas hob with a nod of realisation. A saucepan of water steaming away, and I spot a bottle of milk in a bowl of water. A few seconds of staring, of looking from the pan and milk to Dave sitting silently at the breakfast bar. An urge to say something and fill the silence. Instead, I just nod again and make coffee while feeling spaced out. Like there is no order or sense to my thoughts.

Coffee made, and I lean back against the counter to sip the hot liquid, holding the mug two handed while studying Dave and how he looks so clean and freshly shaved. Even his top is tucked in. I glance down to see I'm just in boxer shorts and suddenly feel very self-conscious that I'm in my undies with a man I hardly know. The fact we slaughtered a raging horde of infected zombie things together doesn't really register. What happened to my clothes? I squint, frown, think on this, and then spot them neatly folded on top of the tumble dryer. I remember we stripped off and put them on to wash, then in the tumble dryer before I went to sleep.

I look at Dave. He stares back. 'At least the clothes dried before the power went off, then,' I say casually, which just sounds weird and forced.

'Almost. I put them outside.'

'What, in the garden? On the washing line? Bloody hell, Dave. Thank you.'

'That's okay, Mr Howie.'

'Dave, you don't have to call me Mr Howie anymore. Howie is fine.'

'Okay.'

He won't call me Howie. I know that.

I head into the lounge to dress. The thought of getting dressed in front of him feels weird. Mind you, everything feels weird. I stand up from tugging my shoes on and spot Dad's road atlas on the bookshelf. My dad loved technology and would always have the latest gadget:

new computer, latest phones, but despite all of that, he would lecture me that society has become too reliant on technology.

'*It has its uses and should be enjoyed, but not taken for granted.*'

I listened but never really took it in. Looking at the atlas now reminds me of what a careful and prepared man he was. Then I get an idea and take the atlas into the kitchen, and start flicking the pages. Dave doesn't say a word but sits in silence.

I find the southeast and rest my finger on my location now. Brighton is east of here. London is north – about two hours on a good day. But then the roads are empty now, so reaching London should be easy; however, getting *through* London will be an entirely different matter. Bloody hell, you'd need a tank.

'Dave?' I ask. He looks at me but stays silent. 'Nothing,' I say, feeling stupid for a second. 'Where could I get a tank from?' I ask, deciding that feeling stupid is the least of my worries right now.

He doesn't even flinch. 'Salisbury.'

'Where's that?'

'I don't know, Mr Howie.'

'Are they hard to drive?'

'I don't have a licence.'

'It must be hard. How about those armoured vehicles?'

'APCs.'

'Yeah, them. They must be like cars to drive.'

'I don't know, Mr Howie.'

'Do they have those APC things in Salisbury too?'

'Yes.'

'Okay, so we need to get into London to get my sister, but I heard an emergency broadcast that said London is infested and to stay away, so I reckon we should get to Salisbury, nick an APS, and get going.'

'An APC.'

'What?'

'You said APS. It's an APC. Armoured personnel carrier.'

'Oh, right. Sorry. We get an APC and try for London. Oh, hang on. I mean *I* need to go to London. I didn't mean to assume that you were coming with me.'

'I'll come with you, Mr Howie,' he says in that flat way.

'Okay. Great,' I say into the slightly awkward silence. 'Er, so Salisbury is here, and we are here. It should take us around two hours to get there, I think, and it's 3 p.m. now. It gets dark at about half nine. So if we leave now, we should make it before nightfall.'

'Okay.'

No questions. No anything.

I nod and finish my coffee.

CHAPTER SEVENTEEN

Half an hour later, and we stand outside, staring at the blood and gore smeared over the front of the Tesco home delivery van. Should have washed it off really.

However, I did think ahead and fill some bags with food from the kitchen. Snack food and a few tins. Dave then put some bedding from the spare rooms in the back of the van, then found a gas lamp from the garage. I should have thought of that really and chide myself to start thinking properly.

I grab my two new axes, and with a last look back at the house, I get into the front of the van and slot the axes down next to me as Dave gets in, with a load of knife handles poking from the top of his rucksack. Another second of silence as I look at them, then at him.

'I like knives,' he says.

I nod and start the engine. Not quite knowing what you say to that. I pull off and start driving away, then realise I don't know where my sister actually lives. 'Arse,' I mutter, bringing the vehicle to a stop, then selecting reverse to go back as the air fills with the reversing alarm. 'Need my mum's address book,' I tell Dave, but Dave doesn't appear to wish to chat.

I rush back into the house and find Mum's old address book. Hard-backed and brightly coloured, with a flowery pattern. The sight of it brings forth a rush of pain inside. I remember this book from childhood, and the sight of my mother's handwriting is almost too much to see.

I flick to 'S'. There it is – 'Sarah, London'. I kiss the book and offer a silent prayer to my mother, still taking care of me. Back outside and into the van. The book goes into my rucksack, and then I think better of it and give it to Dave.

'Can you look after this, please, mate. My sister's address is inside, and I can't afford to lose it. Her name is Sarah – her address is under Sarah, London. If anything happens to me...'

He takes the book like I'm passing him a priceless antique, staring at it for a second before taking a small hand towel from his knife-loaded bag that he wraps the book in like it's a valuable relic.

'Ready?' I ask.

He looks at me, devoid of expression, devoid of anything. 'Yes, Mr Howie,' he says simply, and we set off.

IT FEELS wrong not to be going straight for my sister, but if a little coastal town like Boroughfare can amass a few hundred, then what will a city centre will be like? I think of my own town and the first night, and that cash-in-transit van driving past my house. Who was that? It worked, though. Luring them away like that.

Then I think of the way the infected things group together. It was the same in Littleton. They all grouped together in the village square. Maybe that was the last place they took a survivor down, so they stayed there, hopeful of another one, or maybe a survivor got away from there, and they stayed in the last place of contact, like when I ran through the precinct into the nightclub, they stayed outside those doors for a long time.

But then, in Boroughfare, it looked like more were joining the crowd. There must be something that passes between them. An alert state? So if one senses prey, then they all join in, and the signal passes until they are coming from all around. Can that even happen?

This might be something we could use – draw them together and create a safe passage like the cash-in-transit driver but on a bigger scale. A much bigger scale. How would we do that? I don't know the roads in London well enough to know where to draw them to. We could easily get ourselves trapped or stuck in a far worse situation if we start pissing about, trying to be clever.

I look up at the sky and realise we won't have enough time to get to Sarah today. By the time we have found a suitable vehicle and then get into London, it could be late evening. We don't have satellite navigation, so finding her address in the city will be hard enough. If only I could get a message to her, tell her to wait. Hang on, satnav might work. The mobile networks are down, but do satnavs use the same network systems as mobiles? They all work off satellites and something to do with GPS. Maybe they are still online?

I go through the radio stations in the van, flicking through all of the pre-set ones first and then manually through the frequencies. The message is gone. I didn't make a note of the frequency setting from the Micra. I check FM, MW, and LW but get only static, and so we drive on in a slightly awkward silence. Moving from the town into the countryside, passing fields and meadows. Trees overhead and long, winding country lanes. Birdsong heard outside, and the summer sun bearing down. The odd house or turning for a tiny village. An idyllic Home Counties-type of setting, worthy of picture postcards.

'You hungry?' I ask, opening one of the bags of food. I take an apple and start eating while thinking on this and that, on the infection inside the people, on satellites, and London, and all manner of things. I still feel spaced out and achy, but the normalcy of driving and eating sooths my nerves.

I cast the remains of the apple out the window and catch Dave glancing at me. A few seconds later, I take a banana and scoff that too before flinging the skin out the window, which earns me another sharp look as he takes the waste bag he was using and pointedly places it on the seat between us.

'Sorry, mate, I wasn't thinking. I'm leaving a trail behind us, aren't I?' I say while glancing at the wing mirrors and looking about out the windows. 'They'll be able to follow us. I guess you learnt that in the army?' I look back at him to see his face is still devoid of all expression while somehow managing to imply I am a dick.

'Keep Britain tidy,' he says, facing the front again.

'Right,' I say slowly. 'Sure. Er, Dave, what you said to me before about keeping a firm grip, strike, and move. How do you know that stuff? And the way you use those knives, you must have studied martial arts or something?'

'No.'

'Where did you learn it, then?'

He pauses for a few seconds.

'The army.'

'Wow, why did they teach you all that? I thought it was more about guns and stuff.' Silence. 'So, like, they teach you hand to hand combat and things, then?'

Silence.

I nod and take a breath. 'Dave, the army has probably fallen, mate. Christ, I think the whole country has fallen. Probably the whole world... What I mean is that I'm sure it will be okay if you tell me.'

'I can't, Mr Howie.'

'Why not?'

'I'm not allowed to say.'

'Eh? You're not allowed to say why you can't tell me, or are you just not allowed to say anything?'

'Yes.'

'What the fuck?' I ask, shaking my head at the confusing answer as a sudden cramping hits my stomach, with an urgent message being passed from bowel to brain that I really need a poo.

I look about, thinking I really don't want to squat anywhere Dave can see me and spot the entrance to a lane up ahead. That'll do. I stop the van. Grab some wet wipes and start rushing out as the cramping comes back harder.

'Mr Howie ...' Dave calls. I turn back to see him holding one of the axes out. I grab the handle, offer a wan smile, and leg it off into the lane entrance while trying to clench my bum cheeks. A few yards in. A quick look about. All clear. I tug my trousers and boxers down and squat at the side of the road. The smell is disgusting. My stomach must be upset from the extreme lifestyle of the last couple of days; plus, the sporadic eating. I guess the copious fruit we just ate hasn't helped matters either.

However, and despite the smell and the thought of taking a crap in broad daylight in a country lane, the feeling of relief is amazing, and I'm moaning with the pleasure. I almost sound like one of the infected, and that makes me try and mimic their noise. Groaning while pooing in a country lane at the same time as pondering if zombies need to shit. I bet they just poo in their pants. Dirty infected.

A noise behind me, and I twist round to see an entrance a few metres into the lane that was concealed by the bushes when I first looked. A shuffle, footsteps maybe; then I spot something in the darkness of the shadows and grab the wipes to start cleaning my arse. It might be the end of the world, and I understand we all have to make sacrifices and change our normal behaviour in this new world, but walking around with a shitty arse isn't one of them.

Then the sound comes closer, so I think *stuff it* and yank my trousers up as a black and white farm dog emerges out of the entrance. I freeze and go stock still; my mind filling with images of being chased by a zombie dog, but then my eyes adjust to the gloom, and I can see it looks normal. It doesn't have red eyes anyway, and its head keeps flicking from me to something else set back that I can't see. I swallow, blink a few times, then call out.

'Hello, boy! Who's a good doggy? You're a good doggy.'

I love dogs, always have done. We had dogs when I was younger, ones from rescue shelters, so we had a good mix of crosses and mongrels.

The growl coming low and deep makes me stop, and as the view opens up, so I gain sight of a very fat, middle-aged infected man shuffling slowly towards me in rubber boots, looking every inch the stereotypical farmer. He just needs one of those long sticks, with the crook at the end. I imagine his wife making apple pies and Sunday roast dinners.

Dave comes around the corner, obviously concerned that I have been gone for too long. I point at the entrance, guessing that he can't see them from where he is. He comes down further and joins me, then stops on seeing the infected, and silently draws a knife from his belt.

'I don't think the dog will let you near him, mate. Mind you, he doesn't look aggressive either. Maybe we can try and get him out of that lane. His farm must be close.' Dave looks at me. 'Most farms have shotguns, don't they?'

He nods and walks a bit closer to the dog, who crouches lower and growls more. Dave stops and waits for the infected man to make his way out of the entrance. The dog keeps glancing at his master, then moves position, edging closer to Dave, who backs away just a little at a time.

I drop the axe head onto the raised verge and lean on the handle. Despite the horrible circumstances, the lane is pleasant and quiet. Sunlight dapples through the canopy, causing shadows to dance across the surface of the road. It feels like it is getting hotter. There is no wind and the air is very close.

That makes me look back at the dog and the big tongue hanging out the side. Poor thing must be so hot.

'Wait here a sec,' I say to Dave and rush back to the van to find a bottle of water and a mug, and run back to see them all pretty much in the same position.

'You thirsty?' I ask the dog, crouching down to pour water into the mug. The dog watches me closely, eyeing the water while glancing back to his owner. 'Good boy. Come on, get some water.'

We back away enough for the dog to feel safe and watch as it rushes forward to lap thirstily at the water in the mug.

We skirt them both and go wide to get behind and into a narrow track rutted with wheel marks, and head off, moving slowly uphill. Minutes later, and I'm sweating from the heat and exertion while Dave looks as fresh as anything.

The lane ends at a metal five-bar gate, which is wedged open. A rusty cattle grid lies just beyond the gate. The dark metal poles are evenly spaced, with weeds growing up between them. A few hundred metres to some buildings. Some of them are sheds and barns, long and low, with corrugated roofs. Plant machinery dotted about, things that farmers attach to tractors.

Our raised position means that we can see the fields beyond the buildings. We both wait and stare at the view.

Finally, Dave looks at me and nods, and we go through the gate and onto the driveway. There is a herd of black and white cows standing at the gate in a field adjacent to the buildings. As we get closer, I can see that the udders look full. I had heard that cows will get so used to the routine of milking, they will wait at the gate. I also heard that cows explode if they don't get milked, so I watch them as we pass, ready to duck in case of bovine explosion.

The cows haven't been bitten, and the dog was okay too. The farmer would have access to all types of animals, but they look unharmed.

I had thought of using rotting flesh or an animal carcass to lure them away in London, but it appears the infected people only crave human flesh. If we are going to use meat as a trap, then it has to be human meat and alive too. I force the thought away, disgusted that I'm even thinking of it.

We reach the farmhouse, circling it quietly while looking for entry points or signs of movement. The windows all have heavy net curtains inside in order to prevent the farmhands looking in the house, I guess.

The front door is dark wood and inward opening. I slowly push the handle down, and the door opens a fraction. I look at Dave, nod, and then slowly start to step forward. The axe bangs noisily on the lower half of the door, which remains closed. I look at Dave with an apologetic grimace.

'Sorry. It's a stable door.' I reach in and unlock the bottom half of the door, and we proceed.

The floor is made from flagstones, and there is a flight of exposed wooden stairs ahead of us.

Dave taps me on the shoulder and motions for me to stay still. He moves off to the right into a doorway and is gone from view for a few seconds. He returns and gives me a *thumbs up* signal, then motions, with his hand, towards the door on the left. He goes first, easing each foot down, treading carefully.

He gets to the door, pushes it open, and leans his head in. Without looking at me, he takes both knives in his left hand and raises his right to the side of his head. He makes a fist and then extends two fingers, giving me the V. He makes a fist again and then extends one finger, pointing it to the room, then a fist, and again, he extends a finger and points into the room, more off to the side this time. Then he makes a flat hand and runs it across his throat. Next, he extends all his fingers out straight and reverses his hand so that the palm is facing towards the door; then more palms and fingers are waved about.

I have no idea what this all means.

I think he is telling me that there is someone in there; the rest leaves me clueless. He looks back at me, and I shrug my shoulders, and again, even though his face wears the usual devoid-of-expression look, I could swear he is wondering why he got stuck with me. He then points two fingers directly at his own eyes and motions for me to look. He eases back, and I peek inside. There are two infected in the room.

Ah, so that's what he meant – two of them. Then the hand across the throat must have implied they are dead or infected. I get it, anyway, even though I have no clue what the rest of the waving and pointing was about.

One of them is a fat woman, a *really* fat woman. She must be the farmer's wife, all jolly and large, wearing a white apron over a flowery dress. The other is an adult male, wearing dirty and stained overalls tucked into rubber boots.

They are standing side by side, with their backs to the door, facing out the window. The farmer's wife has a huge chunk torn out of her meaty upper arm, and dried blood splattered all down her dress.

There are bloodstains on the male too, but I can't see any injury from here. They're in the kitchen area in front of the sink. There is another closed door opposite me, so there must be more rooms beyond it as the house extends further than the size of this room.

I ease back and gently pull the door closed. Dave motions with his head for me to follow him, and he starts climbing the stairs. I climb up behind him, looking back at the kitchen door to make sure that I closed it, and walk into the back of Dave, with my head nudging his backside.

'Sorry,' I whisper.

He doesn't reply or even look back.

'I didn't know you had stopped,' I add.

He stays still for a second, doesn't look back, and then carries on going up. I wait for a gap to form between us, then start to follow him to the landing and a corridor stretching off, with closed doors on either side.

Dave motions for me to stay put, then goes left, gingerly working his way down the corridor. I watch how he walks, swinging each foot slow and purposefully – the heel going down first in an almost exaggerated manner; then he slowly moves forward and puts his weight onto the front foot, then repeats the movement in complete silence.

He stops at the first door and listens, craning his head, and then leans in closer until his ear is almost touching the door, his mouth open.

He eases the door open, steps inside, and is back out within seconds. He repeats the action until all of the rooms on that end are clear. Then he creeps back to me and motions for me to move forward. I think he wants me to check my end.

I start forward a few steps, copying his movement and putting my heels down first. It seems to take ages to work my way down. At the first door, I stop and listen, but I can't hear anything above my heart hammering away in my chest.

I lean into the first door, but still can't hear anything. I take hold of the handle and twist it back. The handle squeaks really loudly, and I stop twisting. I look back at Dave, who nods for me to carry on. I keep twisting the handle, which sounds like it's screaming in protest. The door gives, and I push it open too fast, almost tripping in and banging the axe against the frame.

This time I don't look back. I'm too embarrassed to face him. I know that his face will be blank, but he still manages to convey a message through that vacant gaze. I peer into the room – it's all clear.

I move off down the corridor, treading carefully and trying to show that I can do this too.

At the next door, I grasp the handle and hold my breath as I twist. Silence.

I breathe a sigh of relief and start to push the door open, which creaks loudly on the hinges.

For fuck's sake, this is a conspiracy. How did he get all of the silent handles and doors?

I keep pushing slowly. The hinges creaking and groaning. I stop. Pushing slowly is making it worse. If I push it open quickly, the hinges won't grate so much. I heave with force to a cacophony of metallic screams. At least the room is clear.

The final door at the end facing the corridor, and again, I take hold of the handle and push. It opens into a large bathroom: white tiles, white bath, and white shower curtain around the bath, nice and bright apart from the large pool of blood on the floor and the infected woman in the white nightdress standing in the middle of it.

She is fat, incredibly fat, quite possibly one of the fattest people that I have ever seen, and the sight isn't helped by the fact her white nightdress has thin sleeves, which only serve to accentuate the rolls of fat on her upper arms. She's got very long, dark hair, with a wooden-handled hairbrush tangled in the flowing locks.

She slowly turns round to face me, and I see the red, bloodshot eyes. Her wrist has been bitten deeply, leaving a nasty, gaping wound.

I look back at Dave and raise my hand to the side of my head, making a fist. He nods. Then I extend one finger and point into the room. Again, he nods. Then I puff out my cheeks, hold my arms out, and waddle slightly on the spot while motioning to the door behind me. He just stares at me.

I keep waddling on the spot, holding my arms out and pretending to rub my big belly. Dave looks so serious, and after the tension of creeping down the corridor, I let go and start giggling like a schoolboy. Then I pretend to brush my hair and extend one finger, and point it into my pretend hair. Within seconds, I am trying to stifle my laughter, but the farmer's daughter starts waddling towards the door, and I back away.

She is taller than me, and the girth of her is amazing. Puffed cheeks making her mouth look small and pouty.

I back off down the corridor, still trying to stop myself laughing. She makes it to the doorway and gets stuck face on – too fat to get through. She keeps pushing forward though, grunting and straining against the effort.

That's it. I'm gone. Tears of laughter are falling down my face, and I'm leaning against the wall. All of the stress of the last few days has built up, and the sight of the fat woman unable to walk through the door has finished me off.

I try to be quiet at first, but knowing that we have to be silent makes it worse, and I can't stop myself from howling. Within minutes, my stomach is hurting. I manage to get myself under control, then look back at her wedged in the doorway, with her stomach pushing through, but her shoulders and arms can't fit, and she is sort of leaning back and trying to get through belly first. I'm off again, sliding down the wall onto the floor. The laughing is hurting, but I can't stop. I try to look at Dave, but the tears have misted my eyes. I imagine him standing there, stony-faced.

It takes many minutes, but eventually, I get myself under control and get back up. Dave is standing there, impassive as ever, but I swear there is a glint in his eye.

CHAPTER EIGHTEEN

We make our way down the stairs and stare at the kitchen door. There was no sign of a gun cabinet anywhere upstairs. The only place left to check is the kitchen and the room on the other side, but that means going through the room containing two infected people.

'What do you reckon?' I ask. 'We could lead them out again.'

Dave nods, and I check my watch.

'It's gone 5 p.m. already. Shit, we really have to get going.'

'Okay.'

He walks straight past me into the kitchen, disappearing round the door, with two loud thumps following within seconds.

'What the...' I rush in behind him to see the farmer's wife now almost decapitated, with her spinal column showing through her severed neck. 'Fuck,' I gasp and blanch as Dave drags the dead infected male on top of the farmer's wife, showing his OCD for tidiness again, and the humour from a few minutes ago disappears instantly.

The brutal yet reserved nature of this man is staggering. His mind must be so straightforward when he is completing a task, whether it's filling shelves at Tesco or severing the head of a zombie farmer's wife.

A second for my brain to try and catch up as I blink and widen my eyes. Dave stands back, looking down at his work, then over to me.

Silence again. I swallow and nod, then head through the other door into a utility area. An old, stained kitchen top with a deep, white ceramic sink. Dirty pairs of rubber boots up against the wall, and overalls hanging from rails. There are two washing machines, labelled HOUSE and FARM.

There is a back door to the right. To the left is the promised bounty – a large metal cabinet fixed on the wall, complete with a massive padlock hanging from a clasp. The padlock has a thick metal loop, and the clasp has multiple strong rivets securing the cabinet.

'I bet the farmer has the key in his pocket,' I say quietly. Dave doesn't reply.

We start searching the area, checking drawers and the pockets of the overalls. We find keys, but none of them fit. 'Cock it,' I mutter while staring at the padlock, figuring we'll have to break it open. I take a step back and reverse the axe so that the blunt end will be used.

'Watch out, mate.'

Five minutes later, and I'm out of breath, with the metal cabinet bashed and dented but still holding firm and decidedly locked. I even try wedging the blade of the axe into the gap of the cabinet door, but I can't get enough leverage.

'Fucking thing. Any suggestions, mate?'

I look around, but Dave is gone, and the back door is open. I step over, half thinking he's probably seen sense and legged it as far away from me as possible, but there he is, coming back with a sledgehammer and a big metal spike. He walks in without saying a word, hands me the sledgehammer, and sticks the pointy end of the spike into the gap between the cabinet and the padlock clasp, and looks at me with an air of expectation. Not that his expression changes. I heft the big sledgehammer and look at the spike, then back at Dave, then at the cabinet all covered in dinks and dents.

'Um, maybe we should swap,' I suggest, thinking I'm highly likely to miss and bludgeon Dave to death.

We move places in the confined space as I take the spike and realise just how close I am to the cabinet, and start thinking maybe this is a bad idea because Dave could now bludgeon me to death. Then Dave swings and hits the spike, making me yelp and flinch, and half pull back while waiting for the pain to explode. None comes, and I open my eyes to see the spike has been driven in an inch. He hits it again with near on surgical precision. It's a big, heavy hammer too, and he doesn't show any signs of exertion either. A few hits later, and the padlock falls away as I step back, rubbing my arm, now tingling from the energy transference sent through my hand.

I watch Dave as he takes the weapons out and recognise three shotguns from having two big barrels and big, wooden bases or stocks, or bottom bits. Whatever they're called.

There is also a long camouflage bag in the cabinet, holding a rifle that looks very slim compared to the shotguns.

'What is it?' I ask.

'Lee-Enfield point three zero three bolt-action rifle.'

'Is that good?'

'Yes.'

Ask a question. Get an answer. Within seconds, the gun is separated into parts, with Dave's hands working like machines. He checks the separate sections and then puts it back together, and pulls the bolt back several times, listening to the sound. Satisfied, he turns to the shotguns and takes them out of the cabinet, laying them on the worktop.

Two of them have barrels side by side. The other one also has two barrels, but one on top of the other. They are heavy and feel alien to hold.

I push the wooden end of one into my shoulder and look down the barrel. There are two triggers, one in front of the other. I guess it's one trigger for each barrel.

There is a lever, where the metal barrel meets the wooden bit. I push this over, and the shotgun bends in the middle. I remember that shotguns have cartridges, not bullets. The cartridges must just slot in the holes. Then close the barrel and pull the triggers. I've seen it done on television and movies, and it looks simple enough.

There are boxes of bright, red cartridges in the cabinet. They are marked *12 Gauge*. I've heard of that but don't know what it means.

Dave has found a shoulder strap for the rifle and has fitted it on, checking the length and making adjustments until he seems satisfied. I guess he has chosen the rifle, then. After my debacle in the corridor upstairs, he probably wouldn't trust me with a paintball gun.

He next takes a box of shiny bullets, picks up the shotgun with the two barrels on top of each other, and heads out of the back door. I take the other two shotguns and boxes of the shiny, red cartridges and follow him out into the bright sunshine.

He stops in the middle of the central yard area, and I look about at the outbuildings and barns nearby, then watch as Dave holds the rifle and looks down the sights, aiming into the empty barn. He pulls the trigger and listens to the noise. I'm sure they call it *dry firing*.

Dave takes a strip of bullets, all stuck together in a line, and presses them into a hole in the top of the gun. Then he raises it to his shoulder and pulls the bolt back and forth once. He aims into the barn and fires. The sound is really loud, and I was expecting him to be jerked back from the recoil, but he hardly seemed to move. He slides the bolt, and a shiny bullet case springs out. He fires again and repeats the action, with the percussive bangs rolling out across the quietness of the land.

'You try,' he says, holding the rifle out.

He shows me how to pull the bolt back, push the strip of bullets in and how to use the bolt to get the first bullet ready. Then he pushes the butt of the rifle into my shoulder and extends my left hand so it is holding the rifle on the wooden frame underneath the barrel. He then aligns my finger to the trigger and steps back.

'Squeeze gently.'

I pull the trigger. The recoil feels awful, jerking my shoulder back with a violent push. I have no idea what I am aiming for. I do the bolt thing and try again, repeating the action.

The recoil frightens me, and I feel myself bracing in readiness. I end up closing my eyes. I fire three times and hand the rifle back, trying to do what he did and point the rifle down to the ground.

'I'm no good at it, mate. You use it. We'll just waste bullets if I keep trying.'

He nods and picks up one of the shotguns, breaks it, and pushes a red cartridge into each hole, slamming the barrel closed.

He steps forward and again raises the gun into his shoulder. His finger pulls the first trigger, then drops back, and pulls the second one. Both times, there is a loud bang, but he hardly moves from the recoil. I pick up another shotgun and copy his actions, breaking the gun, pushing the red cartridge in, and snapping it closed.

I brace my feet and fire. The first blast feels almighty and slams me backwards. I'm more prepared for the second barrel, and the recoil doesn't feel so bad. I try again, loading and firing, readying for the recoil, and getting used to it.

'Mr Howie,' Dave gets my attention, pointing off to a male infected shuffling from one of the outbuildings, drawn by the noise and action. He is also fat, but this one clearly works and has big, meaty shoulders and arms.

'I thought farmers led healthy lives?' I murmur.

Dave just shrugs and takes the rifle back out of the bag, pushes in another strip of bullets, and raises it to his shoulder. He fires, and the infected man is thrown backwards, hitting the side of the building and slumping down, with the back of his head spread across the peeling boards, with bits of brain and bone dripping down.

The sight makes me feel weird. Like my heart is thumping too hard. I just saw a man getting shot dead right in front of me. We've killed countless with hand weapons, but nothing like this. It was so easy. Dave just lifted the gun and pulled the trigger.

For the first time in my life, I realise why firearms are so talked about. Their power is staggering. I've watched hundreds of war films and seen news reports of war footage, but I guess that I became desensitised over the years. It was just make-believe or footage from somewhere far away. The sheer brutality of it – point and shoot, and you make someone die. I'm suddenly very uncomfortable here, and I want to leave. I want to be back in the safety of the van and moving away.

We load up and head back down the lane, stopping halfway so that I can hop into the bushes and open my bowels again.

Dave looks a little rosy in the cheeks when we reach the van, but I'm melting, with sweat coming off me in buckets. We load the weapons, clamber in, and get going, with the lovely air conditioning kicking in. I want to eat, but my stomach is still gurgling away, so I just drink lots of water instead.

Back to the motion of driving, and my mind starts thinking how the shotguns are really quite heavy and cumbersome. The rifle is good, and Dave handles it beautifully, but I won't be fast enough to keep breaking the shotguns open if we get trapped. That makes me think I'll need to keep my axe with me at the same time as the shotgun.

I start imagining ways to fit the axe head to the end of the shotgun so I can fire, then reverse it, and chop them. I wonder if anyone has invented one. I could have patented it and made a fortune selling it to the crazy survivalists, who kept going on about the end of the world.

Mind you, they weren't so crazy, were they? Are they feeling self-righteous and pious, walking round their communes, patting each other on the back? Maybe one of them even started it? A mad scientist, a fundamentalist, end-of-world theorist doing it on purpose to prove they were right. Cleansing the Earth of all the sin while they sit back and gloat at the genocide they have created.

Fucking fundamentalists.

They're just mentalists; no *funda* about it.

CHAPTER NINETEEN

We are in a town. I was too busy thinking of my new *shotgunaxe* invention to realise we were out of the countryside. I was just following the road, and without looking at the map, I can tell we're in grimy Portsmouth. I should have been paying better attention and avoided the city area.

I've been here a few times. The old part of Portsmouth, with the historic ships, is nice, but the rest just looks horrible, with old, grey buildings and graffiti everywhere.

We used to come shopping here, and I've been for a few nights out with friends, but everyone seemed so aggressive and angry. Blokes with tattoos and earrings and barely clad women with scraped-back hair, big, hooped bangles, and mouths like sailors. Portsmouth is just a small city in the Home Counties, and I could never understand why they all tried talking like *mockney* Londoners, walking about with bandy swaggers.

We are on a wide road, with crappy-looking shops on either side. The metal shuttering on some of them has already been forced open or wrenched off. There are windows smashed and debris litters the place. We spot a few people too, running in and out of the smashed windows, taking armfuls of gear. They look furtive and scared, staying low or hunkering down out of sight until we pass.

We move further into the city, seeing more signs of civil breakdown. Bodies scattered in the road. Burnt out cars and vans. Some of the bodies are clearly infected. Sadly, a lot of them look like normal people. We pass cars still alight and others smouldering, with thick, black smoke coiling up into the hot summer air already stinking of burning rubber and chemicals.

I feel myself tensing up at the sight of it all. At the sinister vibe hanging in the air, at the weird silence where there should be noise and life. A noise to my side, and I snap my head over to see Dave pushing a fresh strip of bullets into the rifle and ramming the bolt back. He grabs the shotguns next, breaking them in turn to load with cartridges.

I stare front and think that places like Portsmouth were always on the brink of civil collapse anyway. Hard places full of hard people.

Dave pulls his Tesco fleece out of the bag and puts it on. It's roasting weather, and I can't understand why he's doing that. He zips it and then loads more of the ammunition clips into the pockets of the fleece. Next, he takes an empty plastic bag and puts shotgun cartridges into it. He leans over and threads the handles through my belt, tying them off. He makes a small, hand-sized hole in the top of the bag. I look down at the bag and feel for the hole with my left hand while slowing down to navigate the obstacles in the road. Cursing myself for coming this way and feeling a growing sense of dread in my gut. Silence in all directions. I look about, trying to see through the smoke to the smashed-in stores as we pass through a narrow gap underneath a concrete footbridge going over the road.

'Ambush,' Dave says; his voice still flat but more urgent, harder maybe. I snap my head up to see the top of the bridge alive with kids and teenagers leaning over, launching rocks and stones that thud on the bonnet and sides. 'Go,' he says, motioning ahead of us. I push my foot down to speed up and hear the sides scraping the debris as we get through.

'Shit,' I spot the barricade ahead running flush to the walls of the junction beyond it. Vehicles parked end on end and more stuff pulled on top – wheelie bins, sofas, beds, cabinets, and all manner of furniture. Worse than that, however, is the huge horde of infected gathered between us and the barricade. There must be hundreds of them.

I clench my jaw while my heart starts racing, cursing myself for coming this way and getting trapped between a huge horde of infected and a bunch of nasty kids chucking missiles about.

The van is strong, and the infected are slow moving, but if they mass in front of us, there will be no way through and too many to go over. I look back at the bridge and see the children running down the walkways towards the van with more missiles in their hands.

'Shit. Look at that lot,' I say as Dave leans forward, peers into the wing mirror, grabs a shotgun, and drops out to run down the side of the van while lifting the gun to aim.

'Dave!' I rush out and round the van to see him aiming towards the teenagers. His face so passive it sends a chill running down my spine. 'Don't shoot them!' I blurt the words out, thinking he'll do it or that the kids will keep coming, and he'll have to bloody do it. Another noise comes to the fore at that same second from the horde of infected all groaning as they turn and start moving towards us as the tension ramps, and the first missiles start getting lobbed towards us, but the distance is too great to risk harm, and the bricks and rubble they chuck just bounces off the road.

We have to get out of here. I glance about, thinking the safest thing will be to drive back under the bridge and hope we don't get hurt by them throwing things down. Maybe Dave could fire a warning shot? Would that work? I twist back to the barricade beyond the infected and realise that someone must have built it, and a barricade is used to keep somewhere safe, which must mean there is a safe place behind it.

'Dave,' I say, pointing to the closest building near the edge of the barricade. 'See those doors? Maybe we can get through?'

He shakes his head at me. 'We'll lose the vehicle and the weapons.'

'Well, we can't bloody stay here…' I trail off as one of the doors set in the wall next to the barricade slams open, and in that split second, I figure someone is trying to help us. 'Dave, see that? Quick!' I set off as a group of people rush through the door. A woman struggling between two men gripping her arms. She screams out, loud and terrified, fighting hard to break free and get back inside, and even from this distance, I can see the men cast fearful looks at the horde as they throw her out, sending her sprawling over the ground. She hits hard, grazing her knees and hands, but springs back up and runs back as the men get through the door and slam it closed.

She pounds hard. Screaming and shouting as the closest infected people start shuffling back towards her, then more, and more. She's empty handed too, with no way to fight them.

'PLEASE!' she screams out, hammering on the door. Her voice cracking with fear and panic. 'PLEASE! IT WAS FOR MY KID. I SWEAR IT.'

'Fucking hell, she'll get torn apart,' I mutter the words. Dave at my side as more of the horde start turning back towards her as she thrashes and begs to be let back in. Screaming that she's sorry.

'I SWEAR! IT WAS FOR MY BABY.'

'We can't just leave her,' I say. I don't know what she's done, but that is wrong, just plain wrong.

I run back to the van and shove more cartridges into the plastic bag, and grab the other shotgun before running back to Dave.

'Dave, you go for her. I'll draw them away,' I say. 'OI! OVER HERE!' I shout loudly as Dave runs behind me.

'Don't shoot me, Mr Howie.'

As if I would. It does make me pause and think, though, and also realise that if I fired now, I'd be shooting towards the woman. 'OI! COME ON!' I shout at the horde and start moving to the side, leading them on. 'HEY! STOP SHOUTING, LOVE! LET ME GET THEM AWAY,' I scream out for the woman to stop shouting, but she doesn't hear me, locked in her cycle of panic and terror, hammering on the door and still drawing the infected towards her.

'STOP SCREAMING. STAY QUIET.'

Holy shit. That came from Dave. A full-on, proper parade square voice roaring out. I look over, amazed that such a quiet man can produce such a noise. Mind you, it does the job, though, and she spins about, seemingly stunned at the sight of me and Dave.

'Stay still and be quiet, let me draw them off,' I call over. She looks terrified and doesn't show any sign of understanding me, but then she doesn't start screaming out again either. 'HEY! THIS WAY. COME THIS WAY.' I shout out again, trying to draw them away. A few turn and head my way, but many still keep going towards her, fixed on their prey.

There's nothing for it. She can't get back in the house, and she's too scared to think to run. Instinct inside. Nothing but pure instinct, and I lift the shotgun, aim at the infected, and pull the first trigger, then watch as the first person is blown back off their feet. I move the aim a little and pull the second trigger, taking another one down. My heart booms, and my hands shake when I start reloading, doing what Dave taught me: lever, break, cartridges out, cartridges in, closed, raise and fire.

I don't notice the recoil this time or the noise. I just see bits of body flying off as the pellets strike them. And at such close range, the effect is devastating.

I move back and keep drawing them away from the woman, not watching my sides enough as an infected man looms at me from the side. An instinctual reaction again, and I slam the butt into his face, making him stagger back as Dave steps in and slices through his jugular with a knife. The rifle on his back, hanging from the strap.

No time to think. No time for thought, and I reload to fire again. Filling the air with shotgun blasts and watching as the infected get blown away. Gunning them down one after the other. Another reload, and I glance over to see Dave fighting through the infected that had almost reached the woman. His knife slicing necks, severing arteries, and spraying bright red blood across the pavement. I reload and notice that the cartridges are the same colour as the blood.

I keep firing into the crowd.

An infected goes down just as I fire; the pellets spread out and knock several more over behind him.

Beautiful.

A gap in the horde, and I spot Dave reaching the woman, but she seems frozen to the spot, looking down at the bloody bodies lying at her feet. I start running over, veering around the slow infected, and jumping over bodies either shot down by me or killed by Dave. Blood everywhere. Thick pools of it on the ground and a few crawlers too, pawing their way over the road, with legs all shot to bits from pellet blasts.

'Is she okay?' I call out as the door opens again, with one of the men reaching out to grab a fistful of hair and yank the woman back inside. Brutal and harsh. 'HEY!' I shout out as Dave lunges at the door, getting his body into the gap before it slams shut. More infected in front of me, and I veer while running, catching sight of Dave pushing hard to get inside; then suddenly, he's gone, and the door slams shut behind him.

Shit.

'Dave?' I shout out, reaching the door. 'DAVE?' I kick at it, then spin to see the rest of the horde all aiming in towards me. Hundreds of them. I aim and fire, sending a few spinning away, then use the butt to hammer on the door.

'Dave. Open up!'

A woman screams from inside; then I hear muffled thuds and male voices yelling. It goes quiet, and I start hammering again as the door opens, spilling me inside as Dave slams it shut behind me.

A front room stripped of furniture. Like someone's lounge emptied out, and that awful droning groan of the horde fades away as I look about at the bodies. Men lying on a faded carpet with their throats cut open, with huge pools of blood already forming.

'What the fuck?' I gasp, looking from them to Dave standing perfectly still, with his hands at his sides, and not a drop of blood on him. Even the knife looks clean. 'Seriously... What the fuck?'

'They tried to grab me,' he says in that flat voice.

'Right,' I say, not knowing what else to say. 'Are they all dead?' I ask, which is a dumb question, considering most of them are nearly decapitated.

'Yes,' he says as calmly as ever.

I spot the woman cowering at the far end of the room; her hands covering her face. Then the interior door opens, and she ups and scarpers quick as you like as the door slams shut.

'Well. This isn't weird at all,' I mutter. 'Did you have to kill all of them?' I ask, looking about the room again. 'Fuck it, let's just go,' again, I trail off as a new sound breaks through that groan of infected. The steady beep-beep of a Tesco delivery van being reversed. 'Wankers, they're nicking our van...'

I burst out through the door into the street, blanching at the size of the horde now cramming towards us as Dave runs out behind me; both of us threading a wide route just in time to see our van reversing away, with kids in the front. Then it stops, and I hear the engine being restarted from one of the thieving little shits stalling it.

'OI! GET OUT!' I shout, running towards it.

Dave stops, and my heart misses a beat when he fires at the van, thinking he has shot a child – a thieving little shit, but still a child.

The front driver's side tire blows out, and the van drops down a little. He then slams the bolt and shoots again – the passenger side tire deflates. The van then stops, and three children get out and start running away.

Dave immediately raises the rifle and takes aim.

'NO!'

He pauses for a second and drops the rifle down, then looks back at me.

'They're just kids…'

'Okay, Mr Howie,' he says as though nothing just happened.

Fuck, this man is cold. I swear he would have shot them as they ran away. The front tires are blown out, and the van is resting lower.

'Grab the stuff. We'll have to run for it.'

Cartridges and ammo are shoved into the rucksacks. Dave goes around to the rear as I pull my rucksack on, fastening the waist and chest straps. The axe is there, but I can't carry it and two shotguns. I take the axe and drop the shaft down between my back and the bag. The large metal head catches on the top of the bag and holds steady. I tighten the chest straps, drawing it closer to my body. It might be cumbersome, but it's better than leaving it here.

Dave comes back with the other two shotguns and the rifle strapped to his back, over the rucksack.

If we go back, we'll get brained by rocks and missiles from the bridge. I move out, looking down to the building to see the door is now shut again. There's no clear way out. I spin around again and look at the row of shops and stores off to the right. We'll have to go through them and out a back door.

'That way,' I say and head off, giving thanks that the windows and doors are already smashed in.

'I'll go in, Mr Howie,' Dave says as we reach the closest one. 'Wait here…' He rushes on by with the rifle up and aimed as I come to a stop and wonder what I'm meant to do. Like cover him or something? I turn around and aim my shotgun about at different things. A wall. A car. A building. Some zombies. That sort of thing.

'No way through,' he says, running back out. We go down and repeat the same thing, with Dave running in, and me aiming at stuff. He comes back, and we try the next one. A hair salon, but even that has been looted. Someone has even stolen one of the big, heavy hairdressing chairs. Unbelievable.

'This way, Mr Howie,' Dave calls out.

'Righto,' I head in and follow through to the back to see Dave battering a back door open, and we squeeze through into a back service alley littered with rubbish.

We start off, following the alley into a residential area of small, terraced houses – a cheap rental area, already rough and grotty anyway, but it is looking even worse now.

There are small streets leading off to the left. They must loop around the back of the barricade, and seeing as Dave has just killed several of them, I think we should try and avoid it.

We keep going until we have passed several of the side streets; then we turn left and head down one of them. We get about halfway down and hear a loud bang from behind us. Dave instantly grabs my arm and drops down, pulling me behind the back of a parked car. I look around to see a group of men holding handguns running towards us as the bullets whizz by, into cars and bounce off walls.

'Fuck, they've got guns. Where'd they get them from?'

Dave doesn't reply but pulls the rifle around, and lifts the rifle to aim as he stands up.

'Dave! What the fuck you doing? They've got guns...'

Dave fires, dropping the lead man, who goes down hard, slamming face first into the ground. Not that he'll feel anything, what with half of his head now missing. The others scatter into the road, dodging behind parked cars as Dave slams the bolt back and steps out into the road, aiming this way and that as he scans the area while I listen to the loud, panic-filled voices of the men shouting at each other.

A head pops up, and Dave fires, with staggering reactional speed, and I see the head explode, with blood and matter spraying out as the guy is flung backwards against another car.

Dave rams the bolt and keeps moving. His movements are fast but controlled; the rifle looks steady in his hands.

'Go down the other side, Mr Howie,' he says, as calm as ever while motioning with his left hand, indicating for me to head down the side we just came up.

My chest is heaving, and I can feel my hands shaking as I set off with the shotgun braced in my shoulder. My vision seemingly coming in strobing flashes. Men shouting. Hoarse, ragged voices, but they sound confused, as though they're all trying to tell the others what to do at the same time.

'I'LL KILL YOU ALL!' Dave bellows out in that drill sergeant voice again. 'I'LL KILL YOUR FAMILIES. YOUR WIVES AND YOUR CHILDREN.'

'Fuck me,' I mumble, feeling the dread myself of his threats and the brutal, awful way he shouts the words. The effect seems to work, though, and the men starburst out to start running. Dave fires fast, dropping one. Bolt back, and he aims, firing again, killing another that sprawls out on the ground. Bolt back, and he turns to aim at the last one.

'Please! Please don't shoot, yeah?'

I reach Dave to see a young man cowering on his knees in the gap between two cars. His hands on his head; his eyes wild and full of fear, with tears spilling down over his spotty cheeks. 'Please, mate! Please don't kill me,' he gabbles the words out in that harsh Portsmouth accent as Dave aims the rifle at his head.

'Are you armed?' Dave demands.

'Please don't shoot, please...' the lad stammers the words out as Dave kicks him hard, knocking him over onto the ground.

'ARE YOU ARMED?' Dave shouts the words out.

'No, no, I'm not. I swear.'

'HANDS ON YOUR HEAD. INTERLOCK YOUR FINGERS.'

'Please, please.'

Dave kicks him again.

'DO IT NOW. HANDS ON YOUR HEAD. INTERLOCK YOUR FINGERS.'

The man responds, putting his hands to the back of his head.

'STAND UP. SLOWLY.'

'Oh fuck... Please don't. Please don't,' he begs as he gets to his feet. He's just a skinny kid, maybe eighteen years old. Tattoos on his arms and neck; the obligatory earring hanging from his ear. Dave looks at me and nods firmly towards the boy. I shrug my shoulders, not understanding what he wants me to do.

'Would you search him, please, Mr Howie.'

'Oh, right... Of course.'

Dave steps forward and pushes the end of the rifle into the boy's neck, which sets him off whimpering again as I step forward and start patting him down. He's only wearing tracksuit bottoms and a t-shirt, and I'm finished in seconds.

'Check the waistband, please, Mr Howie.'

I run my fingers around the waistband. 'He's clear,' I try to sound *military* but just feel silly.

'MOVE.'

Dave pushes the lad over the pavement up against a wall, then turns, and once more nods at me. 'All yours, Mr Howie.'

All mine? What am I supposed to do with him?

'Er. Right. Um...where are you from?' I ask, still trying to sound like I know what I'm doing.

'What?' the boy stammers, still terrified.

'I said where are you from?'

'Carter Street.'

'Is that where the barricade is?'

'Yeah. Don't kill me, yeah? I didn't wanna do nuffin' but he said I had to, didn't he...?'

'Who said?' I ask.

'My dad did, didn't he? That's his brother, innit, my uncle, yeah...'

'What the fuck?' I say, struggling to understand the spew of words. 'Who is?'

The boy nods at the body on the ground, the one that Dave shot first.

'That's your uncle?' I ask. He nods again, fast and shallow. His eyes flicking from me to Dave, but I can still see the feral cunning in them. 'Who's your dad?'

'John Jones?'

He says it like it means something.

'Who is he?'

'John Jones, innit. Like fuckin' everyone knows him, don't they? He runs the area, don't he? He's the fucking boss, innit...' the boy's tones grow more confident as he speaks.

'What does that mean?'

'Everyone knows him, don't they? Like, this is his patch, yeah. Even the pigs don't touch him.'

'And you're his son?'

'Yeah.'

'So he sent you after us?'

'Yeah,' he says, starting to sneer as he talks, puffing himself up.

'Why?'

'Cos of what you did, yeah,' he says, eyeballing me.

'What did we do?'

'You killed his mates. No one does that.'

'His mates? Oh, you mean the men in that room? We were trying to help that woman. Why was she pushed out?'

'She didn't do as she was told. Dad said we got to keep a firm grip of 'em. Stop 'em thieving and fuckin' about, yeah. Like, like, my dad, yeah. He said there's rules, and there's gotta be rules, and if cunts break 'em, then they can fuck right off...'

'What's your name?'

'Jim Jones, ain't it?'

'What wouldn't she do, Jim?'

'Fucking bitch, she thieved, didn't she?'

'I'm sorry, what?'

'The fucking bitch thieved. She stole from my dad, didn't she?'

'What did she steal?'

'Milk.'

'Milk? Why didn't she have her own milk?'

'We got it all stacked in the fuckin' house, yeah. Dad said we needs to ration it and stop the greedy cunts eating it all now...'

'So you took everyone's food and put it in your house?'

'Yeah, fucking right, we did.'

'Why?'

'Cos the greedy cunts will have the lot.'

'Why did she steal milk? Why not something else?'

I already know why she took milk. I heard what she shouted out, but I want him to say it.

A pause. A second's worth of hesitation. 'Dunno,' he says, instantly sulky and petulant.

'Why did she take the milk?'

'I dunno, do I?' he snaps, glaring at me. 'Fuckin askin' me for...'

'Yes, you do, Jim Jones. You do know why, so tell me why she took the milk?'

I can feel anger building in me – the arrogance and cocky attitude is winding me up. I can just imagine this little shit bullying his way through life, knowing his dad is the local big man.

'I don't fucking know, do I?'

'Jim, I will ask you once more,' I say in a voice now very low. 'Why did she take the milk?'

'I fuckin' said that I don't fuckin' know,' he sneers, defiant and angry.

I slap him across the face. Hard and stinging. Then I step in and take a fistful of his hair to yank his head back. 'You listen to me, you little cunt. I don't fucking care who your dad is. Right now, there is me and you, and that's it.'

He squirms in my grip, still cocky, still arrogant, still entitled, and that anger inside spikes again, so I head-butt him square in the face, driving my forehead into his nose. He drops down and puts his hands to his nose, blood pouring out between his fingers, but I wrench his head up again.

My own forehead really stings. I had no idea it hurt that much when you head-butt someone. I want to rub it, but don't want to do it in front of him.

'Why did she take the milk?'

'Her kids,' he gasps, spraying blood as he speaks. 'She took it for her kids, didn't she...'

'You forced a mother out into that lot because she took milk for her kids? You tell me now, why? Why did you do that?'

'Dad said to...'

'Did you help?'

'No, no, I swear I didn't.'

'You're fucking lying to me. Your dad is the big man, so you're the big man too. You fucking helped, didn't you?'

'No, no, I didn't.'

'Lie again and see what happens.'

'I had to... Dad told me to.'

'What happened when she went back in? You killed her, didn't you?'

'*They* did, not me. I swear it wasn't me that did it ...'

'You fucking little cunt.' I punch the boy in the face, then rain blows into him, with fists pounding his head. He drops down, and I kick him several times in the stomach and ribs. I step back, breathing hard. The fury is taking over. 'Get up.'

He staggers to his feet; his face is bloodied and bruised. I take the shotgun back from Dave.

'You are going to lead us out of here, do you understand?'

'Yeah.'

'It's yes, not yeah.'

'Okay, yes.'

'Now walk.'

I push him forward, down the street, and he staggers, then gains his composure, and starts walking slowly.

'Take your clothes off,' Dave says to the boy.

'What?'

'Take your clothes off.' I look at Dave, confused at the strange order. 'It's hard to run away when you're naked.'

'Okay, you heard him – strip off!'

'No, please. Please don't do that.'

Dave shoves the rifle into his face, pushing him hard against the wall.

'Now.'

'Okay, okay.'

The boy starts stripping, taking his shirt off first, then his shoes, and trousers, stripping down to his filthy, once-white boxer shorts.

'Please, I won't run. I swear.'

'Off. Now.'

He slowly bends down and pulls his boxer shorts off, covering his privates with his hands.

'Nice skid marks, Jim Jones. Did your dad tell you to do them too? Try wiping your arse next time, you filthy little shit.'

A few days ago, this act would have sickened me. If someone explained this situation to me in the staff canteen, I would deny that it was right and say no person should ever be treated like that, that we have law and order, and everyone is entitled to respect and dignity.

Not now.

'Hang on, Mr Howie.'

Dave runs back to the body lying on the pavement. I see him pick the gun up and pull the top bit back; then a magazine pops out of the bottom. He checks inside, then takes the gun apart, flinging bits in different directions. He puts one piece in his pocket, then runs back.

'It was empty, Mr Howie.'

We start walking down the road, with Jim covering his bollocks, but Dave makes him put his hands back on his head. He looks pathetic. Just a skinny kid – black tribal tattoos stand out on his pale skin. We reach the end of the road, and Jim turns left.

'Where are we going, Jim?'

'You said you wanted to get out, didn't you? Please, I'll tell you the way. Just let me go home, yeah.'

'You want to go home, do you, Jim?'

'Yeah.'

'What?'

'I mean yes. Yes, please, Mr Howie.'

Fuck it, now he's calling me that too.

'Okay, take us to the barricade at this end.'

'Really?'

'Yes, but do as you're told, or we'll kill you.'

'Okay, Mr Howie.'

We walk on past houses with doors battered in and broken windows. Like a warzone, with blood and gore smeared over walls and cars.

'Did you take all of the food from here too?'

'Dad sent the boys out, didn't he. Told 'em to bring it all back so's everyone has enough.'

'Regular saint, your dad.'

CHAPTER TWENTY

The barricade comes into view. Well constructed and dense too. Stretching from the end of the last house on one side and right across the junction to the end of the next house, sealing off Carter Street. There's also lots of bodies lying broken and dead and left to rot in the high sun. Grotesque and awful. A few infected too, shuffling and groaning off to one side, close to one of the building entry doors.

'Who killed them, Jim?'

'We did,' he says, surly and sulky from being forced to walk naked.

'What with?'

'I dunno, anything we could find.'

'Got any more guns in there?'

He pauses.

'No.'

A look passes between Dave and I.

'So, what are the rules in your street?'

'What rules?'

'There must be rules. Can people leave if they want to?'

'Yeah, 'course they fucking can,' he snaps in that nasty, goading tone. Dave reacts quickly, yanking the bolt back on the rifle as he prods the end into the back of Jim's head.

'Don't lie, Jim,' I say calmly. 'He *will* kill you, trust me. He won't think twice about it.' That's probably very true, and from what I've seen so far, Dave wouldn't even blink.

'Okay, okay. They can't leave, but Dad said it was for their own benefit cos they would just get eaten by the fuckin' zombie things, and then the zombies would get inside.'

'How would they get inside?'

'I dunno... Dad said they would.'

'So how does your dad stop people getting out?'

'He's got the boys watching both ends, ain't he?'

'How do you get in from this end?'

'Through the houses.'

'And I suppose the boys have got the end houses to stay in?'

'Yeah.'

Dave prods him again.

'Sorry, yes, Mr Howie.'

We stop about a hundred metres down from the end of the barricade. I look at Dave and motion towards a brick wall on the other side of the road.

'Get on your knees,' I tell Jim, pushing him towards the wall. 'Keep your hands on your head.'

The lad does as he is told as I clamber over the waist-high wall and prop one of the shotguns down while pressing the other end to the back of his head as Dave gets over and hunkers down.

'John Jones!' I shout out, but my voice cracks and doesn't come out so loud; then I remember Dave shouting earlier. 'Dave, can you shout?'

'JOHN JONES!' The voice is just huge, and I imagine it booming out across a parade square, terrifying new recruits. 'JOHN JONES! COME OUT, OR WE'LL KILL THE BOY.'

Within seconds, we spot faces in the windows of the houses overlooking us. Men seen snatching views as they try and stay hidden. Then one of the ground floor doors opens, and a burly man walks out, looking supremely confident. Swinging his thick arms as he swaggers almost casually and glances at the infected staggering across the road towards young Jim Jones on his knees, with his hands on his head.

'Dad,' Jim whimpers. He cuts off when I prod the shotgun a bit harder and watch the closest infected. An adult male that looks the same type as John Jones, with thick arms and torso and tattoos on his arms. Half of his face is missing, bitten off, and the skin is shredded down to the bone, exposing teeth through the ragged holes in his cheek. Drool hanging from his lips but also coming from the holes too, and his red, bloodshot eyes stay fixed on Jim as he staggers on, jerky and slow, but still closing the distance.

'Fuck. Oh fuck,' Jim squirms as John Jones stops in the middle of the road with arms hanging down at his sides. Tension in the air. Thick and palpable. Dave standing silently. The infected groaning and scuffing their feet as they shuffle forever on. Two of them veer off towards John Jones, who just watches them without expression before exploding with violent motion, lashing out to slam a fist into the closest infected, sending it reeling backwards. He grabs the next one by the throat, seemingly fearless of the risk of infection and throws it down like a ragdoll before stamping on the head, with a sickening display of utter brutality. Like a message is being sent.

Then he looks up; his face flushed, and his eyes set and hard as he moves towards us while lifting an arm to point. 'IF YOU TOUCH MY FACKIN' BOY...'

I raise the shotgun and fire over Jim's head at another infected, blowing it away. Jim drops to the ground, screaming in fear at the noise. If John Jones wants to show force, we can both play that game. I drop the gun back down to aim at the sorry sight of a naked Jim sobbing on the ground. 'Don't fucking move,' I say, looking from the lad to his father.

'Dad, do something!' Jim cries out.

'Shut up, Jimmy,' John snaps, his voice hard and rasping. 'Easy now, boys. What's the problem, eh?' he asks, switching instantly to a charm offensive, smiling as he speaks.

'You killed that woman.'

'Yes. I did,' he says firmly. 'Is that your problem? Yeah, I killed her, and I'll kill others if I have to. There's plenty of people in there, you see. They need protection, and the food won't last forever, will it? I've got kids and families, haven't I. Who's gonna feed 'em and look out for 'em? You?'

'She only took some milk.'

'Is that what Jimmy told you?' he asks with a roll of his eyes. 'The lad's a fuckwit. He ain't all there. Kids these days... They're different in the head,' he adds, tapping the side of his head as though to demonstrate the point. His tone stays calm and natural, easy going, like he's talking to his best mate – the charm oozes off him. 'Now listen, gents. Fair enough, you thought we done wrong, fair play. I appreciate you keeping to yer principles. I admire that in a man, but that woman was a smackhead, and she kept thieving from us. We told her to stop, but she wouldn't listen. I gotta whole street to take care of, and well… It might look hard to you, boys, but there's gotta be order. Now, do me a favour, boys, and let the lad go, eh?'

He sounds so reasonable, so calm and genuine.

'Between me and you, gents,' he says, lowering his tone as though imparting a secret. 'I don't much care for the little shit, but hiss mum, yeah, you know what women are like. He can't do no wrong in her eyes, and she'll give me hell if anything happens to 'im.'

'I'll tell you what, John. I'll let him go, but only if you tell everyone in there that they are free to leave if they want to.'

'Sure, sure, I'll do that. They can go anytime they want. But where to? Have you seen what's going on? They won't last five minutes out here. They ain't like us; they ain't survivors. Those things will tear 'em apart. You must have seen what they're like at night? They change, don't they? Get all fast and angry, eh?'

'Yeah. We've seen.'

'Well, there you go, I'm only protecting 'em till help arrives, just for now until the law gets a grip of it. You boys can see that, can't you?'

Fuck me, he sounds so normal. I imagined some tyrant with a harem and armed bandits surrounding him. Fair enough, he was shouting when he came out, but I *am* holding a gun to his son's head.

'So, let me take the boy in. I'll give him a good hiding for the trouble he's caused you, gents. Then you can be on your way. Or, here's an idea, tell you what, why don't you join us? We got food and plenty of booze…' He takes a step closer, nodding earnestly. 'And we got some nice looking birds in there too, if you know what I mean, gents. Couple of young lads like you, well, they'll be all over you,' he adds with a wink and a sneer, and a flash of his true colours.

'No, you tell those people they can leave if they want to.'

'Or what?' he asks, staring straight at me, unblinking, unflinching.

'Or we'll kill Jimmy.'

'You'll kill him, will you? What, just shoot him dead right here? Go on, then! One less mouth to feed if I'm honest.'

'Jimmy, you tell your dad what we did to his brother and his mates.'

'They shot him, Dad. They shot Uncle Jamie.'

John, Jimmy, Jamie – talk about inbred families.

John Jones' face flushes red. His fists start clenching, and he breathes hard. Then he stares straight at me, and although I'm the one holding the gun, I can see the power in the man and why his son said he was the boss.

'You killed my bruvver? You fucking cunts.'

He takes a step forward, and Dave shoots him in the leg.

'Fuck,' I gasp as John drops to roll on the ground, writhing and clutching his leg.

'DAD!' Jimmy screams out.

'Jimmy,' I shout. 'You run in there, and you tell those people they can leave if they want to. You do that now, or we'll finish your old man off, you got it?'

'You shot my dad...' Jimmy whimpers, scuttling over to his father. His bare arse poking up into the sky as he bends down to him.

'Jimmy, you listen to me. We'll kill him if you don't get in there now and tell them.'

'Go on,' John grunts, pushing his son roughly with blood smeared hands before going back to grunting in agony as I notice Dave appears to have shot him through the kneecap. Just the sight makes me wince, and I catch sight of Jim legging it across the road towards the door just as another man comes out, grabs Jimmy, and disappears inside.

'FACK OFF,' I snap back to see John Jones trying to crawl away from an infected woman staggering towards him

I take aim and shoot her down, watching again as the pellets tear chunks from her body and send her flying back. A few seconds to reload, and I glance to the blood pouring from John's knee, leaving a slick across the road as he tries crawling away, sobbing and crying as he goes.

The sound of breaking glass comes a split second before a deep crack and a chunk of the wall in front of us peppers with pellets, making me and Dave drop quickly from someone firing a shotgun. A second shot comes, hitting the wall, but with a few pellets going overhead, where we were standing but a second ago.

Everything happening so quickly, and once more, I think I should have watched where we were bloody going and avoided the city. Motion to my side, and Dave surges up to his feet, aiming and sending a shot back at the window used by the shotgun man, who falls away out of view. Another shot from somewhere near the top of the barricade. This one strikes the wall with a loud ricochet. Not a shotgun this time.

'Any ideas?' I ask Dave.

'Shoot back, Mr Howie,' he says in a way that would sound sarcastic coming from anyone else. It does, however, seem like sound advice, so I jump up and fire both barrels of the shotgun in the rough direction of the barricade as someone screams out in pain.

'Good shot, Mr Howie.'

'Trust me, that was more luck than judgment.'

A loud crack, and splinters of brick chip off near my head. Whoever is firing from the window is using the rifle now and is getting better with their aiming. Another shot comes, closer again, with more brick chunks flying off.

'Bloody hell. He's getting closer.'

Dave lays down on the ground and starts wriggling along the base of the wall, towards the entrance.

A groan above me, and I twist over with a yelp to see an infected man leaning over the wall. His mouth already opening to bite, with bloodied saliva hanging down. 'Shit!' I gasp out and push the end of the shotgun barrel into the face, and pull the trigger. 'Holy fuck,' I say when his whole head disappears, flinging his body backwards.

'Mr Howie, can you draw him out, please?' Dave asks.

'Eh?' I ask, still wide-eyed from shooting someone's head off.

'Can you draw him out, please?'

'Who?' I ask as the rifle from the building line fires again, tearing another chunk out of the wall. 'Ah, right, you mean him…er…what do I do?

'Give him something to shoot at.'

'Are you taking the piss?' I don't know Dave that well, but I really don't think he's taking the piss. 'Fucking hell… Okay, hang on.'

I take the other shotgun that Dave was using – the one with the barrels on top of each other – and start to raise it up to the wall until the barrel is poking out of the top. Two shots ring out. One of them from the window, which hits the barrel and sends it flying out of my hands. The other shot is a split second after the first and comes from Dave.

'Got him, Mr Howie,' Dave says calmly.

'Thank fuck for that,' I say, not so calmly, peering at the dented barrel of the shotgun. 'He broke your shotgun.'

'You used my shotgun?' Dave asks, looking back at me.

'Err…yeah. He broke it.'

'Right.'

He almost sounds annoyed as he shuffles back and takes it from me, inspecting the damaged barrels.

'Sorry, Dave.'

'It was a good gun.'

'We still have two more. You can have one of these if you want.'

'No, it's okay.'

'Honestly, mate, I really don't mind. I shouldn't have used it.'

'It's okay, Mr Howie.'

'I feel bad now… Shit, I'm sorry, mate.'

He looks genuinely upset. His face is impassive as ever, but just the slightest change in his manner portrays his feelings.

'Honestly, Dave, have one of these. I can't carry both of them anyway. Just take it for now until we get you another one.'

He slowly raises his head and looks at me, then at the shotgun lying by the wall.

'Really, mate, go on, take it.'

'Are you sure, Mr Howie?'

I pass the shotgun along so that the wooden end is just in front of him.

'Honestly, please have it. I want you to.'

He takes the gun and pulls it towards him.

'Thanks, Mr Howie. I'll look after it.'

'It's all yours.'

He busies himself for the next couple of minutes, reloading the rifle first, and then he looks at me before starting on the shotgun.

'Where now, Mr Howie?'

'I don't know. We should get going, I guess. Mind you, I feel awful if the people in there are being trapped by that wanker. Talking of which...' I pop my head up and look over the wall, then straight back down again. 'Or rather, until you shot him in the leg, and he got eaten by a zombie.'

We both raise up and look over the wall.

John Jones is dead. He had crawled most of the way back to the door, but the infected got him. Two of them are bent over him now – one gnawing on his already injured leg; the other on his face.

'He's almost at the door. Why didn't they come out and rescue him? They could have got him in while we were pinned down.'

'I guess they didn't want to, Mr Howie.'

'Hmmm... I guess you are right.'

The door opens, and a still naked Jimmy gets launched out. He looks even more battered and bruised now, with blood pouring from his face, and there are clear, distinct welt marks on his back. Behind Jimmy, another boy of roughly the same age also gets pushed out.

Several men come out behind them, holding long sticks. One of them has a samurai sword.

They start pushing the two boys away, beating them with hard strikes across the legs and back, making the lads scream out, begging them to stop as another man steps out of the doorway, holding a rifle in one hand.

He looks at the boys being beaten and says something to the men. They stop and all step away from the boys. The man with the rifle looks over and starts walking towards us.

Dave is over the wall instantly, rifle up and aimed. The man stops and raises his hands up to his sides, then looks at his rifle, and seems to realise what he's doing. He turns back and hands the rifle to one of the other men, then starts walking towards us again, arms up and palms facing us, a clear gesture to show that he isn't threatening.

He veers around John Jones and the infected munching on him. Several of the other men are on them instantly, beating them with the sticks.

'It's all right. I'm not armed,' the guy says, pausing to spit on the corpse of John Jones before walking on towards us.

I start to climb over the wall, but the axe handle hanging from my back gets caught, and I fall backwards with a gargled yell, then spring back up, and try, and smooth it out by walking through the entrance a few feet up. The guy pretends not to have noticed, but then Dave is aiming a rifle at him.

'Easy, Dave,' I say.

'Okay, Mr Howie.'

Dave lowers the rifle but keeps his hands in the same position, and I have no doubt that it would take him less than a second to shoot the man, who keeps glancing at the weapon, clearly thinking the same thing.

'So you are Mr Howie? I'm John.'

Another John? Carter Street clearly has no imagination when it comes to names.

'Don't worry, I'm not related to that prick,' he motions towards John Jones, then looks to the group of males gazing down at him.

'Derek, you'd better finish him off before he turns into one of them.'

The man with the sword nods and thrusts the blade into the throat of John Jones, then hacks away, ripping the flesh open. More of the men start beating the corpse. They are clearly angry and are whacking the shit out of him.

'As you can see, he wasn't well liked around here,' new John says.

'What happened?' I ask.

'He was a nasty bastard,' he says with a shrug. 'Loved throwing his weight around, but got this barricaded quickly and his mates all tooled up and took over ...'

'His boys must still be in there. What about them?'

'I think your man here did most of them in that room on the other side. Jones went nuts and sent more after you, but only a couple of those came back. I've never seen him so angry. It was bloody great. We took care of the other couple when you lot were shooting each other, and them two there, of course ...' He nods towards Jimmy and the other boy. 'That Jimmy is an evil little shit, untouchable cos of his dad.'

'Who's the other one? Don't tell me. James? John? Jamie?'

He smiles. 'Close. It's Jack.'

Another commotion at the door as a group of women come

steaming out, dragging another woman with bleached, blond hair and orange-looking skin with them, and I watch her fighting back and screaming out. Thrashing and kicking as the women grab her hair and pull her on.

A large, well-built woman breaks away and marches up to the men standing over John Jones' corpse. 'Give me that stick, Terry,' she snaps at one of the guys, who hesitates and looks about for help. 'TERRY, GIVE ME THAT BLOODY STICK.'

She snatches it from his hand and marches back to the thrashing woman, pulling the stick back and striking at the back of her legs. She goes down to the ground. The other women start kicking at her; blows hitting her stomach and back. The woman starts trying to fight her way back up, but is beaten back down and eventually curls up into a little ball.

The women are screaming at her, spitting down. One of them grabs her hair and yanks her head back, then starts slapping her in the face. Jimmy and Jack start running up, but the men move closer, brandishing the sticks, and they stop still – both of them crying and putting their hands over their faces, taking steps forward, then backing off again.

'That's John's wife – she was the worst one. Trust me, she had this coming for a long time.'

I look at the man, and he grimaces at the beating the woman is taking. The large lady drops the stick and grabs at the woman's feet, then starts pulling her shoes off. The other women grasp the idea, and within seconds, the woman is stripped bare. Scrawny, sinewy, and near on bright orange from fake tan.

'That's enough. Leave her be now,' new John shouts.

The well-built woman spins around and screams back at John, 'You stay out of this, John. You saw what she did. Fucking bitch!'

John raises his hands and takes a step back. The large woman is furious. Spittle shooting from her mouth as she screams and goes back to pull the woman onto her feet by her hair. 'YOU CAN FUCKING BEG. GET DOWN AND BEG NOW.'

The woman drops to her knees and crawls around, sobbing and begging at the women's feet.

'Look at those saggy tits. No wonder he kept trying to shag us,' one of the other women says. The rest start cackling, joining in with the humiliation while the fake-tanned woman clutches at their feet, but they kick her away, laughing at her plight, and I look away, unable to watch it.

'TAKE YOUR FUCKIN' MOTHER AND FUCK OFF.'

The boys gather the woman up and start walking her away, hobbling and limping from the beating they've all had.

John turns back to me as the women start heading back inside. A strained silence. Awkward and heavy.

'Er, so Jimmy said people can go if they want,' new John says.

I nod, not sure what to say.

'Great,' he says, nodding. 'Er, so... I think a few might stay now John's dead, and his mates are...you know...'

'Also dead,' I say.

'Yeah,' he replies. 'Where are you from?' he asks with a sudden change of topic.

'Boroughfare.'

'I know it. Is it the same as here?'

'Everywhere is. I heard a radio broadcast saying that London has gone.'

'Yeah, we heard about that. John Jones said someone told him.'

He doesn't mention the other part of the radio message.

'What about the forts?' I ask.

'What forts?'

'The radio message said for survivors to head for the forts on the coast.'

'That fucking shit! He told us the message said that the cities had gone, and we had to wait for help. The fucking wanker... Is that where you're going?'

'Eventually. I'm going for my sister first.'

'Where is she?'

'London. She got a message out, saying she's locked in her flat.'

'Well, I was going to ask you to stay with us. We could do with the extra protection, and we've got plenty of food. John saw to that.'

'Thanks, mate, but I can't.'

'Well, lads, if you change your mind... I guess we'll stick here for today and see about them forts tomorrow. Did they say which ones?'

'No, but I guess any of them will do the job.'

'I might see if we can send someone out to check first.'

'Good idea.'

'Right. Well, I'll let you boys get on then.'

'One more thing, mate. Sorry, but how do we get out of here?'

'To London? Well, that's easy enough...'

'No, er, we've got to run another errand first. Something else we got to take care off. We're heading towards Salisbury.'

He raises both his eyebrows and nods knowingly.

'Ah, Salisbury. Yeah, I understand. Don't worry – I won't say anything. You need to head for Southampton.'

'Is there another way, without going through the towns?'

'Yeah, head north on the London Road, then work your way over, but it'll take much longer.'

He gives directions to a junction, then explains that we have to decide: north through the countryside or west to Southampton, which will be much quicker but will keep us in the towns.

Dave shoulders the rifle and takes the shotgun in his hands. My shotgun is loaded and ready, and I can feel the weight of the axe hanging from my back.

We turn from the barricade and walk away.

CHAPTER TWENTY-ONE

'It will be dark soon, Mr Howie.'

I glance over at him as we walk on through the deserted suburban streets. A heavy silence hangs in the air that's filled with the stench of death and fire. Bodies everywhere. Lying in the road or across doorways. We saw a crawler a few streets back too. An old woman dragging her legless torso along the road. We just stopped, stared, and carried on walking. Flies too. Not too many but enough to start the spread of disease, and these corpses will soon be writhing with maggots.

A few more days, and this will be a very dangerous place, not just with the infected but also from the risk of decaying bodies festering in the baking summer sun. I swallow in the heat, feeling oppressed and hemmed in.

Coming here has sucked the spirit out of me. Up until now I had a purpose, a plan, and somewhere to go. We still have that plan, but the last few hours have taken their toll. Seeing real people being killed, not infected but real, normal people, has left me feeling empty. The world is crumbling at such an alarming rate. Everything we know has been taken away, and men still want to hurt each other.

I'm not some naïve dreamer, and I know what people are capable of, but seeing it happen and the speed it's taking place has left me appalled, with a pervading sense of shame inside me. Shame that we had to do what we did. Shame that I beat Jimmy and made him walk naked back to the barricade. I was no better than them.

The clear lines of distinction between right and wrong have merged. John Jones was an evil psychopath – of that there is no doubt – but in his mind, he was providing protection. Maybe he felt that he was doing the right thing.

He wasn't a James Bond baddie, stroking a cat and laughing evilly. He was violent and nasty, but he had the sense to build that barricade and gather food, and he offered protection to people who couldn't defend themselves.

I guess this was how the world was in times gone by – the strong protecting the weak, but at a cost? The end result was that we took John Jones out, but the people that replaced him could be worse, far worse. Maybe they'll get a taste of power and grow corrupt too. Power corrupts, after all.

At the supermarket, it was common for shop workers to be promoted and enter into the management team. Some of them were hungry for it, and people could see that they were different. Most of the lads always said they wouldn't change, that they would represent the floor workers and do what they could to make it better for them: better hours, better pay, more breaks. For the first few days, they would keep to their word and keep the banter going and sit with the floor workers at break times, but within a short time, they changed.

Just wearing a shirt and a tie marked them out, and before long, the gap was there – evident and clear for all to see.

I know because I did it. I tried to keep in with the lads, stay as one of them, and I swore to myself I wouldn't change, but I did. I made myself get out on the floor with them. When I didn't have my own duties, I would be working alongside them, but then familiarity breeds contempt, and some would try to take advantage, which was uncomfortable at times. I remember the general manager taking me to one side just after I was promoted and telling me to keep a healthy distance from them.

I blink the sweat from my eyes and bring my mind back to the now and this harsh reality of feeling like the buildings are pressing in. It's too quiet. Too hot, and I glance around at the dark windows that look like they're watching us. This city was active, rough, and violent, but it had life, a vibrant life, full of people of all colours and backgrounds. Now it's empty and sullen. It's only been a couple of days. What will it be like in a week, a month, or a year?

Stick to the plan, Howie. Get your sister and get to the forts. The forts are strong and safe and will be full of good people: soldiers, policemen, doctors, and nurses. There will be structure and order.

'I said it will be dark soon, Mr Howie.'

I look at Dave, assessing his quiet demeanour and manner – no chit-chat or witty banter, but then he doesn't show any sign that what we are seeing or doing is affecting him either. Then I think of the giant mound of bodies in Tesco and come to a stop while staring at him. He stops too and stares back. Silent. Expressionless.

'Dave, why are you here?'

He looks about. 'We walked here, Mr Howie.'

'No! I mean... I mean why are you here with me.'

'To get your sister, Mr Howie.'

'No, I mean why did you come? Why go through all of this with me just because of my sister? You didn't have to come. You could walk away any time you want. You worked for Tesco, and that's gone; it doesn't exist anymore. You can do whatever you want now.'

He doesn't say anything but just looks at me.

'So why come with me? Why do this? What about back there? You killed loads of people, Dave. You slit their throats and shot them. You shot them as they ran away. Doesn't that bother you?'

'No, Mr Howie.'

'Why? How can it not bother you?'

'They would have killed us.'

'But it's only because you were with me that it happened in the first place. If you hadn't come with me, you wouldn't have had to kill those people.'

He just stares.

'It's not okay, Dave. None of this is okay, and it'll never be okay. Never again. We stripped a man naked and beat him. We killed people. We took their lives away. Why are you here? Why are you with me? What for? You don't owe me anything. Tesco is gone. It's all gone, Dave. You're free to...to...to do what you want. I'm not your manager now.' I stop from suddenly becoming acutely aware that I'm ranting in the street. Even my heart is going like the clappers. I rub the stress from my face and groan softly. 'Sorry. I didn't mean it like that. Those things didn't happen because of you. I shouldn't have come through the city.' I stop again to sigh heavily, glancing around, then back at him, and although he looks exactly the same, there is a change in the energy about him. Like he's a bit crestfallen.

'I'm not like other people, Mr Howie.'

'No, mate. You are decidedly not like other people...' I say quietly, rubbing my face again. 'How the hell you can do what you do is something else. You're an amazing person, Dave, and I'm glad you're with me. I don't know who trained you or what they trained you for, but it's incredible.' I open my eyes to see him staring unblinking at me as though studying every word I say. 'Okay, look, mate. I'm sorry for sounding off. I shouldn't have. It's just... It's fucking mental. Just know you can go whenever you want. You don't owe me anything. Okay?'

He nods, then goes back to scanning around, eventually looking up at the sky. 'It will be dark soon. We should find shelter,' he says, as though that entire conversation just didn't happen.

'We'll look for a car,' I say, heading off back along the filthy, oppressive street.

We keep going, moving away from the epicentre of the mass civil unrest. There are still signs of devastation here but less so. Another few streets over, and we find some houses that look quite normal, with just the front doors open.

'There's a lot of undamaged cars here. What do you fancy? Sports car? Van? Something executive perhaps? Or shall we go for a four-wheel drive?'

'I don't mind, Mr Howie.'

'Oh, but sir must have a choice. Sir must choose one from our exciting range.'

Silence.

'How about the colour, sir? What colour would you like your vehicle to be? Metallic paint and alloys may incur an additional fee ...'

'How about that one?' Dave asks, pointing to a very old, beaten-up Skoda Fabia.

'You really can't drive, can you?' I say, moving on towards a Range

Rover parked up ahead. 'Now that is more like it. What do you reckon?'

Dave looks back at the Skoda, then at the Range Rover and shrugs. 'I don't mind.'

'You really have no taste, Dave. No taste at all.'

I try to keep the tone light to make up for my outburst a short while ago. There's something about Dave that makes me want to keep my head and wits about me, and I feel a bit embarrassed about having a go at him. 'Let's try in here.'

We move up to the front door of the house next to the parked Range Rover. The door is shut and locked. I knock several times. 'Hello, anyone there? We're not zombies. We promise.'

A terraced house with no obvious way of getting to the rear. I step back and aim a kick at the central panel of the UPVC door that rattles but remains undamaged. 'Like that is it,' I mutter, propping my shotgun down to start kicking hard, whacking the flat of my foot into the door that bounces and flexes, but stays shut.

'Mr, Howie.'

'Hang on, mate,' I gasp, kicking away merrily, but the flexible material absorbs most of the energy from my kicks, rendering me pretty much useless until I give up and bend forward to suck air into my lungs. 'It's no good, mate. We'll have to use the axe or find another house.'

'What about this?' he asks, standing nearby, holding a key in his hand.

'Where did you get that?'

'Under that gnome.'

'Right. You could have told me, though.'

'I tried to.'

Again, I swear there is a glimmer in his eye.

'Shall we, then?'

He steps up and unlocks the door, pushes it open, and waits with the shotgun raised at waist height. He stands still and listens for several minutes. I know what's coming... Yep, here he goes, waving his hands around, twirling, and pointing.

'Dave, if there are zombies, just say so.'

He turns to face me. 'Stay here, and I'll check, Mr Howie.'

'Okay, mate, we really have to practise these hand signals, though. I'll wait here, then.'

He enters and starts checking each room, which takes seconds as the house is tiny, with just two rooms downstairs – a lounge and a kitchen-diner room at the back. He comes back to the front door.

'Would you like me to check upstairs, old chap?'

He looks at me, then at the stairs, then back to me.

'Tell you what, why don't I stay at the door, and you check it.'

He's up the stairs within seconds, and I'm not surprised after my bumbling performance at the farmhouse. I hear him banging about, and then he's back down.

'All clear.'

'I wonder where they went to, then?'

'Who?'

'The people that lived here.'

'They're upstairs.'

'You said that it was clear.'

'It is.'

'Then who is upstairs?'

'The people that live here.'

'Are they zombies?'

'No.'

'Then why haven't they said anything or come down?'

'They can't.'

'Why?'

'They're dead.'

'Shit.'

I run up the stairs into the bedroom and see an old couple in the front bedroom covered in the blankets. The woman snuggled into the man, with her head resting on his chest. Both with dried vomit around their mouths, and I spot the empty pill containers next to the bed.

I stare at them for a few minutes. At how they look so peaceful and serene, and it breaks my heart to see this – an old couple, who made the choice to see the end in peace. Together in death as in life.

I go to turn away and pause on seeing a photograph of young children clutched in the woman's hand, and something about it chokes me up, with tears stinging my eyes, and suddenly I feel like an intruder. I rush out, closing the door quietly while murmuring an apology.

Downstairs, I find the coats on the rack in the hallway and search the pockets until I find the keys to the Range Rover.

We lock the door and put the key back under the gnome; then I think better of it and put the key back into the door lock, and leave it there. The house is secure, and it might just save someone else's life. I feel bad for the old couple, but the living will need it more than them now.

We backtrack through the side streets until we are back in town. It wastes a few minutes, but at least this way we can stick to the directions that John gave us. A heavy sigh, and maybe we can get on and make progress, or at least get out of the city before nightfall. Then I glance down at the display. 'Shit! No fucking fuel. Trust us to pick the only car with no petrol. Cock it. We've got less than hour before it's dark. Keep an eye out for a fuel station.' Then I smack myself in the forehead. 'There's no power,' I add with a groan. 'The bloody pumps won't work without power ...'

'We can siphon it.'

'Do you know how to do that?'

'Yes, Mr Howie.'

'Dave, you're a bloody genius.'

I check the fuel gauge. It's on the right, so the filling cap will be on the right too. I pull the Range Rover up alongside a row of parked vehicles and cruise along until we see one with a cap on my side.

'We need a tube and a jerry can, Mr Howie.'

'Oh, my fucking days, this just gets better and better. Where can we get a tube from?'

'I don't know.'

'It'll take too long. We need to find another vehicle we can take,' I say with a look at the sky. 'And we need to be quick. Keep your eyes open.'

We drive on with panic starting to rise in me. I remember the howling from the infected as night fell and then seeing them switch to fast moving, evil fuckers. I really don't want to be here when that happens. Although having said that, we haven't seen any of them about for a while now.

'Stop. Go back, Mr Howie.'

'What? What did you see?' I select reverse and pull the car back to a junction on the left. 'What am I looking at?'

'Down there.' He points down the road to a recovery truck, with an orange light bar on the top. The back of the truck is lowered down to the ground like a ramp.

'Dave, you beauty. Well done, mate.'

The recovery truck has a double cab and the words POLICE RECOVERY written on the side. I look to the row of vehicles and see a police car parked; the recovery truck positioned ready to start winching it onto the back.

The police car is an old Ford Focus and has seen better days. It must have broken down on Friday night, and they'd called for it to be recovered just as the world went nuts.

I park alongside and get out as Dave moves up to check the cab of the recovery vehicle.

'Mr Howie,' he calls. I follow his voice to see him looking intently at an infected uniformed police officer a few feet away, shuffling towards us with his hands ravaged down to the bone, and blood all over his face. He must have been on the ground, on his back and punching up at them. His knuckles have taken most of the damage, and I imagine him laid out, with infected leaning down into him, punching up repeatedly until they bit into his fists. Poor bastard.

'Dave, you get what we need, and I'll take care of him.' I wait for him to get a little closer, then move away a few steps, keeping him busy while Dave hunts around for whatever we need.

'Got it ...'

He comes out of the cab of the truck, holding a length of pipe and a green, plastic fuel can, and sets to work, syphoning fuel from the police car into the Range Rover.

I keep dancing around the copper, leading him a few steps one way, then back in another direction, figuring just to keep him busy until we can go. Then I realise that if we leave him here, he could infect someone else. I rush back to the Range Rover, grab my axe, and run back while Dave starts pouring the newly filled fuel can into the Range Rover.

'Sorry about this,' I say with an apologetic wince and rush forward to chop down into the infected coppers head. Bursting apart with bone and flesh spewing out as he falls to the floor. I wipe the axe on his trousers and walk back to the Range Rover. Which is when I glance at the green fuel can on the ground, then at the open fuel cap on the police car, and the one word that stops me in my tracks – DIESEL.

I run around the back of the Range Rover, hoping and praying that it has a letter D somewhere in the model type: *TDCi, TDC,* or anything that will indicate it's a diesel engine. Nothing on the back. I open the fuel cap, and my heart sinks – PETROL ONLY.

'Dave, quick. Check the recovery truck! Are the keys in the ignition?'

Dave runs off and sticks his head into the driver's side. 'No, Mr Howie.'

'Bollocks. Fuck it, we'll have to run. Get the stuff quick. We'll have to go on foot.'

'Why?'

'You've put diesel in the car, and it only takes petrol. It's fucked.'

'I'm so sorry, Mr Howie.'

He looks distraught, with the same fleeting look of panic and confusion that he had in the supermarket when I told him he should go home.

'Dave, honestly, it's okay. It's really okay. Christ, look how many times I've fucked up.'

I put my bag on and drop the axe down before tightening the straps. Next, I break the shotgun and check that it's loaded and ready.

Within seconds, Dave is kitted up, the rifle on his back, and the shotgun in his hands. We start off back the way we came, but within a few steps, we stop.

There are several infected shuffling down the road towards us. They must have come out of the buildings on the side. I look over and see more of them slowly emerging.

'Fuck it. Back this way, come on.'

We start running down the road and around the recovery truck, with the light fading fast. We need to find somewhere quickly, but the houses here are all smashed in. Plus, the infected behind will see where we've gone.

'We can't hide here. They'll see where we've gone and surround us.' I'm gasping for breath from speaking while running.

'Okay, Mr Howie,' he says; the fit bastard not showing even breathing hard yet.

We run down a straight road towards a T-junction. The buildings on both sides prevent us from seeing any further than a few metres in either direction. The running causes the axe to slip down and catch between my legs, tripping me over. I fall with a yelp, inadvertently clenching my grip on the shotgun and pulling the trigger, with a deafening bang as I shoot the side of a parked car, with loud, metallic ricochets pinging off.

A second for me to gawp at the shotgun, then up to Dave staring at me. 'Sorry, mate. I shot that car.'

'Keep your hand away from the trigger until you need it, Mr Howie.'

'Righto. Yep. Will do, mate.'

I wince as I get up, with both of my knees hurting from the impact of falling. I take the axe in one hand and the shotgun in the other and set off running again, albeit a bit slower and a bit more carefully now.

We reach the end of the road to the T junction, with one long, grey building ahead of us running in both directions.

'Shit,' I gasp at seeing the left side entirely blocked by a huge crowd of infected a few hundred metres up the road. All of them facing in, towards the big, grey building, but the crowd is too dense for me to see what they are looking for.

We look right, and my stomach sinks again. A set of very high, blue metal gates topped with rolls of razor wire blocking that side off. We can't go back as there are too many infected. We can't go left or right either. 'Fuck. Fuck,' I grunt the words out at our misfortune, clenching my jaw while trying to think what to do as some of the closest infected start turning towards us, groaning and moaning as more seem to notice us.

And then, as if that wasn't bad enough, the last tendrils of light fade, and the shadows drop as daylight sods off and lets the night come down upon us, and the air charges. Everything charges.

The crowd of infected all stop moving. All of them growing still. The sight sends a creep running down my spine, and I spin to see more behind us doing the same. Just standing still, blocking our way out.

I run over to the gates, hammering and tugging to see if they'll budge, but they're solid and strong. The only way out is to climb up, but the razor wire at the top will cut us to pieces.

Dave drops down onto one knee and shrugs his bag off, then opens the main compartment, and takes out a plastic bag full of rifle ammunition, and lays it on the ground. Next, he fills his pockets with shotgun shells, then puts the bag back on.

That's it, then. No way back, and no way forward. I take my cartridge shell bag and fill it up, then tie it off on my belt the way Dave did; the hole ready for my hand to dip into. Neither Dave or I say a word, and strangely, I don't feel that scared either. More annoyed. Irritated even. Pissed off and frustrated at not being able to get where I want.

Then, as one, every single infected looks up to the sky at the same time, with a silence that holds forever. And the darkness grows deeper; the night coming proper. The land growing dark.

They howl as one, and that noise, that awful, terrible, inhuman noise makes the hairs on the back of my neck stand up.

That long, continuous, drawn-out, blood-chilling roar. An immense sound, and my throat goes dry as the fear ramps. Pushing into my mind and gut. Or maybe it's adrenalin. I don't know. My hands and legs are shaking, and I'm bloody glad that I'm not using that rifle; I'd probably miss all of them.

I can feel my knees weakening. I heard this first last night, but I only had one infected in front of me then. Now there are hundreds all letting out the same deep, guttural bellow.

I look to Dave, but he doesn't flinch or do anything other than stare ahead. Even his hands holding the rifle are rock steady, and in this second, in this place, I take comfort from his courage.

'Dave, I just want to say... What the fuck is that?'

He looks at me in puzzlement, but I'm looking over his shoulder at the light on in the window behind him. There is a light on, in a building with power.

Then the light goes out, and the window goes black like the rest.

'That light went on and off – there's someone in there.'

I look deeper into the shadows and see a door secreted in the corner, recessed in a small porch area.

'Fuck me. There's a door.'

I race over and start banging on the solid metal door, using the flat of my fists to rain blows down on it while shouting out. 'HEY! LET US IN...PLEASE!' I scream out while the infected howl, and the world fills with noise.

Then the silence comes as the roaring ceases, and the hundreds of infected all stop at the same time and lower their heads to stare directly at me and Dave. The lolling, shuffling slow things are gone. This is night. These are different. Fixed. Murderous and driven with hunger.

Dave stands stock still. The rifle braced in his shoulder. The entire horde now silent and staring as though all waiting. Everything poised, holding on a knife edge.

An infected male out front. A twitch in his head. A growl coming from his throat, and as he lifts a foot to start running, so Dave shoots him in the face, and the whole fucking lot of them start charging at us. Screeching wildly, and once more, the air fills with noise.

'HEY! LET US IN. PLEASE...' I hammer on the door while Dave aims, fires, yanks the bolt back, and repeats with the pauses in between becoming less as he speeds up. His accuracy is awesome, with every bullet striking a head, but still they charge, closing that distance fast.

Dave pauses with the rifle to lift the shotgun that was resting against his leg and blasts both barrels at the front of the crowd. The pellets spread with a ripple effect as bodies are slammed backwards into the dense crowd, causing more to trip and fall. The effect is marginal. For every one he drops, more are coming, filling the gaps.

I give up hammering at the door and start back towards him, firing my shotgun at them, then breaking the thing open to reload and do it again.

A buzzing sound behind me, on and off, urgent and loud. I glance back, and the buzzer keeps sounding, with a clicking noise coming from the door that signifies the lock being activated on and off.

'Dave! We're in. Come on!'

I rush over and push the door, finding it opens easily, with bright light flooding out. Dave grabs his shotgun and runs for it, rushing through as I spot my axe propped against the metal gates. A reaction born only from instinct, and I dart out to run for it, ducking to grab the handle before running back. Dave holds the door open and fires the rifle over my shoulder as I run back with snarls and screeches sounding out behind me.

'GET IN,' he shouts, grabbing my arm and wrenching me in before slamming the door shut as the infected reach the recessed area and slam into it from the other side. I bounce off a wall from running in so hard and slam back into the door, heaving with Dave to get it closed. Both of us bracing to push as we fight to get it closed; then finally, with an audible click, the door seals shut.

CHAPTER TWENTY-TWO

A brightly lit, small room with a wooden bench on one side fixed to the ground with big bolts. Concrete walls painted institutional beige, all covered in frayed and peeling posters telling people to take their *offences into consideration,* and that they are *entitled to legal advice.* A police station. We're in a police station. The big gates topped with razor wire make sense now. So does the solid metal door. This looks like a waiting area where arrested people are held, and I spot another poster pinned to an internal door.

OFFICERS SHOULD WAIT UNTIL THE CHARGE ROOM IS CLEAR BEFORE TAKING THE DETAINED PERSON THROUGH.

A hatch opens above the poster as I finish reading, with a small female face peering out, twisting side to side to get a good look at Dave and me. 'Are you infected?' she asks in a bossy, high-pitched, squeaky voice.

'No, no, of course not.'

'You're bleeding.'

'Eh?'

'I said you are bleeding,' she repeats.

'I fell over,' I say, turning to look at the metal door behind us and the wild screeches and loud bangs coming from the other side. 'I promise we're not infected. We haven't been bit or scratched. Nothing.'

The hatch closes, and we hear muffled voices. It reopens after a few seconds.

'We need to make sure you are not infected. Strip off.'

'Strip off? Now, just hang on a minute...'

'I'm not arguing with you. Strip off or get out.'

Dave and I look at each other. 'But no... This is a police station, right? You are meant to protect us.'

'Listen to me. You are bleeding, and you are both armed. You won't get through this door, and I can easily unlock the outer door and let them in.'

I nod grimly and cast another look back at the outer door before dropping my bag and tugging my top off. We undress in silence, using the bench to unlace and pull our boots off until we're both just in our boxer shorts, and without trying to look, I notice that although Dave appears to be a small built man, his body is rock hard with lean muscle without an ounce of fat. He looks like someone from a movie, and his thigh muscles look solid as anything.

I look down at my wobbly stomach and untoned body in embarrassed comparison. Actually, maybe my tummy has gone down a bit. Probably through lack of food. I wasn't like fat or anything, just not lean or defined. I tuck my gut in, then push it out, and twist a little to the side, examining my own form while thinking I'm really sure I've lost a bit of weight. Then I look up to see Dave watching me silently, then glance over to the woman peering through the hatch, with my face flushing red.

'Lost a bit of weight,' I say, trying to sound casual and nonchalant. 'Running and...you know...er...'

'Pants off, then,' the woman says.

'Do what now?' I ask.

'We have to be sure you are not bitten.'

'Right. Look, I'm pretty sure I haven't been bitten on my willy...' I say, only realising how stupid the word willy sounds while standing mostly naked in a police detention room.

'Off or out – your choice,' she says primly.

Quietly seething, but with no choice, I take my boxer shorts off and step out of them, covering my privates with my hands. Dave does the same but stands with his arms at his sides without any concern at all.

'Drop your hands and turn around.'

I take my hands away and copy Dave by staring at a spot on the wall for a second before we both do an about turn and face the other way. Another second goes by, and I turn to catch her taking a lingering look at Dave's backside and lift an eyebrow at her.

'Yep, that's fine,' she snaps. 'Get dressed,' she adds, slamming the hatch shut.

'They won't let us in with the weapons, Mr Howie,' Dave says as we get dressed.

'Yeah, you're probably right. Let's see what happens.'

'Well done,' the woman says after opening the hatch a few minutes later. 'Now, if you want to come in, you will have to leave those weapons there.'

'Do we get them back later?' I ask.

She pauses for a minute before answering, 'We'll see about that. Right, put the guns over by that far wall and stand in front of the door. And the bags too.'

We do as told, stacking our kit and guns before moving back to the door.

'Hands on your heads, please, gentlemen, and we'll open the door. Got it?'

'Yep,' I say.

We both put our hands up on the top of our heads and hear the buzz of a lock being turned off, and the door swings in to show a long, narrow room with a high desk to the right side, with a larger space behind it.

Painted concrete walls and floor with two feet-marks set at the base of a long wall ruler measuring up to seven feet. I glance behind the desk to see monitors fixed high showing CCTV images, one of which shows the outside door and the infected throwing themselves at it. Black and white, soundless too, and somehow more sinister. Another monitor shows a man lying on a bench within a cell, apparently fast asleep. Either that or he's dead.

Then I look back to the front at the young policeman aiming a bright yellow Taser at us with trembling hands.

'Don't move, or you'll be tasered!' he says, trying to sound manly and in charge, with a quavering voice.

'Okay, mate, no problem,' I say calmly as he twitches aim from Dave to me.

The woman that spoke to us through the hatch has retreated behind the desk. She looks to be in her mid-forties, with a pinched face and lines in her pursed mouth and at the corners of her eyes. Sergeant's stripes on her shoulders.

'Right,' she snaps, all high-pitched and bossy again. 'If you're coming into my police station, then you will be searched while PC Jenkins covers you with the Taser.'

'Okay, miss,' I say, trying to stay polite and calm.

'It's not miss. It's Sergeant,' she snaps.

'Okay, sorry, Sergeant.'

A silence descends while PC Jenkins and the sergeant stare at us, then at each other, then back to us.

'Um... Who is searching us?' I ask politely.

'PC Jenkins will be searching you.'

'I can't, Sarge... I've got the Taser.'

'Right. Where's Ted?'

'He went to the toilet, Sarge.'

'What about Steven? STEVEN!' she yells out, and a very thin man with large, thick glasses appears at the doorway, dressed in the blue shirt of a community officer as I notice the sergeant and PC Jenkins have black shirts on.

'Yes, Sergeant?' Steven asks.

'Search the prisoners... I mean these men while PC Jenkins covers you with the Taser.'

'Me? I'm just a PCSO. I can't search people...' he says, looking scared witless.

'It's not a request, Steven, and you can search persons under the supervision of a uniformed police officer.'

'Why don't I take the Taser and let Tom search them?'

'He can't take the Taser – he's not had the training,' PC Jenkins says, looking very alarmed at the prospect of his Taser being taken away.

'Oh, but I can search people, can I?'

'Well, yeah, it's completely different. It takes training and skill to use a Taser. It's not a toy.'

'Enough! Thank you. Tom will cover with the Taser, and Steven will search them,' the Sergeant barks out, and they both fall quiet.

Steven moves forward and stops in front of me. I smile at him, feeling sorry for the position he is in and the fact he's clearly terrified.

'Steven, you're in the way,' PC Jenkins says with a huff.

'Eh?' Steven asks, turning to see he's in the way. 'Oh, sorry...er... can you move over a bit, mate,' he says to Dave. 'Then you go back a bit,' he adds, looking at me. I go to move as Dave steps into me, then turns to go back where he was.

'No, that way,' Steven says.

'Er, I've got no aim.' Tom says, moving over as Dave turns and bumps into me again, then goes back the wrong way, and does it again as Steven starts getting stressed, and I glance over to see the sergeant rolling her eyes, and PC Jenkins shaking his head while telling Steven to tell Dave to move.

'I'm trying!' Steven says, tutting as Dave steps towards him. 'No! That way...'

'Can you just search them, please!' the sergeant snaps.

'Steven's in the way,' PC Jenkins says.

'I'm not! He is,' Steven says, pointing at Dave.

'Sorry, sir, I'll move,' Dave gets it wrong again, seemingly confused at the orders and moving into me as I move to block the copper with the Taser while Steven grows red in the face.

'Steven. Get a grip and search these men!' the sergeant yells at him.

'I'm sorry, I'll go this way,' Dave says, stepping around Steven so he's between him and PC Jenkins. 'Is that right?' he asks.

'Oh, my god, this is just stupid.' PC Jenkins says, squeezing his eyes closed in frustration. Which is the precise second Dave spins and snatches the Taser while driving the flat of his hand into the copper's chest, sending him staggering back. Dave moves past him and aims the Taser at the sergeant, then at Steven, then back to PC Jenkins still righting himself as the room falls silent with shock at the speed of the man.

'Now, just you wait...' the sergeant starts to yell at Dave in her squeaky voice.

'SIT DOWN,' Dave shouts. She drops instantly onto her high chair, and I imagine her feet dangling down, not touching the floor. Then I smile as I stare at Dave in admiration.

'Bloody hell, mate, well done.'

'Thank you, Mr Howie,' he replies, moving his aim from one to the other to show he has a clear shot as Steven and PC Jenkins stand slack-jawed and wide eyed, somewhat frozen to the spot.

'Ello, ello, what's going on here, then?' An older man walks in – late fifties, thick set, and bald, with weathered features. A folded newspaper under his arm as he carries two disposable cups of hot liquid and pauses with a brief look about the room. 'Oh, dear... Tut-tut! Well, this seems a bit of a pickle, don't it? Excuse me, mate. These cups are scalding hot; it's these cheap cardboard things. They burn your bloody fingers off.' He moves past Dave, behind the desk and puts the cups down before blowing on his fingers. 'Tea's there, Debbie,' he says without a glance at the silent sergeant, and I notice he's also wearing a black shirt but has the letters DO on the shoulders. He sits heavily in the other chair, groaning as though with pleasure at taking the weight from his feet, and finally looks at Dave, then at me.

'So? What's it like out there? Still hot 'n' horrible, is it?'

'Er, yeah, you could say that,' I say.

'Well, it had to happen, didn't it? So, which one of you has the army voice? I heard it all the way down the block, and I thought to myself there's a voice from the services, if ever I heard one. It took me back a few years, I can tell you.'

'It was him.' I point at Dave, almost feeling like a schoolboy, dropping my mate in it.

'It was you, was it? What were you in?'

'I can't say.'

I bloody knew he would say that.

'Ah, I get it,' the older guy taps his nose and winks knowingly at Dave, then looks at the Taser with distaste. 'You got that off young Jenkins, didn't you? I kept telling him not to keep waving it about. Did he listen, though? No, he didn't. They never do, these young 'uns. Mind you, we never needed 'em in my day.'

'Oh, you're a policeman too?' I ask him.

'No, no, not anymore. I did my time and got out.' He points to the letters on the sleeve of his shirt. 'Detention officer now. Five years army, then twenty-five in the job, and I thought to myself, Ted, it's time to get out, but I keep coming back, like an old fool.'

He speaks calm and easy, but I can see that he is appraising Dave and me constantly. Years of hard situations and having to rely on his wits have left him sharp, and the experience is oozing off of him.

'Ted? I'm Howie, and this is Dave. It's very nice to meet you.' I step up to the desk and extend my hand. It's awkward, but Ted stands up and leans over, dwarfing my hand in his.

'Nice to see someone still has manners,' he says, offering his hand to Dave, who just aims the Taser at him.

'Dave, I think we can put it down now,' I say.

'Yes, Mr Howie,' Dave says, lowering the Taser and putting his hand out to Ted. They shake hands very briefly, and then Dave pulls back and wipes his hand on his trousers.

'I did wash them, you know,' Ted says.

Dave looks at his hand, then back at Ted.

'I'm only joking,' Ted says, deadpan. 'I didn't wash them, really.'

Dave goes back to wiping, and Ted laughs out loud – a nice, deep, hearty laugh.

'Ah, you Special Forces boys are all the same. Trained killers, I'll grant you, but funny buggers, though.'

PC Jenkins' mouth drops open at the mention of Special Forces as his eyes start shining with love hearts. 'Bloody hell, are you SF? I knew you were SF the way you took that Taser off me. Wow! Two SF in here. Are you on operations then? I knew they would send the SF in.'

'We aren't Special Forces,' I say. 'We're just trying to get somewhere and got caught out, that's all.'

'Where are you going?' Ted asks.

'Salisbury.'

I knew it was a mistake the second it came out of my mouth.

'Salisbury?' Tom asks, his eyes now even wider. 'The army base? Wow, that's so cool! Is that where your HQ is?'

'What? No. Look, we aren't Special Forces.'

'Are you like planning a counterattack, yeah? Did they send you to rescue us? Can I have gun? I'd be good with a gun.'

'That's enough,' Ted says heavily, nodding at the young copper. 'You leave it alone with all the questions.'

'Dave, I think we can give the officer his Taser back.'

Dave looks at me, then at PC Jenkins. He checks again to make sure I'm not going to change my mind, then slowly hands it over, turning it so that the handle is facing PC Jenkins, who takes it and looks at Dave like a puppy.

'You can keep it if you want.'

'PC Jenkins, that is the property of the constabulary and not yours to give away,' the sergeant says, clearly feeling confident again now that Ted is here, and Dave has handed the weapon over.

'Sorry, Sarge.' He looks crestfallen, chastised in front of his new hero.

'Can we get our weapons back now?' Dave looks to Ted, not at the sergeant.

'I don't think that will be a problem, will it, Sergeant?'

Ted defers to the sergeant but has made it clear what he thinks. She looks trapped and scared.

'Look, Sergeant. I promise you that we are not psychos or anything. We just got caught out. You've seen what's happening out there. The weapons can stay there if you're sure we're safe in here...'

'Oh, this nick is safe enough,' Ted says. 'It's built to handle terror suspects, so the security is very enhanced. The only way into this part of the building is through the big gates or that outer door. The interior door is solid and can only be opened from this side.'

'Okay, then we'll leave them there for now.'

'Tell you what, gents. Why don't I take you to the canteen for a brew? That all right with you, Debbie?'

'Well, it's time for the emergency strategy meeting anyway, and you two can come.'

She gets up and walks out from behind the desk. Stepping down from the raised area, she looks tiny, shorter than Dave by inches, but with the same, wiry frame. She walks out of the room and down the corridor.

'I'll show you the way. After me!' Ted goes out next, followed by Steven and PC Jenkins.

Finally, Dave and I leave the room and start down the corridor.

The corridor is long, and we pass cell doors on both sides, and every few metres, we have to turn sharp left or right. 'It's designed like that on purpose,' Ted explains. 'Stops anyone being able to shoot all the way down the corridor, and it disorientates anyone trying to escape.'

'Are we leaving this area?' I ask as we reach another fortified door being opened by the sergeant.

'It's okay. The whole building is safe,' Ted says.

The sergeant opens the door with a key and steps out. Steven follows her, then PC Jenkins.

'Tom, where are you going?' she asks.

'To the meeting, Sarge.'

'Tom, you know you have to stay here.'

'But, Sarge...'

'No buts. Stay here to let us back in and watch the prisoner.'

'But that's not fair. Why can't *he* do it?' PC Jenkins points to Steven.

'Don't drag me into this. I'm not trained to look after a prisoner.'

PC Jenkins then stares at Ted, clearly thinking the detention officer should do it, but Ted just lifts an eyebrow and stares down at the young officer. 'Something on your mind, lad?'

'No, I'll stay...' Tom sighs and steps back in, holding the door open for Dave and me to step through.

Ted chuckles as the door closes. 'Keen as mustard and just about as bright too.'

'Did he say *prisoner*?'

'One of our locals,' Ted replies.

'You've got a prisoner with all this going on? Can't you just let him go?'

'Old Harry?' Ted chuckles. 'He don't want to go anywhere – he's homeless. He spends more time in here than at the shelters. Every time it gets too cold or too hot, he breaks something and waits to be arrested, bless him.'

'Bloody hell, does he know what's going on out there?'

'What, him? He's madder than a bucket of frogs. We tried telling him, but he just gibbers on. Nah, he's alright. Wouldn't hurt a fly.'

'So... Why is he in a cell, then?'

'He always has the same cell and gets very strange if someone else is in there. Besides, the door's wide open, and he can help himself to a drink or food. Not that he will. He'll just press the buzzer and wait to be served, the cheeky sod.'

We go up a flight of stairs, and Dave is keenly looking about, taking in all of the exits and windows, checking and rechecking constantly. We head along a carpeted corridor, passing several dark and empty offices on the way, full of blank monitor screens and office swivel chairs.

'Where do you get the power from? The grid went out everywhere else,' I ask.

'There's a generator in the basement. We have to be able to run the cell block in the event of a terrorist attack. We turned everything else off so we don't use too much juice,' Ted says as the sergeant opens a door into a large conference room and switches the lights on, flooding it with bright, fluorescent light.

I walk in after her, feeling better now that we are with the organised authorities. They must have contingency plans and regular updates from the government, and they might be able to help find my sister.

The sergeant is odd, but I guess she is just the "desk" sergeant or whatever they call them. We enter the room, and the sergeant indicates for us to be seated at the large, oval desk. Then she goes to one end and sits down in front of a bunch of hardback files and manuals resting on the tabletop.

'Steven, make everyone a drink, please,' she orders in that curt tone.

'Yes, Sergeant,' he replies, toddling off to the end of the room to busy himself with a kettle plugged into the wall.

Within minutes, we both have a steaming mug of tea in front of us as we hear voices coming down the corridor. I look to the door in expectation of seeing senior officers, but only two people enter, both young women. One with a blue shirt on, and one with a black. I realise now that the blue shirts are for the Police Community Support Officers, and the black shirts for the proper officers. They sit down, and I realise that Steven has made them a drink, and that he hasn't made any more, which suggests there is no one else coming.

'Where's everyone else?' I ask.

'Err, thank you. We'll come to you in a minute. There is an order to these meetings, you know,' the sergeant says, giving me a withering look.

Ted just sits back and drinks his tea.

'Right, everyone's here,' she says crisply, looking about the room. 'Then let us begin. The time is now 22:07 hours, and I am opening the emergency strategy meeting. As the senior officer, I will chair the meeting, and PC Trixey will take the minutes.'

I look to the new female officer; blonde hair pulled back into a bun. She looks very young but very serious and is studiously holding a pen over some writing paper.

'PC Trixey, please record that we have two members of the Armed Forces with us.'

'We're not in the army,' I say.

'Yes, okay, I understand. PC Trixey will note that we have two members of the public as observers. Just note down, separately, that they are Armed Forces. Obviously, they can't officially be here in this meeting,' the sergeant says, making air quotes as she speaks.

'For god's sake. We're not in the bloody army!'

'Er, thank you, Mr...?'

'It's Howie,' I say tightly, rubbing my temples.

'Thank you, Mr Howie, but please stop interrupting the proceedings.'

Bloody hell, why is everyone calling me Mr Howie?

'Now, for the record, also present is PCSO Steven Taylor, PCSO Jane Downton, Detention Officer Ted Harding, PC Terri Trixey and...?' she looks at Dave.

'Dave,' he says.

'Dave what?'

'Just Dave.'

'Oh, of course. Terri, mark that down, will you? Obviously, they can't give their full names for security reasons. Now, on to proceedings. PC Trixey will just go over the minutes from the last meeting.'

PC Trixey flicks to some previous notes made on the same writing paper, then clears her throat. 'The last emergency strategy meeting was held today at twenty hundred hours.' She looks up and glances round at everyone. 'Er, the same people were present at the previous meeting, with the exception of our two members of the public here.' She does the quote things with her fingers too. 'At the last meeting it was required for a full inventory of supplies to be done. There was also an issue with PC Jenkins walking into the female officers' shower room, and consideration to be given to the fuel supply for the generator.'

'Thank you, PC Trixey,' the sergeant says. 'First, I would like to say that in relation to agenda item two, I have spoken with PC Jenkins, who assures me it was an accident and promises that it won't happen again.'

'Fucking pervert.'

'Yes, thank you, PCSO Downton. I have dealt with the matter and made it clear that disciplinary procedures will be instigated if it happens again. Now, in relation to item number one, who undertook the assessment of the supplies?'

'You said that you would ask Tom,' says PC Trixey.

'Ah yes, of course, I did... Well, he isn't here, so we can find out later. What about the fuel for the generator? Who did we task with that one?'

'It was Tom, again.'

'Right, well, we can find that out later too. On to new items. We need to establish a cleaning rota. Any volunteers to draft one for approval?'

'I can do that.'

'Thank you, Steven. Please draft the cleaning rota and submit to me for approval. Once it has been approved, it will be posted in the canteen. Now we also need a sleeping rota so that we make sure we don't all sleep at the same time, like we did last night.'

'I can do that, too.'

'Thank you, Steven. Please draft the schedule and submit it to me for approval. Once it has been approved, it will be posted in the canteen.'

'Tom should go first. He slept all bloody night.'

'Yes, thank you, PCSO Downton, good point. Steven, make sure that Tom goes down for the first night.'

'Yes, Sergeant.'

'Right, well, that just about covers everything. Questions from the floor? Steven, do you have anything?'

'Er. just one thing, Sergeant. Tom keeps eating all of the lasagnes from the prisoners' food cupboard. He knows I can't eat the curry, and I don't like the all-day breakfast.'

'Thank you, Steven. I will speak to Tom and request that he does not eat all of the lasagnes. PCSO Downton?'

'Nothing from me. Just keep that pervert out of the showers.'

'Yes, I've already covered that. Listen, Jane, if this is really bothering you, then you can take out a grievance against PC Jenkins. Just submit a report to me for approval, and I will deal with it.'

'Okay, thanks, Sarge.'

'PC Trixey?'

'Yes, I have a point to raise. At a previous meeting, a decision was taken to limit each person to a five-minute shower each. Now, while I accept that the water supply and power are important, I feel this is victimisation and prejudice. Female officers have longer hair, and it takes more time to wash and rinse out; therefore, I request that the showering time for female officers be extended to ten minutes.'

'Good point, PC Trixey. I am in favour of this. It is true that female officers generally have longer hair and need more time for adequate cleaning. I pass the notion, and this will be effective immediately. Please note that down PC Trixey.'

'Noted, Sarge.'

'I hope that isn't just female police officers. I have longer hair too, and I don't wish to be discriminated against just because I am a community support officer.'

'Very true, PCSO Downton – and a good point raised. Please amend the notes to show that all female *employees* are entitled to the extended shower period. DO Harding?'

'No, nothing to raise, thank you.'

'Thank you, DO Harding. And now the observers... Dave, do you have any points?'

'When can we get our weapons back?'

'Ah, right. A good point for discussion. Mr Howie? Do you have anything?'

'Yes! I bloody do. What kind of shit is this? What the fuck are you lot going on about? Showers, cleaning rota? What the...?'

'Stop right there, Mr Howie. I will not allow the use of profane or abusive language within this building.'

'I DON'T GIVE A FUCK,' I say, slamming my hand down hard on the table, making them all jump, with the exception of Dave and Ted, who both just carry on drinking tea. 'Where's the senior officers? Where's the inspectors and superintendents? Where's the bloody policemen?'

'Er, excuse me. The term is police officer, actually, not policemen,' PC Trixey says, glaring at me.

'I don't give a fuck what the term is, and forgive me for not being politically fucking correct, Miss or whoever the hell you are, but what are you all going to do about that lot out there? The...the...the fucking thousands of zombie things running about, eating people. Other people are killing each other too. Where's the riot squad and the armed officers? Why aren't they here? What about the government? What have they said to you? Have you had updates or been told anything?' I glare at the sergeant.

'No, we haven't been told anything,' she says softly.

'Nothing? No updates?'

'No, nothing.'

'What about your radios? You must be able to speak to each other?'

'They went down with the phones. They work off mobile phone networks,' she says, dropping her eyes.

'Fuck me. What about the old radios that use radio frequencies?'

'They were destroyed when we got the new ones.'

'Jesus Christ,' I rub my temples again.

'You must have secure phone networks, some hotline to your headquarters?'

'This isn't the movies, Mr Howie. We don't have anything like that.'

'Email? You have power. What about emails? Oh, they won't work without phone lines. Policemen or officers, people in fucking uniforms. Where are they all and the senior officers?'

'They've gone...'

'Gone where? Be specific.'

'It was a Friday night. We had a duty inspector, but he left when the troubles started. Some of the officers were out patrolling and just never came back, and those that did left to be with their families.'

'What about your armed officers?'

'We didn't have any on. We don't have enough as it is. The next division was covering our sector.'

'So, this is it? The glorious British police reduced to a couple of community support officers, two infant coppers, and you?'

I don't mention Ted, out of respect. He doesn't seem to notice but carries on drinking the tea. That cup must be bloody deep.

'Yes, this is it.'

'So why are you here? Why didn't you leave to be with your families?'

'We don't have anyone. Steven and Jane are both single. Terri and Tom are new and got posted away from where they grew up. I'm not married and, I have no family.'

'Ted?' I ask, softening my tone.

'Me? Oh no, I'm quite happy here. The wife took my kids to Australia years ago. The job's been my family ever since.'

I lean forward and rest my head in my hands, looking down at the desk as the realisation hits me that this is it. The end of the world.

'We lost the plot a few years ago, I'd say,' Ted says with a long sigh. 'We used to be good at this sort of thing. Oh, we were shit at the community policing, and yeah, we did isolate people, but we nicked more then than we do now, and we were good at major incidents. We always trained and undertook exercises to prepare, but now it's all done from a desk. We, old dinosaurs, tried telling them about the new radios, but they didn't listen. These young 'uns get more training in *diversity* than they do in crime or major incidents now.'

I sit back, rubbing at my chin, which is fast becoming stubbly. 'I guess you couldn't have done much anyway,' I say quietly. 'It spread so fast. I don't know, I was just hoping that there'd be some plan or something, you know? *Hold on. Help is coming* – that sort of thing.'

He shakes his head. 'Nope.'

'So what will you do? Just wait here?' Silence. No one wants to answer me. I look at Dave, but he is devoid of expression as usual. 'Armoury? You must have one, with weapons, firearms?'

The sergeant shakes her head.

'No, we used to, but they centralised it, and all the firearms officers have to go to the divisional HQ to arm up.'

I shake my head slowly, dumbfounded at the turn of events and looking at the desperate people around me clinging on to a world that has already disappeared, trying to use grievance procedures, and making cleaning rotas. Maybe it's better than John Jones and his way, but it's sad, very sad.

'So you have no weapons, no communication, no direction. What will you do?'

'We do have weapons,' PC Trixey butts in.

Dave looks at her.

'In the evidence room,' she continues. 'We seized a load of stuff a few days ago.'

'What are they?' I ask her.

'There's quite a few air rifles.'

Dave carries on drinking his tea.

'And some bullets,' she adds.

'What kind?' I ask.

'I don't know. They all look the same to me.'

'Can we see?' I ask the sergeant.

'Terri will show you.'

'Dave, do you want to go?'

'Okay, Mr Howie.'

He gets up and follows PC Trixey out of the room. The sergeant then asks Steven and Jane to leave us in private for a few minutes, and as soon as the door closes, she turns to me.

'I'm not stupid, Howie. I know how this looks, but they have nowhere to go. None of us do,' she pauses, looking at me. 'But we're safe here, the building is strong, and we can wait it out. We have plenty of food and water.'

I look to Ted who just nods. What else can he say?

'It must seem strange to you,' she continues. 'But they won't last five minutes out there, so we keep on. It gives them hope. Anyway, what have you seen out there? What do you know?'

I recount to them what we had seen so far, but I leave out the bit about Giselle, the stripper, and Marcus. I guess they wouldn't be that interested.

I also tell them about John Jones and the Carter Street barricade, then about the radio message and the forts. They both lean forward and listen intently, asking probing questions. I answer all of the questions as best I can, which doesn't take long, seeing as I don't know much.

Finally, I tell them of my plan to head to London for my sister, then trail off into silence.

'Well, we can't do anything tonight, Debbie.' Ted says, looking at her. 'But those forts sound good, and they'll need a good sergeant.'

'And an experienced officer, Ted,' she replies.

'How will you get there?' I ask. 'You've got a few hundred infected outside your gates.'

'There's an old riot van in the yard outside. We can put the grille down to cover the windscreen and plough through,' Ted answers.

'Sounds good. Mind you, you said you're safe here. Maybe you could just wait it out and hope help comes.'

'No, I, er, I don't think any help will be coming,' Debbie says. 'And I think we need to be with other people.'

'What about you?' Ted asks.

'We have to push on. We'll join you later when I've found my sister,' I sit back and rub my face again, feeling weary to the bone. 'Do you mind if we bed down here for the night and get going in the morning? When they're slow again.'

They look at each other and nod.

Twenty minutes later, we sit in the canteen, eating microwaved ready-made prisoner food with the others, and even Tom has been let out of the custody section.

'What about Harry?' I ask.

'He's alright, fast asleep on his bed; besides, he can't go anywhere,' Tom replies but looks to the sergeant for confirmation.

'He'll be fine for a few minutes, Tom.'

'Thanks, Sarge.'

A change to the atmosphere. A softening perhaps. I know Ted and the sergeant told them about the forts and the plan to leave, and I guess that has eased the tensions a little.

We've even got our weapons back, which Dave is clearly happy about. And when I say happy, I mean he shows no reaction whatsoever other than stripping them down to clean while Tom stays glued to his side, watching every move and asking questions about Special Forces.

'I can't tell you,' Dave replies each and every time, which just seems to excite Tom even more.

It's only been two days since this began. Three if you count today, but it feels like weeks, and if these past few days have been anything to go by, then getting into London will be a bloody nightmare. I eat my fill, drink tea, and grow sleepy until Dave and I are left alone, with thick blankets to use as mattresses, and start settling down, ready to sleep.

The lights go out as they are killed to preserve power coming from the generator, and I sit still for long minutes, looking about the room bathed in moonlight coming through the windows.

Tomorrow, we go to Salisbury, find an armoured vehicle, and head for London. Not the best plan in the world, but it's a start.

I look over at Dave, thinking maybe we'll chat and talk it through, but spot him lying flat on his back, with his hands folded across his front, seemingly fast asleep.

Fair play. It's been a hell of a day, and we've been lucky so far.

How long will it last?

DAY FOUR

PROLOGUE

Southern England, a police station in the heart of Portsmouth. A canteen with two men resting on mattresses made from thick blankets, normally reserved for prisoners detained in the cells. The blankets are rough and cheap, but the weather is hot, so cover isn't needed for warmth.

Howie, the supermarket manager, sleeps deeply. His breathing steady and low.

The second man, much smaller in stature, lies awake. His eyes staring up at the ceiling as he waits for dawn to lift and the new day to begin.

FOR DAVE, life before the army was a confusing mess of memories and images all muddled up in his mind. His first few weeks in basic training had been the same – messy and uncoordinated. He could run and shoot, and do all the things that were required of him, but his interactions with the other recruits were very difficult. They were young lads, pumped up with testosterone and fuelled by the need to constantly impress and show off, and they just confused him; they took the piss and made jokes.

Then they started unarmed defence tactics, and it changed everything.

The recruits were lectured about the need for unarmed combat tactics, and famous stories and accounts of weapons jamming and going hand-to-hand were explained to them.

The instructors drummed into them that this wasn't *king fu* or *karate*, and it wasn't meant to be pretty. They said that the only way to suppress your enemy was to use a massive display of violence. They were, after all, infantry and not ninjas.

They were shown basic blocking techniques, take-downs, and simple strikes, with moves that caused maximum damage with the minimum of effort.

Dave watched and learnt. He was told what to do, and he did it. Being the smallest of the intake, and the fact he never made small talk or joked about made him an obvious target, and the instructors yelled at him more than the others, which only caused to isolate him more from the group. This, though, was normal for Dave.

Each week, they were put through the training and drilled until they were proficient. It was physical, and it was simple. Dave learnt the techniques and worked with each partner in a methodical manner. They had been told not to cause injury to each other, so Dave never did. It was also drummed into them that they were brothers-in-arms, and you never hurt or inflict injury on your own kind.

They were put through their paces and told repeatedly that there would be an assessment at the end that they each had to pass before they could go on to the next stage. The assessment was a new training exercise being trialled.

Some of the regiments still did *milling* – recruits were fitted with large boxing gloves and set at one another for a minute and were not allowed to stop or rest until either one of them was down or the minute ended. The milling was popular, and the army was willing to trial a new method of assessing the skills they had learnt in the unarmed combat training.

Assessment time arrived, and all of the recruits were led into a gym, with rubber matting on the floor. They were in PT kit and sat in a square around the mats. The normal instructors were present, along with various army staff officers and regimental representatives, who had come to see how effective the new trial was. The recruits were told that normal rules of engagement were suspended. They were to attack one another and use any and all of the skills they had been taught for thirty seconds.

The victor would stay on until he was beaten, and they would keep going until everyone had been assessed. They could not stop until either one of them was down or the time ran out.

If the time ran out, and they were both still standing, then the senior officer present would decide who the victor was. Or if they should go again. The victor could choose who the next opponent was.

The idea was to see if the recruits would revert to type and just whack at each other with hay makers, or if the training had been effective, and they would use their new skills. The instructors and army understood that injuries were inevitable, but this was the army, and men had to be trained in the most effective way possible.

The first two recruits were selected at random and duly took their positions in the square. The bell was rung, and they went for each other. Some of the skills were apparent, but they held back too much. The constant warnings of not causing injury during training had run deep, and the bout went the full thirty seconds, with both of them still standing. They were made to go again and were screamed at for not using full force. The time started up, and again they went for it, but were still holding back.

The clock was stopped, and they were told clearly that each and every recruit would stay there until the bout was done to the satisfaction of the instructors. Each time they held back, they would lose a day's R&R and be confined to barracks.

This did the trick, and when the fight started again, the men went for it properly, battering and striking at each other, using the skills they had been taught, along with their natural instinct to punch out wildly. The first man went down, and the other recruit was on him, pummelling his face and body with blows. The bout ended, and the victor was declared. He was pumped up and ready, full of confidence at being allowed to use full force violence. He was told to choose his next opponent and started looking around at the faces.

The recruits were looking at Dave, laughing and calling out his name, eager to see the smallest guy get beaten up. The victor played to his crowd and selected Dave.

Within seconds, they were facing each other, and again, both were told not to hold back. The instructor faced each of them in turn and explicitly told them to use full force.

Dave had learnt that in the army you did as you were told.

The bout started and was over within ten seconds, with Dave's opponent having both his arms broken in two places and a fractured skull.

The stunned silence that followed was only shattered by the instructor declaring Dave the victor and telling him to select his next opponent. Naturally, they didn't know the severity of the injuries at that time, or perhaps they would have ended it there.

The next opponent was a simple decision for Dave, who just pointed to the far left. He was taught to read and write from left to right, so that was his natural instinct when choosing anyone or anything.

Again, the clock was started, and this time it was over in less than ten seconds. His opponent had both knee joints dislocated.

By this time, some of the officers were looking at each other with concern, and the instructors were talking to each other in hushed tones. Then the instructors deferred to a quiet, well-spoken man in civilian clothing, who told them to carry on. He watched Dave intently.

Two minutes later, the assessment was ended to the great relief of the remaining recruits.

All of the recruits that were left were transferred to other training barracks overnight. The instructors were removed from duty, and the whole episode was covered up within hours.

Those officers that were present for the assessment were each spoken to separately and offered promotion if they signed a form, declaring they were not anywhere near the training centre on that date.

The families of the two recruits that Dave had killed were told that their sons died during a training exercise and were compensated heavily for their losses. The quiet, well-spoken man in the civilian clothing, who had allowed the assessment to continue, took Dave with him, and Dave was told that he must never talk about his life or about his training, or any part of his army career.

And Dave had learnt that in the army, you did as you were told.

Years later, his life took another turn, and he went out into civvy street. Finding himself working at Tesco. Dave did as he was told and never gave anyone any trouble. That was until four days ago when he was working the night shift, and a man staggered into the supermarket, covered in blood.

The uniformed security guard rushed forward to help, thinking that the guy was the victim of a horrific and violent assault. He *was* the victim of a horrific and violent assault, but he had been infected and now carried the thing inside that made him into something other than the human being he was just a short time ago, and as the security officer rushed forward, so the guy covered in blood lunged in and took the guard down, biting into his neck as the music from the supermarket speakers played on, and the insomniac shoppers and workers carried on shopping and working.

The infection entered the guard's blood stream, and within minutes, he too was transformed.

The infection needed to survive, and the only way for it to do so was to continuously find more hosts. The infection knew that the quickest way to do this was to bite the host and use the saliva to enter the bloodstream. The infection even learnt to make the host drool to make sure there was plenty of diseased fluid already in the mouth when that bite happened.

The security man died within two minutes, but it was two minutes filled with searing agony that started in his gut and spread out until it consumed him wholly before his heart stopped, and he ceased to live. Then, an instant later, his heart started beating again as the infection took over, replicating and taking over every cell within his body. A few seconds after that, he snapped his red, bloodshot eyes open, with one single urge pulsing through his entire being – to find more hosts. To bite. To gouge. To feast in an orgy of blood and gore.

Dave was at the back of the store, checking that the stock he had just filled was lined up and facing forward perfectly. There was something good about filling a shelf. It was neglected and empty before he got to it. He made it full again and made it tidy. He worked on, heedless to the guard slamming into a woman and taking her down. Cutting her mild yelp off by biting into her throat through the windpipe. Two minutes, and she was dead. A few seconds later, and she sat up, with red, bloodshot eyes and that same urge to bite and feast.

The guard ran on, staggering and lurching, jerky and wild. Bloodied drool hanging from his mouth. Down his jaw, over his clothes. A gaping, awful wound on the side of his neck.

Dave started on the next section. Taking something that was untidy and not right and filling to make it proper. Turning the tins so they faced front and forward, all lined neatly. He paused, stepping back to check his work as the infected guard reached the end of his aisle and stopped dead to slowly turn and look up at Dave.

Dave also turned his head and looked down at the blood covered guard, with a second's worth of nothingness held for an eternity, with neither moving until the guard pulled his lips back to bare his teeth as a chunk of flesh from his neck fell out. Then he charged, staggering, lurching, murderously hungry, and Dave just stared. Unmoving. Unflinching.

It was only at the very last second, just as the beast came in for the bite, that Dave went to work, simply gliding back as the infected sailed by and tried anchoring on the brakes to come back. But by then, Dave was armed with a tin of baked beans in each hand. Sliding his right foot back, lowering his stance, readying for the fight, waiting, holding, assessing, reading his enemy. Reading the motion, the gait, seeing weakness, seeing the path to take.

He moved in fast, slamming a tin up into the jaw, snapping the infected man's head up and back while bringing the other tin in to smash it over into the shelf, making the infected drop and pull more tins down.

Dave stepped back. Thinking his opponent was down. Then it got back up, so Dave beat it down again. Then it got back up, so Dave ditched the tins of beans and broke both of its arms, and sent it headfirst into the solid end of a plinth. Then it still got back up, so Dave broke its legs. Then it gnashed and tried crawling as Dave stared down without any expression at all before moving in the break the neck.

After that, Dave stepped from his aisle and looked left and right as the screams filled the air, with people running this way and that, being chased by other people covered in blood. He watched for a few seconds. Assessing. Learning.

He walked on through the store, peering down aisles to see a woman thrashing on the ground, with two men biting into her neck and body. A man bent over the bench freezer, held down by a fat infected biting into his back. An old woman sitting up with red, bloodshot eyes. Lots of blood too. But then blood had never really bothered Dave.

He reached the end of the store, the homeware department, and was reaching out towards the shelf he wanted when several infected ran by the end of his aisle, stopped, turned, spotted him, howled, and roared, then ran at him. Dave stared. Pulled the brand-new knife from the hook, plucked the sheaf free, and went to work.

For that was Dave's job, and he took great pleasure in following orders.

CHAPTER TWENTY-THREE

DAY FOUR
MONDAY MORNING

'Mr Howie.'

A voice pulls me from my sleep. I can't seem to respond, though.

'Mr Howie.'

There it is again, but I can't grasp a hold of it. The voice is near, yet far away. My sleep is heavy, and I feel like I'm wading through thick liquid, trying to grasp at a lifeline that is being inched away from my hands.

'Mr Howie... Wake up.'

I'm being rocked now. I'm on a boat, and the waves are gently nudging the sides and making me roll.

'WAKE UP!'

I open my eyes to see Dave kneeling by my side; his hand on my shoulder. Ted is standing over me, smiling down.

'That did it. He's awake now. Here, get this down your neck.'

Ted hands me a steaming mug of hot liquid that smells like coffee.

I sit up and take the mug. My head is fuggy, and I drink the strong, bitter coffee in silence.

My mouth feels furry and horrible, and the coffee just adds to the awful mix, but the caffeine kicks in, and within a few minutes, I start to feel more awake.

'There's some cleaning kit for you both. It's the stuff the prisoners use. It's not great, but it'll do the job,' Ted says. I look over and see two sets of things on a table. I raise my mug in thanks to Ted. 'The shower room is just down the corridor. Help yourself and grab some scoff. I'll be back up in a bit. We're getting ready to go.' He turns and leaves as I look at Dave sitting at one of the police station canteen tables, drinking from a mug. Daylight outside, with a bright sun already streaming through the windows.

'Looks like a nice day again,' I say to Dave, who just nods quietly. 'So what have we got there?'

Dave rummages through the pile closest to us. 'Towels, disposable toothbrush, disposable safety razor, disposable cloth, and soap.'

'Is the soap disposable too?'

'I don't know, Mr Howie.'

'I was joking,' I say, standing up and stretching my weary body. Despite the solid sleep, I feel exhausted. My mind is refreshed, but my body has taken more punishment in the last couple of days than in the last ten years. Or possibly ever. 'Oh, my God, I ache from head to toe. Do you?'

'No.'

I shake my head. Of course, he doesn't. The man is a machine. Maybe he's a cyborg, a secret military robot like Robocop? Yeah, that explains it. Dave is a robot soldier cyborg.

No, he's just fit, and I'm not.

I take one of the disposable toothbrushes and discover a pre-loaded plunger behind the bristles that pushes the paste through. A thing of wonder and awe that captures my imagination for a full few seconds. 'We could do with a few more of these. They look quite cool.' Then the pre-loader plunger toothbrush loses appeal, and I sit down at the table opposite Dave and lean back in my chair, with the bottom of the mug resting on my chest. 'So, what's the plan?'

'You said you wanted to find an APC in Salisbury, Mr Howie,' Dave says and looks up at me.

'You still up for it, then?'

'Yes, Mr Howie.'

'I know that I keep going on about it, mate, but this is my issue. I won't be offended if you want to go with them to the forts.'

'No, I'll go with you.'

'Ha, you know I'd get my arse chewed up within the first five minutes of being on my own.'

'Yes,' he says, as deadpan as ever.

'You cheeky bastard! That's it, isn't it? You don't think I'm capable?'

'Yes,' he says, completely impassive while I search for humour.

'Well, personally, Dave. I think I've done all the hard work so far, and it's damn time you started pulling your own weight. I'm not going to keep carrying you.'

'Okay, Mr Howie.'

'Good. Well, I'm glad we got that straightened out. I am going for a shower.'

He gets up to follow me, taking one of the bundles.

'Dave, I think I can shower safely on my own. I won't drown.'

'Okay.'

He keeps following me, so I stop to form a questioning look.

'There's more than one shower, Mr Howie.'

'How do you know?'

'I checked.'

Of course, he did. I bet he could describe the layout of the whole building by now, and the contents of every room too.

Ten minutes later, and I'm standing under a stream of hot water, with the sharp spray needling at my sore muscles. I remember that they said that shower time is restricted to five minutes for males, but seeing as they are all leaving today, I don't think it will be too much of an issue if I take just a few extra minutes. I've brought my disposable toothbrush in with me to scrub my teeth until feel squeaky clean. Then I use the bristles of the brush to scrub at my tongue, which comes away brown from the strong coffee I just drank.

The soap is shit though and barely lathers up. But then it is meant for the prisoners. It's funny, but everyone thinks that prisoners get the best of everything: good food, good bedding, and all paid for by the taxpayer. But this stuff is really cheap and shitty.

Last night was crazy. We got ourselves into a bad situation, and it can't happen again. Getting trapped like that was unacceptable. It was pure luck that we were at the back of the police station. All it would have taken was for the people inside to have been away from the door or not looking at the camera, and we would have been just another couple of zombie infected things.

From now on, we will move and fight during the day, and hide at night. That's it. No deviations. It's already Monday, and my sister will be panicking and might be thinking that no one is coming for her. Two days of solid running and fighting seem like a week to me, so it will be far worse for her, trapped alone in her apartment, with no idea of what's going on.

Dave has finished and is gone by the time I get out of the shower and dry myself off. I get dressed and go back to the canteen to see Sergeant Hopewell, Ted, and Dave talking at one of the tables. Well, Sergeant Hopewell and Ted are talking. Dave is just listening.

'Morning, Howie. Feeling better?' Sergeant Hopewell says to me. Her clipped tone now not quite so formal and direct.

'Yeah, much better, thanks.'

'Good. Right, let's go over the plan. According to your information, the authorities are urging people to head to the forts, the Victorian forts on the coast. Correct so far?'

'Yes.'

'Right, well, we know there are lots of them, but we don't know which ones will be in use. However, we do know that some of them have not been maintained, so they will be in a very bad state of repair but are still possibly defensible. Correct?'

'Er, yeah, I think so.'

'Good, so we also know that some of them have been maintained and kept in use by historical societies as tourist attractions. These may or may not be suitable, depending on the level of work done by those societies, correct?'

'Yeah, I guess that makes sense.'

'So, we don't know which ones are in use or how many there are, or if they are full or will take us. But we have an old riot van outside, and as long as we can get out of here, we have a chance of finding them or at least trying to.'

'Well, I suppose so.'

'Good, right. Now, are you sure that you and Dave don't want to come with us?'

'I can't come, but Dave is more than welcome to join you.'

She looks at Dave, who just shakes his head.

'I thought so. Now listen, we don't have much of a plan, except to get out of here and go, and look for them. But... If all else fails, we will use this place as a fall back. If the forts are no good, then we will come back here and wait.'

'Okay. We'll look for my sister and then the forts. If something goes wrong with that plan, we'll aim for here too. How do we get in if you are not here?'

'Hmmm... There's only one key to the main door, and we'll be taking that with us. We can't really leave it anywhere because of the risk of someone else finding it. Also, we risk the place getting overrun by that lot out there.'

'The building has a flat roof to one side,' Ted interrupts. 'If you can get on the top, then you can drop down onto the internal prisoner courtyard mesh and get in one of these windows. We'll leave it unlocked.'

'That's great. We'll just need a massive ladder, then.'

'Sorry, that's the best we can do. We can't risk leaving it unlocked and letting any Tom, Dick, and zombie in here, can we?'

'No, I suppose not.'

'Don't worry, son.' Ted says, looking back at the sergeant.

'Okay, next we need to get out of here. That lot are blocking the gates, so we need a diversion.'

'Any suggestions?' I ask.

'Well, yes, actually,' the sergeant offers. 'The yard behind the gates keeps all of the marked vehicles – most of them were out on patrol or were taken by the lads to get away. But we have the detectives' carpool in a car park on the other side of the building. If *someone* can get to one of those cars, they could draw those things away from the gates.'

They both lean forward, looking hopefully at Dave and me.

CHAPTER TWENTY-FOUR

The infected gather outside the police station, at the last place their prey was seen.

Hundreds of pairs of arms hang limply as they twitch and knock into each other in the confined space, and hundreds of heads roll back and forth, left and right. Shuffling slowly, with cumbersome feet dragging along the ground. Some of them lurch and spasm as they move, with drooling saliva flinging off to coat those around it.

Flies feast and buzz happily as they lay eggs in the open wounds, drawn by the rancid stench of rotting meat, and it won't take long for those eggs to hatch, and for the tiny white maggots to grow fat and plump as they eat into the flesh they inhabit.

Each life form has a desire to live and will strive for survival. That is nature. That is fact.

Not a great distance away, an infected male lies on the driveway of what used to be his home. His spine broken from being hit by a speeding car driven by a panicked survivor. He should be dead. He was dead. Now he isn't dead. His heart beats.

Within minutes, a small flap at the bottom of the front door the infected male faces opens, and a diminutive cat walks out, sniffs the air, and starts cleaning itself. Its lithe body almost bent double as it reaches around to lick its behind. The cat then walks down the garden path and stops when it sees the body. It pauses. Recognising his owner, but his owner doesn't quite smell right. With effortless grace, the cat jumps up onto the garden wall and looks down at the body. Unsure and hesitant, and the infection within the man looks out through the eyes of the host body at the cat on the wall.

The infection's primary function is to survive. That is the priority of all living things – to survive. The infection also knows that it must evolve to do this.

The infection, without either conscious thought or knowledge of how, enters the host body and takes over the cells within it. That is its purpose: To dominate the host body.

Infecting, replicating, and attacking cells with staggering aggression. The infection then kills the body by stopping the heart. The infection then restarts the heart and brings the host back as it should be. As a carrier. As a host.

The infection has already learnt how to make more blood quickly so that wounds and injuries don't drain that vital liquid away. Then it learnt to congeal faster and seal off the arteries to those wounds, and divert the precious blood away from the leak.

THE INFECTION MAKES the cells work better to replenish the organs and parts of the host needed to make it keep working, and it learnt how to convert fat stores within the hosts into energy in order to survive and find more hosts.

The infection's primary function is to survive, and possessing one host body does not guarantee survival. One body is weak and vulnerable. Therefore, it must seek more hosts. It must seek as many hosts as it can.

It must seek all the bodies to make them into hosts.

The infection also learnt to draw those host bodies together. Creating hordes. Creating super-organisms. For safety. Safety in numbers.

It has learnt to divert more energy into the nasal passages of the host bodies, so they can smell and find each other, with a sense of scent far beyond that of humans.

The infection has also learnt that pushing the host body too much will destroy it faster, so it slows the rate of energy expenditure during the day and works to preserve the body and leave some small functions in order to move towards the prey, knowing it can use the weight of numbers to make up for the lack of pace.

At night, it drives energy into the muscles, ramping their senses, flooding them with aggression and hunger so they can hunt.

It has learnt to make them hunt as a pack too. Forcing the host body to use its vocal cords and drive air out so that it generates a loud roar as the sun goes down so they can find each other. The infection resonates through that noise and bids others towards its furore.

The infection also learnt that the smell of fear is greater at night, and the sound it generates only makes the prey more fearful and, therefore, easier to find.

It has evolved already, but the infection knows that host bodies are controlled by the brain, and the human brain is exceptionally complex.

At first, it pushed signals out hard and fast, and too close together, not understanding the massive, yet intensely subtle levels of cohesion the human host body needs in order to work well. The result was that the host bodies twitched and jerked, going into spasm if the signals were too strong, and was then too hard to control. The infection knows it must understand this brain and learn how to control the electrical impulses.

Outside the police station, the gathered horde moves slowly, conserving energy, groaning from air expelled through vocal cords.

On the driveway of the house it used to occupy, the infected male stares up at the cat, who decides that it misses the rubs and fusses it used to get. The cat can find food and water easy enough, and it can rub against objects, but it likes the strokes and rubs the owner used to give. It jumps down from the wall, landing nearby while making soft noises that it knows makes the owner give it attention.

The infection watches the cat drawing closer. The infection must survive. It must evolve and learn.

The cat stops and stares, then gently reaches forward to sniff the nose of the infected male while purring noisily, and the infected male, despite having a broken spine, lunges quickly, slamming its head down onto the cat, biting into the fur and flesh. The cat squeals loudly, reacting fast to claw and rake at the infected man's face while twisting to get away, biting and screeching in pain. It wrenches free, running off to hide in the bushes. Its heart beating like the clappers. It stops to lick the wound, scared and stunned, sniffing at the bad smell. Pain inside. It cries out and curls up as that pain intensifies, and the infection surges in, taking over cells. It lies down, the breathing becoming laboured until with one last sight. It grows still and dies.

Outside the police station, the horde still shuffle and groan while the infection within them studies the brain and the impulses. The hosts spasm and jerk this way and that, all without cohesion.

Then, in the middle of the horde, one of them grows still and slowly lifts its head. Ceasing the lolling and rolling about. Testing electrical impulses. The head drops. The infection sends one concentrated signal, and the head lifts again. The infection controls those pulses, and the head slowly moves to look first left and then right. Then the infection stops those impulses, and the head drops again.

The infection sends out more defined signals in another direction and gets a reaction; then the infection puts those signals together.

The infection lifts the head at the same time as it clenches both hands into fists; then it lets them go and makes them do it again.

The infection has learnt to make only one host in the middle of many hundreds, in a country of many millions, on a planet of many billions look up while making spasming fists, but it's a start.

In a quiet street, in the south of England, the flies buzzing around a dead cat lying in the bushes near to a now dead infected male with a broken spine.

A beat.

A pulse.

Life restarted, and the cat's eyes open – red and bloodshot.

CHAPTER TWENTY-FIVE

We go down through the police station and emerge outside in the rear yard to see an old police riot van facing the metal gates. On the other side of which many hundreds of infected stare in, back to the slow, dumb, daytime things again.

I was looking for a reaction when we first came out, but they just keep groaning and pressing forward. The ones at the very front are pinned against the gates, and their faces are warped as they are pushed on to the metal bars.

The police personnel have already loaded the van with some equipment, riot shields, and long batons. PC Tom Jenkins even found some old riot armour and a dark blue crash helmet with a plastic visor. He has leg and arm guards on in addition to the crash helmet. The plastic visor is pushed up away from his face, and I can see that he is sweating heavily in the high heat of another scorching day.

'You look like a bloody idiot, Tom,' Terri calls from the van.

'It's the correct PPE in times of civil unrest. You should have some on too,' he replies, looking very uncomfortable.

'What's PPE?' I ask them.

'Personal Protective Equipment,' Terri answers and then looks at the massed infected. 'Will those gates hold them? That must be a hell of a weight pushing in.'

'They're built to withstand vehicle impact,' Ted says, walking over. 'They won't budge unless we want them to.' He stops to stare through the gates, shaking his head sadly. 'There's probably a few of our boys in there,' he adds quietly. 'I hope to god this lot don't recognise any of 'em.'

I look at the concerned expression on Ted's face. The old-timer must have seen many things in his day. Even so, this must be shocking to him. Not that he shows it.

'So,' I say, 'we get to one of the unmarked detective cars and lead those things away to give you a chance to get out. What are you going to do if we don't draw them all away?'

'We can batter through a few,' he replies. 'Wouldn't fancy it with a lot of them, mind.'

'It's a pity we can't thin them out a bit, though,' I say to Dave as he joins us.

Dave walks over to the police kit waiting to be placed in the van and picks up a long, black baton, then walks over to the gates, and runs the end of the baton along the bars. He examines the gates and the hinges, then takes the baton, and starts pushing at the infected through the gaps. Not hard but almost like he is testing something.

I walk over to join him, and despite what Ted said about the gates being very strong, I feel very nervous being this close.

'Bloody hell, they stink.' I put my hand over my nose. The putrid stench of rotting meat is disgusting. The injuries are festering in this heat.

Hundreds of pairs of bloodshot eyes stare back at us, watching every move we make. Drool and saliva hang down from their slack mouths. The closest ones pull their lips back, readying for the bite. Dave is pushing at them with the baton, and I watch as he strains and pushes harder.

'Mate, they are jammed in there,' I remark from behind my hand. He moves up and down, pressing against them at various stages as I glance round to see an old-fashioned diesel fuel pump in one corner. 'We could burn a few of them.'

Dave looks at the fuel pump, then at the infected, and then back to the building.

'Good point,' I say in reply to his silence. 'We'd burn the station down.'

Dave taps at the metal gates again and then looks over to Ted. 'Where is the generator?'

'In that room. Why?' Ted says, pointing to an open door across the yard.

Dave doesn't answer but walks off, tapping the baton against the side of his leg. He disappears into the doorway as Ted looks at me.

'Funny bugger, your mate, isn't he?'

'You kind of get used to him.'

'Tom bloody Jenkins! Stop putting shit into that van, just pile it up, and let me do the loading,' Ted bellows out at Tom, much to the amusement of Steven. 'And you can stop bloody smirking, Steven. Now, the pair of you, get in there and start bringing the food out.'

Steven looks down, embarrassed, and Tom starts to smirk. Then they both begin walking back into the building as Ted shouts after them: 'And make sure that Old Harry gets a wash. He ain't coming in this van if he stinks like one of them,' Ted shouting, jerking a thumb towards the gates.

'You taking Harry with you then?' I ask.

'Yeah, well, we can't just leave him, can we? Mind you, he probably wouldn't mind – he treats the place like his bloody home anyway.'

I stroll over to see Dave inside the generator room pulling black electrical cable from a large reel. He takes the ends and splits the rubber covers back, exposing the bare wires.

'Do you need a hand, mate?'

'Yes, please, Mr Howie.'

He hands me one of the reels.

'Can you feed that wire out until it reaches the gates?'

'Okay, but why?'

He doesn't reply but starts fiddling about with the electrical output socket. I shrug and do as I am asked, walking backwards and feeding the wire from the reel as I go. Then I realise what he's about to do and chuckle at the gruesome thought.

'Do you want me to cut the wire, Dave?'

'No, thanks, Mr Howie.'

He comes out and walks over with a small set of pliers and some electrical tape, and gets to work, cutting and taping bare wires to the metal gate as Ted comes back from loading the van and follows the wires with his eyes.

'Bloody hell, you're going to fry 'em.'

'Don't touch the gates,' Dave says, marching back into the generator room as Ted and I back swiftly away from the gates.

Tom and Steven come out of the police station, followed by Terri and Jane. All of whom stare at the wires, then at Ted and me.

'What's that for?' Terri asks.

'READY?' Dave shouts from the generator room.

'Go for it!' Ted shouts back.

Dave does something inside the room, which causes the generator to increase in pitch from the gentle chugging it was doing before, and I grimace in sickened anticipation.

'NOW!' Dave shouts. The thrum comes louder; the generator chugging noisily as the entire front row of infected go rigid and start convulsing with sparks arcing from the gate.

'Jesus,' Terri mutters, turning away as Tom goes very pale, with Steven clamping his eyes shut.

'STOP!' Ted shouts, and Dave pulls the power as the first row slide down to the ground but are instantly replaced by the next row.

'It'll take all bloody day,' I say to Ted. 'Dave? Cracking idea, but it's too slow...'

'Oh no, it won't,' Ted says, pulling the end of a hose from the wall towards the gates. 'One of you, turn that water on!'

Tom and Steven both dart for the tap and squabble about, trying to get there first.

'STOP PISSING ABOUT AND TURN THAT BLOODY TAP ON!' Ted shouts, shaking his head as a jet of water finally sprays out. 'Turn it on full.'

Ted aims low and starts flooding the bottom of the gates, soaking the tarmac under them as Dave walks out to watch him. Not saying a word or showing any reaction.

'Can I do it, please, Ted?' Tom asks politely.

Ted looks at Tom and hands the hose over, and walks back towards me, rolling his eyes as Tom starts laughing with glee.

'Here, have a drink, you dirty shits!' Tom shouts as he starts spraying the water directly at the rows of infected pushing against the gate.

'Let me try,' Steven says to Tom.

'No! Ted told me to do it.'

'No, he didn't. He didn't say that. Let me have a go.'

'You wouldn't think they were bloody police officers,' Ted mutters.

A few minutes of squabbling and a massive puddle has formed on the ground beneath the gates, seeping backwards onto the floor beneath the massive crowd.

'That's enough, lads.' Ted says, turning the water off. 'Go on, get away from there. Dave? Try it again!'

Dave nods and goes back into the generator room. 'Ready?' he shouts.

'Yep,' Ted shouts as the generator increases in pitch again.

'NOW!' Dave shouts.

Bloody hell. The effect is amazing, with bolts of blue arcs crackling between the gates and the water as the entire horde seem to stiffen and convulse as one. Spasming and jerking but differently from how they were before. Legs locking out. Arms going rigid. Heads bolt up. Veins pushing through skin, and eyes bulging. Then I spot smoke coming from the flesh of those pinned against the gates.

'KEEP GOING!' Ted yells.

Retching behind me, and I look back to see Terri bent over, vomiting on the ground, with Jane rubbing her back, but she too looks nauseous. Tom looks at her, looks at me, looks at the gates, then spews puke on his feet.

'Pussy,' Steven says, seemingly unbothered by the awful sight.

'Piss off, Steven,' Tom gargles between spewing mouthfuls of vomit out.

A flash of light, and I turn back to see one of the infected bursting into flames, with fire licking along the front row; one after the other popping into ignition.

'Shit, look at that,' I say, shaking my head. The flames don't bother me, but the fact they are igniting from electrocution is still quite shocking. 'We'd better watch that the fire doesn't spread too much, Ted.'

'STOP!' Ted shouts out, and Dave powers off the generator.

As soon as the current ends, the entire front of the crowd fall down as one, leaving burnt and smouldering flesh charred on the bars. The ground packed with smoking bodies. Some of them still twitching and convulsing. I raise my eyebrows at Ted, who just looks at me.

'That worked well, then,' he says.

Dave comes out and looks at his handiwork and the big space now cleared. There's more infected further back, but they're tripping over the ones we just electrocuted, which buys us all time to get out.

'Ready, Mr Howie?' Dave asks.

We say goodbye to the others and follow Tom to the other side, to a window overlooking a small parking area filled with rows of small, dark cars.

'Which one we going for?' I ask.

'That blue one there,' he replies, pointing to the closest car before handing me the key.

'Cheers! Right, I guess we'd better get on, then,' I say somewhat awkwardly in that British way of saying goodbye. 'Er, good luck, and it was nice meeting you,' I extend my hand, but Tom looks nervous and still a bit pale from puking while avoiding eye contact.

'I want to come with you,' he blurts.

I look at Dave, who gives a very subtle shake of his head.

'Right. Yep. You know, Tom, we'd love to have you with us. Dave and I were just saying earlier how great it would be if you could come along,' I say as Tom looks up full of hope. 'But we can't, mate. We've seen how much they rely on you, so it wouldn't be fair, and er...wow! So yes, we'd just be selfish taking you away from them,' I trail off while giving a pained expression. 'And I know that you are going to protect your team and make sure that they stay safe.'

He looks hurt but nods.

'Yeah. So, sorry, Dave. We can't take Tom away from his team. They need him. We'll just have to struggle on. Just the two of us. Damn shame, though...' I cut in fast, before Dave can say anything.

'Tom, it's been a pleasure to meet you, mate. Good luck with getting to the forts safely.'

'Yeah, of course. Thanks, and I'll hold that fort and wait for you both as well.'

'Yes, mate, you'll be like a forward reconnaissance advanced recce pathfinder.' I pat him on the shoulder, looking him dead in the eye as I speak before turning to Dave. 'Shall we, Dave?'

'Okay, Mr Howie.'

Tom unlocks the door, and Dave and I walk out into the bright sunshine, with a last look at a very young copper, hopeful and yet also with hurt expression as he waves and slowly closes the door, then opens it again, as though we might change our minds, then closes it fully with another wave.

'What's a forward reconnaissance advanced recce pathfinder, Mr Howie?' Dave asks as we walk on.

'Well, if you need me to keep explaining these military terms to you, Dave, I am going to get fed up pretty quickly,' I reply as we reach the car park. 'But seriously, don't they exist?'

'What?'

'Forward reconnaissance advanced recce pathfinders?'

'No.'

'Whatever. At least I know how to drive.'

'Yes, Mr Howie.'

Dave goes to get into the front and then changes his mind, and gets in the back. He takes both shotguns and the rifle and props them up so they are aiming to the roof. He then winds down both rear windows. I get into the front and look at all of the mess in the foot wells – chocolate bar wrappers and empty cans of soda.

'Messy pigs! Oops, no, I didn't mean to say pigs. Sorry, I didn't mean that.' I scan around, afraid that one of them might have heard me, then remember the whole end-of-the-world thing and realise we're safely alone.

I start the car and back out of the parking space, then drive towards the corner of the building. As we nudge out into the road, we both look left down at the horde. The mass electrocution has definitely thinned them out, but there's still a lot left. I turn right, then stop, and position the rearview mirror so that I can see them.

'Have they seen us, Dave?'

'No, Mr Howie.'

The horde are all still facing towards the gates, with their backs to us. I sound the horn, and a feeble, warbling noise sounds out.

'Anything?'

'A couple have turned. That's it, though.'

'Okay, plan B, then.'

I get out of the car and take my shotgun from the back seat, then open my bag, and get a few more cartridges ready. Dave watches me, then gets out, and does the same.

'Dave, give 'em a nice, big shout, mate.'

'OI!' Dave bellows at them in his drill sergeant voice. A few start to turn, shuffling around, and I fire the shotgun from the hip, emptying both barrels and watching as a few get blown off their feet.

'There's too many,' I say to Dave. 'The van won't get through.'

Dave puts the shotgun back into the car and pulls out two long, straight-bladed knives from his bag, and reverses the grip so that the blades are upright against his forearms.

The sight makes me feel a strange rush of excitement as adrenalin starts pumping through my system. I reload my shotgun, put it back into the car, then draw my axe, and turn to start walking back towards the crowd, with Dave at my side, with nothing said. No plan. No anything. Just an obvious intent.

'Strike and move, Mr Howie.'

'Yep, got it.'

Dave steps off to the right, and I keep left. We walk for a few seconds until we are just over halfway to them; then we both stop, and in the silence, we stand and wait.

This horde almost finished us last night. We were inches away from death when we were saved. They were fast and switched on then, but now they are slow, and we can get some payback. I think of my parents and start to feel the rage building up inside of me again. It's been suppressed for a little while, but I can release it now.

The closest infected have almost reached us now. Those that turned first had a few steps head start from the horde. They can taste the bite, and I can see their lips being pulled back. I fix my eyes on the closest one, an adult male with half his face already torn away. He shuffles towards me; his head rolling, but his red eyes watch me.

I step to the side and launch the axe at his head. The blade bites into the side of his skull, bursting the head open. He goes down, and I attack the next one with an overhead smash, cleaving the skull in two.

I pick my targets and let the rage do the rest.

Strike and move.

I lash out, cracking skulls open; blood and brain matter spraying out. I move away and step backwards to keep my distance.

The blood lust is upon me. The glory of battle surging through my veins, and I unleash hell with my axe, smashing bones, cleaving skulls, and bursting them apart.

Another one to my right. I backswing, and it's knocked away; then I slash to my left and drive the axe blade down into a shoulder bone. Then another one in front of me, and I uppercut the blunt back end of the axe head and obliterate its jaw, sending shards of bone into its brain.

Strike and move.

We draw back slowly towards the car, and they keep coming after us. They are too close now, and we have no view beyond the first few to see if the riot van can get out. But I don't care; this is what I want – this destruction.

I keep hacking away with the axe. The shuffling bodies are slow, and as long as I keep moving back, they can't bite me.

I glance over and see Dave moving amongst them like a ballet dancer. His arms swirling as he spins and pulls the blades across their necks. Arterial blood from the slit throats sprays high into the air as the bodies fall to the ground.

He punches out with the knives, puncturing lungs and breaking ribs with his blows, and more fall down.

Watching him is like watching a master at work. The effortless movements are mesmerising, but I am brought back to reality by a face lunging at me.

I slam my forehead into its nose and use the bottom of the axe handle to bat it away from me. The last time I head-butted someone, it hurt like hell, but there is no pain now. There is nothing other than pure rage.

I strike out at several more, watching them fall and die until there is space around me, with a single infected male watching me. In my bloodlust and fury, I fail to take in that his head doesn't roll, and he is standing as a normal man would stand, head upright and eyes front.

I charge at him, pulling the axe back, visualising the axe going through his spine, and his head spinning away, and I get to within striking range and swing the axe towards him.

His hand raises and grabs the handle, stopping the swing in mid-flight.

We stare at each other, eyes locked, and his hand touching mine. I try to pull the axe away, but his grip is awesome, and he doesn't move. He doesn't pull his lips back or bare his teeth, but just stares at me with those awful, red eyes.

I'm pull back harder, trying to wrench the axe from him, and in my panic, I don't think to just let go of it. His one arm is strong enough to drag me towards his mouth that slowly opens, and just as reason gets hold of me, I let go of the axe. Which is when a knife spins past my head and embeds into the side of his skull, and Dave is there, yanking his head back and slicing his neck open while driving him down to the ground.

'GO, MR HOWIE!'

We run back to the car. Clambering in and speeding away within a few seconds. The rage ebbing away from the surprise of the reaction from that infected man.

I check the mirror as we go, seeing the gates at the far end of the street now wide open, and the riot van gone from view.

At least they got away safely.

CHAPTER TWENTY-SIX

The infected cat slowly gets to its feet and walks a few paces, with shaky legs, and the tail twitching furiously.

Within a few minutes, it gains more control, becoming steadier on its feet until it is moving almost normally. It stops and lies down, and then rolls onto its back, with its legs straight up in the air. Then it twitches several times and spins around back onto its feet. The front legs rise up, and the cat tries walking, just on its back legs, but the balance goes, and the cat falls over. The cat tries this several more times, then gives up, and sticks to using four legs. Then the cat runs and leaps into the air, but lands awkwardly, with legs splayed out. It tries again by running and then leaping, but it lands too heavily on its back legs and again ends up spreadeagled. It keeps trying, running down the quiet and deserted street, jumping into the air until it has mastered the landing.

The cat reaches a wall and looks up. From down here, the wall looks high, but it knows that it must be able to jump up. The cat takes some backwards steps while staring fixedly at the top of the garden wall.

It leaps high and sails through the air. The powerful hind legs propelling it faster than it intended. The cat hits the wall and slides down into a heap at the bottom. The tail still twitching like crazy.

It gets back up and again walks backwards while staring at the top of the wall. More height is needed, so the cat lowers down and again pushes off with its powerful back legs. The power was much better but far too much, and the cat flies over the top of the wall, with a strangled meow, and crashes into a bush on the other side.

It drags itself out of the bush, but a long, thorny stick gets caught in the tail fur. The cat turns around to pull it off, but every time it turns, the stick pulls away. The cat speeds up, desperately trying to catch the stick that is stuck to its tail, spinning around and around in the front garden of the deserted street.

The cat finally catches the stick, but the spinning has made it dizzy, and it staggers about drunkenly until it falls onto one side. When the dizzy feeling passes, the cat gets up and looks back at the wall with narrowed, bloodshot eyes.

It positions itself better this time, launches into the air, and gets to the top of the wall, but the power needed was slightly too much, and its bottom drops down the other side, but it digs in the claws that it just found in its front legs and manages to pull back up.

Once it is stable, the cat raises one front paw and watches as the claws slide out and then retract back in. Then it swaps legs and watches the claws of the other paw. Next, it lifts both front legs to watch them at the same time, but the sudden loss of stability from the front legs causes the cat to tumble and slide back down the wall into the front garden again.

The cat leaps back up and learns to settle its weight down. The tail plays a part in the stability of this animal, and it fights to control the twitching.

Within a short time, the cat detects movement from below and spots a small, black rat face pushing out from between the buttons of the shirt of a rotting corpse, sniffing the air with bristling whiskers. Its head coated in blood from the hole it made by eating through the stomach to get to the juicy insides.

The rat can't believe his luck. He's never seen this much food before, and already his belly is bloated from gorging.

The rat pulls itself out from the gnawed skin and sits on top of the cadaver, basking as the sun dries the wet gore on his fur. He might clean himself in a minute when he's not so full.

The cat watches the rat while a primeval instinct from its once-

living, small cat brain screams out. The infection allows the instinct to take over, and within seconds, the cat has launched off the wall and pounced onto the fat rat. The claws came out mid-flight, readying for the strike, and at the point of impact, the cat sinks those sharp claws into the big, fat rat belly and then bites into the neck. Hot rat blood spurts out over the cat's face. The cat wants to eat the rat, but that isn't the purpose now.

The primary purpose is to survive, and the cat complies, passing the deadly infection through the bloodstream and into the rat's body.

CHAPTER TWENTY-SEVEN

'Did you see that zombie?' I ask Dave as we drive.

'Which one?'

'The one that sat down reading the newspaper. Which bloody one do you think, Dave? The one that caught the axe. It bloody caught the axe as I was trying to chop its head off. They can't do that.'

'Why not?'

'What do you mean, why not? They just can't. They're slow and stupid; they can't suddenly start using their hands and catching things, and...did you see its face?'

'No.'

'It was weird. It looked at me... It actually *looked* at me.'

'They were all looking.'

'No, I mean that it was holding its head up and really studying me.'

'Oh.'

'If they start doing things like that, then this mess just got a whole lot worse. What if they all start doing it?'

'Catching axes?'

'No! Yes, no, not just that. Using their hands and thinking. Fuck me. This is bad, very bad. Did you see any of the others do anything weird, you know, other than coming back to life and eating people?'

He doesn't reply. 'So anyway, maybe it was just a freak, like a professor or something, or a soldier like you, like a martial arts expert.'

'Could be.'

'But his strength, though; that was nuts. If they all get like that one, then we're completely fucked.'

We drive in silence.

Dave gets the wipes out and goes through his cleaning process. First, the weapons, and then he cleans his knives and my axe. Next, he hands me some of the antibacterial cleansing wipes, and I disinfect my hands and clean my face. The used wipes go into an empty bag on the back seat.

We work a route north out of city and into the much nicer countryside as the heat of the day builds until we're both sweltering. These cheap police cars don't have air conditioning, and the blower just sends more hot air into the car.

'Have you been to Salisbury before, mate?' I ask Dave.

'Yes, Mr Howie.'

'What's it like?'

'Big.'

'No, I mean the army place. What's that like?'

'Big.'

Ask a question, get an answer.

'Okay, is the base easy to find?'

'I don't know.'

'I thought you had been there?'

'Just once. It was dark, and I was in the back of a truck.'

'Fair enough. So they train tanks there, then?'

He looks at me, the same impassive expression.

'They don't train tanks.'

'You know what I mean. Do they train people to drive tanks?'

'Yes, and other things.'

'The APS things?'

'APCs – armoured personnel carriers.'

'Yeah, them, sorry.'

'They have barracks and mock-up towns so that the infantry can train too.'

'Oh, right, so there might be soldiers and army people there?'

'Yes.'

Shit, I didn't think this through...as normal. I'm sure the army will let us just walk in and borrow one of their vehicles, or they might just shoot us instead. I was rushing and panicking after I realised my parents weren't coming back, and not thinking straight.

'Right, so if we can't get one, we'll just have to head straight for London and hope for the best.'

'Okay.'

'I mean it's only been a couple of days. It's Monday now, and it only started on Friday. My sister will be safe enough. I'm sure she will. She's just got to stay locked in and wait.'

Dave points ahead to a group of people standing in the driveway of a house at the end of a row of nice, old cottages, but as we get closer, I can see they are not people, not anymore. I start to increase the speed, thinking to just get by as quickly as possible.

'Slow down, Mr Howie,' Dave says, staring intently at them.

'What is it? Do you see something?'

'I want to see if they have changed.'

That makes sense. That last one catching my axe was very worrying. I slow down but stick to the far side of the road, and get prepared to pull away. There are only a handful of them, and most of them look very old and infirm – grey hair and grey skin spattered with dried blood and festering injuries.

One of them is a vicar or priest, wearing a dark shirt with a white dog collar. We slow down to watch them. The heat is intense, and the vehicle engine is the only noise I can hear.

I thought they would be watching the house, and that maybe someone was inside. A sign board outside the house gives it away – the house is the vicarage, and I guess it would be the focal point for a small hamlet like this.

They start shuffling as soon as we pull up, and we both watch their movements closely, but nothing appears to have changed.

'They look normal,' I murmur. 'I mean they look like the other zombies we've met in the day. None of them look particularly clever... or about to start catching axes,' I stop talking as Dave gets out of the car. 'What are you doing?'

'Hang on, Mr Howie.'

He walks round the car and towards the small group, with his knives in his hands. He looks around and then picks up a small stone from the side of the road, and throws it at the vicar's head, striking him in the face.

They don't react but just keep shuffling forward as Dave throws stones and pebbles at their heads.

I examine each of them in turn, their arms hanging limp at their sides, and the heads rolling about. The eyes are still red and bloodshot, and their movements are slow and awkward. Drool is hanging down from their mouths, and the front of their clothing is soaked from the dripping saliva.

Dave moves forward until he is only a couple of footsteps away from the vicar. The vicar, in turn, shows a bit more excitement, and I see his lips pulling back. He lunges forward for the bite, but Dave sidesteps him, and the vicar stumbles and falls to the ground.

Another one lunges at Dave, but again, he darts out of the way, and I watch as the infected staggers, loses its balance, and goes down. For the first few minutes, I watch intently for any signs of different behaviour from them, but there's nothing new. Then I hear the groaning, which sounds almost disappointed from not being able to bite him, and start smiling at the absurdity of it, at Dave baiting, then jumping back, and watching them stumble. It's like an old comedy programme, and I start chuckling.

Then Dave positions himself so he has two coming at him, one from the front and one from behind. He turns so he can see both of them and waits until the very last second as they both lunge, and simply steps back, and they head butt each other with a loud thump.

I burst out laughing and watch as Dave moves around so that another one can come for him, but he smartly gets out of the way, and the infected woman trips on the two bodies and lands on top of them.

I'm almost pissing myself now and keep watching, and laughing until all but one are tangled in a heap on the floor, groaning with frustration as they each try to get up and keep knocking each other down.

The remaining infected man, a big, plump chap, slowly inches towards Dave, who moves backwards and steps over a pair of legs sticking out of the heap. The infected trips and falls into them, and I'm out of the car, applauding Dave and laughing loudly.

'Bloody well done, mate, that was brilliant.'

Dave turns and looks at me, and does something I have never seen him do before. He smiles.

We leave the tangled heap and keep driving, heading west, towards Salisbury. The atmosphere between us now a lot more relaxed. Seeing Dave smile like that was heart-warming. He is so serious all of the time, and to see him play a joke and have fun reassures me that he is human and not a cyborg soldier killing machine.

It's still early, and the day is stretched out in front of us. The road we are on takes us into another village. A few houses either side pass us by, then more houses until there are buildings on both sides. The road signs indicate a lower speed limit, and there are warning signs for children and the elderly, then another one saying *Please Drive Carefully Through Our Village*.

Rural England is sleepy and pretty, but full of more rules and laws than cities. *Don't park here. Use the litter bins. No skateboarding. No cycling. Stick to the footpath only. No ball games.*

I love the countryside and these small places, but they are more like communist settlements than idyllic havens.

'There they are, Dave, all mustering in the village square. I wonder why they always stick together like that?'

'Safety in numbers, Mr Howie.'

'Yeah, probably. How many is that? I reckon about twenty or so?'

'Twenty-two,' he says without hesitation, earning another look from me.

'I'll slow down so we can have another look at them.'

The square is set back from the road, and there is a small collection of shops bordering the village green. None of the infected people are looking anywhere in particular. They're just shuffling around and dribbling on each other until our car comes into view.

'I know it's only a small village, but there's more than twenty people living here. Where are they all?' I ask Dave.

'Locked in their houses or dead.'

'Hmmm, maybe more people heard that broadcast and have headed down to the forts. Even if only a few people heard it, they'll pass the message on, just like we have. There could be loads of people heading down there.'

He doesn't reply.

'What about food and supplies? I know that we told some people to take what they can, but that won't last long.'

I stop the car so that we can watch the infected. Again, they look like the normal, slow, daytime zombies. 'I can't see any with their heads up, can you?'

'No, Mr Howie.'

We both look around, checking the windows of houses, doorways, and any place an intelligent, axe-catching zombie person could hide and watch.

'We were fighting for quite a while before that one reacted, and even then, he just stood there, watching. He didn't actually attack us. Maybe it takes a few minutes of action before they get bright.'

I wait until the nearest infected are almost at the back of the car, then drive forward a few metres. They follow behind the car, and I keep pulling forward every time they get within touching distance.

Before long, they are strung out in a line, and I remember the armoured van that went past my house on Friday night leading them all away, saving my life in the process. I wonder what happened to that man, and I hope that he made it somewhere safe. Who was he? Why did he go past my house? Was it accident or something else?

'Shall I give 'em a little knock and see if that does anything?' I ask Dave.

'Okay, Mr Howie.'

I wait until they are within a few steps of the back of the car, then reverse into them with a loud bang. A few get knocked down, and I drive forward a few metres again, watching for any reaction.

'See anything?'

'No.'

'Me neither. Let's give 'em a few more tries.' The road ahead is clear, so I know that we can get away if one of them suddenly starts running at us. 'Still no reaction. It must have been a one-off then, just a freak thing. Oh, what's that down there?'

We both look down the road and see where the carriageway narrows into one lane and goes over what looks like a bridge.

'Is that a river?'

I drive down, leaving the infected shambling behind us. There is a wide river ahead of us. The water looks cool and inviting in this oppressive heat.

'Must be a movable bridge,' I say. 'Look, it's too low down to let anything other than a small boat get through, and that must be the winch that opens it.' I point to a large, metal wheel that looks well used, with oiled cogs that drive another set of wheels attached to cables that run under the ground.

'Right, it's my turn for some fun.' I look back at the infected still coming down the road behind us and spot more joining the procession. I drive over the bridge and park the car on the other side.

'Dave, would you mind being the bait, please, mate?'

He looks at me for a second before getting out of the car. He then walks over to the edge, where the road meets the bridge, and stands facing the oncoming group.

I move over to the large metal wheel and take hold of the handle that sticks up. I start pushing it and am glad that the wheel moves with ease.

The reaction is instant as the wheels turn the cogs, and I guess some clever machinery happens somewhere, and the bridge starts moving. The two sections move away in opposite directions, creating a gap in the middle. Both sections stay horizontal though, which surprises me as I thought they might lift up. I turn the wheel back the other way, and the bridge closes again.

Dave looks over at me, and I give him a big grin and the thumbs up. He nods back.

'Say when, Dave.'

'Okay.'

We wait for a few minutes as the infected do their slow shuffle down the road. The sun feels nice, and it's lovely to sit here and rest in the silence for a few minutes.

The first reach the end of the bridge and start to cross towards Dave. I wait until they are a few steps back from the middle, and just as Dave gives me a thumbs up, I start moving the wheel. The bridge starts to separate, and the gap forms between the two sections. From my position, it looks quite funny as Dave and the infected swing away from each other.

Then the first one falls off the edge and into the river with a splash, and I burst out laughing and wind the wheel a bit more, making the gap bigger. More of them fall off and land in the water as the first one floats past me. Then another and another.

They don't panic or flap about, but just bob along silently. As the first one passes, I watch it sink down under the water. I turn the wheel more and stare as they keep walking off the end like zombie lemmings. Then the wheel is turned too much, and they stop at the side of the bridge, facing towards Dave. I wait for a few minutes until more of them have built up, then slowly turn the wheel back the other way, and watch the gap get smaller. They hold their position, just staring across at Dave. Then, as the two ends are just about to touch, they all start shuffling as one, and I spin the wheel back, increasing the gap.

They fall off the end, splashing water up the sides of the bank. I laugh and wave at them as they go by until they are all gone, and our fun ends.

I wheel the bridge back together just in case someone needs a quick exit and head back to the car.

'None of them were too bright, were they?'

'No, Mr Howie.'

'Right, time to stop pissing about and get to Salisbury.'

CHAPTER TWENTY-EIGHT

It's said that in modern cities people are never more than a few metres away from a rat at any one time. Rats can survive in almost any environment, and now they can do more than just survive.

The first rat bitten by the cat ran away into the sewers and pipes, smearing its own blood and the gore from the body it feasted on as it went.

The other rats detected that aroma and started following the scent.

Some followed the trail that led out into the road, where more bodies lay ready to be eaten. Some followed the injured rat, detecting the weakness.

The infection took control of that first rat quickly and allowed the instinct to flee to be all-consuming. While the infection stopped the blood flow from the wound, the rat made its way deeper into the underground network of tunnels – the superhighways of the rat world.

Now it sits in a large sewer pipe and waits as the advancing rodents detect that there are many of them going for the kill, and so they rush forward, desperate not to miss out on the chance of a meal.

The infected rat sits still, twitching its whiskers and waiting for the onslaught without knowing a thing, without feeling an ounce of pain, but it does start drooling with saliva hanging from its mouth.

As the first attacking rat comes on, the infected rat leaps and bites into it. Then it keeps leaping and jumping at the other bodies, biting and gnashing its big front teeth, working to draw blood from as many of them as possible. The action sparks a frenzy as the rats are whipped up by the smell of fresh blood, and that infected rat is overwhelmed and consumed.

The infection passes into many more of the rodents, and they, in turn, are made to nip at each other and draw blood as the rat population is quickly taken over.

Up a few metres, on the surface of the world, the cat sits on a wall, watching through red, bloodshot eyes as the street seems to writhe with glistening, black bodies pouring from the drain covers to run and feast on the bodies.

The cat readies, bunching power without knowing a thing or feeling an ounce of pain. It does, however, drool as it leaps from the wall and lands in the middle of the writhing bodies. The instruction from the infection is clear and cannot be denied. The cat bites down, grabs a rat body, and tosses its head, launching the rat through the air. The cat grabs another and keeps going, biting down, and tossing them aside as the infection is passed on.

The rats squeal. They know they are many, and this cat can be taken down. They act as one and surge forward, biting into the cat's legs and body, taking the infection on voluntarily. The cat jumps and leaps, and shakes them off while still savagely biting into them and tossing the still-wriggling bodies away. The injured rats land amongst their own kind, but the frenzy means that anything bleeding is fair game, and they are consumed by more rats.

The infection has learnt to take instant control of this small body and sends the signals down from the tiny brain – bite but don't kill.

Minutes later, the cat lies bleeding heavily from bite wounds all over its body while the infection works to congeal the blood flow, and it lowers its head to rest in peace and to die while all about it, the rats grow frenzied and wild.

CHAPTER TWENTY-NINE

Second Lieutenant Officer in Training of the Territorial Army Charles Galloway-Gibbs looks imperiously over the seated men.

A wealthy, connected, and entitled investment banker by trade, but he couldn't resist the prestige of being a British Army officer, and specifically, being able to wear the uniform, which is why, four months ago, he'd joined the *part-time* TA.

He chose the Intelligence Corp as he had been advised that it was the least likely unit to ever face combat, and Charles Galloway-Gibbs, despite looking like a dashing officer, does not like the thought of combat.

He was looking forward to the officers' day at the gentlemen's club too, just so he could wear the uniform and act very secretive about his part-time role.

'I'm in army intelligence, can't say much about it, of course'.

And the women, of course... Well, the uniform will only make it easier to get them into bed.

But now, life has changed, and as far as he knows, he could be the only officer left in the British Army, and so he swallows nervously and stares at the scared faces of the trainee soldiers in a classroom used for army education sited within the vast military grounds at Salisbury.

'So, let me get this right,' he says, his voice strong, rich, cultured, and nearly always edged with a faint sneer. 'You are all in basic training, is that right?' He gets a chorus of responses from the dozen nervous faces in front of him. 'I see. And none of you have combat experience? Or anything like it?' he asks as they shake heads.

Second Lieutenant Charles Galloway-Gibbs nods slowly and clasps his hands behind his back while thinking and staring at the young men in front of him. All of them young, none of them more than early twenties, and he just learned they are all part of a new government scheme to take unemployed young people and provide them with skills, training, and experience in the part-time Territorial Army in exchange for enhanced government benefits.

'Right. And exactly what stage of training are you at?'

They all start talking at once. 'Wait! You!' he says, pointing to a hard-faced man seated at the front. Short, brown hair and a surprisingly round head. 'You. Name?

'Blowers, sir. Simon Blowers.'

'Tell me what stage you are at, please, Blowers.'

'Sir, we are all new joiners, sir. We've been to assessment and selection and completed very basic training at our regional depots. We are here to undertake our first two-week basic training camp, sir.'

'Right, I see. And none of you have had weapons training?'

'No, sir.'

'Well. What have you learnt then?'

'Sir, basic skills like marching, rank structure, and that kind of thing, but just at weekends, sir.'

'I see, and how did you all end up in here?'

Blowers glances around at the others, hoping that someone else can do the talking, but they all look away as he turns to them.

'Sir, we only got here on Friday afternoon and were just starting orientation and getting to know each other. They took us out into the training ground to show us around... And...' his voice trails off.

'And what? Speak up, man...'

'Well, that's when it happened, sir. We were looking at the urban village training area. There was an exercise going on, and er... Well, they wanted us to be the civilians for the exercise.'

'Keep going, then,' Charles snaps when the man falls quiet.

'Sir, it all went fucking mad. Blokes were running, shooting, and biting each other. We thought it was part of the exercise at first, you know, like fake injuries and stuff, but they were fucking real...'

'Watch your language in front of an officer.'

'Sir! Sorry, sir,' Blowers snaps, sitting up straight to stare directly ahead.

'Well? What happened next?'

'Sir, we waited for a bit. None of us knew what to do, but it got worse, and someone shouted at us to leg it, so we did.'

'Just the twelve of you?'

'No, sir. There was about thirty of us, I think.' Blowers looks around as some of the others nod in agreement.

'Thirty? Well, where are they all, then?' Charles asks, lifting his eyebrows at the soldier.

'I don't think they made it, sir. It was fuck...err...it was dark and confusing, and none of us knew where to go.'

'I told you to stop swearing.'

'Sir! Sorry.'

'So that was Friday night, and now it's Monday. Just what the bloody hell have you been doing since then?'

Blowers looks around again, clearly uncomfortable with the harsh questions being thrown at him by the officer with the posh voice.

'We ran, sir, but the training area is massive. We went into the plain, where they do the tank training. There's loads of hills and valleys, and we just hid.'

'You hid? What, for two whole days?'

'No, sir. We hid on Friday night and kept moving on Saturday, and then hid again in the night. We could hear them all around us, and we lost another few to those...those things.'

'So, you let your comrades fall behind you, did you? You left your brothers in arms to the enemy while you all ran away?'

Charles knows that he would have run too, but he feels braver now that there are more men around him, and he can see the fear and exhaustion in them.

None of them answer; some hang their heads in shame. One or two of them give slight sobbing noises.

'Are you bloody crying?' Charles shouts at them. 'The British Army doesn't cry. Now bloody grow up!' he sneers at them and turns back to the unofficial spokesman. 'And how did you get back here, then?'

'We found the road that led back here and managed to get inside,' Blowers says; his voice hardening a little, making Charles swallow at the change of tone and quickly alter his manner.

'Well, yes, I appreciate you all did your best. That's what the army is all about, isn't it? Doing your best. But please don't forget that you are speaking to an officer.'

'Yes, sir.'

'How did you get in here, with all of that lot surrounding the outside?'

'They're slow in the day. They don't move that quick, and we just legged it through 'em.'

'And in doing so, soldier, you have brought them all directly outside. Very smart, very smart, indeed.'

'Sir, how come you were hiding in here? Where's everyone else?' one of the men from the back shouts out.

There are hushed and silent few seconds while the gathered men realise what he has just said.

Charles stares at the man with what he hopes is a hard look and walks slowly towards him. When he speaks, he hopes it is with a steely edge. 'Hiding, Private? Did you just say I was *hiding*?'

'Er, well...'

'Officers don't hide, Private. I am an officer in the Army Intelligence Corps, and I was gathering intel. That's what we call it, you see, *intel*. I was doing that when you lot burst in here.'

'Oh...'

'And if you ever say I or another officer was hiding again, I'll have you up on a court martial. Do you understand, Private?'

'Yes, sir.'

'What is your name?'

'Tucker, sir. Roy Tucker.'

'Do you understand me, Private Tucker?'

'Yes, sir.'

'Now, are any of you aware if there are any further survivors out there?'

They all shake their heads.

Charles looks at the men. He hasn't told them that he too is still being taught. He hasn't done weapons or combat training yet, either.

'Right, well, you lot look a mess, and you also smell, so go and get cleaned up.' He waves dismissively at them, buying time so he can think of what to do.

He runs his hand down his slicked hair and tries to think what a proper officer would do, then realises that they are all still staring at him.

'I thought I just told you to go and get cleaned up.'

'Sir, what's happening?'

'What's going on?'

'Is this everywhere?'

'Is my family okay?'

'Where's the rest of the army?'

Questions get thrown at him from the desperate men, who have spent the last two days running away from zombie soldiers.

'How the hell would I know?' he answers back.

'You said that you're Army Intelligence, sir, and that you had to report back,' Blowers says.

'Well, that is right...' Charles realises they want answers, and if he is going to lead these men and survive this disaster, he must tell them something. 'I'm sure you are all very worried, but the army will get a grip on this and will all be here very soon, I'm sure. In the meantime, we must survive.'

'So...you've not heard anything then, sir?' Blowers asks.

'Not at this time, Private, but would you like me to report back to you when I do?' His icy tone silences the man, who looks away. 'Now, I don't know what's going on out there. I can't reach or make contact with anyone at this time. The phones are down and the radios too, that includes landlines and mobile phones. We have no choice but to sit it out and wait for help.'

'Help? Sir? Why don't we get the weapons and fight our way out?'

'What weapons, Private Blowers? Where are they kept now? They are not in here.'

'In the armoury, sir.'

Charles panics, desperately thinking of a way not to look inept in front of these *common* men. 'I am not stationed here, and I do not know the layout. I too arrived on Friday for an exercise, so I do not know where the armoury is,' he says stiffly, expecting them to tell him, but they all remain silent. 'So? Where is it?' he asks.

They shrug their shoulders and shake their heads, looking to each other.

'So none of us know where it is, and unless any of you want to go floundering around outside with them, then I suggest we sit tight here,' Charles recovers the patronising tone.

'We could try, sir. They're slow now, and we might be able to find it.'

The same man from the front just won't leave it. He looks tough, though, and Charles falls back on his superior breeding and culture.

'And what will you do when you get there, Private? Do you think that the army just leaves its guns in an unlocked room, where just about anyone can get at them? No, they will be locked and secure, so unless you have the key or the combination, or a bloody big battering ram, then we will sit here and wait.'

'But, sir...'

'Private! I have had enough of your questions. This is bordering on insubordination. What is your name and rank, Private Blowers?'

The man stares back before answering, 'Private Blowers, sir...'

'Don't be bloody cheeky with me, soldier. You are on a charge the minute we get out of here. I don't want to hear another word out of you. I will let this pass, for now, as you are new recruits, but if it happens again, you will be on a charge, understood?'

'Yes, sir.'

'Right, go and get cleaned up. You're all a disgrace to the army in that state, and where are your uniforms?'

'We were being civilians in the exercise, sir, so we had to wear our normal clothes.'

'And your uniforms are where exactly?'

'In the barracks, sir.'

'Right, well, you'll just have to do the best you can until we get rescued. I mean until we get reinforcements.'

Charles walks out of the room and up the stairs of the small admin building and slumps down at a desk, rubbing his temples and thinking furiously.

He was in the officers' mess when it all started. An alarm sounded, and everyone went running off, leaving him alone. He ran too just so it looked good, but he didn't know where he was going, so he darted in this block and hid in one of the dark offices, thinking it could be a terrorist attack, and he didn't want to get involved in anything dangerous, so he sat tight and waited.

Later when he heard voices, he started to sneak out and saw the first infected soldiers. He didn't know that they were infected at the time – they just looked like men with awful injuries. He watched from the shadows of the admin building as they ran at the other soldiers and bit into their faces and necks, killing them. The sight was terrifying, and as more brave men ran into the fray, desperately trying to help, so Charles crept deeper into the shadows until he turned and ran inside to cower under the desk, wishing he was anywhere else but there.

He heard gunshots and screams all during that first night and stayed under the desk, sobbing into his knees and wishing he'd never been so bloody stupid as to join the army.

By Saturday, he had tried every phone in the building, but they were all down. He discovered an old transistor radio and tuned quickly through the frequencies, but got nothing.

He kept hoping someone would come and rescue him, or sort the situation out, but it got worse, with more infected staggering about close to the buildings.

He found some food in a small kitchen area and ate through packets of biscuits, and then found some chocolate bars and crisps. He thought about rationing the supplies in case he was still trapped, but he ate the lot. At least he had coffee until the power went off.

Then he was alone and in the dark, listening to the terrifying roars outside as night fell, and once more retreated back under the desk and hugged his knees, crying and sobbing in fear.

Then, this morning, the raw recruits burst in, and his heart jumped for joy, thinking the cavalry were coming to his rescue. He even had a story prepared – that he had tried to fight, but had been knocked out, and only just come around, and so he staggered out onto the landing to look down at the men, pretending to be woozy until he noticed they were all young men in civilian clothes without a blasted gun between them.

But still, at least he has some men to protect him and keep him safe. Cannon fodder. That's what Daddy always called them.

In the classroom of the building used for army education, the trainee recruits sit still and silent for a few minutes after the officer leaves, stunned at the cold arrogance and patronising sneer of the man.

THIRTY OF THEM started the orientation on Friday evening. Thirty new recruits from different regiments and units all over the south coast. There was a feeling of nervous excitement as they met each other and filed into the briefing tent. The regional training centres were exciting, but this was Salisbury, and it was huge.

The army buildings looked clean, freshly painted and surrounded a large drill square; the roads and paths were straight, and everything was well-ordered. The grass was cut to regulation length, and all of the marker stones were painted a crisp and clean white.

Men and women walked about, dressed like soldiers, real soldiers, wearing proper army clothes. They watched as soldiers saluted passing officers and everyone seemed to know what they were doing.

They were amazed at how many people were here, and just as they were led from the drill square into the briefing tent, they saw soldiers with real guns standing about, smoking and laughing, with faces painted green or black.

There were so many of them, and more arriving by the minute. Several of the units were dressed in brown camouflage instead of the jungle green, looking tanned and leaner than the others.

'Just returned from Afghan or Iraq probably,' Simon Blowers said as they stood around.

'How do you know?' asked Roy Tucker.

'They're wearing desert BDUs, and they're tanned from being somewhere hot and sunny, like a desert.'

The others laughed at this and started making fun of Tucker the way men do when they are together and feel insecure about their surroundings.

'Why are there so many soldiers here all tooled up?' asked another recruit, Alex Cook, a young man in his early twenties, with blond hair and blue eyes.

'Must be an exercise,' said Blowers.

'What are those guns? Are they the SA80s?' asked Tucker again.

'Fuck me, Tucker. What do you think the British Army would be carrying?'

'Well, I don't know, do I?' Tucker replied with an innocent look.

'What unit are you joining, Tucker?'

'Catering corps. I want to be a chef.'

They burst out laughing as the jokes flew thick and fast while someone poked his podgy belly. 'Bloody hell, mate. You gonna leave any grub for the army?'

More laughs and someone from the back called out. 'Tucker, you fat fucker'.

Roy Tucker has been called this all his life – through school and college, and at work in the council office, and although the jibes sting, he laughs along and joins in the banter.

'Fuck you, at least I'll be warm and fed while you lot run around being Rambos.'

The men relaxed into easy banter and excited conversation until a man with stripes on his sleeves walked in and shouted for them to be quiet. As soon as they hushed, an officer walked to the front and addressed the group.

'Welcome to Salisbury, gentlemen. You are at the start of your first two-week basic training camp. You should have all received your uniforms and basic kit from your regional training centres. If you are missing anything, or something doesn't fit, we can get that sorted first thing tomorrow. Now, normally the first night here would be orientation and then a few drinks in the mess to get to know one another. But we have a night exercise taking place, and your arrival fits in nicely.'

He paused to give a wolfish grin, adding a wink as he continued.

'As I'm sure you know, we have tank training and armoured vehicle training at this centre, and the mechanised infantry, regular infantry, and various other regiments train alongside them. This gives us invaluable operational training prior to deployment. Tonight, we have a very large exercise taking place, and we are going to use you as civilians in the urban village training zone. You will be fully briefed as to what exactly is expected from you, but let me say this. This is a remarkable opportunity for you to see the British Army in action. There will be simulated fighting, firing, and explosions, so do try and stay awake, please.'

They laughed and started whispering in excited tones until the sergeant shouted for them to be quiet.

'Now, you will have to excuse me as I am needed elsewhere, but we will get a chance to meet again tomorrow when we begin your basic training. Just one more thing. After the exercise, please do try and get some sleep. Trust me, you will need the rest.'

The officer left, and the sergeant took over, giving the brief for the night exercise. Telling the men to do exactly as they are told the very second they are told to do it.

'They won't be using live rounds, so there's no risk of getting shot, but it will be dark, and there will be lots going on, so if you walk around on your own, there is a real risk of injury. Do as you are told and enjoy the spectacle. We do not allow mobiles or cameras, or you trying to take pictures and using flashes, so all of your phones and cameras will be left here. If any of you are caught with a phone, you will be discharged with immediate effect.'

The recruits were led away and taken by old army trucks down into the training area. All of them buoyed up and excited at the operation and being allowed to be involved.

Within a couple of hours, they were placed in small groups in the houses of the urban village training zone and told to stand around or to sit on the furniture, and wait for further instruction.

The sense of excitement was palpable, and within a short time, they could hear shots and loud explosions coming from the dark grounds all around them.

Then loud engines and heavy vehicles passing through the streets, with men running behind them and taking position. Assault rifles firing with bright flashes from the ends of the barrels are startling in the dark.

The recruits watched as the soldiers started at one end of the street and worked their way down, clearing each house in turn, with more soldiers firing back at them, and massive mock battles taking place with smoke grenades and explosions.

The soldiers worked the house clearance until they found trainee recruits. Treating them like detainees, making them kneel as plastic cuffs were applied to their wrists behind their backs. Then they were led outside, and after some time, the cuffs were removed, and they were led to the end of the street into a "safe area".

It was all very exciting. Hearing the real soldiers shouting and the aggression used, but it was controlled aggression and done with orders shouted from corporals and sergeants.

A short while later, some officers and instructors spoke to the recruits and told them that they will have a "hot debrief".

The recruits all tried to look serious and cool, like they knew what was going on. They were asked to declare any injuries and if they were happy to continue before being back into the houses to do it all again.

More shooting. More vehicles. More voices and bangs, and detonations, and the recruits waited to be found and detained while that shouting got worse and different, like there was more confusion or something had gone wrong, and that got worse as they heard the word *medic* being screamed out.

Simon Blowers watched from a glassless window frame, frowning at the shouts, thinking it didn't sound right.

Blowers wasn't a raw recruit. He'd joined the Royal Marines couple of years ago and got a fair way through basic training until he broke his leg and was told he had to leave. The Marines wouldn't take him back, so after bumming about, feeling sorry for himself, he decided to join the TA, and that short glimpse into military life gave him enough understanding to know something was wrong. And it was at that point, he and the recruits with him saw the soldier fall down in the street, clutching a fake wound to his neck. They even watched as more soldiers rushed to help him, thinking it all to be part of the exercise and that the injury was very realistic.

'Loads of blood,' Alex Cook said, looking seriously impressed.

'Must be a pump,' Blowers said, 'like in his clothes to squirt the blood out.'

'You like squirting,' Alex Cook said, staring deadpan at Blowers. 'Your mum told me. Er, why is the injured guy attacking his mates?'

Blowers looked back out to see the soldier with the injury lunging at the soldiers around him. It looked a bit nuts, but then there was loads of bangs sounding and bright things flashing, so they couldn't see very clearly. But it did look like the injured guy was trying to bite the others, and they, in turn, battered him back down to the ground.

'Fuck me,' Blowers muttered, frowning as he spoke. 'That's a bit realistic...' he added as more soldiers ran past his assigned house. 'Where they going? They shouldn't advance until they've cleared the structures.'

'Dunno,' Alex said.

'Helpful, Alex,' Blowers said.

'Argh, don't call me Alex. It's Cookey,' Alex said, watching more soldiers run by outside.

'Okay, Alex,' Blowers said.

'Oh fuck,' Cookey said, showing surprise. 'Seen that up there?'

'Where?' Blowers asked, following the line of sight up the road to a mass brawl taking place, with soldiers fighting hand-to-hand, and as they watched, so the details became clearer. Soldiers stabbing each other. Stamping and kicking. Hitting and biting. Lots of biting, and even in the poor light, they could see awful injuries that suddenly didn't look fake at all. 'What the fuck...' he whispered as the door to their room burst open, with a soldier staggering in, dripping blood from a ragged wound to his neck. 'Mate, are you all right?'

'I don't think he's alright,' Cookey said. 'Why's his eyes all red? Mate, why's your eyes all red?'

'Fuck his eyes. You seen his neck?' Blowers said. At which point, the soldier charged at them, and at which point, they both yelled out and started running about the room as more recruits ran downstairs from watching out of an upstairs window.

'Fuck! Is he all right?' one of them asked, seeing the injured soldier staggering stiff-legged about the room. 'Oi, mate, are you okay? Is this part of the exercise or WHAT THE FUCK!' he shouted out as the soldier lunged at him, tripping and headbutting his chest, sending him back while the others watched on in shock. 'Fucking careful, mate,' the recruit shouted before feeling the pain of the teeth in his leg. 'Hey! HEY, OI! HE'S FUCKING BITING ME!'

'Fuck, fuck, what's he fucking doing?' Cookey screamed at Blowers.

Blowers reacted quickly, running forward to kick at the soldier's head, forcing him off the recruit. A hard kick too, but it had no effect, and the soldier carried on gnashing and thrashing with immense violence. Blood spraying up, and the recruit screaming while trying to get free. Blowers kicked again, buying a split second for the recruit to yank himself free and turn over to try and crawl away as the soldier lunged back in to bite the lad on his arse cheeks, eliciting more screams of pain.

'You dirty fuck, don't bite his arse. He's biting his fucking arse!' Blowers shouted as Cookey stood in shock for a second before running over to help Blowers kick the soldier down and away. But he kept getting back up, so they kept kicking until he finally went limp, and only then did they realise the bitten recruit was silent and inert too.

'Is he alright?' Alan Booker asked, staring down in shock.

'He's fucking dead.' Blowers replied, checking for a pulse as the carnage ramped up outside.

'Fuck this, I'm out of here!' Cookey said, running for the door, followed swiftly by Blowers. They ran to the end, dodging round fighting soldiers and bodies on the ground.

Shots and loud explosions sounding out as the soldiers try desperately to fight back against the increasing numbers of infected. They spotted the safe zone at the end and some of the other recruits hunkering down and ran towards them.

'What do we do?' Tucker cried out.

'YOU LOT,' a soldier shouted, running towards them. 'EGRESS NOW!'

'What the fuck is egress?' Cookey asked.

'Means get out,' Blowers said.

'LEG IT NOW,' the soldier screamed, waving at them to go as an infected took him down from the side, biting into his neck. Blowers and Cookey reacted quickly, running towards him. 'NO! GET OUT, RUN!' the soldier screamed while fighting, having already seen what happens when you get bit. 'FUCKING RUN. NOW! GET INTO THE PLAINS.'

The lads paused, watching as he drew a knife from his belt and started stabbing the infected soldier in the neck as more infected soldiers lunged in to drop down and bite with screams and howls ripping the air apart.

The two lads backed up and away; then, as one, they turned and ran into the darkness, with the rest of the recruits running with them. More shouts on both sides. More screams. More figures seen running wild and crazed.

'Off the road. Quick. This way.' Blowers said, headed into the darkness of the plains.

They kept running for several minutes, then slowed to a jog until the noise of the fighting and the screams were left behind. A low hill was found, and they dropped down, taking cover to pant heavily; all of them breathing hard.

'What the fuck was that?' asked Roland McKinney.

'I don't fucking know,' Julian Talley replied, gasping for air.

'Is that part of the exercise?' asked Tucker.

'No, it fucking isn't, you thick cunt,' Darren Smith shouted at him, panic in his voice.

'What do we do?' asked Nick Hewitt.

'Let's just wait here and keep low,' Blowers replied as a loud engine roared above them, and a long metal barrel came into view, followed by a huge army tank rising up on the hill behind them, where it teetered on the top before dropping straight towards them.

'Scatter!' Blowers shouted as they legged it off and away in different directions, but one was too slow, tripping over and getting caught under the tracks, pulverised within an instant, with his body bursting apart. 'STOP,' Blowers shouted, waving his arms.

'HEY!' Cookey shouted too. They all did. All of them screaming for the tank to stop while a few retched and wept from seeing their mate bursting apart, but the tank kept going. The top hatch open, with a uniformed guy halfway out, being attacked and bitten by another soldier driving his mouth into his neck. The tank kept going, roaring fast away into the night.

'Did you fucking see that?' Cookey said into the silence that followed.

'We need to keep going,' Blowers said, shocked, stunned, sickened and feeling the panic inside, watching as a few of the lads run at the broken body killed under the tracks. 'He's gone. Leave him. We need to go. Now!' Blowers shouted, running further into the plains.

The others responded, hastening to catch up with him.

'Where are we going?' Cookey asked.

'I don't fucking know. Just keep running.'

After ten minutes, they saw lights and headed towards them. A rudimentary base set up for the exercise, with more tanks parked up, and camouflage netting stretched over a field table covered in maps and folders. Movement in the lights, and the recruits ran forward, shouting and screaming for help. Then they saw soldiers running towards them, and Blowers and Cookey at the front noticed the oncoming soldiers' red eyes.

'Fuck,' they both shouted, one going left, the other going right, as the infected soldiers ran into the group to take down the nearest recruits. Chaos again. Screams and wails, with people running in the dark.

'TALLEY!' McKinney shouted, seeing one of the lads pinned down under a soldier biting into his face.

'Shit,' Talley muttered, running back to help McKinney kick at the infected, battering it away over the grass. 'GET HIM UP!'

Blowers, Cookey, and Nick ran in, grabbing the injured lad up to run on. All of them legging it once more back into the darkness of the plains.

'Gotta keep going,' Blowers said, urging them on.

'My guts,' the injured recruit said, clutching his mid-section. 'Argh, fuck, it hurts.'

'Keep running,' Cookey said.

'Can't. Shit, that hurts so much.'

He dropped to the ground, writhing in agony as the others looked on, not knowing what to do. Everything happening so quickly. Then he simply stopped and grew quiet and still as Blowers and Nick felt for a pulse.

'He's fucking dead,' Nick said, shocked to the core. 'Jesus, he's fucking dead.'

'We have to go,' Talley said as their heads snapped over to the howls coming towards them and the shadowy figures seen in the near distance.

'CPR,' McKinney said, dropping at the dead lad's side to pump his chest. 'Someone blow in his lungs.'

'Fuck!' Talley said, clutching his head in the dark.

'We can't be here,' Darren Smith said as another recruit dropped down to wipe the blood from the dead lad's face before leaning over to create the seal to push air into the lungs. 'FUCK!' Smith screamed out, staggering back as the dead lad grabs at the one breathing into him, who squirms and thrashes, with blood spurting out before being cast aside.

'RUN!' Cookey shouted.

'Fuck this,' Blowers said, running behind the others.

They lost several more during that night. Running with no idea as to direction, and with only moonlight to see by. No phones. No torches. No anything.

On one occasion, the ground dropped down in front of them, and they fell into a small group of infected stooped over a fresh kill. They lost a few from that, and once more, all they could do was run while listening to the screams of their mates, knowing their mates will soon be chasing after them too.

By Saturday morning, they were exhausted, filthy, and very, very lost. They tried resting in amongst the hills, running when they saw infected, resting when they didn't.

During the afternoon, they found a single infected prone on the ground. Alive and groaning, but seemingly unable to get up. The movements slow.

'He's got a water bottle on his belt,' Cookey said, looking at the body as they gave it a wide berth.

'We need to drink. Someone go and get it,' Darren Smith said, his eyes settling on Tucker.

'Why me?' Tucker asked.

'You're in the catering corps, so you're in charge of supplies,' Talley said to him.

Tucker looked around at the faces, hoping for a reprieve, then sighed, nodded, and set off.

'Come up from behind him,' Blowers called out.

'Yeah, I bet you've done that before,' Cookey muttered, earning a few very tired sniggers.

Tucker reached the body and gingerly stretched out to slide the bottle from the infected soldier's belt before standing upright with a look of victory.

'Tucker, watch out!' Talley shouted as the soldier rolled towards Tucker's feet.

Tucker staggered backwards and tripped, going down onto his arse before scrabbling up with a whimper and running back to the men.

Tucker unscrewed the bottle cap and took a sip. The rest of the men watching intently, making sure that he only took a sip before handing the bottle onto the next man.

Talley was the last to drink.

'Is there any left, Talley?' Blowers asked him.

'Yeah, not much, though. We'll save it for later. That okay with everyone?'

They all looked longingly at the bottle but nodded in agreement.

As night fell, they heard what sounded like wolves howling into the night sky. The sound coming from all around them, chilling them to the bone, and so another night of near constant running started again.

The infected soldiers chasing them relentlessly through the hills and valleys, and it's only when one recruit fell down and was set upon, that the others got away.

From the thirty recruits that ran into the plains on Friday night, only twelve remained as the sun rose on Monday morning, and they learnt more survival instincts in those two days than they ever would have during the two-week training camp.

Eventually, after trudging for many miles, they saw the compound buildings in the distance and worked their way over, running between hordes of slow-moving infected soldiers to reach the closest admin building and bursting in, exhausted, filthy, drained, and very dehydrated to the sight of Second Lieutenant Galloway-Gibbs coming down the stairs, holding his head and clutching the handrail. Not that they paid any attention, and as one, they lurched like the infected to find running water to drink deep.

CHAPTER THIRTY

Dave and I stand and look at the lowered metal bar stretched across the road and the small sentry hut next to it.

It's taken us several hours to find the road to Salisbury army training centre, but after many wrong turns and avoiding small groups of infected, we found it.

'It doesn't look like much.' I was expecting something more high-tech than this. 'It looks like something from World War Two. The movies always show army bases behind big, electric gates and cameras, and stuff.'

Dave just looks at me silently for a few minutes, and I shrug back at him.

The metal bar stretches across the road, and the guard hut is just a small, wooden structure with glass windows and a large doorway.

'So, where's the guard?' I ask Dave.

'Should be there,' he points at the empty hut.

We walk closer, leaving the unmarked police car on the road. Dave had told me not to bring a weapon out, and he made sure to leave his knives in the car. We approach the hut and check inside, but it's definitely empty. There is a high wire fence topped with razor wire running off in both directions, and I can see buildings in the distance.

'Where's the switch to raise the barrier?' I ask from the hut

Dave walks over and pushes one end down, and the smaller end lifts up with ease. 'It's manual, Mr Howie.'

'Oh, right. Well, are we driving in or walking? I personally think driving so that we can get away if something horrible happens, which it invariably will. Like literally every half hour.'

We go back to the car and drive through, leaving the barrier up so that we can make a fast escape if we need to.

'Why is there just a single barrier there? It doesn't look that secure.'

'There's always two guards at every entrance,' Dave replies.

'Armed guards?'

'Yes, Mr Howie.'

We drive down the road, and after a few minutes, the buildings come into view. Just basic structures set around a massive drill square, and beyond the buildings, another road going into a vast, open area.

'That must be where they do the tank training.'

'Yes, Mr Howie.'

'Well, I don't see any big vehicles here, so they must be somewhere else out there maybe. Cock it! Look at that.'

I stop the car, and we both look down to the drill square and the hundreds of infected all facing into one building, indicating there must be survivors inside, or that's the place they last saw a survivor.

'I bloody knew it! What did I say? Every half hour something shit happens. Fuck me, are they all soldiers?'

The entire horde are roughly dressed in green and brown camouflaged army uniform. Some are wearing what looks to be battle dress, with helmets on, and twigs and branches stuck in the top. I reel back, amazed at the sight.

'That's a fucking army, a fucking zombie army.' I turn to look at Dave, leaning forward, staring intently at the scene in front of us. 'I can't see another way round Dave. The road just goes straight through them all.'

'Look.' Dave points at the building being surrounded by the infected. A window opens, and a person leans out, waving something white at us.

I get out and wave back with both my arms high up in the air. 'Bugger me, someone's alive.' I look at the horde surrounding them and shake my head, grimacing at the sight. 'We'll have to do something. We can't just leave them there.'

'Okay, Mr Howie,' Dave says from my side, making me jump from not hearing him get out of the car.

'Don't suppose you know Morse code, do you, Dave?'

'Yes, Mr Howie.'

'Really? I was only joking then... We could use the car headlights to signal to them. Would that work?'

'Yes.'

I pull the car around so that the front of the car is facing towards the building and then show Dave how to operate the high beam on the headlights.

It's daylight and very sunny, so hopefully, the infected won't see us; they're all facing the other way anyway.

'Got the idea, mate?'

'I think so.'

He gets into the driver's seat and starts pulling at the headlight stick – quick on and off, then a longer on.

'Okay, all yours now, Dave. Keep going.'

'Okay.'

He pauses for a few seconds, then looks up at me. 'What do you want me to say?'

'I don't know. Oh! Ask them how many there are in there?'

'Okay.' Dave starts pulling at the light stick, and I watch the light flicker on and off, then I look back to the building and watch as the man with the white thing goes back inside.

'SIR, WHERE ARE YOU?' Cookey asks, rushing out of the upstairs room.

'I am right here, thank you, Private Cook,' Charles replies, walking from his office while smoothing his hair down. 'What are you shouting about?'

'There's a car just come down the road, and they've seen us.'

'How did they see us, Private Cook?'

'Blowers waved a hand towel at them through the window.'

'Good lord,' Charlies says, bustling forward into the room packed with recruits to see Blowers at the window. 'What's going on?'

'They're signalling us,' Blowers says. 'I think it's Morse code. They're using the car headlights.'

Second Lieutenant Galloway-Gibbs watches out of the open window, trying not to look down at the hungry faces covered in awful wounds staring up at him. 'Yes, I think you're right, Private Blowers. It does appear that they are trying to signal to us.'

'What are they saying, sir?'

'How the bloody hell should I know?'

'You're Army Intelligence, sir. Every intelligence officer is trained in Morse code.'

Galloway-Gibbs panics, thinking furiously. He can't admit that he doesn't know Morse code, or they'll find out he isn't trained or even fully commissioned yet. 'Yes, of course. Well, some are, but not all of us, though. Things have changed and evolved, Private Blowers, and umm...Morse code training is a specialist training skill that only a few get these days. I put in for it, of course, but you know what the army's like – bloody waiting lists, eh?'

'Right... Sir, well, how do we signal back?'

'I'm in intelligence, Private Blowers, not a signalman. Use your imagination.'

'I found this, sir.'

Galloway-Gibbs turns to see Private Talley holding a torch out in front of him.

'He doesn't know Morse code, Talley,' Blowers tells him.

'Oh...' Talley lowers the torch and goes back out of the room.

'DOES ANYONE KNOW MORSE CODE?' Talley booms out into the hallway.

More of the men appear from rooms, looking sleepy and dishevelled.

'What? Why?' Darren Smith asks.

'There's a car up on the road, and it's using the headlights to signal to us. Does anyone know Morse code?'

'The officer will – he's in Intelligence. I thought they all got trained,' Nick Hewitt replies.

'No, apparently not.' Talley says, rolling his eyes.

'I used to do it at scouts,' Tucker offers.

'Tucker, well done, mate. Come and have a go,' Blowers calls from inside the room.

'It was years ago, though. I don't remember it,' he stammers, suddenly nervous.

'Just try, Tucker,' Nick says.

'Well done, Private Tucker,' Charles says as the nervous lad walks in. 'Where's that torch?'

'Errr... Bloody hell, hang on.' Tucker looks into the lens of the flashlight and presses the on button, then reels back from the retina burn of the bright light.

'Tucker, you fucking idiot. Shine it at them, not yourself!' Cookey says, shaking his head.

'I was making sure that it works,' Tucker replies, then points the flashlight at the car, and starts pressing the light on and off, rapidly.

'So what's he saying, Private Tucker?' Charles asks.

'I don't know yet, sir. I'm asking him to start the message again.'

The car lights go off for a few seconds, then start blinking with short and longer bursts.

Tucker's mouth moves as he tries to keep up with the letters being signalled to him.

'Shit, I lost it. I need a pen and paper.'

'Private Hewitt, go and get Private Tucker something to write with, please.'

Nick shoots out of the room, calling for pen and paper, and returns within seconds, armed with several pens and pads from a nearby office. 'Here you are, mate,' he says, holding them out for Tucker.

'No, I'll call out the letters, and you write them down.'

'Er, yeah... I'm dyslexic,' Nick says with a grimace. 'Sorry.'

'Good lord,' Charles says tightly, adding a deep huff.

'I'll do it, mate,' Alan Booker says, taking the pen and paper. 'Ready when you are.'

Tucker flashes back to the car, asking them to start again.

The car lights go out, and then after several seconds, they start flashing, and Tucker calls the letters out. 'H...O...W...M...A...N...Y. Oh, what does that spell?' he looks at Cookey.

'How many?' Booker responds.

'How many what?' Galloway-Gibbs demands from Tucker.

'I don't know, sir. That's all he sent.'

'How many of us, probably,' Blowers says without looking round.

'Yes, thank you, Private Blowers. I am sure we could have worked that out for ourselves. Well, Tucker, answer the man and make sure you tell him there's an officer here as well.'

'Can't I just tell him there are thirteen of us, sir?'

'No, Private Tucker, you cannot. They need to know an officer of the British Army is in this building, so tell them.'

The officer stares at Tucker just as Talley and Blowers shrug their shoulders. Tucker turns back to the window and starts flashing the torch again.

'HE SAYS thirteen and something else, but I can't make it out, Mr Howie,' Dave says from the front of the car.

'Okay, so there are thirteen of them in there? Wow, that's a lot. Why are they hiding and not fighting their way out?'

'I don't know, Mr Howie.'

'I know there's a few zombie soldiers there, but still, thirteen of them, and especially if they are soldiers… Right, we need a plan.' I look at Dave.

'We could lead them away.'

'No, mate, it's already late, and it will take bloody hours to lure away a group like that. It would be nice to get through them and get one of those APS vehicles, and then come back.'

'APC.'

'Yeah, that's what I meant, but we can't get through them without a fight.'

I sense Dave looking at me. I think I have just used his favourite word, and his ears prick up like a child being offered sweets. I can't help feeling the urge too, though. That feeling of battle is amazing. I start to smile and feel the adrenalin coursing through my system.

'Well, Dave, a fight it is, then.'

There it is again – that tiny, almost invisible smile glint in his eye. It lights him up. How can I say no to such a nice man?

'Are we driving down or walking, Dave?'

'Walk, then we can drop them as we go.'

'Good idea, chum. Walking it is, then. Now, do I take the axe or not. Axe or shotgun, axe or shotgun.' I weigh both of them in my hands, trying to decide.

'Take both, Mr Howie.'

'You think so?'

'You'll need it when we get close. You won't have time to reload.'

'Fair point, mate. Both, then.'

I put the bag onto my back and tighten the straps, then drop the axe down so that the head is resting on the top of the bag, and the handle is hanging down.

'Don't trip up this time, Mr Howie.'

'I won't, mate.'

'And if you do, shoot them and not me.'

'Okay, mate.'

I take the plastic carrier bag that Dave fashioned into a shotgun cartridge holder and loop it through my belt; then I fill it with shotgun cartridges.

'Are you taking the rifle or the other shotgun, Dave?'

'The rifle, Mr Howie...and the knives.'

'I thought you might.'

Dave puts the Tesco fleece on and loads up the pockets with ammunition strips for the Lee Enfield .303 rifle.

'Mr Howie, can I use your bag to put some ammunition in and my knives?'

'Of course, mate, no problem.'

Dave goes behind me, and I feel as he rummages about in the side pockets and puts ammunition in them. I turn my head as he slides his two favourite straight-bladed knives into the elastic mesh at the front of the bag.

'Ready, mate?'

'Yes, Mr Howie. Just stay to my left, please, so I can reload from your bag.'

'Okay, got it.'

We both take a long drink of water and then start walking down, towards the horde.

'WHAT THE BLOODY hell are they doing? Are they mad?' Charles shouts out in surprise as the two men leave the car and walk towards them. 'There's only two of them. They'll be slaughtered,' he says, more to himself than the other men.

'They're armed, though, sir.'

'What, with one gun each? Against hundreds of those things down there. They must be bloody mad.'

At least they are trying, Blowers thinks to himself.

CHAPTER THIRTY-ONE

The road is set higher than the parade square and the building beyond, so we have to walk down a slope. I can't help smiling at the absurdity of it. Two of us armed with one rifle, one shotgun, two knives, and one axe against an actual army of zombies.

'Fuck me, we must be mad,' I say to myself, earning a look from Dave, who appears as calm as ever. 'I guess we should start picking them off and lead 'em over to that big car park so the people in that building can break out.'

'It's a parade square.'

'What is?'

'That big car park – it's a parade square.'

'Fair enough. We can spread them out over the parade square then, you picky bugger.'

We walk for another few seconds until Dave judges the distance is effective for the shotgun; then we both stop again, and he looks at me.

'Ready, Mr Howie?'

'I always ask that.'

'Oh, sorry.'

'That's okay, mate. Ready, Dave?'

'Yes, Mr Howie.'

I raise the shotgun to my shoulder and pause while giving weighty reflection on the fact that I am about to shoot at what was once people. Mind you, I just made a bunch of them fall off a bridge, so screw it. I fire both barrels into the crowd as Dave gets to work with the rifle.

I reload and fire into them again. Dave is firing rapidly, aiming his shots and picking them off one by one. I take a second between reloading to watch his shots, and even from this range, they all look like head shots.

The infected react slowly, turning to start shuffling, with a louder groaning sounding out. I keep loading and firing, and at this range, I am dropping several with each shot. I don't expect to kill them, but at least they are knocked over, which is thinning them out a bit.

We move forward slowly, and as we get closer, I can see just how many there are – several hundred of them.

'MOVE LEFT!' Dave shouts out over the gunfire, and we both start stepping left as we fire.

The horde reacts and starts to follow us. The plan works slowly, and they begin stringing out from the densely packed crowd.

We keep firing and dropping them from the front, and we are doing good work, but for every one we drop, several more shuffle into view.

After several minutes, Dave pats his pockets and shouts, 'AMMUNITION.'

I drop to one knee and keep firing as Dave gropes in the bag and pulls out more clips, then pushes more shotgun cartridges into my belt bag.

'Thanks, mate.'

We maintain this position for a few minutes, with me kneeling down, and Dave standing to my right. The infected are much closer now, and the shotgun pellets have less distance and are therefore less spread out, but the effect at this range is devastating, and they are hammered backwards, with bits of bodies flying off, and once again, I notice the bodies at the front create an obstacle for those following, tripping many over, which, in turn, creates more gaps between them as they struggle to get back up.

'No sign of any super zombies then?' I say to Dave as we both reload.

'Not yet, Mr Howie.'

And then we are back, firing into them and watching as infected soldiers are mown down by the rifle and the shotgun. Heads exploding as the bullets enter their forehead and take the back of the skull out, showering the closest infected with bits of grey matter. Deadly shards of bones from the skulls fly off into more brains and flesh.

'I'M ALMOST OUT, DAVE.'

'MOVE BACK.'

We step more to the left, creating distance from the slow-moving horde. I drop down again, and Dave rummages through the bag and hands me more cartridges.

'THAT'S IT.'

I pick my shots, aiming into the densest part of the crowd, trying to use the full effect of the shotgun, but within seconds, the ammunition is gone.

'I'M OUT.'

Dave fires a few more times, then loops the rifle strap over his shoulder and neck so that it's secure on his back. He runs around to the back of me as I release the chest and waist clips; then Dave pulls the bag down and hands me the axe.

'Leave the shotgun here with the bag. We'll come back for it,' I say to Dave as I take the axe from him.

Dave draws the knives from the front of the bag, and we start moving back to the right, following the path we have just taken. The horde is slow to react, and I can see that they are strung out, coming away from the building. We have killed many of them, and more are wriggling on the ground, tangled with the bodies they have tripped over.

We keep moving until the building is in front of us. The men inside are all staring out of the windows, and I feel that thrum inside building with every second. A violence within me that wants to come out. That wants to fight. My body starts buzzing with adrenalin, but it's not loaded with fear now, not like it was before.

'Ready, Dave?' I ask, my voice low and almost lost.

'Yes, Mr Howie.'

'LET'S HAVE IT, THEN,' I scream out and charge forward, lifting my axe as I go and see Dave lean forward, with his arms out behind him, then leap, and spin through the air, driving the knives into the back of a soldier's neck.

I chop down at my first kill, and the axe slices through his skull. I pull back and move forward again, swinging out and chopping uniformed soldiers down as they lunge forward at me.

'COME ON,' I shout at them, lashing left and right, cleaving a path through the bodies, and within seconds, the blood sprays across my face, hot and wet.

Dave twirls and dances through them, flowing like water and slicing the blades across jugulars, and stabbing through the necks and into spinal columns. I watch two come at him, one from the front, and one from behind. Dave drops down onto his back and sticks the blades up into their heads as they drop to bite, skewering them both before sliding out and carrying on.

My aiming is getting better with the axe, and I use less power and more skill now, judging the blow and conserving energy, and in truth, I can't get enough of it.

'FUCKING LOOK AT THEM GO! Jesus fucking Christ!' Blowers exclaims, on his feet, staring at the two men attacking the infected outside.

'Fuck me, look at the small bloke with those knives! Have you ever seen anything like that?' Talley yells out, equally excited.

'Fuck this, I'm joining in,' Blowers says, starting for the door as Second Lieutenant Galloway-Gibbs blocks his path.

'Stand down, Private.'

'What the fuck?' Blowers asks.

'You will stand down. There is no way those two will reach here. Going out there is just bloody suicide.'

'They're bloody trying, though. Jesus, the things are all slow. We could help. We can attack from the rear.'

'Do not question my orders, Private. Do as you are told.'

Blowers might not have completed his full training in the Royal Marines, but he did meet officers, and they didn't talk to people like this. His face hardens, and he stares at Charles as he swallows while trying to maintain his superior sneer.

'Sir, with all due respect,' Blowers says quietly as every man in the room watches on. 'You can fuck off,' he adds, shoving past to the door as Charles wilts back from the physical contact.

A second and no more. A second for Cookey and Tucker, and Talley, and the rest to share looks before they all burst to chase after Blowers as Charles flinches and moves back away from them rushing past.

'Grab anything you can use,' Blowers yells at them, hefting a long metal pole used for opening the top windows. The men rush around, finding anything that can be used as a weapon: wooden chairs, a coat stand. A couple of them turn the classroom tables over and pull the thick, wooden legs off. Tucker runs into the small kitchen area, wrenching drawers and cupboard open, ignoring heavy pans and sharp things to grab a spatula before running back out into the main area as Blowers shakes his head, then looks at the young lads about him.

'We only met a few days ago, but these fuckers have killed our mates, and those two blokes are fighting to get to us. So we're going to go out there to fuck them up, got it?'

The men nod; faces stern and ready. Terrified to the core. Exhausted too from days of running, but ready and willing. The strain and fear showing as Blowers wrenches the door open and charges out with a roar. Cookey hot on his heels. Nick right behind them. All of them roaring with the charge.

I KEEP KILLING THEM, and they keep coming.

We slowly beat a path towards the building line, but the infected are dense here, and the battle gets harder, and I keep having to move backwards in order to create space, fighting almost back to back with Dave as we slowly get surrounded.

'I'M THINKING THIS MIGHT HAVE BEEN A BAD IDEA, DAVE,' I shout out between swings as more sticky blood sprays out.

'SWAP PLACES, MR HOWIE.' We spin around so that Dave is

facing towards the building, and I can cover his back with the range of the axe. 'Stay with me,' Dave says and starts slashing his way through, carving a path with his knives.

More soldiers lurch at me, and I drive the axe down on them, then swing back out, and knock more down, desperate to get space. Dave is still slashing left, right, and forward, and the body count keeps going up as his arms whirl through the air.

Then I hear loud shouting, and I glance around to see men bursting out of the building, holding a collection of weapons – chair legs, metal poles, and one fat lad clutching a spatula in his hand as they charge into the back of the horde, and we fight with renewed energy as both sides slaughter a path to each other.

I scream out and join Dave at the front, lashing out with the axe, battering, and cleaving the bodies. Within seconds, we get to the men.

'GO INSIDE,' Dave bellows at them, and they react instantly to his drill sergeant voice, falling back and running into the doorway.

One lad stays, fighting with a long metal pole, screaming abuse, and lashing out.

I run up behind him and grab the back of his shirt, and start pulling him back.

'MOVE BACK, GET INSIDE,' I scream at him, and he allows me to pull him back inside the building and slam the door shut.

CHAPTER THIRTY-TWO

We all slump down on the floor, gasping for breath. Even Dave is sweating, albeit lightly, while my chest heaves, and the sweat drips from my nose, mingled with blood and gore. I lean back against a wall and slide down; the axe resting by the side of me as I glance round at the men. Just kids, really. Young men, anyway. None of them look over twenty-one years old. They look terrified and exhausted too.

'Good work, lads,' I gasp. 'Thanks for the help.'

The eager faces look at me, and the fat lad rushes off and comes back a few seconds later with a large glass of water that he hands to Dave.

'Mr Howie first.'

The guys look at me as I realise they're are all in filthy and torn normal clothes and not army uniform.

'Thanks, Dave.' I take the water and down it in one, then hand the glass back, and the lad rushes off to get more.

'Bring two glasses this time, Tucker,' one of the men shouts as he disappears into the kitchen.

Tucker comes back with two glasses of water, and we sit and drink. I wipe the sweat out of my eyes, and my arm comes away all bloody.

'That was fucking amazing,' one of the men says to me; then they all join in, offering thanks and praise to both of us.

I hold my hand up. 'Really, it's nothing. Just trying to help.'

'That wasn't nothing. You killed loads of them. That was fucking awesome,' the lad with the long metal pole says.

'Well, we were starting to struggle at the end there, eh, Dave?'

'Yes, Mr Howie,' he says while looking at me, as though suggesting he wasn't struggling at all.

'Glad you came out when you did.' I catch the glances again as they hear Dave call me Mr Howie, and I try to intercept before the name sticks. 'I'm Howie, and this is Dave.'

We get a chorus of responses, and one of the men stands up in front of me and offers his hand – the same lad I pulled away.

'Thank you, Mr Howie.'

Fuck it, I bloody knew that would happen again, but I'm too exhausted to argue. I'll tell them later.

'I'm Blowers, Simon Blowers,' he repeats the action with Dave, and I watch with amusement as Dave gives a very quick handshake, then wipes his hand down his trousers.

I get to my feet and offer my hand to the next one, and I keep going, knowing they will respond and then offer to shake Dave's hand, and I can't help but smile as he wipes his hand between each shake.

'And who exactly are you, gentlemen?' A posh man comes down from the stairs. Tall, with slicked-back hair and wearing a smart, green uniform. Not the camouflage dress of the soldiers outside.

'Hi, I'm Howie. Nice to meet you.' I walk towards him with my hand outstretched.

He gets to the bottom of the steps and looks down at my blood-soaked hand with disdain.

'Oh, I'm sorry, mate,' I wipe my hand down the back of my trousers and offer it again.

He accepts with a very limp grip. 'Lieutenant Charles Galloway-Gibbs of the British Army Intelligence Corps.' He drops my hand, and I can see that he is itching to wipe it clean but is too well mannered to do it in front of me. 'Now, I asked you a question. Who are you?'

I stare back at him, quizzically. 'I just told you. I'm Howie, and this is Dave.'

'Where are you from?' he speaks slowly, with a patronising sneer.

'I'm from Boroughfare, why?'

'I mean what regiment are you from?'

'I'm not from a regiment.' The bloke is a prick and has irritated me already. The flush of battle is still on me, and I can't help but get bridled by his rude manner.

'You are not from a regiment? Then what, may I ask, are you doing here?'

'We've come to steal an APS...'

'APC,' Dave says.

'We've come to steal an APC, and then we saw you lot in here, so we thought we'd help.'

Dave joins me and stands smartly in front of the officer; then, surprisingly, he salutes.

'Sir,' Dave states, crisply.

The officer looks at Dave and turns to me.

'Not from a regiment?'

'No, I just told you. I'm from Boroughfare.'

'He looks like a soldier to me.' The officer gestures to Dave.

'He was. I'm not.' I speak slowly, angry at the incredibly rude manner of the man.

I turn my back on him and look to the men who are standing around the hallway, all of them watching me with interest.

'There's thirteen of you? Is that right?' They nod at me, and I can see them glancing back at the officer. 'So are you all soldiers, then?'

'Kind of,' Simon Blowers replies. 'TA. We only arrived on Friday for our first two-week camp.'

'Do not turn your back on me. I was talking to you.' The officer speaks from behind me.

'You were speaking rudely to me. That's what you were doing, mate, and after what we just did...'

'Do not call me, *mate*. I am an officer in the British Army, and you do not call me mate...'

I spin around. At any other time, I might have been able to swallow it and remain polite, but the adrenalin is still in me, and I lose my temper and jab my finger into his chest, driving him back into the classroom. 'You're fucking rude, that's what you are...MATE... Now me and Dave here have just fought through a shitload of zombie soldier things to try and help you...'

'DO NOT TOUCH ME! I AM AN OFFICER. YOU, MEN,' he points at the men in the hallway, 'ARREST HIM NOW. HE HAS ASSAULTED AN OFFICER.' The men just stare at each other. 'IF YOU DO NOT ARREST HIM NOW...I WILL HAVE YOU ALL SHOT WHEN THE REST OF THE ARMY ARRIVES.'

A couple of them step forward, clearly scared by the threat, but Dave moves in front of them, and such is his mere presence, they all stop instantly.

'There is no army,' I say. 'There's nothing out there. Every city, town, and village we've been through has fallen. Those things are everywhere. The whole country's gone. There's no army, no police. Nothing...'

The men stare in horror at me.

'What did you think was going on? That this was just here, in this place? No, lads. I'm sorry, but it's all gone.'

A few of them reel back, clearly thinking of families and friends, their homes, and loved ones.

Even the officer goes quiet and stares off into space, and then he looks at me and speaks softly, 'How do you know this?'

'I watched it happen. The whole of Europe got infected within a few hours. God knows how, but it did, and now it's here.'

A tear falls down his cheek, and he slumps down into one of the classroom chairs, looking stricken to the core, and the sight robs the heat from my temper, making me swallow and take a breath.

I pull the door closed and turn back to face the gathered men to see a few crying quietly, and some have slumped down against the walls. The ones at the front don't show a reaction, though, and I note the hard looks on their faces, especially from the one called Blowers.

There is a long silence, and then I look over at Dave, who has assumed his usual expressionless look.

How he isn't covered in blood and bits of body is beyond me. I do, however, spot a single chunk of what looks like a bit of sticky brain on his shoulder. I reach out to flick it free, but it gets stuck to my fingers, and I try to shake it off, but the bloody thing won't go, and I flick at it with my other hand, but it gets stuck to that one instead like a sticky bogey. I keep shaking my hand, but it won't budge, and I start waving my hand vigorously.

'Fuck off,' I mutter at it, shaking and spinning round while trying to flick it off with the other hand, and it again gets stuck to that one. 'Fuck's sake, this is a conspiracy...'

Then I look up and remember where I am, with a dozen or so faces watching me in silence.

'Sticky bit of brain won't come off...' I hold my hand up to show them, then drop my hand down, and wipe it on the back of my trousers. 'Err...is there a bathroom? I could really do with getting cleaned up a bit.'

Blowers steps forward. 'Follow me, sir. I'll show you where it is.'

'Cheers, mate. You coming, Dave?'

A few minutes later, Dave and I are upstairs, standing at washbasins, scrubbing our hands clean.

Blowers went back downstairs, saying he would wait with the others.

'Who is that officer? What did he say he was?'

'He said he is a *leftenant* from Army Intelligence.'

'What's a *leftenant*?'

'It's a lootenant like the Americans have. It's spelt the same, we just pronounce it differently.'

'Why?'

'I don't know, Mr Howie.'

'Is lieutenant a high-up rank?'

'He is a second lieutenant, which means he's just joined. He hasn't got the full marks on his uniform yet, so he must be an OIT.'

'What's that?'

'Officer in Training.'

'So he's a newbie too, just like the rest of them?'

'Yes.'

'He's still a pompous fucking dick.'

Dave stays quiet. I guess his former life means he won't badmouth an officer. I hold back from saying anymore so I don't offend him.

Dave left his bag in the car, and mine is out there too, so instead of his normal ritual of antibacterial cleansing wipes, he is making do with army soap and water.

We scrub and clean the blood from our hands and faces. The front of my shirt is sticky, and I take it off to rinse under the taps. The water runs pink, and I catch my reflection in the mirror, where the blood has soaked through onto my upper body.

I use paper towels from a dispenser and try to clean it off as best as possible. Dave copies me and starts rinsing out his clothes too. First, the Tesco fleece; then, his t-shirt. We wring them out.

'They had windows open up here, didn't they?' I walk out and head across the landing to the rooms where they were leaning out to signal us.

The weather is still gloriously warm, and we drape our tops over the windowsills to dry out.

We slump down into the chairs in the room, and I pick up the bit of paper they used to decipher Dave's Morse code. I show him, and he nods back.

'Is that smoke?' I sniff the air and start to get up. 'Dave, can you smell smoke?' He nods, and we both start down the stairs.

The smell of smoke is strong now, and we can hear voices coming from one of the rooms.

I push the door open and find another classroom filled with the lads all looking guilty. Gathered about a small fire on the concrete floor in the middle made from broken furniture. A large pan of water resting on a metal frame rigged up over the flames. The lads stare at Dave and me standing there, shirtless.

'Tucker rigged this up, sir. We thought you might fancy a brew,' the lad with blond hair and blue eyes says.

'Bloody hell. Well done, mate. That's brilliant. Where did you learn that?'

Tucker swells with pride, and a big smile spreads over his face as the others relax a bit.

'In the scouts, sir. I used the metal frames from the chairs and just bent them up a bit. I won't get in trouble for that, will I?'

'What, for breaking a couple of chairs? You should be more worried about replacing that spatula if I were you.'

A crap joke, and the laughter coming back is weak and forced, but it lightens the atmosphere just a touch.

'What the bloody hell were you gonna do with a spatula, Tucker?'

one of them calls out, and then more join in until Tucker pulls the spatula from his back pocket with a grin.

'I've still got it,' he laughs.

I feel a bit awkward without my top on. I know it's all lads, but still. Dave must have sensed my discomfort because he nipped away, then came back with two lightweight, green camouflage jackets.

'Ah, well done, Dave,' I shrug the coat on and do the zip half up. Dave pulls his on and pulls the zip all the way to the top.

'Where did you find them?' the blond lad asks. Cookey, I think his name is. 'We looked everywhere for kit.'

'Kit gets stolen if it isn't hidden,' Dave answers.

Within a few minutes, we are all seated, and Dave and I get the first steaming mugs of black tea, with Tucker apologising profusely for not having any milk.

'It's fine, mate. Don't worry.' I take an appreciative sip of the tea to show my gratitude and almost scald my mouth in the process.

'So, lads, fill us in on what happened here.'

Blowers starts off, but soon the others join in.

'Thirty of you to start with? Bloody hell, that's awful. I'm really sorry for your loss.'

'What about you, sir? What happened out there?'

I explain about how the event started and then spread across Europe. I tell them what I heard about the forts and London being infested. Then about travelling through Portsmouth and how horrific the devastation was. A few of them look down and start crying again when I mention Portsmouth, and I realise too late that they must be from there.

'Sorry, lads, it's better you know the truth, though.'

After a long pause, only broken by Dave taking repeated sips from his tea, Cookey looks over. 'So... What happens now?' he asks.

'Now? What do you mean?'

He looks at the others, then back to me. 'What do we do now?'

'Lads, I'm not here to tell you what to do. We came to steal an AP...C thing, so we can get through London.'

'Why are you going to London?' another one asks, tall and handsome. 'I'm Nick, by the way.'

I nod in greeting before replying. 'For my sister. She left a message that she's locked herself in her flat, so I'm going to get her and then head to the forts. I say me, but Dave here said he's happy to come with me. We worked together…'

'How are you going to get one, sir? They're all down on the plains for the exercise.'

I look at the lad, trying to remember his name. 'Alan?'

'Sir,' he nods, 'Alan Booker…'

'Well, I guess we'll go down and get one,' I explain.

'Sir, there are hundreds of 'em down there. These ones here were just waiting their turn for the exercise. There's shitloads more down there, far more,' Blowers says.

I look at Dave, who carries on sipping his tea.

'What do you think, mate? I reckon it's worth it,' I say.

'Okay, Mr Howie.'

'Mind you, we've got no ammunition left, so it's down to the axe and the knives again. It'll be a hard one, but there's still a few hours of light left.'

'Okay, Mr Howie.'

A few of the lads watch us intently; some open-mouthed.

'Fucking hang on a minute,' a sudden realisation hits me. 'This is the army; there must be loads of guns and things.'

'In the armoury,' Dave says.

'Fuck it, let's go and get them, then.' I'm all excited and raring to go again.

'You can't, sir. The armoury is fully locked up,' Cookey says.

'Locked?' Dave asks.

'The lieutenant told us.'

'It's not locked,' Dave says.

'How do you know?' I ask him.

'There was an exercise on. It wouldn't be locked. They would need to be ready for resupply.'

'Ha! Even better, then. Right, where is it?' I ask the lads, but they just stare back blankly, and a few of them shrug their shoulders. 'Oh, yeah. I forgot you're all new. Dave, do you know where it is?'

'No, but it won't be hard to find, Mr Howie.'

'Okay, good. We've got a plan. Shall we?' I ask Dave.

'What about us, sir? What should we do?' I look around at the expectant faces. They have no idea where they are or where to go. I don't want to lose valuable time, but I understand that they must be terrified.

'Listen, lads, it's up to you what you do. I know that you've learnt the difference between the zombie things in the day and night. Well, my advice is to avoid them at all costs during the hours of darkness. But during the day, they become slow, and they can be attacked, like that lot out there. We wouldn't have done that during the night. We wouldn't have stood a chance. Having said that, we were fighting a load this morning, and one of them grabbed my axe when I was going for him. He wasn't like the others. He looked more *switched-on*. Maybe he was a one-off, but it's something to keep in mind. Now, if you want to go back to your homes and families, then go for it, but remember what I said. It's a horrible, brutal thing to say, but there are very few survivors. And it's already been a few days, so... Well, it's up to you. But we are all going to need weapons, and we are safer fighting together, so I think we should all go for the armoury, and then you must go where you want from there.'

Most of them nod, and I can see that they are in agreement. It makes sense if we stick together and fight our way through that lot.

'Those of you who are up for it, we'll meet you in the hallway in a couple of minutes. Grab some weapons.' I look at Tucker. 'Maybe something a bit better than a spatula, though, mate.'

I leave the room and head down the corridor, opening doors until I find the officer at a desk; his head resting in his hands.

'Err... Are you all right?'

He looks up. His slicked-back hair isn't so slicked back now; it sticks up in a mess.

'We're going for the armoury, and then we'll try finding one of those big vehicles. You coming?'

He still doesn't reply but just keeps on staring.

'Listen, mate, I know this is all a shock, but you're still an officer, and those lads could do with some leadership. Why don't you come with us?'

Still no reply.

'Well, what are you going to do, then? Just sit here and wait? Mate, nobody is coming. If there is any army left, they will be holed up somewhere, trying to survive like everyone else. Okay, look, I don't have time to waste. If you are coming, then we'll be leaving in about two minutes.'

I leave the door open and walk away.

Dave is waiting for me at the top of the stairs, and I shake my head at him. He nods back, and we both go down. All of the recruits are there, armed with an assortment of weapons, mainly wooden table legs. They all look up expectantly as Dave and I walk down to them.

'Listen, lads, they're slow now, but don't stand and fight them. We just need to get through, that's it. Once we're in the open, we can move much quicker than them. Just watch out for any weirdo super zombies doing crossword puzzles.'

A couple of them smile back with nervous, fear-filled eyes; then every head snaps over to Dave talking.

'Strike and move. Keep moving and keep a firm grip of your weapon. Strike and move. Do you understand me?' Dave barks at them, and I'm surprised at the harsh tone of his voice. He moves into the crowd and shows them how to grip the clubs with both hands. 'Strike down onto the head. Your objective is to get through them, so only strike when you need to but do not hesitate. They lunge at the last second. Do not let them get their mouths anywhere near you. Do you understand?' He moves between them, raising the clubs and adjusting their grips. 'STRIKE AND MOVE. DO YOU UNDERSTAND?' His voice booms into the confined room, and some of them jump from the sudden noise. More of them respond though and shout, 'YES, SIR!'

'I AM NOT A SIR. HE IS A SIR,' and he points to me. 'I AM DAVE. DO YOU UNDERSTAND?'

'YES...DAVE.'

'WHAT?'

'**YES, DAVE!**' they scream out.

'Good,' Dave says and comes back to my side as I lean over and whisper.

'I'm not sir. I'm just Howie ...'

'Yes, Mr Howie.'

'Right. Good chat. Where's my axe?'

'Here, sir,' Blowers hands it to me, and it's been cleaned too.

'Thanks, mate. Now, which way are we going, Dave?'

'The drill square first.'

'The car park. Got it. Do you want to lead?'

He hesitates for a second, which I take full advantage of.

'Too late. I'm closest to the door, so I'm going first.'

'Yes, Mr Howie.'

I look round at the nervous faces and realise just how much I've changed in a few short days. I look at Dave and smile. 'Ready, Dave?'

'Yes, Mr Howie.'

I wrench the door open and charge out into the packed bodies, screaming and roaring with adrenalin.

Dave is right behind me and launches himself straight into them, going off to one side and whirling his knives at their throats as I swing out and smash skulls in.

The third battle today, and I still feel the fury and rage within me as I destroy them one by one. The bodies are packed in here, but the axe and Dave's knives soon clear some space, and we fight out.

I hear more shouts behind me as the recruits spill out of the building, charging into the packed horde. The wooden clubs smacking them down. This feels amazing, having so many fighting together, fighting as one, as a team toward a common goal.

The glory of battle surges through me, and I give a fresh roar and plough further into them. The recruits respond, and I can hear screams and guttural roars from all around me as we take them down.

Dave is spinning and dropping more bodies than any of us, but we surge forward, and the infected are beaten back by the sheer ferocity of the attack.

Fourteen of us charge in, and fourteen of us batter and beat them, killing and destroying anything in our path. This is one of the best feelings I have ever had. We are unstoppable. We are an army come to wreak vengeance.

Within seconds, I am coated in blood again as the snarling faces loom up in front of me, waiting for me to cleave their skulls open. Three of them come from my left, all in a row. I pull the axe back and give a mighty heave, driving the blunt end into the closest one. He barrels into the next, and they all stagger down, only to be clubbed by recruits coming behind me. I glance back and watch the young men fighting. Some of them are clearly filled with the rage of the battle. A few look petrified though and are clutching the clubs to their chests and trying to avoid all contact. One of them is even crying and whimpering, visibly shaking from head to toe. An infected lurches at him. I shout a warning, but it's too late, and he goes down.

Dave and I both run back towards him and attack the soldier, but all in vain. The infected has bitten into the recruit's neck, and blood sprays out over the ground. Another one of the young lads rushes to his side and tries to pull him up.

'IT'S TOO LATE. KEEP GOING!' I shout at him. He stares blindly at me, and I push him forward into the gap created by Dave and the recruits, who have fought their way to the front.

We keep pushing them over to the far side of the drill square and let them flop down on the ground to recover for a few minutes as Dave scans the buildings around the area. I'm bent over, breathing hard.

I look around to the recruits. Blowers, Cookey, Nick, Booker, and a few others are jubilant and high-fiving. Even Tucker looks pumped up. A few of them are silent, though. Silent and terrified.

It's strange how the instinct for survival differs between people. Some, like the officer, will hide or go into shock, unable to process what they have lost and what's going on around them. Others will follow the pack, and even though they don't want to fight, the fear of being left alone makes them move. Then there are those that will fight. Even when they are terrified, they can see what must be done and will do it, because they have to.

Then there are lads like that. Taken into a fight, out of necessity, and they relished every second of it. I can see it on their faces now as they relive the battle and joke about how the heads exploded and the brains came out.

Some of the others are looking up to them and trying to joke along too, but I can see the conflicting emotions in them. They look at Blowers and Cookey and laugh, but then they glance at each other for reassurance. They have just killed what had been people. Soldiers. What they want to be. What they now are.

I look back up at the car and realise what Dave and I did. Examining my own feelings now, I know that as soon as I saw them, I wanted to be in there, hurting them and breaking them apart. We probably could have found a way around them, but I was glad that we hacked through instead. What does that say about me?

That anger and fury I felt when I discovered my parents must have been killed woke something inside me, and I don't know if it will ever go away now.

I realise that Dave has joined me while I was deep in thought.

'You okay, Dave?'

'Yes, Mr Howie.'

'We probably could have found a way around them, don't you think?'

'Probably.'

'But we didn't.'

'No.'

We hold eye contact, and I start to smile at him. 'Let's get them guns, mate.'

He turns back to scanning the buildings. 'Weapons.'

'What?'

'We don't call it a gun; we call it a weapon.'

'You're a picky bugger, Dave. So...which building is it?'

'That one,' he points to the left. There are a row of buildings facing the parade square. They are bigger than the ones on the side, where we rescued the recruits. Dave points at a large building in the middle of them.

'How do you know?'

'The armoury is always central so that everyone can get to it quickly.'

'Right, lads, you ready? We need to move,' I turn to the recruits, who look ready to drop, and it's clear they need food and rest and very soon.

'They need rest,' Dave says.

'We don't have time to rest, Dave. RIGHT. LET'S MOVE IT.'

Dave was right, and we are able to gain entry by simply forcing an external door. I can't help but wonder why the soldiers didn't take weapons from here if they thought they were under attack. But then, it spreads so quickly, and it's easy to look back and criticise after the fact.

The building leads into a hallway, with a long counter and a wall behind it. From the setup, I guess the soldiers line up at the counter and are issued with their weapon.

There is a set of closed double doors behind the counter, and it takes Dave seconds to vault the counter, push the doors open, and disappear inside. Some of the lads are quick to get over. By the time I get through the doors, I can hear whistles of appreciation and surprise.

The room inside is massive and takes up the rest of the length of the building, with metal shelves running down both sides, stacked with guns. The guns look identical and are racked stock down, with the trigger guard facing out.

The recruits spread out along the end of the room, just looking at the awesome display.

Dave is already down at the far end, going through boxes and opening doors to cabinets while I walk down the length of the room, staring at the guns to either side. At the end, I see that Dave has opened a metal cabinet. There are rows of black handles sticking out, and I only realise they are handguns when Dave pulls one out and slides the top back.

'The GPMG are gone, must be out in the field for the exercise,' Dave says to me.

'The what?'

'The general-purpose machine gun. They must have taken it out.'

'Is that one of the big things with a tripod or something?'

'Yes.'

'Oh, well, we clearly don't have enough guns here.' I glance back along the shelves and stare at the impressive sight. 'Dave, how long will it take to show us how to use them?'

Dave pauses and looks back at the recruits. 'To learn how to fire the SA80 will only take a short time, but they need to know about the moving parts and how to clear the weapon if it jams, and how to clean it. That takes longer to explain.'

'Okay, well, it's just gone 2 p.m. now. It gets dark at about 9:30 p.m., so at the very least, we need to be in one of those big vehicles by that time. How long do you need?'

'Depends on them. Some will pick it up quickly, some won't.' I nod and turn to the recruits.

I probably know less than they do, but at least they had an interest when they joined up. I've never even seen an army machine gun in real life, and I need to learn too, but I also need to be moving, and I feel frustrated at the delay. But if Dave can run us through some basic skills now, it will make all the difference when we do have to go back out there. Especially if it goes wrong again.

Which it will. Within half an hour.

'Right, listen up, lads,' I shout over to them, and they drift down to gather around me. 'Dave is going to run through basic weapon techniques. We need to learn this if we are going to survive out there. It will be fast learning, and we don't have time to keep stopping if you don't keep up. You don't have to do this, and it's up to you if you stay or go.' They stare back at me. A couple at the back keep turning around to look at the door, casting nervous glances at each other.

'Lads, honestly, you can go if you want to, but your chances of survival are far greater if you learn this.'

They look completely exhausted and ready to drop. I start to feel guilty as I know I'm pushing them for my own need. There is no way they are going to take this in after what they have been through.

'You lot look worn out. Do you want to rest for a couple of hours and then go through it?'

'I'm okay, sir. I want to do it now,' Blowers says to me.

'Me too,' Cookey affirms, and then a few more of the hard-core group nod and join in. Nick Hewitt. Alan Booker. A quiet lad called Jamie and a few others. The two who were glancing at the door whisper quietly to each other.

'Okay, if you want to do it now, then go over to Dave. I'll be with you in a minute.'

Apart from the two whisperers, they all go over to Dave. I approach the two, and they look at me sheepishly.

'Lads, what's up? You keep looking back at the door.' They gaze at each other, and then one of them plucks up enough courage to speak.

'Sir, we just want to go home. We don't live that far away.'

'That's fine. You can leave whenever you want. I know you had a nasty time on the plains, but I've seen what it's like out there, and trust me, it isn't pretty.'

They both stare back at me. They look like children, but then they are, really. Just boys.

'This is going to sound brutal, but your families might not have survived, or they could be gone from there, thinking you are safe with the army. Make your own decisions but do so knowing what you are walking into and what to expect. If you want to go, carry on, and I wish you luck, but I really have to get moving.'

I go back to the group. It's obvious what the two lads are thinking, and the group remain quiet for a minute, chatting to each other in low voices.

'Sir?' I turn round, and the two lads have taken a couple of steps towards us. I know they have decided to go; otherwise, they would have walked over to us.

'Okay, lads, that's fine. Stay safe and keep moving. Do everything you can to avoid them and make sure you find somewhere safe at least an hour before nightfall.'

They both nod and then stand still, unsure of how to say goodbye.

'If all else fails, head to the forts on the coast. Good luck.'

'Yeah, good luck.' Cookey walks over and offers his hand to them; they shake, and the rest of the recruits go over and also shake hands. Eventually, the two lads break away and leave, closing the door behind them.

CHAPTER THIRTY-THREE

An uneasy silence follows. Nine left, and a couple of those don't look too confident either.

'Right, you lot, ready?' I call over, and they walk back, gathering around Dave. Then the hard work starts, and by hard work, I mean really hard work, with Dave drilling them relentlessly.

First, he hands them a rifle each and makes them sit around him. He shows them the basics of how the weapons fire, then how to load and reload the magazine, pull the bolt, and make the weapon ready. He shows them the safety switch and how to make the rifle single shot only or fully automatic. He repeats it all and makes them do it together, then individually. He then strips the weapon down and reassembles it very quickly, and then makes them do it.

Well, I say he makes *them* do it. I'm doing it too, but for some reason, Dave doesn't make me do it in front of the others. Either on the assumption that I would understand or out of the strange respect he seems to hold for me. I keep up though and understand the basics within a short time.

Dave then runs through weapon cleaning drills. His manner is highly effective too. Without any confusing jargon or rambling on. Succinct and to the point. His expressionless face also serves well as at no point does he appear to be frustrated or disappointed when they get it wrong.

Blowers is very proficient, and from the way he handles the weapon, I suspect he must have had previous experience. Dave seems to notice too.

'You served?' Dave asks.

'Royal Marines. Broke my leg before completing basic. Did weapon drills, though.'

Dave looks at him, nods, then carries on. Making them put the weapon back together, load a magazine, and unload it, take the safety off, select single shot, then fully automatic, then remove the magazine, and put the safety back on. Then he makes them do it one by one while he watches. Most of them get it wrong, but Blowers is on hand to help.

Dave then gathers everyone at the end of the room and explains we'll drill some very basic fire and manoeuvre methods.

'Blowers, to me,' he orders, taking the lad to the side to speak quietly for a minute until Blowers nods and steps back as Dave turns to face us all and drops to one knee, aims, and dry fires his rifle.

He then shouts, 'MAGAZINE!' And at the point he starts to change his rifle magazine, Blowers runs a few metres in front of Dave, takes a knee, and starts dry firing.

'MAGAZINE,' he shouts; at which point, Dave runs past, advancing beyond Blowers, and repeats the same as before, with a very simple method of advance until they reach the far end and turn back as the other lads nod and murmur.

I must admit, they made it look easy.

Dave explains about the danger of having someone in front of you when you have a live weapon and emphasises the point of moving to the side so you are not directly in front of the man who is changing his magazine behind you.

Dave then makes them do it with him, one by one, and they take turns to move a few steps, drop down, and fire then shout *Magazine!* as the next one moves forward.

Then Dave and Blowers each take a recruit and run through the drill, four of them moving up and down the room. Then they take two recruits each. I join in, taking my turn and running with them up and down. Hard work, and we're all sweating heavily.

Finally, Dave tells them all to pair off and practise with their chosen partner. Within minutes, the room is a confusing jumble of noise with loud voices bellowing *Magazine!* and calling each other twats for getting in the way.

'How many are coming with us, Mr Howie?' Dave asks, walking over to me.

'I don't know. Are any of them coming?' I reply.

'It would be good to know so I can split us into teams, ready for when we move.'

'Okay, mate, I'll get their attention and ask.' I shout out for them to come over.

'FINGERS OFF TRIGGERS!' Dave shouts in his drill sergeant voice. 'When at rest, the safety is on, and your finger is on the guard like this.'

They respond, switching the safety on and making a show of holding their fingers over the guards. I glance at Blowers and can see that he had already done it and was resting in the correct manner.

'Right, lads,' I begin. 'In a short time, Dave and I are going down onto the plains to find something big and nasty that will get us through London. We need to know if any of you want to join us. This is a personal thing; it has nothing to do with any of you, but you are more than welcome, and we want to know now if you are coming.'

They nod back at me, then start whispering to each other.

'Sir, if I come with you, will you drop me off after?' Booker asks.

'Yes, of course.'

'Sir, me and Blowers are in,' Cookey says after a short discussion with Blowers.

'What about your families?' I ask them.

'We don't really have any, sir. To be honest, we ain't really got anything to go back to, and Blowers' mum said she won't shag me again unless I pay up.'

'Twat,' Blowers mutters.

'So, you're going to London and then to the forts?' McKinney asks.

'Yes, mate,' I answer.

'Okay, I reckon it's safer with you two. You've travelled this far and stayed alive. I'm in until the forts if that's okay.'

'Of course, it is.' I look to the rest and see McKinney's words have obviously struck a chord as they go silent and absorb what he just said.

'Well, they've got this far, haven't they?' he says. 'They must be doing something right. I've got family at home too, but if everyone is going to the forts, then the best chance of seeing them again is going there.' McKinney shrugs his shoulders and looks down at his weapon. Five seconds later, and they have all agreed to go.

Dave then splits them into two "firing teams". The first is Dave, Roland McKinney, Darren Smith, Roy Tucker, and Nicholas Hewitt.

'We are team Alpha; the rest of you are team Bravo. Blowers is your team leader.'

'Oh, you wanker,' Cookey says, looking at Blowers. 'I haven't got to take orders from you, have I?'

'Oh, yes, my pretty boy, you will do as you are told,' Blowers replies with a wink.

Dave speaks to me quietly, and I nod and go back out to the counter at the front of the building. I find a pen and some paper and go back into the room.

'Lads, I need to take your names down…just in case something happens, and we find your families later.'

I write down the names that I know. The last two I hadn't learnt before were Jamie Reese and Curtis Graves.

The lads then offer me the names of the ones that died on the plains, the one that we lost fighting our way out, and the two that left before we started drilling.

Finally, I check my watch; it's almost 5 p.m. If we leave at 6 p.m., we will still have three hours of daylight, but I don't know how far it is or where the vehicles will be.

'Have any of you got any idea where we will find an APS?'

'APC!' Dave and Blowers chorus at me.

'Yeah, okay. Well, did you see any of them?'

'There was a Saxon near the urban area, Mr Howie. I don't know if it's still there, though,' Blowers offers.

'A Saxon? I'm sure I saw a programme on TV about them. Big things, with massive wheels, big machine gun on the top?'

'Yes, Mr Howie,' Dave answers.

'They're training vehicles here, though,' Blowers says. 'They look a bit different sometimes.'

'Right, we go for that, then. How far is it to this urban area?'

'I don't know. We were taken by truck, and it was quite a long drive. Must be a few miles at least.'

'I was going to give you an hour's rest, but now I'm thinking we should get going. We don't want to be out in the dark, with those things running about, especially after what you said you went through on those plains. Do you think you can manage it?' I direct my question to the group.

They do look exhausted, and I feel like a right bastard for making them move again, but this has to be done now.

Blowers, Cookey, and McKinney nod back and call out that they are ready. I get the impression they are making the others go along with it, and they all start nodding within a few seconds.

Dave then comes over to me and speaks quietly, 'Mr Howie, we need to find the stores building. They need belts to hold the magazines and water bottles.'

'Okay, if you say so, mate. It'll give 'em a chance to rest, too.' I turn back to the recruits.

'Right, the plan is that Dave, Blowers, and I are going to find the stores building, so you get the chance to practise shooting some zombies while we make a run for it.'

A few of them look up, excited at the prospect.

'You each have spare magazines. Do not go forward, just line up outside, and practise single shot only, aim for the head,' Dave instructs them.

We head back out to the front and over the counter. I don't know why we didn't use the side door, but I guess this makes it more dramatic.

Dave and Blowers each have their assault rifles ready. Mine is strapped to my back, and I have my axe. Dave did stare at me when I picked it up. 'Never leave home without it,' I said to him.

We go to the main door and realise that the horde are now all gathered directly at the front, blocking our exit.

We end up using the side door and lead the recruits back to the front, coming out just to the side of the horde. Dave tells them to fire from an angle so they don't shoot the buildings. They make ready but hesitate; clearly none of them want to be the first to shoot. Dave raises his assault rifle and fires several shots into the crowd, getting head shots with each one.

'Fuck me,' Cookey says in awe.

Blowers then fires a few shots, aiming for the head too.

'Pick your shots and take your time,' Dave gives them a final instruction before we move.

We leave the recruits and the sounds of individual rifle shots behind us; they are calling to each other and offering encouragement or comments as they hit or miss. We walk out onto the parade square car park thing and look back.

The recruits are spread out in a row and are firing into the densely packed crowd of infected shuffling and turning around slowly, moving towards the recruits with their slow gait. Every now and then, I see a head explode in pink mist as the bullet hits the mark, immediately followed by cheering.

Smith runs out of bullets first and shouts *Magazine!* loudly.

I look at Dave and see him watching them closely. Smith then drops down onto one knee and changes the magazine. He remains on one knee as he continues to fire into the crowd. The rest follow suit, shouting *Magazine!* and dropping down to change.

We then move off, and Dave identifies the stores building. I have no idea how as they all look the same to me. Within minutes, we are in a similar-structured building, over the counter, and into the stores room.

'What do we need?' Blowers asks me and Dave.

'Belts, magazine holders, and water bottles,' Dave responds.

The room is roughly the same size as the armoury, but there are shelves and units everywhere. There is typical army order here, and it doesn't take long to find a big cardboard box to put all of the belts and other things into. Dave also grabs a load of green camouflage jackets and changes the one he is wearing that is too big into one that fits better.

Blowers comes into view from the end of a unit, holding an army-style, long-sleeved t-shirt.

'Are these any good? Might be too hot in those jackets,' he asks.

We find rucksacks and load them up with belts, bottles, and ammunition pouches, and more with jackets and t-shirts. Then we put the empty bags into the used ones so we have less to carry.

'Fuck it, this is silly. Let's just get the lads up here to grab what they need,' I say to Dave.

I run back outside and over, towards the armoury building.

My jaw drops as I get closer and see the mound of dead infected piled and spread out across the front of the building. There are only a handful left now, and the lads are taking their time to aim carefully for the exclusive head shot.

I call out and get their attention. Yelling for them to come over.

We dump all of the kit outside, and the lads rummage through to get the right sized tops and jackets.

Dave and Blowers then come out, with black and desert-coloured boots in their hands hanging from their laces. Dave hands me a pair of desert boots, then a pair of tan-coloured combat trousers, with pockets on the sides.

'There's only a few of them, Mr Howie. The rest are jungle greens.'

'Thanks, Dave.'

I join the lads in getting changed into army kit – boots and tops. Most of them change into army trousers too but the green ones.

I note that Dave and Blowers are both in the tan trousers too – a hierarchy is developing already, just in this little group, and I understand that maybe it needs to be done, and I wonder if people will ever change.

Once dressed, I turn to see and find myself pausing in surprise at the sight of the lads looking like proper soldiers. All of them chatting, with assault rifles resting across the crooks of their arms, like they saw Dave and Blowers doing. Webbing belts loaded, and the bottles filled from a cold tap inside the stores building. The visual effect is striking, and they suddenly look tougher and harder. Even Tucker looks a bit less soft but not that much.

'Mr Howie and I will take point, the rest of you in two lines, evenly spaced out behind us, covering the flanks,' Dave gives his instructions, and we set off.

One supermarket manager leading an ex-soldier, an ex-trainee Royal Marine, and a group of lads, who only fired a gun for the first time half an hour ago, and we're going into vast plains filled with infected.

What can possibly go wrong?

CHAPTER THIRTY-FOUR

We walk at a constant, brisk pace, and I am sweating freely.

The recruits are spread out evenly behind us in two lines, which took some cajoling and berating from Blowers at first, but Dave bellowed at the top of his voice, and they fell silent, apart from Cookey, muttering to Blowers behind me.

'Why do you get the *Gucci* brown trousers?'

'Cos I'm a section leader, that's why.'

'No, you're a team leader for today, not for always – it's not a promotion in the field.'

'Fuck off, Cookey.'

'You fuck off, Blowers, with your super brown trousers.'

'Ha, go and iron your jungle greens, mate.'

'You're a cock, Blowers.'

'Sorry, what did you say, Cookey? Did you say that you like cock?'

'You know what I said.'

'You said that you like cock. There's nothing wrong with that. It's a modern world.'

'Get fucked, I didn't say anything like that.'

'Yes, you did, you said that you like cock, you like zombie cock.'

'Blowers, you wanker. I'm gonna have a negligent discharge in a minute and shoot you.'

'A negligent discharge?! What? In your pants? Have you seen a hot zombie or something, then?'

'You fucking twat.'

'Watch out lads, Cookey is going to bum some zombies.'

I walk on, smiling at the easy banter behind me.

'Don't they call this tabbing or something?' I ask Dave.

'Yes, Mr Howie'

'Why not just walking?'

'The Romans did it first. A soldier has to show he can march to a place with weight – that's called a loaded march. The word tab comes from tactical advance to battle.'

'Oh.' I fall silent for a moment.

'Dave, did you enjoy showing those recruits what to do?'

'I don't understand, Mr Howie.'

'Well, you were good at it. Did you ever teach when you were in the army?'

'I gave instructions sometimes, Mr Howie.'

'What about that voice? You sound like a proper drill sergeant.'

'When they knew I could shout loudly, they taught me what to say to the enemy to make them scared. Scared men make mistakes.'

'Bloody hell, I think I had better start calling you Mr Dave from now on.'

'No, Mr Howie,' Dave says, casting me a serious look.

'I was joking, Dave. But, mate, I don't know any more than they do, and I know less than Blowers. I guess I don't feel right taking the position of leader.'

Dave goes from constant scanning of the area to looking at me. 'I don't understand people. I don't understand characters and personalities, or when people are upset. I can kill, and I can show how to kill. That's all I can do, Mr Howie.'

'People are just people, Dave. Insecure and scared like the rest of us. People are easy to understand, really.'

He looks at me for a long second before casting his view out to the sides and ahead again.

'People have base needs,' I continue. 'Like needing to eat and drink. Take any of those needs away and people die very easily. But then you have base emotions too – things like love, hate, greed, lust, and jealousy. They are incredibly powerful emotions that drive people to do the most amazing things. And if you mix a few of them together with other, maybe less impacting, emotions like insecurity or distress, then you can have issues, real issues. If you look at history and the evil dictators, I bet all of them had a mixture of those issues going on. Plus, when you couple that with the immediate family around you, then the people, society, and community you grow up in, and the cultural beliefs that are drummed into people when they are young and add all of that to the hierarchy of needs, plus the corruption of power – well, it can make for a deadly recipe. Fascinating but deadly.' I pause to take a breath as the others all fall silent.

'Look at this around us now. Something like this could have been caused by an evil tyrant addicted to power or a belief that his God is the right one, so everyone else must suffer and die. Or it could just as easily be a scientist working in a lab somewhere. Safe and secure, and the most rational person you could ever meet. One day he gets home to find out his wife is cheating, and he is consumed with anger and jealousy, and *bang*, he takes the whole world out for one seemingly small act that would otherwise be a private episode in someone's life.

'In fact, I've heard theories that Adolf Hitler grew up surrounded by wealthy Jews when his family was relatively poor, and so maybe that sparked his intense hatred. A chemical imbalance that sits dormant and then explodes from one random act. Then there is the old cliché of power corrupts. We only have to look at every government that has ever come to power to know that exists. And then, of course, there is communism. What a fantastic notion that everything should be owned by everyone and shared equally. But at a certain point, there will be some bugger stood there, thinking he is doing more work than others, so therefore he is entitled to more than they have. He gets a bit more, and then he always wants more, and if they don't give it to him, he will take it.

'That's why revolutions never really work. You can take a whole bunch of people that have conflicting beliefs, but they unite against a common enemy and work together to bring that enemy down...say, the ruling government. But that just leaves a void, and someone has to fill that void. Someone has to work out the tax rate, fix the roads, and make sure that the hospitals are working, and then, of course, we have security and food to eat. And with the best will in the world, you take a bunch of people and put them in a room together to work out the best for everyone, and they will spend most of the time bickering and arguing. Someone will come out on top, and you are back to the saying of power corrupts again. Then the others get resentful and jealous, and it never really ends, hence the name – revolution.'

It's gone very quiet around me, and I look back to see all of the recruits staring at me with interest.

'That's why you're in charge, Mr Howie,' Dave says simply.

Two hours later, and we are deep into the rolling plains.

The roadway leads directly through the plains as far as I can see. To both sides, there are gently rolling hills and vast, open sections churned up from heavy tracks, with craters pock-marking the ground here and there.

The land is very dry from the scorching summer. It must have been hell trying to cross this land, especially in the dark, and I find a new respect for the recruits. I can't imagine most regular troops being able to do that, but then they are young and lean from hard living in hard times.

We have only stopped once for a rest, and that was called by me when I glanced back and saw the exhaustion on their faces. We took ten minutes to drink water and eat high-energy snack bars that were purloined from a box that Tucker found in the stores building. He must have sneaked them into his backpack when everyone else was putting boots on and making sure they looked like commandos. When he broke them out and handed them round, he was a hero for five minutes, and I could see him grinning from the respect they gave him. After the ten minutes, we were back on, and not one of them moaned.

They have hardly slept or taken on decent food since Friday, and they are still going. Grim determination and fear of being left alone is driving them on.

'EYES ON,' Dave calls from my side.

I snap out of my reverie and look up. Ahead of us, the road sweeps around to the right, and we can just make out the top of a church spire. The atmosphere charges instantly, and I can feel the recruits tensing up and watching left and right as we make our way forward.

There is a low embankment to both sides, and I wave the recruits into the right side to take cover.

'Rest for a minute but stay sharp,' Dave tells them as we shrug off our backpacks and start belly crawling out to the middle of the road and then slowly forward until the bend opens up, and we can see down into the village.

There are houses on both sides of the village – old, brick-built things that have seen far better days but have clearly been patched up here and there to keep them usable for training. The road goes down to a crossroads, and there is a big church on the right.

There is a makeshift area encased by a circle of sandbags just before the village, on the right side. I guess this must be the safe area the recruits were sent to when they were "captured".

The plains roll out far on both sides of the village. It looks like there was once a thicket of vegetation off to the left side, but it's been cut down to open the area up.

From our position, we can just make out the edge of another circular sandbag area situated in the corner between the row of houses ahead of us and the houses on the road to the right of us.

'That's a lot of fucking zombies,' I say to Dave as I look in awe at the largest gathering of infected I have seen yet. The exercise must have been immense judging by the sheer volume of uniforms shuffling about.

The distance is too great to see detail, but I can imagine the drooling mouths and the red, bloodshot eyes, their horrific injuries drying and festering in the high heat, and swarms of flies and insects buzzing in amongst them. The heat coming from them must be intense as there is a haze just above them. 'Oh, yes, that's a lot of fucking zombies,' I repeat quietly as Dave stays silent, assessing the area in front of us. 'Fuck the guns, mate. Let's just go for it with the axe and the knives.'

He turns to me, with that glint in his eye.

'I'm joking, you fucking psycho. Although it would be bloody good fun.'

'Middle of the crossroads?' Dave points, and I follow the straight line to make out the top of something slap bang in the middle of the intersection, surrounded by just about a million zombie soldiers. Yay.

'What's that?' I ask Dave.

'Saxon APC, Mr Howie.'

'Shit, it's completely surrounded. How the fuck are we going to get to that? It'll be dark before we even get close to leading them away, and we really don't want to be out here when that lot turn werewolf on us.' A shiver runs down my spine at the thought of the noise they make as we snake our way over to the group huddled into the side of the road.

'How is it?' Cookey whispers as soon as we get close enough.

'Bad, very bad. The APC Saxon thing is in the middle of the crossroads, surrounded by lots and lots of the infected people. There might be more Saxons somewhere else, but after what you told me about the size of the plains, we would be safer if we just try to get this one. Agreed?'

They nod back at me.

'Right, so me and Dave have previously used the "lead them away" tactic, which would be perfect if we had time. But a group that size would take hours to move away, especially when they are slow like now. On the other hand, we don't want to be anywhere near them when it gets dark. Agreed?'

More nods.

'So we have to attack them. The disadvantages are that they are stacked very deep around that APC, and it's getting late. The advantages are stacked in our favour, though. They are slow moving and packed together, and we have machine guns and lots of ammunition.' I look to Dave. 'Do we have enough ammunition for a crowd that size?'

'I'm not sure. We all brought spare magazines, but they don't die unless they are head shots or the body is so severely injured that they cannot physically move.'

'Bollocks. I wish we had one of those big machine guns. What did you call it? A GPMG?'

'Yes.'

'We could really do with one right now ...'

'Sir, there was one being used,' Blowers cuts in. 'It was on the corner of the crossroads.'

'What?'

'Erm, it was behind a load of sandbags.'

'Yeah. I saw the edge of the sandbags. Are you sure that was it, though?'

'Sir, the sound is unmistakable,' he says.

'Dave, is that right?'

'Yes, the sound is unique, especially if Blowers heard them before when he did his Royal Marines training,' Dave answers.

'Did you hear one before, Blowers?' I ask him.

'Yeah, bloody loads of times,' he says.

'Ah, fucking hang on! Do they use real bullets during these exercises, Dave?'

'No, Mr Howie.'

'Will there be real bullets near it that we can use?'

'No. Back in the armoury,' Dave says.

'Bollocks. Right, that's fucked, then. Unless there's a vehicle around here we can use to send someone back. Other than the Saxon thing, that is ... Lads, did any of you see another vehicle anywhere?'

Lots of shaking heads.

'No, sir. It was dark, and we were in the houses all the time,' McKinney says.

Then I see one of the quiet lads looking at me thoughtfully.

'Go on, mate! Curtis, is it?'

'Yes, sir. Curtis Graves,' he answers softly.

'Okay, Curtis, did you see one?'

'Er, there was a Land Rover just down from the crossroads, sir. My dad had one, and I recognised it.'

'Great. Nice one, Curtis. That's brilliant. Now, where did you last see it?'

'Off that way,' Graves waves towards the village and over to the left.

'Okay, mate. So, on the left side of the village as we look at it from this road here?'

'Yep, er. I mean yes, sir.'

'Come with me, mate,' I say to Graves, and we both belly shuffle out into the middle of the road.

'Fucking hell,' Graves says when he sees the almighty horde.

'Yeah, I know, right? Oh well, fuck 'em, we'll win! Somehow... Now try to describe exactly where you saw it last?'

A sudden noise and groaning comes from behind us, and we look around to see an infected sliding down the embankment, directly into the recruits. They burst away, and Dave immediately dives in and starts striking the head with the butt of his rifle. Some of the other lads join in, and the infected groans as he is pummelled by several rifle butts at the same time.

Dave then whips out one of his knives and slices it across the throat, causing a spray of crimson to spurt out, and Dave rolls the infected over so the blood goes into the ground.

'Fuck me, Dave, can't you go more than five minutes?' I whisper down. He just shrugs. 'Curtis, sorry, mate. Where was it?'

'That's all right, sir. It was to the left of the crossroads and down a bit,' he indicates, with a wave of his arm.

'Okay, let's get back.'

We belly shuffle back to the group, and I shake my head reproachfully at Dave as I look at the infected lying in a pool of blood.

'Dave, I think you and I should go for the Land Rover. The rest of you, stay put.'

'Okay, Mr Howie,' Dave nods and starts getting ready.

'Blowers, you're in charge until we get back. If you hear us firing, then start shooting those fuckers and move slowly back up the road, okay?'

'Yes, sir,' Blowers grins and nudges Cookey.

'Hear that, Cookey, you can't start bumming them until we hear shooting.'

'Fuck off, Blowers,' Cookey grins back at him.

Dave puts his rifle on his back and takes his two straight-bladed knives in his hands. I reluctantly leave my beloved axe and just take the rifle.

'Tucker, look after my axe, mate. Please don't lose it,' I tell him as I prepare to go.

'Yes, sir!' Tucker swells with pride and clutches the axe protectively with both hands.

'Ready, Dave?'

'Yes, Mr Howie.'

We move off, keeping low.

We cross the road and get over the embankment, then down the other side. We move at a fast pace but bent over and aim far left, behind the row of houses. We pass the sandbag safe area, then move further left so we are well away from the road.

Up close, I can see the houses are not really well maintained at all, and none of them have glass in the windows, just empty holes, with shutters held open. The fences to the rear gardens have been relatively well kept, and I guess this adds realism to the place.

Within minutes, we are past the houses and nearing the road, coming into the crossroads from the left. The infected are still densely packed, and we have to go quite far down the row of houses before we see a sufficient gap. We get to the back of one of the properties and start inching forward until we can lean out and peek down the road. The Land Rover is parked to the side of the road furthest away from us. There are infected shuffling and groaning near it, but the gaps between them look fairly decent.

'I reckon we can make that, Dave. You up for it?'

'Yes.'

We dart out and start sprinting down and across the road, dodging around soldiers, who immediately turn and start moving towards us.

I don't engage this time but stick with zigzagging through them until I reach the vehicle. Dave, on the other hand, can't help himself and has already slit a few throats by the time we get to the car. We clamber into the front, and I thank God as I see the key still in the ignition. The diesel engine splutters loudly and immediately gets a reaction as more of them start moving towards us. I turn the wheel hard, surprised at how much force is needed, and I realise these vehicles don't have power-assisted steering. I have to roll forward and then back a few times until I am facing the other way, knocking over a few infected in the process.

Once we're turned around, I drive off and keep going down the road until the row of houses ends. Then I turn left and drive onto the plains, and head back towards the area we left the recruits.

'Well, mate, I think the enemies know we're here now,' I say to Dave, who just nods back at me.

I drive around the backs of the houses, then past the sandbag safe area, and onto the road. The recruits must have heard the engine and are moving out into the middle of the road as we come around the corner. I stop the vehicle but leave the engine running, and jump out.

'Curtis, can you drive, mate? Did you ever drive your dad's Land Rover?'

'Yeah, loads of times,' he replies and starts moving over to me.

'Right, you and Dave get back to the armoury and get the ammunition for that GMPG.'

'GPMG,' Dave says.

'Yeah, that thing. You and Dave get the ammo; we'll start shooting the fuckers from here, got it?'

'Yes, sir.' Graves gets into the driver's seat as I yell one last instruction at him.

'Curtis, we won't be able to hold them for long, so be quick.' The Land Rover roars off, leaving me with the recruits.

'Well, lads, the baddies know we're here. I reckon we should spread out in a line and start shooting them. You up for it?'

'Sir, can I put one on the top of each embankment to watch the flanks and the rear?' Blowers asks.

'Good thinking, mate. Yeah, do that.'

'Cookey, you take the right flank. Smith, you take the left flank, keep a good look out, and make sure you keep checking behind us,' Blowers gives a clear instruction, and they both start scrambling up. The horde are all facing our way now and look immense even from this distance. The army uniform seems to amplify their numbers and make them look even more sinister.

'Fuck it, some still have their NATO helmets on,' Smith shouts down from the top of the embankment.

'Well, there ain't much we can do about that, is there?' I respond. 'Apart from shooting them in the knees.'

A few of the lads snigger, and I can sense the nervous excitement.

I move out to the centre of the road and drop my bag down at my side, then the axe that I retrieved from Tucker. I open the top and make sure there are spare magazines at hand. The lads start spreading to both sides until we are evenly spaced across the width of the road.

'Lads, pick your shots and try to make each one count,' Blowers calls out. I ready my rifle, raise it up to my shoulder, and look down the sights on the barrel. The horde are still some distance away, and headshots will be bloody impossible from here, but from previous experience, I know we will slow them down if we drop the ones at the front and create an obstacle to those behind. I call out my instructions and then lower my sights a little until I'm aiming into the hundreds of pairs of legs shuffling towards us. I fire first and instantly see a soldier get spun back into the few behind him. He goes down, and the next one trips over him.

'Just like that,' I call out to a few cheers. The shots start ringing out, and I watch as infected are dropped and fall to the ground. Most of them carry on moving, but soon, we have created a natural obstacle for the horde.

However, the sheer press of bodies from behind just surges them forward over their fallen comrades. We press on, and I can hear clear gaps between shots as the lads try hard to pick their shots. We work in silence, and many infected are shot down. As they get closer, we can pick out individual details and see the horrific injuries they have already sustained. I raise my aim and start trying to shoot in the general head area. I know that if I miss the one I am aiming for, I will most likely still get one or two behind it.

'MAGAZINE!' I yell out as I start changing the ammunition for my assault rifle, doing as Dave showed us all.

I take a quick glance about and look at the grim faces of the young recruits concentrating and firing their weapons. Cookey and Smith are up top and also firing into the horde.

'Cookey, Smith, keep checking the sides and the rear,' I call out to them, trying to make myself heard over the gunshots.

I see them respond, and both stop firing to look off into the plains and check behind them. I reload, take aim, and start firing again. The horde are incessant, and despite the large numbers we are dropping, they just keep coming at us. I am concerned at how close they are, remembering the super zombie, and suddenly become very wary in case they start charging at us.

'MOVE BACK, LADS! MOVE BACK!' I shout out and hear Blowers repeating my words further down the line.

We all stop firing and start shuffling backwards, either carrying or dragging our kit bags with us. We have to stop as we reach the apex of the bend in the road; otherwise, we wouldn't get a good view of them.

Within a few seconds, we are all back to firing and dropping more and more infected. I can see the effects of the shots now and watch as heads burst apart and pink matter sprays up, torso shots hit home, fresh blood pumps out onto their clothing. After a few minutes, we are forced to move back again, but the bend in the road means we won't get a clear view if we move back any further.

'UP ON THE BANKS,' I shout out.

There is confusion as they all start moving towards the same bank.

'TEAM ALPHA ON THE LEFT AND BRAVO ON THE RIGHT,' I shout again, and they run towards the appropriate side and clamber up, and my heart sinks as I see they are still stacked right back, past the crossroads.

We are soon forced to move further and further up the road, and despite inflicting massive casualties, they don't show any sign of stopping. The light is starting to fade, and I can see that my ammunition is getting very low. There are several magazines left in the bag, but at this rate, they won't last long, and I start to feel very concerned that we will be trapped in the darkness, with low or depleted ammunition. Something must have gone wrong. Dave should be back by now.

'LADS, WE ARE GOING TO RUN OUT INTO THE PLAINS TO THE RIGHT SIDE. FOLLOW ME.'

I hear Blowers, then Cookey repeat the order. and the lads gather their kit, shrugging on bags and moving towards me.

We start moving away from the road and out to the right side, onto the plains. We make distance for a few seconds and then stop for a rest.

'It's going to be dark soon, and we absolutely cannot be out here when that happens. Dave and Curtis should be back soon, but we have to make a plan to get somewhere safe. I reckon we should make it for that church. We go far right and loop around until we come at it from the far side. What do you think?'

'Sounds good, sir,' Blowers responds, and several of them nod at me.

'Okay, let's get moving.' We move out further into the plains, and our fast pace soon leaves the horde behind.

The sky darkens with each second we are running, and I can feel the fear building up within us all. We then turn back towards the village and the general direction of the church. Within minutes, it comes into view.

'Looks clear from here,' I say through ragged breath, more to try and lift their spirits than anything else. Then we get closer and see some of the horde is coming our way from the direction of the village crossroads, spilling out through the buildings, which are well in view now. We slow down and stop for a few seconds, breathing hard.

'If we go into the plains, we'll get separated from Dave and Curtis,' I look to each man in turn.

'We're going to have to fight our way through. There's no other choice. The church is the biggest and strongest building. Are you ready?' They nod back, silent but determined.

'That drill that Dave showed you, we can use that as we get closer. When I say, I want team Bravo to stop and team Alpha to move forward a short distance and fire. I'll go with Alpha, Blowers with Bravo. When we finish firing and shout *magazine*, that's when Bravo moves forward. Got it?' They nod back and start shuffling so that McKinney, Smith, Tucker, and Hewitt are forward with me.

Blowers pulls the rest back a few steps.

'Okay, let's go.'

We start moving forward again, and I see my team start to spread out a little just as Dave showed them. Within a very short time, we are very close, with infected between us and the church, and more shuffling out between the sides of the buildings. A glance up at the sky growing darker by the second. The day is almost gone. The night is coming. *Fuck it! Bad idea, Howie. Very bad idea.*

'ALPHA STOP,' I shout the order as we stop to kneel. 'FIRE,' I yell and start firing single shots. The infected drop down as several of us shoot the same ones, but that can't be helped.

'MAGAZINE,' Smith yells first and starts to change.

Within seconds, we have all shouted the magic word, and I wave my arm forward for Blowers.

'BRAVO, ON ME,' Blowers yells, and they surge past us until he shouts to stop, and they kneel down and start firing again.

I take the opportunity to get some deep breaths to try and slow my breathing down.

'MAGAZINE,' Bravo starts yelling, and I watch until Blowers waves his arm forward.

'ALPHA, ON ME.' We spring up and charge forward, and go past the kneeling Bravo team. I take them about forty metres ahead and shout to stop. We assume the position and commence firing again. We focus on the infected between us and the church, and we still keep dropping many of them, but more are still coming through the gaps towards us, and that bloody sky grows darker with every passing second. We've got minutes at the most before the night comes proper.

I wait until they have all shouted and wave my arm forward. For the next few minutes, we advance slowly towards the church, and the bodies are piling up around and in front of us. As my team change magazines, I yell out, 'IN A MINUTE, THEY WILL ALL STOP AND LOOK UP. WHEN THAT HAPPENS, JUST FUCKING LEG IT TO THE CHURCH.'

We repeat again, advancing but seeing way too many infected to shoot down and more coming. A seemingly never-ending flow. That fucking exercise must have been huge.

Then it happens, and the sun drops fully, ridding the land of light, and every single infected becomes completely still and turns to stare up at the sky overhead.

'NOW! FUCKING RUN!' I bellow and start running towards the church.

There is no order now. We just go for it, legging it towards the church a couple of hundred metres away. The distance is short, but the ground is uneven, and we are all exhausted, and we struggle to keep pace. All of us gasping for air until the sudden, ear-splitting screech from hundreds of infected gives us a fresh burst of fear-fuelled speed.

'KEEP GOING. DON'T STOP!' I urge them on, with the bloody axe banging against my legs again. I reach the church building and burst in through the large, wooden side door.

'Cookey, check that the other doors are closed.'

He runs inside with McKinney as I look back and see most of them are almost at the door apart from Tucker. The poor lad is running but looks ready to drop.

'RUN, TUCKER,' I yell out, and the others join in, urging him to run faster as the howling comes to a sudden and complete stop, with every infected head dropping down, now switched on, focussed, mean, and looking very, very hungry.

'COVERING FIRE,' Blowers yells out, and we drop down onto our knees and start firing into the infected, and the second the first shots hit home, so they charge, and the world once more fills with noise.

We keep firing as they gain on Tucker, picking our shots carefully and aiming for centre mass. Several of them are right behind him as he takes the last few steps to the church.

'INSIDE NOW,' I shout, and we all bundle inside, slamming the door just as Tucker bursts in. We brace the door, and several of the lads throw their weight against it as the infected ram into it from the other side.

'Grab that locking bar,' I shout at Jamie, indicating a thick piece of wood resting against the wall.

We slot the bar down into the metal hooks and slowly ease our weight off. The bar holds, but we can hear the bodies slam into the door from the other side.

'The other door is secure,' says Cookey as he comes back and flops down, breathing hard.

I move into the centre of the room. Just a few rows of wooden pews remain; everything else has been cleared away. Even the stained glass windows are gone, but the gaps are just over head height, and the infected shouldn't be able to get through unless they have learnt to start climbing.

I remember the super zombie again.

'Right, I want two covering each door in case they break through. The rest of you pull the pews over to the windows and start shooting down into them, but save some ammunition in case they get through the doors.'

It's only a matter of time before they bust through the doors. Where the hell is Dave? I curse my utter selfishness of putting so many lives at risk for my own needs. What the fuck was I thinking?

The lads pull pews over and climb up to shoot down outside the windows, but they just keep coming, hammering into the doors that creak and groan.

'Last magazine,' Nick says.

'Same,' Jamie adds, ditching his empty one.

'Save them,' I order as the rest of us fire what we have, sending bullets down, but it's not enough. Nowhere near enough.

'Last one,' Cookey calls out.

'Fuck,' Blowers spits to the side. Anger and frustration in his face. 'Where are they?'

The doors creak, a sound of wood splintering, and the howling seems to grow louder. The tension ramping inside the small, dark church. My ears ringing from so much firing, and I look around at their faces, at how bloody exhausted they look and now fearful too. All of them knowing there is no way in hell we'll get out of this.

'Everyone, in the middle,' I say, more to keep us occupied. 'Pull the pews around us.'

We form a low and flimsy barricade and stand in the middle. Half of us facing one door, half facing the other. My axe next to me, ready to be used when the bullets run out.

Where the fuck is Dave?

We stand in silence, jumping and twitching at the bumps and bangs coming from the doors. The front door starts to make a creaking noise, and we all turn to stare at it. A definite sound of wood creaking and then a splintering noise. Each of us raises our rifles to our shoulders and aims directly at the door.

'This is it, lads, get ready,' I say in a surprisingly strong voice. The wood splinters louder, and the door starts to break inwards as the horde of infected soldiers pile more and more body weight into it. Just as the door seems that it will implode, a sudden fast and loud thudding sounds out, and Blowers immediately cheers.

'GPMG,' he screams out.

We push the pews away and drag them over to the window at the front. Once up, I look out and see a bright, flashing light coming from the corner of the crossroads. It's too bright to see beyond the light, but I know that Dave is standing there, probably smiling to himself as he shoots.

The effect is amazing, and we watch bodies dropping from the larger calibre rounds. Cheering and whooping as the infected peel off from attacking the church and start running towards the noise, only to be shot down by a hail of fire.

A second gun rings out, and I realise that Curtis must be with Dave, watching the flanks and rear. Lights suddenly come on from the Land Rover parked behind the sandbags, and I see Dave illuminated as he rests the front tripod on the edge of the sandbags and fires into the crossroads, shredding everything in his path.

It goes quiet for a second.

'FIGHT YOUR WAY TO THE REAR,' Dave's huge voice shouting out.

'Right, lads, we go out the back and move together as one,' I shout out as we scoop our bags and kit up and go over to the rear doors. I stop to listen and press my ear against the door, but I can't hear anything above the firing outside.

'Cookey, me and you get ready to shoot out,' Blowers says as he and Cookey drop down a few steps back from the doors.

I lift the locking bar up, and me and Nicholas Hewitt take a door each. We wrench it open and stand back, but neither Cookey or Blowers start firing.

'Looks clear, sir,' Blowers calls out.

'Let's go,' I shout, and we surge out.

The area is clear, apart from the bodies of the infected we shot earlier. We move around and start making our way towards the Land Rover, reaching it within seconds to grab ammunition and load back up before moving out to fire into the horde. The noise is something else. The ferocity of it all. The lights from the vehicle giving us sight to aim for but also making the infected look ghoulish and wilder than before.

They seem more ramped too, more aggressive even, moving faster.

We still win, and then it's over, and slowly the guns ease off, and we stand ready, with ears ringing, and throats dry. Spent casings littering the ground by our feet. Dead bodies littering the ground everywhere else. Hundreds killed. Blood everywhere. Smoke hanging in the air. Fumes of shit, piss, and blood too.

'You made it, then,' I say to Dave.

'Yes, Mr Howie,' he replies as deadpan as ever.

'Sorry about the wait,' Curtis says. 'The Landy cut out. We thought we'd have to run but I got it going.'

'Well,' I say, not quite knowing what else to say, 'indeed...'

'That was fucking tense,' Blowers says to Cookey.

'Fucking telling me, mate. Jesus, I thought we were done for. Tucker, you need to start running faster, mate. They almost had you back then,' Cookey shouts out.

'I'm not built for running,' Tucker yells back.

'Built for fucking *eating* is what you are,' one of them shouts, earning some low sniggers.

Finally and after a day from hell, we reach the Saxon APC. A huge, squat thing, with solid sides and enormous wheels. I look inside at the controls and see the front has a driver seat and a double passenger seat. I thought only one person sat up front in these things, but then, someone did say a lot of these down here are training vehicles, so maybe the construction is different.

The controls look just like a normal vehicle, and I'm sure I will be able to figure it out as I go. Thankfully, there is no key needed, and the engine roars to life at the press of a switch. Deep and hearty. Almost beast-like and alive.

There's another GPMG on the top too, which Dave has already loaded with a belt of shiny, big bullets. The rear section is massive, with bench seats going down each side and filled with under-seat compartments and cubby holes.

Dave runs through how to fire and reload the GPMG and tells them that someone must be up there at all times, and as Dave gets into the front with me, I hear them all start bickering about who is going to be first.

I take the driver's seat and marvel at how the Saxon vehicle feels so massive and solid, and strong. It's taken a huge effort to get it too. And for a second, I thought the risk was too great, but right now, inside it, I'm bloody glad we did. Fortune favours the brave and all that. If this won't get through London, then I don't know what will, other than a tank, but we've already discussed that.

'Can we stop at the armoury again and get more supplies, Mr Howie?'

'Yeah, no problem, mate. I reckon we should park up somewhere and get some sleep first. I know that lot must be ready to drop. We'll head into the plains and find somewhere quiet...' I pull away with a hard jerk and stall the engine, then burst out laughing at the jeers coming from the back. I try again, pulling away all jerky and bouncy until I get a smoother motion. We head out into the plains and drive for a solid ten minutes, keeping a rough line with the road, way off to the right.

Eventually, I stop, shut the engine down, and Dave climbs into the back and relieves Blowers on the GPMG, ordering them to rest.

Within minutes, they are all flaked out on the grass at the sides of the vehicle while Dave and I keep watch, and I look down at the filthy, drawn young faces and feel immensely proud to have worked alongside them.

Young, jobless and sent here to get experience, and now, look at them! They are a unit – a fighting unit.

I try to think through everything that's happened today, but I feel very sleepy, and my eyes are drooping. Tomorrow we shall go to London. I just bloody know something else will happen, though. It always does.

DAY FIVE

CHAPTER THIRTY-FIVE

DAY FIVE
TUESDAY

Within an old cottage, deep within Salisbury army training centre, an infected male host stares forward, then starts moving its eyes from left to right while clenching and unclenching his hands as the rate of breathing increases. A few seconds later, and he falls to his knees, screaming in agony as Roger Malin, a corporal within the Royal Tank Regiment, comes surging back into his mind and instantly feels the utter pain of the bite wounds to his neck and arms.

He died. He felt it happen. He was running and fighting with everyone else when the exercise went so wrong. It was dark and chaotic. Nobody knew what was happening; then some lads barrelled into him, biting and savaging him. Roger fought back, punching out, but then a searing pain ripped through his guts, and all he could do was writhe on the ground until darkness came.

Except that wasn't the end. Roger came back, and despite his mind not having control of his body, his brain still recorded what he did, and now, as the dawn rises on the fifth day since the world fell, Roger

Malin screams as the images of what he did since dying come hurtling back.

Images of running. Feeling of insatiable hunger and a rage so deep, so buried inside it became a whole new sense. He bit people too. Soldiers that he knew, soldiers that he didn't know. Young men that screamed out in pain and terror.

The pain too. The injuries on his body, and he paws at his neck, feeling the wounds, seeing the blood. One of his fingers is broken; the bone of the little digit poking out the wrong way. Some of his teeth are missing, and from all those things, he raves in lunacy and staggers about the room, falling over furniture and bouncing off walls.

The pain increases too, ramping far beyond the level of pain he should be feeling from wounds of that type. He falls down to gasp as every nerve ending seems to be set on fire before growing taut as the agony simply becomes too much to bear.

The infection doesn't know how or why it came into existence, only that it is, and if it is to survive, then these losses must be stopped.

In order to do this, it must evolve and learn the human brain, and so it toys with Roger Malin, forcing his mind to stay conscious while flooding every nerve ending with pain beyond anything imaginable.

An instant later, and Roger Malin goes from rigid to relaxed as the infection ceases the pain and starts experimenting with the parts of the brain that release endorphins. The pleasure zones. Finding chemicals to release to make other changes happen, and Roger slowly relaxes and starts to smile as a soft groan escapes his lips.

An amazing feeling of warmth and security cocoons his entire being. There is no pain now and nothing to worry about. Just bliss. Pure bliss.

Then it changes again, morphing from that bliss-like state into something more erotic as Roger becomes unquestionably turned on, with an erection straining inside his bloodstained trousers. He groans again, desperate to fuck, needing to do it, and he ejaculates without touching himself, climaxing, with an orgasmic release that stretches on forever and always.

All across the world, the infection does the same thing many times over. In New York, Paris, Barcelona, Delhi, Singapore, and towns, and cities all over the globe, infected people scream in agony or run about in lunacy while others laugh hysterically while yet more hump the ground and writhe in ecstasy as the infection rushes through brains to test and play, to experiment and learn.

To evolve.

To stop the ones fighting back from killing too many hosts.

The infection even knows the name of one of them.

Howie.

CHAPTER THIRTY-SIX

Deep within the plains, a few miles from the infected male flitting between arousal and glee, Howie stands in the back of the Saxon, turning a slow circle while his upper body pokes out the hole in the roof. A squeak from the GPMG swivelling on its mount as it turns is the only noise, save for the deep breathing of the lads at slumber.

All of them sparked out, fast asleep. Murmurs and whimpers break free now and then, but that's only expected after everything they've seen and done. He glances up, seeing it won't be long until dawn when he can get underway. A nag inside to be moving now. An urge even, but what can he do? Wake them up and force them all on so he can get to London and save his sister?

No. They need rest, so he bites the frustration down and keeps watch while thinking of everything that's happened. Watching the outbreak start on the news, then seeing it in his street. Getting to his mum and dad's house to find them gone, then spending time looking for them, and all the fights and chases he endured while that happened.

He thinks of Dave and how strange he is. A small, quiet man, but so very gifted at warfare and fighting. Howie would be dead several times over if not for Dave. But then, he doesn't chat and seems to struggle with social nuances, which all make Howie think he's maybe autistic or something like that. Functioning, intelligent even, gifted in many ways, but not quite able to read people and situations.

He thinks of the lads too and leans over to watch them sleeping. They look so young. So fresh-faced. He tries to remember all of their names. Simon Blowers, Alex Cook – the lads call him Cookey. Nick Hewitt. Curtis, Jamie, Darren Smith, and Tucker. There's more too, and he winces, struggling to recall the names as a faint groan snaps his head up.

Something there. He's sure of it. He flicks the high-powered light attached by a wire to the Saxon and sweeps it round in a slow arc, stopping when the light goes over an infected soldier crawling over the rough grass. His legs looking mangled and crushed like he's been run over a few times.

Howie grips the machine gun, thinking to shoot it dead, but pauses before firing, figuring it will wake everyone up. Not only that, but a gunshot could draw more. He nods to himself and drops out through the hole to jump from the back of the vehicle, grabbing his axe on the way to land softly on the grass. He walks over to look down, shaking his head in disgust and pity, and not a small amount of hatred too. Hatred for what they are. For what they have done. He thinks of that boy again in the teddy bear pyjamas and brings the axe up over his head as the infected looks up. The head ceases to roll, and it fixes those red eyes directly on Howie. A noise made. Breathy and fast, but enough to make Howie flinch and stumble back on his arse while missing the neck and striking the infected in the head.

'What the fuck...' he mutters, staring in shock at the now dead infected as Dave runs over, an assault rifle in one hand, a knife in the other.

'You okay?' Dave asks, looking from the corpse to Howie.

Howie nods, swallows, and looks at Dave. 'It spoke...'

'Spoke, Mr Howie?'

'It spoke...'

'What did it say?'

'My name. The fucking thing said my name.'

CHAPTER THIRTY-SEVEN

Sarah wakes up slowly as the bright sunlight streams through the smart, black blinds covering her bedroom window.

Dust particles dance and shimmer in the air from her soft breath.

Long, dark strands of hair spread out across the expensive silk sheets of the king-sized bed.

Sarah sits up slowly and looks at her reflection in the mirrored doors of the built-in wardrobes. She stares intently, with a look of concentrated determination, which slowly morphs into sadness. With a long sigh, she shimmies over the bed and stands up, stretching her arms and legs out. Sarah then walks into the en-suite bathroom and reaches for the light switch, but the electricity went out a couple of days ago, and she curses herself for forgetting.

She checks the cold water tap and is pleasantly surprised that clear water still gushes out. She starts to brush her teeth and looks longingly at the large, glass-sided shower cubicle in the middle of the room, then sniffs at her armpits, and pulls her head away from the stale smell of body odour.

There are pans and pots on every surface. Each filled with water and covered with cling film and aluminium foil. Sarah knew that once the electricity went out, she would have to preserve her supplies, so filled every available receptacle from her small apartment. Even the kitchen sink is full of clean water, and she hasn't flushed the toilet for a couple of days now. The warm weather has meant that she's been sweating lightly nearly all the time, especially at night when the air is so still and hot. Her tight, black vest top clings to her body from moisture. Sarah has been washing with cotton cloths and only using the water sparingly, but now, after several days, she longs for a shower. The air is so warm and humid, and she can just imagine the cold water spraying onto her sticky body.

'Sod it,' she says to herself and strips her clothes off, leaving them in a pile on the floor.

Naked, she steps into the cubicle and turns the dial. A powerful jet of freezing water pummels into her skin, taking her breath away and making her squeal. The cold water is pleasant torture, and she soaks herself, watching as goose pimples come up on her arms and legs. She scrubs her body with soap and washes her hair, turning the shower off as the last of the bubbles are rinsed away. She steps out and takes the thick cotton towel hanging from a hook. She walks back in front of the bathroom mirror and stands naked, holding the towel down at her side, enjoying the feeling of the warm air drying her wet skin.

After a few minutes, she is dressed in jeans and a baggy t-shirt and finally goes into the lounge area – a small room with a kitchenette on one end. The apartment was subsidized by her employer – one of the perks of working for a large corporate bank. The downside was that she had to respond to work whenever she was called, and that was quite often during the recession. But even a tiny apartment like hers, in a swish block, would cost a fortune – far more than she could ever afford.

Sarah finally plucks up the courage and steps to the large windows, pulling the blinds up. She slides back the single patio door, steps out onto the tiny balcony that overlooks most of Central London, and glances down onto the streets below. Her heart sinks as she sees the thousands of infected crammed into the streets. Even the road is not visible because they are so densely packed. The only times she has seen crowds like this are for huge royal weddings or the London Marathon.

But these aren't crowds waiting for a glimpse of someone famous. These are hordes of rotting, dirty, filthy infected that want to eat human flesh. Sarah shudders and steps back inside. She closes the door but then opens it slightly in defiance. They are down there, and as far as she is aware, they haven't tried to climb up to her, and the apartment needs fresh air. She walks over to the fridge, and again forgets that the power is gone. It is now empty as she has eaten all of the perishable food and is now on to the tinned goods.

'Sod it,' she says again and steps over to the wall cupboard. She closes her eyes and reaches in. She knows there are some tinned goods inside, and she has been making herself select them at random so that she doesn't just eat the nicer things first.

She feels for a tin and pulls it out, holding it in front of her face as she slowly opens her eyes and peeks down at the tin of tuna.

'Sod it.'

She opens the tin, takes a fork, and sits down on the sofa to slowly munch through the dry fish. Giving up within two mouthfuls and going back to the cupboard. She mooches through the various bottles of sauces and condiments, deciding on an almost empty bottle of barbeque sauce. She shakes the thick liquid down to the cap end before squirting it over the rest of the tuna and mixing it in. She starts eating again, and whilst doing so, her mind travels back to Friday.

A trendy wine bar was what Howie would call it, and Sarah smiles at the memory of her brother making jokes about her whole life being "a trendy gym, a trendy apartment, and a trendy social life". Sarah knew, though, that success in her line of work depended on being able to socialise or network. So she made contacts within all of the communities of the financial district.

Friday evening was the same as any other: calls were made, emails sent, text messages put out, and the in-crowd descended into Central London for drinks and Tapas at Charlie's, which was owned and ran by the sleazy Charlie himself. He was always trying it on with the female staff and customers despite his wife working there. Tapas was appointed with sleek, black, minimalist furniture and exposed, wooden flooring, and photos of pebbles and stones in various poses finished the scene. Sarah knew that it was stomach-churning, fake, and contrived, but business was business, and it had to be done. So she laughed at the right times and gradually made her way through the crowds with her colleagues. A simple, black evening dress was all that she wore. Elegant and classic was how her close friends said she looked, which was exactly the look that she aimed for. Too many of the female financiers showed way too much flesh out of the office, and it just didn't feel appropriate to her. Her dad had always said, *If you want to be taken seriously, you have to act seriously*. And his words had stuck throughout her short career.

Younger than Howie by two years, she had moved to London at the tender age of twenty-three and had been here for two years now. The shine of the city had already worn off, and Sarah knew it wouldn't be long before she wanted out of it. Sarah had seen the desperation of the older people, clinging to their power and fortunes and trying to stay with the in-crowd all of the time. This just made her sad and more resolved to get out when she could.

Smoking had saved her life, and it's not often that people can say that.

Sarah had been addicted for years and controlled the habit by having the odd couple of cigarettes at lunchtime and then after work. So many of the young financiers were health freaks – using the companies' gyms and clubs during lunch hours or after work. They called it "having a sesh". Sarah was amazed at how many of them used cocaine and did so in public, but would then shun the smokers, calling their habit dirty and cancerous.

Taking the opportunity to nip outside and just managing to avoid the grope being offered by Charlie, she talked with her co-conspirator and smoking colleague, Lisa. They chatted as they walked around the side of the building into a quieter side street and both lit up, giggling like schoolgirls, inhaling the smoke, and relaxing with idle gossip.

'Well, that Jonathon tried it on with me last night. I just knew he would, the dirty bugger,' Lisa said.

'He did? What did you do?' Sarah replied.

'What do you think I did? I told him that I'm a strict Catholic girl, and he should bugger off!' Lisa said in a very serious tone, then cackled evilly.

'Oh, you didn't, you naughty girl,' Sarah laughed, waiting for the juicy details of the illicit encounter. A scream came from the front of the trendy wine bar, and it made them both jump. They darted forward to look around the edge of the building. They were just in time to see Charlie standing there in his expensive designer jeans, brown boots, and tucked-in, black shirt, with his podgy stomach pushing against the material.

A very pretty girl with long, blonde hair was shouting loudly at him as he backed away, with his hands raised up in front of him, palms facing her, acquiescent and trying to *shush* her.

'YOU FILTHY BASTARD, YOU GRABBED MY ARSE!' the woman screamed at Charlie, then slapped him hard across the face, causing his perfectly styled, messy hair to get dishevelled. Charlie backed away and begged the woman to keep her voice down. She became angrier and started throwing more haymakers at him. One of the large bouncers stepped forward and restrained the woman, pulling her back.

'YOU CRAZY BITCH!' Charlie shouted and ordered the bouncer to take her down the street.

'He had that coming, the sleazy pig,' Sarah said.

'Oh, he's disgusting. He's always grabbing my arse and trying to squeeze my tits,' replied Lisa.

'I don't know why we keep coming here. It's always the same people and the same thing, and that dirty sleazebag trying to grope anything that moves. He's a sex pest,' Sarah said.

'You know what I heard? He just got back from his brother's wedding in Greece, where he got off with the bride's best mate, and now he keeps going down to see her. Right under his poor wife's nose,' Lisa said.

'Someone should report him to the police. That's got to be sexual assault or something,' Sarah said.

'Oh! Hang on. It's not quite over yet.'

A well-built man with a bald head came storming up the street, straight towards Charlie, who was now talking to his two bouncers. As the man got closer, he pointed directly at Charlie.

'Did you grab my girlfriend's arse? You dirty fucker,' the man shouted as he got closer.

Charlie started stepping back, hiding behind his bouncers. One of them moved forward and extended an arm out to the man – a clear warning to stay back. The man knocked it out of the way and punched the bouncer in the face, causing him to fly back and knock Charlie into a set of tables, spilling the drinks all over the nearest customers. The second bouncer moved in to grab the angry man but got head-butted and sent flying too. Charlie was on his feet and moving backwards, away from the angry man.

'Please, mate, take it easy! Calm down. I didn't do anything. It's all a misunderstanding,' Charlie pleaded, seeing his two bouncers down on the ground, clutching at their faces. Sarah and Lisa were laughing hard, watching as Charlie begged the man to stop whilst backing away into more tables and knocking drinks over. The bald man lunged at Charlie and grabbed him by the front of his shirt, then threw him down onto the floor. Sarah, Lisa, and a half-dozen other previously-groped women all cheered at the sight of the sex pest getting his just rewards. The angry man glanced around at the sound of cheering and smiled awkwardly at first, confused about the reaction. One woman shouted out to cheers and whistles, 'Go on, then. Have him! He's groped all of us, the dirty beast.'

The bald man smiled at the women and bowed his head before walking intently towards Charlie, who was scurrying away on his backside, one hand up in the air, still trying to defuse the situation.

'Please, mate. I didn't do anything. You touch me, and I'll get the law on you. There's CCTV here.' The man bent down and pulled Charlie to his feet by the front of his clothes and punched him once in the face.

The women erupted in cheers and started applauding. People piled out of the main door to watch the action and more joint in by clapping. The man punched him again in the face, and the crowd cheered even louder. Someone shouted 'TWO', and the man pounded him again. The crowd shouted 'THREE'.

The man wasn't hitting him hard but hard enough to stun Charlie and humiliate him. The bouncers were back on their feet now and were starting forward to help their boss. A woman stepped out from the crowd and stood in front of them.

'DON'T DO NOTHING. HE GOT THIS COMING!' the woman shouted at the bouncers in a strong Eastern European accent.

'That's the wife, then,' Lisa laughed as the crowd shouted *'FOUR'*. A loud shout erupted from over the road, and Sarah looked over to see another fight taking place.

'Jesus, this place is getting worse. Look at them going for it.'

Lisa stared over, and they both watched as a man was being attacked on the ground by another man. Some other people ran over and started to pull the man away by grabbing at his shoulders and body. The man was thrashing about and appeared to be trying to force his face into the other man's neck. The attacker then sprung up and launched himself at one of the rescuers.

'Oh, my god, did you see that?' Sarah asked.

'Yeah, that's awful,' Lisa replied. There was a big ruckus going on now across the road as more people tried to subdue the crazy man. He refused to stop and kept lunging his head at more people, biting them, and causing them to jump backwards. The man, who was on the floor, sat up after a few minutes and slowly looked around.

'At least he's all right. I thought he was dead,' Lisa said. The man got to his feet and lunged forward, and bit into the neck of another man. Screams and shouts erupted, and the bald man holding the now bloodied Charlie stopped pounding and looked over at the mass brawl taking place. He let Charlie go, who slumped to the ground, whimpering. The crowd were all silent now.

Some people were running into the melee, and some were trying to escape. One woman, dressed in a smart, black business suit, staggered out of the confusion, clutching her neck, with blood spurting out between her fingers. She staggered across the road and fell, and the bald man tried to catch her and lower her gently to the ground. The man shouted for something to stop the bleeding and pressed his already bloody hands into the side of her neck.

Women were screaming, and men were running about in panic. The fighting got worse, and more people got involved until nearly the whole street was brawling.

Sarah started to take in some of the details. Despite not being experienced in street fights, even *she* understood that biting is not a normal action.

'We should get out of here,' Lisa whispered to Sarah.

'What? Christ, yes. Let's go,' Sarah responded, shaking herself. Sarah and Lisa started down the main road but quickly saw that the road ahead was also blocked by people fighting. They turned round and tried to go the other way, but that too was blocked.

'What the fuck is going on?' Lisa shouted.

'I don't know. Quick, down here.' Sarah grabbed her hand, and they started back towards the entrance to the side street that they were smoking in just a few minutes ago. They passed the front of Tapas again, and Lisa screamed as she saw the bald man being pulled down by the woman in the smart business suit.

The woman was biting into his neck, gouging the flesh away, and hot, crimson blood was pouring down her face. They scurried past and entered the darkness of a quiet street. Both stopped halfway down to take off their high heels and run in bare feet. They burst out of the street, into another main road also swamped with cafés, restaurants, and wine bars, and hundreds of screaming people covered in blood and clutching facial and body wounds. Sarah and Lisa ran down the pavement, dodging around people fighting. Blood spurted out from an arterial bleed, soaking Lisa on her face and bare arms. They continued to run, narrowly missing being attacked by inches. Within a short distance, they reached Sarah's apartment block.

'Come in with me, Lisa. You can't stay out here on your own,' Sarah said, panting heavily.

'I can't, Sarah. I've got to get home!' Lisa broke away and started running down the street.

'I'll call you when I'm home,' she yelled. Sarah watched her run, then turned to go into her own block, but movement to her left caught her eye, and she saw a man staggering into view. His shirt was blood-soaked, and half his face was torn away. He saw Sarah and started directly towards her. Sarah fumbled at the numbers on the key-coded entrance lock. Her fingers moved too fast, and she had to press "clear" and start again. Finally, she pushed through the door and slammed it shut behind her.

In the foyer, Sarah pressed the button to call the lift. While waiting, she peered at the front door and watched the man through the glass staggering past the door; then, he stopped and walked towards the plate glass.

Sarah pulled back and urged the lift to move faster. The doors opened with a loud ping, and Sarah got inside and waited for the slow climb to her floor. She didn't hear or see anyone else and got safely into her flat.

She then pulled her mobile phone out of her bag and cursed that she forgot it was on silent. The screen flashed with missed calls from "Home". Her parents had been calling her again and again. She pressed the phone and waited for the connection. Her dad answered and let out a loud sigh.

'Sarah, thank God, you're okay,' he said.

'Dad, what's happening? There's loads of fighting, and people being attacked, and a man had his face hanging off,' Sarah babbled into the phone.

'Sarah, listen to me. The phones will be down soon. Something bad is happening everywhere. I don't know what it is, but you stay in your flat, okay? You must lock yourself in and wait for us.' Howard spoke slowly and firmly, making sure she takes it all in.

'Dad, what? What's going on. Are you and Mum okay?'

'We're fine, Sarah. Your mother's right here. We are going to get Howie, and then we'll come and get you. Wait there, do not go out or leave the flat.'

'Is Howie okay, Dad? Is this everywhere? I've been out in town, and it was awful.'

'Yes, Sarah, it's everywhere. Now, you must stay there.' The line went dead.

Sarah panicked and yelled into the phone over and over again, 'DAD? DAD! DAD!'

She pressed the "END CALL" button and tried to call them back. She kept trying again and again, then called Howie, but got no dial tone, and then she worked her way through her call list, one by one.

All around the world, people screamed into their phones, desperately trying to make contact with their loved ones. The huge numbers crashed the networks, and the engineers were busy fighting for their lives like everyone else and couldn't bring the systems back online.

Sarah had never had a landline connected; the mobile signal in most of Central London was always brilliant, and the building provided secure wireless connection.

Sarah tried using her computer, but the Internet was down too. After hours of frantic calling and texting, she gave up and sank onto the sofa, curling up and sobbing. After some time, she remembered the television. She had rarely watched any TV. Sarah flicked through the channels, but each one was either blank or showing a static image apologising for the loss in broadcast.

Those were the events of Friday. Now it's Tuesday, and there is still no sign of her family.

Sarah finishes the tuna and discards the empty can into the waste bin. She is feeling a little stir-crazy, and yesterday sneaked out to knock on her neighbours' doors, but there was no reply, and she ran back inside her own apartment.

She knows that she has to keep mentally alert and that regular physical exercise releases endorphins into the system. She grabs her iPod and changes into a pair of shorts and a sporty vest top. Naturally very slim and lithe. Regular workouts in the company gym helped keep her fit and toned. Selecting her gym playlist, Sarah commenced exercising, again cursing herself that she had the shower first instead of waiting.

For the next two hours, Sarah punishes herself with hard physical exertion: running fast on the spot, then doing star jumps, squat thrusts, push ups, and sit ups; then, she makes use of the kitchen worktop for dips. Loud dance and rock music blares directly into her inner ear, pushing her to work harder and faster. Eventually, she flakes out, crashing down to the floor, gulping air down, and pulling the small, white speakers out of her ears.

As she recovers, she tries to think how many apartments there are in the building. There are many floors, maybe twenty or twenty-five, and most of the apartments are small so the developers could make more money.

So maybe four apartments per floor, apart from the big, luxury ones at the top. That would make it around one hundred apartments in my block. There must be someone else alive in this building, and there should be a decent amount of water storage to supply the apartments.

Which must mean there is plenty of water, so I can have another shower!

Sarah runs for the bathroom before she allows any doubt to creep in. Again, having showered under the pleasantly cold water, she gets dressed and makes her mind up – she is going to go out of her apartment and see if anyone else is still here. What harm can it do? Sarah selects a large knife from the kitchen drawer and starts towards the front door.

'Sod it,' she exclaims as she slowly opens her front door.

CHAPTER THIRTY-EIGHT

'Oh, who did that?' Cookey exclaims and bursts out from underneath the Saxon, clutching his nose. 'Tucker, was that you? Stinky fucker!' Cookey shouts again after taking a few steps away.

Tucker chuckles to himself and then lets rip with another loud fart, causing more of the recruits to burst away from the rear of the vehicle.

'You dirty fucker,' Darren Smith yells as Tucker carries on laughing.

I start giggling myself from my spot at the top of the Saxon vehicle. Dave took the last look-out during the night, and I got another couple of hours' sleep before the sun finally came up.

'What time is it?' Nicholas Hewitt stands and stretches out.

'Just gone 6 a.m.,' I say out loud so they can all hear.

'You lot feeling any better today?' I get a mixed response.

'Right, we need to make a move. Load up, and we'll go back to the main buildings and find some food.'

'Hang on. I need a piss,' Simon Blowers calls out and runs out from the Saxon, stopping after a few metres and relieving himself onto the grass.

Within minutes, he is joined by all of us, in a row, pissing in the warm summer morning. Contented sighs and long groans sound out as bladders are relieved.

'I'm bloody starving,' Tucker says.

'No surprise there, then,' Cookey says to a cackle of laughter.

'Stop talking about food. I feel like my throat's been cut,' Curtis Graves says.

'What? You didn't even do anything last night, Gravesy. You were pissing about, driving that Land Rover all night while we were fighting for our lives,' one of them shouts, and then they are off again, bantering and jibing.

We slowly load back into the Saxon, and I take the driver's seat. The Bedford 500 6-cylinder engine roars to life, and I engage the first gear and pull away. The Saxon is a big, squat-looking thing with massive tyres and can hold up to ten soldiers in the rear. From looking at the controls, I can see it has two-wheel and four-wheel drive capability, but I leave it in normal at the moment.

The ground is hard and compacted from the scorching hot summer, and the Saxon makes light work of it until we reach the smooth surface of the road that leads back into the main area. I familiarise myself with the vehicle while we go over the low bumps, causing the lads in the back to bounce around. I think back to the night before when the zombie said my name. I theorise that it must have been just the body expelling air, and in the eerie night, my imagination made it sound like my name.

'You all right, mate?' I say to Dave.

He is sitting in the passenger seat of the cabin.

'Yes, Mr Howie,' he replies, deadpan as normal.

'You hungry too, mate? I'm famished.'

'Yes.'

'So, what do we need to do? Get some food and go to the armoury. Anything else?'

'I don't think so. More ammunition and a bit more kit from the stores would be good.'

'Okay, mate. Food first, though. We could split up and use the two teams we had yesterday – one for cooking and one for getting the stuff.'

'Okay, Mr Howie.'

I'm sure most of the lads are doing the same as me and thinking only of food and their stomachs. We follow the road for several miles. The plains are massive and stretch out on either side as far as the eye can see. Eventually, we drive into the main building area. Bodies littering the ground everywhere. Flies and insects are buzzing between the cadavers, and I realise just how much of a disease risk all of the corpses across the country are.

'Right, everyone out,' I call as I bring the vehicle to a stop on the large parade square.

'We will split into two teams. Tucker, you're on team Alpha, aren't you?'

'Yes, Sir,' he replies but looks worried.

'Team Alpha will come with me and get the grub ready. Team Bravo are going with Dave to get what he needs from the stores and the armoury. Right, who knows where the, er, food place is?'

'It's called the mess, sir, and it's over here.' Tucker starts off immediately, followed by the members of our team.

'STOP RIGHT THERE!' Dave bellows out in his drill sergeant voice, and everyone freezes, including me. I look around, trying to identify the threat; my assault rifle already raised up. I see Blowers and Cookey are doing the same.

'WHERE ARE YOUR WEAPONS?' Dave shouts, and I realise that half the recruits have got out and started moving off, with their rifles still in the Saxon.

'GET YOUR WEAPONS AND KEEP THEM WITH YOU AT ALL TIMES!' Dave's voice does the trick, and they scramble back to the Saxon and gather their weapons, looking sheepish and embarrassed. I nod at Dave, and he nods back.

'See you in a bit, mate. Say, an hour? Will that be long enough?'

'Yes, Mr Howie.'

We set off to the "mess", and I wonder why the army has to have such weird names for everything.

The mess looks like most of the other buildings from the outside. The door leads into a corridor, which opens into a large, canteen-style dining room with long tables and benches. There is a long serving counter at one end; hot plates and cold cabinets are dark and cold.

Tucker walks down the room, rubbing his hands.

'I don't know what they'll have left. I guess the meat might be off by now. What day is it? Tuesday? We'll see. There might be something decent we can use. I'll go and have a look.' He's in his element now .He is the official cook and food supplier for our band of misfits. I follow Tucker into the kitchen area, which is spotless and very modern-looking: huge ovens, multiple sinks, and various equipment are around the sides. There are lots of work surfaces in the middle. Tucker walks through, taking it all in.

'Have you done cooking before, then, Tucker?' I ask him.

'I was joining the Catering Corps, sir. I love food and always have done loads of cooking as you can probably tell,' he jiggles his large belly and laughs.

'Ah, here we are ...' He opens two large metal doors that lead into a huge walk-in chill room.

'Won't all that be off now, mate? If the power's been off for a few days,' I ask and follow him inside.

'The army uses a different power supply to the normal grid. It's gone now, but I was hoping it stayed on long enough to keep this lot chilled. Plus, these are very well insulated from the heat outside, so it takes a while for the temperature to rise.'

I see what he means. Although the power is definitely out, the chilled room is decidedly colder than the kitchen or the outside.

'Now, let's see. They must use the LILO method, so we just need to work out where that starts,' Tucker says as he starts rummaging through boxes and packets.

'The what, mate?' I ask him.

'The LILO method means Last In Last Out. Which means they have a system to see when the freshest stock is added, so they use the oldest stock first.'

'Ah, I see, that makes sense.'

Tucker identifies the freshest line and starts pulling boxes out into the kitchen. I call the rest of the lads, and we start a chain, piling it up on the work surfaces until there is a considerable mound. I start poking through and see boxes of red meat, beef, and whole chickens. I smell each of them in turn, but they all seem quite fresh. Tucker walks back into the kitchen as I'm sniffing.

'They must have had a delivery of new produce on Friday, so we're lucky – this lot is still good,' he says.

'Are you using all of it?' I ask him, surprised at the pile of goods.

'Might as well. It will only go bad otherwise.' He stops and stares at the pile, and immediately starts separating them.

Tucker is, by far, the least fit of the recruits, and he gets a lot of stick for it, but watching him now, he looks focussed and very happy.

'Anything we can do, mate?' Roland McKinney asks Tucker.

'Oh, yes, the power is still on!' Tucker exclaims as he turns a dial on one of the gas hobs. Then he checks if the oven is working.

'Right, Roland, can you grab some of those pans and fill them with water? Darren, if you start cutting these up into small chunks,' Tucker thrusts a box at Darren and moves on to Nicholas Hewitt.

'Nick, could you start chopping the veg, please, mate.'

'Anything I can do, Tucker?' I ask him.

'Err... No, sir. Thanks anyway, but we can manage.'

I leave them to it and make my back out of the building and across to the parade square. The Saxon looks massive. It must be over two and a half metres in height and over five metres in length. I feel more optimistic about our chances of getting through London, but again, the delay concerns me. These lads didn't have to come with us into the plains yesterday. I know they said that sticking together increases the chances of survival, but getting that Saxon was my objective, and I did it to rescue my sister. I put them in danger for my own ends. In the church when the ammunition ran low and we were seconds from being invaded, not one of them moaned or said a word, but they stood together and prepared for the worst. So the least I can do now is give them some time for food and rest. I meet Dave at the Saxon, and we watch the recruits bringing boxes of ammunition out. Dave takes the magazines out and stows them in compartments in the vehicle. Then he does the same with the spare rifles and ammunition for the GPMG, then more clothing, and finally some NATO helmets.

Once loaded, we head over to the mess and walk into a wonderful aroma – a mixture of meats and sauces that sets my mouth watering at once. Tucker has done an amazing job. There are bowls and trays of food in the middle of one of the tables.

A few minutes later, and we are all tucking in, piling plates with food and shovelling it into our mouths without manners or etiquette.

There are laughs and jokes around the table as everyone eats their fill.

Dave stays quiet and eats an enormous amount of food for such a slightly built man. We sit back, relaxed and content, and drink strong coffee.

'So, I'm going to head to London with Dave. I promised I would drop some of you off on the way...' I let the question hang in the air.

'Sir, if it's all right with you, I'd rather stick with you two until you get to the forts. I haven't really got anywhere else to go,' Blowers speaks first; his voice steady and decisive.

'Yes, mate, of course, but going to London is going to be hard. Are you sure this is what you want to do?'

'Yes, sir. I think Cookey feels the same way. We talked about it earlier.' Blowers looks to Cookey, who nods in affirmation.

'I won't last five minutes on my own, and besides, someone has to do the food and make the brews,' Tucker offers.

'That's great, mate, thank you,' I say to Tucker. 'McKinney, what about you, mate?'

'Well, I want to see my family, but I know they would have headed with everyone to the forts if they haven't...'

'I understand,' I interject to try and save him the hardship of having to say it.

'But there's no point me trying for home on my own. Especially after seeing what they are like at night. So if it's okay, I want to come with you, too.' McKinney looks down at his empty plate, clearly uncomfortable, with feeling like he has to ask.

'Lads, Dave and I would be more than happy to take you all with us. You've proved yourselves. Trust me, it's not me doing you a favour, it's the other way round.'

'I'm going to head off, sir, if that's all right,' Alan Booker offers suddenly.

'No problem, Alan, where you heading to?' I ask him.

'I'll try home first and then the forts if that fails. I live in the other direction, so I'll find something to take. Save you having to drive away from your direction.'

'Alan, after what you've done for us, mate, it's really not an issue if you need a ride somewhere,' I say to him.

'Nah, thanks anyway. I can take something to use,' he says but looks sheepish, and avoids eye contact.

'How will you take something, Alan? Even Dave and I struggled to find transport at times. It's not as easy as you would think.'

'Nah, it will be okay. I sort of know how to take cars without keys if you get my meaning.'

'Ah, a misspent youth, eh, mate? Well, it's a pity to lose you. Feel free to change your mind.'

'Thanks, Mr Howie. I really appreciate it.' Alan is the only one that wants to leave. The others try and convince him to stay, but I can see his mind is made up.

Half an hour later, we are driving out of the gates and down the road.

Alan insists on being dropped off at the main junction, and he gets out with his rifle, ammunition, and rucksack. There's a silence after he goes, and we drive on quietly. The recruits have been through so much together in such a short space of time, and the loss hits them hard.

Cookey makes an effort to crack a joke, but it falls flat.

'Now, are the rest of you sure that you want to come with us?' I shout back to the lads. 'Because there's going to be a lot of zombie mother fuckers that need killing. Dave and I did want to keep them to ourselves, but seeing as you lot have helped out, we are willing to share them, but not if you're going to be holding back.'

A few muttered responses.

'Oh, yes, a whole lot of zombies that want to eat brains...' a few chuckles this time.

'BRAINS... I MUST HAVE THEM BRAINSSSS...' I groan the words out and then look across at Dave.

'EAT DAVE'S BRAIIINNNSSS...' A few more laughs, especially when Dave looks at me with his usual deadpan expression.

'COOKEY NO HAVE ANY BRAAAINS TO EAT, THOUGH...' They laugh properly this time and start ripping on Cookey, who takes it well and abuses them back.

The tension is broken, for a little while at least.

CHAPTER THIRTY-NINE

Sarah treads softy down the carpeted hallway, creeping forward and stopping at the first door. She knocks gently and listens, with her ear pressed to the door, and after a few seconds of silence, she tries the door handle and is not surprised to find that the door is locked. She moves down the corridor, checking each door, knocking, and listening, and then slowly pushing the door handle down. Sarah hasn't heard any noise from the neighbouring flats since the *event* began, which is unusual because she can normally hear the muted tones of the televisions, music being played, or the tones of voices.

She realises that she has never heard anyone from above or below her apartment, so has nothing to gauge whether the occupiers will still be there. Her floor is finished quickly. There is no noise, and all of the doors are locked. Out of habit, she moves towards the lift doors and goes to press the "CALL" button, only remembering at the last second that the power is out. She moves to the fire door and slowly pushes it open, looking down into the stairwell. The apartment block is modern and finished to a high standard. The developer went to the extent of carpeting the emergency stairwell and having brass rails fitted.

Some of the more health-conscious residents used the stairs for a daily workout. The carpet is light brown, carefully selected to absorb moisture and street dirt from the boots of delivery drivers. The developer also thought to add glass panes to each fire door so that natural light filters into the stairwell.

'Up or down?' Sarah whispers to herself.

Living on the 14th floor meant she was just over halfway up. She stands still for some minutes, considering which way to go. In the end, she chooses to go up, knowing it will be quicker for her to run back down the stairs if she has to escape anything. The memories of seeing the infected bite into the living makes her shiver with fear as she starts to ascend the stairs, keeping to the central, carpeted section to deaden her footfalls.

There are two sets of stairs between each floor, and she is at the next landing door very quickly, crouching behind the door and listening, then raising herself up slowly to peer through the glass pane and out into the corridor. The view is exactly the same as her floor: carpeted corridor, with four apartments, two on each side, and a large picture window at the end. She creeps out until she is through the doorway and gently closes the door behind her. She repeats the actions from her floor, moving from door to door. Each apartment is quiet, and the silence only serves to add to the tension and fear she is feeling. She moves stealthily back to the stairwell and climbs up to the 16th floor.

By the 19th floor, she is more nonchalant, and the knife is held down at her side rather than up and ready. She still tries the handles, but her movements become less stealthy and covert, and she spends less time at each door. By the 20th floor, the knife is in her back pocket, and she walks normally down the corridor and knocks loudly at each door before trying the door handle, not bothering to listen this time.

Thinking that there is clearly no one there, the whole block must be empty. She makes her way back down the corridor and into the stairwell.

Up the stairs and onto the 21st floor. Again, she knocks and tries each door handle, but there is no sign of life.

'Where is everyone?' she mutters. She goes back into the stairwell and climbs further up. Her thigh muscles still aching from the two hours of exercise.

Feeling hot, thirsty, and sweaty, she reaches the 21st floor and pushes the door open before stepping into the corridor.

Thinking of a cold drink and another cold shower, she reaches the first door, and her fist freezes mid-air as she goes to knock. The door is wide open. Her heart starts beating faster, and her breath catches in her throat as she looks down at the bloodstains beneath her feet. She looks back down the corridor to the stairwell door and curses herself for not noticing the red, smeared footprints on the light-coloured carpet. Deep red, dried blood smears are all over the high gloss, white, wooden stairwell door. She slowly follows the bloody footprints on the carpet and looks towards the end of the corridor. Her heart skips a beat as she sees the man that is facing her. He has drool coming from his mouth, and his eyes are all bloodshot, like he has a serious disease. His skin is drawn and tight against his face, and Sarah can see that his normally dark, black skin has gone shades paler, almost grey.

The man rocks gently as he stares at her, and his head rolls about, seemingly uncontrolled. He is dressed in white shorts and a once-white vest top that is now heavily stained from blood and saliva.

The man groans and starts to shuffle slowly towards her. His movements are slow and jerky as he moves. He slowly spasms and twitches, flicks his arms out, and causes his head to jerk to one side.

Terrified, Sarah stands still, watching the man shuffling towards her. Then she comes to and darts forward into the open doorway with a squeal, slamming the door behind her and running into the lounge area.

The apartment has the same layout as hers, but with different furniture and décor, which makes it feel surreal. She pulls the knife from her pocket and turns back to face the door, listening intently; her heartbeat thudding in her ears.

An old, infected woman shuffles on thick carpet slippers into the lounge. Saliva dribbles from her old and puckered mouth and coats the front of her nightgown. She inches towards Sarah. The bloodshot eyes staring at the tender skin of Sarah's bare neck.

Sarah's heart is pounding, and the blood rushes through her temples, deafening her senses. She waits for the sound of the man against the door and tightens the grip on the knife handle, but a sudden noise behind her causes her to spin around. She screams as she sees the old woman; a massive, ragged gash in her neck. She lunges at Sarah, with her lips pulled back.

Sarah yells and jumps backwards, at the same time thrusting the knife forward, plunging the sharp blade directly into the old woman's chest. The infected is knocked back but then continues forward again. Sarah backs away, staring at the knife handle embedded in the woman's chest.

She is trapped in the short corridor between the lounge and the front door, and within a couple of steps, her back is pressing against the door.

The old woman keeps coming; each small, shuffling step bringing her closer and closer to Sarah, who stares in horror at the skin that is torn away from the open neck wound.

Sarah waits until the old woman is two or three steps away and lunges forward again, grabbing the knife handle and pulling it free. She stabs, plunging the knife back into the woman's chest, but again, gets no reaction.

The dead woman is pushing against Sarah and has again pulled her lips back to reveal worn-down, old, yellowing teeth.

Sarah stabs furiously in a blind panic and then uses her hands to drive the woman away.

The old woman falls to the floor from the power of the blows, and Sarah yanks the blade free and staggers back to the door. The elderly infected slowly sits up and starts bending forward to stand.

'Oh, fuck off,' Sarah cries out, and without thinking, pushes the door handle down, and pulls the door open.

The infected man is standing in front of her, and Sarah screams again and lashes out with the knife, slashing him across the face. His skin peels apart like dried fruit, and blood seeps down into his mouth, turning the saliva pink.

Sarah feels the old woman against the back of her leg and spins around to see the woman reaching towards her. She stamps down on the woman's head and drives her face hard into the floor, feeling the crunch as the nose is broken and teeth are knocked out.

The man staggers in, spitting bloody drool, and Sarah stabs out hard and fast, puckering his chest and abdomen. She moves backwards but gets stuck by the old woman's body.

In desperation, she raises the knife high in both hands and drives it into the skull of the man as he lunges forward for the bite. The blade forces through the skull into the brain, and the force of the blow drives the infected down onto the floor. Whimpering and full of panic, Sarah jumps over his body and dashes out into the corridor. She screams loudly as she sees another infected coming out of the next apartment, shuffling towards her. Sarah backs away down the corridor, unarmed. The knife still embedded in the man's head. She backs down to the stairwell door and turns to run away, suddenly seeing another ravaged and bloodied face staring at her through the glass pane from the stairwell.

'FUCKING HELL!' Sarah moves away from the door.

Turning round, she sees the old woman crawling out of the apartment doorway into the corridor. The other infected man advances slowly, and Sarah hears the door being pushed open behind her.

With a yell, she slams her body into the door, sending the infected behind it flying backwards. She spins around, trapped again, desperately trying to think of a way out. She looks down at the wall and the bright red, plastic case of the fire hose and instantly starts tugging at the large door to open it up.

The door stays shut, and Sarah loses valuable seconds, fumbling to open the clasp.

The stairwell door starts to open, and Sarah kicks out hard, slamming the plate glass into the face of the infected. Blood spurts out from his broken nose, coating the glass pane. Sarah pulls at the hose and the heavy metal head, yanking it free of the reel. The large, red metal head has arrows depicting ON and OFF.

Sarah fumbles with the tap head, and in her panic, twists it the wrong way. The door swings open, and the infected lunges into the corridor. Sarah swings the heavy metal hose head and batters him across the face, forcing him to spin into the wall behind him. She twists at the tap and hears as water surges through the hose, sending it rigid, but no water comes out. She pulls the lever and gets thrown backwards onto the floor by the sudden release of the water shooting out of the end. The hose dances and bangs against the walls, forcing gallons of water out into the corridor, soaking everything. Sarah is drenched within seconds and has to fight against the powerful spray to take hold of the metal head. She picks it up and turns it back towards the stairwell door, straight at the man. The powerful jet of water knocks him back through the door and into the stairwell. The door swings closed, causing the water to spray back and soak Sarah again. She spins round on her backside and directs the jet at the next male, again hitting him from close range at centre mass and knocking him clean off his feet and down onto the floor. The old woman has crawled close to her victim, and Sarah forces the jet of water directly into her face. The woman's skin is pummelled and forced back as she gargles and chokes on the water, but she keeps crawling forward. Sarah leans over with the hose so that it is right in front of her, and the jets force the infected woman's head back as the water is pumped down her throat.

Finally, the old woman dies again as her lungs fill with water, and her stomach lining expands from the sudden fluid intake. Sarah gets to her feet and switches the lever off. The sudden loss of pressure causing the hose to drop down a few inches as she turns back to the stairwell door.

Sarah marches forward and kicks the door open to see the infected man just getting to his feet, balancing on the edge of the top step.

'Fuck you,' Sarah shouts and pulls the lever back.

The powerful surge of water takes the infected clean off his feet and down onto the next level. Sarah pulls the hose through and slowly steps down the stairs. Her feet squelching in the sodden carpet. Sarah directs the hose at the infected, spraying it across the short landing and down the next flight of stairs. A look of grim determination on her face. The hose extends far enough for Sarah to jet the infected out of the next door and into the corridor of the 20th floor. Then she rushes forward, spraying it further down the corridor, buying herself time to run back to her own apartment. Tears streaming down her already-soaked face.

Sarah sprints to her door, lurching through and slamming it behind her. Then she slumps down, sobbing and soaked through. Her mind races at what she has witnessed. When this first happened, she'd suspected it was a mass breakdown of civil order and general violence that had happened recently in London and other English cities. Then she spoke to her father, who said it was everywhere. Sarah has been running his words through her mind ever since. What did he mean by *everywhere?*

He couldn't mean worldwide. Surely not the whole world? Zombies and vampires are make-believe, something invented for the movies. They can't exist. Something so frequently seen on television can't just happen, but all the things I have seen must be believed. Zombies have risen and are roaming the land.

Sarah sobs for a long time, unleashing the pent-up misery and isolation of the last few days; crying hard for her family, friends, and the people she had seen being taken down. Tears course down her cheeks, and her body heaves as the sadness pours out of her. Eventually, wet through and shivering from shock, she staggers to the bathroom and pulls off her soaking clothes. She uses the thick cotton towel to dry her body, moving like a robot, without expression, thinking only of what she'd just witnessed a few floors above her, thinking of the decaying bodies that stank of death, with greying skin and saliva drooling out of their mouths, the red, bloodshot eyes, and the horrific injuries on them. She had stabbed that woman again and again, but still, she kept coming, and Sarah replays the action in her head, feeling as the knife bit into the rib bones and jarred her wrist, the suction of the skin as she pulled the knife out, and the fresh blood spurting from the injuries she had caused.

The thoughts and images become too much, and her stomach heaves as she drops down, with her head in the toilet bowl, puking up the tiny tuna meal she had forced down. She stays there for a long time, retching and sobbing into the toilet.

CHAPTER FORTY

We sit in the Saxon, with the engine switched off. We only left Salisbury a short time ago, and we have already passed through several small villages as we progress through the country roads. The first village centre only had a handful of infected in the centre. All of them gathered, once again, in the heart of the village, shuffling and groaning in the scorching sun.

'They're not getting much of a tan, are they? Considering how long they've been out in this heat,' I say to Dave, who is sitting next to me, staring at the mini horde as we drive past.

'No, Mr Howie,' he replies.

'You'd think they'd be burnt to buggery by now.'

'Possibly.'

'But then, there's something in the body, isn't there, that causes the skin to get tanned? I guess dead people just don't tan very well.'

'Pigs do.'

'What?'

'Pigs can get sunburnt.'

'No way! Pigs can't get a suntan.'

'They can.'

'Well, I always thought that cows explode if they don't get milked.'

'Do they?'

'I don't know. I heard that they did.'
'Oh, I've never seen one explode on its own.'
'Well, maybe it's not true then. Hang on! What do you mean – not on its own?'
'Well, I haven't.'
'So have you seen a cow explode, then?'
'Yes.'
'How did it explode?'
'I blew it up.'
'You blew a cow up?'
'Yes.'
'Why? How did you blow a cow up?'
'I put explosives on it and blew it up.'
'You did what?! You can't go around blowing cows up.'
'I had to.'
'Why? Why on earth did you have to blow the poor cow up?'
'To kill the cow herder.'
'What? You blew a fucking cow up just to kill a cow herder?'
'Yes.'
'That makes no sense. Why didn't you just kill *him*?'
'I did.'
'No. I mean, why didn't you kill him some other way like shooting or stabbing, or strangulation, or something other than blowing him up?'
'It had to look like an accident.'
'A fucking accident? Oh, yeah, 'cause cows are always exploding where I live. How on earth can you make an exploding cow look like an accident?'
'He was a courier for explosives.'
'Oh, I see. Well, I guess that makes sense then, I think?'
'He carried explosives for the insurgents, so we rigged the cow to blow up and took him out.'
'Oh, where was that, then?'
'I can't say, Mr Howie.'
I knew he was going to say that.
'Fuck me, look at that lot!' I shout and hear the recruits scrambling forward to try and peer out the front.

'Zombies ahead,' Tucker shouts from his look-out position on the GPMG.

'No shit, really, Tucker? Where are they?' Cookey yells back.

'Ahead,' Tucker shouts down.

'I was being sarcastic,' Cookey calls out.

'What?' Tucker yells.

'I SAID I WAS BEING SARCASTIC,' Cookey bellows out.

'You want some elastic? Try my bag. There might be some in there, mate.'

'Oh, for fucks sake,' Cookey groans.

'Give up, mate, it's a lost cause,' McKinney offers.

So here we are, sitting in the Saxon, looking at a massed horde blocking the road ahead of us. The village doesn't look that big, with just one main road going through a collection of shops and houses. There is a village green off to the right, bordered by a metal fence, and the horde is gathered up against the fence. They start slowly turning around to face us.

'Well, that's a shitload of zombies,' I say to Dave.

'It is, Mr Howie.'

'Do you think that the A P C will get through them?'

'Might do, Mr Howie,'

'Right, lads, buckle up,' I call back.

'TUCKER, HANG ON TIGHT,' I yell up.

'What?' he yells back.

'Ah, he'll be all right.' I restart the engine and push my foot down, making the engine scream with power.

I slowly lift the clutch, and the vehicle shoots forward and...stalls.

'Not a word!' I say as I hear sniggers coming from behind me and try again, going a bit easier with the clutch this time. The vehicle surges forward, gathering speed quite quickly. We plough into the front of the horde, and the hard, metal, square front detonates their heads and bodies, sending them spinning off and knocking more over.

I plough through and feel a slight bump as the massive tyres crush the infected beneath us. The vehicle hardly rocks on the suspension, and within seconds, we are through them, leaving a trail of broken and squashed bodies behind us. The lads all cheer and whistle, and I can hear Tucker shouting something. I stop the Saxon and look over at Dave.

'Did you see that? Fucking brilliant. This thing is awesome,' I sound like an excited child, babbling away. 'They were smashed apart, and we hardly felt a thing.'

'Yes.'

I use the wing mirrors to look back and see the mangled remains and those not-so-injured picking themselves up off the ground.

'Would be a shame to just leave them there, mate,' I say to Dave with a grin.

'Do you want to go back again?' he asks me.

'Yeah, we could, or we could do it the old-fashioned way.'

Dave turns to look back at the recruits in the back.

'Blowers, get those bayonets from the box and show the rest how to fit them on.'

'Yes, Dave,' Blowers answers promptly and somehow makes the word "Dave" sound like "Sarge". I reach down to the floor and lift my axe up. It is all shiny and clean, feeling nice and heavy. I test the blade with my thumb and jerk my hand back from the unexpected sharpness.

'I sharpened it,' Dave says.

'Bloody hell, thanks, mate. You still got the knives, then,' I say as he suddenly has them in his hands. I didn't even see where they came from.

'I put new blades on these too,' he says, staring along the sharp edges.

I can hear the recruits talking quietly and then clicking noises. One of them yelps.

'I fucking told you it was sharp, didn't I?' Blowers says with a scorn. Then, after a few minutes, he shouts out that they are all ready. I feel the adrenalin start pumping, and the anger is knocking at the door, waiting to be let out. I pull the axe and climb down from the high driver's position. The infected are shuffling closer to us, and I hold the axe down at my side as I walk around the front of the vehicle to meet Dave as he climbs out.

The lads jump down and walk back towards us, holding their rifles carefully due to the massive, nasty-looking blades at the end.

'Safeties on,' Dave says to them, and they all look down to check the side of their weapons.

'Strike and move, use the weight of the weapon to drive them back with repeated stabs to the chest and torso. Use the butt of the weapon for blunt trauma. The bayonets are sharp and will slice through their jugulars easily. Be very careful if you have to fire the weapon in close confines. The round will rip through the body and come out the other side,' instructs Dave. An impressively long speech from him.

Finally, Dave turns to me and nods. I start to walk towards the encroaching infected and stop.

'Ready, lads?' I ask the young recruits.

'Yes, Mr Howie,' they nearly all mutter. I turn and stalk towards the infected. The last few metres, I stare hard at the nearest one, a large-built male, and I feel my eyelids twitching, my mind filling with the image of my beloved parents being bitten by one of these foul things. The axe is down at my side as I step closer. Time slows, and I feel my right fist clenching, and before I have any idea what I'm doing, I have slammed my hard fist into the side of the infected man's head. I follow through with a punch and slam him across the road. He staggers but stays on his feet, and I'm on him before he can react, punching again and again with my right fist. The blows send him down onto the ground, and I go still. Waiting. Breathing. I feel them surround me. I feel their presence, and I close my eyes in anticipation.

The danger of being so close to these evil things thrills me. The infection they carry is all around me. Their teeth are being pulled back, and they step and shuffle closer and closer.

I open my eyes and scream into the air as I spin the axe up and around, slicing through skin and bone. I drive the cutting edge towards necks and feel the sharpened blade bite and slice through their evil, tainted, infected skin.

I step backwards and drive down a massive, overhead strike, cleaving through a skull and watching as the brain bursts out and the head implodes. My senses are heightened, and I feel one lunging at my back. I step back and drive my elbow into his face, dropping him instantly. The axe is alive, an extension of my body. We are one, and we destroy those that stand before us. I chop into heads and necks, slicing faces off, biting the vicious blade into collarbones and spinal columns as they fall at my feet. I plough forward, swinging and killing. A quick glance over, and I see Dave moving like water through them, his arms spinning with grace and beauty. A strange man, with an amazing gift, moving like a ballet dancer – his whole body poised, flexing, bending, and stretching with each killing blow. He darts forward and plunges the knives into the chest of an infected woman. His arms a blur as he rapidly stabs and then slices through the jugular, and drops down to avoid the spray that soaks into the eyes of the next one, blinding him. Dave spins around the back, dragging the blade after him as he lunges forward, driving the point of his other knife into the throat of the next one. I go back to work and cleave my way through the bastard horde, the evil, foul things that walk this earth after their natural life has expired. I kill and maim, and leave broken bodies behind me. Then I break through into a clearing and rejoice as I see a fresh and densely packed group ahead of me. The anger has only just warmed up. It has stretched out and flexed muscles and is now ready for the proper workout. I look back and see Blowers driving into them with a look of pure fury on his face. Cookey by his side. The banter and easy jokes gone now as they tear the infected apart. Tucker is screaming with hatred and fear, hacking away. McKinney, Smith, and all of them are in amongst them, and the bodies fall down with hacked and bloodied injuries. I turn back to the horde ahead of me just as Dave gets to my side. We stare at each other, words not needed, and we charge together, roaring into battle. Dave launches himself high into the air and comes down into them. His knives doing the deadly business of sending them back to the hell from whence they came. My axe is breaking them apart.

I pick my targets one by one.

A neck gets cleaved, and the head drops down. I swing the blunt end back, and I crush a skull. I drop the axe low and strike up into bollocks, destroying his chances of ever breeding. I spin and swing the axe behind me, chopping an arm off at the shoulder. Then I go low again and take a leg off at the knee joint. This doesn't kill them, but it pleases me to maim and hurt, and make them fall down onto the bloody and slick ground. We keep going, chopping, slicing, hacking, and destroying until one dirty infected remains, and we gather round him.

Silent faces.

Hard breathing.

The male turns around and around, unable to decide which one of us to try and bite.

Me, Blowers, Cookey, McKinney, Smith, Tucker, Graves, Reese, Hewitt, and Dave stand around this one remaining filthy, dirty, evil fucker.

We stare hard at him, and I see the anger inside each of them. There is glory here, glory in battling alongside brave warriors such as these. Dave steps forward and takes the male by the back of his hair, wrenching his head back and pulling him off his feet. I raise the axe high, driving it down into the exposed neck. As the blow lands, the recruits pile in, and the infected is punctured by eight sharp points from eight sharp bayonets.

'That was fucking beautiful,' Cookey says quietly to nods and murmurs of agreement from all around him. We use wipes to clean the blood from our weapons and skin and then load back into the Saxon.

'At least you didn't try and kiss them this time, Cookey,' Blowers says.

'Fuck you, Blowers. You were stabbing them in the willy,' Cookey retorts.

'The willy? Are you ten or something?' McKinney joins in.

'You were stabbing them in their zombie willies.' Tucker laughs loudly at the infantile language being used.

'You can all get fucked!' Cookey shouts, and the abuse goes on. I drive the Saxon away from the village, away from the devastation and the bodies lying festering in the sun.

CHAPTER FORTY-ONE

The infection watches the one called Howie and his fighters kill many hosts, and the infection watches through the eyes of many hosts to see when they will reappear so it can send the rats into them.

The infection urges the rats on, knowing the small rodent bodies cannot withstand the pace for long; therefore, it must act fast before they perish.

CHAPTER FORTY-TWO

We enter another small village and find a horde gathered outside a florist. The once beautiful flowers in the window are now wilting.

This horde is small in numbers, compared to the previous one. Maybe a dozen of them, at most. I see a child in the group this time. A couple of days ago, I would have blanched at the thought, but now I've hardened, and they are not children any more. They are infected, and they must be dealt with like any other infected.

'Can we stop, please, Mr Howie,' Dave says to me, snapping me out of my thoughts.

'Yes, mate. Why? What's up?' I ask him as I bring the huge Saxon to a halt, causing the recruits to cram forward.

'Practise,' Dave says simply and indicates the small horde.

'Okay, mate.'

The recruits clamber out and gather around Dave at the back of the vehicle. I look at the horde, itching to go for them and take them all out.

'You did well with the last lot, but you were clumsy and slow. We are going to practise on these,' Dave informs the recruits as I lean on my axe.

'Take off the bayonets, and I will show you some basic techniques for using it as a bladed weapon.' The recruits do as instruct and remove the bayonets from the end of the assault rifles. 'Weapons back in the Saxon, and follow me.'

They place their assault rifles back in the Saxon and then walk with him towards the horde.

The sun feels uncomfortably hot.

The infected have turned towards us and started their slow shuffle, but I parked well back to give us time to arrange ourselves, so there is no immediate rush. The recruits gather around Dave, holding the knives self-consciously out in front of themselves, glancing at each other and at the horde.

'Now, you can stab them in the chest, but that won't kill them. It buys you time, and the weight of the thrust can drive them backwards, but it is not a killing blow. Do you understand?' Dave asks and looks at them in turn as they nod.

'The only sure way that I have found of killing them is the neck and head. Even after repeated stabs to the chest and abdomen, they still fight back, so they don't die like normal people, but they do bleed. The bleeding is different, though. A few stabs that would normally render a man lifeless within seconds do not seem to affect them in the same way. The way round that is to cause them a massive loss of blood that even they cannot cope with. Now watch!' Dave walks towards the horde, holding his knives down at his sides. The nearest infected is an adult male, middle-aged and fat. He is wearing a pink, frilly dressing gown that is open, and his wobbly bits dangle as he shuffles along.

'Now, take it easy, Cookey. I know what you are looking at,' Blowers mutters to a few sniggers.

'Yeah, you're just jealous cos he's bigger than you,' Cookey retorts. Dave turns back to look hard at the lads, who fall silent under his intense gaze. Then he simply walks up to the infected and stabs him once in the chest, and leaves the knife embedded in. He quickly steps back as the male bares his teeth and lunges forward.

'See here? This one is now stabbed through the chest with a long-bladed weapon. This would normally drop even the strongest of men, but he does not even flinch,' Dave calls out, and the recruits watch with interest as the male continues to shuffle forward, with the knife handle sticking out of his chest. Dave steps in and stabs with the other knife, driving that one down into his lungs.

'So now, he has two knives in his chest. I have punctured one of his lungs, but still, he does not react, nor does he slow down,' Dave points at the infected.

He then steps forward and pulls both blades out, causing the infected to stagger forward a little from the pressure of the pull.

'Now, a lot of the damage from stabbing is done when the weapon is removed. The embedded blade can cause a seal around arteries and capillaries, and the removal of the weapon breaks that seal, but here we see that although there is blood loss from the wounds, it is far more reduced than with a normal person. Their blood congeals much faster than ours, which means that they can withstand injuries such as this.' Dave turns back to the recruits to make sure they understand. Most of them nod and murmur with interest.

'So a stab will only be of use if it has a single purpose to drive them back, like this,' Dave lunges with frightening speed and stabs repeatedly into the chest and abdomen. His arms blur, and although I have seen him move in several battles now, I am still amazed. The infected is forced backwards from the many punctures and eventually falls down onto the ground. Dave steps away and faces the recruits, not in the slightest out of breath.

'He is still alive.' Dave scratches his head and stares down at the infected trying to rise back up. 'The repeated wounds have not killed him, so we have to look to the rapid blood loss.' Dave steps forward and sweeps his blade across the male's throat, stepping behind him and facing back to the recruits. 'See the arterial blood spraying out? There is nothing known that can congeal, stop, or replenish that amount of blood loss in that short space of time.'

The recruits watch the bright red jet of blood spurting out in waves from the throat, soaking the pink dressing gown and the ground beneath. Within seconds, the infected rolls over and becomes still.

'So, we go for the throat or the brain, but the brain is protected by the hard casing of the skull and requires a significant use of force.' Dave steps to the next one and lightly taps the point of his knife into the skull.

'The skull has to be thick to prevent injury to the brain. So, here I am, hitting the skull with light force, and other than causing minor puncture wounds, I do not affect the brain at all. Now, as I increase the force used, you will see that even a significant amount does not penetrate the bone.' Dave keeps walking round the adult female, digging the tip of the knife into her head.

'Now, in order to penetrate and drive into the brain, you must apply direct force. Do not sweep or slash. Drive the point of the weapon directly into the top of the head.' Dave pulls his arm and slams it down, causing the knife to dig into the skull. Then Dave lets go, and the body falls to the ground, with the knife still stuck in the head.

'Blood is slippery and can easily cause you to lose grip on the handle, and you need a similar amount of force to pull the knife back out. You can see that with a wet handle and the weight of the body dropping, you could lose your grip and then have no weapon.' Dave bends over and grabs the fallen female by the ankle, dragging her over to the recruits.

'I want each of you to feel how hard that blade is stuck in.' The lads all gather around the female's head and take it in turns to pull at the handle, remarking to each other in serious tones how really hard it is stuck in there. This has got to be one of the most surreal scenes I have ever witnessed. A group of eighteen-year-old lads standing round a dead zombie in a quiet village in southern England, discussing how well the knife is stuck in her brain.

Dave then puts a foot on her shoulder and pulls the knife out, then leans down, and wipes the blood on the back of her nightdress.

'Right, I want each of you to try it out,' Dave says as he cleans the blade.

Blowers, Cookey, McKinney, and Smith all move forward to do as Dave says. Tucker hesitates; then, he too moves into the crowd. I watch the lads dodge around and through the horde. Blowers and Cookey both go for the same infected and start arguing about whose it is until Tucker grabs the back of the head and slices cleanly through the neck, dropping the body before smiling and walking back to Dave. They both stare after him, open-mouthed.

A determined look crosses Cookey's face, and he stalks off to viciously pull a head back hard and gouges down into the flesh, sawing away until he almost decapitates it from the body. Eventually, they are all dead, apart from the child, who drools and starts toward Dave. The rest all watch with mixed looks of horror and revulsion. Dave starts forward with his knives, but before he has taken two steps, I have rushed in with the axe and sliced clean through the neck. The body falls slowly to the floor; blood pumping out onto the hot tarmac. I stare back at the recruits until they all look down to their feet or off into the distance.

'It's not a child anymore. They are not people. They will kill you and turn you into one of them. Don't hesitate next time.' I walk back to the vehicle, with a mixture of feelings. Guilty because it was still a child's body, and everything we are ever taught in life is to protect children at all costs – they are the future. Even though I told them it wasn't a child, it has left me feeling numb.

The fuel gauge drops steadily, and I realise the biggest flaw of having a vehicle this size is that the fuel consumption is so high. We will need to refuel before too long. Dave looks at me, having followed my gaze. I can see that he remembers the last time we tried to refuel by putting diesel into a petrol-only tank. We almost got caught by a massive horde as night fell.

'Don't worry, mate, I'll make sure it's the right kind this time.'

'Thanks, Mr Howie.'

Before long, we pass through yet another village, but this one is devoid of life. I slow down so we can look closely, but there are no bloodstains or broken windows. Nothing. This doesn't feel right. Every village we have passed through has had some zombies in it.

'Who is on look-out?' I call back to the recruits.

'McKinney,' Reese shouts back as he is the closest to my end.

'Ask him if he can see anything from up there.'

Reese stands up and speaks with McKinney, who yells down.

'He said no, sir. He can't see anyone.'

'Strange,' I say, and Reese continues leaning forward to look out of the front window.

'Certainly is quiet,' he murmurs.

'What's up?' one of them calls from the back.

'We're going through another village, but it is completely dead, if you'll pardon the expression. There's no one here,' Reese calls back to them.

I hear more of the lads shuffling along to try and glimpse out of the front windows.

'Can I open the rear doors to look out?' one of them shouts. It sounds like Blowers, but he must be at the back, and the vehicle is loud.

'Good idea,' I shout out, and the message gets relayed.

I suddenly hear more noise from the massive wheels going on the road. We drive out of the village and into a country lane. There are wooden signposts stuck into the verge, advertising a Farmer's Fete this weekend. Then, as the road bends around, I see the top of a large, white marquee in a big field off to the left. As we get closer, I can see the tops of cars and vans parked in the adjacent field and a gap in the hedge connecting the two fields. The signposts indicate to turn left for parking. I slow down to try and get a better view, but the hedgerow is too high. I hear McKinney shouting, and I decrease the speed even more, waiting for the message to be relayed.

'McKinney says they are all in the field by the ten. Loads of 'em, sir,' Reese leans forward and tells me.

'Well, we've got to have a look, really,' I say to Dave as I stop the Saxon.

'There are bloody loads in there, sir,' McKinney says as I clamber up onto the roof. I stand up and look over the hedge, and see a large, flat field, with the big, white marquee off to one side. There is a roped-off circular central area and then some smaller tents, and marquees around the outside. This explains where all of the village infected have gone – they are all here. Hundreds of them have gathered in and around the large marquee in various types of nightclothes or completely naked. From a distance, it looks like some weird sex party or a fancy dress shindig, with everyone coming in their pyjamas.

'Fucking look at that,' I mutter to myself. 'You don't see that every day, now, do you?'

'No, sir,' McKinney answers.

'Well, we can't stop and kill every zombie we see, but I feel bad if we just leave them here for some poor, helpless soul to wander into,' I say to McKinney.

'Do you want me to use this, sir?' I look at McKinney, and he taps the top of the GPMG.

'Dave, how much ammo do we have for the GPMG,' I shout down and then see Dave is already climbing up onto the roof.

'Oh, sorry, mate, I didn't mean to yell.'

'That's okay, Mr Howie. We've got loads,' Dave says.

'All yours then, McKinney,' I say to him and move off to the side so I am well out of the way.

A large grin forms on McKinney's face, and he yanks back the lever and aims the gun into the middle of the horde. He hesitates for a few seconds and glances at me again.

'Mate, you don't have to do it. Someone else will...' I say to him.

He shrugs and lets rip with the heavy machine gun.

The noise invades the quiet air, and the infected immediately start falling as they are torn apart by the heavy calibre weapon. The recruits all look up at McKinney, and I know some of them will be jealous that he has the chance to use it and kill so many. Movement catches my eye, and I see Dave waving at me, pointing to the GPMG. I shout out for McKinney to stop firing. Once silent, I shake my head from the sudden cessation of noise and look down at Dave. He has got a large metal container out from the back of the Saxon and opens the lid. The things inside are instantly recognisable. I've seen them a thousand times on movies but never in real life.

Hand grenades. Dave gathers the recruits around him, apart from McKinney, and shows them how to remove the pin and keep hold of the lever, then pulls the arm back for a long throw. Dave leads them all up the lane and into the car park, then through the gap in the hedge until they are in the field and staring at the already reduced numbers of infected.

I can see Dave talking to them but cannot hear what he is saying. From his movement, I guess that he is telling them to throw it far and then find cover.

There is a large tractor, with an evil-looking, giant metal contraption fitted to the end. Dave leads them all over so that the tractor attachment is between them and the infected. He then pulls the pin out of his grenade and uses a big overhead sweep of his arm to launch the grenade into the middle of the packed crowd, shouting 'GRENADE' as he does so.

The explosion that takes place a few seconds later is a lot bigger than I'd expected, and I see several bodies blown up a few feet into the air, and many more drop down from the shrapnel ripping through legs and stomachs. Dave then makes them all take turns to throw a grenade each and shout 'GRENADE' as they launch it.

McKinney and I watch with *oohs* and *aaahs* like a fireworks display as the grenades explode and cause devastation to the horde. The infected closest to the exploding grenades are obliterated with each loud percussive bang. The lads finish lobbing their grenades, and I can see that they are smiling and laughing at the carnage that has been caused.

Dave gives me a thumbs up as they leave the field, and it's safe for McKinney to continue. The GPMG starts up again, and within seconds, they are all dead or at least down, and unable to get back up from their awful injuries.

'That was fucking amazing. Did you see them explode? I fucking love blowing stuff up,' Darren Smith says excitedly as they walk back to the Saxon and load up into the rear.

'Are we going to stop at every village on the way, sir?' Blowers shouts to me.

'It would be nice, but we don't have the time, mate,' I reply, thinking how everyone is calling me sir or Mr Howie now. I'm just a shift manager for a supermarket. How the hell did I end up leading a squadron of zombie killers across the country?

CHAPTER FORTY-THREE

The infection recognises this group of resisters that keep cutting it down. It watches the one they call Howie.

The infection controls billions of hosts across the world, so this handful of losses does not impact it greatly, but the infection feels the loss. Although it does not have emotions or feelings, it has an understanding that they must be stopped.

The infection continues to experiment on the few host bodies across the world that it keeps isolated to practise with. Those few hosts, separated from the hordes, suffer incredible amounts of torture as the infection floods them with the chemicals it learns to produce.

The hosts scream in pain and collapse on the floor when the pain becomes too much. They break down and cry when they are filled with a sudden overwhelming sense of sadness and loss, weeping uncontrollably and pounding their fists into their heads in desperation.

Then they start giggling with glee and laughing uncontrollably. The chemical flow is switched again, and the laughing stops. They become serious and stare hard into the distance as the infection pumps the blood and makes them feel anger; then, the anger increases until they are filled with a burning rage.

The infection knows this is something it can use. The practise hosts are pumped full of this hormone and are released from control to do as they wish, and they move with lightning speed to pound and destroy anything near them. Those that are alone turn on themselves as the blind fury possesses them. They gouge their skin and bite their fingers off, then pummel their own bodies with vicious blows, breaking ribs and knee joints. Some of the control hosts are near other host bodies, and they turn on them with an amazing ferocity. They attack and kill with incredible strength, and the infection allows them to continue, watching through many eyes.

The infection has found something here, something it can use, but it has to learn to harness this power. So, as the first control hosts are killed by their own demented actions, the infection takes more control hosts, and in every land, there are single hosts that step away from the hordes they are with to stand alone.

CHAPTER FORTY-FOUR

Sarah wakes on the sofa. The sobbing and crying had left her feeling drained, and she slept fitfully for a few hours, with horrific images coursing through her sleeping mind. What she experienced has shocked her to the core, and a deep feeling of sadness, loss, and desperation overwhelms her. She doesn't know how long she can keep going, unable to leave her apartment and struggling to survive on just the few tins of food she has left. She paces through her apartment, which helps her to think and forces her mind to work rationally. She can now use work skills to break the problems down into small chunks.

'What do we know?' She starts speaking to herself as she would at work when faced with a difficult or complex matter.

'I'm on the 14th floor, and I only saw them on the 21st floor. There were no signs of them on any floors between here and the 21st floor. Now there is one on the 20th floor. He did not see which floor I ran to, so unless he can smell me, he cannot find me, and I was soaked with water, which will remove any smells. But then I did leave a water trail behind me. Okay, so he *could* find me. But there were no signs of them on the other floors. I have only a few tins of food left but plenty of water, so I can survive, but it will get very hard. Priorities! I need more food. Even if they are infected with whatever this is, they cannot survive forever without food or water . They have been outside in the street now for days, and I haven't seen them eat or drink anything. So I need to eat and wait for them to die, or just fuck off, and leave me alone. But in order for me to survive, I need food, and that means going back out there for more supplies.' She stands still as she realises what must be done. She nods to herself with quiet resolution.

'I have to get more food. Going up is no good, so this time I will go down. I also need weapons.' She rushes into the small kitchen and goes through her cutlery drawers. Waving knives and rolling pins about, she practises with each item, but the knives are no good – stabbing at them seems ineffective. She moves from room to room, looking for anything that could be used. Eventually, back in the kitchen, she finds a large, wooden broomstick that had been left by the previous tenants. She always thought it was odd to have a wooden broom in a tiny, carpeted apartment. Sarah takes the broom and holds it up. It isn't heavy, but it is long. She rummages through more drawers and pulls out a roll of brown parcel tape that she used to secure her moving-in boxes. She takes a long-bladed kitchen knife and tapes it securely to the end of the broomstick handle. She then moves into the lounge and practises lunging and stabbing with it. It isn't perfect, but it will have to do, and she knows that she has to leave now and try again, or the fear will become too much, and she will never be able to leave.

She walks to the door and extends her hand, grasping the handle and pausing to calm her breathing and her rapidly beating heart. She then yanks the door open and jumps out into the corridor like an Amazonian warrior, holding the broomstick out in front like a spear. She faces one way and jumps around to face the other side of the empty corridor. She gets to the stairwell, and each step brings more fear, but the courage grows after each step is taken.

Sarah peers through the glass pane. There is nothing but silence all around. The only signs of her prior encounter are the wet stains on the carpet, but even they are drying quickly in the hot air. Sarah breathes deeply and starts down the stairs, taking each step slowly to make sure her footsteps are masked from noise by the soft carpet. She reaches the door to the 13th floor and again looks through the window, into another empty corridor. She advances slowly, and this time, she opens the fire hose cabinet and pulls the metal head free, making it ready for use. Walking down the corridor, with the spear waving in front of her, the bristle end is just behind her back, and she has to keep twisting it so the flat end doesn't catch on her hips when she pushes the bladed end forward.

She stops at the first door, listens quietly, and only when she is sure there is no noise does she try the handle. *No knocking this time*, she tells herself, *move silently and do nothing to draw attention to yourself.* All the doors on the 13th floor are locked and secure. Sarah was surprised when she discovered the apartment block had a thirteenth floor. A lot of developers still go straight from twelve to fourteen – out of superstition. Sarah descends each floor in turn. Each time, she unlocks the fire hose and pulls the head free in preparation. At the 9th floor, she listens at the first door, hears nothing, and tries the door handle. Moving on, she listens and tries the door handles for each door. At the last one, she pauses for a second as she holds the handle down, resting her head against the door. The tension, fear, and concentration are exhausting, and she rolls her shoulders to ease the pain building across them.

'Who's there?' a voice says softly from the other side of the door, and Sarah opens her eyes wide, suddenly very fearful and not wanting to release the handle in case it gives her away; then, she realises the stupidity of this thought process.

'Hello?' the voice calls again. A soft male voice, full of fear.

Sarah releases the handle and steps to the side, not wanting the person on the other side to see her trough the peephole.

'I saw you move. Who is it?' the voice asks, still soft and very scared.

'I live on–' she pauses, not wanting to give away her floor.

'I live on the 18th floor. I was looking for other people and food,' she says softly, still not wanting to draw too much attention to her location.

'Are you alone?' the voice asks.

'Yes,' she replies. Sarah hears the sounds of the locks being rotated, bolts and chains being removed and pulled back. The door slowly opens, and a man comes into view.

'Hello...Charlie,' Sarah says to the battered and bruised face of the wine bar owner, and he smiles through swollen lips.

CHAPTER FORTY-FIVE

Another bland and boring village, another horde, and again, we stop the Saxon well back from them; the engine switched off to save precious fuel.

The crowd are gathered at the front of some shops on the main road.

'Don't they get bored?' I ask Dave.

'I don't think so,' he replies.

'It doesn't look like they're focussed on anything specific, does it? They're all just aimless.'

'Yes, Mr Howie.'

'I reckon about thirty or so?'

'Twenty-eight.'

'Oh, okay. So, what is it this time? Rocket launchers? Flame throwers? Or are we going for samurai swords?'

'Sniper rifle,' Dave says and gets out of the Saxon to walk around the rear of the vehicle.

'Of course, it is. Why wouldn't it be? I didn't even know we had a sniper rifle,' I mutter to myself as I climb down. The recruits have piled out and are stretching in the sun and chatting quietly.

Dave comes out of the back doors, holding a long bag, which he places on the ground, then unzips the full-length zip. He removes a long, green-coloured rifle. The stock is folded, and Dave pulls it out to its full length and then fixes on a long tube to the end of the barrel. He checks the magazine and fixes it to the bottom of the rifle. Finally, he walks over to the middle of the road and lies down, facing towards the horde.

'This is a L115A3 long-range rifle. The scope is a standard day scope, which increases the magnification by 25. There are five rounds in the magazine. The weapon has an adjustable bipod so the rifle can be settled while you locate the target. This bit here is a cheek piece...'

'What does that do?' Tucker interrupts him to groans from the rest of the recruits.

'You rest your cheek on it,' Dave answers without expression. He waits for a moment, then goes on. 'The suppressor at the front reduces the range, but it also reduces the noise and flash, which thereby serves to keep the sniper concealed and increase his survivability.' Dave pauses to extend the bipod and make minor adjustments as he looks through the scope towards the gathered horde.

They have noticed our arrival and have turned to shuffle towards us, but the distance means it will take them quite a long time to get near us. I keep my assault rifle ready just in case any of them decide to start sprinting.

'The rifle fires an 8.59-millimetre round. This is heavier than some sniper rifles, but it means the round is less likely to be deflected over long ranges. The range is six hundred metres for a solid strike, but it will fire over one kilometre and still be effective.'

The recruits murmur at this, and I'm shocked too at the great distance this thing can cover.

'So, we settle down and breath nice and slowly so we are not jerky. Each movement is slow and controlled. You have to take into account wind speed, but in weather like this and over this distance, that is not an issue. Locate your target and keep your breathing controlled. When you are ready, you squeeze the trigger, do not snatch at it as you will jerk the rifle and ruin your aiming. Squeeze and fire.' The rifle makes a coughing noise, and I watch a head explode in the middle of the horde as the body drops down amongst them.

'Okay, Mr Howie, would you like to try?' Dave asks me.

'I'll try, mate, but you know what I was like with that last rifle.' I go over and drop down to lie flat. I snuggle my shoulder into the end of the stock and rest my cheek on the cheek piece. I always thought that you put your eye right against the scope, but Dave shows me to look through it and locate the target. I choose a fat one, front, centre. His head is wobbling less than the others due to his fat neck.

'Breath gently, identify the target, and move slowly to make adjustments if you need to,' Dave instructs. 'When you are ready, squeeze the trigger.'

I keep the head in sight. It sways from left to right, and I keep focussed on the middle of the sway, breathe slowly, and squeeze the trigger.

The end coughs, and I watch as the head explodes, and the bullet rips through, taking the back of the skull off and going into the chest of another behind the fat one. They both fall down, and the recruits cheer and applaud as I get back to my feet.

'You got two. Well done, sir,' McKinney says, and the rest join in.

I grin back at them, and Tucker hands me my rifle.

'I'll go up on the GPMG while you take your turns,' I say to them, then climb in through the back and up through the hole. I check all around to make sure there aren't any sneaky ninja zombies trying to creep up on us. Dave settles each recruit and goes through the same instructions as he did for me. Blowers first, then Cookey. Tucker struggles due to his larger size and just pulls the trigger quickly, and gets up. Reese goes next and lies down next to the rifle. He calmly settles himself down and stays still for long seconds, making very minor adjustments. He hardly seems to move, and even from this close distance, I cannot see him breathing. He takes the shot, and the round strikes centre forehead, taking the back of the head off in an explosion of blood and brains. He'd aimed for one of the infected at the rear of the group, deliberately choosing a more difficult target. The lads all cheer for Reese, and he responds by going bright red.

'Try another one,' Dave says as Reese starts getting up. He nods and settles back down.

'That one at the back – the small woman in the pink thing,' Dave says.

I look over and see a small-built infected woman at the rear of the group. She is shuffling the same as the rest, but her head is wobbling quickly and erratically.

Reese settles and pauses for long seconds, then squeezes the trigger. The woman drops immediately, with her head blown apart.

'Fucking good shot, mate,' Cookey says and bends down to pat Reese on the back.

'That was very good, mate. Well done,' Blowers says. Reese blushes even more as Dave watches him closely.

'Let him do another one,' McKinney calls out, and the others all shout in agreement.

'Okay, I want you to take the one on the far right with the white shorts and then the naked one on the far left,' Dave says, 'but I want them both shot within ten seconds of each other.'

Reese nods and identifies both targets through the scope, sweeping from right to left, then back again. He aims for the male on the right with the white shorts and takes the shot. The infected drops as before, and Reese racks the bolt and sweeps over to the left, and pauses just for a couple of seconds, then takes the second shot. This one strikes her in the mouth, and the infected gets thrown backwards as the bullet explodes through the back of the skull.

'Sorry, I missed the second one,' Reese says apologetically as he stands up.

'You rushed, and sliding the bolt threw you off a little,' Dave says to him.

I'm amazed at the criticism. Two headshots like that were amazing, but Reese nods at Dave.

'Yeah, it felt rushed. I adjusted my position as I reached for the bolt, and I didn't need to,' Reese explains. Dave allows the rest of the recruits a go. Nearly all of them miss head shots, and they all seem flat after Reese's amazing efforts.

'Jamie, you finish them off,' Dave says to Reese as the rest of them stand back.

Reese nods quietly and goes to drop down.

'Go on top of the Saxon,' Dave tells him, and Reese obliges in silence as he clambers up, and the rifle is passed to him. I drop down from the GPMG hole and climb out to join the others.

'I will number them for you, starting from the front and always moving from right to left as they go back, got it?' Dave calls up.

'Got it,' Reese affirms quietly.

'Front, centre, large-built male is one. Two is the female with blonde hair. Three is the old man in the striped pyjamas,' Dave continues to count them out, showing Reese his method of selecting multiple targets.

'Ready?' Dave calls.

'Yes,' Reese replies softly.

Dave waits a few seconds, then calls out, 'ONE.'

Reese takes the shot, and the large-built infected drops.

Dave calls out, 'TWO.' And the blonde gets blown away.

Dave calls out, 'FIVE.' And Reese instantly adjusts to identify the target and drops it.

Dave keeps going, calling out random numbers.

Reese only gets one wrong, but all of them are headshots.

There is utter silence, apart from the numbers being called out and the coughing noise from the rifle.

The last one drops to an outburst of loud cheering and clapping from all of us. Even Dave claps and smiles at Reese as he gets down.

'Very good,' Dave says to him simply, and I see Reese swell with pride from the praise.

'So, we have a sniper in the team,' I say to Reese and shake his hand.

He looks down, clearly uncomfortable.

'Right, let's get loaded and gone from here. Time is ticking, and we need fuel,' I call out, and the lads all load up. I get into the driver's seat and look across as Blowers gets into the passenger seat.

'Dave is showing Jamie how to strip and clean the rifle, so you've got me for a bit, Mr Howie,'

'Okay, mate, no worries.' I start the engine, and we pull away, driving straight over the bodies and crushing them into the road.

The country roads give way to more urban areas, and despite the fuel getting lower, I keep the speed up as we drive through the towns. The signs of devastation and severe civil uproar are everywhere just like in Portsmouth: burnt-out cars and vehicles, shop fronts smashed in, and bodies everywhere. Some of the houses have been burnt out too, and there are more signs of fire-damaged buildings the deeper we go.

Dave has swapped with Blowers now and is sitting up front with me again. Curtis Graves is on the GPMG, and the rest of them stay quiet. The villages were quaint, but we didn't really see signs of just how severe the outbreak is. But here is different. It's gritty, and it reminds me that a whole lot of people live in this country, and every single one of them has been deeply affected by this event. The tragedy is everywhere – in the roads and streets, in the smashed-in buildings, with their front doors hanging open. Bloodstains and smears are all over the roads and on road signs, and metal railings. The bodies that we see are festering and already rapidly decaying in the hot summer sun.

'We'll take the motorway into London,' I say to Dave.

'Okay, Mr Howie.'

The road leads us through the centre of the town, and we see the high street stores have been looted, debris and everyday items litter the ground. There are very few infected, though. Just a couple here and there, shuffling along and slowly turning to watch us as we drive past. A man runs out in front of the road ahead of us, waving his arms and shouting loudly. I didn't see where he came from; although, it must have been from one of the shops or buildings. I slow the vehicle down, and he stays in the middle of the road, trying to stop us with his physical presence. I slow to a full stop, with him standing just a few feet in front of us. He walks around to my side and looks up as I open the window slightly.

'Thank god. I knew the army would come,' the man shouts. He is middle-aged and dressed in suit trousers and an office-style shirt, now filthy with grime.

'We're not the army, mate. We're just using this vehicle,' I say to him.

'Well, you've got a man on the top with a machine gun,' he shouts back.

'Er... Well, yes, but we're just trying to get somewhere.'

'You have to help. I got trapped trying to get supplies, and I can't get back to my family. I tried to go back, but they're surrounded by those things!' the man shouts in desperation and indicates a side street. Tears are streaming down his face, and he looks petrified.

I glance over to Dave, who shrugs his shoulders.

'How far away are they?' I ask him. I don't want to keep stopping, but he's clearly desperate.

'Down there, not far, honestly, just down there.' He moves from foot to foot, pointing back to the side street off to the left.

'Okay, hop on the ledge and direct us.'

The man climbs up, holding onto the wing mirror and balancing on the driver's step. I drive forward, and the man keeps waving to the side street and shouting, 'Down there, down there!'

I turn in and drive down the road for a few hundred metres.

'Down this road.' The man waves to a residential street, and I see a handful of infected immediately outside a terraced house.

'Bloody hell, mate. There's only a few of 'em. I thought you said there were loads.'

'There is loads. Look at them! I'll never get through them.'

'Are you being serious?' I look at the man incredulously.

'What? How am I supposed to get through them!' he cries.

'What about weapons? You must have armed yourself.'

'Well, I've never really believed in violence, and I don't like weapons,' he says defensively.

'Oh, but it's all right for us to use our weapons?' I shout at him.

'But you're the army...'

'We are *not* the bloody army,' I cut across him. 'You are not going to survive very long without weapons and being willing to bloody use them.'

'But–' he tries to stammer.

'No *buts*, mate. You said you have a family in there – kids and a wife?'

He nods.

'So *man up* and defend your family.' I push the door open, and he falls off the ledge. I take my axe and walk towards the five zombies that are shuffling around his front door. The recruits are bursting out of the Saxon and running towards us with their knives, and Dave is already at my side as I walk up to the closest one and behead him as he turns round.

I follow through with the swing and take another one down. Dave has already dropped the other three by the time the recruits get close, and they all stop, looking disappointed, and slowly turn, and walk back towards the vehicle. The man is staring open-mouthed at Dave and me and then at the bloodied bodies on the ground.

'What's up, mate? Was that too violent for you?' I say as I walk past him to the Saxon.

We drive back up the side streets, onto the main road. I glance back once in the mirror, and he's still standing there, gaping. His arms hanging at his sides.

We enter the featureless and empty motorway and keep driving towards London. We have no satellite navigation, just a road atlas. Getting into London will be easy enough, apart from the millions of zombies, but finding where my sister lives will be extremely hard.

At least we don't have to worry about one-way roads, no entry signs, or traffic build-ups now, and we won't have to pay the London congestion charge. Mind you, I imagine there will still be someone sat in their offices, clocking the vehicles and sending out letters to their home addresses. A city the size of London should have lots of survivors holed up, so maybe they have already started cutting the numbers of infected down.

That radio message said that London was infected and to stay away, but that was a few days ago now. I imagine driving through an empty city centre, with piles of zombie bodies stacked up neatly, ready to be burnt.

It won't be like that, but a man is allowed to dream.

'There's some services on this road,' Curtis Graves calls out.

'Thanks, mat. How do you know that? I guess you've been here before then?'

'We used to go to 4x4 vehicle shows and take our old Land Rover. Dad always worked out each service station so we could stop if it broke down,' Graves says.

'And did it break down?'

'Rarely. They tend to go on forever, especially the old ones. You just need a few tools and a working knowledge, and they are easy to fix.'

'How far up this road, mate?' I say, looking down at the fuel gauge that is now only a little bit above the red line.

'Only a few miles, not far.'

'Do any of you know how to get fuel out when there is no power?' I shout.

'I know they either have to press a button inside the kiosk to allow the fuel out, or it's done on an automated system when the cameras have had time to record the registration number,' Nick Hewitt shouts down to me.

'What about now, with no power in the service station?'

'I don't know, but some of the main services have to have backup generators in case of power outages so they can still get fuel to the emergency services and stuff,' Hewitt shouts.

'Curtis, is this service station a large one?' I ask him.

'Yes, sir, it's the only one for quite a while.'

'Okay, we'll aim for that then. We have to get fuel, and Dave has experience with generators.' I cast him a glance as I remember him electrifying the metal gates outside the police station.

'Dave and Curtis, can you two go for the generator? Nick, I want you to try and find out how to activate the pumps if we manage to get the power back on. Darren, you take the GPMG, and Jamie, go up top with the sniper rifle. The rest of us will spread out and keep watch, got it?'

I get a chorus of yeses from behind me. I glance over and see Dave staring at me, and although his face is blank, I can tell he is thinking of something.

'What?' I ask him.

'Nothing, Mr Howie.'

'Was that a bad plan? Change it if you want to, mate. Sorry, I should have checked with you first.'

'It's a good plan.' He looks back to the front.

'It is a very good plan.'

CHAPTER FORTY-SIX

Sarah stands in the apartment's entryway, with the front door directly behind her, staring at Charlie. Her makeshift spear is lowered but is still pointing towards him, and he keeps glancing nervously at the large blade taped to the end.

'I didn't know you lived here, too,' Charlie says.

'Or you,' Sarah says.

'You been here long?' he asks.

'A little while.' She watches him gingerly touch his bruised and battered face. His lips are still swollen, and the bruising has gone a sickening shade of yellow.

'It still hurts,' he moans.

'Does it?' Although this is the first person she has seen in days, Sarah is not overwhelmed with joy to see the sleazy bar owner.

'So where is your wife?' she asks.

'Err... I haven't seen her for a few days,' he mumbles quietly and looks away.

'Doesn't she live here with you?' she asks him, puzzled.

'Err, well, she did, kind of.' He looks very uncomfortable.

'You left her there when all this was happening? You left her on her own?' she demands; her voice rising slightly.

'Well, it was all going mad, and someone had to stay and lock up. I needed to get changed after that crazy man attacked me for no reason.'

'That crazy man was the boyfriend of a woman you groped. I'm surprised it didn't happen a long time ago,' Sarah shouts.

'What woman?' a tall girl with long, straight, black hair asks. She has a slight accent.

'Oh, hello,' Sarah says, surprised.

'Hello. What woman?' she repeats.

'I'm Sarah. Nice to meet you,' Sarah says.

'Hello, Sarah. I'm Vivien.' The woman is strikingly beautiful with high cheekbones, but with a surly, pouty face. 'What woman?' Vivien looks to Charlie and then back at Sarah. Charlie visibly squirms under her gaze.

'Excuse me, Vivien, I don't mean to be rude, but Charlie was just telling me how he left his wife at the bar when all of this happened.'

'Not my problem,' Vivien shrugs.

'He left her to die,' Sarah says, shocked at the coldness of the woman.

'Like I said, not my problem,' Vivien says again, pouting.

'So, how did you get here?' Sarah asks the woman.

'Charlie got me from the hotel on Friday night,' she replies expressionlessly.

'The hotel?' Sarah asks.

'I was staying in a hotel near here. Charlie came and got me, and we came here.'

'You fucking scum! You left your wife to die and went to get your girlfriend instead?' Sarah shouts at Charlie.

'I didn't know what was happening. I was coming home to get changed and picked Vivien up on the way...'

'You were beaten up for groping another woman, and then, when the whole world erupts, you slink off to get your mistress from the hotel she is hiding in to have a quickie at home?' Sarah shouts loudly now, gripping the spear hard.

'What woman? You said there was a fight at the bar!' Vivien shouts at Charlie, erupting in anger.

'You fucking cunt, you said there was a fight, but a man beat you up for grabbing his girlfriend? You dirty fucking animal!' Vivien screams, her accent getting stronger with the instant rage.

Sarah stares in shock at the sudden outburst.

Vivien turns and walks into the bedroom and slams the door. She reopens it a few seconds later and stands there with her arms folded.

'You fucker. You got me in a hotel, waiting for you, and your wife at home, and you were touching some other woman? You disgust me. Filthy fucker!' Vivien shouts; her face contorted with anger.

'No, Viv, I didn't. I promise I didn't. It was all wrong – just some mad bloke,' Charlie pleads with her.

'You can fuck off with your promises. You make empty promises, always empty promises.'

'Viv, please...' he looks at her pleadingly.

'I gave up a life for you, a home with a decent man. I gave up my job and my studies and got into debt. I had a life, and you promised me you would take care of me. I even had to pay my own fucking hotel bill, you cheap, dirty man!'

'Err, excuse me. Have you seen what's going on out there?' Sarah interjects.

'I don't fucking care!' Vivien screams.

'Well, I do. As far as we know, the whole world has fallen. That creep left his own wife to die, and now you're arguing about him touching up another woman?'

'Who the fuck are you to talk to me? Don't talk to me, you fucking whore. You're all whores in this country!' Vivien screams. The veins in her neck bulging out, and suddenly, she isn't so beautiful.

'Okay, listen, Vivien. Those *things* are in the building, and if you don't keep your voice down, they will come here,' Sarah says, with a firm, level voice.

'This is your fault,' Vivien turns back to Charlie. 'This is all your fault, you fucking prick, and now we're going to die in this shithole.'

'Now, listen to me, you bitch. You made your choice, and now it's too late, so don't fucking moan at me,' Charlie retorts in anger.

'What!? I'm moaning, am I? You promised me a life, and this is what I get? You cheap bloody man.'

'Viv, you're a cheap bitch that fell for it. That's your fault. What did you expect from me? I'm fucking married, for god's sake.'

Vivien runs across the room and starts pummelling his body and face with her fists. Her long, black hair flying about.

Sarah slowly backs away, fearing the loud noise will draw the infected. She quietly opens the front door and checks the corridor, then pulls the door closed behind her. The sound of the raised voices and glass smashing can still be heard as Sarah reaches the stairwell and goes down to the next level.

The noise will draw those things, but it will also mask any noise she makes, so she moves onto the next level, trying door handles and then thinking to check under the floor mats. The next couple of floors are all locked and secure, but then she gets lucky and finds a shiny key under a mat outside a door. She quietly listens and then slides the key in, gently pushing the door open. Once again, the apartment is a replica of hers – the layout and the room sizes are the same, just the décor is different. She eases forward slowly, making each step land softly and shifting her weight from foot to foot. The lounge is clear. She checks the bedroom and bathroom, which are also empty, and breathes a sigh of relief as she rushes into the kitchen and checks through the cupboards. The various tinned goods get swept into a bag that she finds in a drawer, plus some rice cakes and unopened cartons of orange juice. Within minutes, she is back outside and replaces the key under the mat, just in case the owner returns and also in case she gets stuck away from her apartment again.

Back in the stairwell, she climbs up and pauses when she reaches Charlie and Vivien's floor. She slowly peeks through the door, and her heart sinks as she watches the infected shuffle along the corridor, towards the still raised voices.

Sarah shakes her head at the blind stupidity of it all and begins making her way back to her own apartment. On the next floor up, she has to dart back down and hide as an infected shuffles through the door and into the stairwell; the slow and heavy footsteps resound on the carpet as the cumbersome thing drops down each step. The infected moves slowly, and Sarah keeps backing further down, staying out of sight until it follows the sound of the voices and enters the corridor.

Sarah wastes no time and sprints up the stairs until she reaches her own floor, where she checks that it is empty. Then she runs back into the safety of her own apartment, heady, with the sense of victory at the accomplished mission and the gained supplies.

CHAPTER FORTY-SEVEN

We drive down the slip road to the services, following the long, narrow route until we reach a fork in the road. I take the right path and drive into a service station. Several rows of fuel pumps with green and black handles are stretched across the centre. The pumps on the far end look bigger, and I guess they are for commercial-sized vehicles. I aim for those pumps and stop before I reach them.

'Which side is the fuel cap on?' I ask Dave, and he jumps out and checks both sides.

'Your side,' he shouts up.

'Cheers, mate.' I slide the Saxon alongside the pumps while Dave waves me forward and then holds his hand up.

'Okay, lads, let's go,' I shout out, and the rear doors are thrown open. The recruits pile out. Curtis runs to Dave, and they both set off towards the rear of the building, carrying their assault rifles at the ready. Darren Smith is already up top on the GPMG, and I watch Jamie clamber up with the sniper rifle and then start sweeping the area through the scope. Blowers then directs Cookey, Tucker, and McKinney to take a side each. They respond quickly and spread out. I watch them rack their bolts back and make ready. Within seconds, everyone is where they should be, and I glance over to see Nick Hewitt trying to force the doors open.

'Is it locked?' I shout to Nick.

'Yep, locked up tight,' he calls back.

'Fuck, I wasn't expecting that. I can't believe it's still locked and hasn't been looted yet,' I join him at the electric doors, which are shut tight and secure.

'I'll get the axe, hang on.' I run to and from the Saxon, and then I take a big swing and strike the glass in the middle, holding my head away to avoid any flying glass. The axe has dented the glass, but that's it. I strike again and again, but the glass holds tight.

'Security glass,' I say to Nick. 'Try shooting it.'

I step back and turn round to face the other direction.

'NICK IS GOING TO SHOOT THE DOORS,' I call out so the others don't panic when they hear the shots. Nick aims and fires once. The round makes a hole in the glass pane, but otherwise, no damage. I use the axe to strike at the bullet hole, hoping it has weakened the structure, but it holds fast.

'Fuck this. Hang on, mate.' I run back to the Saxon, climb into the back, and start checking through the various storage sections until I find a nice, long, thick chain, with a hook on one end. I find a hole at the bottom front of the Saxon and attach one end of the chain, then stretch it across to the doors and wind it through the bar handles several times. Once back in the Saxon, I engage the reverse gear, and the chain pulls tight. I apply slightly more pressure to the gas, and the doors are pulled clean off and get dragged a few feet until I stop and drive back to where we were. Hewitt runs straight into the shop area, and I see him make for the counter. Curtis comes running round to the front, towards me.

'We've got it ready. It should be on in a minute or so, sir,' he yells as he gets closer.

'Well done, mate. We just need Nick to figure out how to turn the pumps on now.'

CHAPTER FORTY-EIGHT

The infection tracks the group through the countryside and towns and watches the one they call Howie using the axe and the other smaller one cutting throats.

The infection watches them as the smaller man teaches others to use knives to kill the hosts, cutting into their necks.

The infection sends the rats to find them, and soon, the black bodies are popping up to fix their gleaming, black eyes on the small group.

CHAPTER FORTY-NINE

'Fucking look at the size of that rat!' Cookey shouts, and we all turn to see a big, fat, black rat sitting on the top of a waste bin, off to the side of the fuel station.

'That's fatter than you, Tucker,' McKinney shouts.

'Fuck off. We like our food, don't we, my lovely?' Tucker shouts towards the rat.

'Argh, they're disgusting. I fucking hate rats,' Blowers says.

'Must be full up from chomping on all of those bodies,' Tucker says with gruesome relish.

'Ah! Tucker! That's fucking gross, you dirty bastard,' Cookey shouts at him. I watch the rat watching us. There is no fear in it, and I guess that they have evolved and gotten braver.

'That fucking thing is watching us,' Blowers says with disgust.

'Jamie, do you think you could hit that rat from up there?' I shout over to him. He nods and lies down on top of the Saxon, aiming towards the litter bin.

I hear a slight cough, and the rat is blown apart in a burst of pink and black fur. We all cheer, and Jamie gives a slight nod and carries on scanning the area.

'He's morphing into Dave,' I mutter under my breath.

THE INFECTION WATCHES the group and the one they call Howie walking back and forth. The smaller one has gone out of sight, but they are all holding those long things that kill the hosts so easily.

The rat sits and watches the group, fully controlled by the infection as it takes in the area. The rat is made to piss down the sides of the waste bin so that others can track its location. Another one pops its head out from some bushes further back and watches the rat on the waste bin.

Then another one climbs out from under a drain cover and watches the one in the bushes.

More start popping out all around the area, watching the others and marking the site, pissing where they stand so that the infection can use their powerful sense of smell. Within minutes, there are rats throughout the fuel station site. Their red eyes almost glow against the darkness of their fur. The scent markers work, and rats from miles around are sent surging towards the location. A scent trail is laid by each rat as it gets closer to the smells left by the preceding rodents. Survivors fighting for their lives against the rats invading their homes are suddenly dumbfounded when the rats turn as one and start running away. They look out of their windows and peek holes to see a thick carpet of black bodies all running in one direction. The motorway that Howie and the recruits used just a short time ago is slowly filling with sleek, black bodies and fat, black bodies – first, in ones, then twos, then small groups until they are piling in from the sides, the drain covers – all pushing towards one direction. Slowly, the infection is able to watch the group from many different eyes, but it holds the rats back and waits. The infection has learnt to resist the urge to send these small hosts in. It must wait until there are enough to overwhelm them.

'GOT IT,' Nick Hewitt bellows from behind the counter.

'Well done, mate, nice one,' I say from the end of the aisle.

I had just taken cans of warm drinks out to the lads, carrying them in a basket and letting them select the ones they wanted. Then, while I was waiting for Dave and Nick to figure out how to get the power supply to switch to the generator, I stocked up the back of the Saxon with more chocolate bars and snacks.

The room suddenly fills with light, and the chilled cabinets start up with a clunk and a whirl. The pumps outside make a noise, and I watch the lads all turn to look at them and start smiling.

'Is the pump ready, Nick?' I ask him.

'Um, hang on, sir. I'm just figuring it out.'

'How do you know about these things? Have you worked in fuel stations before?'

'No, sir. I just like technology and electrical stuff, computers, that kind of thing. I love figuring out how stuff works.'

'Oh, right. I thought all of you were unemployed?'

'We were. I was.'

'How come if you can do this kind of thing? There must have been employers out there desperate for blokes like you.'

'I'm dyslexic, sir.' He looks up at me with a grin. 'The army was going to help with that. Well, they were going to... Anyway...'

'Bloody hell, didn't they do that at school?'

'Not really. They thought I was pissing around and just not trying, and by the time they figured it out, it was too late really, and I lost interest. I was bunking off all the time. Oh, here we are. Right. That should be it.'

'Have you done it?'

'I think so. Try it now and give me a shout if it doesn't work,' he says as I leave the store and cross to the pumps.

I unwind the fuel cap and sniff the hole, just to be sure it's diesel and not petrol. I wouldn't have thought these things would run on petrol. That would cost a fortune, but after the last time we put the wrong fuel in, I double check. I press the lever in on the black handle and feel the vibration as it starts to pump fuel into the tank. I give a thumbs up back to Nick, who returns the gesture and starts walking out from behind the counter. Then he stops and goes back, and slides up the metal shutter that hides the cigarette display. He looks over at me, gesturing towards the tobacco display. From his manner, it appears he is asking if it's okay to take some cigarettes.

Bless him. He doesn't have to ask me.

I give him another thumbs up and nod vigorously, showing that I don't mind. The fuel pumps steadily into the tank as I watch Nick load up bags with all of the cigarettes, tobacco, papers, and lighters and stroll back outside.

He goes over to the lads and shows them the contents, and I'm surprised when Blowers, Cookey, and McKinney all take a packet and light up.

Tucker declines and walks over to the Saxon as Dave walks back around from behind the building with Curtis.

'Do you want a packet, sir?' Nick asks me.

'Nah, you're all right, mate. I gave up a little while ago. Would be a shame to start now – right at the end of the world.'

'Okay, lads, do you want any smokes?' Nick calls up to Jamie and Darren on top of the Saxon.

'Yeah, I will in a minute, mate. Best not smoke here, with all this fuel about,' Darren calls down.

'Probably a good idea,' I say.

'Is it okay if I go over to the side for a smoke, sir?' Nick asks me.

'Yeah, mate, no problem.'

Dave walks up and watches the fuel handle. Curtis joins Nick Hewitt and Blowers chatting away and takes a packet of cigarettes, opens it up, and lights one. They all stand chatting, blowing smoke into the air, and I notice they keep their observations up and are constantly scanning the area.

'Fuck me. They nearly all smoke,' I say to Dave.

'Squaddies, Mr Howie. They nearly all smoke.'

'I thought soldiers had to be super fit.'

'There's a difference between being fit and being healthy.'

'Have you ever smoked, Dave?'

'No, Mr Howie.'

'I used to, but I gave up. Watching them now makes me want one, though.'

'Are you going to have one?' he asks me.

'God no, far too expensive. I can't afford them anymore.'

'True, they do cost a lot,' Dave answers, missing the joke. 'Or you could just sign for them, seeing as you're a manager…' he says, *not* missing the joke.

'Bloody hell, Dave. Did you just make a joke?' I ask him, shocked at his reference to when I met up with him in the supermarket and tried to get him to take some clean clothes from the clothing section. He had refused, saying he had no money, and I told him I would sign for them.

Dave just gives a slight smile, but his eyes are glinting.

'Well, mate, you *are* changing. Becoming an instructor, smiling, and even making jokes now. I just don't recognise you anymore. You've changed. You're not the person I met.' I smile at him. He looks puzzled and stares at me.

'I am,' he says.

'I was just joking, mate.'

'Oh, okay.'

'SIR!' Jamie Reese shouts out loudly from his position above us on the Saxon.

'What's up, Jamie?' I lean back to look up at him, but he is facing the other way.

'Sir... There are lots of rats all around us.' Reese says.

'Rats? I wouldn't worry, mate. They're just getting brave now that all the people are gone.'

'I don't think so, sir. Maybe you should look.' He sounds concerned, and I get Dave to hold the pump lever down while I clamber up top.

'Where, mate?' I ask him once I'm next to him.

'Everywhere, sir. Have a look,' he says. I take the rifle and look through the scope. I scan from left to right.

'You're too high, sir. Look down to the bottom of the bushes, at the edge of the car park,' Jamie says.

I can just see the top of the main services building where the shops and cafés are. I lower down to the bushes. As I focus and watch, I see black shapes emerging and then staying still. I sweep along the bottom of the bushes and can see hundreds and hundreds of rats, all looking in our direction. I keep sweeping and see more emerging every few seconds, and my heart misses a beat as I notice their small, beady, red eyes.

Zombie eyes.

Zombie rats.

They don't move, though, but just squat still, watching all of us.

'Everyone, back in the Saxon right now, but do not run,' I shout out.

I hear footsteps as the lads all start heading back. All of them quiet, and I can tell by the noise they are walking fast.

The pump switches off as Dave extracts the nozzle, and I hear the clunk as he rests it back on the stand. More and more rats are coming into the perimeter, and I sweep the scope over to the access road and almost shout out when I see a thick, black carpet of undulating bodies sweeping towards us.

'Smith, get that gun aimed on the access road leading in. Is everyone loaded up?' I shout down.

'Apart from you and Jamie, yes. What's going on?' I hear Blowers say.

'Lads, there are thousands of rats watching us and more are coming. They are wild zombie rats. Jamie, I want you to get back inside, mate.' I hear movement as Jamie drops down to the rear and climbs into the back.

'Smith, you drop down, mate. I'll take the machine gun. Curtis, can you hear me?'

'Yes, sir,' Graves replies.

'Get up front, into the driver's seat and get us out of here,' I say, trying to keep my voice level and calm. I glance over and see that Darren Smith has dropped back down.

I lower the sniper rifle and ease myself into the hole, and take over the GPMG.

I pull the lever back and aim directly at the entrance to the access road. Movement catches my eye, and I look over to the shop area. The fuel pumps are covered by a large, flat roof to keep customers dry when they are filling up. The store building also has a flat roof – only inches away from the edge of the fuel pump roof. Black bodies are running and jumping onto the fuel pump area roof.

'Shit, they're above us. Quick, Curtis, get us out of here!' I shout down.

The engine starts, and I hear Curtis grinding the gears as he tries to select first. Then I hear skittering noises directly above me as the rats' tiny claws scratch against the top of the metal roof. I look back to the hedgerow just as thousands of rats burst out and start running directly towards us. More are coming from the other side, and within seconds, the ground is covered by the rodents as they surge forward.

'NOW, CURTIS!' I bellow, and then realise that if I open up with the GPMG, I run the risk of hitting the fuel pumps, which would blow us all sky high. The Saxon starts forward and rolls away from the fuel area. The rats are already close to the vehicle, and I move around in a circle to see them come from all directions. Curtis increases his speed and turns to go back down the access road, which we came up on. The tyres start hitting the rats, and I hear popping noises and crunches as they are squashed under the giant wheels.

'KEEP GOING,' I yell and wait until we are clear of the fuel pumps before opening up with the GPMG.

The rats' bodies are small, but there are so many of them that I can't see the road surface now. The heavy calibre machine gun rips through them, sending bodies flying into the air. But for every rat that is torn apart by the machine gun, several more appear.

I spin around to face back towards the pumps and see them pouring around the sides of the building, all heading our way. Now thousands of rats with red, bloodshot eyes surge towards us, and as we clear the end of the flat roof, I see bodies dropping down onto the top of the Saxon.

'FUCK! THEY'RE ON THE TOP!' I scream out and feel the Saxon give a burst of speed as Curtis tries to shake them off.

Several of them fall off, but a few remain and start walking towards me, rocking with the motion of the vehicle. I can't shoot them as I don't know if the rounds will penetrate the armoured vehicle from this close range, and the gun won't aim down that low anyway.

I open fire on the fuel station and pour rounds into ground level.

Bodies get burst apart and blown away, and I see mini explosions of blood as the large bullets rip through their bodies. I keep firing, and the rounds hit the fuel pumps. I aim for the one we were using. As we get onto the access road and are crushing hundreds of rats beneath us, the fuel pump explodes into flames with a massive bang. Thick, black smoke billows up and rolls across the flat roof and over the sides. The fuel in the pipes gets set alight, and within seconds, the other pumps are exploding, sending scorched bits of rat bodies past me from the pressure wave.

Each pump goes with a massive *bang*, and a huge fireball erupts upwards, incinerating the flat roof within seconds. The structure collapses from the sudden, intense heat, which sends more flames and smoke billowing out the sides. Another huge fireball explodes, and this one is much bigger than the previous. The remains of the roof are launched high into the sky, and jagged chunks of metal fly off in different directions.

One large chunk is sent wheeling through the air, directly at us, and I drop down just as it bounces off the rear and goes spinning over us, landing directly in the path of the Saxon.

Curtis slams the brakes on, and we all go flying forward, then off to the side as he steers around the obstacle.

'There's fucking thousands of them,' I shout out above the noise of the engine screaming and the huge explosions behind us.

Just as I move back towards the GPMG hole, a big, fat, black rat drops down onto the floor of the Saxon. We all shout and scream, and start stamping down with our boots, but the speedy body darts and weaves through us.

Another fat body drops down, and now we are trying to stamp down on two of them. Tucker's big boot gets the first one, which explodes under his foot, bits of blood and fur spraying out.

'Fucking got him,' Tucker yells with victory.

'Get that other fucker, then,' Cookey yells as we keep trying to stamp down and kick it. The rat is darting about very fast and trying to leap up at our legs, the long, yellow teeth bared and gnashing with ferociousness.

'Yeah, got both of the fuckers,' Tucker yells as his massive boot crushes the next one.

'Thank fuck for that. I fucking hate rats.' Blowers sinks back onto the bench seat just as several more rats drop down from the hole and start running around the back.

'CURTIS, WE HAVE TO STOP!' I shout out as we all dance up and down, stamping our feet.

'THEY'RE EVERYWHERE, THOUGH,' Curtis yells back.

'HEAD FOR THE SERVICES BUILDING. FUCKING QUICKLY, TOO.'

We all jolt as the Saxon goes in a straight line and speeds up, bouncing over the kerbs and lane dividers. We keep jumping and slamming our feet down as a rat jumps onto the front of Darren's trousers and starts climbing up his legs, onto his stomach.

Blowers punches out hard and strikes the rat in the middle of its body. The rat drops down, but the blow is hard and knocks Darren back onto the benches.

'Sorry, mate,' Blowers shouts.

'It's okay,' Darren yells as he gets up, winded but still dancing on the spot.

'ALMOST THERE. MAKE READY,' Dave bellows at the top of his voice, and we all try to pick our assault rifles and bags up as we bounce up and down; black bodies scurrying and jumping at our boots.

'BRACE,' Dave yells, too late, as Curtis slams the brakes on, bringing the Saxon to a grinding halt.

We all go flying, and I drop down onto my hands and knees. A rat launches at my face and is kicked aside by a black boot.

'THANK YOU!' I shout as I get back up, and we all scrabble to get to the back doors, bursting out onto the concrete just a few feet away from the front doors.

'GET INSIDE,' Dave yells, and we all start running to the doors. Dave gets there first and slams into them, but bounces off.

'LOCKED,' he yells and starts kicking at the doors. I get to his side and glance back to the car park. We have gained a few seconds, but the rats are pouring across the car park. I start hammering on the doors and see someone moving around inside. A man appears, running towards the doors, but stops when he sees several armed and crazy-looking men yelling at him.

'OPEN THE DOORS,' Dave shouts, but the man walks a bit further, then stops, and stares back at us. A terrified look on his face. Dave steps back and aims his assault rifle directly at the man.

'I CAN SHOOT YOU FASTER THAN YOU CAN RUN. OPEN THE DOORS, NOW.'

The man jerks forward and pulls a set of keys out of his pocket, and fumbles with a lock. Eventually, he opens the door, and we burst in, roughly pushing him aside. We all try to get at the doors at the same time and slam them shut. The keys are still in the lock, and I manage to turn them and pull them out just as the rats slam into the glass panes from the other side. We all jump backwards and aim our assault rifles down into the writhing mass.

'DON'T SHOOT. YOU'LL BREAK THE GLASS,' Dave shouts, and we all slowly lower our weapons, watching with horror and disgust as the rats throw themselves at the doors.

Several of them stretch their mouths wide open and try to bite at the smooth glass, but all I can see are hundreds and hundreds of pairs of red eyes.

'We need to seal the building up,' I say to the recruits. 'Team Alpha, take the left side with Dave. Team Bravo, the right side with me. Make sure every door and window is closed and locked.'

Dave, McKinney, Smith, Tucker, and Hewitt all run off to the front left side of the building, straight into the café area. To the right is a convenience-style shop, and I start into it with Blowers, Cookey, Reese, and Graves. We sweep around the edge of the building, kicking in doors and shouting clear when we have checked the area.

The convenience store has a storeroom and small staff canteen. Both have doors and windows leading to outside, but all are checked and found to be locked securely. We move out of the shop and down the wide, central aisle. The next room on the right is a small amusement arcade, with darkened fruit machines. I watch the lads sweep the rooms, but the room is sealed internally, with no other doors. As they come back out, I hear a woman screaming and see her running out of the restrooms, which are directly ahead of us.

'There's a rat in the toilet,' she screams and doesn't even take in the armed men walking towards her.

I see a Burger King off to the right, a long counter and seating area with tables and chairs, with several people all standing up to look at us.

'There are thousands of rats trying to get inside this building. We need to seal every point of access,' I shout at them, scaring them witless, and a woman faints and falls onto the floor.

A young child starts screaming and is picked up by another adult female.

'Blowers, you check in there with Cookey. Jamie and Curtis, with me to the toilets.'

'SIR,' they all shout.

I run ahead to the toilets. One wide access in, the males to the right, and the females to the left.

'Jamie, you take the right side. Curtis, with me.'

We split up as Curtis and I burst into the ladies' toilet. The first cubicle door is open, and a fat, black rat is climbing out of the toilet bowl, using its front paws to pull itself up. I run into the cubicle and slam the lid down hard, crushing the rat dead. I lift the lid and use my foot to push it back inside, then slam the lid down again.

I hear Curtis yelling and slamming the lid down in the next cubicle, and I move out and around to the next one after that. I see one rat already on the floor, scrabbling towards me. I take a running kick and splat it against the rear wall. The body hits it, slides down, and remains motionless on the floor. The next rat drops out of the bowl onto the ground, and I stamp down, crushing the wet, shit-smeared body. I move from cubicle to cubicle, pulverising rats as they appear.

'Curtis, I'll hold these. You find something heavy to put on the lids,' I shout to him. I position myself a few feet back so that I can see all of the cubicles and then run forward to crush or kick them as they appear.

I'm kept busy as they keep coming until I pick the dirty, wet, dead rat bodies up and throw them into the bowls to try and block them. I keep doing this until each bowl is filled with dead rats; then, I put the lids down, but can still hear them fidgeting and moving about. I push the flush buttons for each bowl, trying to drown any infected rats that are still down there. Curtis bursts in with Blowers and Cookey, each of them carrying a heavy, long, cylindrical waste bin. We put the heavy metal bins on the lids and step back to see if the rats can get out. After a couple of minutes, I am satisfied that they can't, so I push the already dead rats out of the way and get the lid up.

'Burger King is clear, sir,' Blowers says.

'Thanks, mate. What about the men's toilets?' I ask Jamie.

'We did the same thing in there. They were trying to come up through the bowls, too.'

'Okay, let's see if the others are all right.' We leave the toilets and make our way into the central area. Dave and Team Alpha are already waiting for us.

'All clear for the minute, Mr Howie, but it won't last long,' Dave says as we join them. Nick has pulled out a packet of cigarettes, and the lads start lighting up, after Nick looks at me for approval.

'Crack on, lads. I think we need a few minutes' rest after that,' I say to them as they light up, taking deep drags. 'I know what you mean, Dave. We always had rats in the supermarket. The fuckers will get through anything for food. This place has air-conditioning, so there will be vents. Also, the drains will need sealing up.'

'Okay, Mr Howie,' Dave says.

'Mr Howie, are those fucking things zombies too?' Tucker asks me.

'They certainly look like it, mate. I don't plan on getting bitten, though, so I cannot be exactly sure, but look at those eyes.'

'Yeah, but why are they coming for us, Mr Howie?' Smith asks me, and they all look to me for an answer.

'I don't know, but it bloody looked like that, didn't it? They were watching us for ages before they started to attack. There's people here they could have come for, but mind you, we *were* out in the open, and they were locked in here.' I shake my head, trying to make sense of it all. 'What a fucking day,' I add and rub my forehead.

We are all sweating heavily from the hot weather and the frantic exercise we have just done.

'I am parched. They must have some fluids in here. Let's look.' I turn and start walking, amazed that I have used the word *fluids* instead of saying *drink*. Bloody Dave! He is rubbing off on me.

'Er... Hi!' a voice says meekly, and I look up to see the man who unlocked the doors walking slowly out of the entrance to Burger King.

'Hi, sorry about that. We didn't mean to barge you out of the way like that,' I say to him. 'Cookey, you're on first watch on the front doors. Hewitt, you watch the toilet entrance. We'll bring you some drinks,' I say to the lads and then walk up to the man, and extend my hand.

'Hi, I'm Howie,' I say to him, and we shake hands.

'Tom. I was the night manager when this happened. There's quite a few others in here too,' he says, nodding towards Burger King. 'Are you guys the army?'

'No, mate, these lads had just joined up when Dave and I found them at Salisbury. We were there to take that huge vehicle.'

'So, that means you *are* the army, then?' Tom says.

'Well, they are newbies, really, and so am I. Dave is the well-trained one. He was in the army.'

'But...you're in charge of them?'

'I guess, but they're just lads, really. We are on our way to London.'

The man nods at me.

'You'd better come and meet the others,' he says, and I follow him into Burger King. The lads are already behind the counter, going through cupboards and pulling out bottles of water.

'Mr Howie!' Tucker calls out and throws a bottle of water over as I go past the counter.

'Cheers, mate.' There are about eight or nine adults in here, plus one small child and a baby. They are all clustered around some tables in the middle. The people look very tired and frightened and keep glancing over to the lads behind the counter. I realise how terrified they must feel, seeing us all in full action. I nod at the group.

'Hi, I'm Howie. Sorry about the noise and bursting in like that, and please excuse the lads; they're just getting a drink. We are not here to hurt anyone, I promise. We're just trying to get away from the thousands of rats that are chasing us.'

They all start talking at once, and Tom holds up his hand to quieten them.

'Mark, why don't you go first,' Tom says, indicating a man who is still wearing a smart business suit, although the shirt top button is undone, and his tie is pulled down slightly.

Mark stands up and glances round at the others before speaking.

'I think I speak for all of us when I ask just what the hell is going on here?' He has a strong, cultured voice.

'What do you mean?' I say to him, puzzled at the question.

'Well, you're the army. I think we have the right to some answers.'

'We are not the army. I—'

'But you are dressed like soldiers and are carrying military assault rifles. Plus, you are driving around in a tank,' Mark continues.

'APC,' the lads chorus.

'Yes, I know how it must look. Dave was in the army, and we are wearing army clothes as ours were covered in blood.'

'So, just who are you, and why are you here?' Mark demands.

'I'm Howie. That's Dave over there,' I indicate Dave, who just stares back blankly. 'And the other lads are the recruits we met at Salisbury. My sister is in London. I'm going to try and get her, which is why we've got the big vehicle. Didn't any of you hear that broadcast on the radio?' They look at each other in confusion, then back to me with eager faces.

'What broadcast? Has the government released a statement?' Mark asks.

'I don't know about the government, but I heard a broadcast on a car radio. It said that London was infected and for survivors to head to the forts on the South Coast.'

'Well, just who put the broadcast out? Who sent it, and what else did they say?' Mark says; his tone becoming more forceful.

'I don't know. It didn't say. It was just a looped message on a random frequency. Didn't any of you go through the radio frequencies?' Some shake their heads, and others just stare back at me blankly. 'Don't any of you watch the movies? In horror movies, they go through the radio frequencies and search for government messages.'

I am dumbfounded at the amount of people I have met so far that have not bothered to do this.

'I don't think any of us have scanned the radio, but...what's this about rats?'

'We were getting fuel when we saw hundreds of rats staring at us. Now this whole area is covered in them. They've got the same red eyes as the zomb– The *strange* people have.'

'I told you, Mark, that they were coming up through the toilet,' the woman who ran screaming earlier says. She too is wearing a smart business suit and has the same cultured tones as Mark.

'Yes, thank you, Cynthia,' Mark says without even looking at the woman.

'Listen, we need to secure this building and make sure they can't get in,' I say to the group.

'How will they get in?' a woman holding the child asks; her face pale and drawn.

'Rats can get in anywhere – through air vents, drains, and with so many of them in full force, they can chew through most materials.'

'Oh, my god, they'll get in and kill us! They'll kill my babies!' She starts panicking, clutching the child closer to her.

'No, we'll secure the building and figure something out. Even if it means just waiting until they go away or die.' I turn to Tom. 'Tom, we need you to explain the layout of the building to us and identify any rat entry points.'

'Okay. Now?' Tom asks.

'Yes, mate. Lads, gather round.'

'Now, just wait a minute. I think we were talking,' Mark says with a condescending tone.

'No, mate,' I say, cutting him off. 'We have to do this now before it's too late. We can talk more later.' I make a point of turning away from him and looking at Tom.

'Is there a flat roof?' I ask Tom.

'Yes, it's quite big actually,' he replies.

'Okay, we need to get someone up there. Is there access from inside the building?'

'At the back, there's an access ladder.'

'Jamie, you've got the rifle. I want you up top, but we need a way for you to communicate with us down here.'

'There's a couple of skylights in that central area, sir. We could open them so that Jamie can shout down,' Blowers says.

'Tom, will they open without being forced or broken?'

'You just need to undo the latches. This place is open twenty-four hours a day, seven days a week, so they're not a security issue,' Tom replies.

'Okay, good idea, Blowers. Jamie, do that then, mate, crack open one of the skylights, and shout down to make sure we can hear you every twenty minutes so we know you're all right, got it?'

'Yes, sir,' Jamie Reese replies.

'Right, we keep two in the middle area at all times, watching the front and the rear, and then a couple on constant patrol around the building, checking all of the rooms. The rest of us will make the building secure. Tom, does that shop stock Sellotape?'

'What?' Tom asks.

'Or brown parcel tape?' I say to him.

'Oh, right, yes, they do. We had to get some of our office supplies there if we ran out.'

'Right, okay, if any of you want to help, that would be great,' I look at the group seated in front of me. An old man and woman quietly look at each other.

'We'd be glad to help you, young man,' the elderly chap says.

'I'll stay here with Mary and help to look after the children,' the old woman says, indicating the scared woman clutching the child; a baby in a removable car seat sleeps next to her.

'Tucker, we need to get moving. While we start getting the building secure, you go through the supplies and see how much food and drink we have.'

'Yes, sir,' Tucker responds and shoots off towards the counter.

'Dave, can you come with me, Jamie, and Tom, to look at the roof?'

'Yes, Mr Howie.'

We go through to the back of the building into the utility and office areas. Tom explains that they have daily deliveries, so the only stock will be what is in the shops and cafés. We stop at a metal access ladder that leads up to a small landing and a door. Tom ascends first and unlocks the door with his set of keys. We follow up and step out of the door into the bright sunshine, ready to respond in case the roof is covered with rats. The sides of the building are sheer, and unless the rats start stacking boxes, it will be unlikely that they can get up here.

'All of the wiring and pipes are underground, so there are no attachments to the building anywhere,' Tom says as we walk around the perimeter.

The view is much worse than I thought it would be. The ground level is thick with rats stretching out across the car park all the way back to the still burning fuel station.

'At least now we know who caused that,' Tom says.

'Yeah, sorry about that, mate. Bit of a desperate situation,' I apologise, watching the thick, black smoke pluming up into the sky, sending a massive smoke signal to every infected in the area.

'We can expect more visitors now,' I say to Dave, who nods. The rats are climbing on top of each other at the edges of the building; each one desperately fighting and squirming to get inside.

They are on all sides of the building now, and hundreds more are still pouring in from all directions. We get to the central skylight and undo the clasps on the sides. The top can be fully removed, but that would be dangerous – rats might descend very quickly like in the Saxon.

'Just crack it open a few inches so we can slam it down if we need to,' I say.

'Cookey? Nick? Can you hear me?' I shout down.

Two faces appear underneath me, grinning up.

'Loud and clear,' Cookey shouts up.

I move away a few feet.

'How about now?' I call out.

'Yep, still good.'

I move over to the edge of the building and call out again.

'Yep, we can hear you fine,' Cookey shouts up.

'Okay, Jamie, all yours. Shout down every twenty minutes so we know you're still alive.'

'If I see any of the *people,* can I fire on them?' Jamie asks me. I look to Dave, and we both nod.

'Yes, mate, but let us know first, so we don't all jump out of our skins.'

'Okay, Mr Howie.'

Bugger, he *is* slowly turning into Dave.

Back downstairs, I see that Blowers has already divided them all into teams and sent them off into various sections to secure the building.

'I told them to tape up every possible entry point,' he says.

'Well done, mate.'

I watch as Dave walks down the aisles and stops to pick something up from the shelf. Then he walks over to the counter, to a tray of cigarette lighters. He raises a can of hairspray and presses the button as he sparks the cigarette lighter, and a long flame shoots out from the nozzle of the can. He looks over to me and smiles.

'I knew we'd have flame throwers at some point,' I jokingly groan. 'Bloody good idea, though, mate. Let's hand them round to everyone. But they might burn the building down. Maybe we should put them at key points so we can spray into the drain openings and toilet bowls in case they break through.'

Dave nods in agreement, and we start walking through the building, watching the recruits and the people from Burger King taping up every air vent and drain cover. Darren Smith is stretching tape across the gap just a few inches back from the front door.

'It won't stop them, but it might buy us a bit of time, sir,' he says as we stop to help.

'Tom, we need a safe, secure place we can all go to in case they get through.'

'The storeroom or the office? The office has the cash safe in there, so it's the most secure, just very small,' he replies.

'Will we all fit in there?' I ask him.

'Probably not, so we could use the office *and* the storeroom if we make the storeroom fully secure.'

'They are connected by the corridor, aren't they?' I ask him.

'Yes, so we could fall back to the storeroom first and then the office if all else fails,' Tom replies.

We walk through to the back area. The old chap from Burger King is working with McKinney, taping up the air vent. I check the rear access, a double, metal door with safety bars on the inside and thick-looking bolts on the top and bottom.

'We should keep these doors clear. They look strong, and even rats can't chew through metal quickly.'

I explain the plan to the old man and McKinney and then work with them to secure the room completely. The door leading into this area from the main building is only a single wooden door. There are some stock cages in the storeroom, and I work with Dave and McKinney to pull the cage off the wooden base. Once free of the wooden base, the metal cage stretches out. It's fine mesh, and we jam it against the door.

'That should hold them for a bit longer if needed.' We remove the mesh barrier and rest it to one side. We hear shouting and run into the main area to see Nick booting a rat against the wall.

'Coming from the ladies' toilets,' he yells, and we run in to see thick, black bodies straining to lift the lids, with the heavy waste bins on top. The dead rats I put in the bowls have just given them something to stand on and get leverage.

I grab a can of deodorant and a lighter and charge into the cubicle.

Just as the lid lifts and two of them squirm halfway out, I ignite the spray, keeping the button pressed down, and push the flame throwers at the bodies.

The rats squeal and start thrashing. The jet of hot flame incinerates their small bodies within seconds. Remarkably, they keep trying to fight their way out rather than dropping back down into the safety of the bowl. I kick out at the flaming bodies and stamp them down onto the floor so that I can crush them underfoot. I rush out and see Dave doing the same thing but holding the flame directly on their heads so the fur burns away. He scorches them to death amidst squealing and thrashing.

'We need someone in both toilets all of the time,' I shout out as the last of the rats is destroyed by fire and stamping.

'I'll do these ones,' McKinney offers. We go back out into the main area. Cookey and Nick Hewitt are still there but looking in our direction with concerned faces.

'All clear for now. Cookey, can you keep watch in the men's toilets, mate? Nick, you watch this area and the front doors,' I shout over to them.

'He'll bloody like that,' Blowers shouts from off to the side somewhere. 'Cookey likes hanging around in the gents' bogs, don't you, Cookey?' he adds as the lads all start sniggering from their various positions. I even hear Jamie chortling from above us on the roof.

'Get fuc—'

'Language, lads,' I shout out and cut Cookey off before he offends everyone in the building. Cookey grins and walks off to the toilets.

'Oi, Nick! You got any more smokes, mate?' Cookey yells, and Nick throws him another packet. We keep walking around the inside edge of the building, checking, and re-checking the access points.

Nearly all of the tape is used up. There's just a few rolls left over. The storeroom is searched, but no more tape is found. I find Tucker in the other café, the one by the services company. He is sorting through boxes of food and making piles.

'Tucker, can you get some supplies into the storeroom and office at the back? They are our fall-back points,' I say to him.

'Got it,' he responds and starts loading boxes with bottles of water and snacks.

'Also, mate, in your official capacity of stores man, can you get those first aid kits on sale in the shop and stack them in there too? Get some dressings and stuff to the lads as well and make sure they've all got water and something to eat.' Tucker nods and starts moving off.

'Oh, and Tucker?' He turns back to face me.

'Sir?'

'Thanks, mate, good job.' He smiles and walks off, and Dave stares at me again. 'What have I done now?' I ask him.

'Nothing, nothing at all, Mr Howie.'

'It's going to be a long night. I can bloody feel it.'

'Yes, Mr Howie, it will be.'

CHAPTER FIFTY

The rats sat and waited until the numbers were strong enough to attack and be sure of a victory. The infection felt the pull of the rodents as their urge to attack and bite the resistors was growing. But the infection held them back and waited for more to arrive. It watched from the thousands of pairs of eyes and picked up on the scent trails from thousands of pairs of noses until sufficient numbers were present.

Then, as the one they call Howie got on top of the vehicle, they commenced the attack, pouring across the small fuel station forecourt and throwing themselves at the vehicle. Many died instantly from the giant wheels crushing them, but still, they poured in, and the infection knew they would be taken now. The vehicle started moving, but the infection had planned for this, tapping into some of the memories and images from the human hosts and starting to learn basic tactics. It sent rats up onto the roof so they could attack from all directions. As the vehicle rolled under the roof, the infection pushed the bodies over the edge to drop down. Some held on, but many were thrown off as the vehicle went faster, and then the one they call Howie used a loud tool to fire metal at the rats, and the station exploded. The infection felt many of the rodents scorched and blown to pieces by the massive explosions, but still, it sent wave after wave of rats after them. The infection moved the rats from the top of the vehicle and made them drop down into the inside, where it could see and smell the potential hosts. But those resistors were quick, and the infection failed to send in enough rats to finish them off. It kept the rats moving and leaping at the bodies, but the boots were too thick, and the rats' small teeth were unable to penetrate. The resistors were lucky as they had no idea how many times the rats sank their teeth into the edge of the thick leather boots before being kicked away or stamped upon.

The infection watched as one of the rats gained purchase on the front of one and started to climb up to the soft skin of the stomach, but another one struck out and killed it.

Then it got more rats inside, and the potential hosts stopped the vehicle and ran into the building. The rats were urged on and whipped into a frenzy, but the resistors got inside the building. The infection sent the rats against the walls and glass and forced them to bite into anything soft enough to damage. It found pipes and access tunnels and sent the rats along and into the toilets just as it had done so many times before, but the resistors were there again and repelled each attack, killing the rodent hosts. Through the eyes of the rats, the infection saw the huge plume of black smoke rise high into the clear, blue sky. Every host across the county stopped and stared into the sky, searching for the sign. The infection saw the thick, black smoke through many human host eyes and sent those towards it, but they were too slow, and the shuffling would take them too long.

The infection knows that it can speed them up, but they will become weaker and unable to repair the already badly damaged and decaying bodies.

The infection calculates this risk and allows more energy to flow, and the hordes of infected suddenly start forward with renewed speed towards the smoke signal.

CHAPTER FIFTY-ONE

We keep pacing around the building, checking and re-checking. More rats escape from the toilet bowls but are quickly dispatched by the flame throwers used by Cookey and McKinney. They shout to each other with a running tally, competing with the number of kills they both get. Tucker has distributed water and snacks amongst the recruits, and I keep rotating them around so they don't get bored, apart from Cookey and McKinney, who are too intent on their competition to leave their posts. The people that were already here are moving about, chatting with the recruits and making suggestions until they all gather back in the seating area of Burger King. Dave and I join them after taking another walk about and checking each area.

'How are we going to get out?' I ask Dave quietly, away from earshot of the group. 'They are too small to take on easily, and there are fucking thousands and thousands of them now.' Even Dave seems stuck for once and looks thoughtful. 'Maybe they will die quickly, but we can't risk just waiting here. They'll bite their way through soon enough, mate,' I say to him. He doesn't respond but just looks at me. 'There must be something we can do to reduce their numbers or get back inside the Saxon and lock the top down.'

'We'll never get through them,' Dave says.

'Okay, what about fire? But that risks the building and us too, or we could try poison? But we don't have buckets of rat poison.' I keep making suggestions, negating each one as I think of it.

'How about electrocution? We did that at the police station.'

'There's no power here, Mr Howie. I did think about that.'

'Okay, mate, do you know what we need?' I ask him.

'What?'

'An exploding cow,' I smile at him.

'We don't have any cows here, Mr Howie.'

'I know. It was a joke, Dave.'

'Oh, okay.'

'The grenades would be no good. We're too close to the building,' I say thoughtfully.

'They're still in the Saxon,' Dave says.

'Oh, well, there's that idea gone.'

'CONTACT,' Jamie shouts from above us.

The people in Burger King all stand up and look about, terrified.

'Quick, upstairs,' I say to Dave, and we run to the access ladder in the back area and climb up onto the roof.

'What've you got, Jamie?'

I race towards the front edge where he is standing, aiming the rifle.

'Look.' Jamie points almost dead ahead, and I peer out over the car park to the hordes running towards us.

'It's not nighttime, and they're running. Why are they running?' I shout out, alarmed.

'They're coming straight for us, sir,' Jamie says.

'Start shooting them, mate.' I run across the roof to check the other sides, and I am horrified to see more of them coming across the car park. More are on the motorway and even coming across the fields behind the services building.

'Fuck me, there's loads of them.' I check my watch.

'It's about an hour to sundown, but they're running now. Something has changed.'

'What's going on?' a voice shouts up through the skylight.

'Zombies, coming from all sides, and fast,' I yell down.

'But it's daylight,' the voice shouts up.

'That's what I said. Get the others up, quick as you can, but keep Cookey and McKinney in the toilets, and Hewitt on the main area beneath us.' I move back to the front and see Jamie taking aim and firing at the oncoming masses. His aim is brilliant. Even from this range and firing at moving targets, he still drops them.

'Are you getting head shots from here?' I ask, surprised as they fall down and stay down.

'No way, not from this distance and the speed they are moving at,' Jamie replies and fires again, with a *cough* sound from the rifle.

'But they are staying down!'

'Are they? I haven't looked. Hang on,' Jamie says and sweeps the scope back to the ones he has already shot down.

'You're right. They are staying down, not even moving,' he says.

'They must be weaker. A body shot like that wouldn't stop them. It might drop them down, but they would keep coming.'

I make my SA80 assault rifle ready just as Tucker, Blowers, Curtis Graves, and Darren Smith come out onto the roof, one at a time.

'Jamie is killing them from this distance with body shots,' I say as I take aim and hear the rest of them rack their rifles and make ready.

'Spread out to cover all sides,' Dave says.

I aim at the centre mass of a large-built female staggering and wobbling across the car park. I fire and watch her drop as she is struck somewhere in the middle of her body. I keep watching, waiting for her to start twitching and trying to get up, but she remains completely still.

Next, I aim for the middle of a group and fire into them. One of them drops and is instantly trampled under the feet of the others. I hear rifles popping all around me and the coughing noise from the sniper rifle held by Jamie. I keep firing and feel a deep satisfaction as they are dropped on the spot.

There are more moving fast, though, and they are already halfway across the car park. The rats pay them no attention, and the infected just stagger through the black bodies, treading them down or kicking them aside as they lurch forward. Even when the human zombies drop from being shot, the rats don't try and eat them. They just keep surging forward.

'Shit, look at that lot,' Blowers calls out, and I look over. He is facing the motorway, and I see a densely packed horde charging down it towards the slip road. They are really crammed together at the front and then spread out to a long tail further down the motorway.

'There's more coming across the fields at the back, too,' Tucker shouts.

'Fuck me, they don't like us much, do they?' I shout out.

'Rats and zombies all coming for us. Doesn't it just make you feel special? Jamie, can you start dropping them as they come into the access road from the motorway, mate?'

'Sir,' Jamie confirms and moves over to the corner of the building so he can cover the car park entrance to the access road and the motorway. He puts his bag down at his feet, and I see it's full to the brim with boxes of bullets.

I move over to the skylight and shout down, 'Get one of those people up here to help Jamie reload the rifle magazines.'

I watch Hewitt run towards Burger King, and I go back to the front and take aim. There are hundreds coming for us now and thousands of rats. We keep firing, taking single shots and manage to keep them back from the building, but their numbers are huge, and it's only a matter of time before they get to us.

'How can I help, young man?' I turn to see the old man coming up the ladder and onto the roof.

'Can you reload a rifle magazine?' I ask him.

'I did National Service. I can't imagine it's changed very much. I might be a bit rusty, but I'm sure I will soon pick it back up,' he says with confidence.

'Dave, can you show him what to do? We need to keep Jamie firing.'

'Yes, Mr Howie, on it now,' Dave responds and takes the old-timer over to Jamie, and shows him how to push the bullets into the magazine and stack them up on the low wall next to Jamie. We keep shooting, and they keep dropping, but more are coming, and we still have the rats to deal with. We are getting good results, though, and the car park and surrounding areas are soon littered with bodies.

'Here they come!' the old man shouts as the massive horde from the motorway staggers out of the access road and spreads into the car park, running towards us. I turn and fire into them as do Dave and Jamie.

Our shots are good.

Dave stops firing and drops down to the bag at his feet. He pulls out a black pistol and hands it to the old man.

'Can you use this?' he asks.

'Oh, yes, I was a good shot a few years back,' he replies, taking the gun and examining it with steady hands.

He takes seconds to figure out how to push a magazine in and slide the top back.

'When they get closer, start using it,' Dave says simply and goes back to firing at the massed horde charging towards us. I keep shooting into them, but the numbers are too high, and they are relentless. They get halfway across the car park, and the old man raises the pistol and starts firing. Sharp cracks fill the air as the handgun fires, and his arm hardly moves from the recoil.

He drops several with his first magazine and starts reloading, checking to make sure Jamie has enough magazines before he continues firing.

Despite our constant firing, they reach the front of the building and slam into the glass doors with a loud bang.

'Tucker, get down and support Nick in case they get through,' I shout, and Tucker runs towards the ladder. I switch the assault rifle to fully automatic and lean over to look down at the already packed horde and squirming black bodies jumping up between them.

I then press the trigger and watch as they are cut down from the rapid fire, but thirty or so rounds last seconds, and I'm reloading and firing again.

The old man is leaning over and firing into them too.

'They're at the sides,' Blowers shouts.

'Which side?' I yell back as I change magazines.

'Both,' he shouts back, running between the two edges and looking down.

I glance at the Saxon and the GPMG sitting dormant on the top, wishing we had it now.

'At the back, too,' Smith yells out.

'How are those doors looking?' I yell towards the skylight.

'They're holding, but they won't last if they keep coming,' it sounds like Nick shouting up.

'Tucker, get those people into the safe area and make Tom keep them there.'

'Yes, sir,' Tucker shouts, and again, I go back to firing down into the increasing horde.

They are staring up at us. Pale, drawn, decomposing faces that are rapidly becoming less human in appearance. The bodies pile up as we shoot them, which creates a natural obstacle for the others, but they are frenzied and claw, and rake at the bodies to get to the doors. The groaning noises they emit are a lot more aggressive now, and they almost sound like they are growling.

'What's got into them?' I shout out as I change magazines again.

'I don't think they like us very much,' Blowers says as he fires his weapon down at the sides.

I look up and see more coming along the motorway and from all around. Dave runs off and slides down the ladder, heading underneath us to the shop. He returns a few minutes later with a basket full of bottles of spirits and a roll of kitchen towels.

'I'll help with those,' the old man says and starts working with Dave to open the bottles and stuff thickly twisted paper towels in the top of them. Dave steps up to the edge of the building and lights the first one. He waits for it to catch alight and launches it high into the air. It smashes on the ground in the middle of a group charging across the car park. The flammable liquid ignites, and flames shoot out as the liquid bursts away. Several of the infected are set alight instantly, and they stagger forward but drop down within a few steps.

'They really are much weaker now,' I yell out as the old man hands Dave a flaming bottle. Dave launches it, and again, it hits in the middle of a group, bursting into flames that shoot up and ignite the infected. Dave continues with the deadly cocktails until there is a line of fire across the car park. The infected run straight through it, and many are set alight and fall down within a few steps, but many more make it through and get to the front of the building.

'THE MALE TOILETS ARE GONE!' Cookey yells out, and I glance down to see him holding the door shut.

'IS THAT BECAUSE YOU BUMMED THEM ALL?' Blowers shouts, and I can't help but burst out laughing.

'YES, IS THAT A PROBLEM?' Cookey yells back.

And I snigger as I fire my weapon down into the horde again, blowing heads apart and watching the bits of skull and brain matter fly off.

The doors are getting overwhelmed now, and the zombies are already several deep and growing.

'Dave, drop some straight down on them. We'll have to risk it. The building is metal and glass, so we might be all right. They'll be through there any second.'

Dave leans over the lip and pulls his arm back; then, he launches a bottle straight down, which explodes and bursts into flames, sending smoke straight up at us. Dave grabs another one from the old man who has lit two, and they both lean over and throw them down. The liquid flames up instantly, and infected drop like flies to lie in the flames. The rats squeal and scurry about, with more frantic movements, and I see many of their bodies on fire too.

Daylight fades and turns to night as more pour across the car park towards the building. As the last of the light fades, they all stop and stand perfectly still.

'Here we go,' I mutter under my breath. 'Mind you, they can't get much worse, can they?'

They all stare up at the sky and start to roar into the night, just as they have done each dusk so far. We take advantage by shooting many down, firing into them as they roar. I feel anger building up in me, and I roar back at them, 'COME ON, YOU FUCKERS!'

Dave joins me, and we roar with defiance at these things that are refusing to let us be.

Blowers and Jamie join in. Even the old man shouts, and I hear the lads underneath me screaming with defiance. The adrenalin courses through my system.

You are many, and we are few, but we will kill you.

We are righteous, and you are evil, and we will destroy you.

We roar at each other, masses of infected. A small group in a motorway service station, but right here and now, I wouldn't change sides for anything in the world.

The infected stop roaring, but we continue. We scream every bad word ever known to us at them.

Dave's drill sergeant voice is the loudest of all. 'I AM DEATH,

AND I COME FOR YOU!' he bellows, and it sends a tingle down my spine. I let rip with every ounce of being and scream as they charge. As one, we stop roaring. As one, we lower our weapons and aim. As one, we fire.

We cut them down as they charge towards us; weapons on fully automatic now. Jamie has ditched the sniper rifle and has taken up his assault rifle, and is firing into them with deadly accuracy. They keep coming, and they keep dying as we scorch them and tear them apart with our bullets.

'DOORS!' Cookey bellows from underneath us.

'MOVE BACK,' I shout, and we start moving back to the ladder and dropping down onto ground level.

'Are they all in the safe area?' I ask Cookey as I move into the main area.

'Yes, sir. Tucker has taken them, and that Tom bloke said he would keep them in there,' Cookey answers.

'Where's Tucker now?' I ask him.

'He's staying with them to make sure they don't lock us out.'

'Bloody good idea. Christ, look at that lot,' I say as I look towards the doors and see a solid press of bodies squished against them.

The pressure is so much that the ones at the front are pushed hard against the glass, and I can see the black rat bodies running between their legs and feet.

'The toilets went then?' I ask Cookey.

'Yeah, we got fucking loads, though. The bodies were stacked right up, but just too many of them coming out. The doors are inward opening, though, so they can't push their way out.'

'Who won the competition?'

'McKinney, the bastard,' he grins.

The rest scale down and come to join us staring at the doors when a sudden realisation hits me.

'Fuck, the roof is probably the safest place. Why don't we get them all up there? At least we can still fight back,' I spin round to Dave.

'Mate, you hold up here with Cookey and McKinney. The rest of you, come with me.' I run back to the safe area and into the storeroom. Tucker is just inside, closest to the door. They all jump up and stare at me with terrified faces.

'Change of plan. We need to get everyone on the roof as soon as possible. You have to move now,' I say to them.

'But hang on, we were told to come in here, and now we have to go up there? Surely this is safer?' Mark, in the business suit, starts moaning.

'Shut up, we need to get moving now, quickly. Get those children up first.' I run forward and snatch up the baby, and start moving back towards the ladder.

I make Smith go up ahead of me, and I climb up one-handed, holding the baby with the other arm while the mother screams and chases me, holding the other child. I pass the baby up to Smith, who takes it like it's a bomb about to go off.

'Quickly, pass me that child now,' I say to the woman.

'No, don't take my baby,' she screams in blind panic.

I drop down and push her to the ladder, and force her up the first few rungs. She climbs up, clutching the child. I force them up, apart from the old woman, who, due to her age, takes a little longer. Mark is right behind her and goes to push her up faster, causing her to slip down.

'Fucking hurry up, or we'll all die, you old cow,' Mark shouts at her.

Blowers steps in and punches him hard to the side of his head, causing him to smack against the wall and slide down. Blowers then stands over him, watching him intently.

'The rest of you, get up. This man and I will wait till last,' Blowers says through gritted teeth.

Mark stares up at him, with a look of horror on his face, but stays down on the floor.

'DOORS ARE GOING,' Dave shouts from the main area.

'Blowers, get up there quickly, and you,' I shout to Blowers and point at Mark, the last ones to go up. I run back to the internal, wooden door leading out into the main area and see the glass doors slowly buckling inwards, the glass cracking noisily as the pressure builds.

'Get back to the ladder and up to the roof now,' I shout, and Cookey and McKinney sprint past me. Dave and I kneel down just a few feet from the internal door leading to the back area and the ladder.

'You next, Dave.'

'No,' Dave states.

'Fine, then we'll both stay here,' I say stubbornly, and we both raise our rifles and take aim at the doors. 'Are you going or what?' I say after a few seconds.

'Nope,' he answers.

'Okay, be like that.'

'I will, Mr Howie.' We both watch the doors, both of us being unwilling to be the first to break away.

'They'll be through those doors any second now, Dave.'

'Yes.'

'So you'd better get going, then.'

'You really should go, Mr Howie. I'll cover.' The glass fractures, and doors start buckling further open. I glance over to him, and he looks back at me as I grin. He smiles slowly back at me.

'Ready, Dave?' I ask him, turning back to the doors.

'Yes, Mr Howie.' The doors burst open, and the infected start pouring in. We open fire on fully automatic, cutting them down in droves and sending them back to hell.

They surge forward: zombie men, zombie women, and zombie rats.

Just as they reach us, I lean over and slam the wooden door closed, and brace it with my back.

'I've got the door. You go now,' I shout at Dave pushing against the door next to me.

'Dave, I've got the door. Get up that ladder now.'

'I've got the door, Mr Howie. You go.'

'I got to the door first, so it's mine,' I shout back at him over the thumps and bangs.

'No, Mr Howie,' he grunts, straining at the door.

'Right, I didn't want to have to do this, but you said I was in charge.'

He shoots a look at me.

'So if I'm in charge, then I'm ordering you to get up that ladder.'

He stares at me for a moment, then says, 'Okay, Mr Howie. Move quick, though. The door won't hold.'

'I know, mate. Now go!' I shout.

He releases and sprints to the ladder, and starts climbing up fast. As soon as he gets halfway up, he shouts down, 'NOW.'

'COMING,' I shout back and jump away from the door, and start sprinting towards the ladder.

The door bursts open behind me, and I hear them charging into the room.

During those milliseconds of running, I work out that if I grab that ladder, they will be on me before I can climb up.

Dave or anyone else up there won't be able to shoot down because I will be in the way. Dave will most likely drop down and try to fight them all, and get killed in the process, and Dave is the strongest chance they all have for survival.

All it will take is one bite or scratch, and I'm done for, and they are moving fast now. There is no way I can go for the ladder. It just can't be done.

Time slows down as I reach my hand out to grab it, then pull my arm back at the last second. I race forward into the storeroom, slamming the door behind me. I lock the door and push the bolts in at the top and bottom as I hear Dave bellowing my name and the growling of the infected as they impact on the other side of the door. The door is solid wood and will hold for a bit. Plus, the door isn't that wide, so they won't be able to get that many bodies across it. But they can press in from behind, and eventually, the door will go. I pull the opened cage sides down across the door and pile boxes and items in front of it. Sweating and breathing hard, I step back and look round. Tucker has left some supplies down here, and I smile as I realise that even during those frantic few minutes, he managed to get some of the supplies up onto the roof. I sink down onto the top of some boxes and change magazines in the assault rifle. Next, I pick up a bottle of water and take a long drink before I settle down to listen to them thrashing against the door, trying to get to me. I hear muffled shots. The lads must be shooting down onto the horde below. I feel numb and suddenly very alone. I know that if I had gone for the ladder, I would never have made it, but already there is doubt in my mind that maybe I could have gone for it. But they were right behind me, and I only just managed to get this door closed. One bite, that's all it takes.

DAVE SCREAMS as Howie runs past the bottom of the ladder. He is at the top, aiming down with his rifle, ready to drop them as Howie climbs.

But he went straight past and into the storeroom.

Dave hears the door slam shut, and his mind calculates that Howie got into the room safely.

'MR HOWIE,' he bellows and then listens.

'MR HOWIE,' he shouts again.

Still nothing.

'GET ON THOSE SIDES AND KILL THEM.' Dave turns away from the ladder and storms over to the front of the building.

The people from Burger King are huddled in the middle of the roof, cowering down, while the recruits and the old man fire down.

'SMITH, WATCH THAT LADDER,' Dave bellows and starts firing down into the crowd. Howie told him he was in charge and Dave had to go. In Dave's mind, things are black and white, right or wrong. There are leaders, and there are followers. Even at the supermarket, Dave admired Howie as he reminded him strongly of some of the best officers he had served under. Hardworking, kind, and considerate, but also not a fool. He was always willing to make conversation and show a genuine interest in his staff. These traits are rare in an officer, and Dave admired Howie for them.

Dave knew he had been without a purpose when they attacked the supermarket that night. He'd fallen back on his years of training and natural instincts to protect the base, to protect the place that recruited and paid him. Then Howie showed up, and instead of panicking or screaming, he showed those traits even more. He'd stood next to Dave when they started to attack again.

Over the last few days, Howie has shown what a natural and strong leader he is, sticking to the primary objective but being flexible enough to adapt and overcome whatever is in his path. Doing the right thing at the right time and doing something that the army had never done with him – Howie encouraged Dave to be human, to joke, and to smile. And during that first battle when they charged the infected in Boroughfare town centre, Howie didn't allow the anger to control him.

He channelled it and made it work for him. He was clumsy and took unnecessary risks, but Dave could see the battle lust in his eyes and knew that Howie was a man to follow.

Since then, Dave had protected Howie. Howie took the recruits and showed them kindness and respect, and by doing so, he became their natural leader too. He protected them during the battle to get the Saxon and knew how to get them safe before the night came, and even after that, when most men would weep or break down, Howie took the time to check on the recruits' welfare and make sure they were all okay, then joked with Dave. Dave knows those are very special traits. He has been in countless war zones and on countless operations and can see when someone is good.

Howie is good.

Howie is his friend and his leader. To Dave, killing is a skill that comes naturally. He doesn't relish it or dream of it. Killing is just something he is able to do easily. He is small and can move quickly, and is able to coordinate his movements to achieve maximum efficiency. Only with Howie, has he felt that bloodlust, that feeling of fighting alongside a fellow warrior and defeating something evil.

Dave begins to feel something he very rarely feels, and it's inside, growing and gnawing at him. The assault rifle in his hands becomes something weird and strange, something that doesn't belong to him, and he stops firing and lowers the weapon down gently, then stands still to examine this feeling inside him, trying to block it out, but it pushes up inside of him and tries to take over his mind and body.

Dave blocks it and tries to focus, but it screams inside of him, it demands to be released, and it will never go away until it is let out.

'BLOWERS!' Dave shouts; his voice rising above all the noise and weapons firing.

'YOU'RE IN CHARGE!' Dave lets the feeling out.

He releases it to purge into his blood stream and pump around his heart. He closes his eyes as the pressure builds and threatens to overwhelm him. Then the feeling is in control of him, and he opens his eyes and draws his knives, one in each hand, with the back of the blade pressing up against his forearms. Dave looks down into the horde and leaps from the building, straight into the middle of them, as that feeling takes over completely. That feeling is anger.

Dave is angry.

※ ※

I SIT IN THE STOREROOM, feeling sorry for myself, sorry that I'm separated from the others. Then I think of Dave. He has the address book in his bag, and I know nothing will stop him from finishing what we set out to complete. I feel bad for ordering Dave away from the door like that, but he is a special man, and the recruits need him more than they need me. I can laugh and joke with them, but it's Dave that has given them the skills to survive, and he can carry on showing them and protecting them. Under Dave's tutelage, the recruits will prevail, and I know my sister is in good hands with them, too. They will fight together or die together, and they have already shown the commitment and camaraderie they have built up. I feel proud to have fought with them, and I feel especially proud to have fought alongside Dave. I know he struggles with day-to-day living and is unable to see irony or sarcasm, and cannot work out the things people mean when they say something different. But then I think back to some of the little quips he has made, and it shows that even under the most extreme event known to mankind, people can still evolve.

The building is surrounded by rats and infected, and they all want to kill us. The lads can fight them off for a while up there, but the infected have proven they can wait longer than we can fire, and there seems to be an endless supply of them. But the rats and infected are trying to get *into* the building and are all facing inwards. Not the other way. I get to my feet; my blood starting to pound in my ears. My sister stands the best chance of survival if Dave can get to her. Those recruits stand the best chance of survival if Dave takes them, and those survivors we found here stand the best chance of survival if Dave is alive to lead the recruits.

If I can get to that GPMG, I can even the odds, and even if a rat bites me, the infection won't be instant, and I can still fight through or lead them away. It's a chance worth taking, for Sarah, for the recruits, and for those people.

Dave must survive, and if that means I charge out to my certain death, then I will do it. I've been lucky so far, and I admit to myself that is mostly down to Dave, and if he could keep a clumsy fool like me alive, he will be able to do it for them.

I draw the long bayonet from the scabbard on my belt and fix it to the end of the rifle, wishing I had my axe with me. One magazine in the rifle, and then the knife on the end, and that's it to get me to the Saxon. Fuck it. I do this for Sarah, for the recruits, and for Dave, and I kick open the rear doors and burst out to find a whole load of nasty zombies on both sides.

The door had swung hard and knocked two of them off their feet.

I run forward as they immediately turn and start chasing me. I outsprint them and run down the back of the building, and see more of them pressing into the sides of the building. I run out and away from the building, and into the car park, then turn, and drop down on one knee, and fire the assault rifle into the infected closest to me.

They drop down from each shot, and I thank the Lord for whatever has made them weaker. I run on as more of them start running after me, and I see more turning away from the building, coming towards me. I turn right and start towards the front of the building. The rage and anger building inside me. I get to the corner and see the Saxon immobile a few feet from the building. Hordes of infected are facing away from it, towards the front and surging into the open doors of the services building. I run forward, desperately trying to reach the Saxon before they see me, but the ones chasing me must send some signal or make noise because they turn and start towards me. I drop down and fire the remains of my magazine into them, tearing them apart and watching them fall and get blown backwards.

Out of bullets, I start charging towards the Saxon, roaring with anger. The top of the roof at the front of the building lights up with sustained firing. The bright muzzle flashes startling against the night sky. The recruits shoot down at the zombies as they run towards me, and I know I've been given a chance now, and I take it, sprinting flat out to reach the Saxon.

Rats are scurrying around my feet, and I feel bodies being crushed and kicked as I sprint over them. I reach the Saxon and race around the front to climb into the open driver's door, but there are infected waiting for me. I charge into them as they come for me and slam the butt of the gun into the closest face.

I whip around and thrust the bayonet through the throat of the next one as I catch a glimpse of my axe handle poking out from the edge of the Saxon. I kick the infected away, leaving the bayonet and rifle stuck in his neck, and reach out to grab the handle. My hand closes around the shaft, and I draw it towards me like an old friend. I step back with my axe, my faithful and trusty axe. I know that if I try to climb in now, they will be on me, so I step to meet their charge and swipe the axe into them. The heavy blade bites into flesh and sends them slamming into the side of the vehicle. I pull back and use the blunt end to knock the next one down, and I keep going and smashing them aside as they charge at me.

Suddenly, there's a gap, and I climb into the Saxon and slam the door closed. I dive over the back of the driver's seat and into the back. The rear doors are open, and an infected appears and starts clambering in, with his teeth bared. I step forward and lash out, with my boot connecting to his face and pulverising his nose. Another one charges towards me, and I slam the axe down on his head, breaking his skull open. I overextend and fall out of the back doors and onto the ground. An infected is inches away from me, bending forward as he lunges for the bite. I press backwards, up against the open rear door of the Saxon and realise I have nowhere to go. The infected man's head then bursts apart from a round fired from an assault rifle held by someone on the roof.

That had to be either Dave or Jamie firing. Either that or one of them is trying to kill me. I clamber back inside the Saxon, pull the doors closed, and move towards the ladder that leads up to the GPMG. A fat, black rat drops down as I look up.

'JUST FUCK OFF,' I scream and pick the thing up with my bare hands, and launch it hard against the metal rear doors; the body exploding on impact. I climb up and see another rat on top of the machine gun, and punch it in the face, sending it flying off the side of Saxon. I rack the bolt back and spin around to the front of the building, and the huge horde charges towards me. My face splits into a grin as I pull the trigger.

DAVE DROPS down into the horde, using their bodies to break his fall, and instantly, he is up and spinning about. The absolute anger and rage burns through him and makes him fight faster than he ever has done before.

His arms spin, and his legs kick out as he drags the deadly, sharp blades across throats and slices open the arteries. He pushes forward, using the knives to puncture the backs of infected too slow to turn, and plunges the knives into their necks. With amazing athleticism, Dave cuts through the horde, slicing them apart and tearing flesh open with each precise sweep of the blades. He roars into the night, and they charge at him. He spins and ducks, and leaps through them, killing them swiftly and dispatching them with gruesome finality. Two of them charge at him, and Dave drops his upper body down but raises the knives high and wide, and pushes through the middle of them, slicing their necks open as he pulls the blades past him. He pulls his arms forward and thrusts the points through the necks of the next two, dropping them instantly, and he keeps driving forward, killing anything in his path.

The anger and the desperation to rescue Howie overwhelms and consumes him.

The perfect killing machine, trained only to destroy with ruthless efficiency, allows the rage to spur him on, and those skills become more deadly than ever before.

Dave fights his way into the building and down the main area, working his way through countless infected. The bodies drop behind him as he whirls and dances through them.

Fighting and killing to get to Howie. Fighting and killing to rescue his leader and his friend. Dave reaches the door and pushes against it hard, bellowing out, 'MR HOWIE?'

The door is locked and barricaded, and he hammers on it with brutal strength as more infected enter into the main area behind him.

Blowers drops down from the ladder and fires into the oncoming infected, then joins Dave in beating at the door.

Between them, they force the door open and push the barricade away, bursting into the room to find Mr Howie gone and the rear doors wide open. They charge out into the night and continue fighting their way around to the front of the building. Dave uses his knives to rip them apart, and Blowers uses his bayonet and butt of the rifle to cut, slice, and slam them down. Rats pour out after them and jump at their legs as they fight and keep moving; both of them roaring and growling with ferocity and fury. Just as they reach the corner of the building, the GPMG starts firing, and they both turn and run out to the car park, then duck down to get to the side of the Saxon.

Mr Howie is on the heavy machine gun, firing into the front of the building and cutting down anything that moves.

※ ※

I KEEP FIRING and tearing them apart. For each one I kill, I know that I give the others a fighting chance for survival.

My mind is blazing at the destruction I am causing before me as the bodies are ripped apart, brains and heads bursting apart, and limbs being taken off.

Blood, bone, and bits of body fly everywhere, and even the rats are squirming to get away from the deadly hail of bullets. I hear shouting and turn to look down at Dave and Blowers crouching by the side of the Saxon. I grin down at them and wave for them to climb in, and watch as they pull the driver's door open and disappear inside.

I turn around and aim towards more coming into the car park from the access road, and together, with the recruits firing from the top of the roof, we slaughter them all.

'MAGAZINE!' I yell as the GPMG clicks empty.

'LET ME DO IT,' Dave yells from below me, and I drop down, grinning at him stupidly as I reach the bottom.

He grins back, and there is a look of relief on his face as he stares at me.

'Where did you two come from?' I ask them.

'Dave jumped off the building and killed 'em all to get back inside,' Blowers says.

'Fuck me, bloody hell, mate. I would have stayed there, with my feet up, if I'd known that.'

'Good to see you, Mr Howie,' Dave says as he climbs up to change the ammunition box on the GPMG.

'You too, mate, and you, Blowers. Did you leap off the roof too?'

'No, I came down the ladder like a normal person,' he says, grinning at me.

'I'll take over,' Dave shouts down, and the machine gun starts up again. I tap him on the leg to get his attention, and he stops firing.

'Is the front clear? Me and Blowers will make a run for the ladder and get back on the roof. Are you okay here, Dave?'

'Yep, all clear. I'll be alright here,' he shouts and starts firing again. We open the doors and climb out, slamming them shut again as we run towards the front of the building, jumping, clambering, and slipping on all of the broken and mashed-up bodies. The rats are still running about, but they seem less directed now and slower. Many of them are dead. We get to the ladder and climb up onto the roof. The recruits are all waiting for us, smiling and cheering as we come up to them.

'Well done, lads. I think we got most of them now,' I say to them.

'We? You did most of it, sir. How did you get to the Saxon?' Tucker gushes; his face red and sweating as he hands me and Blowers a bottle of water each.

'Ah, you know, just sort of legged it and hoped for the best. Jamie, was it you who shot that zombie that was about to bite me?'

'Yes, sir,' he says.

'Bloody good shot, mate. Well done. You saved my life.'

He blushes as the lads pat him on the back.

'How's it looking now?' I ask them and walk around the sides of the roof, looking down.

'We got nearly all of them,' Cookey says.

'Just a few left to get, and the rats, of course.' Looking down from the roof, I'm amazed at the huge amounts of torn and broken bodies lying about covered in blood. The front is a mess – corpses everywhere. I look over and see Dave scanning around with the machine gun, looking for something to kill. Jamie has got the sniper rifle back and is also sweeping the whole area. The rifle giving little coughs as he fires into the night. Within a few minutes, we are relaxing with bottles of drink and munching on chocolate bars as the lads regale each other, with how many kills they got.

I walk over to the central area, to the group we found in Burger King.

'Everyone okay?' I ask them.

Tom stands up and looks at me.

'So you got them all?' he asks.

'Yep, pretty much. The rats are still down there, but they are getting slower, and some of them are just dying where they stand. If they keep going like that, they should all be dead by sunup, and we can get rid of any that remain.'

'So what happens now?' Tom asks me, and the others all look over.

'Now? Well, we rest here for the night and move out in the morning, I guess.'

'What about us? We have lost our safety,' he says, looking down at the ground. I get the impression he has been forced to speak like this and is feeling ashamed.

'You weren't safe here for long. It was only a matter of time before they found you or before looters came for what was left inside. When daylight comes, you should find vehicles and head for the forts. Stick together and avoid the towns and cities, and you will be okay.'

He nods and turns back to the group, and they start discussing things with lowered voices. I walk away, feeling like I'm intruding on their discussion.

'You staying there, Dave?' I shout down to him.

'Yes, Mr Howie, for a bit, anyway.'

'Okay, mate, we'll get someone down to take over in a bit.' I arrange for the lads to take shifts, and I do the first one.

Walking slowly around the edge of the roof and peering out into the darkness, I can't believe we came through this again. The odds were overwhelming, but we stuck together and backed each other up. I feel shocked but humbled that Dave leaped off the roof to try and rescue me while I was charging out into a horde that size to try and keep him alive. We really must coordinate our heroic efforts next time, or this bunch could have ended up with neither of us.

We only made a few miles again today. But tomorrow is a new day.

We have a full tank of fuel and a straight road into London. What can possibly go wrong?

DAY SIX

CHAPTER FIFTY-TWO

Day Six
Wednesday

The sun rises and promises yet another scorching day. The humidity has been high all during the night, and the people on the flat roof of the services on the motorway between Salisbury and London have had a broken sleep, twitching and crying out from the horrors they have witnessed and the fear they have faced.

They sweat heavily and slowly strip down to the barest of clothes, just enough to cover their modesty, but they are still desperate to be rid of the restrictive and sweat-soaked clothing.

There is no breeze, and as they lie below the low wall running around the edge of the flat roof, they feel the pressing heat even more. Throughout the night, they get up and move about, breathing heavily and longing for air conditioning. They are listless and lethargic, and any conversations are held quietly and are restricted to the minimum amount of words possible. Those people on the roof each think of the lives they once had, of the things they did, and how they took so much for granted, getting bogged down in the mundane existence of day-to-day living, dreaming of better cars, bigger houses, more money, better phones and computers. Convincing themselves that this is what life is about – achieving and getting more things that will make them happy. Not one of those people now wishes they had more money to get the latest iPhone or had a chance to drive a Ferrari. Even the previous excited dreams of winning the lottery now feel unimportant. They all dream and wish they had spent more time with their families, had taken more effort to tell their loved ones how much they loved them. Petty family squabbles that seemed so important at the time now feel stupid and as petty as they really were.

Lives full of regret and remorse, dreams unaccomplished, and hopes taken away, all for something they played no part in and had no concept of.

This living nightmare is a thing of movies and stories, too farfetched to have ever been taken seriously.

Soft living in safe places have made most people unfamiliar with the struggles of life that many of their fellow humans suffered. War, disease, and poverty had never really affected any of these people on the flat roof, but now, the conditions they survive under are so extreme they feel sorry for themselves, and nearly all of them point the finger of blame elsewhere.

The government, fanatics, crazy people did this.

Why weren't more control measures put in place?

Why didn't someone do something and stop this?

The need to blame someone almost overwhelms some of them, and they fail to realise the time for blame has gone. There is no structure left and no authorities to call up or email, and demand answers from.

There will not be any parliamentary enquiry or difficult questions raised at the next session of the Prime Minister's Questions. This has happened, and the only thing that matters now is survival. Those clinging on to their past lives and waiting for the horror to end are living in denial and will quickly perish, simply for not facing reality and taking the necessary steps for survival.

Food, water, warmth, and security – nothing else matters now, and any hope that life will soon return to normal is false.

Tucker grows into his role of welfare and supplies coordinator and, ambling around the various sweaty bodies, distributes bottles of water, and urges them to drink and stave off any risk of dehydration.

Jamie Reese periodically sweeps the area through the scope of the sniper rifle, taking his time to drop infected latecomers that appear staggering towards the building. The suppressor on the rifle gives a polite cough and causes no reaction from those scattered about. Simon Blowers and Alex 'Cookey' Cooke spend a short time chatting and verbally abusing one another before falling silent and drifting off to sleep. Nicholas Hewitt chain-smokes cigarettes while lying on his back, staring at the stars.

Darren Smith leans against the edge of the look-out hole in the Saxon armoured personnel carrier, slowly circling around to check the perimeter.

Curtis Graves sleeps a few inches away, on the top of the vehicle.

Roland McKinney sits closest to the group of survivors they found in the services, playing marbles quietly with the young child. The mother sleeps fitfully nearby; her hand resting on the car seat within which her baby sleeps.

Finally, out in the wide car park, which stretches around the front, sides, and rear of the services, two men stand and stare at the smoking remains of the fuel station they blew up just a few hours before.

'That's got to beat the exploding cow,' Howie says.

'It does, Mr Howie,' Dave replies.

'Have you ever taken out a fuel station before then?' Howie asks, and Dave stops to ponder the question.

'Not a fuel station, no,' Dave answers.

'You say that like you've done something similar,' Howie says.

'A refinery.'

'No way. You blew up a refinery?'

'Yes.'

'Bloody hell, bet that was big.'

'Yes.'

'How did you do that?'

Again, Dave ponders the question and looks at Howie before finally answering.

'It's not that hard really. There are pressurized gas and oil pipes everywhere, and this one didn't have decent fail-safes and safety measures that most should have, so a few explosives, and the rest went naturally.'

'I bet that was a big bang.'

'Yes, we were told afterwards that it was seen from space.'

'No way. That must have been massive. How did they know where to look?'

'Who?'

'The astronauts?'

'What astronauts?'

'The ones in space that saw the explosion.'

'It was an imaging satellite.'

'Oh well, that's still impressive.'

Howie looks back towards the services building and wipes the sweat from his forehead.

'That's a lot of bodies,' he says.

'It is, Mr Howie,'

'Must be the biggest amount we've killed yet.'

'Salisbury was a lot,' Dave replies.

'True, maybe about even then. Mind you, if we add the rats too, then this is the biggest yet.'

'Yes.'

'Those rats didn't last long, did they?'

'No, Mr Howie.'

'Why did they start dying off? And the zombies that came for us were much weaker than we've known before. Most of them were dropping from one shot. Do you know, mate, it felt like they were coming for us, like it was for us specifically, like we were targeted.'

'Could be. We *have* killed a lot of them.'

'Do you think that's it, that we've angered them somehow with the amount we've killed?'

'Could be. It's basic strategy to take out your strongest enemy.'

'Is that what we are now, an enemy? Bloody hell, we're just trying to survive.'

'Not really, Mr Howie. Those people are trying to survive...' Dave points up towards the top of the services roof.

'So what? Because we've attacked a few of them, they're going for us now?'

'It's a bit more than a few, Mr Howie.'

'True, yeah, maybe we have pissed them off. We have killed a shitload of 'em,' Howie laughs.

'I think that's most likely.' Dave nods, giving one of his rare smiles.

'Been bloody good fun, though. It seems that every half hour something happens, and we just react...normally.'

'By killing them,' Dave answers.

'Yeah, by killing them, by killing all of them. That's a normal reaction, isn't it?' Howie says, still laughing.

'I don't think so, Mr Howie. I think most people have run away and hidden.'

'Well, we don't really have that option, do we, mate?'

'No.'

'London will be far worse, especially if they are targeting us. There could hundreds of thousands or even millions. Bloody hell, when you think of it like that, it's quite scary.'

'Only *quite* scary?' Dave asks.

'Well, maybe a little bit more than quite scary but nowhere near full terror. I'm not scared of these fuckers. I hate them.' Howie's voice hardens, and his face takes on a determined look.

'Fear is healthy. It keeps you alive,' Dave offers.

'Yeah, I guess so, but I still fucking hate them. No, hate isn't strong enough. It's more than hate, but I don't know what to call it... I wonder what it's like,' Howie continues after a few seconds of silence.

'What?' Dave asks.

'Do they have any memories or thought processes? Do they know what's happening to them? Maybe they're trapped inside the body, like when you hear about people going through surgical procedures and being awake the whole time. Maybe they are like that, aware and conscious, but just not in control.'

'So, who is controlling them?'

'Whatever the virus or infection is. It's a horrible thought, being aware of what you are doing and not being able to stop it. It can't be that. Surely they would give some sign.'

'You said one of them spoke your name on the plains that night.'

'I forgot about that. None of these did it, though, so I must have been mistaken. Nah, they ain't aware of anything. Nasty fuckers, but that change last night is still worrying. It's good if they get weaker –

it'll make them easier to kill, but not so good if they all start chasing us about during the day too.'

'No,' Dave agrees.

'Bloody hell, it's hot already. I've never known it to be so hot and humid,' Howie moans as he wipes yet more sweat from his forehead.

'It is unusual.'

'I've got a headache coming. I only get them before a storm, though, but that sky is as clear as anything. We'd better get back on the road. No doubt something else will happen as soon as we get going.'

Howie and Dave walk slowly back towards the services building, stepping over the many bodies of zombie people and zombie rats. Towards the front, the bodies are packed so deep they have no choice but to step on them, and their boots sink into the soft, torn flesh, coating their feet in sticky gore. They climb the ladder and reach the roof. Most of the people are already awake from the oppressive heat. Tom, the manager in charge of the services building, approaches them as they walk across the roof.

'Going to be another hot one, then?' Tom says.

'Scorcher! Feels oppressive, though, like a storm is coming,' Howie answers.

'Could be. It might break the heat a little,' Tom says.

'I don't know if that's a good thing. It might give them some refreshment too,' Howie says.

'So I guess you lot will be off soon, then?' Tom asks.

Howie nods. 'What about all of you? Are you going to head for the forts?' he asks.

'Yeah, I think so. Well, we can't really stay here now, can we?' Tom says with a reproachful tone.

'Tom, you weren't safe here. They would have come eventually, and like I said before, if not them, then looters would have come,' Howie answers him.

'Well, we did okay for quite a while before you lot came,' Tom says.

'Since Friday, Tom, you hid since Friday, and what's that? A few days? How long do you think you would have lasted?'

'We had food and drink...' Tom responds.

'Yeah, and how long before someone else wanted it or the fuel that we took. This isn't going to go away. This isn't a temporary glitch. Everywhere we've been, it just looks worse and worse. There's no police, no army, no government. It's all gone. This was safe for a few days, but believe me, after the things I have seen, you wouldn't have lasted a week here.'

'Yeah, well... Maybe, maybe not. It doesn't matter now, does it? We have no choice,' Tom says bitterly, which adds to the frustration Howie already feels.

'I think they've done a sterling job,' the old man, who helped them fight off the hordes during the night, stands and speaks, loud enough for them all to hear. 'I saw them last night, how fast they moved, and the way they attacked, and those rats. We wouldn't have stood a chance without these boys. We owe our lives to them.' The old man stands proud and looks to the group gathered around him.

'They wouldn't have come if it wasn't for them,' Mark says, still dressed in his business suit but now sporting a bruised face thanks to the punch he got from Blowers during the evening for trying to manhandle the old man's wife out of the way of the ladder.

'Claptrap, utter claptrap, and you know it,' the old man barks at him with a sudden ferocity. 'You are soft and have no idea what war is like. I've served my country, and those things are like nothing I've ever seen before. They would have come, and they would have killed every one of us: me, you, and the children,' the old man storms at them. The children's mother clasps the children to her tightly at the mention of a threat.

'We need to toughen up and get with it to survive this thing. Where were you last night, Mark, when they were attacking? I'll tell you. You were cowering at the back while the big boys did the dirty work for you. I'm an old man, and I was up here with them.'

'...and very glad we were too,' Howie interjects. 'He's right, though. You need to toughen up and get a grip on reality. This is not going away. The quicker you accept it, the greater chance for survival you will have.'

'Great speech. Well done,' Mark says sarcastically, rising to his feet and clapping his hands together slowly.

'It's the truth. You've been holed up here, and you've done well to survive this long. But this place is a beacon to anyone moving along that road, and they *will* come here to find supplies. They might be nice, and it could be a good thing, or they might not, and they could take what they want, *anything* they want,' Howie says, his voice rising.

'Oh, so the heroes come and rescue us from the bad men, destroy our safety, and then piss off to leave us to rot. Thanks very much. Thanks for nothing,' Marks retorts with a condescending sneer.

'Now, you stop that! Do you hear me?' the old man shouts at Mark. 'These boys risked their lives last night. That man jumped off this roof to fight them!' pointing at Dave. 'This man fought through all of them to get to that machine gun,' the old man points to Howie. 'If they hadn't risked their lives and fought so bravely while you cowered at the back, then we wouldn't be having this conversation because we would all be dead or worse – we would be one of those things.'

'Oh, piss off, old man. Did it remind you of your service days?' Mark shouts, and the old man lashes out and punches him hard to the same side of the face that Blowers had struck the night before.

Mark falls back but stays on his feet. He rubs his head and steps towards the old man, with an angry look on his face but stops dead as the lads and Dave all step forward at the same time. The silence holds for a second until Mark drops his head and backs off, prompting the lads to do the same with Mark casting a quick hard glare at the old man.

'I saw that,' Blowers says.

'What did you see?' Howie asks.

'He gave the old chap a look.' Blowers stops and stares hard at Mark.

'A look? What are you on about? I was just watching where I was going,' Mark says with that same instant shift back to being the victim.

'No. I think we all know what will happen if we leave you with this group,' Howie says. 'You're a bully. And a coward.'

Silence descends on the group as they all watch Mark. Even the other woman, dressed in a business suit and clearly with Mark, just stares at him and slowly shakes her head.

'I think Mark will be staying behind, seeing as he likes this place so much,' Howie says clearly for them all to hear.

'You can't do that,' Marks shouts in alarm.

'Watch me. You three, you're on him. Make sure he stays here,'

Howie orders with a nod to Blowers, Cookey and Nick. 'Everyone else get ready to go.'

The three lads step in close as Mark protests and struggles to hold his temper in check, giving the lads and everyone else murderous looks.

'Fuck me, you need therapy mate,' Cookey says with a shake of his head.

'He does. Talk about anger management,' Nick says.

'Just fuck off!' Mark snaps. 'You can't just leave me here!'

'Oooh. Yeah. So? I think we can,' Cookey says with a look to the other two.

'I mean. I'm pretty sure that's exactly what we are fucking doing,' Nick says.

'You fucking can't!' Mark shouts.

'Can't or cunt?' Cookey asks, quick as a flash.

'Did he just call you a cunt?' Blowers asks with a glance to Cookey.

'I heard cunt,' Nick says.

'I said cunt!' Mark shouts then flushes red at his own mistake. 'Can't! I said CAN'T!'

'Jesus, fuck me,' Cookey says as the lads burst out laughing. 'What the fuck is wrong with you?'

'He's raging,' Nick says.

'He's fuming,' Blowers says.

'He's gonna go on Facebook and leave an angry post,' Cookey says.

'WHAT? IN CAPITALS?' Blowers says loudly and slowly.

'I can't even spell post,' Nick admits. 'Dyslexic,' he tells Mark. 'But at least I'm not a cunt.'

CHAPTER FIFTY-THREE

'This is for you,' Howie says as he hands a pistol and ammunition to the old man with them and everyone else turning to face up to the roof at the sound of the three lads laughing as they start clambering down the ladders with Mark's head appearing at the top, screaming abuse.

The old man tuts with a heavy sigh as he takes the gun and deftly checks it over. Sliding the magazine out then back in and checking the safety.

'Fucking brilliant!' Cookey says as the three lads run past, all of them laughing hard as they reach the Saxon.

'Squaddie humour,' the old man says with a wink at Howie. 'It can get hard at times, but squaddies need to vent. Let them have fun when they can, but don't be afraid to pull them into line. They clearly respect you.'

'That means a lot. Thank you,' Howie says. 'Right, we've got to be off. It was nice meeting you. Hopefully we'll see you at the forts,' Howie says as he shakes hands with the old man.

'Fuck me, look at that one. He's a bit late for the party,' Darren Smith shouts, and they look over to see an infected slowly emerging from the access road into the car park. His slow and awkward shuffle bringing each step down heavily.

'I'll sort him out,' Darren shouts and starts jogging towards him with his knife drawn.

'Jamie, see if you can drop him before Darren gets there. It'll wind him right up,' McKinney urges as Jamie pulls the sniper rifle out of the bag and raises it up to peer down the sights.

'Wait until he's just a few feet away, make him run all the way there,' Cookey says. Jamie lines up the sight and waits for Darren to get within a few feet, then squeezes the trigger just as Darren starts to lift his knife up.

The infected is blown backwards, away from Darren, who stops and turns back to the group, then sticks his middle finger up. The lads all cheer and start laughing as Darren starts walking back to them.

Eventually, the people from Burger King are in the cars they arrived in, loaded up with supplies, sourced with help by Tucker, and they move out in a small convoy, leaving Howie, Dave, and the recruits standing around the Saxon.

'So, what was so funny?' Howie asks as the recruits all stare past him while laughing hard, prompting Howie to turn and see Mark now in the entrance on the ground floor stripped down to his urine-stained boxers.

'Where the bloody hell did his trousers go?' Howie asks as he starts to smile at the ridiculous sight.

'Don't know,' Nick gasps, gripping his sides, which ache from laughing.

'Right, well, let's get off before this gets any weirder,' Howie chuckles as he climbs into the back of the Saxon and inches over into the front and driver's seat.

'Bye, Mark,' Cookey shouts.

Nick slams the doors closed to a fresh outburst of laughing. Mark stares at his trousers trapped in the back of the door and watches as the Saxon slowly pulls away.

CHAPTER FIFTY-FOUR

Darren nears the body and starts to lift the knife just as Jamie Reese squeezes the trigger of the sniper rifle, and the bullet parts the air before it as it flies and strikes the host in the forehead.

The bullet strikes and takes the host clean off its feet as the head is thrown backwards. The saliva sprays out, and one tiny invisible drop sprays high into the air and spins towards Darren, landing on his bottom lip.

Darren doesn't even feel it and turns and sticks his finger up at the laughing lads, and starts walking back towards them, while smiling as thinking he would have done the same thing. He licks his lips and starts jogging while shouting abuse back at the others.

And inside of him, the infection gets to work and starts surging through Darren's body – except this host is genetically different to others. The infection is already inside of Darren, but it's a different strain. The same but not the same. The two strains merge and mix and mingle and create something entirely unique and wholly different.

It still takes the body over, but because of the existing strain within the host, within Darren, it changes the way it happens, making it go slowly without the sudden waves of agonising pain that would make the host drop and scream or gasp in pain.

That doesn't happen.

Instead Darren feels a minor gurgling and few stabs of discomfort as he reaches the Saxon and clambers inside to his seat, then leans over to lift an arse cheek to fart. Prompting the others to shout and jeer.

'I've got wind!' Darren says with the infection inside of his head and body, seeing through his eyes.

But not the infection that was already within Darren, and not the infection that just entered him either.

Those two have merged and become one.

A new strain.

A new version.

CHAPTER FIFTY-FIVE

'You all right, mate?' Tucker asks Darren, seeing him grimace.

'Trapped wind,' Darren replies as the pain eases off, and he settles back to rest on the journey as the deadly infection quietly consumes his body from within.

The Saxon armoured personnel carrier moves along the now empty motorway, passing fields of wheat and crops left untended and wilting in the strong sun. The strong, bright rays bounce off the bare tarmac, keeping a permanent heat shimmer just ahead of the heavy vehicle, and Howie has to squint due to the bright glare bouncing back at him. Beads of sweat slowly slide down his face, and even Dave looks red in the face for once. On a normal day, it would take only a couple of hours to reach London, but without traffic hold-ups, accidents, or the normal day-to-day congestion, they move swiftly.

The rural fields slowly give way to the urban sprawl of Greater London. The houses by the side of the busy main roads are blackened from the constant daily smog of the exhaust fumes. The houses look run down and uninviting after the beauty of rural England. Their fronts made even worse as the signs of devastation slowly start to appear. At first, they see doors hanging off houses and windows smashed in. Some of the buildings are burnt out, and some still smoulder as the fire slowly eats away at them, threatening to flare up and reignite. As they pass further into the urban mess, they see burnt-out vehicles and signs of extreme civil disorder. Debris litters the road and streets, and the front gardens of houses have their contents strewn about. Then the bodies start to appear. A few cadavers litter the roadside, but within a short distance, they increase dramatically. Bodies torn apart from horrific injuries tell a tale of extreme violence. Bodies still clutching bats, knives, and sticks lie still in pools of congealed blood. Swarms of flies buzz around them and spread disease from corpse to corpse. The rotting flesh is already falling apart, and the rate of decay increases as the high temperature slowly cooks the bodies and provides ideal breeding grounds for the writhing maggots eating them away. The rats would have slowly eaten everything in sight until just bones were left. But the rats were taken by the infection. The world's greatest scavengers have been used up, and now their bodies add to the decay.

As the group venture deeper, the visible signs become worse. There are bodies everywhere, and nothing is left undamaged. The area looks like a war zone, with the road pitted and scarred from running pitch battles, and bodies left where they fell.

The Saxon follows a clear route through main roads, and the numbers of dead increase with every passing minute.

The recruits all fall silent and lean forward to peer out of the windscreen at the horrifying scenes before them. Even Howie and Dave remain silent and watchful as they pass through.

'MOVEMENT,' Cookey shouts from his position as look-out on the general-purpose machine gun fixed to the top of the Saxon.

'Where?' Howie shouts back, easing some of the speed from the vehicle.

'OFF TO THE RIGHT. SOMEONE SAW US, THEN LEGGED IT,' Cookey shouts down.

'Okay, mate,' Howie calls out.

'I suppose we're going to see more people here. I think I'd run away too if I saw us coming,' Howie remarks to Dave, who nods back but remains silent as usual. The main road continues towards the city. Traffic lights and pedestrian crossings now dull and lifeless.

Houses give way to cheap shops that could not afford the higher rent and rates nearer the city. These too have been looted, trashed, and burnt out, and the contents thought useless to the looters have been cast aside on the pavement and road.

'Fuck me, it's hotter than hot,' Howie says to Dave as he breathes in the heavy air.

The heat is made to feel worse by the increasingly oppressive scenes in front and to the sides of them. Thick, black smoke plumes into the air from a raging fire that is off to the left, but still, they keep going forward, further into the densely populated city.

'WHAT THE FUCK IS THAT?' Cookey shouts down in alarm.

Dave leans forward and stares at an object leaning against a lamppost further ahead, down the road.

'Is that a body?' Howie asks.

'Looks like one, Mr Howie,' Dave answers.

'What the fuck?' Howie questions as they draw nearer and get a clear view of an adult male hanging, with a rope round his neck. The top of the rope is looped over the top of the street light curvature.

'Is that a zombie?' Howie asks to no one in particular.

'There's another one.' Dave points to a second body hanging in the same manner but on the other side of the road.

'Who's done that?' Howie mutters to himself. As the road sweeps around the next bend, there are bodies hanging from every lamppost, twisted and gruesome. Some of them are clearly infected from the state of their injuries and the sickening pallor of their skin; some are not so clear. As they drive on, Cookey looks to each body with morbid interest and can't help but take in the macabre scene unfolding in front of him.

Fear creeps up his spine as he tightens his grip on the handles of the machine gun.

'This is interesting,' Howie says to Dave. 'I bloody said it, didn't I? Every half an hour something happens.'

'You did,' Dave replies.

'Someone has been very busy here,' Howie says.

'Some people. One person couldn't do this,' Dave remarks as he looks to the bodies hanging high up the side of the lampposts. The road sweeps around the next bend only for the scene to become more horrific.

A large stately building is on the left, with wrought iron gates and an iron fence running alongside the pavement.

Each iron spike of the fence has a head impaled on it; each wearing a myriad of expressions. One of them is even smiling. Most have their eyes open, but not all of them have the red, bloodshot eyes of the zombies.

'This is fucking gruesome,' Blowers says in the silence of the Saxon.

'Where's the bodies?' Tucker asks as he takes in the impaled heads.

'The road signs are covered,' Dave says to Howie.

'What?'

'The road signs are covered or painted over, look.' Dave points to a large sign that once would have depicted the route ahead but is now covered in a layer of black spray paint.

'Same over there, Mr Howie,' McKinney points to another sign off to the left.

'Are you following the road map, Dave?' Howie asks, alarmed that they will become lost.

'I am,' Blowers says. 'We need to just keep going straight on and follow the signs for the city...'

'Well, that might be a bit difficult now, mate. Any other ideas?' Howie says more calmly.

'Just keep going straight. I think I know where we are on the map, and we just stick to the main road. I remember they put the letter C on the roads that lead into the city,' Blowers says.

'But what if they've covered them up too?' Tucker asks as the recruits in the back all stare at him.

'What?' Tucker says, looking back at them.

'Then we just follow the covered-up bits,' Howie calls out.

'Oh, yeah, course,' Tucker says sheepishly.

'Why cover the road signs?' Howie asks.

'To make people get lost?' Tucker states.

'AHEAD, ON THE RIGHT,' Cookey shouts, and they look ahead to see a junction on the right is blocked by several burnt-out cars pushed end to end.

They pass slowly, expecting to see a barrier formed beyond it, just as Howie and Dave saw in Portsmouth, but the road is clear and empty behind the cars. Another junction on the left has the same thing – burnt-out cars stacked to block the entrance. The Saxon continues on the main road and soon comes to a large roundabout with three exits: one on the left, one ahead, and one on the right.

The left and right are both blocked up with vehicles. The road is wide, and many vehicles have been pushed together to fully block the exits.

'Looks like they've been pushed there and then burnt out,' Howie says as he looks to the vehicles all melted and fused together in one big clump.

'Same on both sides,' McKinney states.

'Good job we need to keep ahead, then,' Howie jokes, but it falls flat in the tense environment.

'Do you think this is being done on purpose to keep us going ahead?' Curtis Graves asks.

'They wouldn't know we were coming,' Blowers replies.

'Whoever has done this couldn't know we were going to be coming along today,' Howie says confidently. The Saxon keeps a steady pace, not too fast that Howie wouldn't have any reaction time but not too slow to make them an easy target either.

'I haven't seen any zombies yet,' Howie says after another few tense moments of driving in silence.

'No, none,' Dave replies flatly.

'This is getting creepy,' Tucker says.

'Getting creepy? It's been fucking creepy for a long time,' Blowers says.

'Are you all right, Smithy?' Blowers adds, looking to Darren.

'Yeah, mate, why?' Darren asks him.

'You look pale, mate, and you're very quiet.'

'Nah, I'm all right, just tired, that's all,' Darren says to him as the recruits all look at him with concerned expressions. 'Honestly, I'm fine – just feeling tired. Didn't get any sleep last night.' Darren smiles. The lads all turn to face forward again and see more junctions blocked off with burnt and molten vehicles.

'SMOKE AHEAD,' Cookey bellows out, and within seconds,

they see thick, black smoke billowing up into the air further up the road.

'Make ready with your weapons, make sure you've got magazines in your pouches and your water bottles are full,' Dave says to the recruits.

'Already done, Dave,' Blowers says and again makes the word *Dave* sound like the word *sarge*.

'What is that?' Howie asks as they drive closer and closer to thick, black smoke.

A distinct smell hits them before they get close enough to see what is causing the fire – a smell of roasting, rotting meat.

'Ah, that's fucking gross,' Cookey shouts.

'Tell him to come down and close the hatch,' Howie calls out, and the message is passed to Cookey, who drops down and seals the hatch shut with a sigh of relief.

'That fucking stinks up there,' Cookey moans, then takes a long drink of water. They reach the area of the smoke and see a large public park on the right side of the road. Open gates lead into a big, green area with football posts and a children's play area. A massive mound is burning in the middle of the green area.

'I guess that explains where all of the bodies went,' Howie says as they slowly drive by.

Dave rummages around the switches in the front and finally flicks one on. A whirring noise starts up, and cool air is pushed out of the vents.

'Ah, that's fucking better,' Cookey remarks as he wipes sweat from his brow.

'Is that to just circulate the air in here?' Howie asks Dave.

'Yes, Mr Howie.'

'Not too long, then. It'll burn more fuel,' Howie says to groans from the lads in the back.

'We don't want to have to blow up another fuel station, do we?' Howie calls out.

'Would it be bad if I said yes?' Nick jokes as the others snigger.

'You're all just delinquents,' Howie replies as they keep going. The Saxon continues on the main road, which goes into a nicer area with big, Victorian brick buildings on both sides. There are coffee shops and expensive boutiques on nearly every corner. Every one of them is looted and smashed in. The junctions are still boxed off, and soon they start to see vehicles positioned on both sides of the road, end to end. Large vehicles, vans, and trucks are parked and blocking both sides, leaving just a wide, single lane running down the middle of the road. The parked vehicles narrow the road, and they see a large truck parked across the road ahead of them. The trucks on both sides now have cars stacked on top of them, forming high walls and a dead end ahead.

'Perfect ambush position,' Dave says quietly.

'We're okay in here, aren't we?' Howie asks him.

'From most things, yes. Small arms won't be a problem,' Dave replies.

'What about the tyres?' Howie asks.

'Run flat,' Dave replies.

'Okay. At least we can back away if we need to,' Howie says as he brings the Saxon to a halt a few hundred metres back from the truck parked across the road. They sit in silence.

The cool air blows into the interior and gives them a blessed few minutes of relief from the intense heat. Slowly, they see movement between the gaps on both sides. Shadowy figures move fast between the vehicles, then more movements up high as people on the other sides climb up the vehicles. Within minutes, they see barrels poking out of the gaps and aiming directly towards them. The barrels waver for a few minutes as the people on the other sides position themselves; then, all goes quiet.

'Has this thing got a public address system?' Howie asks, and Dave starts rummaging around the front again, opening small doors.

He pulls out a truck-style microphone, with a large button on the side. Howie takes the handset and stretches the cord over, presses the switch on the side, and taps the front of the microphone.

'Nothing. Must be a switch somewhere,' Howie says to Dave.

'That one there, Dave,' Nick Hewitt leans forward and points to one of the switches.

Dave presses it, and Howie again taps on the handset. A loud thumping noise sounds from the hidden speakers set around the vehicle.

'Here goes,' Howie says quietly and presses the switch.

'HELLO? ANYONE THERE?' Howie's voice booms out into the quiet air.

'WE ARE NOT LOOKING FOR TROUBLE. WE JUST NEED TO GET THROUGH.'

Nothing happens, so Howie again presses the button, 'WE JUST WANT TO GET THROUGH. WE DO NOT WANT ANY TROUBLE.'

'How many can you see, Dave?' Howie asks quietly.

'At least twenty on both sides, and more moving round behind them,' Dave murmurs.

'Looks like we got a reaction,' Howie says as a figure is seen crawling under the truck parked ahead of them.

The person crawls out and slowly gets to his feet.

'There's more behind him. Weapons trained on us,' Dave murmurs again.

'Bloody hell, mate, you've got good eyes,' Howie says, squinting into the gloom and just making out some movement under the truck. A very strange looking man stands up and slowly starts walking towards them. He is tall and very thin, with long, straggly, blond hair hanging limply down. Black sunglasses adorn his pale face, and he's dressed all in black, with just a flash of white socks as he bounces towards them. The man has sets of keys and other objects hanging from his belt.

'Looks like a fucking day-release patient,' Cookey mutters behind them as the man slowly walks forward, towards the Saxon. The man stops a few feet back from the front of the vehicle and slowly lifts his hand up to wave at them and smile.

'What the fuck?' Blowers states. Howie waves back and indicates for the man to come closer.

The man steps forward again, and Howie waves him around to the driver's door, then cracks the window open a few inches.

'Hello, mate,' Howie says through the window, trying to keep his voice friendly.

'Hello,' the man says in a high-pitched voice and stands staring up at Howie.

'Erm, is everything okay?' Howie asks, unsure of how to proceed.

'Yes, fine thanks,' the man says.

'So, is something wrong with the road?' Howie asks, and the man shakes his head. 'Erm, it's just that there's a big truck parked across it, and we can't get through,' Howie says.

'Big Chris put the truck there. I helped him, though,' the man says to Howie.

'That's great. It's a…err, good truck. It's just blocking the road at the moment.' The man nods back at Howie. Howie, in turn, looks over at Dave, who shrugs.

'He's a fucking nutter,' Blowers says quietly.

Howie turns back to the man. 'I'm Howie. It's nice to meet you.'

'I'm Damien,' the man says simply.

'Hi, Damien, I would get out to shake your hand, but I don't want to get shot by your friends.' Howie smiles and nods up at the trucks parked to the sides.

'Oh, they won't shoot you,' Damien laughs with glee and claps his hands.

'That's great. Did this Big Chris send you out to speak to us?' Howie asks.

'Yep, he said I was the messenger,' Damien nods seriously.

'Well, that's great, Damien. Did he give you a message, then?'

'Yep.'

'And, er, what is the message, mate?'

'Oh, yeah, ha! I forgot to tell you, didn't I?' Damien slaps his own forehead and laughs again. 'Big Chris said to ask you what you want.'

'Oh, can you tell him we just want to get through,' Howie says.

'Okay.' Damien stands still, smiling up at Howie, not moving.

'Er, and also that we don't want any trouble, and it would be very nice of him to let us go through,' Howie adds.

'Okay,' Damien says and remains rooted to the spot.

'I was just thinking, Damien, that I forget messages too if I don't hurry and relay them. Maybe you should hurry so you don't forget?' Howie says kindly.

'Oh, yeah, sorry.' Damien turns and runs back to the truck, like a child, with his arms up in the air. He gets to the truck, bends over dramatically, and looks to be shouting through.

'Jesus, he's a bit special,' Cookey says.

'Relation of yours, is he?' Blowers asks to a few sniggers.

'Fuck you,' Cookey retorts.

'He's coming back,' Cookey adds as Damien runs back to them to stand by the side and stare up at Howie again.

'Hi, Damien,' Howie says.

'Hi,' Damien replies.

'Did you tell them our message?'

'Yep.'

'Okay, that's great. Thanks, mate. What did they say?'

'Big Chris said to ask you where are you going?'

'We are going into the city. Can you tell him that, mate? We just want to get through and be on our way.'

'Okay,' Damien replies and again stands still.

'You'd best rush, mate, before we forget our messages,' Howie prompts, and Damien runs off back to the truck.

They watch him bending over and then start back towards them before being called back and bending over again; then finally, he runs back to stand beside the driver's door.

'Hi,' Damien waves up at Howie.

'Hi, Damien. What did he say?' Howie asks.

'Big Chris said the city is gone, but I don't know where it's gone. He didn't say that,' Damien says, looking confused.

'This is going to take all day,' Howie says quietly to Dave. 'Maybe I'll just go and talk to them.'

'I'll come too,' Dave says. Not a question but a statement.

'Dave, it might be best if you stay here and watch my back,' Howie says, concerned that if they both get shot, it wouldn't leave anyone to get to Sarah and would also leave the recruits on their own.

'Okay, take Blowers,' Dave says.

'Blowers, you happy with that?' Howie calls back.

'Yes, sir. Out the back or over the seat and out with you?' Blowers asks.

'Hang on just a second,' Howie says and turns back to Damien.

'Damien, can you tell Big Chris that we will come and speak with him. Make sure you tell him we are not armed. Can you do that?'

'Okay,' Damien says excitedly and runs back towards the truck, and bends over to shout the message through, pointing back at the Saxon.

Howie presses the button on the handset microphone still in his hand and speaks into it.

'TWO OF US ARE COMING OUT. WE ARE NOT ARMED,' Howie's voice booms in the enclosed area.

'I fucking hope he's not like that fucking bloke in Portsmouth,' Howie says to Dave.

'Me too.'

'What bloke?' Blowers asks as he puts his rifle down and prepares to climb over the driver's seat.

'Tell you later, mate. You ready?' Howie asks.

'Yep.'

Howie slowly opens the door and climbs down to stand beside the Saxon. His hands clearly up.

Blowers slowly climbs out and stands next to him. He sees Howie's arms up and raises his too.

'Nice and slow, mate,' Howie whispers, and they walk towards the parked truck. They both hear as the driver's door of the Saxon is closed behind them. Howie looks up at the barrels moving along with them.

'They got a lot of guns,' Howie says quietly to Blowers.

'Yeah, they bloody do, and they're all pointing at us,' Blowers replies under his breath.

They stop a few metres back from the truck and wait in silence. Then Damien stands back up and walks over to them.

'Big Chris said you can go through and talk to him.'

'Thanks, mate. Do we go under that?' Howie asks, pointing to the truck.

'Yep, follow me.' Damien turns and walks to the truck, and drops to all fours before crawling underneath it.

'Oh, well, we're here now,' Howie shrugs and starts after him.

Blowers follows, and they drop onto hands and knees to crawl under the vehicle. The smell of oil and rubber fills their noses as they proceed into the shade.

They emerge into bright sunlight and look up to see many men staring down at them, all of them armed with various weapons: shotguns, handguns, rifles, and even a few machine guns. One man stands in the centre. He is about average height but is very wide, with massively powerful shoulders and thick arms.

Howie looks up at him and notices that he isn't pumped up like a body builder, just a naturally big man, clean shaven, with short, dark, tidy hair. The big man gives an easy smile as they get to their feet.

'Just stand still for a moment, please. We need to be sure you're not armed,' he says in a firm but polite voice. Two men move forward and pat Howie and Blowers down. They are thorough and take the time to check side pockets and waistbands. They move away and nod to the big man, who takes a step forward.

'So, which one of you is the boss?' he asks in the same, polite tone.

Blowers speaks first, indicating Howie, 'Mr Howie is.'

'Nice to meet you, Mr Howie. I'm Chris.' They shake hands, and his giant mitt dwarfs Howie's hand, but his grip is surprisingly light.

'Hi, it's just Howie. Good to meet you. You must be Big Chris,' Howie says, smiling and trying to avoid the name Mr Howie from catching on again. 'This is Blowers.' Chris shakes hands with Blowers and turns straight back to Howie.

'So, you must be the army, then?' Chris says politely.

'No, mate. We just kind of borrowed one of their vehicles.'

'In army clothes? With this one calling you Mr Howie?' Chris enquires, with another rueful smile.

'Like I said, mate, it really is a long story. We're just trying to get through, but the truck is in the way.'

'I tell you what, Mr Howie. It's a hot day, and we're all melting out here. Step back in the shade with me and have a drink. Then you can tell me that long story.' Chris turns and walks away from them, making it clear they are in his backyard now.

Howie glances around to see the truck has enough room to roll forward but not backwards, and the rows of vehicles are stacked up here too, forming another narrow roadway.

They fall in step next to each other and follow Chris further down the narrow lane. The armed men wait for them to go past, then turn and follow behind them; a few staying behind to man the gateway.

The narrow lane ends suddenly, and a wide road and pavement are ahead of them. Chris leads them to a typical London pub. Hanging baskets filled with flowers droop from iron railings. Wooden benches with sun parasols stretched taut over them offer a shady relief from the sun's strong rays. Howie and Blowers exchange a glance and then stare at the people already sitting at the benches and other seats nearby. There are families with children playing in the road, and people walking about, some with purpose and others chatting amiably. The people stop and stare at the uniforms worn by Howie and Blowers. Although they are not in army greens, they both have tan-coloured combat trousers and black tops on, with utility belts hanging from their waists. Howie nods back and smiles at them as he passes. Blowers picks up on this, and soon he is offering nods and smiles to the people too. They seem comforted to see Big Chris with them, and within minutes, they return to what they were doing, and the scene switches back to normal. Which is strange as this road looks normal, with normal people dressed in normal clothes, and nobody walking around with horrific injuries. The people look clean, and the road and pavements are free from litter. None of the buildings here have been looted, and the windows are still intact. Armed men and women patrol through the crowds, and Howie watches people stop and talk to them, chatting...normally. No signs of oppression or forced captivity. The street stretches away, and they see more people walking about or sitting in the shade.

'This looks like a movie set,' Howie whispers to Blowers.

Chris leads them to a wooden bench and nods at the people sat round nearby. They nod back, and when they see Chris take a seat and motion for Howie and Blowers to sit down, they start moving away.

'It's all right. You don't have to leave,' Chris calls out, and Howie watches them closely for signs of forced behaviour, but they smile back naturally and politely make room.

'Sit down, lads, get out of that sun for a minute,' Chris says, and they both sit down opposite him.

An adult woman strolls out with three bottles of water and hands one to each of them before smiling and stroking the back of Chris's neck. He smiles back sweetly, and she strolls off back inside the pub. Chris takes a long drink and looks at Howie.

'So, about this long story?' he asks.

'Mate, I'm sorry, but this is staggering,' Howie says, looking about. 'Not what I was expecting at all.'

'What were you expecting?' Chris says with a slight smile.

'I don't know, some kind of enforced camp or something,' Howie says, still looking about at the idyllic scene.

'It looks nice, doesn't it? Took some doing, though, I can tell you, but we've got more people arriving every day, and we try to squeeze them in, of course, but we got to be careful we don't get too big, but we can always expand out a little if we need to.'

'It's amazing, Chris. How many people have you got here?' Howie asks, genuinely impressed.

'Hmmm, I think the last count yesterday was just over two thousand,' Chris answers as Howie's mouth drops open.

'Bloody hell, two thousand?' he exclaims.

'Well, that was yesterday, but more have arrived during the night, and more today, so it has gone up a little,' Chris explains.

'I don't know what to say. I went through Portsmouth, and some bloke had formed a barricade, but he was keeping the people against their will and stockpiling all the supplies for himself and his mates. Right nasty bugger he was,' Howie says.

'Oh, don't get me wrong, lads, we have strict rules here. I won't pretend otherwise, but no one is held against their will. They can come and go as they please. People are going out all the time, going to their houses to get things they want, or trying to find family and friends. We have a procedure, though, and no one gets back in without going through it.'

'What procedure is that? If you don't mind me asking, mate.' Howie says, adding the polite bit on the end in case he sounded too demanding.

'It sounds harsh, but we have sterile viewing areas, where they have to strip off, but only so we can check them for bites and scratches, and we only use same-sex vetting,' Chris says.

'We had to do a similar thing when we took refuge in a police station. It seemed horrible, but it makes sense.'

'So, let's talk about you for a minute,' Chris says politely. 'You're saying you are not from the army?'

Howie explains how he and Dave started out and how they met

the recruits along the way. Chris listens patiently, asking pertinent questions at key points and going over certain bits again until he is sure he understands it.

'So we got this far and then found your truck blocking the road, and if we can't get through, then I guess we'll have to go around.'

Chris leans back against a wall and finishes the bottle of water.

'I see. Well, it all seems to make sense. Of course, we have to be careful we don't let a load of armed soldiers in here without finding out who they are first,' Chris says.

'Honestly, we're not soldiers,' Howie protests.

'Lads, you're driving an army vehicle, carrying army guns, and dressed like soldiers. He called you Mr Howie, which shows me there is some element of control and discipline within your group. So you *are* soldiers,' Chris explains clearly.

'Yeah, I guess so,' Howie agrees reluctantly.

They sit in silence for a moment.

'What about you? How did all this come about?' Howie asks, eager to find out.

Chris leans forward to speak, but Howie interrupts him.

'Mate, I'm so sorry, but I just realised my lads are sat in the vehicle out there, and it's sweltering. Can they come through?' he asks.

'Well, they can but not with their weapons,' Chris says, looking directly at Howie.

'I understand. What will happen to the weapons and vehicle if they leave it there?' Howie asks.

'I can guarantee that it won't be touched. I can have one of my men drive it in, and you're welcome to have your men near it but not in it, and I will have my men nearby too,' Chris says firmly.

'I understand, Chris, but we can't afford to lose that vehicle or weapons. It's the only chance we've got of getting through to the city,' Howie counters.

'Sorry, Howie, family is important. I understand that, but I've got over two thousand people relying on me for safety and security, and I don't think they'll be impressed if I let a bunch of armed soldiers in here.'

'They're just lads, Chris, only eighteen years old, apart from Dave.'

'Dave?' Chris asks.

'You'll meet Dave. He's, er, different. An exceptional man, just a bit different,' Howie says, and Chris leans back, staring at Howie as he thinks.

'Tell you what, let me and some of my men come out and check you all over first. The slightest whiff of bother, though, and well, I think you'll know what will happen. Is that fair?' Chris offers.

'Sounds more than fair to me,' Howie says, looking at Blowers, who nods in agreement.

A few minutes later, the truck is being pulled forward to save Big Chris having to crawl under it. Damien is still near the Saxon, staring at the windscreen from a few feet away.

'Who's he?' Howie asks as they walk out towards the Saxon.

'Damien? He's all right, can be a bit of a pest, but he's good at this sort of thing. He hasn't got a confrontational bone in his body, so he's ideal as a messenger for anyone that looks a bit naughty,' Chris chuckles.

A few armed men walk behind them, holding weapons ready but aimed down to show they are not a threat, yet. Howie is impressed by the control and discipline.

Back at the Saxon, Howie walks with Chris and holds his hand up to Dave, motioning for him to come out.

Dave opens the driver's door, and Howie calls for him to come out unarmed. Dave pauses for a few seconds, then puts down his rifle and pistol.

'Chris, this is Dave. Dave, this is Big Chris,' Howie introduces them and smiles as they shake hands, and Dave quickly wipes his hand down his trouser leg.

'Lads, come out the back but leave the weapons inside for a minute, make sure none of you is armed,' Howie calls out and hears shuffling noises as the lads move to the back of the Saxon, and the rear doors open.

They climb out stiffly, with red, sweating faces.

'That thing's an oven,' Cookey moans as he steps down.

'I left the air on for you,' Howie answers him.

'Dave switched it off, worried about the fuel,' Cookey says but is careful to show respect when mentioning Dave.

The lads walk around to the side as Howie introduces them one by one. Chris takes the time to shake hands with them all, then excuses himself, and walks around the back to look in the rear doors, coming back after a few minutes of close examination.

'Okay, Howie, you can come through, but it would make me feel a lot better if the weapons stayed in the vehicle,' Chris says finally.

'I'm not sure, mate. It all seems genuine, but like I said, we can't afford to lose them,' Howie states.

'I understand. I guarantee they won't be touched by anyone inside. I'll have my men guard it,' Chris offers.

'How about a few of yours and a couple of mine?' Howie says, smiling at Chris. 'That way, we both feel better.'

Chris laughs with genuine amusement.

'If that makes you feel better, then okay, but I don't know what a couple of yours will do against the many we have in there,' Chris laughs.

'Ah, keeps the lads busy if nothing else,' Howie chuckles back to the groans from the recruits.

'Okay, come on through, then. I'll get the truck pulled forward.'

'Curtis, can you drive it through? Blowers and Cookey, you're first up on guard duty. Get your weapons now, but for fuck's sake keep them lowered and fingers away from the triggers, got it?'

They nod back as Curtis climbs back into the vehicle and through to the driver's seat.

Blowers and Cookey both collect their weapons and hold them ready but lowered as instructed.

CHAPTER FIFTY-SIX

'You happy with this, Dave?' Howie asks as he falls into step with Dave.

'If you are, Mr Howie,' Dave replies.

'It looks really nice inside. Wait until you see it.' They walk through the gap left by the truck and down the narrow lane. Dave and Howie follow Chris, flanked by some of the armed men. The Saxon is following slowly behind them, with Blowers and Cookey just in front of it.

Howie glances back and catches them walking at a steady pace, looking about and smiling at the other armed guards. *They do look like real soldiers,* Howie thinks and is glad he chose those two to take first guard. Their easy manner and banter will show them in a non-threatening light.

The lane ends, and the lads all stare in amazement at the surreal scene in front of them. They follow Chris over to the wooden benches outside the pub, and within minutes, they are sitting down in the shade, drinking bottles of water.

'Thanks for that, Chris. They won't be any bother to you, I promise,' Howie says in earnest.

'They seem good lads. Young, though.' Chris rubs his chin as he stares at the recruits.

'So, you were saying how all this came about,' Howie reminds him.

'I was. Well, I was born and raised here. I know pretty much everyone, and they know me. I was in this boozer when it started, and we got some rough lads that drink in here; lads that can handle themselves. If you know what I mean. So we were able to keep them away. More people joined us in the pub, and we fought out and cleared this street here first. Then, as more people arrived, we pushed out and kept gaining ground. We didn't attack them as much as remove them. I worked on the principle of securing ground and preventing them getting back in. We used local resources to form barriers and barricades, and over the next few days, we found ways of getting our people in and out safely. Then a couple came back bitten and risked everyone else, so we put the vetting procedures in place. We are lucky as we've got a few doctors and nurses, and ex-army medics with us. They are setting up a little hospital. We send foraging parties out during the day, with strict instructions not to engage unless absolutely necessary. Their primary function is to gather supplies: medicines, equipment, fuel, food – all the things we need to survive. Even the doctors have no idea how long this will last, so the plan is to keep secure and try to wait it out,' Chris finishes.

'And you're in charge of all this?' Howie asks, and Chris ponders the question.

'Yes, I am. But only in the sense of putting the right people in the right places and making sure the area is secure. Lads, I come from a hard background. I served in the Forces and then fell into some not very nice things. I've had all sorts of jobs, and I guess I was just in the right place at the right time when this happened.'

'What were you in?' Dave asks; the first time he has spoken since they sat down.

'I was in the Parachute Regiment, but that was years ago. I did some other stuff with other departments and worked overseas for a while, helping teach guerrilla tactics. Like I said, I came out and did some naughty things, and served a bit of time. What were you in?' Chris returns the question to Dave.

'I was Special Forces,' Dave answers, and Howie almost spits his drink out in surprise. Dave has always answered *I can't say* when anyone has asked him that.

'I thought you were,' Chris says. 'I met a few of them, worked with a few too. Mind you, most Special Forces never say they were Special Forces,' he says, staring intently at Dave.

'I don't normally, but I can see the regimental tattoo on your arm, and you wouldn't get that without actually serving. The Regiment lads would never let that happen. I've met your lads before, and they all have that same look about them too,' Dave responds, holding direct eye contact with Chris.

'How many exits have you noted?' Chris asks without looking away.

'There are four immediately obvious. One, the way we came in, but your people are still on those high sides, providing a perfect ambush site, so that exit is negated. My assumption, from the way these people are walking about, is that the exit points are secured with armed men. Two, these buildings are deep and would lead out into the area you have not secured, and you would be using the natural building line as a barrier. Those windows and doors would lead out. Three, these buildings have connecting roofs, which could be used to move from one to the other, to a non-secure area,' Dave finishes, still staring back.

'What's four?' Howie asks.

They both remain silent for a few seconds before Chris replies, 'I'm four – you take me, and you could walk out untouched.' He slowly smiles.

'You have a mixture of weapons and have used the rifles as sniper points, keeping the shotguns further back to make use of the power and keep a clear firing line. The armed people patrolling this area are made up of services and police. The services people hold their weapons in a permanent state of readiness, with the fingers stretched over the trigger guard. The police walk differently, with a steady tread due to the fact they spend long periods on patrol. You covered the road signs to keep people *or those things* confused as to where they were going. You strung the already dead bodies up and the heads on spikes to show any possible other survivors that you were not to be messed with and to send a clear signal to any potential invaders,' Dave says flatly to an enormous grin spreading across Chris's face.

'Okay, okay, well done. You've convinced me,' Chris laughs and finally breaks away from Dave's intense stare.

'I see what you mean,' Chris says to Howie, nodding towards Dave. 'The heads and hanged bodies send a strong signal, but most of them were dead already. Like I said, I don't go actively looking for them.'

'Are they stacked up at the exits?' Howie asks.

'Some of them are. Massive crowds of them. A few of our exits have been kept quiet, though, and we use our people to lure them away when they get too many.'

'So what have you heard about the city?' Howie asks.

'It's a few miles from here and completely overrun. Where is your sister?'

'Canary Wharf,' Howie replies.

'That's going to be hard, very hard. None of us have ventured that deep. I know most of the roads that way are infested.'

'Well, we have the Saxon and plenty of ammunition, so we should get through,' Howie says, watching Chris, who seems deep in thought.

'Have you thought about your route in?' he asks eventually.

'We have a road atlas. We'll work from that,' Howie replies.

'Right... I'm thinking of something here. We might be able to help each other out,' Chris says slowly.

'Come with me. I want you to meet someone.' He gets up and starts walking away from the bench.

Howie and Dave shrug at each other and follow him out from under the shade of the parasol and into the hot sun again.

'Stay here, lads. We'll be back soon,' Howie says as the recruits all start getting to their feet.

'Are you all right, Darren? You don't look well, mate.' Howie stops in front of him, looking with concern at the pale and sweating face of Darren Smith.

'I'm fine, Mr Howie. Just this heat, I think,' Darren replies, wiping at his forehead.

'Get plenty of fluids, mate. You might be dehydrated. Stay in the shade, too.' Howie walks off with Dave, following Chris down the street, past the big Victorian buildings and the groups of people walking through the area. They reach a side street and see the end is fully blocked off, with stacked vehicles and other items forming a high and substantial barricade. Armed guards watch from over the barricade, out of open windows, on the adjacent buildings.

'If we don't make it to the forts, this wouldn't be a bad second choice,' Howie says to Dave as they follow Chris further up the street.

'Seems nice, Mr Howie,' Dave agrees.

Chris stops at the doorway to a large building and pushes the door open. Two armed guards are outside, leaning against the wall, smoking cigarettes.

'Come in here, lads.' Chris walks into the gloom of the building, followed by Howie, then Dave.

They enter a reception area, with wooden flooring and doors leading off to both sides. A woman appears, wearing a white lab coat, with a stethoscope hanging from her neck.

'Hi, Chris, everything okay?' she asks, with a genuine smile to the big man.

'Hi, Doc. Yeah, everything is fine. Just showing these lads about. Is Doc Roberts about?' Chris replies, smiling at the pretty doctor.

'He's around here somewhere. Make sure you clean your hands if you go in.' She disappears through another door.

'This is the hospital we set up. We've got operating rooms and triage points through those doors. It's very basic but okay for now. Come with me.' Chris opens a door to the right and walks through. Howie and Dave enter a wood panelled room, with rows of beds on both sides. The beds are occupied by sleeping figures swathed in bandages and dressings.

'The beds are valuable and only the most seriously injured use them,' Chris explains quietly as they walk down.

'Stop right there, please,' an older man, wearing a white lab coat, calls over in a firm voice.

'Clean your hands,' the man gestures for them to go back, waving his arm.

'Sorry, Doc,' Chris calls out and takes them back to a desk next to the door they came through, picking up a large bottle of antibacterial hand wash and applying it liberally on his hands before offering the bottle to Howie.

'That's Doc Roberts,' Chris says. 'He's in charge of the hospital.' He smiles as the older doctor approaches them.

'Good to see you, Chris. Everything all right out there?' Doctor Roberts asks, raising thick, grey eyebrows over bright, intelligent eyes.

'Yes, Doc, this is Howie and Dave. They arrived a short time ago from the south. It's as bad down there as we thought.'

'Hmmm, I thought it would be. Good to meet you.' The doctor nods at them.

'You too, Doctor. Have you any idea what's causing this?' Howie asks.

'Not a clue,' the doctor says. 'The infection can enter from saliva or blood, and once it's in the body, it takes everything over. None of us have ever seen anything like it before. But we don't have the equipment or the means to start examining it properly.'

'Which is why we have come to see you, Doc,' Chris says.

'These lads are going to Canary Wharf. There's a few of them, and they're armed to the teeth, too. Might be a good chance to try for that hospital you mentioned...?'

'Excellent, I will prepare a list immediately. Ideally, I want to send someone with you, but I cannot afford to risk losing any trained people,' the doctor replies instantly. 'We need equipment, surgical implements, and as many medicines as you can find. I'll get on it now. My list will be ready in ten minutes.' The doctor turns and walks back down the room and through another door.

'Well, that's that, then,' Chris shakes his head as he leads them out of the hospital and back into the street.

'Chris, we don't have time to do a hospital raid for you,' Howie says politely. 'If we can get Sarah and bring her here, maybe we can go back, but I have to get her first.'

'No, that's not what I'm thinking. I think we could join forces and go with you. That armoured personnel carrier will be an ideal support vehicle, and if we combine our forces, we should get through a lot easier.'

'So how would it work?' Howie asks as they walk back down the street towards the pub.

'The hospital is on the way, well, just a very minor deviation, but if you help us get to the hospital, we'll go with you to your sister. We combine the strength of our forces and work together,' Chris explains.

'Why that hospital? London is huge, and there must be other ones closer.'

'Doctor Roberts helped design it, and he was in charge of it. It's brand new, and he knows every piece of equipment in there and the exact layout too. Plus, it received a huge funding allowance for infectious disease research, so he wants some the equipment from that area in particular.'

'It does make sense, I guess. How long will it take before you're ready to go?'

Chris stops to consider the question, nodding his head from side-to-side.

'An hour or so.'

They agree to meet near the Saxon, and Howie returns to the pub and calls Blowers and Cookey over.

'We've got a plan,' Howie says once they are all grouped round.

'We are heading into the city, to the Canary Wharf area, where my sister lives. Chris said the area will be overrun, but we have the Saxon and weapons, with plenty of ammunition.' They nod back at him.

'Chris wants to do a raid on a special hospital on the way. There's a doctor here who got some funding for an infectious disease research lab. He wants to join forces, and we'll help him with the hospital, and he will help us get to Sarah. I've said yes, but I'm open to any questions or concerns from you guys,' Howie finishes and looks to each of them.

'I'm happy,' Cookey offers first.

'With men's arses,' Blowers mutters to a few chuckles.

'I'm in too.'

'Me too,' Hewitt says.

'We are coming back through here on the way back, though?'

'That's the plan, Nick. It looks nice here, doesn't it? I was thinking this would be my second choice if the forts don't work out.'

The recruits nod.

The extreme contrast from the incredibly degraded urban area, the battles, the violence, and the utmost upset they have already faced is stark against this calm area full of normal-looking people going about normal lives, and it reminds each of them of what they've lost.

'Lads, this is a personal mission for me to save my sister, and I've said from the beginning you don't have to do this. Any of you can stand down and stay here, or choose to do what you wish, with no comeback from me. You're all young, and your lives have already been devastated enough. You don't have to keep going with this,' Howie says in earnest.

'Nah, I'm still in. We've come this far. It would be a shame to stop now, and besides, there's still a shitload of them fucking zombies to kill,' Hewitt is the first to speak his mind.

'I'm with Hewitt,' Cookey adds.

'In more ways than one,' Blowers says.

'Stop with the fucking gay jokes, you dick,' Cookey says, exasperated.

'You want dick?' Blowers retorts with a smile.

'Before them two get going again, I want to say I'm in too,' Tucker holds his hand up.

'And me,' McKinney adds. The rest add their affirmation with nods and grins.

'You lot must be fucking mad,' Howie says, grinning back at them. 'But I am glad you're on my side, though. I wouldn't want to face you lot in a fight.'

'Fucking right,' Cookey says with firm conviction.

CHAPTER FIFTY-SEVEN

Darren Smith works alongside the recruits, unloading the weapons from the Saxon and stripping them down for cleaning under the watchful eye of Dave. He sweats heavily, but then the weather is scorching, and everyone else sweats too.

His skin flushes red, and at times, he feels dizzy, but then the others also look flushed, and after everything they've been through, Darren puts it down to stress, heat, and the constant action.

A NEW STRAIN.

A new version.

Darren's heart beats strong and healthy. Sending infected blood throughout his body. Changing every cell while resisting the urge to take control. Instead, it allows Darren to think and act freely, and in so doing, it sees where Darren is.

Inside a commune packed with potential new hosts.

The infection, even this strain developing within Darren, is young and still learning, but even it fathoms there must be pockets of survivors like this everywhere. Whole swathes of potential new hosts that need to be turned and taken. Because that is the primary driving force within the virus. The absolute need pulsing through all of the hosts: To take more hosts.

The infection also starts feeling the reactions with Darren when Howie speaks. It observes the chemical reaction that invokes a change, and it recognises the thought processes that fly through the mind as Darren listens intently.

Darren deeply admires and respects Howie and the small man called Dave that is always next to him. Darren feels a great sense of loyalty to this them, and the infection picks up on this and knows it can work to learn how to use these chemicals and feelings to control more of the host bodies and make them feel loyalty towards a leader just like the lads do with Howie.

It hears the one they call Howie talk about Sarah and a place called Canary Wharf, and the city, and the infection scours through billions of memories and thought processes to work this out. It slowly develops an understanding of the route they will take, of the path that lies before them and the end destination.

Within Canary Wharf and the surrounding streets, and neighbourhoods, all of the hosts stop and turn to face the route Howie and the resistors will take.

Those on the outskirts are sent shuffling in that direction, and other survivors are amazed and greatly relieved to see hordes of hosts moving in one mass filing towards another area.

The infection has already once made the mistake of making them move too fast too soon and weakened the feeble bodies, but now it will keep them slow, repairing until the time is right.

The infection has learned to plan ahead, and it will do it right this time.

CHAPTER FIFTY-EIGHT

Sarah wakes up late on Wednesday morning. Her head aching as she lifts it from the pillows. Her hair is splayed out and messy, and her throat feels dry. She slowly rolls to the edge of the bed and pushes her legs over the side. Her feet knocking into the empty wine bottles left by the side of the bed.

With a groan, she looks at the several bottles lying throughout the room and slowly remembers the righteous decision she made to get smashed. Not a heavy drinker anyway, the alcohol had a rapid effect on her due to her empty stomach, which now heaves in complaint at the harsh chemicals forced into it the night before. She runs to the toilet and just manages to lift the lid as she vomits into the bowl, retching and dry heaving until nothing but bile comes up.

She sinks down and rests her pounding head on the cool tiles of the floor, regretting every single gulp of wine she took. She started off listening to thumping rock tracks on her iPod, but as the alcohol took effect, she selected the slower songs until she was wallowing in self-pity, listening to power ballads over and over.

She doesn't even recall getting into bed but gets flashbacks of dancing naked in the tiny apartment after stripping off her clothes in the sultry heat of the evening. Sarah lies on the floor, with sweat pouring off her body, and the rancid taste of bile in her mouth. She slowly gets up and crawls to the corner shower cubicle, closing the door behind her. She reaches up and twists the water flow on, giving a scream as the freezing jets of water soak into her before sliding down to lie on her side and let the water cleanse her.

CHAPTER FIFTY-NINE

Howie drives the Saxon slowly down the main road, nodding and smiling at people as they step out of the way.

Armed guards walk in front and to the sides of the vehicle, reassuring the residents of the commune that all is okay with their presence.

'I like that Chris bloke,' Howie says to Dave.

'He seems okay,' Dave replies.

'Nice place, this.'

'Yes, Mr Howie.'

'So how come you decided to be open about your military background?' Howie asks.

'It served a purpose. We needed him on our side, and the Parachute Regiment always worked well with our lot.'

'So, it was a tactic?'

'Yes, Mr Howie.'

'Smart move, mate, and that stuff about the exits was clever too, and the way he realised he was the fourth – that was impressive.'

'Thanks, Mr Howie.'

'No, mate, I mean it. This heat is getting worse. There must be a storm coming.'

'Maybe.'

'I've never known it so hot. Even the road surface is melting.'
'I can see.'
'Have you known it hotter than this?'
'A few times,' Dave replies.
'Where?'
'The jungle is hot and humid. It just saps the blokes and drains them. The desert is different – dry heat, with no escape.'
'What do you prefer, heat or cold?' Howie asks.
'I don't mind. I did service in cold places and hot places. It doesn't bother me too much.'
'You must have a preference?'
'Not really, Mr Howie. How about you?'
'I thought I loved the heat, but I'm having doubts now. Sitting on a beach in Spain with a cold beer is slightly different than running around the country, killing zombies.'
'I guess so. Never been to Spain. Well, I went to Gibraltar once. Does that count?'
'Gibraltar? That's a British place, but it's in Spain, so yeah, I guess it does. Where did you go on holiday?'
'I didn't.'
'What about downtime or when you had time off?'
'I stayed at the base or went back to get ready for the next mission.'
'Bloody hell, mate. Never had a holiday?'
'No, Mr Howie.'
'Well, maybe after this ends, you should take one.'
'This won't end,' Dave says flatly.
'It has to end sometime. One way or the other,' Howie says, quietly staring dead ahead.

The end of the road sees a repeat of the entrance area – vehicles piled high on both sides to form solid walls, and another big truck parked across the gap.

The road they travelled down to get here was surprisingly long, and Howie realises how much effort and work Chris and his group have put into securing space and then keeping it secure. This is just the main road, though, and the safe area extends out to both sides, taking in side streets and more buildings to house the increasing number of people living here. Howie realises this cannot be sustained, after the devastation they've witnessed. This place looks ideal, but with increasing numbers of displaced refugees, there will be increasing numbers of problems.

The food they can source from raiding parties will last for a while. The city housed millions, so finding food for a few thousand will be easy enough for a while, but after that, they will need renewable supplies.

The water supply is another thing, maintained by experts who clean and sanitize it with chemicals, and keep the flow going. Who will do that now? Who will secure a constant supply of fresh water, not just for drinking but for bathing, and cleaning too?

Children will need milk and fresh food, and education, and as nice as this environment seems now, unless they start long-term planning, they will soon perish.

These people will settle into their new lives, and the pain and loss they have suffered will fade. After that, they will become like any other society – greedy, selfish, wanting more, and questioning those in charge.

Chris rules the roost now, but it won't be long before someone else emerges and challenges him. At the moment, they look to him for safety and security and are thankful for the efforts he has taken and the control measures he has put into place. Will he be able to maintain that calm exterior when he's challenged, or will power corrupt and turn him into a despotic tyrant, enforcing his rule with an iron will?

The truck is already pulled back to reveal the stretch of road on the other side. Chris is positioned next to another large truck, looking up and speaking to someone in the cabin. There are a few four-wheel drive vehicles waiting on the road, and more vehicles parked up – vans, sports cars, and motorbikes.

There are more vehicles piled high on the sides here too, but the road is wider, and Howie realises this is still a sterile area but used now as a car park for the commune's small fleet of various vehicles. There is another large truck parked further down the road, forming the end of the barricade. The other side must be the unsecure area. The Saxon rolls up behind a four-wheel drive vehicle, which is immediately behind the truck. There are plenty of men here with automatic weapons. Some dressed in part-police clothing, and some in a mish-mash of army and civilian clothing.

'They've kept the best weapons for this lot,' Dave remarks, looking around at the armed groups.

'Where did they all come from?' Howie asks.

'Most of them look like police issue; although, there are some military weapons in there too.'

Chris walks over to them, and Howie jumps down to meet him at the front of the Saxon.

'You all ready?' Chris asks.

'Yep, what's the plan?' Howie asks as another man carrying a black machine gun walks up to join their group.

Dave slides out of the Saxon and comes round to join them too.

'Howie, this is Malcolm. He was in the Regiment with me,' Chris introduces them as they shake hands.

'I was thinking, Chris, we either need the weight of the truck at the front to plough through them or the main fighting vehicle, which will be the Saxon here,' Malcolm says.

'If the truck is the main vehicle to bring supplies back, then it should be kept safe and protected in the middle,' Dave says in a firm voice.

'Is this the Special Forces guy?' Malcolm asks Chris.

'Can't you tell? You're getting old and rusty, mate,' Chris jokes.

'Piss off, you fat bastard,' Malcolm fires back as Chris laughs.

Howie watches the exchange and can't help but be reminded of Blowers and Cookey.

'He's right, though,' Chris says.

'We need the hospital supplies, and the truck is the only vehicle it will all fit in. I think we'll keep it in the middle and use the Saxon as the point vehicle. How much ammunition do you have for the GPMG?' Chris asks Dave.

'Plenty, I took all of it from Salisbury.' Dave answers as both Chris and Malcolm raise their eyebrows.

'All of it? Fucking hell, mate, you going to war?' Malcolm asks.

'Yes,' Dave answers to an uncomfortable silence broken by Chris coughing politely.

'So that settles it, then. The Saxon in the lead, with the truck behind, and then the four-wheel drives behind them as support vehicles.'

'How many people do we have?' Dave asks.

'You have your lot in the Saxon. That's ten, isn't it?' Chris asks.

'Yeah, eight recruits, Dave, and I.'

'We got two in the truck cabin. One is the driver, but he's got no experience of weapons, so we've put a bloke in there with him. Then four in each of the four-wheel drive vehicles behind the truck. I'll be in the first one with three lads, and Malcolm in the second with another three. All of them are handpicked and have served in the military or the armed police,' Chris explains.

'Signals and communications,' Dave says.

'We got some shortwave radios that we got from some bouncers. They will work for a few hundred metres, but that's it. The Saxon is Alpha, the truck is Bravo. I will be Charlie, and Malcolm will be Delt. Keep it simple. You happy?' Chris asks the small group.

'Yep,' Malcolm answers, and both Howie and Dave nod in agreement.

A very large-built, muscular man with a bald head and a tight, black t-shirt approaches them, carrying small, black radios. He hands them out to each of them.

'They got fresh batteries. Use channel one,' the man says in a very deep voice.

'How long will they last?' Howie asks.

'They lasted all night on the doors, and that's with constant use, so they will be good for the day,' the man answers before walking off. As he turns, Howie sees a small machine gun hanging from a strap across his back, previously hidden by his immense girth.

'Did he serve with you, too?' Howie asks as the man walks away.

'Yeah, good bloke. Looks like an animal, but he's as calm as they come,' Malcolm answers.

'Er, what about the route? None of us know London very well,' Howie asks.

'You got that road atlas handy?' Chris asks, and Dave runs back to pull it out from the front of the Saxon. Chris takes a red pen from his pocket and marks along the roads.

'It's pretty much a straight run up to Tower Bridge. I suggest we plan an RV just before the Bridge and go from there,' Chris says, handing the atlas back to Dave.

Howie looks at the marked route, which does look like an easy run.

'Right, we'll go round to the front. Shout when you're ready to move off,' Howie says.

'One more thing. Our ammunition is good, but it won't last forever, so we'll be relying on your lads and the GPMG to do most of the shooting,' Chris says before walking off with Malcolm.

'You happy with the plan, Dave?' Howie asks, relying on his military skill and tactical sense.

'Yes, Mr Howie, do you want me to be ComsOp?'

'Er, if I knew what that was, I would answer you.'

'Communication Operative.'

'Oh, you want the radio?' Howie asks as he hands the small device with the stubby aerial to Dave.

Dave accepts it without a word.

Howie drives the Saxon around to the front and pulls in ahead of the truck while explaining the plan to the lads in the back.

'So we're going right into the city then?' McKinney asks.

'Yes, mate. At least we get to see some sights – Tower Bridge, maybe Big Ben, spot of lunch in Covent Garden, take in a show in the West End, then into Soho for some fun.'

The lads cheer at the idea and start talking about how many beers they would drink and how many women they would pull.

'*This is Charlie. Radio check, radio check. Delta, are you reading me?*' the radio crackles to life in Dave's hand.

'*Delta receiving loud and clear, Charlie.*'

'*Charlie to Bravo. Radio check.*'

'*Bravo receiving loud and clear, Charlie.*'

'*Charlie to Alpha. Radio check.*'

Dave answers in a crisp, clear voice, '*Alpha receiving loud and clear.*'

'*Roger that, Alpha. All units loud and clear. Radio check complete. Alpha will maintain point. Bravo to keep a close distance but be ready to hold back in case of contacts. Ready when you are, Alpha,*' Chris's voice booms through the radio.

'Alpha to Charlie, do you want notice if we establish contact?' Dave asks into the radio.

'Charlie to Alpha, yes, if you have time, but all units, be aware in case Alpha opens up without notice, do not run into the arc of fire.'

'Roger that, Charlie. Moving out now,' Dave answers and looks to Howie, who slowly drives forward.

The truck blocking the road starts up and gently pulls forward to reveal the clear road beyond.

The Saxon pulls out and proceeds down the road at a slow speed until the follow vehicles are clear of the barricade, and then gently increases the speed.

'Who's up top?' Howie asks Dave.

'Hewitt.'

'Blowers, make sure that Hewitt shouts down before he opens up on anything. We just want to get there and back quickly.'

The signs soon start appearing. First, some debris on the road; then, bodies lying festering in the high heat. Corpses of rats and people lie where they dropped. Windows of houses are smashed in, vehicles are burning, and there's blood everywhere. The already hardened people within the vehicles look out to the extreme scenes, and despite being in countless war zones, each of them feels a sense of loss and pain at the things they see. Hewitt half pokes out of the hole in the roof of the Saxon, holding onto the handles of the GPMG tightly, partly for balance but also for comfort. After all, he's an eighteen-year-old man in charge of a heavy calibre machine gun while riding as point vehicle for an armed convoy, undertaking a daring raid and rescue mission.

The Saxon reaches a junction, and Dave indicates to take a right turn. Within minutes, they start to see infected all shuffling in the same direction that they are going.

'AHEAD, SIR,' Hewitt shouts down.

'The priority is to get there, but fucking look at this lot. Why are they going in the same direction as us?' Howie calls out.

'I don't know. They're not even turning to look at us,' Dave answers.

'Dave, let them know we're opening up, and someone tell Hewitt he can crack on and slaughter as many as he can,' Howie calls out.

'*Alpha to all units. Large groups ahead and to the sides. We will fire on them, over.*'

'Hewitt, Mr Howie says to crack on and get as many as you can,' Blowers shouts up.

'Thank fuck for that,' Hewitt mutters and racks the bolt back to engage the chain. A grim smile forms across his face as he squeezes the trigger slowly. He feels the pressure as the trigger depresses under his finger, and the machine gun comes to life, spewing hot lead into the backs of the infected as they shuffle in front of the Saxon.

The massive bullets rip into them, shredding their bodies and ripping them apart as the general-purpose machine gun roars with vengeance.

'Sir, can we open the back doors and shoot them down?' Cookey shouts out.

'Fucking do it, kill 'em, kill them all!' Howie bellows. The rear doors burst open, and recruits lean out to fire left and right at the slow, shuffling infected, ripping them apart and wreaking revenge.

'What the fuck are they doing?' Chris shouts from his position as passenger of the four-wheel drive vehicle.

'Having fun, by the looks of it, Chris,' one of the men in the rear says.

Chris spins around to see them both grinning, and he shakes his head as a slow smile spreads across his face.

'Fuck it, why not?' he says as he winds the window down and points the end of his assault rifle out. The Saxon leads, with the recruits taking it in turns to man the GPMG and slaughter the infected from the top position. The rest take turns to shoot from the rear doors, yelling and cheering as they take them down. The ones closest to the back doors are gripped from behind by the recruits further in to save them from falling out. The passenger of the truck is leaning out of the window, firing down into the hordes as they pass. Both of the four-wheel drive vehicles have barrels pointing out of the windows, firing into the dense hordes. There are thousands and thousands of infected slowly staggering into London, strung out in long, shuffling queues.

'MY FUCKING TURN. BRACE YOURSELVES,' Howie bellows.

'BRACED!' Blowers shouts back as the recruits all grab a hand-hold, and the ones closest to the doors step back inside. Howie gently veers to the side and inches closer and closer to the infected strung out ahead of them.

The solid-plated, heavy Saxon clips the first one, who gets spun off, taking out more infected next to him.

The Saxon holds a steady course as Howie slams its front right wing into the backs of the horde, pulverising them and sending them splattering off. The vehicle takes the punishment without hesitation, and they leave a broken and bloody trail of mashed-up zombies behind them.

Howie pulls off to the left, creating a bloody slick behind the Saxon. He keeps going for several minutes as the GPMG starts up again, and through the view of the windscreen, he sees bodies burst apart, blood spraying high and slamming into the thick glass screen. The recruits resume their killing from the rear doors as they slaughter every one of the infected that they can hit. Many escape the deadly firing, but many more are cut down and left to rot on the road.

'AHEAD!' McKinney shouts from his position up top.

Howie and Dave both lean forward and peer down the road to another junction completely blocked by a massive horde. They are trying to walk into a smaller side street, but the immense size has clogged them at the junction, and more join the back of the crowd, pushing forward.

'It feels like they know where we're going,' Howie says to Dave.

'I agree,' Dave answers.

'We're definitely being targeted.'

'Looks like it, Mr Howie.'

Howie brings the Saxon to a slow crawl just back from the massed horde, all facing the other way at the junction.

'*Alpha to all units. Road is blocked ahead,*' Dave transmits over the radio.

'We'll have to take them out,' Howie says, staring at them, and his left hand drops down to touch the top of the axe handle sticking up. Dave catches the movement and looks at Howie.

'*Alpha to all units. We're going to take these out,*' Dave says, still staring at Howie.

'Charlie to Alpha. Are you using the GPMG? We can't hear it. Is there a problem?' Chris asks.

Dave pauses to look at Howie, at the darkness starting to seep in across his face. Dave notices Howie's breathing has become slightly faster as he stares intently at the horde facing them.

'Alpha to Charlie. Negative. We are doing this the old-fashioned way. Standby.'

CHAPTER SIXTY

Dave drops the handset next to me, but all I can see are the hundreds of infected stacked up in front of us. They are targeting us, going to our location, somehow knowing where we are heading, and trying to get there ahead of us. They have taken my mother and father, and now they threaten to destroy the rescue attempt of my sister. No, this isn't a rescue *attempt* – this *is* a rescue. I will get to her, and I will find her. These things will clearly do everything they can to stop me, but I will prevail.

My breathing increases, and I feel *him, or it,* inside me. He went away after the last battle, but now he's back, and he wants another payment.

I pause at the door; my hand resting on the handle. I know what will happen if I open the door. I can see what will happen. I want that to happen. I want it more than anything. My hand grips the axe handle, and I look across to Dave, who is staring at me intently.

I twist slowly in my seat and look into the rear of the Saxon – eight young faces stare at me with grim expectation.

Eight faces watch me, and I see those eight faces struggling to contain the violence that is threatening to burst out.

Eight young faces that have seen more violence and destruction than most see in a lifetime: Blowers, McKinney, Cookey, Smith,

Tucker, Hewitt, Reese, and Graves all stare back at me. No one speaks, for we can all hear the anger and the rage, and the fury knocking at the doors.

Our hands rest, waiting for the second when we can open the door and unleash hell.

I look back to Dave slowly and stare into the killer's eyes. I nod to him once and watch as he slowly draws breath in.

'FIX BAYONETS!' Dave shouts at the top of his voice – a drill sergeant voice, a parade square voice that booms around the buildings, and the horde starts shuffling around to face us.

'Ready, Dave?'

'Yes, Mr Howie.'

'Ready, lads?'

'YES, MR HOWIE!' they shout, and I'm out, flying through the air, with my glorious axe in hand.

Dave has done the same. Both of us leaving our assault rifles in the vehicle as I swing my axe in preparation, and Dave turns his knives back against his wrists so that the blades rest up against his forearms.

We pause as the recruits pile out of the back and stand behind us. A thin line, with me and Dave out front. The horde turns and starts their shuffle towards us. We wait. They shuffle and groan, and we wait. I hear clicks as bayonets are fitted. I turn to look and see a few of them have left their rifles in the vehicles and are just holding their long, deadly bayonet knives down at their sides. Jamie Reese has one in each hand like his idol, Dave. They shuffle, and we wait.

Chris bursts out of the four-wheel vehicle and starts walking forward past the truck. His men join him just as Malcolm and his group run to catch up.

'What are they doing?' Malcolm asks.

'They said the road was blocked,' Chris replies.

'Why aren't they using the GPMG, then?'

''I don't know. Fuck me!' They all stop to stare at Howie and Dave standing in front of the recruits.

Howie holds a long-handled axe down at his side. Dave has a long-bladed knife in each hand. The lads stood behind them, with a collection of knives and rifles fitted with bayonets.

'Crazy bastards...' Chris says in a shocked voice and looks back to his men all staring forward at the small group of men facing down a massive horde that is slowly shuffling towards them.

I am Death. I come for you. For every innocent man, woman, and child you have taken. I come for you. For every life you have ruined. I come for you. For my parents you have already taken. I come for you. For my sister, who still lives. I come for you. I am Death, and I come for you.

I roar as the fury explodes out of me. I hear Dave unleash his anger, and his voice joins mine, and together, we roar our defiance and rage at these evil things.

Behind me, I hear doors opening as the anger is released and comes forward for his payment, and together we stand, and we scream at them.

We draw breath, and we roar our rage into the air. I charge forward, with my axe held out to my side. I charge at the solid wall of infected who want to bite me, who want to kill me, but I am Death, and I come for you all.

They bare their teeth as one as we slam into them. Ten men against hundreds of vile creatures, but we have righteous glory on our side, and we will not be defeated. Dave drops down and charges forward into the massed line, steaming through them and using sheer momentum to split them apart. The gap he creates is filled by screaming recruits, who pour into the front line, slashing, hacking, and tearing flesh apart, roaring with anger, roaring with fear, and driving forward.

Bayonets slice through necks and split throats apart. Chest cavities are punctured again and again as the lads use the simple techniques shown to them by Dave.

They work together, and they work alone.

Jamie has watched Dave fight and has taken to this new skill like a duck to water. His arms blur and wave through the air as he fights into the horde with desperate fury.

I scream as my axe whirls, decapitating the first one in front of me. I lash out to the left and right, driving them back and embedding the sharp blade into their heads. Skulls are cleaved apart, and brains burst out, but this isn't enough for me, not by far, and I keep swinging as the glory of battle surges through my veins.

Bodies drop in front of me, and the heavy, blunt end does as much damage as the sharp blade as I bludgeon and shred them. Two line up for the lunge, and I take a massive swipe and cleave through the first neck, and bite deep into the next one. The axe head jams into the spine, and I drive my forehead hard into the zombie's face and drop him down, leaving my axe free. I use the handle end to lash backwards into the nose of another one lunging at me, and I smash his face in. More are coming, but I want them to. I want all of them to come. I spin around with a huge strike and take out several at the same time, and I drive forward into a gap and turn to hack them from behind. Arms are torn off, and legs are cut through as the bodies continue to fall.

'They must be fucking nuts,' Chris says quietly, watching with horrified shock.

'Ten men against an army,' Malcolm muses.

'Hardly seems fair...' the big, bald-headed man says from behind them as he pulls the strap of the machine gun over his head and rests it down on the ground, then draws a massive knife from a sheath on his belt. More of the men take their weapons off and draw bladed and pointed weapons from various pockets. Chris watches them and feels the urge of battle calling. He slowly lowers his weapon and reaches behind him to draw two deadly-looking knives out.

'Watch the weapons.' Chris stares hard at the truck driver, who stares back in absolute terror buts nods vigorously. The men start stalking forward, rolling shoulder joints and twisting their necks to warm their muscles. Chris starts walking faster, and they all move to keep up. Chris starts jogging, and they all do. With a hundred metres to go, Chris turns to grin at Malcolm.

'Just like the old days, eh, mate?' He doesn't wait for a response but charges forward, screaming at the top of his voice. The others join him. The experience of their age showing as they spread out into a line and charge into the fray.

I hear screaming behind me and hack down the closest infected to create space so I can turn. I look back to see Big Chris and his men charging towards the horde. Rifles gone, and all of them holding weapons to fight hand-to-hand. They roar as they strike, and I feel a fresh surge of adrenalin rip through me. I scream out with a primeval roar, and I hear my men, my warriors, take up the voice and join me. More voices join in, and now we are not ten men.

We are more, and we will slaughter every one of you. We are Death, and we come for you.

I swing the axe around with fresh energy and take them down. I split them apart and bodies fly before me.

Dave is fighting off to my side and going deeper into the horde, and I fight my way towards him, savaging the creatures as they lunge for me. A strong uppercut, and I cleave into the pelvis of one of them. I kick out and send him back to the hell he came from. I swipe out to my right and take another two down. We fight, and we push forward, and the bodies rack up behind us. I get to Dave's side, and together, we clear a small space. Blowers and Cookey burst through and join us in the slaughter as our ground grows larger. Jamie Reese is next and doesn't hesitate as he plunges at the line of zombies encroaching on us. The recruits pile in until we are all in the small clearing. A loud roar sounds off to the side, and I see the big, bald man charging through them with his head down, using his almighty size and strength to drive them apart.

He bursts into the clearing just as Big Chris and his men get through, until we are all there. We wait for a second, drawing breath. None of us speak, and we gather around in a tight circle, shoulder to shoulder. The infected gather around us and slowly inch forward, saliva drooling down their mouths.

We wait for them to draw closer, and then, as one, we roar out and charge back at them. The circle is made much wider as the infected fall back from the furious onslaught. We keep to the circle and let them come to us. We rip them apart as they step forward. Brains and bones are splintered onto the ground, innards of stomachs fall out from the vicious stabs and slashes, and we work on in silence.

This is our ground now. This small circle right here is our ground.

It is holy and sacrosanct, and these evil demons, spawned from the devil himself, shall not touch it.

You shall not live nor breathe the air in our circle while we hold it, and to the last man, we shall fight you.

The circle grows wider and wider as we slaughter them. They

keep coming, but we move amongst the front line, keeping them in the roughly circular shape around us.

Dave and some of Big Chris's men move beautifully with their knives and blades. Experienced and tough, they do what their country told them to do. They do what their country demanded of them, and they did it without question, and when the time came to return to normal life, they were the freaks and the killers that people avoided.

Dave has always done what was required, and despite all the glory and praise it brought him, he was alone in those battles, and he was alone when the fighting ended. But these men can now use those skills they honed for so long. They can use the skills and the tactics, and the outright violence they were so encouraged to have. Throughout time, men have stood together in battle, and they have fought for what they believed was right and proper. Now they fight for survival, to protect their loved ones and destroy this common enemy.

The recruits fair well. Their youth, vitality, and streetwise nature make up for their lack of knowledge and experience. But they have already proved they are capable by surviving in the plains through the first weekend, and now they just get better.

I can now judge the amount of force needed and can preserve energy to sustain myself during the long minutes of battle. Fighting this way is a paradox. It seems to go on for hours, but then it's over in minutes, and one by one, we stand down and stagger backwards. Chests heaving for air as we look about at the sheer devastation we have wrought. We have hacked them down until the road is clear, and just one small group remains. Still, they shuffle towards us despite the huge losses brought to their kind. We look to one another to see who will go for them, but Dave is already there, dispatching them with cold efficiency, slicing their throats open until the last one drops, with blood spurting from his jugular. Then Dave drops down to wipe his knives on the bodies. I look around at the men – all of them covered in gore, with blood still dripping from their weapons. I look down at myself and see I am also covered in filth.

'The road is clear now,' I say to Chris and start back towards the Saxon as the recruits slowly follow me.

Chris and his men turn and walk back to their vehicles, each of them nodding respectfully towards us as they pass.

Before long, we are driving again. The lads in the back cleaning themselves off with wipes.

'Fucking hell, Jamie, you took a few down, then,' McKinney says to the quiet lad, and I imagine him blushing furiously.

'He bloody did. Well done, mate,' Blowers adds, and I know Jamie will now be extremely uncomfortable but grinning back at them.

'Better than Cookey, anyway. I saw him trying to grope their arses instead of killing them,' Blowers says.

'Fuck off, Blowers. I stabbed loads,' Cookey retorts.

'Yeah, but not with your knife, though,' Tucker cuts in to guffaws of laughter.

'Oh, don't you start too, Tucker,' Cookey groans.

'Feel better?' Dave asks me.

'Yes, mate, much. You?'

'Much better, Mr Howie, much better.'

CHAPTER SIXTY-ONE

The infection watches Howie through the eyes of Darren. It allows Darren to be himself, and feels adrenalin coursing through his system. It feels the nervous energy, fear, and thirst for vengeance flood through Darren – a mixture of chemicals that causes a massive reaction.

Dave's voice calls loudly, and they charge. The infection watches the two come together and can feel Darren fight with fury and power, using his body as a tool to cut the hosts down.

The infection watches Howie, Dave, and all of them work, and it watches, and it learns.

The hosts are cut down until just a few are left, and the infection watches with cold detachment as the small one slaughters those few precious, remaining hosts. It feels the exhaustion flood through Darren's body, and it knows that it could release different chemicals to make this feeling go away, but by doing so, it would draw unwanted attention, so it stays almost dormant, and it watches as they get further into the city.

CHAPTER SIXTY-TWO

Sarah slowly gets dressed, feeling dizzy and light-headed as the aftereffects of so much alcohol purge from her system.

Last night saw an explosion of emotions: anger, hurt, loss, isolation, fear, and desperation. But today, she feels flat and numb, void of emotion, with a dull headache, and an upset stomach. In a way she feels a bit better, drained, but somewhat relieved that those emotions came out. Despite the heavy drinking and crying, she coped with them and is still here. She could have plunged to her death from the balcony or cut her wrists, or run crying through the corridors, screaming for someone to help her, but she didn't. She remained in her apartment and kept to herself.

After dressing, she walks through the lounge, to the kitchen, and instead of her normal method of putting her hand into the cupboard with the tins and taking the first one she touches, she opens the doors and looks through the selection, choosing fruit salad, canned meat, and small potatoes.

Today she needs sustenance and fuel to help her think a way out of this.

The time for depression and self-pity is over. Now is a time for action.

THE CONVOY DRIVES FURTHER into London, going past well-known places and delving further into the grotty inner-city areas. These places were rough already before the event. The red brick of Victorian England mixes with the greys and browns of post-war Britain. Urban decay, with millions of people living hard lives in one of the world's fastest moving cities. New buildings of glass and steel, sporadically placed, only serve to make the rest look like the grimy places that they have come to be. There was constant civil disorder here before, caused by huge numbers of disaffected, young people left with a weak education system, a poor social structure, and zero employment opportunities. People who were left to grow in an area that didn't want or need them and didn't know what to do with them.

Infected slowly shuffle through the streets and roads. All of them still heading in the same direction as the convoy, but instead of the open, main roads, they use side streets – routes drawn from the memories of local hosts; although, the team doesn't know this.

Howie drives the Saxon, with Dave next to him, and both of them peer out of the toughened glass at the passing streets. The battle left all of them tired, and even the boastful laughing of the recruits soon drifts into silence as they each clean their weapons and clothing from the gore and splattered blood. The convoy passes over the distinctive red and yellow curves of Vauxhall Bridge and the famous River Thames sliding slowly underneath. A tourist boat has broken free of its moorings and has drifted down to rest against the high walls. Its sides scraping along the concrete embankment.

'We are over the River Thames,' Howie calls out as the lads move forward to see out of the windscreen at the grey-blue water.

'Oh, I would like to swim in there. It looks inviting,' Tucker says with a sigh, sweating heavily from the heat.

'A swim would be fucking lovely,' McKinney answers.

'I wouldn't swim in that filth,' Cookey calls out. 'Probably get bitten by a mutant turd,' he adds to sniggers from the others.

They cross the Bridge and head into the main road on the other side, travelling through Lambeth, towards Tower Bridge.

'There's shitloads of them again,' Howie says to Dave, looking at the long queues of infected walking along the same route.

'Get Jamie on the GPMG to start cutting them down,' Howie calls out.

'Alpha to all units. Large numbers in front. Opening fire on them now,' Dave speaks into the radio.

'Charlie to Alpha. Roger that. Are you sure you don't want another knife fight instead?' Big Chris asks, and Howie smiles broadly.

Jamie opens up on the GPMG, firing into the long, drawn-out queues.

'It's like culling, really,' Howie remarks.

'What is?' Dave asks.

'Shooting them like this.'

'Why is it like culling?'

'We're reducing their numbers, culling the density of them.'

'Oh.'

'More we get now, the less we have to deal with later.'

'Or the angrier they will get,' Dave replies.

'Speaking of angry... Did I see you a bit angry back then?'

'A little,' Dave admits.

'A little? Looked like a lot to me. Jamie is doing well.'

'He is.'

'He takes after you.'

'Do you think so?' Dave asks.

'Oh, no doubt. Did you see him with the two knives?'

'Yes.'

'Who do you think he learnt that from?'

'Well, I guess from me...'

'No guessing needed, mate. He is now Mini Dave. But he's got some skills, though.'

'He moves well, just needs to plan ahead a bit more and hone his use of force.'

'Show him, then,' Howie says.

'Okay, Mr Howie. You still like the axe?'

'No. I *love* the axe! Knives are too fiddly for me. I like the power and strength of the axe.'

'Like a Viking.'

'Yeah, I'm gonna grow a big beard and put plaits in it, and have a horned helmet.'

'Speaking of axes...' Dave points out of the window to a row of shops. One of them clearly a large DIY and garden store.

'Does anyone want an axe?' Howie shouts out jokingly but hears a chorus of approval.

'Seriously?' Howie asks.

'I want an axe. I'm no good with the knife, and the rifle feels... I don't know. It feels too cumbersome,' Nick shouts out.

'Dave, let them know we're having a quick pit stop, and someone, shout up to Jamie about the plan.' Dave speaks into the radio as Howie slows the Saxon down. Jamie concentrates his fire on the infected that are anywhere near the DIY store, cutting them to pieces and clearing some space.

'Right, let's be quick,' Howie shouts as he jumps out of the vehicle.

'Those not going for a new weapon, make a cordon round the vehicles,' Dave calls out as he gets down and holds his assault rifle at the ready.

The truck pulls up behind them, and after a few minutes, Big Chris and his men are stepping over the bloody bodies and walking towards the Saxon.

'What's going on?' Chris calls out.

'Mr Howie and a few of the lads are getting some hand-held weapons,' Dave replies and nods to the DIY store.

'Lads, if you need anything, you've got five minutes,' Chris says to a few of his men, who oblige with smiles.

The DIY store door gets kicked in by joint, choreographed kicks from Howie and Blowers and soon bursts open in a shower of glass. The lads pile in and all start heading towards the hand tool section.

'What about a sledgehammer?' Cookey calls out.

'Tried it, not bad, but it's very heavy and gets tiring after a few minutes,' Howie replies. 'I tried two lump hammers as well, but their range is too short. The chainsaw was good, but it was petrol-driven and ran out of juice too soon,' he explains and realises that everyone has stopped to stare at him. 'What?' he asks defensively as they turn back to the shelves. He finds the axe section first and starts looking through the racks.

'Oh my, look at this beauty,' Howie whispers to himself as he pulls off a long-handled axe with a double-bladed end – each blade covered with a leather sheath.

'It suits you.' Howie looks up to see the massive, bald-headed man standing next to him, staring at the axe.

'Do you think so?' Howie asks.

'Oh, yes, very you.' The man mountain nods firmly.

'There's another one left if you want it,' Howie says, pulling the last of the double-bladed axes from the section and handing it over to the big man.

'Oh, that feels nice,' he says appreciatively, weighing it in his giant hand.

'The single-bladed axe was good with the sharp end and the blunt end, but this is much better,' Howie says, admiring the metal blades.

'I've always been a knife man myself,' the big man says. 'But I saw you with the axe back there, and I thought that I've got to try one.'

'They are good. I tried the knives, but I lack the precision and finesse they need. I like the power of slamming them down with these things,' Howie says.

'Yes, I can see what you mean. Tell me, do you use a constant, swiping action or more of a chop?' he asks.

'Well, it depends on the situation. A good swipe will clear space and take a few down, but a solid chop down into the head is lovely. Even better, if you chop or slice down, is the uppercut into the groin, but the head can bite into the bone and get caught,' Howie explains, going through the motions of the swipe, chop, and uppercut as he describes.

'Ah, yeah, I can see that. I suppose a foot into the stomach pushes them off then?' he asks.

'Yeah, that does it. A big guy like yourself could do some awesome damage with one,' Howie says.

'To be honest, I've always wanted to try it, but the army would get a bit funny if we all started carrying them around with us, I reckon.'

'Yeah, I can see that,' Howie says.

'Bloody hell, are there any more of them left?' Blowers asks.

'No, sorry, mate, we got the last two. Plenty of the single-bladed ones, though. Don't dismiss them. I was just saying that the blunt end can do a good amount of damage too,' Howie explains as Blowers pulls them out and hands them around to the others.

'Do you keep the end covered all the time?' the big man asks.

'Not really. I clean it after each fight, and I know Dave keeps a knife sharpener, and he sharpens it for me,' Howie answers.

'Right, good point.' The men all stand in the aisle, taking practise swings and commenting on each other's pose and grip until Big Chris enters to stand in the doorway.

'When you lot have finished fucking about...' he shouts out.

'Sorry, mate, my fault. Just getting a new axe,' Howie says as they all start to leave, carrying long-handled axes back out into the sunshine.

Soon the Saxon, leading the convoy, heads off towards Tower Bridge.

The convoy continues along the main road, going through the Elephant and Castle roundabout and off towards Tower Bridge Road. The exodus or *invasion* of zombies, is even more prevalent on the road to the Bridge, with massive numbers stretched back in solid lines, seven or eight deep. The general-purpose machine gun does a good job of cutting them down, but the thickness of the lines means many on the inside escape uninjured and continue on their slow shuffle.

'*Charlie to Alpha.*' The radio crackles in Dave's hand.

'*Alpha receiving. Go ahead, Charlie.*'

'*Charlie to Alpha. This area looks too hot for RV. I suggest we move to a quiet side street. You choose.*'

'Roger that Charlie. Stand by,' Dave answers.

'This place is crawling with 'em,' Howie mutters but loud enough to be heard over the constant thumping of the machine gun above them.

'Over there, sir,' Blowers points, leaning forward to indicate a side street, with a constant stream of infected going past the entrance.

The Saxon slows down, and Howie peers over to see that the road looks wide enough to take the truck and is quiet enough to move down.

'We'll go through here. Get Jamie to stop for now,' Howie calls out, and the machine gun ceases firing as Cookey yells up.

'*Alpha to Charlie. Side street identified. Moving in now,*' Dave reports to the others as Howie turns the wheel and ploughs through the lines of infected. The solid front end of the Saxon easily squashes some and shoves the rest out of the way.

'Bloody hell, they didn't even slow down,' Howie shouts as he looks in the side mirror to see the infected still slowly marching forward, not breaking pace to turn or look. The Saxon is followed by the truck and then the two four-wheel drive vehicles as they proceed a safe distance down the quiet street and finally pull over.

'Blowers, get some lads out front and to the sides, mate,' Howie asks as he drops down from the cabin and walks back along to meet Chris and the others.

'Will do,' Blowers calls out as he and the recruits pile out of the back and spread out as directed.

They meet near the front of the truck: Big Chris, Malcolm, Howie, and Dave. A few of the others are standing nearby but clearly distancing themselves from the immediate group.

'That bridge will be full up,' Malcolm says, rubbing the back of his neck.

'We can get through them easily enough,' Howie replies.

'We can, but there are thousands heading that way. They seem to know where we're going, and I don't like that fact one bit,' Big Chris says.

'How can they know?' Malcolm asks, and they both look to Howie, who shrugs back at them.

'I don't know. It seemed they were coming for us last night at the services too, like we were being targeted, but I don't know how,' Howie says, thinking hard.

'Unless they're going into the city for something else?' Malcolm asks.

'Not likely. Every time we've met any hordes, they turn and come for us. These aren't doing that. They're intent on getting somewhere. This could get very messy if we are anywhere near this place at sunset,' Howie replies.

'We can get through them, no problem, but then we have to stop at the hospital, with this lot still coming behind us. Even the GPMG can't cut that many down, and we don't know how many are coming from other directions,' Chris says.

'What choice do we have?' Howie asks.

'Lift the bridge,' Dave says quietly.

'Lift the bridge?' Howie asks.

'Of course. Tower Bridge lifts. We could raise it up after us,' Malcolm says excitedly.

'How will we do that? Does it need power? Do you know how the controls work?' Howie asks, liking the idea.

'Mate, we were Para-Reg...' Malcolm smiles.

'It must have a separate power supply in case of blackout or something, and the controls can't be too complicated,' Chris muses, rubbing his chin.

'So we get across and then work out how to raise it to stop this lot getting across. Then we just have to worry about the rest on the other side,' Howie says, looking between them all.

'Yep, that's about the size of it,' Chris nods.

'Okay, where do you want us?' Howie asks.

'Keep the Saxon at the end of the bridge, on the other side to keep them back while we work out how to get the thing lifted, with the truck behind the Saxon,' Chris says.

'Are you leaving a unit there so we can drop it again for the egress?' Dave asks.

'I think we'll need everyone for the hospital and then Howie's sister,' Chris replies.

'Okay,' Dave says.

'Everyone happy?' Chris asks, looking between them all as they nod and depart back to the vehicles. The vehicles all move off and follow the side streets around until they come back out onto Tower Bridge Road, again using the front of the Saxon to mow down the chain of infected trudging across the junction. The last stretch of road brings the bridge into view; the massive towers rising up high into the blue sky.

'Hold off on the GPMG until we get across. We'll be wasting ammo if we can get that bridge lifted,' Howie calls back and hears the machine gun stop.

'Who's going to lift the bridge, Mr Howie?' Nick Hewitt shouts out.

'I don't know. One of the others,' Howie replies. 'Why? Do you fancy a go?' he adds, remembering Nick's passion for mechanical and electrical things.

'I'd love to,' Nick shouts back.

The Saxon powers through the middle of the road, entering the bridge. The road is so clogged with infected the Saxon has no choice but to plough through them, sending them scattering off to the sides. Still, they keep dead ahead, and none of them turn to look or alter course.

'This is fucking freaky,' Cookey says in the quietness of the Saxon.

'It ain't right, is it?' McKinney responds.

'Why aren't they turning or doing anything else? They're just heading the same way as us,' Tucker says.

'It's eerie. They must know something we don't,' Darren Smith says.

'You feeling better now, Smithy?' Howie calls out on hearing his voice.

'Yes, thank you, Mr Howie, much better. Guess I was just tired or had a bit of heatstroke or something,' Darren replies.

'Or *cockstroke*, in Cookey's case,' Blowers says.

'What? How did you make that connection?' Cookey exclaims. 'Smithy's talking about heatstroke, and you turn it round to a gay joke.' He shakes his head.

'Just comes naturally, mate. You either got it or you don't,' Blowers says in a modest voice.

'You're a prat! Tucker, you got anything to eat, mate? I'm starving,' Cookey asks.

'Yes, mate, I got loads of stuff from that services shop.' Tucker pulls out a carrier bag and hands it around as the lads dig in for snacks.

'Be quick, lads. We're almost there,' Howie shouts as he hears packets being ripped open and loud munching noises. The Saxon roars over the central part, between the towers, and through to the north side, pulling to a halt where the normal road joins the bridge.

'Clear the area and keep them off the bridge,' Howie shouts as he jumps down with his assault rifle.

The lads spread out and open fire as they continue to proceed off the bridge, still heading towards the city. Despite the firing and the stationary positions, none of the infected turn or change direction, but continue onwards, away from the bridge. The truck pulls behind them, and Howie glances back to see the four-wheel drive vehicles stopping by a structure on the bridge, with glass windows going round it.

'That must be the control room,' Howie shouts to Dave as the recruits fire into the backs of the infected.

The end of the bridge is cleared, and the lads all turn and start on the oncoming infected that are streaming down the bridge, towards them.

'*Charlie to Alpha. We are at the control room, but it's going to take longer than we thought.*'

'*Alpha to Charlie. Received the last. Do you need support?*' Dave answers.

'*Negative, they're just going straight past us, not even looking. It's very weird.*'

'Dave, tell them I'm coming up with Nick,' Howie shouts. 'Nick, you're with me in the Saxon.' The two of them jump in and drive the short distance back to the control room. The infected shuffling around them without so much as a glance.

'This is fucked up, Mr Howie. What's going on?' Nick asks.

'I don't know, mate,' Howie replies as the Saxon comes to a halt. They get out, readying themselves to fight through the infected, but none of them stop, look, or even bare their teeth as Howie and Nick stand and watch them.

Howie reaches out and pushes one on the shoulder, forcing him to stagger off to the side and knock into several others.

'Nothing,' Howie says.

'They fucking stink,' Nick says, covering his nose at the stench of decaying flesh.

They run over to the side, weaving through infected but still being guarded in case they turn and attack, and they eventually find their way to the control room.

Some of the armed men from the four-wheel drive vehicles are standing outside, vigilantly watching the hordes shuffle past.

'Bloody hell, that's a lot of buttons,' Howie says as he gets inside and looks at the complicated array of switches on the control panel.

Nick's eyes light up, and he rushes forward to start examining them. 'This is awesome,' he says quietly as he looks over the panel.

'It's more complicated than we thought,' Big Chris says to Howie.

'Just give him a few minutes,' Howie motions to Nick, who is absorbed, muttering to himself.

'I can't believe they haven't turned on us,' Howie says, looking out at the infected going past.

'Something's not right,' Malcolm says.

'Maybe that's it – they've given up and stopped eating people,' Howie jokes. The awkward silence that follows is only broken by Nick's loud exclamation. 'You got something, mate?' Howie asks, relieved by the distraction.

'Yep, got it. There's a power supply and a series of safety switches that have to be done in the right order before the hydraulics start lifting the bridge,' Nick says excitedly.

'Bloody kids. Too much Xbox, if you ask me,' Malcolm jokes.

'Right, you ready, Mr Howie?' Nick asks, and Howie feels a touch of pride at being asked instead of Big Chris or Malcolm.

'Yes, mate, go ahead.' Nick presses and flips a series of switches, then starts pulling back on a small, black lever. An alarm sounds outside, and the bridge starts to lift smoothly, separating in the middle as both sides lift.

The action is surprisingly quick, and the men watch as infected start staggering faster as the bridge lifts; then, gravity takes over, and they start tumbling into the backs of each other, causing a concertina effect as the momentum picks up.

The men smile and laugh as the infected are sent plummeting down onto the road surface.

'The other side are still walking off the edge,' Nick laughs, watching a number of black and white monitors above the control panel. The men wait for a minute as some of the infected pick themselves up and start their shuffling again. Many stay on the ground in a tangled mess of arms and legs. Before long, the hordes have shuffled off down the bridge, and the men leave the control room to slowly walk behind them.

'If this keeps on, we'll have an easy time at the hospital and then going for your sister,' Big Chris says as he stops by the door of his four-wheel drive.

'I bloody hope so,' Howie replies. 'But knowing what seems to happen to us every half hour, I very much doubt it,' he adds before walking back to the Saxon with Nick.

CHAPTER SIXTY-THREE

The infection pushes the hosts towards the city, using roads, streets, and the underground rail network. Hosts pour down the steps onto the platforms and drop down onto the inert rail lines, shuffling through the darkened tunnels to emerge closer to their destination. Never has London seen such a densely packed crowd before, all moving as one without aggravation. No fights or pushing and shoving. Just host bodies all being told to move to this location as they slowly pile into Canary Wharf and the surrounding streets until every inch of pavement and tarmac is covered. The bodies still have the craving for flesh, but this is overcome as they move slowly past Howie and the resistors. The temptation to turn and lunge for the bite is almost too much to control, but the infection holds them back and waits. It knows how the resistors can fight back now, and unless the numbers are overwhelming, the hosts can be cut down too easily. On the bridge, the infection almost decides to make the host bodies move fast and go for the attack, but the big vehicles are nearby, with one of the resistors sitting on that devastating machine gun, so it sticks to the plan and waits for them to come.

CHAPTER SIXTY-FOUR

Sarah finishes her meal and drinks plenty of water to rehydrate after the heavy drinking the night before.

Then she carefully fills her pots, pans, and receptacles while the water supply still works, thinking there must be a massive tank at the top of the building to keep a building that size supplied.

Dressed in jeans and a t-shirt, with her hair pulled back, she looks serious and determined – determined to do something to help her situation but not knowing what that should be. She opens the patio doors and steps out onto the balcony, and takes a sharp intake of breath as she looks down.

There had been crowds of them on the road and pavement below, but now the whole area is covered in them. The street below her is packed, and she can see into side streets further up and the junctions at the end of the road. There are infected bodies packed in like sardines, shuffling and rippling like one giant snake. The intense heat and stillness of the air sends putrid and fetid odours wafting up on the thermals created by the packed bodies, and Sarah almost gags as she covers her face and mouth with her hand. The strong sense of purpose and determination ebbs away as she realises there is no way out of the building.

The sheer amount of them could push through the main front

doors with ease if they put their minds to it, and she steps back as she realises they could be at her door within minutes, if they chose. She slowly pushes the patio doors closed and realises that from her position on the balcony, she can't see the main doors, and they could already be inside now. She creeps over to her front door and rests her ear against the cool wood, intently listening for any noises, but there is only silence.

CHAPTER SIXTY-FIVE

'*Charlie to Alpha.*'

'*Alpha receiving. Go ahead, Charlie.*'

'*We have identified a secondary route using side roads. Slow down and let us take the lead from here.*'

'*Roger that Charlie. Slowing down now for you to take lead position.*' The four-wheel drive vehicle pulls out from behind the truck and shoots past the slowing vehicles, slotting in front of the Saxon. The men in the rear of the vehicle look back and nod to Howie and Dave in the front.

Howie nods back and raises his hand as Dave keeps scanning the area.

'Bloody hell, this is packed with 'em,' Howie says.

'It is, Mr Howie,' Dave replies.

'And it's getting worse the further we go in.'

'It is.'

'Here we go,' Howie says as the four-wheel drive turns a sharp left, mowing down several infected crossing the junction and sending the bodies spinning off. The rest keep going across as the Saxon takes a turn to run some over, too.

'They don't know the Green Cross Code, do they?' Howie says.

'The what?' Dave asks.

'The Green Cross Code.'

'What's that?'

'You've never heard of it? Everyone knows the Green Cross Code,' Howie says.

'I don't,' Dave replies flatly.

'Lads, you've heard of the Green Cross Code, haven't you?' Howie calls out.

'What's that?' voices shout from the back.

'Well, you're all just youngsters really. You must have heard it at school, Dave?'

'No, Mr Howie,' Dave answers.

'What did they say as they taught you to cross the road, then?' Howie asks.

'Look left and right,' Dave answers.

'Well, yeah, but what about the big bloke in the cape?'

'Superman?' Dave asks.

'No, he had a green cape, I think.'

'Superman had a red cape, Mr Howie.'

'I know that Superman had a red cape. I meant the Green Cross Code man – he had a green cape, I think.'

'I don't know him,' Dave says.

'No, hang on, he didn't have a cape. He had a white top, with big shoulder pads, and a big, green cross on his chest,' Howie says, looking across at Dave, who shakes his head.

'The Green Lantern wears green,' Dave says.

'Yeah, I know he does, but I'm on about the Green Cross Code man.'

'The Incredible Hulk was green too,' Dave adds.

'I know. But he isn't the one I'm on about,' Howie says.

'The Incredible Hulk? I never liked him that much,' Tucker says, leaning forward to join the conversation.

'Why not?' Dave asks.

'I was always into Batman,' Tucker says.

'Early Batman or late Batman?' Curtis Graves cuts in.

'Oh, has to be early Batman,' Tucker replies.

'No way, the last Batman movies were the best,' Curtis replies.

'Batman didn't wear green,' Dave adds.

'Spiderman is the best one,' Cookey says, leaning forward too.

'Yeah, I like Spiderman, but I never liked spiders, so they always put me off him,' Tucker replies.

'Spiderman didn't wear green either,' Dave says.

'Iron Man was the best!' Hewitt shouts out.

'He wasn't a superhero. He was a normal bloke in a special outfit,' Tucker replies.

'Well, Batman was too, then,' Curtis says.

'No, Batman had special powers,' Tucker says.

'No, he didn't. He was a normal bloke, who just did loads of training,' Curtis retorts.

'The Thing from The Fantastic Four was my favourite,' McKinney calls out.

'The Human Torch was the best one,' Blowers joins in.

'They didn't wear green,' Dave says.

'The Green Cross Code man wore green,' Howie says.

'Mister Fantastic was way better than any of them,' Curtis replies.

'You're telling me that being a bit bendy, like Cookey, is better than being able to burst into flames?' Blowers asks indignantly.

'What can you do with fire other than make things hot?' Curtis asks.

'Well, you can set things on fire, for a start,' Blowers says.

'And?' Cookey asks.

'That's cool enough,' Blowers says defensively.

'I got a plastic lighter in my pocket that can do that,' Hewitt says.

'Yeah, well, he could move fast too,' Blowers shouts.

'So would I if I was on fire all the bloody time,' Tucker laughs.

'I liked Wonder Woman,' Jamie Reese joins in to a stunned silence from the rest.

'She was bloody gorgeous.'

'Yeah, very pretty,' Blowers agrees as most of the lads nod.

'Fair point, mate. She was a crumpet,' Cookey says.

'She didn't wear green,' Dave says.

'Have you got a favourite one, Dave?' Cookey asks.

'Yes,' he replies.

'Who?' Howie asks.

'Wolverine.'

'That figures,' Howie says as the lads all nod in agreement. 'Is that the hospital?' he adds as they come onto a wide road leading to a large, modern-looking building.

'Yes,' Dave replies as the large sign "Canary Wharf Hospital" comes into view.

'Yeah, thanks for that, Dave,' Howie says. The access road leading to the hospital is long and goes around the back of a large visitors' car park, with a surprising number of cars still parked there. The access road then leads on and curves off into large ambulance bays outside a set of immense double doors.

'*Charlie to all units. We are going with Bravo to the side entrance to gain access as directed by Doc Roberts. Alpha, you cover the front unless we call for help. Delta, you check the rear and then go to the far side.*' The units all respond with affirmations, and the four-wheel drive vehicle and the truck drive on down the access road and bear left, disappearing down the side. The Saxon pulls up tight to the front of the building.

'Can you ask Darren if he's got a good view from up there or does he need it moved?' Howie asks and hears Darren reply that he can see fine.

'Right, lads, spread out across the entrance here and keep a good eye out,' Howie says.

'Where are they all?' Tucker asks, leaning forward to look out of the windscreen.

'I don't know, mate. I guess this is off the main road or the centre, or wherever they are going, but it won't take them long if they want us,' Howie replies and gets out of the vehicle with his assault rifle, checking his webbing belt pouches for magazines.

The recruits climb out from the rear doors and start moving out to form a wide line spread across the front, facing out onto the main road.

'You like that sniper rifle, then?' Howie asks Jamie as he walks down the line, checking the lads are all okay.

Jamie has the rifle up and is looking through the scope, down towards the building line; the SA80 strapped to his back.

'Yes, Mr Howie,' Jamie answers.

'You're getting very good with it too, mate,' Howie says.

'Thanks, Mr Howie.'

'You'll be giving Dave a run for his money soon, mate. Especially if you carry on like that, with the double knives.'

'Oh, do you want me to just use one, or the bayonet on the rifle instead?' Jamie asks, concerned.

'No, no, mate, it was a compliment. Even Dave said how well you did with them,' Howie says as Jamie blushes bright red and stammers a thank you. Howie walks down to the end and stands next to Dave.

'It's very quiet, Mr Howie,' Dave says in hushed tones.

'Oh, you've said it now...' Howie groans.

'*Charlie to Alpha. Multiple contacts inside. Requesting immediate reinforcements. We are on the second floor, at the rear of the building,*' Chris's voice booms out. The sound of gunshots loud in the background.

'See what I mean. You had to say it, didn't you?' Howie admonishes jokingly.

'Blowers, you hold out here. I'll take Jamie, McKinney, and Dave with me. We've only got one radio, so stay safe and get back inside the Saxon if it gets too much,' Howie calls out.

'Yes, sir,' Blowers answers as Jamie and McKinney rush over towards the front doors to join Dave and Howie.

'Jamie and Dave at the front as you're the best shots. Me and McKinney will go behind and cover the rear, er...if that's okay with you, Dave?'

'That's fine, Mr Howie,' Dave answers respectfully.

'Okay, let's go!' Howie says as they push the doors open and enter.

'Use the rifle for now but be prepared to swap for the assault weapon if it gets hot. Single shot to the head and watch out for our guys,' Dave advises Jamie as they take the lead and start moving down the wide, central corridor and past the reception desk. The interior already looks looted, with debris littered everywhere, and dried blood stains smeared down the polished and gleaming floor of the new hospital. Waiting room chairs are strewn about, and the contents of the desks look to have been thrown out into the main room.

'Looks like someone tried to fight them off,' Howie remarks as they step around the items on the floor.

Dave pauses and raises a hand up in the air, first, in a clenched fist and then with one finger raised, then points off to the side.

'Oh, not this again,' Howie mutters as they pass the area where Dave was indicating and see a dead body halfway out of a toilet door. The face is bitten away, and a large pool of congealed blood is under the head. They walk down the central corridor, passing doors and waiting areas on both sides. Signs hang from the ceiling, giving directions to the various departments.

As they get towards the rear of the building, they hear the sound of muffled gunshots and start moving faster. Dave and Jamie walk in front – Dave with his assault rifle raised to his shoulder, and Jamie with the sniper rifle. Howie and McKinney keep scanning to the sides and checking the rear as they progress quickly but quietly. The sniper rifle coughs as Jamie sweeps to the right, and an infected falls out of a concealed side corridor; the back of his head blown away. Jamie racks the bolt and continues moving forward, hardly breaking stride. Two more shuffle around from the end of the corridor towards them and are quickly dispatched by a single shot to the head each. The quiet noise of the sniper rifle suppressor is deadened by the loud retort of the assault rifle fired by Dave. The infected are both blown backwards as the four men keep stepping forward to the end of the corridor and identify the stairwell doors. Dave enters first, sweeping up the stairs, with his rifle aimed high, then takes each step carefully, but still moving with speed.

'Clear,' he says quietly but clearly as the others follow him to the door leading onto the second floor. Dave and Jamie pause for a second at the double doors as Dave pushes gently to test they open inwards. He nods to Jamie and indicates for him to check right and he will check left, then turns to show Howie and McKinney to cover the front.

Then Dave nods, and he and Jamie push the doors open and burst out into the corridor. Dave turns immediately to face left, and Jamie to the right.

Howie and McKinney step forward to the long corridor facing them and the several infected shuffling in the other direction. They both open fire, using single shots. Once the corridor ahead is clear, Howie looks across to see Jamie and Dave have both dropped several each.

'Alpha to Charlie. We are on the second floor at the rear stairwell. Confirm your location,' Dave says into the radio.

'Charlie to Alpha. We have got most of them down. Hold there until we make our way back to you,' Chris answers.

'Roger that. Holding position at the rear stairwell doors, on the second floor.' The four of them stay in position, occasionally firing as an infected appears from one of the many side entrances that branch off.

Eventually, they hear banging noises from the corridor ahead of Howie and McKinney.

'Charlie to Alpha. We are approaching your position now. Be aware, be aware.'

'Roger that, Charlie, acknowledged.' The noises increase as Big Chris and several of his men run into view from a side entrance. Each of them carrying large items and boxes in their hands. Their weapons strapped across their backs or shoulders.

'There were loads of them up here,' Chris shouts as they draw closer.

'Are you all okay?' Howie asks.

'Yeah, no injuries. Bloody close call, though. We went into a wrong room, and it was packed. I mean fucking *packed* with them. They couldn't get out until we opened the bloody doors; then, they just started pouring out of everywhere,' Chris answers as they stop by the stairwell doors.

'Did you get everything?' Howie asks.

'Nope, we have a load more to get yet. Can we borrow two of your blokes to cover us while we carry this lot out?' Big Chris asks.

'Dave, do you want to go with Jamie? Me and McKinney can wait here.'

'Okay, Mr Howie,' Dave answers as he and Jamie go down the stairwell, ahead of the group, leaving McKinney and Howie on the second floor. Several minutes pass in silence as they wait for the group to come back.

'Looks like they got them all,' Howie mutters.

'Yep, erm...would you mind if I had a smoke, Mr Howie?' McKinney asks politely.

'Smoking in a hospital? You'll get in trouble for that, mate,' Howie jokes.

'Oh, okay, I can wait,' McKinney answers.

'I was joking, mate. Crack on if you want.'

'Thanks, do you want one?' he offers, and Howie is very tempted despite having stopped smoking before the zombie invasion.

'No, thanks, mate, if I start now, I will never bloody stop, and I'm already too unfit for all this running about,' Howie says. Will power winning over temptation. McKinney lights up, and Howie smells the smoke wafting over, further tempting him. They hear the others coming up the stairs.

'Smoking in a hospital? You'll get in trouble for that,' Big Chris calls out as he walks off.

'That's what I said,' Howie mutters quietly and waits in position until they come back past them again, carrying equipment and boxes.

'I think it's pretty clear up here now. How was the front?' Chris asks as he moves past them again.

'Quiet when we left. No sign of them anywhere near us,' Howie answers.

Darren Smith grips the GPMG from his position as look-out on the Saxon, slowly moving left to right, looking for movement. He is completely unaware of the infection inside him alerting all the hosts in the area to their location.

The main road runs left to right beyond the car park in front of them, and the building line is beyond the road. Big, tall office blocks are mostly joined together to form a continuous line, but some walkways, alleys, and side streets connect the main road to the hospital area. Blowers, Cookey, Graves, Tucker, and Hewitt are stretched out in a line across the entrance, smoking cigarettes while watching the perimeter.

'They're taking a while,' Cookey calls over to Blowers.

'Probably had to get a lot of stuff,' Blowers replies.

'CONTACT,' Darren shouts from behind them.

'Where, Smithy?' Blowers shouts back as they all start looking more intently.

'Building line, small alley off to the left,' he shouts back as a single adult infected slowly emerges from the shade.

'There's only one of them,' Hewitt calls out.

'Who wants him?' Blowers offers.

'Let me try for a head shot,' Cookey says as he raises his assault rifle and aims down the sights.

'You'll never get him from this distance,' Hewitt says as Cookey pauses for a few seconds, then slowly squeezes the trigger.

The rifle fires, and the bullet flies through the air, straight at the infected, and straight past him, going into the wall a few feet beyond.

'Ah, fuck it,' Cookey says as the rest start laughing.

'Let me try,' Hewitt calls out and repeats the same action as Cookey, aiming at the shuffling infected creature's head and firing after a few seconds' pause.

'Ha, you fucking losers,' Blowers laughs as the shot misses.

'I'll show you how it's done.' Blowers takes a few seconds to line the shot up, then fires the rifle. The bullet just clipping the zombie on his upper arm, making him spin around and bang into the wall behind him.

'I fucking got him,' Blowers exclaims.

'No, you didn't. He's still coming,' Darren shouts over as the infected turns back towards them and continues shuffling.

'My turn,' Tucker says and lines the zombie's head up between the sights, and fires. The round strikes the infected in the centre of the forehead, and the back of his skull explodes in a pink cloud as he slumps backwards onto the ground.

'Fucking hell, Tucker. Well done, mate,' Hewitt shouts out.

'Did you bloody see that?' Tucker's mouth drops open as he lowers the rifle and looks over at the others.

'Good shot, mate,' Blowers says.

'He was a lot closer, though,' Cookey adds.

'Fuck off, he was shuffling slowly. He did about four steps in total, and he got knocked back by Blowers' shot,' Tucker shouts.

'Nah, he was a lot closer, almost halfway, I'd say,' Hewitt joins in, laughing.

'He fucking was not. He was still in the same place,' Tucker yells back, offended.

'They're joking, mate. It was an awesome shot,' Blowers says. 'Even if he was a lot closer,' he adds.

'Oh, piss off, you wankers,' Tucker pouts.

'OH, SHIT, TO THE RIGHT,' Darren shouts, alarmed, as a massed horde start shuffling into view, coming from a side street to the right.

'That's a lot of zombies,' Cookey mutters, looking at the front of the thick horde.

'LEFT SIDE TOO,' Darren shouts again, and the lads look to see another horde coming out of a side street.

'MAIN ROAD TO THE RIGHT,' Darren shouts again as another huge horde comes into view on the road they had just driven along a few minutes ago.

'This is going to get interesting,' Blowers says. 'Let's pull back a bit so we are out of the firing line,' he says, and they pull back towards the Saxon.

'That's enough, lads,' Darren calls out when he's sure he can fire at the hordes over the top of them.

'Oh, well, best get on with it, then. Smithy, you take that lot on the road to the right. We'll take the other side street to the right. They're both closer than the left side.'

'Okay, mate,' Darren says and turns the heavy machine gun to face into the horde, and opens fire on them.

The GPMG bursts to life, spewing rounds into the front of the horde, who start dropping instantly. Blowers and the rest start firing single shots into the front of the horde coming from the right side street. The effect is less dramatic than the GPMG, but they still start to wither away at the front of the horde.

THE INFECTION WATCHES SIMULTANEOUSLY *through Darren's eyes and the eyes of the hosts as they start towards the resistors.*

The weapons are doing their deadly work already, and many hosts are being cut down. The infection has the whole area packed with hosts, but the losses are too great already, and it knows they will be cut to shreds before they get anywhere near the hospital.

'FUCK ME, THEY'RE MOVING FASTER,' Blowers shouts, unheard over the constant firing of the machine gun behind him and the assault rifles to both sides.

The hordes have increased their pace, not by much, but there is a definite increase from the slow shuffling to an almost normal walking pace.

'Fuck it, they're getting faster,' Cookey yells out.

'I just said that,' Blowers shouts back as they continue to fire into the hordes, and instead of picking their shots carefully, they now fire directly into the front of the crowd, hoping that any shot will drop them or slow them down enough to buy time.

Inside the hospital, at the rear stairwell, on the second floor, the thick walls and dividing rooms suppress the sounds of firing from the front of the building. Howie and McKinney hold their position, waiting for the others to load more equipment and medicines into the truck.

'I never liked hospitals,' McKinney remarks.

'A lot of people don't, mate,' Howie replies.

'Too clean and sterile, and full of sick people.'

'True, but where else should the sick people go?' Howie asks.

'I spent ages in them when my mum got sick – different hospitals all over the place,' McKinney says.

'What was wrong with her?' Howie asks.

'Heart problems. She died a few months ago,' McKinney says quietly.

'Oh, mate, I'm really sorry about that,' Howie says.

'Thanks, Mr Howie, but it was probably for the best. Got to be better than going out in all this mess and turning into one of them.'

'Yeah, maybe. Still, tough thing to have to deal with.'

'Yeah, Dad didn't cope very well, started drinking a lot, and just went downhill,' McKinney says in a soft voice.

'That's awful, mate, but I guess grief will do that.'

'Yeah, I guess,' McKinney replies.

'How do you think the others are getting on out front?' he adds, trying to change the subject.

'I bet Blowers is taking the piss out of Cookey, and Hewitt is smoking a shitload of cigarettes,' Howie says as McKinney laughs, a little forced, but at least he laughs.

Malcolm bursts through the doors behind them, panting from running up the stairs.

'Lads, there's shitloads of firing coming from the front. You'd better get back,' he says as Howie and McKinney start running down the stairs and back along the corridor, towards the main entrance.

The sounds of the GPMG and the assault rifles get louder as they approach. They burst outside, into the bright sunshine and the sight of several hordes walking at a steady pace towards them. Most of them are already halfway across the road and getting closer to the edge of the car park.

'They've got faster again,' Blowers shouts as Howie gets to his side.

'I can see. Shit, Dave still has the radio,' Howie says as he and McKinney start firing into the encroaching hordes.

The ground is littered with bodies torn apart by the constant fire rate, but the supply of infected seems endless. Darren moves around to start on the hordes pouring in from the side streets and alleys to the left – tracer fire flashing through the air, and shiny, spent casings jingling onto the ground. Within minutes, they reach the edge of the car park and are soon starting to cross.

Darren adjusts again and concentrates on the ones getting closest, bursting them apart, with the large rounds ripping into them.

'MAGAZINE,' Darren yells as the machine gun clicks empty.

'Fuck it. Focus on the ones getting close,' Howie yells as they start shooting into the car park. Dave and Jamie come running around from the side of the hospital and see the immense crowds surging across the road and car park towards the hospital. Jamie runs to join the others, switching from his sniper rifle to the assault weapon on his back. Dave runs to the rear of the Saxon and climbs in, going straight to one of the compartments and pulling out a canvas bag. He then jumps down and runs around to stand behind the others. Reaching into the bag, he pulls out a hand grenade, pulls the pin, and throws the grenade high into the air. It spins and lands in a cluster of cars.

'GET DOWN!' Dave's voice booms out as they all drop down onto the ground.

An immense explosion rips the air apart, followed by several more as the fuel tanks of the vehicles explode from the shrapnel and the heat, and fire of the grenade. Chunks of metal fly off into the air, taking out more of the infected in the car park, and a huge fireball scorches up into the sky as the fuel burns up.

Dave gets back to his feet and throws another one at parked vehicles, and the others all drop down again, covering their heads with their arms as the explosion booms out. Then the fuel tanks go again, creating another enormous fireball. The GPMG starts up again after Darren changes the magazine, and then the zombie slaughter continues.

'*Alpha to Charlie. We have heavy contact. Repeat. We have heavy contact, holding for now. How long will you be?*'

'*Charlie to Alpha. A few minutes is all we need. Keep holding them.*'

Dave puts the radio back into his pocket and selects another hand grenade, this time throwing it directly onto the massed hordes coming across the main road. The effect is amazing as a large circle of infected are thrown away from the blast, spinning and crashing into more of the infected around them. Dave keeps throwing the grenades, carefully selecting his spots to create the most damage. The combined efforts of the GPMG, the assault rifles, and the grenades being thrown keep most of them at bay, dropping huge numbers. The sides of the buildings, side streets, and access points are thick with infected walking towards them, and slowly, they gain ground, inch by inch. The body count climbs swiftly higher, and the attackers are forced to clamber and climb over their fallen comrades. Darren continues to fire, choosing the densest parts of the crowd to achieve the maximum amount of damage.

At first, it was thrilling to be able to cut so many of them down, and then it became a job, a necessity that had to be done for survival. But now there is another feeling, a feeling that sends signals to his brain, suggesting that maybe he is doing the wrong thing. These were people, they look like people, and he is killing them without mercy. These were people who had children, mothers and fathers, brothers and sisters. Normal people, with lives, and he is just slaughtering them. Darren starts to see the effect of the deadly fire and becomes aware of the bodies being ripped apart and torn limb from limb. Tears start forming in his eyes and slowly drip down his cheeks. He tightens his grip on the trigger as he battles within himself. He knows that this has to be done in order to survive, but slowly that feeling gets stronger, like a voice in his head, gently telling him to stop.

The voice of his father, telling him this is wrong. Darren releases his grip on the trigger and freezes, unable to resist the voice any longer, and stops watching the advancing horde.

'SMITHY! WHY HAVE YOU STOPPED?' Howie shouts over but gets no response as Darren just stares ahead with a frozen expression. 'SMITHY, YOU HAVE TO KEEP FIRING. THEY'RE GETTING CLOSER,' Howie yells; his voice taking on an angry tone. 'BLOWERS, GET ON THAT GUN,' Howie orders as Blowers runs to the rear of the Saxon and climbs into the back.

'Smithy, mate, get down,' Blowers calls up.

He gets no response and calls out again, tugging at Darren's legs and yelling louder and louder.

'Smithy, for fuck's sake. You'll get us all killed. Get down now, or I'll fucking move you myself,' Blowers yells up.

He is forced to strike the back of Darren's knees, and his legs buckle as he drops down from the look-out hole.

Blowers grabs at his shoulder and pulls him away, dumping him on the floor of the Saxon. He climbs up through the hole and takes position on the GPMG, instantly opening fire on the hordes now back in the car park and gaining ground. Howie's face creases with concern for Darren, but his main priority is the thousands of infected pouring across the road towards them. The pause between Darren stopping and Blowers taking over has allowed them to get so much closer, and they are spread out across the whole of the area now. The weapons cannot cut them down quickly enough.

'*Alpha to Charlie. We are being forced back. We have to move. Repeat. We have to move,*' Dave shouts into the radio over the constant firing all round him.

'*Charlie to Alpha. Roger that. We have enough. Move out. I repeat, move out.*'

'BACK TO THE VEHICLE,' Dave shouts out, and they all move backwards, still firing as the closest infected reach the edge of the car park only a few metres away. They turn and run to the rear, covering each other as they clamber in and then over Darren, who is lying on the ground. Cookey and McKinney pick him up to push him into a sitting position as Darren stares blankly ahead.

Howie climbs into the driver's seat and fires the massive engines up, pulling away just as he hears the rear doors slam. Howie drives the Saxon straight into the closest infected and lets the solid metal plating and huge tyres create a gap as they are mowed down and forced apart.

The GPMG is still firing away above him, and it cuts them down in droves. Howie forces the vehicle onto the road and then straight through them, engaging the four-wheel drive capability to keep the power high. The Saxon bounces as it climbs and drops but does not slow down, taking the obstacles with ease.

'We'll tuck in behind the truck,' Howie yells out to Dave.

'*Alpha to Charlie. We are behind Bravo. We will hold this position.*'

'*Roger that Charlie. Moving out now.*' The truck pulls out, following the two four-wheel drive vehicles, and heads away from the hospital. Within a short distance, the hordes are left behind, and Blowers releases the trigger on the GPMG.

'Is Smithy okay?' Howie calls out.

'Smithy! Darren, mate, are you okay?' Tucker leans forward, waving his hand in front of Darren's face.

Darren slowly comes to and focuses on Tucker.

'Wha–what happened?' Darren stammers quietly.

'You froze up, mate, stopped firing, and just froze,' Tucker says gently.

'Jesus, I don't know what happened. I don't remember,' Darren says, shaking his head.

'Shock, mate, it's just shock after everything that's happened. Take it easy. Here, have some water.' Darren takes the bottle and drinks slowly at first, then gulps it down, and belches loudly. He smiles back at Tucker.

'I'm so sorry. I don't know what happened,' Darren says, looking at the concerned faces of the lads staring back at him.

'Don't worry, mate. You were feeling rough earlier,' Tucker continues in the same gentle tones.

'I'll be okay. I am sorry. It won't happen again.'

'Don't worry, mate, just relax for a bit,' Howie calls back as he follows the truck into the maze of side streets.

CHAPTER SIXTY-SIX

Sarah's head pokes out from the line of the door, peering out down the corridor, looking left and right. No sign of any zombies, no noise either, so she gently creeps out to move down the corridor to the stairwell door. She leans forward to look through the glass pane and pushes the door open to listen for any sounds. Satisfied, she enters and steps down the stairs, checking each window of the doors as she goes.

She gets down to the level that Charlie lives on, inches her way to the door, and looks through the window. Her breath catches in her throat as she sees the corridor is packed with infected all clustering around Charlie's front door.

Silly, bloody fools, she thinks to herself. *Their shouting has drawn every infected from the building, but then, if every infected is in here, then the rest of the building might be clear.* She keeps to the stairs, moving quickly and checking each window. She didn't intend to come this far and didn't bring a weapon, but the urge to check the ground floor is strong, and she wants to see if they are through the main door yet. At the ground floor, the door doesn't have a window, so she crouches down to push the door open and peer out from a few inches above the floor. The lobby is clear, but she can see to the main doors at the front. The glass is opaque, but she can spot the hundreds of silhouettes on the other side – just a dense, gently moving mass, blocking the light, casting the lobby into shadows. She closes the door and gets back to her feet, biting her bottom lip as she wonders what to do.

There must be a rear entrance? The fire safety officials would have insisted on it, surely.

Quietly cursing herself for not knowing the layout of her own building, she crouches down again and slowly crawls out of the door and into the lobby. Moving slowly and watching the front door, she moves towards the ground floor apartments. She reaches the corridor leading to the flats and looks to the fire escape door at the end. This door has clear glass and leads out onto a small, grassed area that looks clear. Sarah moves down the corridor and reaches the door. There is a safety bar on it. *Simply push and walk out.* She tries to peer to the left and right. Both sides look clear. To the front is the small lawn, separating this block from the next one.

She pushes the bar down. The door opens silently, and she breathes in almost fresh air. It is tainted by the acrid aroma of the infected that walk around a few metres away. This is it, the way out. But if she steps out now, the door will close behind her, and she will be stuck, weaponless.

Sarah eases back inside and heads over to the stairwell.

Climbing back to her own floor, she heads inside her flat and starts preparing to escape. If they are massed to the front, she might be able to find a way out of the city, going in the other direction.

It's a crazy plan, and she knows it, but she also knows if she waits, she will go mad within days or just become trapped. At least this way she is doing something of her own choice.

CHAPTER SIXTY-SEVEN

'Did you get everything you need?' Howie asks Big Chris and the others.

They have stopped in a quiet street to discuss the next phase of the plan. Armed men and the recruits stand out on point duty at either end of the small fleet of vehicles.

'Not quite. Doc Roberts gave us a massive list. We got most of it, though, and loads of medicines from the pharmacy department,' Chris replies.

'At least that's something then. We can always try more hospitals away from the city later if you need to,' Howie says, and Chris recognises the genuine offer.

'We've worked well together so far, Howie. Your lot did a good job of keeping them suppressed,' Malcolm says.

'It was bloody close for a moment or two. One of our blokes seized up. He just froze, poor lad,' Howie says, dropping his voice down.

'It's normal, Howie. They're just kids. The basic training would have assessed them to see what they were like under stress, but they never got that far, did they? It happens sometimes, and those things are still people, *sort of*, and that will play havoc with a young mind that's already suffered from all this,' Chris explains calmly, the voice of experience. Howie can see how he came to be such a natural leader.

'Just take it easy with him and keep an eye on him, maybe get one of the other lads to pair up with him or something,' Malcolm offers.

'Yeah, I'll get one of them to stick close to him in case it happens again. I do feel for them, but there's no hiding from this. It's happening, and there's nothing we can do to stop it.'

'Right, so where does your sister live?' Big Chris switches back to business.

'Dave, have you got that address book?' Howie asks, and Dave pulls it from his bag and hands the brightly-covered, small hardback book over to him.

Howie flicks through the pages. His heart twinging with pain from seeing his mother's handwriting again and the names of relatives now gone.

'Millennium Towers, just off Westferry Road,' Howie reads out and looks up to see Chris and Malcolm examining a road atlas.

'I got Westferry Road. It's this big, straight one here,' Malcolm traces the road with his finger.

'Any idea which street it is?' he asks.

'Smithson Street. Mum wrote it down the side,' Howie says. His head down.

'Yeah, got it. Right, we can go straight down Westferry. It looks long and straight, or we can work in from the back roads,' Malcolm says.

'We can get to Westferry Circus roundabout and recce from there. If Westferry Road is no good, we can go round, but there's this bloody big bit of water in the middle and only one other road leading over it at the other end,' Chris says.

'Try for the roundabout then and see what it's like, I guess,' Howie says.

'Okay, slight change to the formation. Saxon up front as lead vehicle Alpha. I will take second position as Bravo, and the truck third as Charlie, with you, Malcolm, bringing up the rear as Delta again. This gives us two lead support vehicles and offers greater protection for the truck,' Chris says, looking around at them.

'If the truck is that valuable, send it back now and don't risk taking it further into their ground. We've still got three vehicles left,' Dave says.

'He's right, Chris, the truck is big and strong, and good for ploughing through them, but we can't risk losing it now. I think we should send it back. All those things were coming this way, so it should have an easy ride home,' Malcolm says, looking directly at his old friend.

'Howie, what do you think?' Chris asks to Howie's surprise. He is just a supermarket manager, not a military strategist, and he feels honoured to be asked his opinion.

'I have to agree with Dave and Malcolm. The truck's contents could save many lives. Sarah is my sister, but she is only one person.'

'Okay, agreed, we send the truck back, which makes the Saxon Alpha, me – Bravo, and Malcolm – Charlie. We head on this route to the roundabout and see what happens from there,' Chris says, and they part company.

Howie and Dave walk back to the Saxon, with Howie hoping he can remember the new call signs.

He thinks of Sarah and the long days she must have been waiting in her apartment.

'I hope she's all right, mate,' Howie says.

'Me too,' Dave replies.

'Gonna be a hell of a scrap getting through them.'

'Not the first one, though, is it, Mr Howie?' Dave says, giving one of his rare smiles, and Howie laughs.

'No, mate, I guess not.'

The vehicles drive back to Tower Bridge and escort the truck to the control room. The main road is still clogged with infected, but they plough through as Tucker uses the GPMG to cut them down as they go. Back at the deserted bridge, Hewitt goes into the control room and lowers it. The two halves drop down until they connect, and the road is normal again.

Rows of infected that got stuck from the bridge going up, start shuffling across again as Hewitt raises it a few inches to watch them struggle walking up hill. He waits until they almost reach the middle and raises it higher so they all tumble back. He laughs loudly as he watches the monitors above the control panel.

The others all hear him laughing and cram into the small room to watch him do it again.

'That's fucking funny,' Blowers laughs, wiping tears of merriment from his eyes. Big Chris and his men have crammed in and are laughing too. Hewitt lowers the bridge and examines the control panel more intently. The infected all start forwards again, trampling over the increasing numbers of squashed infected as they go.

'Ha, watch this,' Hewitt shouts out.

The infected walk over the first half of the bridge, and just as they get to the middle, Hewitt raises the closest half, which lifts up a few feet and blocks them from walking forward. The momentum of the infected is too great, and the first few rows get crushed as more keep trying to walk forward. Everyone in the control room laughs as Hewitt lifts it another foot or so, and they watch the infected getting crushed on the monitors. Hewitt then drops the bridge back down to normal level, and they all fall forward as the barrier holding them in place is suddenly taken away. The room erupts in laughter as the infected all fall forward onto their faces, and Hewitt raises the Bridge again to stop them coming on to this side.

'Hang on, I've got another one,' Hewitt laughs as he waits for the bodies to press against the slightly raised nearest section again.

The bodies keep pushing forward. Hewitt raises the nearest half of the bridge, and the bodies tumble forward and down into the river as the barrier is once again released.

Howie bursts out laughing and looks at Dave as they remember doing something similar with a smaller bridge in one of the villages they passed through.

The bodies keep pushing forward and stepping out onto thin air, as they are pushed from behind by the pressing horde.

'They just keep going,' Hewitt says, bent over double, laughing as they keep walking and shuffling forward, and dropping down into the river with a splash.

Big Chris, Malcolm, and the big, bald man are all laughing hard at the ridiculous sight. Even Dave smiles as he watches the spectacle, until the last one falls off the edge and down into the River Thames.

'That was bloody brilliant,' Chris says, with an enormous smile, showing his white teeth.

They all laugh and then start applauding Hewitt as he turns and takes a mock bow to them, laughing himself.

But Darren is at the back, watching the hosts fall off the bridge. He smiles along with the joke, but inside, he feels different.

This isn't funny, and they shouldn't be doing this.

Suddenly, he feels very alone. He smiles and goes along with it, but his eyes are not laughing.

The truck moves off along a now clear bridge, and the men file back to their vehicles, laughing and joking. Howie gets into the driver's seat as Tucker shouts down, 'What were you all laughing about, and why did the bridge keep going up and down?'

'Nick was playing with the zombies on the other side, making them fall into the river,' Blowers calls up as he settles into the back of the Saxon.

'THAT WAS BLOODY FUNNY,' McKinney says.

Howie had taken McKinney to one side as they walked back to the Saxon.

'McKinney, can you do me a favour, mate?' Howie asked him.

'Yes, Mr Howie,' McKinney replied.

'I'm worried about Smithy. Can you pair up with him and keep an eye on him just in case he freezes again?'

'Yeah, no problem, does he know you've asked me?' McKinney asked.

'No, I don't want to make him think we're watching him or anything like that. Just keep an eye out so he doesn't get hurt or something,' Howie says quietly as McKinney nods and climbs into the back of the Saxon.

'RIGHT, YOU READY FOR THIS, DAVE?' Howie asks as he starts the engine and turns the Saxon in a wide arc to drive back down the bridge.

'Yes, Mr Howie,' Dave replies as they move off slowly, waiting for the two four-wheel drive vehicles to catch them up.

They head back onto the main road to follow the route they

agreed on. Within minutes, though, the road is full of infected, back to shuffling slowly and again moving in the same direction as they are.

'They're ignoring us again. What is going on? They were going nuts for us at the hospital, and now they're not even looking at us,' Howie says.

'Maybe they know where we're going and want to use their speed only when we are static,' Dave answers.

'As crazy as that sounds, mate, it does make sense. They ignored us all the way here and only came for us when we stopped at the hospital, and they did speed up. That could have got very messy if they had started running.'

'Maybe moving faster makes them weaker,' Blowers adds from behind them.

'I've been thinking that. At the services, they were running, and we were putting them down with ease. Did you notice if they were weaker today?'

'No, not really,' Blowers answers.

'But if they only just started moving, and it was only a bit faster, it might not be enough to make them weaker that quickly,' Dave says.

'Okay, that makes sense, but how do they know where we are or where we're going?' Howie asks into silence.

'It can't just be a coincidence. We are specifically going for Canary Wharf, and they are certainly heading that way now,' Howie adds. 'They haven't attacked Chris's commune in large numbers or with the ferocity they've shown us.'

'We've killed many of them, Mr Howie. That's the only link. We've cut them back, and they don't like it,' Dave says.

'Well, do you know what I think about that?' Howie asks. 'I think fuck 'em. I'll keep killing 'em every chance I get until the last one fucking drops,' he spits out the words, with venom in his voice.

Darren listens intently. A feeling of alarm inside him from Howie's words. He respects this man deeply and would follow him anywhere. But now there is doubt creeping in. Howie wants to slaughter every one of them, and that isn't right. They don't deserve that, do they? The voice in his head, the voice of his father speaks out, telling him this is not right. Howie has no right to do this. If he left them alone, they might have left him alone. Howie is leading them all to danger, with his reckless actions, and will cause the death of all these people.

The voice carries on, and Darren sits quietly in the back of the Saxon, with his mind deep in conflict.

'Bravo to Alpha.'

'Alpha receiving. Go ahead, Bravo.'

'The road looks almost blocked. Can you make it through?'

'Affirmative, we are moving through them without issue.'

'Roger that. We will close the gap and travel right on your tail to keep a solid line. Bravo to Charlie. Close up on our tail and keep a solid line.'

'Charlie to Bravo. Roger that. Closing up now, nose to tail.'

'Bravo to Alpha. We are nose to tail on you now. Bravo out.'

Dave climbs out of the passenger seat and gets Tucker down from the GPMG so he can climb up and look out.

Once up top, he scans the road ahead and the solid lines of infected traipsing in the same direction as them.

The front of the Saxon pushes them aside or knocks them flat, and the Saxon rocks with the constant bumps from the bodies it runs over. The power of the vehicle is immense, and they force an easy enough path through. Dave drops down and pulls out another canvas bag full of grenades from a compartment, then climbs back up to the look-out position, resting the bag between his body and the edge of the hole.

'Alpha to units. Be aware, be aware, grenades being thrown behind the convoy, be aware,' Dave speaks into the radio and hears both units confirm their acknowledgment. He then looks back to see Big Chris's vehicle within inches of the back of the Saxon and Malcolm's vehicle within inches of Chris's, keeping a solid line to prevent the hordes from slipping between the vehicles and isolating them. Dave pulls out a grenade and pulls the pin. He looks at the sides, the front, and then back at the rear and the solid mass of infected swarming into the wake left by the vehicles.

He pulls his arm back and launches the first one high in the air. It lands far beyond the back of the last vehicle. Within a few seconds, a muffled explosion booms out, and bodies are seen flying up into the air. Dave can see a wide circle form as the deadly shrapnel rips through the densely packed bodies. He repeats the action, launching grenade after grenade behind the vehicles, and before long, he can see a distinct gap forming behind him.

Each grenade takes out several infected immediately, but the shrapnel takes more down with horrific injuries, and those bodies are sent hurtling into others. Dave empties the bag of grenades and looks with satisfaction at the huge holes now forming behind them. He then turns and grips the GPMG, and focuses it on the ones in front of him. He takes a practise sweep from left to right, aiming directly in front of the Saxon; then, nodding to himself, he squeezes the trigger and sweeps back right to left, aiming directly at head height and watching as skull after skull explodes like a row of melons. Brains and bones burst up into the air.

Dave extends the aim and keeps going, focussing to keep the machine gun at head height, and take as many heads off as possible.

'Fucking hell, look at that,' Blowers shouts from his position in the front passenger seat, next to Howie.

They hear the muffled pops of the grenades thrown by Dave and then the sudden *whump, whump* of the machine gun above them. The closest infected are all mown down by the hail of bullets, and Dave starts on the next load, taking heads off with each accurate sweep.

'He's getting bloody head shots with a heavy calibre machine gun!' Blowers shouts as the lads all pile up front to watch the work being done by Dave. All of them cheer as the heads pop like fireworks, one after the other. Dave keeps the motion going, sweeping steadily side to side and cutting down swathes. He extends his range and is soon taking them out at the sides too. A look of intense concentration is on his face as he aims directly at the heads and sweeps the bullets across to see head after head popping open and the bodies slumping down. The shooting to the sides means that Chris and his men see the awesome display being put on by Dave, and they cheer and shout as they watch the skulls bursting open in precise lines.

'Only fucking Special Forces would do something that crazy,' Chris mutters to himself but can't help grinning at the sight of the craniums being popped open. They reach the Westferry Circus roundabout and wait in situ as Dave continues with the machine gun, sweeping low at first and taking the closest ring out, then lifting the aim higher and higher with each sweep until there are almost concentric circles of decapitated bodies lying all around the vehicles. Eventually, he stops and climbs back down into the Saxon to a roar of cheers from the recruits. He gives a slight smile as he climbs back to the front seat, respectfully vacated by Blowers.

'*Bravo to Alpha. Nice display.*'

'*Charlie to Alpha. Likewise.*' Small words, but big compliments, coming from such hardened and battle-experienced men.

The Saxon sits on the exit road to Westferry Road, facing in the direction they need to go, at a solid, massed gathering of infected stretched out as far as the eye can see. It is an undulating carpet of bodies, once killed and now brought back to semi-life, with a hunger for human flesh. They hold position and don't move an inch towards the Saxon. Howie gets out of the Saxon and walks around to the front, staring hard at the blocked road. His eyes move along the front row, sweeping across the horde. Dave joins him, and they look ahead silently. The recruits come out to stand to the sides of them, one by one. Big Chris and his men, Malcolm and his men, all step out of their vehicles and walk forward to the front of the Saxon, and stand with Howie. They stare at the lines ahead of them.

An enemy holding position in readiness for battle.

Thousands of enemy infected waiting for these few to try and take them on.

They know these things can now move fast if they want to, that they can change within a split second and become deadlier than the slow, shuffling things they have faced already.

'How far up is it?' Howie asks.

'Third on the left,' Malcolm replies.

'They can move fast now, and they can change. They *will* change, and they will come for us.'

'Do you have a plan?' Malcolm asks.

'Yes,' Howie replies.

'What is it?' Chris asks.

'To go and get my sister,' Howie replies.

'How?' Chris says.

'Go in there and get her out,' Howie replies.

'There's a lot of them,' Malcolm adds.

'There is,' Howie replies.

'Listen, you've all helped me get this far, but this is my issue. None of you have to do this with me. You don't have to risk your lives for this.'

'You'd go on your own?' Chris asks quietly.

'Yes,' Howie replies instantly.

'No, he wouldn't,' Dave speaks with a firm voice.

'Not without me either,' Blowers says.

'Me too,' Cookey adds. Howie looks back to the lads standing to the sides of him. They look to him and nod firmly.

'All of us,' Blowers speaks for the group.

'Okay, how?' Chris asks.

Howie looks back at the Saxon, then to the horde waiting for them.

'We'll charge them,' Howie says.

'The other vehicles won't get more than a few metres into that lot,' Chris says.

'Then we all go in the Saxon,' the big man with the bald head says.

'Good plan. I'm in,' Chris adds.

'Me too,' Malcolm says.

'Fuck it, let's load up, then,' Chris says as they all turn and walk back to the Saxon in silence. Howie sits in the driver's seat, slowly increasing the pressure on his right foot and making the engine roar loudly.

Big Chris clambers through and gets up on the GPMG. His large frame barely fitting into the hole. The Saxon surges forward. Howie working through the gears as the engine increases in pitch, racing towards the waiting hordes. Big Chris opens up on the GPMG, sweeping across the front ranks and cutting them down with a deadly hail of lead. The ranks get cut down from the ferocious firing, but they hold position as the bullets rip through them. At the last few hundred meters, Chris aims directly in front of them, making small movements left and right, chopping them down and creating a hole for the Saxon. The Saxon slams into them with enormous power and speed. The impact jolts each man inside, but Chris braces his powerful legs and absorbs the blow into his large frame. His hands never leaving the machine gun. He spins around, cutting them down, then sweeps back to the front, and works to carve a hole for the Saxon. The vehicle ploughs into the bodies, and Howie selects the four-wheel drive to keep the vehicle surging forward.

The huge tyres keep their grip and bounce over bodies, crushing them into a pulp. The vehicle keeps going further and further into the bodies, and the engine screams as Howie applies more power with his foot, forcing the heavy vehicle to slam them down or send them spinning off to the sides. Within seconds, they are deep into the horde and ramming the infected away as they keep pushing towards the third junction on the left. The first one passes, and the Saxon powers on, taking each body down with ease. The GPMG spews a hail of rounds into the bodies in front of the vehicle as they gradually work closer and closer. They pass the second junction, and suddenly, the massed horde surges forward into the path of the Saxon. The bodies push and press, and the gaps between them close up as they become a solid object. The third junction gets closer and closer as the vehicle keeps going, punishing the infected for daring to be in the way.

The infected keep pushing forward, forcing more and more bodies into the path of the vehicle. More bodies push them from behind too, and the zombies stretch away for miles in every direction.

The Saxon reaches the junction and starts to slow as the sheer weight of bodies prevents it from advancing. Howie pushes his foot flat to the floor, and the Saxon's engine scream out. They gain ground, inch by inch, slowly crushing the bodies in front of them. The GPMG sends a withering hail into the infected, and they drop down, allowing the Saxon to keep pushing forward, but the horde is relentless and keeps pushing back.

A solid object against an immovable force.

The competition goes on as the machine gun rips them apart and creates small gaps for the Saxon to push into.

'You'll blow the engine,' a voice shouts from the back, and Howie is forced to ease off.

The sudden reduction in power brings the Saxon to a halt, jammed in a sea of infected pushing closer and closer into them.

'I'll cut down a gap; then, we're out and fighting for it. Make ready!' Chris yells down and commences firing again, moving slowly around in circles to create an ever-increasing gap around the Saxon.

He spins, and the constant rain of bullets shreds the infected to pieces. The bodies rack up and form a barrier to those behind, and he keeps spinning around as the circle surrounding the Saxon gradually grows more and more.

'Make ready,' Chris bellows as the men inside the vehicle prepare for their big moment.

CHAPTER SIXTY-EIGHT

Sarah empties her gym rucksack on the bed, sending white socks, deodorant, and a small make-up bag tumbling across the crumpled bed sheets.

She grabs two bottles of water – the only two actual water bottles she has in the apartment – and pushes them into the bag.

Next, she goes to the cupboard and looks at the tinned food. Tins are heavy, and too many will slow her down. Plus, the bag isn't that big, and also, they will clunk together and make noise as she moves.

But she needs food, and everything else has been eaten. After minutes spent deciding, she finally chooses three tins and takes them to the bag, then runs back to take the tin opener from the drawer.

'What else will I need?' she mutters quietly, having learnt years ago that talking to herself calms her down and helps to rationalise her mind.

'Water, food – got them. What about clothes?' She puts in clean panties and a pair of socks, then pulls them out, chastising herself. Within minutes, she puts them back in and stands back to stare at the bag, waiting for inspiration to strike her.

'That's it, then. All I need: water, food, and clean pants,' she mutters again and closes the bag up before shrugging it on her back, feeling uncool for using both straps, then laughing at herself for the ridiculous thought. She gathers up her homemade spear – the broomstick with the long knife attached to the end – and walks towards her apartment door, pausing to listen before she opens it. A noise. Some kind of bang. She drops her head down to listen harder. There it is again – a muffled, constant thumping. She moves away from the door and back into her apartment, and the noise gets louder. A fast, banging noise that's familiar but not quite there in her head yet. She moves to the patio door and slides it open. The noise floods in, and she looks down onto the solid crowd of infected jammed into the pavement. Her eyes follow the line of them, realising they are all facing in the same direction, down to the main road. They are all facing and pushing towards Westferry Road.

She leans out to try and see down to the junction and gasps as she takes in the amount of infected crammed into the area. Every single one of them is pushing towards the main road. She waits, leaning over the balcony; the *broom-spear-stick* still in her hand.

Slowly, the noise gets louder, until an army-type vehicle comes into view. Even from this distance, she can see the outline of the giant vehicle and someone standing halfway out of the roof. Bright flashes flare out from the top of the vehicle, and she realises that the man is firing a machine gun into the zombies. Her heart races as she watches the desperate struggle, the vehicle inching forward bit by bit as it gets closer to her junction. It looks like it's trying to turn into her road, then comes to a halt as the pressure of the bodies forces it to a stop.

The man on top spins around, and Sarah watches a space slowly being created around the vehicle as the machine gun cuts them down. Hope is surging through her, but it starts to ebb away as she realises that the vehicle is stuck and can no longer move forward. Sarah watches as the firing stops, and the man drops out of view. Then, another man climbs out and stands on the top of the vehicle. He is followed by the first man again.

It looks like the man standing up is holding a large bag. He rests it down, and she watches as he takes something out of it, then throws it high into the air. Sarah hears a loud bang and sees bodies flying upwards. The man throws something again, and after a few seconds, she hears another loud bang, and more bodies are shot up and away.

'Grenades, he's throwing grenades,' she whispers quietly.

The man is throwing them down into her road and making a point of making them land at different points. Each throw is followed by a loud explosion, and she watches as gaps start forming where the bodies are blown away, and more are felled by the blasts. The machine gun keeps firing, and more and more of them are cut down. The machine gun appears to be focussing on keeping them away from the vehicle while the grenade man is launching the explosives down her road. Slowly, the gaps get bigger as more damage is reaped on the infected. She wants to scream and wave to tell them she is here, but she can see the hopeless situation they are in, and she watches in silence, willing them to break free somehow.

CHAPTER SIXTY-NINE

The anger bursts inside me, filling me with rage and cold, hard fury. We are stuck in an ocean of never-ending, infected zombies. I fucking hate them. I fucking hate zombies. I hate the way they shuffle and groan. I hate the way they move fast without warning and change the rules as they go along. I hate their decomposing flesh and their rancid, putrid breath. I hate the drool that drips from their mouths and their red, bloodshot, dead eyes. Everything around me slows. The firing above my head becomes a slow *thump-thump,* and I see shiny, spent casings spinning down gently past the window. I see a grenade rolling, end over end, through the air until it drops down out of sight, and an eternity passes before the slow explosion erupts ahead of me.

Bodies are floating through the air, limbs detached and flying off, and drops of blood are strung out and arcing high. My eyes follow another grenade that spins in the air above me, going down into the road. As I follow the trajectory, I see the tall apartment blocks further up the street and the outline of a person standing on one of the balconies facing towards us.

My eyes fix on that spot, and I feel the person is staring straight at me. Suddenly, it's not just anger inside me, there is hope too. I snap back to reality as I realise there is a gap in front of us created by the GPMG spinning around, and I engage the gears and push the Saxon, and bounce high over the many fallen bodies. Just in those few metres, we gain enough speed to slam into the crowd and send them backwards.

The grenades thrown by Dave have created gaps that we can use to our advantage by pushing the infected back. We gain a little more distance, and I see Chris is firing directly in front of us again. He has created small gaps for the Saxon to power into. Little by little, metre by metre, we gain ground, and I keep looking up to see the person still watching us from the balcony.

I select reverse gear and slam the Saxon back into the crowd behind us, crushing yet more of them and gaining a little space in front to gather some speed before I use the front as a battering ram to drive further into them.

The machine gun and the grenades do an amazing job of making little pockets of space, which I use to force them back. The vehicle is tonnes of solid steel, with more weight added by the number of people inside, and although the crowd is incredibly dense, they cannot withstand the force of the vehicle repeatedly hammering them.

The progress is painfully slow, but at least we have progress.

'PULL BACK AND HOLD FOR A SECOND,' Big Chris yells, and I change into reverse to force the Saxon backwards, impacting on the crowd that is surging forward to fill the gaps.

'HOLD,' Chris yells, and the GPMG remains firing directly ahead of us, making little sweeps left and right at the same width as the vehicle.

The bodies are decimated right in front of me, torn limb from limb and cut in half as the rounds slice through them with ease. Chris holds the firing position as a large hole is made, with fallen bodies lying like felled trees on the ground.

The GPMG clicks empty as Chris shouts, 'NOW!'

I push my foot down hard, and the vehicle pulls ahead with amazing speed, crushing the bodies under the huge tyres. We bounce up high from the impact on so many corpses, but the vehicle slams back down and keeps pushing forward. That extra speed we used has gained the momentum to drive us further ahead than I had hoped for, and I look up to see the person waving from the balcony as we get closer and closer. Then we are close enough to see the front of the building and a large plaque reading "Millennium Tower", and that hope inside me gets stronger with every inch of ground we gain. The horde surges forward, moving with speed as they slam into the front of the Saxon. The bodies pushing hard against each other to make a solid wall.

Something is wrong with the GPMG as it doesn't resume firing from running empty. I try to pull back, but the Saxon moves inches before losing power – such is the force of the bodies pushing against us.

'We're bogged in,' I yell out. 'We'll have to fight through on foot.' I clamber out over the seat and try to get in the back, but there are too many people, and no room to manoeuvre.

'Get a few on the roof to shoot down, then more at the back. Doors ready,' Dave yells out as some of the recruits and Chris's men clamber up through the GPMG hole and start firing down into the surrounding hordes.

I glance back through the windscreen and can see the infected are stretching their arms up now and trying to reach up to the men on the top. Their teeth bared. Almost angry expressions on their rotting faces.

'When I shout, push those doors open and fire out,' Dave yells down.

'Get to the back, two lines, with front line crouching, and rear line standing,' I yell out as they try to organise themselves in the confined space, pushing and shoving until they are formed up and ready.

One of Chris's men at the front shouts for the rear line to move backwards so the hot casings don't land on them.

'Make ready,' Dave yells down, above the constant firing of assault weapons. 'We're making a bit of room at the back. You'll have time for one round of firing to cut more down, and then we have to charge them,' he adds. I see the big, bald man work his way back to me, with his axe in his hands.

'When they stop firing, we'll burst out with the axes and try to clear them back,' he says to me.

'I'll go with you,' Blowers adds, grabbing his axe.

The rest of the axes are stacked up and ready to be taken by the others.

'Us three first and then this lot behind us. We're heading for Millennium Towers. It's just up a bit and on the left,' I shout out so they can all hear me, and I hear Dave repeat my words to the lads on the top. The firing continues, and I see knuckles going white as the men in front of me grip their weapons tightly; faces serious. They stare forward with fear and terror, but above all else, they have courage. The courage to face down an enemy that outnumbers them thousands to one. The courage to stand firm and not fold or back away. Hardened men, tough men relying on each other and their natural-born instinct to fight and survive.

They have a reason to fight, a purpose, something to believe in, and we stand together, ready to charge to our deaths if needs be, ready to lay our lives down for the right to live how we want.

We repel the idea of these foul things that have tainted this earth and caused the deaths of so many innocent people.

'I don't know your name,' I say to the big man with the bald head.

'Clarence,' he replies, looking me dead in the eye.

'Good to meet you, Clarence.'

'You too.'

Dave lightly drops down onto his feet and draws his knives. He holds them, with the blades upright and reversed to press into his forearms. The action sends a fresh surge of adrenalin through me, and I see Blowers grip the handle of his axe. A dark look crossing his face. That action by Dave has preceded every fight so far, and it signifies our readiness for battle.

Our willingness to do battle.

Our right to do battle and do so on our terms. For we have taken the fight to them today. They are thousands, and we are few, but we came for them.

They stood and waited, and we charged them.

This battle was ours for the choosing, and we took that choice. My breathing gets faster, and my chest rises. My hands were shaking a little, but now they are steady, and my legs feel firm and strong. My grip won't fail me, and I know what needs to be done.

A sensation within me; a tingling inside my stomach. Hairs on the back of my neck prickle as I hear it once more knocking on the door to my soul.

'What do you want?' I know what it wants.
'I want to come in.'
'Why?'
'Because you need me.'
'I rely on you too much.'
'You can't do this without me, Howie.'
'Maybe this time I can.'
'Without me, you will die, and Sarah will die because of you.'
'I can't keep using you like this.'
'Why not?'
'The more I use you, the more you want.'
'You can't get through this without me. You know that. You have no choice, but my costs are mounting, and payment is due.'
'It's too much… But I want you. I need you.'
'Then let me in, Howie.'
'I want to. I like it when you come in.'
'So?'
'That's the problem. You're addictive, and it's dangerous.'
'But you wouldn't have got this far without me.'
'I know that.'
'So let me in.'
'Do you want to come in?'
'Yes.'
'What if one day I can't shut you out again?'
'Worry about that later. You need me now more than ever.'
'Okay, but this has to stop soon.'
'I understand, but not now.'
'Come in. You're not alone? Who are they?'
'You've met them before – Rage, Fury, and Wrath.'
'Bring them. Bring them all.'
'You are right. I am addictive, aren't I?'
'Yes.'
'But you need me, don't you?'
'Yes.'
'You need all of us.'
'Yes.'

'Open the door wide, Howie, open it wide, and leave it open this time. I think we'll be coming back quite often...'

'NOW,' Dave shouts the word so loudly that every zombie for miles must be able to hear him. The back doors are thrown open wide, and the firing commences as eight men open fire with fully automatic assault rifles – four crouched and four standing, shoulder to shoulder, jammed in tight, and deafening each other. The immediate ground at the back of the Saxon is already clear from the men firing from the roof. The split-second timing works perfectly as the men in the rear and the men on the top all fire into the packed horde. The effect is devastating as the first few ranks are cut to pieces and the force of the rounds drives them backwards into the infected behind them. I hear the guns click empty, and the men burst two to each side as they create a gap wide enough for one man to go through. I am that man, and I run through them and launch myself high out of the back doors, with my beautiful, double-bladed axe wide out to my side. I land with my feet planted apart and sweep in a wide arc as I slice through several necks extended in front of me. I take a step forward and swing backwards, cleaving more of them open with the deadly blades. My voice roars as I take those first swipes, and I feel the glory of the first death from my hands sweep through me.

I scream out and plunge forward, swinging the axe around with fearsome power and speed. I hear voices behind me, and the recruits and men are pouring out to charge into the lines of infected.

You are thousands, and we are few, but we fucking charge at you with axes and knives.

We fucking take you on with the weapons we hold, and we will defeat you.

I hear the glorious sound of Dave roaring at full volume, and I lift my voice to join his.

I see him off to my side as he launches himself fully into them. His arms spinning with grace and supple power as he bends and flexes to slice their throats, then drops down to cut through Achilles tendons, and they fall from their weakened legs.

Clarence stands back and swings his double-bladed axe high above his head. A Viking warrior, a berserker of gigantic size, and he steps forward with long strides. His almighty power sweeps the axe through many bodies as he swings out and then back again as he takes another big step. We roar, and we fight, and more of our voices join in, and we take the fight to them. My two-headed axe doubles my ability to kill them and take them down. Bodies fall about me as we fight our way through. We arrange ourselves, with the axes to the front, and Dave takes them down to fight a path through. The others behind us keep our backs and sides clear as they hack and cleave the bodies down. They push forward, but we fight harder than they can surge. They try to surround us, but we keep fighting, and we make progress through these evil things as they fall under our righteous blades. The battle is brutal, but we fight and power on, and each step we take brings us closer to the building. I glance up and see a figure waving down and screaming at us. I raise my axe high and bellow a cry. A cry of war, a cry of violence, and for a second, my comrades join me, and we raise our weapons up and scream into the air.

We are coming. We are fighting for you.

We will kill every one of them to get to you.

We are coming, and we bring death with us as we slaughter, hack, chop, cleave, slice, cut, and kill the infected.

Two sides fighting, but our small size means they can only present a limited front, and we can fight that front, and we do. We cut them down in droves and keep pushing as our hands and arms become slick from the blood we spill.

※ ※

SARAH WATCHES the men climb on top of the army vehicle, and they start firing down, keeping the fire pouring onto the infected at the rear.

She watches with bated breath as the rear doors burst open, and a withering fire from within is directed towards the infected. They burst apart and are sent flying back from the almighty hail sent their way.

The second the firing ends, a man launches himself from the back of the vehicle, swinging an axe above his head. Sarah's mouth drops open as she realises they are taking on thousands of infected in hand-to-hand combat. Men surge from the back of the vehicle, and they bravely charge into the lines. Even from her high position, she can hear the men roar as they offer challenge to the infected army. The men from the top jump down, and they too charge into the melee. The effect is mesmerising. These men, these few men kill many of the infected as they fight to gain a circular shape. Men with axes take them down, and others work to the sides and the rear as that tiny, clear circle of men starts to move through the infected throng. These men are killing machines, and they move with deadly purpose. Each of them advancing with speed and power, and the killing goes on as they leave a bloody wake of broken bodies behind them. Sarah watches the man in the front centre swing his axe. A giant of a man next to him cleaving the bodies down.

She screams to tell them she is watching. Their brave actions have not gone without witness. The man in the front centre looks up and raises his axe high in the air to her. He roars, and every one of those brave warriors stops and holds their weapon high, and roars their defiance as they look up at her. Then, as one, the weapons drop back down, and they fight with renewed purpose to slaughter the infected. They have seen her.

They are coming for her.

Howie.

It must be Howie.

Her heart races as she runs to the front door, not bothering to stop, look, or listen, and she charges down the corridor and into the stairwell.

As she gallops down the stairs, an infected staggers out from a door in front of her, and Sarah rams the point of her spear deep into its throat.

'FUCK YOU!' she screams as she pulls the spear out, then continues running down the flights of stairs.

WE KEEP MOVING FORWARD, and our fighting shape holds. We suffer our first loss as one of Chris's men slips on the bloody ground and falls down.

We all turn to help, but it's too late, and the infected drop down on him, burying their faces into his stomach and legs.

He screams with impotent rage, and Dave drops down to slice a blade deep across his throat.

'Sorry,' Dave whispers in his ear and then is back up, fighting.

The loss hits us. We fill with rage and fury and fight with a consumed anger that burns our hearts.

We have lost one of our own to you, and for that, you will pay with hundreds now.

We won't stop until you all die and cease to be on this earth.

'ALMOST THERE,' Dave bellows. His enormous voice drowning the grunts and growls of the men as we fight.

We push out harder now, in sight of the doors that lead into Millennium Towers. I look up and see the doors burst open, and a woman comes out, screaming with fury. My heart soars as I see my sister Sarah marching out, holding the end of a hose like a machine gun.

'SARAH,' I scream, and she stops to stare straight at me.

Just a few lines between us now, and we hack them down. I thought Dave was fighting with awesome speed before, but he goes into overdrive now. His arms spinning with fury as he cuts a path through them and breaks free to race towards Sarah. My world is complete. The toughest, bravest man I have ever known is now by my sister's side. She is safe and will live as I know that small man will kill anything to protect her. He is my friend. Sarah will live. She will survive, and I smile, staring hard at them as I begin to laugh.

'I WIN, YOU FUCKERS!' I scream out and charge, with every ounce of strength I have, as the hose opens up.

Sarah steps forward slowly as the immense jet of water sluices into the horde and knocks them down.

We burst sideways as Sarah walks further towards us. The power of the life-giving water is with us. The clean water is on our side, and that simple thing repels them and forces them back as they lose their grip and slide down.

We fight to the sides, and one by one, we burst out of them. Then, as one, we turn and form a line in front of Sarah.

They keep coming, and we kill them. The power is on our side now as they fight to gain ground, and we fight to protect what we have taken.

Dave stands by her side. His knives held ready as he stares with deathly calm at the horde.

The powerful jet pushes them back as we start to retreat, and I see Clarence take the hose from her and walk closer to the horde, using the extreme power of the water to send them staggering backwards.

'Howie,' Sarah yells, and I rush to her and wrap my arms around the only surviving member of my family.

'Sarah, thank god, you're okay,' I shout back over the noise. 'We need to get out of here,' I glance back at the horde and then to the building.

'We can't lose that vehicle. We'll never get out of here alive without it,' I shout to Dave.

'Then we fight back to it, Mr Howie,' Dave says, loud enough for them all to hear. The men and recruits all stop to stare back at me, looking at Sarah and nodding to her.

'We have to fight back,' I shout out loudly. 'That vehicle is ours, and we must take it back.'

Big Chris stares at me, then looks at the horde.

'I hate to say this, but you're right. We have to fight back. Get your sister in the middle, and we'll fight the way we came in,' he shouts, with a ferocious look on his face.

'Sarah, get in the middle. Dave, stay by her side.'

He looks at me and nods once, taking a step to stand just in front of her.

'FORM UP,' Dave bellows, and the men drop back to form a ring around Sarah. She looks to me in horror.

'We can't go into that lot!' she says, terrified.

'We have to, Sarah. There's thousands of them all round us. The only hope is to get back to our vehicle. Just stay with Dave.'

'Who?' she asks, confused.

'Sarah, this is Dave. Dave, this is Sarah. Now, let's go.' I take front centre position again, and we start to step forward as Clarence drops the hose to fall back into step by my side again.

Within seconds, we are back in amongst them, fighting and slicing our axes into their soft, decaying bodies. We have our prize. We have the chalice we came for. We are warriors, and all that we need is something to believe in. To protect those that need protection, to have that principle, and to fight for it with every breath we take. Not one of us flinches or questions this. For in our hearts, we know the reason we are here. To stop the evil from taking her.

We fight you to give her life, and we will carry on to be sure that happens.

Our shape holds as we battle on. They can push as hard as they like, for all they do is force the ones at the front onto our deadly blades and axe heads. Clarence swings the axe with his almighty strength, and heads are sent spinning in the air as he chops through necks. Dave sticks by Sarah's side, taking small lunges if one pushes through a gap left by the men at the sides. Our tactic works, and once again, we make progress, slowly gaining ground back to the Saxon.

Darren fights with courage and bravery. The infection pulling back to watch him during this battle.

AS THE SAXON powered closer and closer to the building, the infection made a conscious decision to watch from within and learn from his natural reactions. Darren feels his uncertainty leave him, and once again, he feels the surge of adrenalin as the last seconds before the battle slowly tick away. He fires from the back of the Saxon and then moves aside to watch with pride as Howie launches out to attack them single-handed.

He slots the bayonet on his rifle and bursts out with his mates and the other men to charge into the infected. Feeling hatred and glory, he fights to follow Howie and Dave. They saved him and gave him respect and protection, they made sure he was okay, and they did so many small things that grew a deep sense of respect in him. For that, he fights, and the infection learns the mixture of chemicals pouring into Darren's system that make him feel like this.

Darren hacks away at the infected and grimaces with determination as they fall under his blows and swipes. He aims for the throat and thrusts deep into their necks. The infection floods every host in that area with an image of Darren and makes it clear that they should not touch him. As they gain ground, Darren feels invincible as he cuts down host after host, not realising they lunge at him but hold back from biting. Several chances present themselves as his increasingly reckless bravery leaves him open, but they suppress the urge to bite as Darren becomes the safest man on earth at that moment.

They start fighting back towards the Saxon, and the infection plans for the next phase. It floods Darren with adrenalin and a feeling of confidence. Darren laughs as he attacks them, feeling that he cannot be touched. The infection increases the flow as Darren surges into them for the attack. The infection has learnt what chemicals to release to flood a body with that same feeling of love, pride, and devotion towards another body, and it keeps Darren safe as they fight their way back to the vehicle. Within a few metres of them reaching the vehicle, the infection pulls them all back and makes every infected step away and leave their path clear.

WE FIGHT ON, getting closer and closer to the Saxon, when they suddenly pull back and step away from us. Mid-swing, they move as one, and there is open space in front of me as the axe rotates and almost takes me over with it.

'What's going on?' Blowers shouts in alarm.

'They're pulling back,' Tucker shouts, with victory in his voice.

'No, it must be something else. We haven't won this,' Big Chris shouts.

'STAY TOGETHER AND KEEP IN FORMATION,' Dave shouts as we move through the clear path towards the Saxon. A noise. I look over to see Darren laughing with unrestrained glee.

'We've fucking beaten them. The fucking pussies are giving up,' he shouts.

Dave glances at me, and I shake my head.

I look over to McKinney and put my fingers to my eyes, then point at Darren.

'Watch him,' I mouth, and McKinney nods and steps closer to Darren.

'Ha! You fucking losers. We win. We fucking win,' Darren screams out.

'Darren, calm down, mate,' I call out as we keep stepping towards the Saxon, only a few metres away now.

'Why? We've won. We've fucking won. We're untouchable. We can't be beaten,' Darren shouts louder and laughs. We get to the Saxon. The rear doors still open.

Dave climbs in first as I help Sarah up.

Dave goes straight to the GPMG to try and get it working again. The lads and men start piling in as Darren stands away from us all.

'COME ON, THEN. COME AND FIGHT ME,' Darren goads them and holds his rifle above his head.

'Smithy, get back here, now,' I shout out, but he's too far gone.

'FUCKING COME ON, THEN. COME AND TAKE ME, YOU CUNTS,' Darren screams and drops the rifle, and charges into them.

'SMITHY, STOP,' McKinney shouts and runs after him.

'NO, STOP,' I shout, but Darren runs and starts attacking them, taking swipes with his bayonet and thrusting forward to stab them.

McKinney catches up with him and tries to pull him back. McKinney tries harder, and Darren swings out hard, knocking McKinney to the ground.

'DARREN, STOP,' I shout and start forward as the horde approach and start grouping round Darren.

'YOU FUCKERS,' I shout and charge forward.

The infected drop down onto McKinney, who is trying to crab away. Within seconds, he is swamped with them biting into his legs and stomach. I reach them and swing the axe out to cut them away. McKinney screams from the pain of the bites. I kill those on him, and they draw back again. I drop down to McKinney's side and watch as the blood pours from his mouth. I look down at his savaged body and see his innards spilling out of the ragged wound to his stomach.

'Mr Howie. I'm sorry, Mr Howie...' McKinney whispers as more blood cascades out of his mouth.

'It's okay, mate, I'm sorry. You've fought so bravely. You are so very brave.' I feel tears spilling down my face as I cradle his head in my hands.

'Please... Don't let me become one of them,' he whispers.

'You'll be okay. We can get you help,' I weep as I speak, trying to offer him some comfort.

'Don't let them take me,' he says again, imploring me as Dave lowers at my side with his knife in his hand.

'Don't you fucking touch him,' I snarl at Dave. 'Don't you lay a hand on his fucking head,' I scream out as strong hands grip me from behind and pull me away.

'DON'T FUCKING TOUCH HIM,' I scream at Dave, who stares back at me. I see a tear spilling down from his eye, but I keep yelling.

'Take it easy,' Clarence's deep voice fills my ear as he pulls me back.

'DAVE, DON'T FUCKING DO IT. DON'T YOU FUCKING DARE,' I scream, and I see more tears fall down Dave's eyes.

He drops his head and cradles McKinney in his arms. He holds him close as I scream and fight to break free.

Dave gently sweeps his blade across McKinney's throat, and I see the red blood pouring out from the open artery.

'DAVE, NO,' I scream, and my legs go out from under me.

Clarence grips me hard and pulls me back, and I hear Sarah's voice but can't make out any words. Dave gently places his hands on McKinney's face, and I watch as he closes McKinney's eyes; then, he slowly stands and looks at me. His cheeks wet from the falling tears. Seeing McKinney die and then Dave crying breaks my heart, and I feel myself being pulled into the back of the Saxon. Dave climbs in beside me.

'Where's Darren?' Tucker asks in a quiet voice.

'They took him,' Clarence says. I hear sobs breaking out around me, and I watch as Dave's face remains expressionless, but he is still crying.

'I'm sorry, Mr Howie,' Dave says quietly, staring down at the floor. I see the hardest man I have ever met crumbling in front of me from that simple act to fulfil a dying man's wish, and I fight my emotions back under control.

'No, Dave.' He looks at me, with fear in his eyes. *'I'm* sorry,' I say gently, and I hear more sobbing break out around me. The rear doors are pulled closed, and the engine starts.

The road must be clear because we pull away, and I feel the motion of the vehicle. Sarah drops down at my side, and she holds me as I fight to keep the tears from coursing down my face.

Dave and I stare at each other as we drive away.

※ ※

DARREN IS PULLED *into the horde and fights with fury, still thinking he can take them all on, but as Howie weeps over McKinney, so the infection breaks cover within Darren's body and surges to take control, making Darren gasp with the first wave of agony in his guts.*

He staggers to the side. Overwhelmed by the pain. Gasping for air. Looking for help but seeing only infected on all sides. He tries to scream, but his voice doesn't come. Only a soundless gasp as the infected move in. He clamps his eyes shut. Expecting to be torn apart and feels the hands on his body.

Holding him gently. Lowering him down until he's blinking up into a sea of faces and red, bloodshot eyes. Confusion in his mind. In his eyes. His heart slows and he dies right there. On that street while engulfed by infected.

His life now over.

A second in time and they open again and Darren Smith, now feeling no pain at all, stares out through his own red, bloodshot eyes. His heart beating once again but now in the true state of being.

He slowly gets to his feet with thousands of infected, gazing at him with devotion and love.

He feels different. He feels very different. Strong. Confident. Fearless.

Something else too.

An urge inside. A pulsing urge to find Howie and kill him.

DAY SEVEN

CHAPTER SEVENTY

Day Seven
Thursday

High above the surface of the earth, water vapour forms in the troposphere. White clouds expand and cast shadows over the already darkening land. Those clouds form and move with the wind and soon cover the once vibrant city of London.

The already grim-looking streets and buildings appear more despondent as long shadows form over the bloodstains and the rotting corpses that litter the ground. The abnormally high temperatures of the last week have scorched this normally wet land. Swarms of flies and insects drift around the streets, moving from corpse to corpse, laying eggs. Those eggs soon hatch in the perfect breeding ground, and the corpses look alive as thousands of fat, white maggots writhe and burrow their way through the skin. The first drops of rainfall drop through the warm air to land on the windscreen of the Saxon armoured personnel carrier driving through those grim city streets back to Tower Bridge.

By the time the Saxon reaches the bridge, sheets of rain are covering the surface with spray. Visibility is instantly reduced, and the Saxon slows to a stop. One by one, the men climb out from the vehicle and stand under the purifying downpour, letting the water cleanse them from the dirt of battle. Crimson pools form at their feet as the blood is sluiced from their skin and clothes. They hold their heads back, open-mouthed, and drink the cascading, cool water. They wipe their hands, pull fingers through their hair, and then wring their clothes out to rid themselves of the filth and gore. The three losses they suffered are heavy on their minds and hearts, and their tears blend with the rain as they cry silently. Now they can grieve and mourn those losses. They know more hardship awaits them, and later, there will be no time for mourning.

Sarah stands close to the doors of the Saxon, sensing the bond between these men and realising this experience is not hers to share. She watches Howie closely and can already see the change in her brother. The goofy, playful, sweet-natured man is now more like a hardened soldier. She doesn't know how he came to be here or what happened along the way, or why the men follow him, but she saw the reaction Howie had to the dying lad and felt the emotion in all of them as they watched him die.

Sarah held Howie as he wept in the back of the vehicle, and she looked around to see them all with tear-filled eyes, and that small man called Dave – he stayed by her side throughout the battle back to the Saxon. The way he moved was extraordinary. It's clear to Sarah that there's a deep connection between her brother and Dave.

Now, standing at the back of the vehicle, arms crossed, and sheltering from the rain, she watches them as they stand in silence, letting the rain pour down on them.

                                                 ❧ ❧

'WHAT THE FUCK HAPPENED, DAVE?' Howie asks.

'I don't know, Mr Howie.'

'I thought we'd all be slaughtered. Why did they suddenly stop? And what happened to Darren? He just charged them on his own, and I told McKinney to keep an eye on him and stay close, and now he's dead,' Howie says, holding his hands to his forehead. 'It was like

Smithy was possessed or something. Did you see how he was fighting?' he asks Dave.

'McKinney?'

'No. Darren. Did you see him?'

'Yes, Mr Howie.'

'And?'

'And what?'

'Fuck me, Dave. Darren! Did you see how Darren was fighting? He seemed different.'

'He was overextending himself and lunging too far forward.'

'Yeah. Sorry, yes. He was doing that,' Howie says. 'And he said he felt sick. But like. I mean. Did it look like they were holding back on him? The infected I mean. On Darren. They stopped and moved back, didn't they? I thought. I don't know. It felt like they weren't holding back on me or you or anyone else. They took McKinney down in seconds. So why not Darren?'

Howie looks down to the water, thinking back to just a short time ago. Darren had become very strange, screaming abuse at the infected and goading them to fight him.

Howie also remembers seeing McKinney on the ground, with infected biting into him, and then Howie was there with his axe, knocking them back.

'I didn't *see* Darren being attacked, but that doesn't mean he wasn't,' Howie says.

'Is this a private conversation?' Big Chris asks as he walks up to them.

'Chris, did you see what happened to Darren?' Howie enquires.

'The infected got him,' Chris answers, confused at the question.

'But what did you see?' Howie asks, staring hard at the big man as Malcolm and Clarence walk over to them. 'Lads, come over here,' Howie calls out to the rest all moving in closer. Sarah with them. Staring intently at her brother.

'Listen, I'm sorry for what happened back there. Both of our groups lost people, and watching McKinney die like that was truly awful.' Howie watches as the recruits' eyes drop down.

'I know it's painful, but did anyone see what happened to Smithy?' Howie asks.

'He went fucking nuts and got McKinney killed,' Cookey says, and Howie watches a few of them nod in agreement.

'We need to think about this clearly. He was sick, right?' Howie asks. 'Then he felt better, and then he was laughing and shouting as we fought. I haven't seen him do that before, but you know him better.'

'No, he never did anything like that before,' Blowers says.

'And then right at the end, when he charged them on his own, what did you see?' Howie asks, sweeping his eyes over them all.

'Sir, he ran forward, screaming, then he started attacking them,' Jamie says. 'They didn't react, though. They just stood there and took it; then, McKinney tried to pull him back, and he got pushed off; then, he tried again, and Darren knocked him down. Then they went for McKinney, and Darren got pulled in.'

The rest of the group all stare at Jamie, as the lad blushes from the sudden attention.

'Jamie, you saw all of this?' Howie asks.

'Yes, Mr Howie. They didn't bite him or anything. They just grabbed him, and he was gone.'

'Did anyone *see* Darren getting bitten?' Howie asks the group.

'What's this about, Howie?' Chris asks, with a serious expression.

'You think he's one of them?' Malcolm finally voices the unspoken thoughts.

'I don't know, but he was sick; then, he went nuts, and they didn't go for him,' Howie shrugs.

'Fuck me...' Blowers says, reeling from the idea.

'No way,' Tucker adds as though it can't be true.

'He stopped firing on that fucking GPMG at the hospital too,' Blowers adds.

'He did what?' Chris asks, turning to Blowers.

'While you lot were inside, we had a contact at the front. Darren was on the gimpy and just froze up. I had to drag him down to take over.'

'But anyone infected drops to the ground in agony. I've seen it too many times,' Clarence says. 'Are you? Are we? Okay. Be clear. What are you saying here?'

'I'm just saying we have to consider all possibilities,' Howie says as even Chris, a veteran soldier, blinks at the ability of Howie to absorb and process and understand the things that are happening.

'So worst case scenario. I'll just say it. He's one of them?' Chris asks.

'If he *is* one of them, does that mean anything to us?' Cookey asks.

'Ye,' Chris replies with a blast of air as he shares looks with the other soldiers. Blowers grasps it too. What it means and the risk they are now under. 'He knows our numbers, strengths, where we're heading, the route we took, the access and egress points.' Chris explains

'So why aren't they attacking?' Blowers asks.

'I don't know. They just stopped attacking us and let us go,' Howie says. 'Hang on. Let me think this through. So, they knew where we were going. They massed in the exact place we were heading for, and if Darren *was* one of them, that explains how they knew where we were going. Which is very fucking scary cos it suggests a form of intelligence.'

'Expanding on that,' Chris says. 'That theory might suggest they pulled back as a tactic because they gained what they wanted.'

'Er. Bit lost. What was that then?' Cookey asks.

'Darren,' a few of them say at once.

'What for? Why would they want Darren?' Tucker asks.

'If he was the only one infected, then it would have to be him,' Howie says.

'I don't buy it,' Nick says. 'They're mindless fuckers. They were walking off that fucking bridge, for god's sake.'

'No. Actually. It makes sense,' Sarah cuts in as they all turn to stare at her. 'Those things were outside before you came, but nowhere near the numbers they are now. They must have known where you were going and flooded the area, ready for you, and if they knew that Darren lad was infected, then why *not* take him – he's one of theirs.'

'They came for us at the service station,' Howie says. 'They sent loads after us, and those people said they had gone unnoticed before we arrived, and we already said it was like we were being targeted.'

'Then they know about *our* place,' Chris adds.

'Your place?' Sarah asks.

'They've rigged up a sort of commune a few miles out. There's about two thousand survivors there,' Howie says.

'So if this Darren knows about the commune, are they safe?' Sarah asks.

'We've left them alone though. We thought maybe that's why they weren't going for us,' Chris says.

Howie nods while thinking. 'I think we need to accept they're changing, or evolving. We've seen them change at night and now during the day too. They can get faster when it suits them.'

'Howie,' Sarah says urgently, cutting into the chat with a tone that makes them all turn fast, following her gaze to where the bridge meets the road now blocked with infected standing silently.'

'Fuck me, they did that quietly,' Chris says as the tension ramps instantly. All of them startled at seeing thousands of infected staring at them having moved on mass in perfect silence. No howls either. No snarls. No anything. All of them like sentinels with their heads up and fixed and staring directly to Howie and his small group.

'This isn't spooky at all,' Cookey says with his voice falling to silence as they watch the front lines of the infected part to allow someone to slip through who walks slowly and steadily, crossing the line from the road onto the bridge and coming to a stop. His head up. His arms at his side. His red eyes staring at Howie.

'That's Darren,' Blowers says quietly. The others can see him too. Darren Smith. Right there. Staring back at them.

'Look at the way they're formed up, ,' Malcolm says, stepping forward to peer through the rain at the perfect spacing between each infected.

'What's he want?' Tucker asks. 'Maybe he's hungry or something.'

'What the fuck?' Blowers says, giving Tucker a look.

'Fuck it. I'll go and ask him,' Howie says, walking off as the rest of the group follow in his wake. 'Wait there. I'll go on my own,' Howie calls back as Dave joins him at his side.

'Okay, Mr Howie,' Dave says, ignoring him.

They walk across the bridge, through the rain, coming to a stop a few steps away from Darren with Howie staring at the lad's red, blood-shot eyes.

'Mr Howie...' Darren says with a sneer, drawing the sound out.

'What the fuck happened?' Howie asks.

'Happened?' Darren asks with a casual mocking air. 'Nothing has happened, Mr Howie. Why?'

'Are you a fucking zombie?' Howie asks, blinking at the lad. 'Cos. You know. The red eyes and the massive zombie army literally right behind you,' he adds, leaning out to look at them then back to Darren. 'Which isn't spooky at all.'

'That's what I said,' Cookey calls from a little way back. 'Alright, Smithy? Why are your eyes red?'

'Why do you think, bellends?' Darren asks, holding his hands out.

'So?' Howie asks slowly. 'Are you saying you are a zombie then?'

'Clearly.'

'Hmmm. But so. You're still talking?' Howie says. 'Mate. Okay, listen. Jump back in with us and we'll get you back to that doctor in Chris's commune. Maybe he can help or, I don't know.'

'Make me into a test subject? Strap me to a chair? Poke things in me.'

'You might like that!' Cookey calls.

'Not now, Cookey!' Howie says, turning to give him a look then glancing back to see Darren's features growing dark and hard. 'Whoa. Take it easy, Darren. We can fix this.'

'Fix what?'

'This!'

'This what?'

'Your red eyes, mate! And being a zombie.'

'Why?'

'Fuck me. I'm so confused,' Howie says. 'I'm offering to help you.'

'I feel great,' Darren says with an instant casual switch. 'I feel fucking wonderful. WONDERFUL!' he shouts then grins widely. 'So yeah, I don't need help.'

'Okay. Er, then what do you want?' Howie asks.

'You,' Darren says simply, quietly, staring at Howie unblinking in the rain.

'What for?' Howie replies.

'All of you. I want all of you. But especially you, *Howie*.'

'What for, Darren?' Howie asks.

'To peel your fucking skin off.'

'Fuck me. That got dark,' Howie says.

'You've killed too many of my kind,' Darren says.

'Your kind?'

'MY KIND! MY KIND!' Darren screams with the veins pushing through his neck and forehead.

'Your kind? You killed them too. Mate, what is this?'

'I didn't kill my kind,' Darren cuts in.

'You fucking did!'

'That was before!'

'Before what?'

'BEFORE! Before I was perfect. Now I am perfect. I am. I AM! I AM ALIVE!'

'Oh fuck, fuck, fuck,' Howie mouths, seeing the change in the lad.

'But you. You,' Darren says, lowering his voice as he stares with palpable hatred at Howie. 'You made me kill them. And your *fucking cunts* only kill them because of you.'

'Darren, mate.'

'Just because they killed your parents. Oh poor Howie lost his mommy and daddy. Poor Howie is all alone, so he decides to kill every living thing to try and rescue his whore sister.

His fucking whore sister, dirty cunting WHORE SISTER. He killed everything and risked the lives of everyone to rescue his dirty, fucking cunt of a sister just because his parents died.'

Howie stares in horror, watching Darren shout and laugh as he paces between Howie and the massed mob behind him.

'Oh, look, here come Howie's heroes, a shambling fucking mess. Look at them,' Darren laughs. 'Oh, no, Howie's heroes have come to get me. Oh, no, someone save me. Maybe your dirty, cunt, whore, slut sister will come and rescue you, Howie,' Darren screams with every ounce of effort he can muster. His face flushes red. Spittle flying from his lips as the rain lashes down.

'Oh, hi, Jamie,' Darren waves with vicious cheer to the others standing a few metres back. 'Have you fucked Dave up the arse yet? You know you want to. Oh, and there's Tucker, the fat fucker. Hey, Tucker, how many pies have you eaten yet, you fat roly-poly cunt? Ha! That's fucking funny – Tucker, the fat fucker,' Darren throws his head back and laughs then twists to glare at the infected behind him. 'That was funny. Laugh then!'

They laugh as one. Thousands of them erupting into instant forced, fake laughter and giving voice in a way that sends chills down spines.

Darren slowly looks back at Howie with a gleam of spite and clicks his finger. Instantly ending the laughter. Plunging them back into a hard and heavy silence. All of them seeing a thing happening first hand. A swift and awful evolution of the infection.

'Oh, and there's Nick, thick cunt, who can't read or write. Can you, Nick? You never got past Spot Goes To The Beach, did you, mate?'

'Yes, Darren,' Nick replies quietly.

'Yes, Darren,' Darren mimics Nick in a high-pitched voice. 'And then there's Blowers and Cookey. What a pair of utter cunts, fucking playing at soldiers. *Yes, Mr Howie, and no, Mr Howie, and can I suck your cock, Mr Howie?*' Darren shouts as he walks back and forth, spittle flying from his mouth. Then he stops and stares directly at Dave.

'Hello, Dave,' Darren says with a mock friendly tone. 'How are you, Dave?' Dave remains void of expression. His cold, hard eyes staring directly at Darren. 'Oh, are we playing the staring game, Dave? Okay, mate, let's do that.' Darren takes a step forward and stares hard into Dave's eyes. Dave doesn't flinch. He doesn't move a muscle, and no hint of emotion escapes his cold eyes. 'You fucking runt,' Darren screams in fury as Dave stares back without moving. 'You just want to fuck Howie up the arse. You want to do a reach around with Howie while his dirty cunt sister licks your arse.' Darren says and starts thrusting his pelvis back and forth while stretching one arm out with a masturbation motion,

'That's fucking brilliant,' Howie says with a snort of laughter. 'What the actual fuck?'

'Don't fucking laugh at me! I've got an army!' Darren screams and clicks his fingers and the horde, as one, all take a step forward in perfect synchronicity, stamping their feet down with a solid whump of noise.

'Can you make them dance too?' Howie asks.

'I don't think you should be mocking me, Mr Howie,' Darren says through gritted teeth.

'What do you think, Dave? Should we be taking Darren seriously?' Howie asks. 'He has got such a big army behind him. Chris, did you ever see such an impressive army, mate?' Howie asks, drawing the big man into the conversation.

'They're the biggest and bestest I ever did see,' Chris replies, scathingly.

'And the uniform is the best we've seen yet,' Malcolm adds as the lads take in the torn ragtag clothes and the injuries on show.

Darren takes a sudden step forward, with his fists clenched and his horde moving in time with him as he locks eyes with Howie. 'I'm coming for you,' Darren says quietly. 'And I'll turn every person I can find along the way.'

Night hits, and as one, the infected look to the sky and howl into the air. Thousands of voices filling the night sky, sending shivers down the spines of all the men that watch them. They start to back away, but Howie stands his ground for a few more seconds, watching a slow smile form across Darren's face. Then Howie leans forward and stares hard at his former friend.

'Roar,' Howie says simply and walks away, showing his back to the horde and praying they don't cut him down.

'Am I the only one that wants to fucking leg it?' Cookey says as they all walk steadily back to the Saxon.

'No, I certainly do,' Big Chris adds.

'So why are we walking, then?' Tucker asks.

'Don't give them the satisfaction,' Clarence rumbles.

'FUCKING RUN!' Howie shouts as he sprints past them, causing them all to break out and start running. Howie dives into the back of the Saxon and clambers through to the driver's seat as the rest climb into the rear.

'They're fucking running at us,' Blowers shouts as he pulls the rear doors closed with a slam.

Howie starts the engine and pulls away with a jerk, sending them all lurching backwards, and Sarah falls into the laps of the men. Soon, she gets her balance and stands back up, suddenly becoming aware of the big men in the confined space and the very wet t-shirt that she is wearing.

'Err, does anyone have a spare top?' Sarah asks sweetly. A dozen tough men start scrabbling about in the tight confines.

'Here you go, Miss,' Clarence speaks first, holding out a dry top to Sarah as the others all stare daggers at him.

'Is that my top?' Nick asks, recognising the clothing.

'I don't know, is it?' the massive man stares innocently back at Nick.

'Maybe not,' Nick adds, looking up at Clarence.

'Chris, does that truck driver still have one of the radios?' Howie shouts back.

'Yes, but they're only short-range things. Do you think they'll go for the commune?' Chris shouts.

'I'm sure of it. Is that GPMG working now?' Howie yells.

'I'll get on it,' Dave replies and climbs up to start working as the Saxon speeds up through the dark city streets.

No streetlights come on, none of the shops are illuminated, and there is no warm light spilling from houses or apartment blocks anymore. The rain clouds cover the night sky and cast the streets into absolute darkness.

The powerful headlights shine out like beacons in the darkness, and the infected surge towards them like moths. The solid, plated front of the Saxon hardly rocks as they plough through body after body. The infected bare their teeth as they lunge to the front of the vehicle.

'Should we be shooting them down from the back doors?' Tucker asks.

'No, we're going too fast, and it's not worth it for dropping just a few of them. We need to get back as soon as possible,' Chris says, with worry clearly in his voice.

'How secure is it, Chris? Will it withstand a mass attack?' Howie shouts back.

'No, we can hold against a few of them at a time, but we've only been going a few days. A big push would get them through easily.'

'Can we make it more secure?' Howie asks.

'If they're coming for us with large numbers, we'll have to bug out. We can't repel 'em, and we don't have time to secure it more,' Chris shouts back.

'How soon can they make ready to leave then?' Howie asks.

'It'll take hours. We don't have enough vehicles, and we've got kids and sick people too.'

'I don't think we'll have hours, Chris. They move fast at night, and *he* knows where it is now. He can send them in to attack it.'

Chris looks to Malcolm and his men. They have families and friends at the commune. Fighting huge hordes of the infected in hand-to-hand combat is one thing, but now there is a direct threat against the people he offered safety and security to.

'Are those forts big enough for all of us?' Malcolm calls out.

'I don't know. It depends how many have already gone there and how full they are. They are big, though. Especially the main one,' Howie replies.

'Is there anywhere else we can go, easy to defend and hold many people?' Clarence asks.

'Probably loads of places, but I don't know of them,' Howie shouts back.

'We need to make a decision, Chris. We'll have to move out as soon as we get back,' Malcolm says.

'Okay, we'll go for the forts. Women and children into whatever vehicles we can find. There's still space in the truck we can use,' Chris says.

'They've probably started to unload it already,' Clarence joins in.

'We'll have to take essential equipment only and use the rest of the space for people. We've also got the trucks that we used as barriers across the access roads,' Chris says, thinking as he goes along. 'Right, Malcolm, I want you to arrange the vehicles, get those trucks ready and lined up on the exit road. Clarence, I want you to sort the hospital out. Don't take any shit from Doc Roberts and make sure he only takes essential items,' Chris barks out.

'Got it,' Clarence nods.

'Howie, can we use the Saxon at the rear access road to cover if we get the GPMG working again,' Chris asks.

'I'll get it working,' Dave calls down.

'Okay, Saxon at the rear, with Nick on the GPMG. Jamie as sniper. Blowers, Cookey, and Sarah, I want you with the vehicles to help load the people up. They will be scared and confused, so be nice but get them moving,' Howie calls out to nods and yells of affirmation. 'Chris, do you have a stores area?' Howie asks.

'Yes,' he replies.

'One of our blokes excels in that area. Can you make use of him to help organise?'

'Yes, definitely,' Chris shouts back.

'Tucker, that's you.'

'On it,' Tucker shouts back.

'Dave, me and you will stick with Chris to work from a central point. We stay put so everyone knows where we are so they can come to us. That okay with everyone?'

Sarah watches as the men and lads all shout out in acknowledgment, then she looks at Chris, a naturally big man, with a dark beard and very white teeth – he has an air of natural leadership about him. He and the older men are clearly ex-soldiers. When they took their tops off in the rain, she saw the scars on their bodies – bullet holes and knife slashes, long healed but still very visible. Clarence is a huge manmountain, with muscles on top of muscles, but with a kind face. Then she looks to her brother. Less than a week ago, he was working nights in a supermarket. Always a kind man, fun loving and very caring, but now there is a hardness to him, and these men respond to him and listen to what he's saying. Her brother is giving orders in a manner that just makes them want to follow him.

She had watched as he stayed at the front, fighting towards her, and then went back again, swinging that axe with a look of pure fury and hatred on his face, and these battle-hardened men and young lads are following him.

She can see the difference in him, the way he uses humour and kind words, but then gives an order that leaves no doubt it will be followed, and the thing is, it all makes sense. He shows respect to Big Chris, knowing that the big man is the leader of his group, but Sarah suspects that even if he hadn't shown that respect, they would have still accepted what he said. Life has changed, the whole world has changed, and her brother has changed the most.

He walked alone towards a huge horde of infected back on the bridge. Maybe he did feel fear, but he faced it and walked towards it. She knows he came for her, and now that he has saved her, he could turn tail and run far away, but even now, he's accepted the responsibility of trying to save those other people. They are nothing to him, and these young lads don't hold any loyalty to them or Howie. But they accept what he says without question.

She feels an immense sense of pride in her brother. She felt pride in him before, just for being a good person. But now... Now he shines with a glowing light. He is amazing.

'He's a good man,' a rich voice intones, and she snaps out of her reverie to see Clarence smiling at her.

'What?'

'Your brother, he's a good man, a natural leader,' he repeats.

'Yeah, I guess he is,' she smiles back at him.

'HOLD ON TIGHT,' Howie yells as the Saxon slams into a horde gathered in the road. The impact at such high speed sends the Saxon rocking on its suspension, causing them all to slide and fall in the back.

A huge hand shoots out and grabs Sarah round the waist to prevent her falling back.

'Thanks...again,' Sarah says to Clarence.

'THERE'S MORE,' Howie bellows, and the Saxon rocks and jolts as it slams into body after body, pulverising them instantly from the raw power of the impact. The Saxon careers through the streets as Howie negotiates the bends and turns. Infected launch themselves into the oncoming vehicle, screaming as they run and lunge forward, only to be splatted against the front like flies. 'BIG GROUP,' Howie yells as the lights pick up an oncoming horde running full tilt at the Saxon. Howie pushes his foot down hard, and the big engines roar out into the night as the vehicle surges forward. Howie grips the wheel and growls deep in his throat.

'BRACE!' he screams as they impact. A horde of infected play chicken with an armour-plated military vehicle. The result is devastation, with bodies exploding as they strike the corners, and skulls imploding on the solid metal being driven into them at speed.

'They really don't like us anymore,' Howie shouts back as they continually slam into the living corpses.

'Have we done something to upset them?' Cookey asks.

'They got fed up with you touching them,' Blowers says to loud groans from everyone else. He smiles around at them. 'What?'

'Please don't start that again,' Tucker whines.

'Hey, don't tell me, tell Cookey. I'm only saying what I see,' Blowers replies.

'Blowers, you are homophobic, and I find it offensive,' Cookey says in a serious tone, causing a few of the others to burst out laughing.

'Homophobic! Me?' Blowers says back at him.

'You are homophobic, and you offend me, and you could offend some of these new people with those nasty comments,' Cookey says, retaining his serious tone, to more laughs.

'Who am I going to offend?' Blowers laughs back at him.

'Me,' a rich, deep voice says from behind him.

Blowers turns to stare up at Clarence, who, in turn, stares back down with a very serious expression.

'You?' Blowers asks. 'You're not gay,' he adds.

'Aren't I?'

'Err, are you?' Blowers asks, looking up at the huge man. Clarence stares back in silence, a silence that is only broken by the thumps and bangs as the Saxon hits more infected. 'Err. I'm really sorry. I didn't mean anything. I...was just, um...' Blowers stammers, unaware of Big Chris, Malcolm, and the other men all smiling behind him.

Blowers keeps going for several seconds, stuttering and stammering his words while staring up at the imposing face of Clarence.

Clarence bursts out laughing, like a braying donkey, with his deep voice, and they all erupt as Blowers glares around at them.

'Piss off, I knew he wasn't gay,' Blowers shouts out.

'You shit yourself, mate,' Cookey says, wiping tears from his eyes. Even Sarah laughs at Clarence's deep braying.

'Never seen you nervous before, Blowers,' Nick laughs at him.

'Yeah, very funny, very funny,' Blowers mutters and starts laughing himself.

CHAPTER SEVENTY-ONE

The Saxon drives through the night until it reaches the road leading to the rear of the commune. Within seconds of arriving in the area, the infected suddenly stop attacking them, standing still, but leaning forward to scream and bare their teeth as the vehicle roars past them.

'Why are they holding back?' Sarah asks, leaning forward to look through the windscreen.

'We're right near the commune. They must be waiting to gather more numbers before attacking,' Howie shouts back. 'There's no other reason I can think off.'

'The entrance is in sight. Chris, are we safe to go straight in?' Howie yells.

'Yes, they'll recognise the vehicle,' he shouts back.

'GPMG is sorted,' Dave says as he drops back down. 'I've cleaned it the best I can, too.'

'Right, if they're starting to mass, we need to move very quickly. Nick, get on that GPMG – you're with Jamie here. The rest need to get moving,' Howie shouts as the vehicle pulls up in front of the truck parked across the road.

Big Chris jumps out of the back and shouts for the truck to be moved as he strides forward. Within seconds, the gap opens, and the Saxon pulls through.

'We'll leave it here, Curtis. You stay with them, mate. They might need a driver for it,' Howie says as they all get out and start moving off to their allocated positions. Chris is surrounded by people coming to greet them. He silences them all by holding his hands up in the air.

'We will be attacked very soon,' he says loudly and simply. 'We have to get everyone out, and we need to do it now. Get those trucks turned around and every vehicle we have down to the front.' Chris turns to a few of his men. 'I want you to start sweeping down. Do it quickly but thoroughly. Get everyone you can find to help you, get them all to the front ready to get on the vehicles. Women and children first. No stopping to get toys or clothes. We will be overrun very soon, and we must move quickly. Do it now,' Chris urges as they start sprinting away. He turns back to the guards still standing by the access point, 'You lads, you heard what I said. We've got the Saxon here and a couple of lads with it, but I need you to stay and hold this area. Take this radio and keep me updated if you get contact, got it?'

They nod back and turn to stare out. Nick climbs up through the look-out position and turns the machine gun around to face back down the road. Jamie and Curtis sit inside the back of the vehicle, facing down the road, with their rifles aimed and ready. Howie, Dave, and Big Chris start striding down the main road as his men move quickly ahead of him, darting in and out of the buildings. All down the wide main street, people start running about with panicked looks, grabbing at children and pulling them along. As soon as Chris comes into view, they aim straight for him.

'I'm sorry. I don't have time for this. Get ready and get down to the front,' Chris repeats over and again; his voice staying calm. The truck they used to transport equipment from the hospital in Canary Wharf back to the commune is resting on the main road. The rear doors are open wide, and half the equipment has already been carried into the makeshift hospital. Howie looks over at the building as they pass and sees Doctor Roberts with his shaggy eyebrows peering out at them.

'Chris, what's going on?' Doc Roberts walks swiftly towards them; his long, white coat flapping out behind him.

'Doc, we're going to be overrun very soon. Get loaded with whatever you can grab and get down the front,' Chris calls back.

'Right,' the doctor calls out without breaking stride – a man used to processing information very quickly and reacting without panic. He turns to stride back inside the hospital, barking orders to people as he goes.

They reach the pub on the corner amidst scenes of bedlam – people shouting and torches flashing as men run back and forth. The refugees scurry towards the assembly point, all of them clearly terrified. Children scream and cry as desperate parents cajole and snap at them to move faster and keep up. Armed men and women run through the masses towards Chris, taking instructions, and are told where to position themselves. Howie assists where he can, diverting questions from terrified residents and urging them to move quickly. The truck from the rear entrance point drives slowly past them, followed by more vehicles taken hastily from the commune's gathered collection.

'I think you'll be needing these.' A woman appears next to them, carrying a tray with three steaming mugs of coffee and a small pot of sugar . She puts the tray down on one of the wooden bench seats outside the pub, and Howie sees Chris smile for the first time since they got back.

'Thanks, love, are you ready to go?' Chris asks gently, drawing the woman into his arms.

'I'll be ready when you are,' she replies, smiling up at him.

'I suppose there's no point in asking you to get down the front, is there?'

'I suppose you know the answer to that,' she replies quickly, but still with the smile. 'How was it out there?' she adds.

'Bloody awful,' he replies.

A man marches towards Chris. Howie steps out to intercept him, trying to give the big man a moment of privacy.

'Hi, can I help you?' Howie asks in his best supermarket manager's voice.

'I want to know what's going on. We were told we were safe here...'

'*CONTACT AT REAR ENTRANCE,*' Dave's and Chris's radios boom out.

'Chris to rear entrance. What have you got there?'

'Lots of zombies. They are staring at us from the end of the road. Looks like they are getting ready. Permission to engage.'

CHAPTER SEVENTY-TWO

In London, Darren walks with a fast pace through the streets, towards the commune, at the head of a huge army all walking with purpose. The infection floods them with chemicals that make them aggressive and angry, making them growl as they stalk through the streets, feeling the ever-present urge to break free and race forward to take the resistors down. The hosts ahead of them hold and wait for the head of the army to pass, staring at Darren as he goes by.

Darren doesn't look at them but stares ahead, with a determined glare on his face, fixed on images of Howie dying painfully and that whore sister of his being ripped apart, and Dave being slowly tortured and begging for his life with his dying breath.

Darren also conjures up images of Blowers and Cookey being made to humiliate and degrade themselves with disgusting sex acts before being turned into hosts. Jamie Reese having his eyes gouged out. Tucker being force-fed human flesh. One by one, he thinks through his former comrades and dreams of ways of torturing and killing them slowly.

The infection inside him revels in the power and the sudden organisation using this host has brought.

Darren learnt skills of survival, strategy, and tactics from Dave and holds his army in the shadows while figuring a coordinated and focussed attack on many points that will be far harder to repel.

Darren also knows that the increasing numbers standing just close enough to be seen will send fear and dread through the people in the commune. They will be panicked and make mistakes, and be far harder to control.

Not like his loyal subjects, who are easy to control and bend to his will. But those people, those feeble people, will panic and scream in fear, which will only make his hosts fight harder to get at them.

The infection has also learnt that the more speed he applies to the hosts, the less power and strength they have. Even at night, if the infection can hold them at a steady pace rather than an all-out, reckless charge, they will have greater energy for the killing and the taking of more hosts.

CHAPTER SEVENTY-THREE

Big Chris, Howie, and Dave stand outside the pub, receiving a constant flow of intelligence from the eyes and ears placed all around the perimeter. The infected are massing at nearly every access point, but they hold and wait. This knowledge spreads like wildfire through the area, and people start running and screaming in panic, fearing they will be attacked at any minute.

'That fucker knows what he's doing,' Howie says bitterly. 'Maybe we should open up on them, start cutting the numbers down.'

'I think we should. Better than waiting for them to go for us,' Chris says.

'No, we'll keep loading the people up. If they attack now and break through, we'll get overrun. Every minute they hold off buys us time,' Dave says firmly.

'Chris to all units and access points. Do not engage until they attack, do not prompt them to attack, hold positions, and wait.'

'I'm going down the front to see how they're getting on,' Howie says, feeling frustrated. He walks off, with Dave stepping beside him. 'Mate, this is nuts,' Howie says, shaking his head. 'Fucking Darren. Did you see him back there? He was fucking demented and twisted up, poor lad. Don't get me wrong, though. I'll fucking kill him the first chance I'll get, but still...'

'Still what?'

'You know, we knew him. He was one of us, and that doesn't just go away. Have you ever had anything like this happen before? I mean, have you ever had one of your own side turn against you?'

'Yes, Mr Howie.'

'What did you do?'

'I killed them,' Dave says.

'Jesus. Ask a question,' Howie says as they reach the end of the row of vehicles and sees Blowers and Cookey urging people into a line and then sending them forward to the vehicles.

'How's it going, lads?' Howie asks as he walks up.

'Bloody nightmare, boss,' Blowers says. 'Everyone's going crazy. We got them in a line here and send them forward to Sarah at the vehicles. She's helping them get loaded and shouting when the next one is ready,' Blowers replies.

'We got loads into the first truck. If we can get them down here, we'll shift them a lot quicker,' Cookey adds as he waves the approaching people into the line.

'MOVE OVER TO THE LINE, PLEASE. WE WILL GET YOU AWAY VERY SOON,' he yells out.

'*Howie to Chris. We need the trucks down front. We've got too many people here waiting for vehicles,*' Howie says into the radio.

'*Chris to any units listening. Get those trucks down to the front as a priority,*' his voice returns on the radio.

'*Clarence to Chris. I'm on it now. Doc Roberts has got half his truck filled. I'll get them down to you now,*' Clarence's deep voice booms out. Within minutes, the huge, bald man is walking down the road, ahead of two trucks. He steps aside and waves them towards the front of the vehicle line. Sarah steps out of the vehicles and stands in front of the first truck, waving her arms high to stop it.

'HOLD IT THERE. BLOWERS, COOKEY, GET THOSE PEOPLE INTO THE BACK OF THIS ONE FIRST,' she yells out with a calm and confident voice.

'GOT IT,' Blowers shouts back.

'Your sister takes after you then, Mr Howie,' Blowers says with a smile.

'She's bossier than me, mate. She'll be running the show within an hour,' Howie laughs back.

'OKAY, LISTEN UP, PEOPLE. WE NEED TO GET YOU INTO THE TRUCK. WOMEN AND CHILDREN FIRST. STAY CALM,' Cookey shouts out as the crowd starts surging towards the rear.

Howie walks around to see Clarence and Sarah at the back doors of the truck, helping people up. A constant surge against them as the panicked people try to clamber in.

'MOVE BACK AND WAIT,' Clarence shouts out to no effect, and Howie nods at Dave.

'YOU WILL WAIT AND MOVE CALMLY,' Dave's voice booms out into the air, silencing the entire area as everyone turns to look.

'Cheers, Dave,' Clarence rumbles with a smile as he and Sarah return to helping lift people up into the back.

Questions are thrown at them, and children scream as they are pushed up into the darkness of the back of the truck. The first vehicle gets filled, and Sarah rushes to the front to wave it on while Clarence waves the next one in.

The rear doors are already open, with Doctor Roberts standing there, still in his white lab coat.

'My staff are already in here. We'll stand across the back to protect the equipment,' Doc Roberts says, not so much a question as a statement.

'We're doing well,' Sarah calls out, 'considering how many people are here and the lack of time.'

'*Chris to all units. The access points are reporting mass numbers now. Get them people out, do it now,*' the urgency in his voice is clear. '*I'm sending more vehicles down now.*'

On cue, headlights appear down the road, and the sound of diesel engines of vans and small delivery trucks fill the air. The group waves them down and sends the people into the back of them. The waiting crowd has thinned down considerably, which makes it easier to manage the loading.

Latecomers run down to the area to join the people cramming into vehicles. A small truck then appears and pulls up next to Howie and Sarah. Tucker's face peers out from the passenger window.

'Supply vehicle, Mr Howie,' Tucker says.

'Bloody hell, mate, that was quick,' Howie answers, impressed.

'They were well organised. Well, sort of, they are now, anyway,' he laughs. 'Is it okay if I stay with this vehicle? They will need an armed escort.'

'Good idea, mate. Get in the middle somewhere. Don't be the first or last vehicle in the convoy,' Howie yells as the vehicle rolls forward. There are many vehicles stretching back into the main street, loaded with refugees. Headlights shine into the night, casting deep shadows and making the guards cover their eyes as they look up and down. Deep roars split the air from all around them – deep, and guttural, and truly terrifying.

'Here they come,' Howie calls out as the hairs on the back of his neck stand up.

The roaring ends as the sound of gunfire erupts from all the access points at the same time. Small arms automatic weapons spitting out alongside the distinctive sound of the GPMG at the far end.

'FORM A LINE ACROSS HERE,' Howie bellows out, pointing at armed men and indicating a section of road back from the refugees, who are still waiting to get loaded.

Men and women run into position and stand across the road, facing out with grim faces and shaky hands.

Cookey and Blowers run in the middle. Now experienced and hardened from the battles they have faced, they stand still, calmly. Both of them feel the exhilaration and excitement that comes the minutes before the fighting starts. Without speaking, they take magazines from their bags and lay them down face up on the road in front of them, checking their rifles and assuming a kneeling position.

The experienced ex-soldiers and police officers look down to see their actions and copy them.

Within minutes, there is a line of armed men and women stretched out, kneeling in front of spare magazines, weapons ready.

'Cookey,' Blowers says.

'Yes, mate,' he answers.

'Don't try and bum them this time.'

'Ah, that's not fair,' Cookey says.

'Well, maybe just one, then.'

'Okay, mate, just one, I promise.'

'Thanks, mate,' Blowers replies as the rest of the men and women look at them, seeing them joking with easy banter, knowing what they are about to face.

Howie looks at them with an immense sense of pride.

'Clarence, you and Sarah keep loading those vehicles. We've got seconds now,' Howie shouts back at them from position behind the line. Dave standing at his side.

'*Rear access point to all units. We are getting overrun. We are pulling back. We will move slowly down the main road. There are fucking thousands of them.*'

'*Chris to all units. Start pulling back towards the vehicle form-up point, staggered fall back, keep them suppressed.*'

'*Malcolm to Chris. We are running out of room in the vehicle form-up point. We need to start pulling out, but once we start, we are not stopping.*'

'*Chris to Malcolm. Roger that. Chris to Clarence. Are we loaded and ready?*'

'*Clarence to Chris. We are not loaded, but we are almost there. Clarence to Malcolm. Start rolling out slowly, keep it slow. We'll throw them in as you move past.*'

'*Malcolm to Clarence. Roger that. We are starting to roll out now. I need guards to the front.*'

'*Chris to all units. Get guards to the front in support of Malcolm on point position.*'

'*Clarence to Chris. I cannot spare any guards from my position. Can you take them from the access points?*'

'*Chris to Clarence. That's a negative. They are doing a fighting withdrawal. They are swamped.*'

'*Howie to Chris. We can send every third person from our line and move them to the front. That gives you about four guards. Is that enough?*'

'*Malcolm to Howie. Roger that. Just send two. We will work on speed and momentum. Get that Saxon to the front when you can.*'

'*Howie to Malcolm. Roger that. Two guards on way to you now.*'

'Chris to rear access point Saxon. Did you copy the last from Malcolm?'

'Rear access Saxon to Chris. Roger that. Fighting retreat down the road, and then we move to point position.'

'Blowers, get two from the line and send them to the front, in support of Malcolm until the Saxon can take point,' Howie shouts out as Blowers jumps up and motions to two people within the line.

They are both much older than the nineteen-year-old Territorial Army recruit, but they accept his orders without question and sprint down towards the front of the vehicles. Howie stands, watching back down the road, then turns to see Clarence and Sarah pushing people into the backs of vans and small trucks and shouting at the drivers to move on. The fleet starts to move slowly, being held by Malcolm at the front.

'MOVE,' Clarence's voice booms out as he starts picking people up to push them into vehicles. Sarah lacks the physical strength, but her strong character and force of personality achieves the same aim, and she shouts, bellows, and urges them into the vehicles.

'HERE THEY COME,' Blowers shouts from the line.

Howie spins around to see the Saxon slowly rolling towards them, the GPMG firing constantly from the top.

'WE HOLD THIS LINE!' Howie shouts out.

'LET THE SAXON THROUGH, AND WE HOLD THIS LINE UNTIL THOSE PEOPLE ARE LOADED. WE WILL NOT FAIL. WE WILL HOLD.'

'YES, SIR,' Blowers and Cookey chorus back.

'DO YOU HEAR ME? WE HOLD THIS LINE.'

'YES, SIR,' voices from the line shout back at him as Howie feels the adrenalin start to surge through his system.

He spins back to look at Clarence. They make eye contact, and Howie raises two fingers to his own eyes and then points at Sarah. *You watch her for me.* Clarence nods once and goes back to pushing people into the vehicles.

'WE ARE NOT SCARED. WE DO NOT FEEL FEAR. WE ARE GOOD, AND THEY ARE EVIL, AND WE WILL NOT FAIL. WE WILL HOLD THIS LINE!' Howie roars out. The Saxon draws close and flashes the headlights. Cookey and Blowers move to the side and create a gap for the Saxon to pull through.

Once the back of the vehicle passes the line, they close up and return to a kneeling position. Howie and Dave run to the line and take up positions between Blowers and Cookey, kneeling down and looking up to the solid wall of infected marching towards them.

'FUCKING HAVE IT,' Howie shouts and opens up with his assault rifle.

The GPMG pauses as Nick bellows, 'MAGAZINE.'

The line opens up as every weapon starts firing. Bright muzzle flashes light up the dark sky, and the oncoming horde starts dropping. Bullets rip through the infected, tearing them apart. They drop many and keep killing as they get closer and closer.

'MAGAZINE,' Blowers shouts, and within seconds, he has expelled one and snatched one from the ground, rammed it home, slammed the bolt back, and he opens up again.

'WE ARE COMING IN,' Chris shouts down the radio as Howie sees groups of men and women running into the main road from the side junctions, firing behind them.

'CEASE FIRE,' Howie shouts. 'WE ADVANCE ON ME.' Howie pauses for a second to allow the men and women to grab the magazines in front of them.

Howie paces forward with deliberate steps, watching as the line walks with him.

The guards from the access points run down the road, with Big Chris leading them, turning to fire back as the side junctions become stacked with infected marching out to meet the main horde.

'HOLD,' Howie shouts, and they all drop down again as the access point guards stream past them.

'FIRE,' Howie shouts, and they again open up on the horde, giving the retreating access point guards a few seconds to move back to the Saxon.

'PULL BACK,' Chris shouts out, and as one, the line stands to start stepping backwards, each man and woman firing as they go.

Voices shout '*MAGAZINE*' as they eject and ram new ones home. The fire rate is devastating, and the front ranks of the zombie army are torn down under the deadly hail of bullets.

'HOLD,' Howie shouts as they reach the back of the Saxon.

'ARE YOU READY, NICK?' Howie shouts behind him.

'YES,' Nick shouts down as the GPMG opens up.

One heavy calibre machine gun and two lines of men and women firing automatic weapons slaughter the oncoming infected. They are shredded as they walk, and the massive fire rate devastates them.

'ATTACK FROM THE REAR,' Dave's voice booms out, and Howie spins to see infected surging into the vehicle area.

'CHRIS, GET THOSE VEHICLES MOVING NOW,' Howie screams as he leans into the Saxon and draws his axe out. He pauses and grabs the other double-bladed axe, and starts running towards Clarence, who is fighting them with his bare hands.

The huge man grabs them as they swarm at him, throwing them aside as he roars and screams with violence.

Dave is at Howie's side; his knives drawn. Cookey and Blowers run on the other side of Howie, bayonets in hand.

Howie looks ahead and watches Sarah pushing the last few people into the backs of vehicles. They run faster, seeing more going towards Sarah as she pushes the last one into the vehicle and slams the rear doors closed.

'SARAH, GO WITH THE VEHICLE,' Howie bellows out. She turns back to see four infected striding towards her, and she backs into the vehicle, becoming trapped against the closed doors. The infected spread out in a line only a few steps away from her.

Howie screams and sprints with all his strength.

A deep roar drowns every other noise as Clarence picks a zombie up and throws him high into the air, then charges the line of four infected, with his shoulder dropped down. The man mountain powers into the first one and drives through the rest, scooping them up on the way. Clarence bowls them over so they are underneath him; then, his arms pull back and start piling in massive punches to the zombie heads beneath him.

Clarence roars, and those fists lift up and drive down again and again as he pulverises the skulls. They don't stand a chance, and the big man kills them all, then stands up to run back to Sarah. He lifts Sarah by her waist and opens the rear door of the van, pushes her in, then takes a small, black item from his back pocket and presses it into her hand before slamming the door closed.

'MOVE NOW!' Clarence slams his hand on the side of the vehicle, causing it to rock on its suspension, and the vehicle pulls away with squealing tyres.

Finally, he looks back at Howie, and they nod once to each other as Howie hands him the axe. They turn to face out, towards the oncoming infected, both holding their axes, with faces drawn with intensity. Howie launches forward and starts driving them down, swinging the blades through their heads and necks. Brains burst apart and blood pours out from necks as Dave whips through them, slicing them apart.

Jamie comes running in, with his knives held the same way as Dave. He drops down and starts slicing into the backs of legs, cutting through tendons and ligaments. Infected drop down from the deadly wounds to writhe on the floor, only to be stamped on by Clarence's huge boots. The vehicles slowly pull away as the men fight amongst them, battling to keep the infected away from the vehicles and the people within them. The last vehicle leaves the compound. A row of bright, red lights reflecting off the wet ground, and headlights dimming as they draw away into the inky night. The small group backs away towards the line behind them, keeping pace with each other and fighting out as the infected come at them sporadically.

Howie slashes out, swinging the axe in a vicious uppercut and driving the blade straight through the thrusting chin of an infected male, bursting his face apart in a spray of blood, bone, and teeth.

They reach the Saxon, and Howie looks out to see the carpet of slaughtered infected.

'They're pulling back,' Chris shouts over as the group take position around the Saxon.

'I'm not surprised. You've bloody killed 'em all,' Howie shouts back to see Chris give a big grin. His white teeth gleaming in stark contrast to his dark beard.

'The Saxon can't fit us all in. We need more vehicles,' Howie shouts. His voice is drowned out by the weapons firing all around him. He walks around to stand near Chris and repeats his concern.

'There's a couple of vehicles we might be able to use at the end of the barricade. We left the keys in the glove boxes of the ones we might need,' Chris replies.

'But they're all piled up. They'll be fucked,' Howie says.

'No, there's some right at the beginning. I know which ones. We'll have to work our way down there,' Chris says. 'There's not so many of them now,' he adds, looking up the road.

Howie looks up to see small groups still advancing, but nothing like the volume that was coming just a few minutes ago.

'CEASE FIRE,' Chris calls out. The ones closest to him hear and respond immediately, but the GPMG keeps going, and the ones further down the line do not hear.

'CEASE FIRE,' Dave bellows. The firing stops immediately as they all turn to look at him.

'KEEP THE GPMG GOING AND MOVE ROUND THE SAXON TO KEEP GOING DOWN THE ROAD,' Chris orders as they start regrouping.

'Curtis, are you okay to keep driving, mate?' Howie shouts over.

'Yes, Mr Howie,' Curtis responds and clambers into the back and through to the driver's seat. They start grouping around the Saxon as Nick aims the fire into the last few groups of infected struggling over the fallen and mashed-up bodies on the road ahead of them.

The GPMG falls silent after a short time as Nick calls out the all clear.

'MOVE OUT, STAY CLOSE TO THE VEHICLE,' Howie shouts, and the Saxon starts moving, with the armed men and women standing shoulder to shoulder around the vehicle.

They inch down, sacrificing speed for the ability to stay together as one unit.

'CONTACT,' someone shouts from driver's side of the Saxon, and weapons fire as the infected are cut down.

'TO THE REAR,' Jamie shouts, and more weapons open up as infected continue to push out from the darkened buildings and run into the road towards the vehicle.

'KEEP GOING. YOU'RE DOING WELL,' Chris shouts out, and step by step, they move slowly down the road.

The constant contacts keep them busy as they fire into infected pushing in from the sides and the rear, and then, as they near the section, where the truck was used to block the road, they start coming from the front.

'NICK, FOCUS ON THE FRONT. WE NEED TO KEEP OUR ROUTE CLEAR.' Howie shouts out. Nick spins around to face the road ahead. His face grim from the constant use of the machine gun.

The recruits and guards shout out directions as they spot infected flitting through the shadows.

The contacts suddenly cease, and silence descends, only broken by the low rumble of the heavy diesel engine of the armoured personnel carrier.

'Why have they stopped?' Nick shouts out, spinning around to get a full view.

'I can't see them anywhere,' he adds.

'They're still there,' Jamie calls out. 'They're keeping pace with us in the shadows.'

'Dave, can you see them?' Howie asks.

'Yes,' Dave replies. A small child walks slowly out from the shadows, towards the passenger side of the Saxon. She wears a long, white nightgown, and her flowing, blond hair gleams in the moonlight. She shows no sign of injury. She stops just ahead of the vehicle and holds her arms out, offering an embrace.

'Come here, darling,' one of the male guards shouts out and rushes forward. The girl looks normal and terrified as she holds her arms out and glances around behind her.

'DON'T!' Howie yells. The guard scoops the girl up and starts running back with her, but he screams as the girl sinks her teeth into his neck, savagely tearing the soft flesh apart with a violent gnashing.

Her face is instantly soaked as the artery is opened, and the hot, red liquid spurts out. Two more guards rush forward. One of them grabs the girl and starts pulling her away. She wraps her arms around the first guard's head, clinging on as she devours the flesh with frenzied biting. A small horde of infected then rush out from the shadows, taking advantage of the distance the guards have created between themselves and the Saxon.

They are on the guards instantly, pulling them to the floor and sinking teeth into the flesh. Screams erupt as more guards rush forward to beat them away.

'STOP,' Chris shouts as they are set upon by more infected surging out of the darkness.

'CUT THEM DOWN,' Dave booms out and opens up with his assault rifle, firing indiscriminately into the melee of fighting bodies.

More guards scream out as they see their comrades being cut down by Dave. More rush in, flying into the frenzied attack. Their screams rip the air apart. One of the guards lunges at Dave, desperately trying to stop him from shooting down his mates. Blowers steps in and pushes him away. The guard staggers but lashes out with his fist, knocking Blowers back. Cookey strides forward and slams the stock of his rifle into the guard's face, dropping him instantly. Clarence grabs the back of his collar and drags him around to the back of the vehicle and launches the unconscious form into the rear.

'NICK!' Howie shouts out.

Nick grimaces and slowly shakes his head as he aims down to the struggling mass of bodies. Some of the attacked guards are clearly still alive.

'Fuck it,' Nick mutters and squeezes the trigger. The GPMG roars as it fires solid rounds into the mass of bodies, cutting them down instantly.

Sobs sound out from the guards as the infected and their friends are killed by the firing.

'KEEP IT TOGETHER,' Howie shouts. 'STAY WITH THE VEHICLE.'

Shots sound out from the driver's side as the infected show more intelligence by attacking that side with force while the resistors are focussed on the passenger side. Nick spins around to see a mass of infected coming from the shadows at full pelt.

He opens fire, trying to shout a warning at the same time.

The infected impact within seconds, and more guards are taken down as their assault weapons become useless in the close quarters combat. The brawling bodies are right at the side of the vehicle, and Nick pushes the machine gun over, but can't get the angle to fire down. Dave runs around the back of the vehicle, throwing his assault rifle into the rear as he passes the open door, then draws his knives from the back of his waistband.

Within short steps, he reaches the scrabbling line.

The first guard is pinned against the side of the vehicle, with infected savaging her face. She screams and thrashes, but the body weight is too great.

Dave steps behind them and draws a knife across each of their throats before spinning around to drive the two blades into the neck of a lunging infected female, then steps back as the zombie falls beside him. He works along the side of the still moving Saxon, cutting down infected and injured guards alike. At the last one, he spins through the air, slicing the throats open of the remaining infected as his blade comes to rest millimetres away from the throat of the last guard.

They keep walking sideways, keeping pace with the vehicle as the guard tries to push himself backwards into the solid metal side of the Saxon.

'ARE YOU BITTEN?' Dave shouts into his face, terrifying him even more.

'No, no, they didn't get me,' he stammers back.

'I AM WATCHING YOU,' Dave says and promptly pulls away. 'THIS SIDE IS UNGUARDED,' he bellows out.

Howie comes around the side from the front and looks back at the fallen bodies as the Saxon slowly advances down the narrow lane of the stacked vehicles.

'Fuck me…' he mutters, taking in the now unguarded side of the vehicle, apart from Dave and one shaking guard, who keeps glancing at Dave with a terrified expression.

'Are they all gone?' Howie asks.

'Yes, Mr Howie,' Dave answers as he stalks next to the vehicle; his knives upturned against his forearms.

'LOAD UP NOW,' Howie shouts out as Chris appears from the rear of the vehicle.

'What the fuck!' Chris's mouth drops as he looks back at the fallen bodies.

'We need to load up and go,' Howie shouts down, aware they will now fit in the vehicle as so many of the guards have been taken down.

Chris nods back in silent agreement.

They load up, one by one, covering each other as they work back down the side of the vehicle and into the rear doors of the moving Saxon. Howie is the last to load and pulls the doors closed.

'ALL IN,' he shouts.

'Catch up with the convoy, Curtis! Someone, take over from Nick, give him a break,' he adds, sinking down onto one of the side benches in exhaustion.

The Saxon increases in speed as Curtis works to catch up with the fleet. The vastly reduced numbers are exhausted from the sustained battle. The remaining few guards weep and sob at the loss of their fallen friends. Howie looks up to Blowers and Cookey, both sitting forward, with their heads down. Nick is slumped, leaning back with his eyes closed.

Jamie and Dave are both sitting straight; eyes open and staring ahead out of the windscreen. Howie ticks them off in his mind as he goes. The mother hen counting the brood: Curtis driving, Tucker with the supply vehicle, and Sarah in the back of the last vehicle. He looks over at Clarence, the big man taking up the space of two people with his enormous frame, leaning back with his eyes closed. Howie remembers him saving Sarah and offers a silent prayer of thanks that he was in the position to react so quickly. Other than Dave, none of them would have been able to take so many down with their bare hands and walk away unscathed. Finally, he looks to Big Chris. They lock eyes. Two leaders, who have suffered losses and taken the responsibility of so many lives and have fought to keep those people safe. One – a former soldier and criminal, the other – a supermarket manager. Something passes between them – a meeting of minds, an unspoken contract that they will do anything to ensure the survival of the people that have trusted them with their lives.

CHAPTER SEVENTY-FOUR

Sarah stands, with her head resting against the inside of the door. The last image as the doors were slammed was of Clarence staring hard at her and a scene of utter carnage behind him, and of Howie sprinting towards her, carrying two axes. She realises that she is holding something in her hand. The inside of the van is pitch black, and she feels around the object. It feels like a knife handle, but there is no blade. Her fingertips brush against a small button on the side. She looks back up to the door as she realises what he gave to her. She tucks the item into her back pocket as she turns around. The motion of the vehicle and the gentle sway as it turns increases her sense of fear. Any notion of space and dimension disappears, and she stretches her arms to press her hands against the insides of the vehicle.

She feels the heat from the bodies pressed tightly into the back of the van, and sweat starts to form on her face. Then she feels something small pressing into her and reaches down with a hand to feel a small head with long hair.

'Hey, it's okay,' Sarah says softly as the small body flinches away from her hand.

A tiny hand reaches up to touch hers. Fingertips brushing gently, then gripping tightly.

'Mummy?' a small voice says.

'No, I'm Sarah. Where is your mummy?' she asks.

'I don't know,' the child whimpers.

'Hey, everyone, there's a small child here missing her mummy,' Sarah calls out to the darkness.

'Who is it?' a female voice answers from somewhere near the front.

'What's your name, sweetie?' Sarah asks the small child.

'Patricia,' the small voice replies.

'Her name's Patricia,' Sarah calls out.

'What's her mum's name?' the same female voice answers.

'What's your mum's name, sweetie?' Sarah asks.

'Jane.'

'Her mother's called Jane,' Sarah says.

'I don't know her. Does anyone else?' the female voice calls out to no reply.

'What about your daddy? What's his name?' Sarah asks Patricia.

'I don't know,' Patricia whimpers; her voice small and weak.

'Come here, angel,' Sarah says as she drops down low and draws the small girl into her body. The child throws her arms round Sarah's shoulders, squeezing tightly.

'I wanna go home,' Patricia says quietly.

'I know, sweetie, but we'll be okay. It won't be dark for long,' Sarah replies, rubbing the girl's back.

'Is there a light in here?' the female voice from the front calls out.

Sarah listens to the rustle of hands feeling alongside the sides and roof of the van, scrabbling about in the pitch dark.

A feeble light switches on from the front.

'Hey, look over there,' Sarah says softly. The girl turns slowly to see the very soft, yellow light illuminating the many faces packed into the van, all of them women.

A few of them smile down at the girl hugging Sarah.

'See, we're not in the dark anymore, and soon we'll be able to get out. We just have to wait,' Sarah assures the girl.

'Will those things get us?' Patricia asks, with fear in her small voice.

'No, sweetie, they won't get us,' Sarah says as Patricia pushes into her shoulder to cover her face.

'Do you promise?' Patricia asks.

'I promise. I know the men looking after us, and they're very, very brave. They won't let anything happen to us,' Sarah says.

'Will they stop those things?' Patricia asks.

'Yes, they will stop them, and they will keep us all safe. I promise. They're big and strong, and brave, and we're in here, and those things can't get us in here.'

'How do you know them?' one of the women asks.

'My brother is one of them,' Sarah replies.

'One of the guards?' another asks.

'No, Howie is with the army vehicle. He's in charge of them,' Sarah replies with pride.

'HOWIEEEEEEE,' a woman screeches out from the far corner of the vehicle. Heads turn at the sudden noise as the voice screeches again. 'HOWIEEEEEEEE.'

A commotion breaks out as another woman screams.

'She's biting her. She's one of them!' a voice shouts out.

Sarah catches a glimpse of an old woman sinking her teeth into the neck of a younger woman and blood pumping out.

The packed bodies try to push away as others try to push in to stop the attack.

'GET HER OFF!' Sarah screams out as a hand reaches out to grasp the hair on the back of the head of the old woman, pulling her away with a violent yank.

The attacked woman drops to the floor as women start pummelling into the freshly turned zombie, and she goes down in the packed confines. The women screaming with fear. Feet start stamping down, desperately trying to kill the old woman.

'SHE GOT ME,' one of the women screams out as her ankle is bitten into.

She drops down to beat her away until more boots and shoes can stamp down on the old woman's head and neck.

'IS SHE DOWN?' Sarah calls out.

'Yeah. Where's the other one that she bit?' another voice shouts in panic.

'She's on the ground. She's not moving,' someone answers.

'Kill her. She'll come back as one of them,' the first voice shouts. In the dim light, Sarah makes out women pushing and scrabbling to get away from the fallen woman. Some of the braver ones fighting to get to her. None of them able to move much because of the small space. The woman with the bitten ankle screams and sobs as she clutches her ankle.

'I've been bitten. I've been bitten,' she repeats over and again. Sarah pulls the girl closer; her hands going around her chest in a protective embrace.

'Go behind me, sweetie,' Sarah whispers in her ear and pushes the girl around.

Another scream pierces the air as the savaged woman rises up and lunges, sinking her teeth into the closest leg.

Hands start beating at her as the van erupts in panic.

The air is filled with screams, and the van rocks from the pushing and pulling as the women fight to get away. More of them fall down from vicious bites as zombie teeth tear flesh apart. Women start slipping over as the wooden base of the van becomes slick with the spilled blood. More women are bitten and go down onto the ground.

Sarah watches as the bodies fight and writhe on the ground. She slips her hand around and draws the handle from her back pocket, feeling for the small button. She holds it down at her side, with her finger pressed gently on the button.

The driver of the van hears the screams and bangs clearly. His hands grip the steering wheel as pure terror grows inside him.

He leans forward to stare at the red light of the vehicle in front. He knows he's the last in the fleet, and if he stops now, he will be left behind, defenceless in the dark streets of London, surrounded by the infected.

The bangs and screams increase as he drives, and hot tears start spilling down his face. He beats his hands against the steering wheel, imagining the scenes breaking out just inches behind him.

Instinctively, he reaches for the radio and presses the on switch. Static fills the air. The driver finds a CD in the cubby-hole of the dashboard and tries to force it into the CD slot; his hands shaking.

The CD refuses to budge, and it takes minutes for him to realise there is already a CD in the player. He throws the CD down onto the floor, frantically pressing buttons as the screams and bangs get louder from the rear. The driver finally presses the right button, and loud rock music bursts out of the speakers. He twists the volume knob until the sound is so loud it comes out distorted. He looks up to see he has drifted off to the side in his panic to fill the van with noise. He overreacts and yanks the steering wheel hard. The van swerves over and then back again as he fights to get control.

Sarah watches as the fight breaks out in front of her; then, she lowers down to speak into the girl's ear, 'Put your hands over your eyes, sweetie, and keep them there.' The girl does as she is asked and pushes her small hands over her tightly closed eyes. 'I'll be right back. I promise,' Sarah whispers while watching the unfolding mess in front of her.

Half the women in the van are bitten, and the rest are fighting like troopers to protect themselves, falling and tripping over the bodies wrestling on the floor.

An infected woman stumbles backwards, having been thrust by a large built woman at the front. The zombie stumbles into Sarah, who reaches around to grip her around the neck, squeezing tightly. She presses the small button on the handle – a shiny blade sliding out instantly, and Sarah digs this into the throat of the woman while gripping hard. Blood pumps out, covering her hand and arm. She pushes the body away just as the large woman sends another one her way. Sarah steps forward and grabs the zombie, pulling her head forward as she sticks the knife deep into her throat, then twists the handle left to right and back again, tearing a ragged hole in her windpipe. Loud rock music booms out from the front, drowning out the screams, grunts, and groans of the women trying to kill each other.

Sarah drops the woman down and lunges for the next one as the van swerves violently, causing all the women to fly into one side, landing in a crumpled heap, with Sarah at the bottom of the pile.

Pinned to the floor by bloodied bodies, she thrashes her legs, frantically trying to prevent any of the infected from biting her ankles. The bodies fight and writhe about as Sarah struggles for breath under the heavy weight. The van swerves again as the bodies slide across the slick floor to ram into the other side. Sarah is now free and rises up to see red, bloodshot eyes pushing towards her.

She yells as she sticks the blade into the throat, missing and stabbing the woman through the cheek instead. She pulls the small handle back and lashes out again and again, swiping the blade back and forth across the throat. Another one pushes her head out of the mess of limbs, and Sarah rams her foot into the face, feeling bones crunch underfoot.

She tries to roll away as the van swerves again, and they slide back across the floor to pin Sarah against the side.

Once more trapped under the bodies, she fights to draw her legs into the foetal position, hoping the press of bodies will protect her. She feels the blade sinking into the back of another woman pressing into her, with no idea if she is stabbing a zombie or another survivor. She tries to pull the knife away, but her arm is pinned into position as the body writhes on the blade. Another swerve sends them back across the floor, and Sarah loses grip on the knife as they slam into the other side. She crabs backwards as a body drops down on her; blood pouring from a deep bite wound to her neck. Sarah cranes her neck, trying to keep her face away from the blood, and she rolls hard to displace the body, pushing it aside as she gets back to her feet.

Another zombie comes from the right, and Sarah ducks down and moves behind to wrap her arms round her neck. Sarah squeezes with all her might as the body staggers forward, arms flailing. A woman in front of them turns around to bite into the mass of bodies, and Sarah sees the knife sticking out of her back. She reaches out to grab the handle as the zombie pulls away. Sarah squeezes hard and pulls her upper body backwards, forcing the zombie to fall down. Sarah slams her booted feet down again and again on the face just as the one, with the knife stuck in her, turns to Sarah with bloodied teeth bared.

Sarah slams her fist into the side of its face, snapping the head away, then sidesteps, and finally gets a grip on the knife. She pulls it out and forces the blade into the side of the zombie's neck, sawing and hacking away until a large, ragged hole forms in the soft flesh. She turns to see an infected stalk towards Patricia, still cowering in the corner, with her hands over her eyes. Sarah dives forward onto the floor and grabs the ankles, pulling them back as hard as she can. The zombie slams down face forward into the floor as Sarah clambers over its back to grab the head and slam it down again and again into the hard flooring.

Remembering the knife in her hand, she repeatedly stabs into the rib cage, breaking bones and puncturing the lungs. The body eventually goes still as Sarah rolls off to find another one bearing down on her.

She lifts her feet up and takes the weight of the zombie body on its chest. Her boots push into the zombie's breasts as she tries to force it away. The zombie is heavy, fighting forward, and Sarah feels her legs starting to buckle. She rolls to the side as the body falls down, just missing her.

She slams her arm down and forces the blade into the back of the neck before the zombie can roll or turn towards her. Sarah keeps fighting as they are bitten and turned, one by one. She fights out with desperation until she is side by side with the large built woman from earlier. The large woman wraps her arms around an infected, pinning her against the side of the van.

'STAB HER,' the woman yells as Sarah lunges forward with the knife to slice open the infected woman's throat.

They back away as the body slides down onto the already crowded floor. The large woman thrusts her arm out to grab the hair of a zombie about to bite Sarah from the other side, yelling a warning as she fights to pull the infected woman away. Sarah sticks the small blade deep into the exposed neck. They keep going until the last one drops down onto the top of the gory pile of corpses. Both of them soaked with blood and filth.

They back away until they are both standing protectively in front of Patricia. Sarah hands the other woman the knife and drops down so she is eye level with the little girl.

'Sweetie, I want you to turn around and face the other way now.'

'Can I take my hands away?' Patricia answers.

'Yes, but only when you've turned around.'

'Did those things get in here?' Patricia asks. 'You promised they wouldn't.'

Sarah looks up to exchange a glance with the other woman.

'Just turn for me, Patricia. There's none of them in here now. It's safe,' Sarah says as she turns the girl around.

'I'm Mary,' the large built woman says when Sarah stands up. 'Nice to meet you. Do you want your knife back?'

'Yes, if you don't mind,' Sarah replies. 'Nice to meet you too, Mary.'

'You're better with it than me. I'll grab 'em, and you stab 'em,' the large woman jokes.

'Deal,' Sarah replies as they stare down at the bodies piled in front of them.

CHAPTER SEVENTY-FIVE

'There they are,' Curtis says to Howie, who is now in the passenger seat.

'Nice one, mate. Just need to get to the front now,' Howie replies.

The taillights disappear around a bend in the road but soon come into view again as the Saxon speeds up.

Curtis drives up close behind the last van, the one containing Sarah, Mary, Patricia, and the pile of zombie bodies.

They flash headlights to alert the driver they are going around as Curtis pulls out to start overtaking them. One by one, they drive past the fleet of vehicles. Howie giving a wave or a thumbs up to the drivers while wondering how they will feel when they find out most of their guards have been wiped out.

'Which fort are we heading for?' Chris calls out from the back.

'There's quite a few of them, but I reckon we should go for Fort Spitbank. It's the biggest one that I know of, and it's been maintained,' Howie shouts back.

'Have you been there before?' Chris asks.

'Yeah, but years ago. We went with school and then a couple of times later. It's huge, and the rear wall goes straight onto the sea. From memory, it had open, flat land all around it too.'

'Let's just hope it's not full, then,' Chris says. The Saxon weaves its way past the fleet of vans, cars, and trucks until it eventually reaches the front. A long convoy snaking out of London, into the pitch black of the countryside. Howie checks and rechecks the map, planning ahead and making sure they stick to major roads so the big trucks can fit through.

'Malcolm to Chris. We are being flashed by headlights from behind. There must be an issue. Can we find a safe area to pull up?'

'Chris to Malcolm and all units. Roger that. I know this road. There is a section ahead with high concrete walls on both sides. We will stop there.'

'About a mile or so further, Howie, you'll see big walls on both sides. We want to stop there,' Chris shouts forward.

'Got it, mate. Curtis, make sure you keep to the middle lane so we have equal distance on both sides,' Howie says.

'Okay, Mr Howie.' Within a few minutes, the Saxon is slowing down as they enter into a very long, straight section of the motorway. High concrete walls create a tunnel effect from the headlights and the dark sky.

'Who's on the GPMG?' Howie asks.

'Jamie,' Blowers answers.

'Right, I want us out, down the sides, keeping watch, and Curtis, I want you to drive forward a short distance so Jamie can get a good view of the sides. Everyone ready? Good, everyone out, then,' Howie shouts as he jumps down and runs back to meet Chris.

They stride down the left flank of the convoy, pausing as Malcolm jumps out from the front vehicle to meet them.

'What's up?' Chris asks him.

'I don't know. We were getting constant flashes from behind,' Malcolm replies. They walk to the next vehicle and shout up to the driver. He leans out of the open window, with a cigarette hanging out his mouth.

'Everything all right?' Howie calls up.

'We're fine. We were getting flashed from behind, so I passed it on.' They walk to the next vehicle to find Tucker climbing down from the passenger door and stretching out.

'That looked a bit nasty back there, Mr Howie,' Tucker says.

'It was, mate, was it you flashing?'

'Nope, came from behind,' Tucker replies. They walk down the fleet of vehicles, with each driver giving the same response. With only a few vehicles left in the fleet, Howie looks to the back to see the driver of the last vehicle running towards them, waving his arms in the air.

'That's Sarah's vehicle,' Howie yells as he starts running forward. Big Chris and Dave sprinting beside him.

'They were screaming and banging. I didn't know what to do. I didn't want to get left behind,' the driver sobs as they run past him.

Howie twists around the back of the van and wrenches the rear doors open to see Sarah standing, facing him, covered in blood. A small knife is held tightly in her right hand. Her left hand grips the fingers of a small girl, who is also holding hands with a large built woman. The three of them drip with blood and gore.

'Sarah... What the fuck?' Howie stammers as he jolts forward, picking the girl up to pass back to Chris. As Sarah and Mary step down, Howie's mouth drops open as he looks at the utter scene of carnage in the back of the van. Dead bodies are strewn about and piled up. Thick pools of blood shimmering on the floor and smeared up the sides. Dead eyes, both human and zombie, stare blankly. Dead mouths gape accusingly at him.

'What happened?' Howie says to the women.

'One of them turned, and it just sort of exploded from there,' Sarah replies calmly.

'This is Mary. Mary, this is my brother Howie.' Howie stands speechless as Mary calmly says *hello*.

Dave then steps forward to peer into the back of the van. He gazes at Mary and Sarah, then down at the small knife, then finally back to the bodies.

He looks at Howie and nods, clearly impressed at the work completed.

'Who is the girl?' Howie eventually asks when his brain catches up with the sight before him.

'Patricia. She lost her mum,' Sarah replies still in a calm voice.

Mary steps forward to take the child from Chris, who is also standing with his mouth hanging open.

'We'll come with you,' Sarah says flatly.

'We don't have a lot of room,' Chris starts to say.

'She said we're coming with you.' Mary glares at Chris.

'Yeah, fine, no problem,' Chris replies, holding his hands up.

The vehicles move off again. The Saxon in the lead, with Sarah and Mary sitting in the hastily vacated seats, using wet wipes to clean themselves and Patricia of the blood and filth.

Hardened and battle-experienced men watch them with keen interest. They work with purpose, chatting with the small child as though nothing had happened.

Before the women arrived, Chris had got to the vehicle ahead of them and whispered what they had seen inside the van. Clarence had moved quickly to Sarah on seeing the state she was in, asking her again and again if she was okay.

'You can have your knife back now,' she offered as the huge man fussed around her.

'No, you keep it. In fact,' Clarence said as he unbuckled his belt and removed one of the large sheath knives from it before handing it to Sarah, 'you'd better have a bigger one.'

'How does it go on?' Sarah said, taking the big knife and pulling it from the sheath to admire the weapon.

'Here, let me,' Clarence said as he unbuckled Sarah's belt and pulled it free from the loops. Then suddenly, realising what he was doing, he looked down to see her smiling at him.

'Oh, sorry, I didn't mean to...' He blushed bright red to Sarah's delight.

'What didn't you mean to do?' she asked mischievously.

'Err, undo your belt...' he stammered.

'But you *did* undo my belt,' she replied.

'Yeah, but you know...'

'I know what?'

'I, err, well, didn't mean it like that.'

'Like what?' she asked innocently and laughed as he went even redder.

'I'm only joking. Thank you for the knife,' she said, touching him on his massive forearm as his face split apart with a huge grin.

Howie had taken over the driving, seeing Curtis looking tired and drawn, and suggested he get some rest in the back.

'Did you see those bodies?' Howie asked Dave as they continued driving.

'Yes, Mr Howie. I was there,' Dave replies.

'Oh, not this again. I meant, did you see how many there were?'

'Yes. I was there.'

'Do you do this on purpose?'

'Do what?'

'Answer each question literally.'

'How do I answer that?'

'What?'

'You asked me if I answer each question literally, so in order to give you an answer, I would have to be literal, which would then suggest that I do, in fact, answer each question literally.'

'You never cease to amaze me, Dave.'

'Thanks, Mr Howie.'

The crowded Saxon settles into near silence as they travel towards the coast. The exhausted survivors try to sleep in whatever space they can find.

Patricia dozes fitfully, snuggled into Mary in one rear corner while Sarah rests in the other.

The others find space where they can. Clarence and Chris both remain standing near the front, leaning in towards Howie and Dave and chatting in muted tones.

'Have you seen any yet?' Chris asks.

'Nope, not one. Fuck knows where they've all gone,' Howie replies.

'Can't be a good thing,' Chris says.

'Darren knew all along we would be heading for the forts, but I don't think I ever said which one,' Howie says.

'So there's no doubt they're going to be coming for us, then,' Chris says.

'He'll come. It just depends how long it takes him, and we haven't seen any for a long time, so I reckon they're massing again,' Howie says.

'Or waiting for him to pass through so they can join in,' Chris says.

'Jesus, there'll be thousands of them if he collects them all on the way,' says Clarence.

'More than that,' Chris says.

'I was wondering if he would try to use vehicles. He's obviously got control over the rest of them somehow.' Howie says.

'Yeah, and if he can tap into their memories and knowledge, then it wouldn't be hard to get the keys for the vehicles and move down here quickly,' Chris interrupts.

'He'll come on foot,' Dave says in his normal, flat tone.

'How do you know?' Howie asks.

'They've been going for a week now, with no sign of slowing down. They're decaying but still moving. I haven't seen any of them eat or drink, so they don't need sustenance, which also means time is not relevant to them. He held them outside the commune until he thought there were sufficient numbers, but he held himself back away from harm, which shows he has awareness for his own safety. They also massed in Canary Wharf when we went for your sister, so the biggest single tactic deployed by them is high numbers. Logistics for any army on the move is difficult at the best of times and will be even harder using vehicles...'

'Not if they have collective intelligence,' Howie cuts in, 'and it does look like they have. Darren snapped his fingers, and they all started laughing; then, he made them take a step forward perfectly, in time. With that kind of power and control, they could find it easy.'

'I don't think they will,' Dave replies. 'That would mean having every one of them have access to a vehicle and be ready in the right place, at the right time to slip in with the main fleet. Even if they share intelligence, that is an extremely hard thing to organise. A forced march is the best way for them to pick them up as they go.'

'So, if they have a collective intelligence or consciousness, then they would know the route they are taking and would just have to wait at those points,' Chris says.

'Yes,' Dave responds.

'So why not get vehicles and wait at those points?' Howie asks.

'Their motor skills have got better, but during the day, they shuffle and become slow, and are not able to control their own bodies that well. We saw them increase speed during the day, but that made them weaker. Darren will have no choice but to keep them moving at a set pace that can cover ground but will conserve energy to prevent them weakening,' Dave explains clearly.

'Okay, so how long will it take to walk that distance?' Howie asks.

'They can go as the crow flies, in a straight line, so that would be about fifty miles or so,' Clarence says.

'If they shuffle along like they do during the day, then a couple of days at least. If they move fast the entire time, it could be as little as sixteen to twenty hours, but we know that weakens them. But if they have enough, err, people, I guess, then they might not worry about being weaker,' says Chris.

'People,' Howie laughs.

'Yeah, I know. I don't like the other word, though,' Chris replies.

'What? Zombies?' Howie asks.

'Yeah, it seems like a movie or something when I use that word,' laughs Chris.

'What do you think, Dave?' Howie asks.

'About the word zombies? It doesn't bother me.'

'No,' Howie laughs again, 'about the speed they'll move at.'

'Oh, sorry. I don't think time is an issue for them, so they will do what all big organisations do.'

'Which is?' Clarence asks after a lengthy pause.

'They will work out the best speed to make the best distance using the least amount of fuel, like airlines do or shipping companies,' Dave replies.

'Sounds ridiculous when you say it like that,' Howie says, 'but I guess that's about right, though.'

'Well, we have no answer to the question, then. We don't know when they'll turn up,' says Chris.

'In short, nope,' Howie replies.

'Brilliant. We have a huge army of dead people marching through the country specifically looking for us, and we're heading for a hundred and fifty-year-old fort somewhere on the coast, with a handful of men able to fight. I like those odds,' Chris laughs.

'Stuff 'em,' Clarence says in his deep voice.

'Stuff 'em? What kind of an insult is that?' Chris laughs, looking at the huge man-mountain.

'Well, there are ladies and a child present, and I didn't want to be a potty mouth,' the deep voice rumbles as the rest burst out laughing.

'Potty mouth!? That's even worse,' Howie says, laughing. 'I just watched you take four of them down with your bare hands.'

'Yeah, well, there's no need for foul language in the presence of ladies,' Clarence replies defensively.

'I think your sister has an admirer, Howie,' Chris says, wiping tears of laughter from his eyes.

'No, just hang on,' Clarence tries to interrupt, going red in the face.

'Oh, really, you fancy my sister, do you?' Howie asks, pretending to be offended.

'No one said anything about me fancying your sister, Mr Howie,' Clarence says.

'Oh, he's *Mr Howie* now, is he? Trying to win him over, are you?' Chris laughs again as Howie bends forward, trying to stop laughing so loud.

'No, he *is* Mr Howie. Everyone calls him that,' Clarence says in a more defensive tone.

'So, you don't fancy Sarah, then?' Chris asks, unable to stop goading him.

'No, of course, I don't,' Chris replies, going even redder.

'Where's your knife, then?' Chris asks innocently.

'My what?' Clarence replies. His voice going higher as Howie starts to laugh harder.

'Your knife. I gave you that knife years ago, after you broke that cheap thing you had.'

'Well, err, well, she only had that little knife.'

'That little knife that you gave her, and now you've given her your big knife. What's next? The axe?' Chris says between laughing.

'Oh, just fuck off,' Clarence finally snaps; his voice louder.

'Language, please, there's a child back here. Keep that potty mouth for later,' Mary calls out as Howie and Chris burst out laughing even more. Even Dave chuckles as Clarence drops his head into his hands, groaning.

'What's so funny?' Sarah asks, clambering over the legs of sleeping forms to get to the front.

'We were just talking about Clarence,' Chris replies, still chuckling.

'Oh, what about?' Sarah asks, stretching.

'Chris...' Clarence growls and tries to turn away from Sarah; his face bright red.

'Just about the knife he gave you,' Howie cuts in, tears streaming down his face.

'Oh, that was sweet. Thank you again, Clarence. You'll have to show me how to use it, though. It's very big,' Sarah replies, smiling at him. 'Howie, are you all right?' she asks as Howie's body heaves with laughing, bent forward enough to be almost biting the steering wheel.

'Fine, I'm fine,' Howie whimpers.

'Clarence was just saying how he wants to show you some moves,' Chris says innocently.

'That's great, thank you, Clarence,' Sarah says, placing her hand on his shoulder.

'It's no problem,' Clarence replies.

'Are you okay? Your face is very red,' Sarah says with concern. 'Are you coming down with something?' She presses the back of her hand to his forehead.

'No, no, I'm just very hot in here,' Clarence replies very softly.

'Okay, well, I'll leave you boys to it and try to get some more rest,' Sarah says as she clambers back down the Saxon.

'Okay, we'll be quieter now, Sarah,' Chris smiles as she goes, then looks down at Clarence bent over, resting his head on the back of the seat. His face now beetroot-coloured, but his forehead tingling from where she touched him.

'Poor Clarence, are you okay?' Chris says in a sweet voice and puts his hand on Clarence's face.

'Fuck off, you wanker,' Clarence whispers.

'Oh, poor Clarence. Come here, you big teddy bear, and give me a cuddly wuddly,' Chris laughs as he tries to wrap his arms round Clarence's huge shoulders.

'I said fuck off, Chris,' Clarence whispers as he starts laughing, trying to squirm out of the manly embrace.

'So, how do you feel, Howie, about Clarence showing your sister some moves with the knife?' Chris asks.

'Me? I'm fine with it, mate. You carry on,' Howie replies, still chuckling.

'Really?' Clarence looks over at him as Chris laughs again. 'You don't mind, then?'

'No, mate, but Dave's the one with the knife skills. Maybe he should do it,' Howie says. 'What do you think, Dave?'

'I think your sister would like Clarence to do it,' Dave replies, showing a rare ability to pick up on a social situation.

'Cheers, Dave,' Clarence says softly.

From the motorway, the convoy takes a slip road to pass through rural villages as the night sky starts to lift. The lush landscape of rolling hills, wooded copses, and cultivated fields soon becomes flat, open heathland – the first signs they are nearing the coast. The Saxon leads the vehicles through an industrial zone, with large hanger-style buildings signed for marine engineering. Expensive looking powerboats and luxurious yachts loom high on giant stands dotted about the area.

'This is the road to the fort,' Howie reports back to the rest. 'As far as I can remember, this is the only road in.'

The convoy drives through the industrial units and into a country lane bordered with high hedges. Within a few minutes, they enter a housing estate full of large, detached houses. The road passes through the middle of the estate, which abruptly ends with lines of dwellings stretching out on both sides, bordering open heathland.

Howie explains that the landscape changed abruptly one hundred and fifty years ago when the fort was constructed to allow the defenders a wide view of the entire area. Thickets of trees and undulating hillocks had been flattened, and now the area remains wide open.

Lights shining in the distance are the only sign of the fort ahead of them.

'Can you slow down, please, Mr Howie,' Dave asks.

'Do you see something?' Howie replies as he slows the vehicle down, causing a long line of red brake lights to shine out behind him.

Dave looks to the rows of buildings stretched out on both sides, then out to the flat land. The sky getting lighter with each passing minute.

'Is the fort down there, where the lights are?' Dave asks, pointing down the road, away from the estate.

'Yep, you can see it clearly during the day,' Howie replies.

'Okay, thanks, Mr Howie,' Dave says, apparently satisfied.

'Chris, can you hear me?' Howie calls out.

Chris lumbers back to the front and leans forward. 'What's up?' he asks.

'Chris, when we get there, we need to make sure we are isolated if we discuss anything,' Howie whispers just loud enough for Chris and Dave to hear.

'We don't know how long Darren was infected before he turned, and we don't know anything about the people here,' Howie adds as they both nod, understanding.

'How do we know none of us are infected?' Dave asks.

'Well, I know I'm not,' Howie replies.

'Darren would have said that too,' Dave says.

'True, so how can we be sure?' Howie asks.

'Check for bites and scratches, any open wounds?' Chris says quietly.

'How about we get Doc Roberts to check us over to be sure?' Howie suggests.

'Sounds good. I'm okay with that,' Chris replies.

'Dave, that all right with you?' Howie whispers.

'Yes, Mr Howie,' Dave nods.

They drive forward on the straight road as night transforms to morning. The rain clouds of the previous day have now drifted away, leaving a beautifully clear sky. The flat grassland rises into steep embankments that stretch out to both sides, with the road cutting through the middle of them.

Once past the grass banks, they see another stretch of flat grassland, then another high, steep embankment, which drops down into a wide ditch on the reverse side. The ditch is cut deep into the earth and is at least ten feet in width, with sheer sides.

'So we've got the first high bank, flat land, then another high bank dropping down into a deep ditch, then more flat land,' Chris voices his thoughts out loud as he takes the scene in.

'It looks like the banks stretch out to both sides of the spit. So does the ditch. Is that an outer wall or just the main wall?' he asks Howie.

'Err, I think it's an outer wall,' Howie replies, trying to remember. 'From memory, the rear of the fort has a high wall that drops down straight into the sea. The land was dug out, so the sea is very deep straight away, with no beach. I think there's a rear access point, though,' he explains.

'The rear wall runs the length of the rear section and then curves back round with the natural lay of the spit. The front section here isn't a straight wall. It has two sections that jut out. One on each side where the wall starts coming back inland, and then there's the long, straight bit we can see here,' Howie finishes.

'We'll need a good look around as soon as possible,' Dave says.

'Ah, you mean we need an advanced recce reconnaissance pathfinder,' Howie jokes.

Dave smiles back at him, remembering the previous conversation of a few days ago.

'Hello, we've got company.' Chris points up to the high walls to see heads moving about, peeking over, and then dropping back down.

Howie brings the Saxon to a halt a few metres back from the gates.

'I'll go and say hello,' he says, opening the door and dropping down to stretch his arms out and arch his back.

'Ah, that feels nice,' he mutters. Dave jumps down and walks around to join him at the front.

'Well, we made it, mate,' Howie says as they walk towards the gates.

'We did, Mr Howie, and we got your sister,' Dave replies.

'It's all good in the hood, mate. Apart from the zombie army coming to eat us.'

CHAPTER SEVENTY-SIX

They stop a few feet back from the gates, looking at a single door cut into the solid metal plates. A small hatch opens from the inside, and a pinched face looks out.

'Are you bitten?' a high-pitched, female voice calls out.

'Oh, yes, we are bitten all over and completely infected,' Howie smiles broadly. 'I'd recognise that voice anywhere. Hello, Debbie.'

'You have to strip off again,' the voice laughs back from the hatch.

'Now stop being a pervert and trying to look at Dave being naked and let us in. We're gasping for a brew,' Howie says, laughing. The single door swings inwards, and Sergeant Debbie Hopewell walks out, looking neat and tidy and still wearing her all-black police uniform.

'Hello, Mr Howie,' Debbie smiles as she reaches them; genuine pleasure on her face.

They hug briefly.

'It's good to see you, Debbie. I somehow knew you'd be at the front gate,' Howie says.

'Well, we can't just have anyone at the main entry point now, can we?' Debbie says, turning to Dave and giving him an awkward hug, which makes him blush bright red.

'Let me guess. You had a meeting and got it submitted in triplicate, and posted the rota on some wall, somewhere,' Howie jokes.

'Oh, yes, there must be order, Howie,' Debbie smiles back.

'Hello, 'ello! There's a couple of ugly faces I wouldn't forget in a hurry,' a loud voice booms out into the quiet morning air.

'Ted! Hello, mate, it's good to see you,' Howie calls out as he steps forward to shake hands with the former policeman.

'You too, Mr Howie. Hello, Dave. You've kept him alive, then?' Ted says, looking at Dave but nodding towards Howie.

'Hello, Ted.' Dave leans forward to shake his hand but stops midway. 'Did you wash your hands this time?' he jokes.

'Bloody hell, someone's taught him a sense of humour,' Ted says as they shake hands.

'So you made it down here okay, then?' Howie asks them both.

'Easy run, really. We just kept going despite young Tom whining that he needed to pee,' Ted replies.

'You should have seen the state of the place, though,' Debbie cuts in.

'Absolute bedlam. People arriving every few minutes. There was no order, no rationing, no lists, nothing. It's taken days to get things shipshape,' she adds.

'Well, we've got a couple of thousand tired, scared, hungry, and thirsty people crammed into these vehicles,' Howie says, turning back to look at the vehicles and seeing Chris, Clarence, and Sarah walking towards them.

'We'd better get them inside, then. They'll have to come in on foot. We don't have the room for the vehicles,' Debbie responds in a business-like fashion.

'Ted, Debbie, this is Chris, Clarence, and my sister Sarah. Chris had set up a safe area in London, but it got overrun last night as we left,' Howie introduces them as they shake hands with polite greetings.

'Right, we need to get the people out and filing in here,' Howie says. 'No room for the vehicles, though. Have you set up a vehicle area?' he asks.

'Not inside. I made them take the vehicles out and put them into the estate,' Debbie replies. 'We have kept a few for patrolling and gathering supplies, though,' she adds.

'Okay, how do you want this done?' Howie asks.

'We're recording the names, date of birth, and last address of everyone entering and then allocating them a specific place inside the compound. We also record any specific skills such as butchery or carpentry, that kind of thing,' Debbie replies.

'We've got doctors, nurses, and some hospital equipment with us,' Chris adds.

'Brilliant, we're desperate for medical personnel. Right, I suggest you get them out of the vehicles and have them line up in front of the gates. I'll get some people out to distribute water while they wait,' Debbie says. They depart from the brief meeting as Debbie and Ted head back inside to prepare for the incoming refugees.

Howie and his small group walk back to the Saxon, and Howie calls the recruits and guards over. Chris calls out on the radio for all guards to make their way to the front. Within a few minutes, the small force is all assembled in front of Howie and Chris. Doctor Roberts and a few of the medical team stand to one side.

'Right, they've got enough room for everyone, but we have to line them up for details to be taken. We need a perimeter set up, and Curtis, I want you to take the Saxon and go to the rear, keep sweeping back and forth across that area. Nick, I want you on the GPMG. Blowers and Cookey, you're both at the gates, being nice to people again. Sarah, would you mind going with them?' Howie asks.

'No problem, I'll take Mary with me,' Sarah replies.

'Be on the lookout for anyone with cuts, bites, or any open wounds,' Howie continues.

'What if we see any?' a voice asks.

'They need to be isolated, but do it quietly, with no fuss, and do not create panic,' Chris cuts in. 'Doc, can you set something up inside to check people over as they enter?'

'Yes,' Doc Roberts replies curtly and moves off with his team.

'Jamie, I want you up high somewhere with the sniper rifle,' Howie says to the quiet lad as Jamie looks about.

'Go in and get up on the inside of the outer wall,' Dave says to him.

'Right, spread out, stay sharp, and get those people out,' Howie calls out as they depart. Jamie runs back to the Saxon and draws the sniper rifle from the protective bag. He loops the bag over his shoulder and starts jogging towards the gate.

'Tucker, we'll get that supplies vehicle up front for unloading. Can you get inside and see what the situation with supplies is like? I would imagine Sergeant Hopewell would have a tight grip on it,' Howie tells him.

'Okay, Mr Howie, I'm on it now,' Tucker replies and starts striding after Jamie to the gate. Doc Roberts and his team walk past, carrying armfuls of equipment and soon disappear into the gate too.

'Mr Howie!' a voice calls out.

Howie turns to see Tom Jenkins and Steven Taylor walking towards him, both of them with huge smiles.

'Hello, Tom. Hi, Steven, good to see you lads again,' Howie smiles as they shake hands with genuine warmth.

'I knew you'd make it,' Tom says excitedly, looking back at the armed guards. 'Wow, you got more soldiers with you. Are they SF too?'

'Err, no. Some of them are ex-soldiers, police officers like you, and some army recruits we, sort of, found,' Howie says.

'Wow, and you're in charge of them all,' Tom looks at Howie with awe.

'Well, I wouldn't say that...' Howie starts.

'Yes, Mr Howie is in charge, with that man over there,' Dave says flatly, pointing at Big Chris.

The vehicles are slowly unloaded. Scared and terrified survivors drop down from the trucks and squint in the bright sunlight, or slowly emerge from cars to stretch wearily.

Howie watches as Sarah and Clarence work their way back along the fleet, telling the people to move down to the gates, where Blowers and Cookey are standing, smiling and joking, with their assault rifles strapped to their shoulders. Howie, Chris, and Dave stand near the front, watching the Saxon drive off, with Nick waving at them from the top, smiling as they go back down to the rear.

'They're good lads, those recruits,' Chris says.

'Very good, considering what they've been through,' Howie replies. 'Bloody brave, too.'

'We need to start thinking about defence,' Chris says, turning to look at Howie.

'No time like the present, then,' Howie replies as they make their way over and finally step through into Fort Spitbank.

They step into the shadow of the gate and pause for a few seconds to allow their eyes to adjust. The outer wall behind them stretches off in both directions, with a gap wide enough for a few vehicles to drive abreast before the inner wall looms up.

'Bloody big walls,' Chris mutters.

'Good job, really. We should just close the door and hide,' Howie replies to see Chris smiling back at him.

'Well, we could, but where would the fun be in that?' says Chris.

'Hello, gentlemen,' a voice calls out from behind them.

They turn to see an old man walking towards them, wearing a blue jumper marked with the *English Heritage* badge. A cravat is tucked into the front of the V-neck jumper. Grey roots show in his thinning, dyed ginger hair.

'Hi,' Howie responds as the man draws closer. They shake hands, and Howie watches as the man turns to Chris and Dave. Dave wiping his hand immediately after the shaking.

'So, which one of you is Mr Howie?' the man asks, looking at them each in turn.

'Err, that'll be me,' Howie says.

'Name's Hastings, Roger Hastings, as in the famous battle,' the man smiles at Howie.

'Oh, err, nice to meet you, Mr Hastings,' Howie replies.

'Oh, now, call me Roger,' the man beams back at him.

'How did you know my name?' Howie asks.

'There's been some talk of you in here. Quite some talk of Mr Howie and Dave rampaging round the country, killing off the heathen infected,' Roger talks quickly, with an effeminate voice.

'Oh, err, really? Well...' Howie stutters, unsure of how to respond.

'I think there's quite a few of the people you've met already in here. I keep hearing stories of the famous Mr Howie and Dave, and here you are in the flesh,' Roger speaks, waving his hand as he talks.

'Now, Roger, they've only just arrived, so take it easy with them,' Ted calls out, walking over to them. 'Howie, this is Roger Hastings. He was the principal guide here for the guided tours. Apparently, he's been here since the place was first built,' Ted adds, smiling at Howie.

'Oh, stop it, Ted, you big brute,' Roger simpers, smacking a limp hand on Ted's old but still solid shoulder.

'Excuse me for interrupting, but your doctor has set up an initial screening room just off to the right, inside the inner wall. The people are getting processed fairly quickly, and we should have them all inside quite soon. Debbie has got a few of her team getting details as they come through,' Ted says.

'Thanks, Ted, appreciate the update. How many people are already here?' Howie asks.

'You'll have to ask Debbie for the official figures, but with your lot coming in, I'd say that puts us to maybe seven thousand,' Ted replies.

'Seven thousand?! In here? Bloody hell,' Howie exclaims, looking at Chris, who looks equally stunned.

'Word spread quickly. People met up on roads and told each other about it, and well, they just kept coming. It slowed right down yesterday and the day before, but obviously, now we've got a lot more coming in,' Ted shrugs his shoulders.

'Listen, I need to get back and help Debbie before young Tom and Steven drive her mad. I'll leave you in the capable hands of Roger for the full experience,' Ted winks at them as he turns away.

'Thanks, Ted,' Howie calls out.

Ted waves back at them.

'Are you all ready?' Roger asks, hand on hip and head cocked to one side.

Howie glances at Chris, then looks to Dave, who is staring wide-eyed at Roger.

'Err, yeah, I guess so,' Howie says.

'Okay, boys, follow me, please,' Roger says as he starts to walk towards the inner wall.

They follow behind, exchanging glances and shrugging shoulders.

Stepping away from the gated section of the outer wall, they walk through a large gap in the inner wall and enter the Fort proper. The sight that greets them is staggering, and they stop to take in the view. Ahead of them lies the interior of the Fort – open land, with the thick inner wall running around the entire perimeter. The wide, open, grassed area of the Fort is thick with tents and marquees. Some wooden structures have been hastily erected amongst them. Tents of all sizes and shapes have been placed into the grounds. At first, it looks to be a mess of canvas and modern tents, but Howie quickly realises there has been order in the layout.

'Right, gents,' Roger drops the effeminate speech as he launches into full tour guide mode. 'Initially, we were using the buildings built into the Fort walls. As you can see, there are doors and gated entrances built into the inner wall. Within those doors and gated entrances are many rooms and tunnels. They were originally designed for ammunition storage, food and supplies, also barracks, sergeants' and officers' quarters. There were hundreds of soldiers based here. They had to live and work within the Fort, so everything they needed was within these walls. There is even a fresh water well here.'

'Does it still work?' Chris cuts in.

'Oh, yes, we've been using it constantly. They knew what they were doing back in those days. The site was very carefully chosen. They would have needed fresh water in the event of a siege, which they fully expected,' Roger continued.

'Anyway, we were using the buildings and rooms within the Fort walls as accommodation until we started getting more and more people arriving. Some of those people were surveyors and architects, so we were able to start designating the grounds to be used. We have sectioned off small areas, to the best of our ability, so we can keep walkways and avenues running between them.'

'It looks impressive,' Howie comments.

'It took some doing, but Sergeant Hopewell was very good at getting the right people into the right roles. We were cooking from a central point, but as the population grew, we had to separate that into several smaller cooking points. Each person or group that arrives only gets entry on the basis that they hand over their supplies to make sure the distribution is fair.'

'Has anyone refused?' Howie asks.

'A few got upset, which is understandable, but we were able to convince them to leave the supplies outside and step in to see it was a good set up and they were not going to be robbed. Most of them are just glad to get somewhere safe.'

'I can imagine. So have you got many supplies, then? A population this size will need a lot of food,' Howie says.

'Well, as soon as we got some organisation in here, we started sending out armed foraging patrols. They were tasked to gather supplies and avoid contact at all costs. They have been bringing back tents, sleeping bags, wet weather clothing, bedding, food, medicine, and anything that will help us. They've been raiding every outdoor and camping shop for miles. In terms of food, we are okay, not brilliant, but with careful rationing, we have been able to make sure everyone at least gets something,' Roger explains as they walk into the grounds and stroll down the wide central path.

People scurry about or sit, looking forlorn, outside of tents. They all stare at Dave, Howie, and Chris as they walk through, and Dave picks up on some nudges and whispers.

'Are the Fort buildings in use now?' Chris asks.

'Sergeant Hopewell uses one as admin offices, and there is a larger section of rooms built into the south side that have been taken over as a hospital. The rooms are the biggest, cleanest, and most recently repaired. In fact, most of the rooms and sections built into the south side are being used. We have the supplies section in there and the armoury.'

'The armoury?' Dave asks immediately upon hearing his favourite word.

'Yes, we have sourced some items: shotguns, rifles, and quite a lot of ammunition. It's where we stored the black powder for special events,' Roger explains.

'Black powder?' Dave asks again.

'The Fort has retained some of the original cannon and armaments, which one of the historical societies still uses for events and public displays.'

'How much black power do you have?' Dave asks, staring hard at Roger.

'Quite a lot,' Roger replies.

After a brief pause, while Dave soaks in that information, Roger continues, 'So that's the south side. Over towards the east section, we have the visitors' centre, gift shop, and café. We are using that as a meeting place and information point.'

'This is great, Roger. Really very good and well organised,' Howie says, genuinely impressed.

'We're not even at the start yet,' Roger replies, immediately back in his camp voice as they enter the visitors' centre.

There is a quiet calm inside the building, and Howie recognises the young lady sitting behind the reception desk, speaking to a few people.

'Hello, Terri,' Howie calls out to the female police officer that he met in the police station.

'Mr Howie, wow, I heard you arrived,' Terri smiles sweetly, rushing around the desk and running to hug Howie.

Howie responds, slightly embarrassed, as the pretty, blonde girl squeezes him tightly.

'Err, so how have you been?' Howie asks, unsure of what to say after the display of affection. He had thought of Terri Trixey as stuck up and prudish when they had first met.

'Well, apart from Tom and Steven being a pain in the arse, we've been very well,' Terri smiles back at him, finally releasing him from the hug.

'Hello, Dave, lovely to see you too.' Terri turns on Dave, stepping forward to embrace him. Howie holds his laugh in at the look of pure terror on Dave's face as he squirms uncomfortably.

'Terri, this is Chris,' Howie introduces them. 'Chris, this is Terri Trixey. She's a police officer from Portsmouth.' They shake hands formally; then, Terri immediately turns back to Howie.

'I heard you brought loads of people with you?' Terri asks.

'Yeah, Chris was in charge of a sort of commune in London that got overrun, so we managed to get them out and down here. Listen, we need to have a look around with Roger. Can I catch up with you in a bit?'

'Yes, of course, come back for a coffee as soon as you've finished,' Terri smiles at him.

'Err, right. Yes, of course, a coffee sounds nice,' Howie says.

'She seemed nice,' Chris smiles at Howie as they step away. 'Going for a coffee later, then?' he jokes, putting emphasis on the word coffee.

'Piss off, Chris. You did that with Clarence and my sister. Don't bloody start on me,' Howie laughs at the big man.

'Right, gents, up here, please,' Roger cuts in, back to business.

He leads them up a flight of metal stairs, across a small landing area, and then up onto the top of the inner wall.

'The Fort was commissioned in the 1850s and completed in 1858. The Fort was designed primarily as a motor battery with over fifty mortar placements, which could be angled to fire both out to sea and inland. The smaller sections we will see are for the mortar placements. These are primarily on the south and north walls. The larger sections are for the RMLs, which means–'

'Rifled muzzle-loader,' both Dave and Chris say in unison.

'Very impressive,' Roger responds. 'These forts, especially the larger ones like this, used new techniques and equipment that had never been deployed before. Those small metal rails that loop in the half circle around this section were used for the loading of the cartridges,' Roger keeps the information flowing as they slowly walk around the walls to the south side.

'The ground at the rear of the south wall was dug away, so the sea comes straight up to the side of the wall. It gets a bit shallower when the tide goes out, and over the years, the sediment and mud have built back up, but it's still pretty deep down there.'

'How deep?' Chris asks.

'At high tide, it's well over head height. At low tide, it's probably chest height,' Roger admits.

'We'll have to have look-outs posted at the rear, then,' Howie says.

'Why? Are you expecting trouble?' Roger asks.

Chris gives Howie a warning look.

'We'll talk later, mate, let's keep going,' Howie replies.

'As you wish,' Roger says.

'After the threat of French invasion finished, the Fort was used as public grounds and then re-commissioned for the First World War. By 1920, it had passed back into public control. Then the Fort was re-commissioned in 1939 for the outbreak of the Second World War. During this time, the Fort was taken over by the Navy and re-named HMS Spitbank. It was mainly used as an anti-aircraft site, but there were also radar installations, and due to the close proximity of the sea, it was used for the designing and testing of landing craft. Then, in the early 1950s, it again passed into public hands. English Heritage acquired the site during the late 1980s. By that time, most of the interior had fallen into disrepair. Work conducted by English Heritage and the historical societies brought it back to the present glory you see today.'

'You said that you had cannon,' Dave says once Roger has finished speaking.

'Yes, we do. Two on the south wall and two on the north wall. They are not the originals but the type they would have used in that era,' Roger replies.

'And they can be fired?' Dave asks.

'Yes, they can, but only by members of the historical society, but none of them made it here, and I don't think anyone else has the knowledge,' Roger says.

'I can work it out,' Dave says.

'Cannons are very difficult to use,' Roger says, with a concerned expression.

'I wouldn't worry. Dave likes blowing things up. Did you know he once blew up a cow?' Howie says lightly.

'A cow?' Roger asks, aghast.

'Oh, yes, you should hear some of the stories Dave has told me, incredible really,' Howie says, looking about nonchalantly.

'Oh, really, sounds fascinating,' Roger says, back to the camp voice. They reach the north wall and stand looking out. The view takes in the vista of the flat land stretched out in front of them. From the other side, it appeared that the outer wall was higher, but the design was well thought out, and the inner wall is raised slightly higher to allow a clear view, but with the ability to drop down to a lower section. Two sections of the front wall jut out, with large, flat platforms situated on top of the inner wall. A huge cannon rests on each buttress; the wide, dark mouth facing out to the flat lands.

'Big cannon,' Howie remarks.

Dave examines the cannon closely, feeling along the surface and peering at the rear end. Finally, he stands back up and nods.

'Roger, I apologise for being rude, but can you give us a few minutes, please,' Howie asks.

'Why, yes, of course. Call me when you're ready.' Roger walks off a respectable distance and turns to face the other direction.

'They'll come from that direction for sure,' Howie remarks,

looking out to the houses in the distance. 'And I wouldn't be surprised if they come round the back, too,' he adds.

'If the tide is low enough,' Chris says.

'But that's only a matter of six hours or so... Priorities. We need to make everyone aware of what's happening. We don't tell them details of how we plan to deal with it, just what the threat is. We know Darren was turned for a while before we knew about it, so we have to assume any of these could be turned too. I think we'll tell everyone what the threat is; then, we make secretive arrangements,' Howie says.

'It's actually an old tactic,' Chris explains. 'In olden days when kings suspected a traitor, they would give each general a set task. Some of them would be fake tasks and some real. All of the generals were told not to discuss their tasks with any of the others.'

'Can we do that?' Howie asks.

'No reason why not,' Chris replies.

'Right, so we've got a massive zombie army coming for us. What do we do?' Howie asks, staring out over the walls.

'Thin the numbers down before they get here,' Dave replies. 'And we keep thinning the numbers down until we can either meet them equally in battle or they leave.'

'I don't think they will leave, and the numbers will be huge by the time they get here. We need scouts out there so we get notice of when they arrive. We should gather all the weapons in and see which ones will be best, make sure ammunition is distributed evenly. Dave, these cannons can be fired, but I guess they don't actually fire cannonballs. Can we use something else?' Howie asks.

'Grapeshot – lots of little metal things that will spread out like a shotgun,' Dave replies.

'Good. How about the GPMG? Can we get that up here to fire down, or is it better on the vehicle?'

'There's a long slope over there. We should be able to get the Saxon up here,' Chris replies, looking back towards the south wall. Howie turns to see a long, wide, grassed slope leading up from ground level to the top of the inner wall.

'Perfect, we can get the Saxon up here, with Jamie sniping. See if he can take Darren out early in the game,' Howie says.

'If we organise quickly, we can dig pits, use spikes and caltrops. If there is enough black powder, we could rig something up in the housing estate, too,' Dave says.

'Caltrops?' Howie asks.

'Sharp, metal spikes hidden in the ground that pierce the feet. It won't kill them, but it will cause horrible injury and slow them down,' Chris replies for Dave.

'I like it, and the spikes?' Howie asks again.

'Put them in the ditch and cover them with something or dig pits and cover them up,' Chris explains. 'They're called Punji sticks.'

'Punji sticks? Sounds nice,' Howie says. 'Oh, like the sharpened bamboo canes?'

'Yeah, wood or metal will do it.'

'We've got a lot to do and not much time to do it in. If you're both happy, we'll get everyone together, tell 'em what's happening, and sort who can do what according to skills and materials we have available. Once we've done that, we'll set up in one of those rooms and use runners to tell them what we want done,' Howie says; the confidence and natural leadership showing in his voice.

'Agreed,' Chris responds, and Dave nods firmly.

'Roger, thanks for that, mate. We need to get everyone together. How can we do that?' Howie calls out.

'Everyone? That's a lot of people,' Roger replies in a business-like manner rather than the camp one.

'Yep, I know, but it's very important. The Saxon has a loudspeaker on it. Can we get that inside and everyone gathered round somehow?'

'Right, yes, of course. Leave it with me. I'll get some people on it now,' Roger replies before scampering off back down to ground level.

'It's gonna be a big fight,' Howie says after a pause.

'It will be, Mr Howie,' Dave replies.

'How many of these fights have you had so far?' Chris asks.

'A few,' Howie replies.

Chris looks to Howie and Dave to see the dark looks on their faces.

'There's gonna be a whole lot of them,' Chris says softly.

'Fuck 'em. We'll win,' Howie says in a firm voice.

CHAPTER SEVENTY-SEVEN

I stare out at the flatlands and look to the housing line in the distance. Dave is by my side. Chris a few steps away.

I hear noise behind me and turn to see Clarence and Malcolm climb up to stand with us. No words are spoken. We look to the view before us, and each of us thinks of what is to come. After a few minutes, I hear more noise behind me. Blowers and Cookey are coming to tell me they have been relieved by some of the Fort's guards. They are joined by Tucker, chasing after them noisily to try and catch up. They sense the mood and join us, looking out, spread out in a line. I almost don't hear the stealthy Jamie until he is standing at the end of the line; sniper rifle hanging from his shoulder. We stare at what we know is coming our way. What we know is coming to wipe us out. The hatred they have for us, *for me* is incredible, and thoughts pass through my head that maybe if I offered myself to them, they would leave the rest alone. But I know that isn't true. They won't stop until every last one of us is taken and turned. Can I do this? Can I fight these things again? Maybe we should turn and run, but the sea is behind us, and there is nowhere to run to. We could take boats and ships and sail away, but more of them will be there to meet us, wherever we go. We don't have boats or ships for several thousand people. Running is useless. Even if we used every vehicle we could find, they would seek us out. We need food, water, warmth, and rest. They need nothing.

Injuries hurt us. Blood loss makes us weak. Nothing less than death stops them. My head spins. I feel like I'm drowning. I'm in too deep, and I can't go anywhere or do anything else now. I dragged Dave across the country to get Sarah, and I picked those lads up on the way. Why did they follow me? I'm not a leader, not a soldier. I can't do this. Self-doubt and fear grow in me. I had Sarah to fight for before. I had something to keep me going, but she is safe now, and without that driving motivation, I don't know if I can do this again. The cost is too much. If I fail, then they all fail. They all die. I think of McKinney. Poor McKinney. He followed me, and I let him down. He died because of my mistakes. I taunted them and fuelled my revenge by killing too many. The loss of my parents provoked me, and I went after them. Poor McKinney followed me and did what I asked, and I watched him die. I held his sweet face, and he knew he was dying. I feel sick, weak, and pathetic. But then I look to my left and to my right, and I see those men and boys staring out, the fixed eyes, the set expressions. No words are spoken. No words are needed. I look behind me to the people going about mundane tasks in the Fort: washing clothes, playing with children, and walking between the tents. Smoke drifts up lazily from the cooking points.

The people look like normal people, trying to make sense of their worlds torn apart and destroyed. They are not safe. Sarah is not safe. None of us are safe. The Fort won't protect us forever. At some point, they will get through, and then we will all be taken.

The men beside me look resolute and ready, but I feel anything but that. I don't feel ready for this. We turn and start walking back down the slope. Each step feels heavy and wrong. I feel fake. These battle-hardened men keep looking at me like I have the answers. These are soldiers that have fought in proper wars. They were trained and taught tactics and strategies. I am a supermarket manager. I don't belong here on this slope, with these men. I belong down there, with the other survivors. Who am I to take this on and show the way? Who am I to think I could even breathe the same air as these professionals?

As we stride down, the people of the Fort stop and watch us. The sounds of the camp all cease, conversation stills into silence, and children stop playing. The new arrivals lining up for checking all stand and watch. We are higher than them. We stride like warriors. They know we have fought and will fight again, but they don't know what's coming. They look up, and I see many faces looking directly at me. Don't look at me. I am nothing. I shouldn't be here, let alone out in front, with these men following me. I can't do this.

Chris can lead. He's a proper leader, and he should take this from now. Not me.

We keep walking, and I notice Dave glancing at me, but I feel ashamed, and I can't look back at him. The others walk in silence behind us. We get to the bottom and then have to walk through the camp to get to the front area. I can't help but look to the people standing, watching me as I pass. Their faces look drained and old. Their skin is taut and tight from the lack of food and sleep. Dirty children, with unwashed faces, stand and stare at the heroes as they pass. The heroes led by a phoney, a fake, a nothing.

I can feel my leg swinging with each step. I am aware of each step and the thousands of eyes standing in silence to watch me. I understand that Roger has spread the word that we need to speak to them all, but suddenly, I am not the man to do it. The pressure of so many lives depending on me is too much. Just Dave and I running round quiet streets was one thing. Nothing can touch Dave, and there was no risk to him, so there was no pressure. All I had to do was get to London and get Sarah, but I made the recruits think I was something special, that I could lead them. I made them believe in me. We reach the Saxon, and I see Curtis Graves standing by the open driver's door. He nods at me as I get closer and respectfully moves out of the way, showing deference to the leader, showing that he was in my place, but now that I am back, he will stand aside.

I am a joke, and none of these men should show respect to me. I turn to see the thousands of Fort occupants walking towards us, crowding around the Saxon to hear what we have to say. My stomach flips, and I feel sick. My throat is instantly dry. There are thousands of eyes all watching me, waiting for me to speak, and more are coming. The new arrivals move away from the line. I recognise some of their faces from the night before. I see Sarah pushing through the crowd to stand by the side of Clarence. Clarence is a man-mountain. He looks the part, big and tough. He should do this. He has a deep voice and looks hardened from years of fighting. Chris is a big man too and looks like a leader. But they both look to me. Chris has shown deference too. He could step forward and do this, and these people would listen to him and believe in him. Why has he stepped back? Why is he doing this? Can't he see I'm a fake and out of my depth? Leaning into the Saxon to draw the handheld microphone feels like swimming through mud. My hand reaches out through treacle to switch the microphone on as Nick drops down from the look-out hole, on position with the GPMG.

'You should climb up top, Mr Howie, so they can all see you,' Nick smiles at me as he clambers out of the rear doors. I pull the cord and realise it is very long, long enough for me to climb up on the top. I wish it wasn't. I wish I could sit in here, hide away, and close my eyes, and they would all go away. But instead, I persist in continuing my farce, and I clamber out onto the front of the Saxon and then up onto the top. I stand up straight, and my legs feel like they will buckle as I look out at the thousands of faces all staring at me. The whole fucking lot of them are staring at me, watching, and waiting for the promised speech, the news they have been told I will deliver.

I lift the microphone to my mouth. My thumb hovers above the button. I look down. Dave is looking out to the crowd. Everyone else is watching me: Cookey and Blowers, Tucker, Sarah standing next to Clarence, Chris and Malcolm, with arms folded and legs apart.

Jamie, Curtis, and Nick stand together. They are closer to the Saxon than the rest, separating themselves from the main crowd. I hesitate as my thumb starts to depress the button. I freeze. I can't speak. I look at Sarah, and I see a proud look on her face. Her brother is standing on top of a military vehicle, addressing a crowd of thousands. Why can't she see I'm a fake. She must see I have frozen. What do I say? What do I tell them?

There is a massive army of infected zombies coming to eat you, but don't worry – I'm here, and even though I have no training or skills, I will protect you.

Fuck off. Get off, Howie! Get down and let a real warrior do this, I scream at myself as I feel the panic rising within me. I scan the crowd as the fear threatens to consume me. Faces old and young are waiting patiently. It feels that I look at each and every face in that crowd, and they see me for what I am. I look down and see Dave staring at me.

His eyes lock on mine. He knows I am freezing. He can see right through me. Our eyes lock, and something passes between us. A warrior born to fight staring at me hard, passing a message. His gaze is intense, so intense. He nods at me just once, and that's enough.

I look back up at the crowd and press the button down. My voice booms out, strong and confident, 'There is an army of thousands of those things coming for us. Tens of thousands, maybe more. They are coming, and they won't stop until every last one of us is dead and turned into one of them.'

Concerned expressions abound. This isn't why they came here. This isn't what they were expecting.

'They are coming, and nothing will stop them from getting here. The army has gone. The police are gone. There is no government, and no one is coming to save us. Behind you is the sea, and there is nowhere left to run. This Fort is strong, but they will get through, and they will kill every last one of us.' Fear and panic grips them, and tears start streaming down faces as parents clutch their children close.

'We have all lost loved ones. Just in one week, we have lost everything we knew. Our friends and families have been taken from us, and now they will come and try to kill us. The way of life we had is gone and will never come back. All that remains is what we have here and now. This is it. There is no rescue party coming, no fighter jets or warplanes that will wipe them out. This isn't a nightmare that will end. This *will* happen.' I wait and let those words sink in. They need to know how bad this is.

'We are few. Compared to the size of them, we are tiny. But there is one thing we have that they don't. We have life. We have life within us, and if you want that life to continue, then we have to fight.

One week ago, I was the same as you, living normally and working towards the future. But in that one week, I have changed. I decided not to just wait and let them come for me. I fought back. I met Dave, and then together, we fought back, and since then, we haven't stopped killing them. These brave, young men you see in front of me, they joined Dave and me, and together, we fought back, and we took them down. We took them down for killing our families and taking away our loved ones. We did not run away and hide. We went to them, and we fought, and we are still here. We learnt that if we stand together, we can survive.

We went to London, and our small group joined with Chris. Then, together, we fought against thousands of them. One small group of men took the fight to them, and we walked away from it. We lost men, but only a few, and for each one of ours they took, we took down many of theirs. We showed them we are not scared, and we do not fear them. Our small group took hand weapons and attacked them. They are dead already, and they don't feel pain. Blood loss doesn't hurt them like it hurts us. If we bleed, we get weak. They don't. The only way to kill them is by a massive loss of blood or by taking out the head and the brain. We learnt that, so we adapted, and we took them down.' I can feel my voice rising.

'Now we are here, with you, and this is clear – if we hide, they will find us. If we run, they will catch us. If we stand still and let them, they will take us. So what else can we do? I'll tell you what I want. I want to show them we will not hide and we will not run, and we will not stand still. We will fight. We will take as many of them down as we can. We may lose, but to the last man, we will fight back. They are infected. They are evil. They do not have the right to walk amongst us or take our air. They have taken everything from us, but this place, this place here, this is ours, and they will not take it from us without a fight. These men in front of you have stood on the line and survived. On this occasion, we got beaten back, but many times before, we took ground from them, not only surviving but winning.

When they come, we will be ready. We will prepare and do whatever it takes to make ready. Not one person here will sleep or rest until we are ready. There is no choice in this. Every man, woman, and child must be prepared to fight. There is no hiding away and letting the bigger boys fight for you. We will meet them, and we will fight them, and the last one standing will go down fighting!' I roar out at the crowd.

Chris smiles and turns to stare out at them. Clarence follows his lead, and I see all of them turn to face the crowd. I see defiance creeping in, firm looks as expressions harden. Men cross their arms, and women lift their heads to stand proud.

'We have the right to be here, and they do not. This will be hard. Harder than anything you can imagine, but we will work and prepare, and then we will meet them and show them no fear, for we shall stand proud. What do we need to do this? We need tools, weapons. We need to know who can make things, fix things – engineers and mechanics. We need foraging parties to go out and bring us the things we need to prepare. We need you to listen to the instructions we give and accept those instructions without argument. We need you to work and toil, and then, at the end of that, we will need warriors, fighters, brawlers and, scrappers, and most importantly…we're gonna need buckets of coffee to keep us awake.'

I get a few smiles and nods from this.

'We can do this. We few here at the front have shown that we can fight back. We did not roll over and accept it. We are humans, and throughout history, we have fought with each other. But now, at this time and at this place, all differences are set aside, and we stand together, and we fight together, and if needs be, we will die together, but they will know that we did not weaken, and we did not run.'

I see the change in them – faces look ready, men look to one another, with pride on their faces, and women stand straight and true, ready to fight to protect their own.

'Stand with us and show those things that we are not to be touched.' I nod once, firm and strong, and start to clamber down, to an explosion of cheering.

CHAPTER SEVENTY-EIGHT

'Thanks, Dave,' Howie says quietly after jumping down from the Saxon and sidling over to the small, quiet man.

'What for, Mr Howie?'

'You know very well what for,' Howie smiles at him.

'I don't know what you're talking about,' Dave replies.

'Okay, mate, thanks anyway,' Howie says again, still smiling at the glint in Dave's eye.

There is a sudden excitement and air of action within the group. Howie's words have stirred them, motivated them, and given the opportunity, they would charge out of the Fort now and attack the zombie army with just forks and spoons.

'Good speech, Howie,' Chris calls out over the noise from the thousands of voices all speaking at the same time.

'Thanks, mate,' Howie replies.

'Seriously, I've heard some corkers before. Normally from some officer, who will be safe in the base when we charge out, but that was good. You told them the truth and then got them going,' Chris says, closer now, but still having to raise his voice.

'Yeah,' Howie says, feeling just a little embarrassed.

'Honestly, Howie, it was good. Typical British spirit that was,' Malcolm joins in.

'Well, I had to tell them something,' Howie says, 'and the microphone is still there, mate. You can have a go if you want.'

'No, no, honestly, it was good stuff,' Malcolm laughs.

'Hey, Howie, that was great.' Sarah appears at his side, still accompanied by the giant Clarence.

'Thanks, Sis,' Howie replies, uncomfortable with all the praise that is being heaped on him. 'Right, we need somewhere private to work,' he says to Chris and Dave. They both nod in return, and Chris strides off to find Roger.

'Why the secrecy?' Sarah asks, concerned.

'That lad, Darren, he was turned for some time before we knew. Any one of these could be the same, so we can't risk everyone knowing exactly what we are doing.'

'Oh, that makes sense...' Sarah looks around, staring at the many faces.

'It's possible. There's too many here to check everyone, and Darren wasn't bitten or scratched that we knew about,' Howie says. 'So for safety's sake, we have to assume any of them could be.' He looks around at the crowd. Their faces suddenly look sinister – plots being hatched and plans being made.

'Howie, Roger has a room for us that we can work from. You ready?' Chris calls out, walking towards him.

'Yes, mate, I'm ready. Who are we taking with us?'

'I was thinking you, me, and Dave definitely. I would like Malcolm and Clarence too if you're okay with it. Any of yours?' Chris answers.

'Blowers is good, but then we'd have to ask Cookey too. That pair are joined at the hip. I think we'll get them initially, then stick them on the door to prevent anyone else walking in. That sound okay?'

'Hmmm, maybe we should just go with you, Dave, and me, then.' Chris rubs his bearded chin.

'I know what you mean, but Malcolm and Clarence are good, experienced blokes. It would be good to have their input,' Howie replies.

'What if they're infected, though?' Chris asks.

'True, any of them could be. Fuck it, any of us could be, for that matter,' Howie says.

'Okay, so we get Doc Roberts in with us initially. He checks us over first, then a visual check on each other, and we crack on?' Chris suggests.

'Yep, sounds good to me. We need everyone to meet over at the south wall, so we can talk quietly,' Howie replies.

'You go. I'll round them up and send them on,' Sarah says.

'Thanks, Sarah. Are you sure you don't mind doing that?' Howie asks.

'No, it's okay. I'll get Clarence to stand over them while I smile sweetly,' Sarah laughs, leading the big man away, with her hand on one of his meaty arms, and his face going bright red again.

It takes many minutes to walk to the south side of the Fort and the rooms set aside by Roger. Survivors stop to shake hands with Howie and Chris at every few steps, patting them on the back and calling out as they pass. At first, Howie tries to move on quickly, but after the first few people, he gets a mischievous glint in his eye.

'Hey, don't just thank me. Dave and Chris here did as much as me,' Howie replies, then watches as the people move on to offer handshakes to Chris and Dave.

Chris takes it in his stride, smiling good-naturedly and making comments while looking them in the eye, inspiring confidence, and looking every inch the warrior leader. Dave, on the other hand, looks aghast at the many hands being thrust in front of him, knowing that to refuse would cause offence but clearly hating the idea of touching so many people.

'Don't forget to smile, Dave,' Howie calls out as they work their way through the crowd.

Dave glares back as he frantically wipes his hand on the back of his trousers between each handshake.

Howie and Chris both laugh as they watch Dave trying to smile. The corners of his mouth turning up and showing teeth, which looks very strange on the normally impassive face. Eventually, they break through to the far side as Dave pulls a bottle of antibacterial spray from his pocket and starts cleaning his hands.

'Sorry, Dave, I couldn't resist it. Your face was a picture,' Howie laughs as Dave offers him the spray bottle.

'It's okay, Mr Howie,' Dave says, vigorously rubbing his hands.

'Is it here?' Chris asks, looking at the south wall looming above them. Several doors set into the wall are spread along the ground floor.

'I don't know. Where's Roger?' Howie replies.

'Coo-eee, gentlemen, over here,' Roger calls out, leaning out of a doorway further up and waving an arm at them. They walk up and enter the door. The room is big and square, with a solid-looking, old table in the middle. Large, rolled-up sheets of paper lie on the top of the table. Howie looks up to see a single electric bulb hanging down.

'You've got power?' Howie asks as Roger turns the switch on.

'These rooms have a dedicated generator supplying power. You can't turn all the lights on at the same time, but it will mean you can work privately, with the door closed if you need to,' Roger replies. 'Through that door are more rooms. Some of them have old camp beds and chairs if you need to rest. Let me know if you need anything.'

'This is great, thank you, Roger. Where will you be?' Howie says.

'Just a few doors down. That's where Sergeant Hopewell is working from, and the hospital is further down,' Roger replies. 'Oh, there's more of you,' he adds, backing away from the door as the recruits and more of Chris's men start piling in. They chat quietly as they wait for everyone to arrive.

'Nick, can you nip down a few doors and see if Sergeant Hopewell and Ted are there, please, mate,' Howie asks.

'No worries, Mr Howie,' Nick calls out, disappearing out of the door.

Howie looks amongst the group crowded into the room. The recruits are chatting to each other and now mingling more with Chris's men and women left from the commune. Howie thinks of the losses they took last night, and the image of McKinney flashes back into his mind.

'We can grieve later,' he mutters.

'Did you say something, Howie?' Chris asks.

'No, mate, just talking to myself,' Howie replies.

'First sign of madness,' Chris smiles as he looks back to the room.

'Don't even joke about that,' Howie laughs.

'What are those, Dave?' Dave has unrolled some of the large sheets and is bent over, studying them.

'Maps and plans of the Fort and surrounding areas,' Dave replies.

'Hello, what's all this, then?' Ted booms out as he strides confidently into the room, followed by Sergeant Hopewell and Terri, who immediately smiles at Howie.

'You never came back for that coffee,' Terri admonishes him.

'Hi, Terri. Err, well, kind of been busy,' Howie replies, feeling Chris and a few of the others watching him.

'That's okay. I heard your speech. It was amazing,' Terri says, staring with big, blue eyes directly at Howie. Her pink lips revealing perfect, white teeth as she smiles again.

'Oh, yeah. Err, thanks Terri.' Howie feels himself starting to blush.

'Hi, I'm Sarah, Howie's sister,' Sarah steps forward, becoming aware of her brother's discomfort. They start chatting as Howie discreetly steps over to Chris.

'I don't know you very well, Howie, but I've not seen you nervous before,' Chris says quietly.

'I always get nervous around pretty girls,' Howie whispers back as Chris throws his head back, laughing loudly and drawing attention from the whole room.

'I've seen you charge into thousands of those things,' Chris says, still unable to use the word zombies, 'and then give a rousing *gung-ho* speech to thousands of people, and you get nervous round one pretty girl?'

'Shush, keep your voice down. Oh, bollocks, I think she heard you,' Howie mutters, seeing Terri staring over at him.

'I think we're all here,' Malcolm says as Doc Roberts enters the room, with his white lab coat flapping open.

'Thank fuck for that,' Howie mutters again, grateful for the reprieve. 'Can someone close the door? Thanks. Right, most of us know what's coming our way, and these people will be looking to us for confidence and reassurance. I know we're all tired and have had enough, but without us, they don't stand a chance. The plan is that a few of us will be working from here and sending out instructions for what's needed.'

'And we expect you to see them through,' Chris steps in.

'From now on, only those with a reason are to go up onto the walls, and I expect each of you to try and make sure that happens. We know that people can be infected and either not know it or hide it very well, so we will be taking every precaution to prevent all of our plans from becoming known. If you are given a task, please do not question it or discuss it with anyone else.

Debbie, we will need a list of skills, and we are going to need runners too – people that can run out and pass messages, or find the people we need,' Howie says.

'Okay, I've got more lists than you will ever need, and I'm only a few doors down. Also, we've got a pool of bored, older kids that need something to do. We can use them as runners. I'll organise that and have them nearby,' Debbie replies.

'Good, we also need guards on the gate. I don't want to tell the people out there what they can and can't do, but for now, we need to restrict who goes in and out,' Chris continues after Sergeant Hopewell finishes. 'There's some rooms back there to relax in or outside, but stay close and wait for further instructions. Has anyone got any questions?'

'Weapons, sir. We've got some, and the people out there have some too, and I think there's probably some more knocking about. Are we going to centralise them and work out who has what?' one of Chris's men shouts out from the back.

'Good point. We'll cover it and make sure they are distributed to the right people and in the right place,' Chris answers.

'We're going to need sleep. We've been going all day yesterday and all night. If we work through the night and then fight tomorrow, we'll be dropping like flies,' a man says from the front, half-dressed in a police uniform.

'Try to sleep when you can, rest when you can, but ultimately, tough shit. If they come and we're not prepared, we'll die. Simple as that,' Howie replies quickly and without humour.

An awkward silence follows, with the armed men and women looking down at their feet, avoiding Howie's intense stare.

'But...Mr Howie, we're exhausted. We've been fighting and going for a long time. We can't keep going like this,' the man whines, rubbing his forehead.

'Okay, mate. I'll tell you what. Why don't you fuck off and get some sleep, then? Go and sleep, and feel sorry for yourself, and whine that no one is giving you a suitable rest period. Even better, we'll send someone to the massive zombie army and ask them nicely to please wait so we can all have a nice sleep,' Howie's voice rises as he speaks, and the darkness spreads across his face. '*I'm sorry, zombie army, but we're tired, and you're pushing us too hard.* Get this, mate, we are all going to die and become brain-eating zombies if we don't do whatever it takes.'

'Yeah, I get that, but listen, there's only so much we can take before we just drop,' the man carries on, oblivious to the whining tone of his own voice.

'MAN UP AND DEAL WITH IT, OR DIE,' Dave's voice booms out, causing everyone to jolt backwards. The man goes to speak again, but Dave steps forward with lightning speed and stands nose to nose with him.

'WHAT? DO YOU HAVE SOMETHING ELSE TO SAY?' Dave shouts at him.

'No, nothing,' the man replies, avoiding Dave glaring at him and staring down at his own feet.

'DO YOU WANT TO DIE?' Dave bellows.

'No.'

'DO YOU WANT TO LIVE?'

'Yes,' the man replies quietly.

'MOANING AND WHINING IS MORE INFECTIOUS THAN THOSE THINGS OUT THERE. IF I HEAR YOU MOANING AGAIN, ME AND YOU WILL HAVE AN ISSUE. IS THAT CLEAR?'

'Yes,' he mutters. 'I'm sorry, I didn't mean to whine. I lost some good mates back there, and I'm in shock, but you're right, and I apologise to you and everyone else in here,' the man says, turning back to face the room with a look of shame.

Another one of Chris's men steps forward and rests his hand on the man's shoulder, nodding gently at him.

'Debbie, can you get on to those lists and have the runners ready? Tucker, would you mind arranging for some food and cleaning supplies to be brought over?' Howie asks, breaking the silence.

'Yes, of course. Is there anything else?' Debbie asks.

'No, that's it. Get some rest while you can but stay close,' Howie says.

The door opens, and Debbie files out first, followed by Ted.

Howie turns to see Terri coming back into the door. The sunlight catches her golden hair, framing her soft skin and casting an angelic halo about her. Howie finds his breath catching in his throat as she smiles at him. *She is beautiful*, he thinks, staring at her with an open mouth.

'You'll catch flies,' she says quietly.

'What? Eh?' Howie says, snapping back to reality.

'Sarge said for me to stay close and act as your liaison officer,' Terri says. 'Are you okay, Howie?'

'Yep,' he replies too quickly.

'Now, I wouldn't do this for anyone else as I'm not a bloody secretary, but I'm going to get you some strong coffee and stay here while you drink it, got it?' she says seriously.

'That sounds lovely, Terri. We need to speak to Doc Roberts for a few minutes anyway,' Howie replies.

'Did someone say something about coffee?' Chris calls out, looking up from the maps on the table.

'I'll come with you,' Sarah interrupts, knowing what the men need to do.

They leave the room, and Howie calls out for Blowers, asking him to prevent anyone coming in from the back rooms for a few minutes.

Blowers nods once and turns to face the other way, standing with his arms folded and blocking the door.

'Doc, shall we?' Chris asks.

'Shall we what, Chris? You asked me to come here, but I don't know why?' Doctor Roberts snaps back in his usual, clipped tones.

'Doctor, we need to make sure, as best we can, that none of us three are infected. Darren, one of my lads, was infected for a while before he turned, and we can't risk any of us three turning while we are planning,' Howie explains as the doctor holds a hand up to stop him talking.

'Right, got it. I understand, gentlemen. You are going to be planning the defence from here, and if one of you is infected, then you could potentially let the other side know about the plans. Is that it?'

'Yes,' Howie and Chris say in unison.

'There is no sure way of checking without blood tests, but we don't have time for that. There are some tell-tale signs we have learnt: an increase in body temperature and increased heart rate. I'll do the best I can and check you visually. Strip off,' the doctor commands.

Howie and Chris shrug at each other and start to slowly peel their clothes off. Dave doesn't hesitate and is stripped naked within a minute. Doctor Roberts starts with Dave, checking his temperature first and then listening to his heart rate. He examines his eyes closely, shining a bright light into the pupils, then into his ears. After that, the doctor conducts a very close visual check, examining each inch of skin to check for scratches or open wounds.

'Turn round,' the doctor orders and starts checking Dave from behind. First, his back, then down to his buttocks, and then his legs.

'Bend over,' the doctor commands, shining a torch into Dave's backside.

'I can see that light shining out your mouth, Dave,' Chris jokes.

'Clean and healthy, as far as I can tell. Chris, you are next.' The doctor drops down onto his knees to examine Chris's legs, and after a few minutes, the doctor pauses and stares over at Dave. Howie and Chris realise the same thing and both stare over at him.

'You can get dressed now, Dave,' the doctor says quietly as the door opens, and Terri steps in, holding a large, metal flask.

'Oh, my god,' Terri fumbles with the heavy flask, staring at the three naked men standing behind the table.

Howie and Chris both quickly cover their privates as Dave spins around to face the other way.

'Err, I'll leave this here,' Terri says, flustered, as she walks further into the room and places the flask on the table, glancing at Howie as she does so.

'We're just being examined by the doctor,' Howie says feebly.

'All at the same time?' Terri says, then sees the doctor crouching down, examining one of Chris's kneecaps.

'Oh, hi, Doc,' she says and smiles at Howie trying to cover his bits with both hands. 'I'll leave you to it.' She smiles and walks out as Chris bursts out laughing.

'That wasn't funny,' Howie groans to the sound of Blowers stifling laughter from the doorway.

'I think she enjoyed it,' Chris laughs.

'Stop laughing and stand still please, now turn round, and bend over,' the doctor orders, oblivious to the interruption.

CHAPTER SEVENTY-NINE

'They have to approach from the front. The Fort is built onto this spit,' Chris says, running his finger around the outline of the land on the map. 'They cannot attack from the sides or rear in any great numbers, so at least we know to expect a frontal attack.'

The three of them pore over maps, drinking strong coffee, after being left with explicit instructions from Doctor Roberts to report any changes in body temperature and to watch each other closely.

'Okay, so we know which way they are coming. We've got a large, open, flat land in front of us with two big banks, one of which drops down into a type of dry moat. Before that, we've got the housing estate,' Howie continues, describing the area.

'If I can use that black powder, I should be able to rig up some traps within the housing estate,' Dave cuts in.

'What sort of thing?' Howie asks. 'I don't think we've got any cows to blow up.'

'I'll have to have a look round and see what's there first, but the large numbers they're bringing means they will have to funnel through the estate,' Dave replies.

'Cows?' Chris asks, puzzled.

'Dave once blew up a cow to take out an enemy target,' Howie explains.

'Oh, was that you? We heard about that,' Chris says.

'And a refinery too,' Howie adds.

'You did the refinery? We were on standby for that. Christ, that went up, didn't it? You should definitely rig the estate, then,' Chris says.

'How many will you need?' Howie asks.

'Just one other. Jamie?' Dave replies.

'Yeah, good idea. How about you take a few more and place them for spotters, put them out as far as you can,' Howie says.

'Okay, Mr Howie, we'll take a couple of vehicles and use one of them as the furthest obs point. Do they have any spare radios here?'

'Check with Debbie. Those radios that we used yesterday, will they reach into the estate from here?' Howie asks.

'Not likely,' Chris replies, shaking his head.

'Dave, see if you can source some more. We will need constant radio contact with you, and make sure you can get back quickly if it goes bent,' Howie says.

'Okay, Mr Howie,' Dave replies, gathering his backpack and assault rifle before heading out the door to find Jamie, who is sitting patiently in the sun.

'You're with me,' Dave says to him.

'Okay,' Jamie replies, instantly on his feet and ready.

Howie walks into the back room to find several of the recruits and Chris's guards dozing quietly.

'Blowers, can you get Cookey, Nick, and Curtis to come in, please, mate,' Howie asks, keeping his voice low.

'On it, Mr Howie,' Blowers replies, instantly awake and alert.

Within minutes, he rounds the others up and leads them back into the room with Howie and Chris.

'Lads, between the four of you, I want to make sure the tops of the walls stay clear from anyone else. Curtis, I want you to get the Saxon up onto the inner north wall. The slope is wide enough to drive up. Position it so that the GPMG can fire down onto the flat lands. Nick and Curtis, you take the Saxon and swap round between manning the GPMG and making sure no one else goes up on the wall. Blowers and Cookey, I want you both on the front gate, making sure no one goes outside. Blowers, find a couple of Chris's guards and get them positioned at some of the access points up onto the walls to politely discourage anyone from going up. Got it?' Howie asks.

'Yes, sir.' Howie gets a chorus of replies as they ready themselves and move out of the room.

'So that's Dave and Jamie taking care of the estate and putting spotters out, and then the walls and lookouts taken care of. What's next?' Howie turns to Chris.

'Weapons,' Chris replies and steps out of the door to call Malcolm inside.

'Malcolm, find Roger and get a suitable place to work from. Get an inventory of all the weapons we have and ammunition. Do it as quickly as you can. Also try and find out if there are any gunsmiths anywhere near here that we can raid or make use of,' Chris says to him.

Malcolm nods back and is gone within seconds. Chris disappears into the back room and drags two chairs over to the table, placing one on each side.

Howie pours more coffee, and they sit down, examining the maps closely while drinking the strong java.

'I remember reading historical novels about cannon firing grapeshot...' Howie says. 'If Dave can get those cannons working, we can use them from the tops of the wall.'

'Good idea. Chains, nuts, and bolts – anything will do for them,' Chris replies, leaning forward to look closely at him. 'Listen, we can go for a siege situation and pick them off bit by bit. Maybe we don't have to go out and meet them face to face, Howie.'

'It won't work, Chris. If we bed in and one of these thousands of survivors in here turns, all it would take is for them to infect a couple. Those couple get a few each, and within minutes, we're attacked from inside and outside, with nowhere to go. I honestly think we should do what we can to reduce their numbers and pick them off, but then we end it, once and for all,' Howie replies, staring back at him.

'I do agree with you, and I think it's the right thing to do, but I want to be sure we know what we're getting into.'

'I know, mate. I think we need to choose our ground. We can use the estate and flat lands to lay traps and pick them off. The banks and the deep ditch we can use too. That open land between the ditch and the outer wall, that should be our ground,' Howie says, indicating the area on the map.

Chris nods, looking down at the area Howie traces with his fingers.

'It gives us some cover from the cannon firing overhead. Plus, we get to use the banks and ditches to slow them. It's a big enough area.'

'There it is then, our ground,' Howie says quietly. They both stare down at the map, just marks on paper showing the outline of the Fort walls and the positions of the embankments and ditch.

'Who'd have thought it. One hundred and fifty years ago this was built to protect us from the French, and now it's being used again to stop a zombie army,' Howie chuckles.

'I hate that word,' Chris mutters with distaste.

'We could dig some ditches along the edge of the flatlands, by the estate, then put the spikes down in the longer grass and then something after the first bank...' Howie says.

'If we put vehicles on this side of the first bank, they wouldn't be seen until they're coming down the sides,' Chris cuts in.

'Okay, so a load of vehicles set to explode; then, they go up the second bank, and they've got the deep ditch. Fuck it, let's fill it with petrol and blow the shit out of 'em,' Howie laughs.

'Why not? As long as we're far back enough, it's a good idea,' Chris replies seriously.

A knock at the door interrupts them, and Terri walks in.

'You're dressed, then?' she asks lightly.

'Dave asked me to give you this. He's got one and said to tell you the spotters have them too.'

'Ah, that's great. How many more have we got?' Howie asks.

'I don't know. Malcolm came in and took all the radios into one of the other rooms further down,' she replies.

'Okay, Terri, have we got any diggers or plant machinery here?' Howie asks, taking the radio.

'I'll find out. The sergeant has lists of everything,' Terri answers before smiling at Howie again and heading for the door.

'That coffee was really nice, by the way,' Howie calls out. She turns and smiles back again before closing the door behind her.

'*Howie to Dave,*' he speaks into the radio, holding the big side-button down.

'*Dave receiving. Go ahead, Howie.*'

'*Radio check. Receiving you loud and clear.*'

'*Dave to Howie. Roger. Loud and clear this end. Out.*'

'Right, let's go and find Malcolm, and see what he's got,' Howie says.

They step out into the bright sunlight to find guards lazing about, stretched out in the warm sun, leaning against the wall, or chatting to each other and the survivors.

Howie and Chris stroll down until they reach Sergeant Hopewell's office. They see her sitting at a desk and looking up at Terri.

'Hi, Mr Howie.' Howie turns to see Tom and Steven walking towards him from the main camp area.

'Hey, mate, everything all right?' Howie replies.

'Yeah, the sergeant's got us patrolling the camp to show a presence. Everyone keeps asking us when the fighting starts or if they can have weapons,' Steven answers.

'Steven, Mr Howie was asking me, not you,' Tom says petulantly.

'No, he wasn't. He was asking both of us,' Steven fires back.

'I'm the policeman. You're just a community officer, so leave the serious stuff to us.'

'No, Tom, you *were* a police officer, but Mr Howie said there isn't a police force anymore, so if there isn't one, how can you be a police officer? Ha, we're both the same now.'

'No, I've been trained more than you,' Tom says defensively.

'Trained in what? How to take a statement? Custody procedures? That doesn't really help us now, does it?'

'I've got more unarmed defence training than you, Steven.'

'No, you don't. We both got the same. You just got taught how to use your baton and pepper spray. I know because we partnered up for the training, you bloody idiot.'

'Lads, listen, I think it's probably fair to say that you're both the same now, but you're both very valued, and it's good you're going round the camp and letting people know you are here,' Howie says diplomatically.

'Ha, fuck you, Tom Jenkins,' Steven shouts triumphantly as Tom stares at him in horror.

'I'll leave you to it, lads,' Howie chuckles and steps into the office. Terri and Sergeant Hopewell both stare out, shaking their heads.

'They'll never bloody change, that pair,' the sergeant mutters.

'They seem good lads, though,' Howie laughs.

'Did you find out about the diggers or plant machinery, Terri? Oh, hi, Sarah. I didn't see you there.'

'My job was mainly administration, so I thought I'd put myself to good use. Besides, Patricia here was feeling a little lost, so I said she could stay with me,' Sarah replies, indicating the girl sitting further in the room, drawing on some paper.

'Where's the other woman that was with you? Mary, wasn't it?' Howie asks.

'She's getting cleaned up, then is coming over here,' Sarah says.

Howie turns back to see Terri standing at a desk loaded with thick piles of paper.

'Bloody hell, that's a lot of lists,' Howie says.

'Language, Howie,' Sarah warns.

'Sorry, err, so...about the diggers?'

'Right, so we have compiled a list of all the people within the Fort: name, date of birth, and last known address. We added work skills and any former military training or firearms experience, pistol or rifle clubs, that kind of thing. We have divided and subdivided the interior of the Fort into sections and allocated people into those sections, so we know roughly the area they should be in. We also appointed a contact person within each section that we can go to then and find out where the section residents are. The idea is that each resident of each section reports to the section contact where they will be in case they are needed. We have also listed every vehicle in the area and if they are usable or if we have access to them with keys. We categorised each vehicle into commercial or non-commercial, with a reference to how much fuel the vehicle has, and of course, which fuel type. So, in answer to your question...' Terri pulls a clipboard from the pile and starts flicking through the lists.

'You've listed the people that have military experience or firearms knowledge?' Howie asks.

'Yes,' Terri answers without looking up.

'Can you get that list to Malcolm? He's setting up an armoury here, somewhere. I don't suppose you recorded what kind of firearms they have previously used, have you?' Chris asks.

'Of course, we have,' Terri replies, still not looking up. 'We'll get that to him straight away. Ah, here it is. Yes, we have access to three diggers, and here's a cross-reference to the people that can operate them.' Terri looks up and smiles; her blue eyes twinkling.

'Wow, that's great,' Howie says, amazed at the volume of work they've undertaken already. 'Can you get those digger drivers to us as soon as possible?'

'Of course, *Mr Howie*,' Terri says mock demurely as she steps outside.

'Can I have three runners in here, please?' Terri calls out.

Within seconds, three slim teenage boys run into the room, almost standing to attention in front of Terri, who runs her finger down the list of vehicles and then starts flicking through the pages of names of the Fort occupants.

'I need you to find George Kimberly from Section 2, Martin Aylesbury from Section 7, and Mark Donovan from Section 18. Bring them back here as soon as possible, thank you.' Terri looks up with a stern face, nodding at the boys to get moving.

They run into the thick crowds and weave through the tents and structures.

'That's brilliant,' Howie says, watching the lads sprint away.

'Is there any kind of blacksmiths here or workshops?'

'There's workshops, quite well equipped too, from what Ted told me,' Sergeant Hopewell replies.

'Terri, can you also find engineers, mechanics, and metal workers and send them up to us?' Howie asks.

'Of course, leave it with me. I'll get more of those runners out,' she replies, examining her lists.

'Those runners are great,' Howie says admiringly.

'Oh, those boys all like our Terri here. Especially when she smiles at them,' Debbie says without looking up from the papers in front of her.

'I bet they do,' Howie says, then instantly blushes as he realises what he said. 'I mean, err, I'm sure they do. Shall we go and see Malcolm, then?' he says, turning to Chris, who is smiling broadly and leaning against the wall.

'Or we could stay here and watch you trying to pull your foot out of your mouth,' Chris replies.

'Very funny. Thanks for the list, Terri. Err...we'll be off, then,' Howie says, turning to see Sarah leaning back in her chair, watching him with amusement.

Howie steps out, rubbing his face, groaning softly to himself. Chris comes out, shaking his head silently. They walk down a few steps to find an armed guard outside a set of solid-looking metal gates that lead into a tunnel.

'Is Malcolm in here?' Chris asks the guard.

'Yes, Chris, down there, to the right.' The guard opens the gate to admit Howie and Chris.

They enter the short tunnel and turn right into a large room. Natural light trickles in from barred windows set into the wall. Long workbenches run down one side, and weapons of all types are stacked up next to boxes of ammunition. Malcolm and Clarence work their way through the weapons, checking and clearing.

'Hi, Chris, we've got quite a lot here, really,' Malcolm says, straight to the point. 'We've got some decent rifles, which will be good on the walls, for longer range. We've separated the assault rifles; though, some of them are only 9 millimetre. No good for longer range. There's loads of shotguns, too.'

'How about ammunition?' Chris asks.

'You can never have enough rounds,' Malcolm replies. 'We've got quite a lot, but it'll soon go if we get into a period of sustained firing.'

'Did you find out if there are any gunsmiths nearby?' Chris asks, picking up one of the rifles from the bench.

'There's a few, actually. All in a ten-mile radius,' Malcolm replies.

'Clarence, can you get some people together and a couple of vehicles – vans would be good. We're going to need a foraging party. See Sergeant Hopewell next door. I bet she's got a list of them somewhere,' Chris says to the huge man.

'Got it,' Clarence rumbles, putting down an assault rifle.

'What else do we need?'

'Any kind of weapons you can get: guns, knives, swords, axes, anything we can use. Also, we'll need nuts, bolts, and short chains to make grapeshot for the cannon.' Chris explains.

'Clarence, try and get some more arrows too,' Malcolm calls out.

'Arrows?' Chris asks, looking about.

'There's quite a few competition-level archers in here. Have you seen the range and power on modern bows?' Malcolm replies, indicating the end of the bench and the modern bows racked up next to a pile of arrows.

'Fair enough, get whatever you can, Clarence,' Chris says.

'On it,' Clarence replies and steps out of the room.

Back in their planning room, Howie and Chris sit down and go over what they've already set in motion, discussing the finite details. There is a knock at the door.

'Come in,' shouts Howie.

'Hi, we were asked to come here?' A middle-aged man enters, followed by two younger men.

'Hi, thanks for coming. Excuse me asking, but who are you?' Howie stands, holding his hand out to the closest one.

'I'm George,' the first man answers. The other two introduce themselves as Martin and Mark.

'Ah, you must be the digger drivers, then?' Howie asks.

'Yeah, we are. Not just diggers, but anything like that really,' George answers.

'Do you know each other?' Chris says, watching the men closely.

'I've known Martin for years. We worked together before, err, before this. We only met Mark here, though.'

'When did you arrive?' Howie asks.

'Saturday afternoon. We heard the broadcast and came straight here. Me and Martin didn't have far to come. We live near each other, too. Well, we *lived* near each other...'

'Mark, when did you arrive here?' Chris takes over the questions.

'Sunday morning, sir,' Mark answers in a polite tone.

'I apologise if this is an insensitive question, but did you come with your families?' Chris asks.

'I've got my wife and son with me, sir,' Mark says.

'We've got our wives and children here too,' George adds.

'Have any of you been bitten, scratched or had any direct contact with those...'

'He means the zombies. Have you had any contact with the zombies?' Howie finishes off for Chris.

'No, sir, I saw them, but we hid in the house and then got down here quickly. They were in the street when we left, but it was daytime, and they were slow,' Mark says first. Howie looks to George and Martin.

'Well, we had a spot of bother getting out of our road. There was a couple of them in the way...' George says nervously.

'What did you do?' Chris asks.

Martin and George look at each other, then back at Chris.

'We, err, well, we ran them over with the van,' George says after a pause.

'You were all in one van, and you ran them over? Did you make contact with them physically, get any blood on you, or get cut, bitten, or scratched, or did any of your families?' Chris says, staring hard at them.

'No, sir, nothing like that. The van got blood on it, but none of us did,' George says as Martin nods in agreement.

Chris looks to Howie, nodding once.

'Okay, sorry about the questions, but we had to be sure none of you were infected or ran the risk of being infected. We have a task for you, but before we say anything about it, would you all be willing to have a full medical examination?' Howie asks.

They each nod and reply that they would agree to the exam.

CHAPTER EIGHTY

After the men are thoroughly examined by the doctor, Chris starts to explain.

'Okay, gentlemen, we need some trenches dug into the ground near the housing line, but we want to do it so we can hide them afterwards or, at least, cover them up so they're not easily visible. Is that possible?' Chris asks. The three men look to each other, thinking, until George takes a small step forward, nominating himself as the unofficial spokesman.

'It depends on how deep and how wide?' George replies. 'The grass is long enough out there to cut some down and lay the cuttings across the top. That would cover it and blend in somewhat, but only if it's not too wide or deep.'

'We want it roughly two yards wide so it's not easy to step over or jump and deep enough to put either some spikes in or some flammable material,' Howie replies.

'Oh, I get it. Like a trap for the zombie army,' Martin cuts in. 'Yeah, that can be done. For spikes, you would want a decent drop in there for the body to be impaled, though.'

'Yeah, a few inches wouldn't do it. Unless they were razor sharp, that is; otherwise, you'd need a couple of feet, at least,' Mark adds.

'I reckon we could dig 'em out about three feet deep and a couple yards wide and be able to cover them over. It won't be pretty, but I reckon we know what you want, and we'll do the best we can,' George says earnestly as Martin and Mark both nod.

'Good, we'll have some guards go out with you to give you some protection. We need to do this now, though. The most important thing is that you do not mention a word of this between here and getting outside the gate. That is vitally important. Is that clear?'

'Sir, we won't say anything, but could you let our families know we'll be back a bit later? They'll only worry otherwise,' Martin replies.

'Of course, we will. Chris will show you on the map exactly what we need, and I'll be back in a minute,' Howie says, ushering the men over to the table.

Chris indicates the area of flatland immediately in front of the row of houses.

'We need it all the way across the entire width of the spit. Will three of you be enough to do this?' Chris asks.

'Yes, sir, the digging won't take long. Cutting the grass and laying it across will take the longest. Err, may I ask how you are going to fix the spikes in?' George asks.

'We're going to speak to engineers next and ask them to arrange it,' Chris replies, looking at the experienced man.

'That's a long strip you're planning, sir, right across the width of the spit, and the spikes will need to be driven in quite a way to hold fast, but done without blunting the ends, especially if you're using metal. Also, where will you get the spikes from?'

'There's a workshop here. We'll find some engineers and mechanics to try and sort them out. You think spikes will be hard to do, then?' Chris asks, openly taking their advice.

'Not impossible but certainly difficult. We've got enough people here to do it, but if you're concerned about some of them being infected, then it will be bloody hard for you to trust that many to go outside,' George says.

'Okay, good point, we'll see if it can be done. Where are the diggers?'

'Over on the west side, stacked up between the two walls. We managed to get quite a few vehicles in the gap.'

'That's good thinking. Keeps them safe,' Chris says.

'I've got runners telling your families you're busy for a little while. They can go to Sergeant Hopewell next door if they've got any concerns, and I've jacked up some guards to go with you. I've had to use some of your people, Chris. Mine are all tucked up, but I've briefed them to what's needed,' Howie says, coming back into the room. 'Whenever you're ready.'

Howie leads the men out of the planning room and down towards the gate, stopping to speak to Blowers and Cookey, who are leaning against a post, smoking cigarettes, and drinking coffee. Their assault rifles are strapped across their shoulders, allowing the rifles to rest at the front.

'Lads, how's it going?' Howie asks as he walks closer.

'Mr Howie, sorry, we're just having a coffee,' Cookey replies guiltily.

'No worries, lads, you don't have to apologise. I know you'll stay alert. Has anyone tried to get in or out?'

'Nope, we've had a lot of people come and ask us questions,' Blowers says, stubbing his cigarette out.

'How do they seem when they're speaking to you?' Howie asks.

'Nervous and pumped up, to be honest, sir, like they want to be doing something rather than just waiting,' Cookey replies.

'Okay. Just to let you know that we're taking these chaps out into the flatlands with some plant machinery in case anyone questions the noise or anything,' Howie explains as Cookey opens the small walk-through gate for them.

They step into the wide lane between the inner and outer wall. The concrete walkway is now covered with a cropped layer of grass. They turn left and walk down into the area that runs between the two walls. The plant machinery and other vehicles coming into view as the lane bends to the left. Several armed guards, recognised by Howie from back in the commune and already spoken to, follow at a discreet distance, with their weapons gripped and ready.

Howie pauses to let the three men walk on to their vehicles.

'Okay, so you know what they're doing. Keep a close eye on them and make sure they don't leave their vehicles and go into the estate. We've got a couple of our people already in the housing area, so be very careful if you have to venture in. In fact, I would say don't go in there unless absolutely necessary and make sure you let us know on the radio, got it?' Howie says to the guards, who nod back as the nearest of the diggers starts up with a noisy roar.

'We might be sending more people out, but I'll let you know if we do,' Howie says, leaving them to it and walking back to the gate. Once inside, he walks slowly back towards the south wall, thinking of the plans they have put in place. A visual image forming in his head.

We've got spotters out front, so we should get notified when they arrive. There could be infected already in the estate, watching us, but we can't afford the time or people to sweep it clean, and Dave is in that area, rigging some traps up. The zombie army has to come this way, so they have to go through the estate. Dave blows some of them up and slows them down. Then they push into the flatlands and into the trenches, with either spikes or something else to hurt and hamper them. After that, they have to negotiate the first bank and, hopefully, a load of vehicles set to explode, then the second bank, and the deep ditch. After that, we're on our own. How many will they bring? Will they be armed? Fuck, what if they're armed? We'll be slaughtered. Nothing we can do about that. I suppose we can fall back into the Fort if we have to, but it won't take long for them to get through. Mind you, we've got the Saxon up top, with the GPMG. We can put more rifles and weapons up there and hopefully the cannon with grapeshot if Dave can sort them out.

Thinking all this through, Howie realises how much they're relying on the quiet man, leaving him to rig the estate, which must be a hell of a task, then needing him to work out the cannon too. If they didn't have Dave, they would be at a loss. Howie knows he would have been dead a long time ago if not for Dave. Thoughts race through his mind as he slowly paces back towards the south wall, oblivious to the many people, who stop and stare at the man with the dark hair and dark features. There is something about his manner and appearance, the way he walks slowly, planting each foot in turn, the faraway look on his face that puts them off from disturbing him. A few of the less sensitive ones step forward to interrupt his thoughts, only to find strong hands placed on their arms from the more astute people, holding them back and discreetly shaking heads.

Children go quiet as Howie walks through the camp. His mind racing with a thousand images and thoughts, but his face is stony and grave. Eyes down and subconsciously avoiding trip hazards and guide ropes stretched out from the many tents. To Howie, it's like a movie in his mind – an image of grotesque, decaying forms racing through the estate with sharpened, yellowing teeth. The traps fail to go off; then, they leap over the pits and surge too quickly past the non-exploding cars, only to fall on the weak lines, devouring and wiping them out instantly.

Keep them coming, keep them running after them until they eventually fall down and die again.

But then he has an overwhelming desire to fight them. To stand on that line and face them down. Howie thinks back to the feeling of battle, the horror and the fear, the blood and gore, the knowing that at any point, he could be taken down and killed, only having his own strength and speed to rely on. The feeling of glory, the sense of doing something that is right, standing with his people and fighting with them, charging into almost certain death, but doing so knowing you're all in it together.

The pull of that feeling is hard to ignore, and Howie accepts that there is a big part of him wanting that final showdown.

Take as many down as you can, Howie, and then fight them. They don't think of fairness or equal sides, so hurt them, cut them down, and do what it takes, because that fight will be the end.

Howie snaps back to reality, to find that he is in the middle of the camp. There is silence all around him. Howie lifts his head and nods once to the mass of people who stand and stare at him before walking towards the south wall and back to the reality of planning the impossible.

CHAPTER EIGHTY-ONE

'You, you, and you two, come with me.' Dave points to several of the guards nearby, handpicking the ones he had seen fighting: serious men with calm expressions, fit, and athletic. They get up and make ready without question.

'Get some fluids and food, meet us at the gate,' Dave says, walking away towards the Saxon. Jamie following behind him.

They reach the Saxon just as Curtis and the rest come out of the planning room. Dave opens the rear doors and climbs in, rummaging through the bench seat cupboards to pull two heavy, bulging canvas bags out. Dave then exits the Saxon to see Jamie staring at the bags.

'Grenades,' Dave explains.

'Okay,' Jamie replies.

'Leave both of your rifles here, take this, and put it on,' Dave says, handing Jamie a pistol pouch, with belt loops at the rear, and the black stock of the handgun poking out. Jamie hands over the two rifles. Dave slides them into the rear as Curtis arrives at the vehicle.

'We're leaving our rifles here. Take care of them,' Dave instructs Curtis.

'Yes, Dave,' Curtis replies, still making the name *Dave* sound like the word *Sarge*.

'Ammunition,' Dave says, handing Jamie spare clips for the handgun.

'I've never used a handgun before,' Jamie says.

'I'll show you,' Dave replies.

'Okay,' Jamie says, looping the heavy pouch onto his belt, to his right side.

'Ready?' Dave asks.

'Yes, Dave,' Jamie replies. They walk towards the gate in silence, each carrying a bag full of grenades over one shoulder. Two quiet men, with pistols strapped to their sides, walking silently through the camp. They reach the gate and wait in silence for the other guards to catch them up.

Ted appears, smiling.

'Going anywhere nice?' Ted asks.

'No,' Dave replies flatly.

'Oh, right,' Ted pauses; the smile slowly disappearing.

'We need some vehicles,' Dave says.

'Okay, how many do you need?' Ted asks.

'Three,' Dave replies.

'Anything in particular?' Ted asks.

'No,' Dave answers.

Ted walks away into a nearby room, selecting keys from a key cupboard.

'Can you drive?' Dave asks Jamie.

'Yes,' Jamie replies.

'Good,' Dave says. Ted returns, handing the keys over as the four guards reach the gate. Each of them with a rucksack on their backs.

'The vehicles are between the walls, to the left,' Ted says as they step through the gate.

'Okay,' Dave answers.

'Funny bugger, that one,' Ted says to himself, closing the gate behind them.

They walk down the lane until they reach the vehicles. Dave stopping to look at the keys, then at the vehicles, trying to figure out which key fits which vehicle.

'You're going on point duty. You each get a radio. One of you has to go to the furthest point out that the radio will reach. Keep checking in on channel two until you lose signal, then come back. The other two I want on the sides and out as far as the radios will reach. Got it?' The guards nod back as they take the radios and switch them to channel two, using the small dial at the top.

'The one furthest out takes one of the vehicles. The other two – out to the sides. One gets a vehicle, and you arrange where the other gets dropped off and the pick-up points in case it goes bent. We keep the other vehicle. You will be there for some time. I will try and get relief for you, but that may not be possible. You are the advance contact points. Without you, we will not have advance warning of when they come. Do not engage and give away your positions. Report back at the first sight and pull back to the Fort. Got it?' Dave says. They each nod. 'Stay alert,' Dave says, handing all of the keys to one of the guards.

The man sorts through them, then hands a set to Jamie. 'For that one,' the man points to the first vehicle.

'You get the vehicle ready,' Dave says to Jamie.

He nods in return and walks over to get into the driver's side, adjusting the seat and checking through the controls. Jamie glances out to see Dave speaking intently to the other men. Finally, they nod back, with very serious faces, and break away, heading for their vehicles.

'Okay,' Dave says, getting into the front passenger seat.

Jamie starts the engine and pulls away slowly. They get to the big vehicle gates on the outer wall; then, Dave gets out and pushes the gates open, waiting for the vehicles to drive through. Jamie pulls over to allow the other two to drive on down the road.

Dave closes the gates and gets back into the vehicle.

'Where are we going?' Jamie asks as he pulls away.

'Into the estate. We're going to set some explosives,' Dave answers. 'We also need to sweep as we go.' Dave thinks of all that Mr Howie and Chris have to contend with. He didn't need to ask if they wanted the area swept. They have enough to think about. Jamie drives down the long, straight road, past the banks, and then through the flatlands, finally reaching the housing estate.

'Drive down to the right,' Dave instructs as Jamie turns the wheel, going down the road between the two rows of houses – one row on the flatlands side.

'Park at the end,' Dave says. Jamie pulls the car up at the end of the cul-de-sac. They get out and walk around to the back of the vehicle. Dave pulls his pistol out and indicates for Jamie to do the same. Dave then shows Jamie how to load the ammunition clip and pull the sliding top back to engage the first round.

'They kick quite a lot. Use a two-handed grip. Same as the sniper rifle – squeeze and fire,' Dave says.

'Can I fire here?' Jamie asks.

'Yes, they won't hear from this distance,' Dave answers. Jamie raises the pistol and copies Dave, firing once. The loud retort sounding out into the quiet air.

'Good, you anticipated the kick without dropping or lifting the weapon. Two shots per target, like this,' Dave says, lifting his own pistol and walking towards the front door of the nearest house. As he steps onto the garden path, he fires two shots very close together. The rounds strike the door at mid-height, millimetres apart.

'Got it,' Jamie says, walking towards the same door and firing twice into the same height as Dave hit. Both rounds hitting within millimetres.

'Good, we call it a *double tap*. Aim for the head if you can and be ready to reload quickly. Don't be afraid to put it away and go for bladed weapons if you need to.'

'Okay,' Jamie answers.

'Show me a reload,' Dave instructs and watches Jamie eject the clip, catch it with one hand, drop that same hand down, and swap for a fresh, full clip, and slam it home, racking the top back – all within a second or two.

'Sorry, that was slow,' Jamie apologises.

'That's okay, you'll get faster the more you do it,' Dave answers. 'We'll do the first house together.'

'Okay,' Jamie replies. They move up the path until they reach the front door. Dave steps close to the front door and stares at Jamie.

'How many windows to the front?' Dave asks.

'Two on the ground level, two on the first floor,' Jamie replies without breaking eye contact.

'Describe them,' Dave asks.

'The ground floor, far left appears to be a lounge window. Net curtains restrict the visibility, but the curtains are drawn back, which indicate the people are either not at home or were not home when the event happened. The other window looks similar, so it might be a dining room. It does not look like a kitchen,' Jamie replies.

'Upstairs?' Dave asks.

'The far left has partial net curtains, drawn back, but there is no view of the inside from ground level. The right side is the same, but the curtains are half drawn across.'

'Are the windows closed, or are any of them open?' Dave asks.

'I think they are all closed,' Jamie replies.

'Okay, it's your first time, so I will allow for that, but in future, remember this – we don't *think*, we know. Got it?'

'Yes, sorry,' Jamie replies.

'Good, now the door. Tell me about it?'

'Wooden, inward opening, and hinged on the right,' Jamie replies, looking straight at Dave.

'Good, how many locks, and where are they?'

'Central lock on the door handle to the left. Letterbox is situated at standard height. I was unable to tell if there are any further locks.'

'Good, how can we tell if the door has further locks?' Dave asks.

'I don't know. Pressure?'

'Yes, push against the door, next to the door handle. Does it yield?' Dave asks and watches Jamie push hard.

'No,' Jamie answers.

'Now push at the top of the door. Does it yield?'

'Yes, slightly,' Jamie answers, then pushes at the bottom. 'The base yields too. No locks on the top or bottom.'

'Good, so we know that to force entry we aim for the central lock. Now, do we use a shoulder or a foot?' Dave asks. Jamie considers for a split second.

'A shoulder will risk injury, and I don't think people our size could generate enough force. The foot?' he asks.

'Correct. Men the size of Clarence and Chris can use shoulders as they have huge amounts of power and strength. Men our size do not, so we use our feet, but before we do that, what should we do first?'

'Look for a key?' Jamie replies.

'Good, and also...' Dave pushes the handle down, and the door opens slightly, 'we check to see if it's actually locked first.'

'Got it.'

'Room clearance,' Dave says as they step into the hallway. 'Working together we clear as we go. One remains at the door, facing out. The other enters. We do not lean around corners, with our weapons held out ready to be taken off us. Got it?'

'Got it.'

'Good. We walk in fast, with the weapon held ready to use. We face forward and sweep. Like this,' Dave says as he enters the first room on the right, pushing the door open with his foot and stepping in.

He holds the pistol in the two-handed grip and sweeps the room rapidly. The gun rising and falling as he looks up and down, left to right.

'Got it,' Jamie says.

'You do that one,' Dave says, nodding towards the lounge door opposite them.

Jamie mimics Dave, pushing the door open with his foot and sweeping the room; the weapon tracking his facial direction.

'Good, now, if we both proceed to the ground floor rear, we leave the stairs behind us, and we do not know if upstairs is clear. So one holds at the point of risk while the other advances. I'll hold while you clear the rest,' Dave says.

'Okay,' Jamie replies, stepping down the narrow hallway and entering the kitchen. He disappears from view and is gone for several seconds. He walks back out, with the weapon slightly lowered but still held correctly.

'Clear,' he reports.

'Good, stand behind me,' Dave asks as Jamie walks to stand behind him.

Dave raises one hand and makes a fist.

'This means hold,' Dave says, then extends one finger.

'This means one target, two for two targets, three for three. All of the fingers extended means multiple targets.'

'Got it.'

'Good. If I point the finger like this, it means the target is that direction. If I point one way, then another, it means one target that way and one target the other.'

'Okay.'

'Good, we'll stick with that for a minute. Going upstairs, we keep the weapon raised to strike the target at the top, taking into account the height difference. Place your feet to the sides of each step. There is less chance of creaks that way.'

'Okay,' Jamie says as Dave lifts his weapon and advances up the stairs quickly and surely, reaching the top and pausing to sweep down the hallway.

'Corridor ahead, loops back to the front bedroom. Another room on the right. Appears bathroom at the end. I'll hold. You clear the front,' Dave says quietly, stepping aside to allow Jamie to move along the few steps to the bedroom.

He walks inside and reappears within seconds. 'Clear,' he reports quietly and moves on to the next bedroom. He repeats the action, then moves along to the bathroom. 'Clear.' He then returns back to Dave; weapon lowered.

'Good,' Dave replies.

They exit the house and move outside, to the next one, trying the door first but finding it locked, and no key to be found.

'Aim your strike next to the lock. Do not expect it to burst open on the first hit,' Dave says, watching as Jamie steps back and powers his right foot into the door.

Jamie watches as the strike hits, then adjusts his stance, and pauses for a second, appearing to draw power, then drives his foot forward again, with lightning speed. The strike is perfect, and the door pops open, causing the frame to splinter from the solid brass lock being forced in.

'Good, now we move faster. Go. I'll hold,' Dave orders.

Jamie walks forward, kicking doors open and sweeping the house, room by room, reporting "clear" after each one.

Jamie takes the lead on the stairs, leaving Dave to hold at the top. The house is cleared within minutes, and they walk back out.

'That was good, but we have a lot of houses and not much time, so do it faster,' Dave says.

'Okay,' Jamie replies.

The next house is cleared within two minutes, and they exit again, moving across the lawns to the next one.

'My turn. You hold,' Dave says as he kicks the door in and enters swiftly, striding from room to room, with quick, jerky, but controlled movements. He clears each room, then moves straight up the stairs, and clears the rest. He is back outside in under a minute.

'Your movements are much faster than mine,' Jamie says as they walk to the next house.

'Years of practise and drill, but you do not have that luxury. Your turn,' Dave says as they reach the door. Jamie checks the door handle, locked. He pressures the top and bottom, steps back, and kicks the door hard, forcing it open on the first kick. He enters as the door is still swinging open. Jamie strides into the first room, again mimicking Dave as he checks the four corners and moves back out, then moves on to the next room. They exit the house in just over a minute, again moving down to the next house.

'Better. Keep that pace but stay alert,' Dave says, testing the door handle and finding the door unlocked.

'You go again,' Dave says as the door swings open.

Jamie strides into the lounge on the right, then back out, and across the small hallway, and into the dining room. He exits and clears the kitchen at the back before moving back and climbing the stairs, pausing at the top for a split second to allow Dave to reach the top step.

Jamie advances towards the front bedroom, pausing at the door, with his head cocked to one side. He raises a hand and makes a fist, then extends one finger, and points to the door. Dave moves up close behind Jamie and listens. He taps Jamie on the shoulder once and waves his extended hand forward, then about turns to watch the rear.

Jamie steps forward and pushes the door open with his foot. Walking into the room, he observes an infected standing on the other side of the double bed. The pistol already tracking with his eyes. He fires two rounds very close together into the forehead and is already moving to check the rest of the room as the zombie slumps to the ground, leaving a massive blood and brain spatter on the wall behind him.

'Clear,' Jamie says, exiting the room.

Dave enters the bedroom and moves across to look down at the body, then heads back out into the hallway.

'Good shots. The second was slightly off, though,' Dave says.

'I know. I started to turn away to continue the sweep too quickly,' Jamie replies.

'If you are satisfied that the first shot is enough, then you can start the move,' Dave says.

'Okay, I will keep to the double-tap for now to practise if that's okay,'

'Okay,' Dave replies.

Jamie clears the rest of the rooms, and they move on, working house by house, clearing each one in under a minute, then crossing the road to start on the other side. They work back towards where they started.

'Now we work alone. You start with this one, and I do the next. You leapfrog and do the next one, and I leapfrog after you. Got it?' Dave asks.

'Got it. Same method?' Jamie says.

'Yes,' Dave answers.

'Okay.' Jamie walks to the front door and pauses until Dave has reached the front door of the next house. They nod to each other, and in unison, they check the door handle, the top and the bottom, then step back, and kick the door, entering as the door swings open. They work from house to house, double shots ringing out sporadically as they find infected in rooms. The street is cleared within ten minutes, and they each exit their last house, both changing clips and re-holstering their weapons as they walk back to the vehicle.

'How many?' Dave asks.

'Three, you?'

'You know how many I had.'

'You had two.'

'Good.'

'What now?' Jamie asks.

'The next street behind this one,' Dave answers.

'Okay,' Jamie replies. They move down the central road until they reach the next junction. Once again, two rows of houses run along on each side.

'You take that side. I'll do this side. Meet back here,' Dave says.

'Okay.'

Ten minutes later, they meet back at the junction. Dave ahead of Jamie, but only having to wait for under a minute.

'How many rounds did I use?' Dave asks.

'Eight,' Jamie answers. 'Four targets.'

'Good.'

'Two more streets, and we can start on the explosives,' Dave explains as they walk further down the road.

'Lead point to Dave,' the radio crackles on Dave's belt.

'Dave to Lead point. Go ahead.'

'Lead point to Dave. I am positioned approximately two miles away from your location, testing transmission strength.'

'Dave to Lead point. Transmission strong. Can you move further?'

'Yes, will do so now. Out.'

'Dave to East point. Are you in position?'

'East point to Dave. Roger that. In position now. West point has retained the vehicle.'

'Dave to East point. Received. Dave to West point. Confirm you have retained the vehicle, and are you in position?'

'West point to Dave. Confirm I have retained the vehicle. Confirm I am in position.'

'Dave to West point. Roger that. Dave to Lead point. You are now North point. Received?'

'North point to Dave. Roger that.'

'Dave to North point. Switch to channel one and check signal strength to the Fort before you move any further.'

'North point to Dave. Roger that. Doing now.' Dave switches the dial on the radio back to channel one and listens for the transmission.

'North point to Fort. Radio check.'

'Fort to North point. Are you forward observation point? Your signal is weak but readable.'

'North point to Fort. Answer yes. I am forward obs point. Likewise, your signal weak but readable. I will hold this position. North point to Dave. Did you receive the last?'

'Dave to North point and Fort. Roger that. Received the last. North,

East, and West points will hold those positions and maintain channel one. Dave out.'

Dave turns to Jamie. 'Explosives,' he says simply.

CHAPTER EIGHTY-TWO

'Did you hear that last transmission?' Chris asks as Howie enters the planning room.

'Yeah. Dave's got the spotters in place?'

'Yep, at least we've got eyes on now, so we'll get an advance warning,' Chris replies. 'You okay, mate?' he asks, taking note of the expression on Howie's face.

'I'm fine, mate, was just thinking it all through as I walked back,' Howie replies.

'There's a lot to think about,' Chris concedes. 'But all we can do is try, Howie.'

'I know, mate, any news on the engineers?'

'I spoke to Sergeant Hopewell, and she's sent runners out. Did the digger drivers get away okay?'

Howie nods back, staring down at the plans on the table. 'Where do we put the soil that they dig out?' he says.

'They seem experienced men, Howie. I'm sure they will figure it out and put it somewhere…out of sight,' Chris replies.

'Wouldn't they need dumper trucks to carry it away?'

'Hang on,' Chris says, reaching for his radio.

'*Fort to guards with the digger units. Fort to guards with the digger units,*' Chris repeats several times.

'Digger guard to Fort. Sorry, it's noisy here. Go ahead,' a voice booms out; the sound of loud engines in the background.

'Fort to digger guards. Make sure the soil taken out is disposed of, out of sight.'

'Digger guard to Fort. Repeat your last, please.'

'Fort to digger guard. MAKE SURE THE SOIL TAKEN OUT IS HIDDEN FROM SIGHT.'

'Digger guard to Fort. You want us to work all night?'

'Fort to digger guard. ANSWER NO. I WANT THE SOIL FROM THE HOLES HIDDEN.'

'Digger unit to Fort. Roger, will do.'

'Bloody hell, they're going to wake the dead,' Chris says, shaking his head and putting the radio down on the table.

'Bit late for that, mate,' Howie jokes.

A knock, and Terri enters, immediately smiling at Howie. 'There are some engineers here for you,' she says.

'Ah, great,' Howie replies, stepping to the door and finding several men waiting outside. 'Come in, chaps.' Howie smiles at them, opening the door wide. They walk into the room, looking about with a keen interest at the interior, and then head straight to the plans on the table.

'I'm Howie. This is Chris. Nice to meet you all,' Howie says, politely shaking hands with the men, one by one.

'Sorry, is this the room for the engineers?' A middle-aged woman appears at the door, leaning in.

'Yeah. Hi, I'm Howie. Come in.'

'Hello, I'm Kelly,' the woman replies, shaking hands with Howie, then Chris.

'So are you all engineers?' Chris asks once the handshaking has stopped.

They all nod at him.

'Good, forgive us for being blunt, but we need to get straight down to the point. We need some sharp spikes to be made that can be embedded into the ground,' Chris says.

'Also, we want some very small, sharp objects that can be hidden in the long grass, out in the flatlands,' Howie adds.

'You mean caltrops?' Kelly asks straight away and leans forward to examine the plans on the table.

'Yeah, those,' Howie replies, surprised at her direct manner.

'What about the spikes? How many and how deep are they going in?'

'The spikes will be put into a hidden trench the width of the spit,' Howie explains.

'We can use sharpened, wooden spikes for that. Getting the material and fashioning them will be relatively easy. The hardest part will be getting them in. You'll need a lot of people for that if you want it done quickly,' Kelly answers.

'We can get more people. That's not a problem. What about the caltrops?'

'Right, the first problem is materials. We'll need lots of metal, but then most metals can't just be bent into shape. They might be brittle and snap. We might have to heat them and then, of course, make them sharp. That will need power tools, and you'll want them over a large area, so we need lots of them.' She finishes speaking, then looks expectantly at Chris, then to Howie.

'There's a workshop here. I'm sure we can rig some of the generators up for you,' Howie replies, impressed.

'Can we take metal from the fittings and fixtures if we need to?' one of the other engineers asks.

'Take what you need, do whatever you need to do, but get it done as fast as possible. We will have to put some guards with you to make sure you don't go off and tell other people what you're doing,' Chris says, resting his hands on the desk and leaning forward to emphasise his point.

'Excuse me?' One of the engineers steps forward. 'What was that about guards and telling other people?' He is middle-aged, with blond, swept back hair.

'We cannot run the risk of anyone else knowing what our tactics are, so for now, you will work alone,' Chris replies.

'Are you telling us or asking us?' the man asks politely.

'Listen, I'm sorry it sounds harsh, but it's the way it has to be, I'm afraid,' Chris says to the man, equalling his polite tone.

'We were told we could come and go as we needed to as long as we were checked when we come back in.'

'That was then. The situation has changed,' Chris says.

'So we can no longer come and go as we please?' the man asks.

'No, I'm afraid not,' Chris replies.

'Tell me, what will happen if we do?'

'Do *what* exactly?' Chris asks, still maintaining his polite tone.

'If we try to leave or if we try to tell other people of what we are doing?'

'You will be stopped,' Chris says curtly.

'How?' the man asks; his cultured tones not slipping.

'By any means deemed necessary,' Chris responds.

'I'm sorry? You mean that if we try to leave or speak with the other people in the camp, we will be killed?' The man leans forward, staring intently at Chris.

'If that is necessary, yes,' Chris stares back.

'I thought this was a democracy, not a—'

'I will stop you there,' Chris interrupts pointedly. 'This is *not* a democracy, and while I understand your concerns, I can only respond by saying there is no alternative. If those *things* coming here find out about our plans, we will lose the best chance we have of reducing their numbers before they get to us. We do not know if anyone in the camp is infected, so we cannot run the risk of people knowing what we are doing. It really is that simple.' Chris speaks calmly, looking at each of them in turn as his diplomatic skills shine through.

'Gentlemen, and lady, of course,' Chris inclines his head to Kelly. 'There is a huge zombie army coming for us. This is a fact. We have to do what it takes to cut their numbers before they get here. While Howie and I have the skills and knowledge and are prepared to meet them face-to-face, we need your skills and knowledge to try and even the sides. You are trained engineers. You have skills that we simply do not have, and we need your help. But it must be done in a controlled environment,' Chris explains, looking to each of them in turn.

'I agree,' Kelly responds immediately and with passion.

'We all heard what Howie said earlier, and we know the risks involved. We'll get on with it and do what we can to help.'

'Okay, I understand, but I'm a little uncomfortable with being treated like a slave or having some tyrannical despot ordering me about,' the man replies directly to Kelly.

The atmosphere becomes instantly charged, and a silence follows his comments.

Chris is clearly struggling to contain his temper, and Howie has to bite his own anger down.

'I don't understand what your concerns are?' Kelly asks slowly and clearly.

'My concern is being told this was a safe place and now finding out we are captives to be used as they see fit and without any form of redress, and being told who we can and cannot talk to,' the man replies.

'We can manage without this man. I think the rest of us understand your need for secrecy, and we are happy to comply with that request, is that so?' Kelly asks the group in general.

'Yes, completely. I am amazed at you, Donald,' an older man with glasses responds, looking at the outspoken engineer.

'I have the right to question their motives,' Donald replies.

'You do, but we all know the situation, and it would appear you are happy to accept the safety of this place without undertaking any of the risk involved in keeping it safe,' the older man says.

'That is not the case at all,' Donald responds, still maintaining a polite and calm manner.

'Donald, we are not on site now, discussing the plans with the architect or planning officers. We are in the middle of an event of global proportions, and if we want to live, we have to accept that and deal with it,' Kelly says.

'I do accept it, but I still maintain the right to question the methods used. This could be one step away from some kind of communist regime, where we are being controlled, and I simply will not accept it,' Donald replies.

Chris looks to Howie, with a discreet shake of his head. Howie walks to the door and over to the police office.

'Debbie, we've got the engineers. We've told them what we need doing, but one of them is refusing to agree not to tell anyone else,' Howie says. Sergeant Hopewell looks up at him with a concerned expression; eyebrows raised. 'Look, we don't know if anyone else in the camp is infected, and we cannot risk people finding out what our defence tactics are, so we are controlling the access points...'

'I know all of this, Howie,' Debbie interrupts him.

'I am concerned...'

'Detain him,' Ted says firmly from the back of the office.

'You have to Howie, you can't run the risk of him telling people or causing dissent,' Sarah adds.

'How would we detain him?' Howie asks.

'Leave it to me. There's a secure room back here that he can sit in for a few hours,' Ted replies, taking a thick, black belt from a hook and fixing it around his waist; handcuffs and black pouches hanging from it.

He takes a police flat cap and puts it on. The peak low to his eyes. Instantly transformed from genial Ted to official policeman.

'Where is he?' Ted asks.

'In the planning room. I think his name is Donald,' Howie answers.

'Lead the way, then,' Ted says, with a voice full of authority. They walk back to the planning room, with Howie leading the way. Ted puts a hand out as they reach the door.

'Which one is he?' Ted asks quietly.

'Err, middle-aged, with blond hair, sort of swept back,' Howie replies.

'Let me go first and do the talking, understand?' Ted says, not giving Howie a chance to reply as he steps into the room, pausing for dramatic effect as all eyes turn to him.

Ted keeps a stern, impassive face. Eyes staring out from underneath the peaked hat. He looks at each person, taking them all in. Years of experience in his manner and an aura of authority ooze off him. Ted nods and steps over to the blond man.

'Sir, are you Donald?' Ted asks. His eyes staring intently at the man.

'Yes, I am,' the man replies, clearly shocked at the arrival of a fully uniformed police officer.

'Sir, I need you to understand what I am going to say to you. We will remain calm, and we will not react in an undue manner. Is that clear?' Ted says.

'I'm sorry? What?' Donald replies.

'Sir, as far as we know, this Fort is the last safe place in the country. We have no knowledge of any other surviving colonies or places such as this. Therefore, this Fort may represent the country. Therefore, this Fort also represents the concern of the nation as a whole. I am led to believe that you are causing dissent and refusing to comply with the requests being made to you. I am therefore detaining you in the interests of national security. You will come with me, where you will be held in a safe place, without fear of abuse or assault.'

'What? You can't do this!' Donald shouts, with a horrified look on his face, and steps away. Ted steps forward and takes a firm grip of the man's wrist, pulling it behind his back and fixing one end of a handcuff on.

'Sir, this *is* happening. These men are doing what is necessary for the protection and survival of all of us. They and we do not have time for inconsiderate and selfish people like you. Put your other hand behind your back, thank you. Now, you will come with me and be quiet about it.' Ted spins the handcuffed man around and marches him towards the door. 'Once outside, you will not scream or shout, and you will not cause distress or alarm to any other persons within this camp,' Ted says smoothly, and with such firm authority, the man complies instantly.

Ted steps through with Donald and turns back to close the door, winking at Howie as he does so.

'Bloody hell,' Howie mutters.

'I'm sorry about that,' Chris starts to say but is cut off by Kelly holding her hand up.

'Don't be,' she says. 'Extreme times call for extreme measures. I know he'll be looked after.'

'It did need to be done, I'm afraid. I've met Donald on a few jobs, and he's always like that. Very contrary, which normally can be dealt with, but as you say, extreme times and all that...' the older man says calmly.

'To business. Where is this workshop?' Kelly asks.

'Follow me. We'll find Roger and get him to lead the way,' Howie replies.

A few minutes later, they find Roger and follow him around the edge of the camp to the west wall and a set of large, wooden double doors.

Chris had found three guards from the dwindling numbers and briefed them fully, and Howie had grabbed a couple of runners and asked them to stay close.

Roger opens the doors up and steps aside as the group files in. Long, wooden workbenches run down the sides, with old, battered metal cabinets filling spaces and gaps. Hand tools are pinned to walls, with the black outline of their shape etched on, showing their intended space. The smell of grease, oil, and coffee is in the air.

'The power tools are in that room in the back. It's kept locked, but the key should be in the top of that set of drawers,' Roger explains, pointing to a metal filing unit in the corner.

One of the engineers opens the door and pulls out a single key on a large ring. The rest move slowly down the room, examining the various tools with professional interest.

The rear door is unlocked, and the engineer doing the unlocking takes out a small flashlight from his pocket to illuminate the dark interior. The other engineers join him, each taking out a small flashlight as they enter the dark room.

'Bloody engineers, always so practical,' Roger jokes.

'Is there a generator here?' a voice shouts from the back room.

'Yes, there's one here. We can get more for you if you need. We always had plenty of power as we're so isolated from the main power supply,' Roger says, walking forward and leaning into the dark room.

'Well, where is it, then?' the voice calls out.

'You're the engineers. You figure it out,' Roger answers with mock indignation. 'This is not my usual environment,' he adds.

'Got it. Hang on, we'll get some power going,' another voice calls out.

A few seconds later, a deep rumbling noise comes from the back room, and the darkness is dispatched with illumination from the bright strip-lighting overhead. Murmurs of agreement and satisfaction reach them as the engineers mooch through the various tools and equipment.

'Have you seen up there, Howie?' Chris asks.

Howie follows his gaze to a suspended roof, adding extra storage to the room. Piles of long metal rods are stacked up in one end.

'Perfect. I love it when a plan comes together,' Howie jokes and looks to see Chris staring blankly at him.

'What plan?' Chris asks. 'The whole plan or just this bit?'

'It's from The A-Team,' Howie says.

'What's The A-Team?' Chris asks with a puzzled expression.

'You are fucking joking, right? Christ, you're worse than Dave,' Howie mutters.

'Of course, I'm bloody joking,' Chris smiles. 'So, which one am I?' he asks.

'Hmmm... I would say Hannibal, but with that beard, it's got to be BA,' Howie replies.

'No way. Clarence has got to be BA,' Chris responds.

'Yeah, fair one. Well, Dave is definitely Murdoch,' Howie says. Chris chuckles. 'But you can't be Hannibal as that would only leave Face, and I'm not being Face,' Howie says firmly.

'What? Face was great,' Chris says, shocked.

'In the movie or series?' Howie asks.

'Both,' Chris replies.

'Well, you be Face, then, if you like him so much. I'll be Hannibal,' Howie says as they start walking back to the planning room.

'No way. I can't be Face. You're much better looking than me,' Chris replies.

'You'll have to be Face. I'll be Hannibal.'

'Nope, shave your beard off, and you'll make a great Face,' Howie says.

'I pity the crazy fool, who tries to shave my beard,' Chris growls in a deep voice as Howie bursts out laughing.

'I pity the crazy fool, who tries to make me be Face,' Howie growls back as they reach the planning room door, entering to drink more coffee.

'What's next?' Chris asks.

'*Clarence to the Fort,*' the radio bursts to life, with Clarence's deep voice booming out.

'That is, I guess,' Howie replies.

Chris smiles as he answers the radio, '*Chris to Clarence. Go ahead, BA.*'

'*I AIN'T GETTIN' ON NO PLANE,*' Clarence's voice booms

back, making both of them laugh. '*Clarence to Chris. We are on way back, will be with you in a few minutes.*'

'*Saxon to Howie or Chris. Confirm we can see convoy of vehicles coming from the estate.*'

'*Chris to Clarence. Roger that. Hold at the gates. We'll come to you.*' They down the now cold coffee and head back out of the door, walking through the camp, smiling at people as they walk past or stop to stare. Ted falls in and joins them.

'How's our man?' Howie asks Ted.

'He's all right. He's asking for a lawyer, so we told him your sister is a lawyer, and he's trying to make a claim of unlawful arrest now,' Ted smiles.

'Fair one,' Howie replies.

They arrive at the gates to find Blowers and Cookey still there, joking with each other.

'Lads, how are you?' Howie asks.

'Yeah, we're good, Mr Howie. How's the plans coming on? We've still got loads of people coming up, asking if they can help,' Blowers says.

'Slowly getting there. It seems to be taking ages, though. You two okay down here?'

'Yeah, fine. We've got coffee on constant flow, and there's a toilet in there,' Cookey says, smiling.

'What more can a man need?' Howie says.

'Err, some women, some steak, no zombie army coming for us, maybe a television, and an Xbox, some popcorn...' Cookey replies.

'Oh, listen to him. Women, he says... You wouldn't know what to do with one, other than sit and talk about curtains and flower arranging,' Blowers cuts in.

'We could sit and chat, with our legs folded up underneath us, wearing thick woolly jumpers,' Cookey adds.

'What's wrong with woolly jumpers? I've got woolly jumpers,' Chris interrupts, with a look of serious intent.

'Ha, nice one...' Blowers laughs.

'Who's laughing?' Chris asks. 'I'm not.'

'Yeah, right, you got me like this before,' Blowers laughs, trailing off as Chris remains poker faced.

'You are joking, aren't you?'

'Do I look like the kind of man who wears woolly jumpers?' Chris replies as his face splits apart with a big grin.

'Well... Now that you come to mention it...' Blowers jokes.

'You cheeky bugger,' Chris retorts. 'Have some respect and get that bloody gate opened up.'

CHAPTER EIGHTY-THREE

Clarence steps out of the armoury and walks to the police office, thinking through all the items he needs to find.

'Hello,' he says, finding Sergeant Hopewell behind the desk. 'Howie and Chris said to speak to you. I'm taking a foraging party out.'

'What do you need?'

'Gunsmiths and hardware stores,' says Clarence.

'Hi, Clarence,' Sarah smiles, walking into the office with Terri. Clarence starts to blush. 'Hello, Sarah,' he rumbles.

'Hello...Sarah,' Sarah mimics, trying to copy his deep voice.

'I don't sound like that,' Clarence chuckles.

'No, you're far worse. I'm only joking,' Sarah says, putting her hand on his forearm and making him blush even more. 'What are you doing here?'

'I'm taking a foraging party out. Chris and Howie need some items,' he says as a look of concern passes across her face.

'Are you taking many with you?'

'Yeah, there'll be a few of us.'

'Okay, well, you take care and make sure you come back. I still need that knife training, remember?' she says.

'Um, okay, I will,' Clarence replies, aware of Terri and Sergeant Hopewell watching them.

'Here you go. There's a list and a map with them marked on,' Sergeant Hopewell says, handing him some papers and a map book.

'Thanks. Vehicles? Do you have any?' he asks.

'Check with Ted down at the gate. He's got all the keys.'

'Thank you. See you soon,' Clarence says, turning to walk out of the room.

Sarah follows him out.

'Clarence,' she says, turning him back to face her and seeing his red, flushed face.

'You don't have to blush every time I talk to you.'

'I can't help it,' Clarence murmurs, looking down at his feet and then slowly back up, at her face, and her beautiful, dark eyes looking at him steadily.

'Well, just promise me you'll come back safely,' she says, looking up and holding his gaze.

'I will...' Clarence starts to say as Sarah steps in close and stretches up on her toes to kiss him on the cheek.

'Come back,' she whispers, with soft breath on his face, squeezing his arm. 'You'll catch flies again,' she laughs.

Clarence starts to walk away. His mind whirling and spinning from the kiss she gave him, still feeling the warmth on his skin and thinking he will never wash that bit of his face again.

After a few steps, he realises he's forgotten to get more men and turns back towards the planning office and the groups of guards resting outside.

'I need a few to come out with me,' Clarence says, stopping in the middle of them. They look at each other to see who will go. Two men and two women eventually step forward.

'Services or police?' Clarence asks as they walk in a tight group towards the gate.

Two of them answer services, one – army, the other – Navy. The first two explain they are police from the armed response teams, with one of them having previous military experience.

They chat amiably amongst themselves as they walk to the gate, meeting Ted and arranging to take four vehicles out.

Clarence rides shotgun in the first van, and the others have one vehicle each. It takes a while to sort through keys and walk down to find vans that can be taken out from the clogged-in fleet wedged into the alley between the inner and outer wall, but eventually, they are out and driving down the road and through the estate. They stop at a large multi-chain hardware superstore on the edge of a town. The streets and villages they pass through show signs of the devastation and decay of urban life. There are burnt-out houses and rotting corpses, vehicles abandoned and left at angles, and embedded into walls. Bloodstains and broken glass litter the ground. The superstore looks remarkably normal, almost surreal, like it's an early morning bank holiday.

'You two, stay out front. You two, with me,' Clarence says, taking the two armed police response officers with him, knowing they will be better trained in close quarters fire and manoeuvre tactics.

'What do we need?' the female officer asks him.

'Nuts, bolts, chains, and anything that can be fired from a cannon. Also axes, hammers, scythes, and anything that can be used as a weapon,' he replies.

'Cannon? Are we using those old things in the Fort?' the male officer asks.

'We're going to try,' Clarence says. 'You two, go for the nuts, bolts, and chains, and I'll do the weapons.'

'Roger,' the woman replies. The hardware store doors hang open, smashed and ruined from a previous looting. At least someone else has made the effort to gain entry and save them the time of having to do it. They find rows of trolleys inside the large entrance area, and each take one and move off into the wide aisles flanked on both sides with high shelving units. There is surprisingly little damage inside the store. Dried bloodstains and debris littered around the entrance area indicate that something happened here, but no bodies or corpses remain.

Clarence looks down the ends of the rows of aisles and looks at each of the large signs. He finds the one marked Hand Tools and heads that way. He aims for the section with the axes and starts scooping them up and placing them into the trolley. He also finds sledgehammers, pickaxes, scythes, and even long-bladed machetes.

Within a few minutes, the trolley is full. He wheels it outside and asks the guards to start loading before heading back in and filling a new trolley with more items.

He passes the two police officers heading outside, with trolleys full of buckets and metal objects. They nod at one another, just like normal people mooching around the DIY store at the weekend.

Loaded up, they set off away from the store. The female police officer drives the lead van, with Clarence examining the map and giving directions to the closest gunsmith.

'I haven't seen any zombies at all,' the woman states quietly.

'Must be hiding,' Clarence rumbles and goes back to his map reading.

They keep on through the quiet, rural roads, passing fields and woodland, and then head back into expensive residential areas of large, detached houses, eventually finding their way into a small market town.

'That's it, over there,' Clarence says, pointing towards the only shop that looks fortified and solid.

They drive closer and find a window display of air rifles and pistols, binoculars and hunter-style clothing.

'Someone had a go at getting in,' the woman driver says, looking at the half smashed-in door.

Despite the quaint appearance, the shop had been well secured against such raids, and the door appeared to have withstood the half concerted effort to get in.

'There's blood everywhere out the front. Something happened here,' Clarence says.

'Turn the van round and back in close to the door,' he adds, getting out to examine the door closely.

He walks over to the next van.

'Did you get any big chains?' he asks. A few minutes later, and the van is revving loudly, with a thick chain stretched from the tow bar back to the door handles.

'NOW,' Clarence shouts, and the van accelerates quickly, powering away from the shop.

The chain springs up as the pressure pulls it, and the door is out of the frame, with a loud noise of wood and metal tearing.

'Easy when you know how,' Clarence mutters, stepping through the ragged hole and entering the small shop, seeing rows of shotguns and rifles chained to a display cabinet behind the long counter and boxes of ammunition stacked up in a glass display case.

'Bingo,' the ex-army man says, walking in to see the goods on display and holding a set of bolt croppers. 'I came prepared,' the man adds, walking around the counter.

He grips the thick chain in the mouth of the bolt croppers and starts squeezing, then squeezing harder until his face goes red from the exertion.

'May I?' Clarence steps forward, taking the handles from the now sweating man.' Clarence takes a handle in each hand and gives a sudden, overwhelming push on each, driving the handles back together and severing the chain.

'Yeah, well, I weakened it for you,' the man jokes.

'And I thank you for doing so,' Clarence replies, smiling, long used to the never-ending comments about his strength and size.

He reaches up and starts selecting the shotguns and rifles, twisting at the waist to turn and lay them on the counter.

'There's some good weapons here,' the ex-solider remarks, checking through the various rifles.

'Hu-huh,' Clarence replies, distracted and thinking about Sarah, her dark hair and eyes, the way she speaks and laughs, and that kiss. Wow, that kiss. She actually kissed him. He, the massive, bald-headed freak of nature, being kissed by someone so beautiful and graceful.

Clarence pauses, holding the last shotgun and staring off into the middle distance.

'You all right, Clarence?' the woman asks from behind him, making him start back to reality.

'Yep, never better,' Clarence grins hugely to her as he turns back to the counter.

'So, what's her name?' she adds.

'Her name?' Clarence replies.

'The only thing that can make a man smile like that in the midst of all this chaos is a woman. So, what's her name?' she repeats.

'Sarah,' Clarence rumbles quietly.

'Oh, Mr Howie's sister?' the woman says lightly. 'She's very pretty.'

'She is,' Clarence confirms, still smiling.

'We need bows and arrows too,' he adds, remembering why they are here. They prise open the ammunition case and unload all of the boxes into plastic bags found behind the counter.

One corner of the store is dedicated to archery and crossbows.

'There's loads here, Clarence. Do you want them all?' the ex-soldier asks, examining the longbows, compound bows, and dozens of packets of arrows.

'Yeah, get everything,' Clarence replies.

'And the crossbows?'

'Yes, I don't know anything about archery, so take everything.'

And everything is taken. The only thing they leave are the air weapons, on the basis of firing small lead pellets at a massive army of infected zombies will not have that much of an effect.

Within an hour, they find the next gunsmiths. This one is located in a much bigger town and already plundered, and looted extensively. Zombie corpses are everywhere.

They drive on through the town, weaving past the debris, until they reach a supermarket fuel station on the town exit road.

'Stop,' Clarence calls out.

The van slows to a stop, causing the following vehicles to brake suddenly.

'Pull into the garage forecourt,' Clarence instructs, staring hard to the side of the fuel station.

The van turns slowly and heads into the fuel station.

'Look there,' Clarence points to a set of large, wooden gates.

'Good spot, Clarence, very good,' the driver says admiringly, seeing the top of the fuel tanker just peeking out over the gates.

'Do you think it's full?' Clarence asks as they get out and walk over.

'That's almost too much to ask for,' she replies.

They find the gate locked with another thick chain and padlock. Clarence turns to see the ex-soldier jogging towards them with the bolt croppers.

'Do you want me to weaken it for you first?' the man asks light-heartedly. Clarence grunts back and snaps through the chain easily, wrenching the chain and lock off. The gates get pulled open to reveal the all-white fuel tanker. After checking it out, they are jubilant to discover it is, indeed, full.

'Does anyone know how to drive it?' Clarence asks.

'I can. I was in the traffic department and did my heavy goods vehicle training,' the woman police officer answers.

She walks in and steps up on the metal plate to open the driver's door. A body falls out on top of her, making her scream. The rest race forward to see the corpse rolling off to one side, and the woman on her arse, having been pushed back.

'Is he dead?' the woman asks in shock.

'Dead or infected?' the ex-soldier jokes, moving forward to punt the head of the corpse with his boot. The body rolls over to reveal normal human features. Dead but normal. 'Nah, he's normal dead,' the ex-soldier remarks.

The woman police officer gets up and climbs gingerly back into the cab.

'Check him for keys,' she says, going through the controls.

Clarence bends down and pats his pockets to find a set of keys, and passes them up to her.

She inserts the key and starts the engine. The fuel tanker rumbles to life, spewing out a cloud of black smoke, which quickly dissipates.

'I'll take the van. You drive this behind me,' Clarence shouts up.

They start back to their vehicles, and all stop and wince as the gears are crunched painfully behind them. They turn back to see the woman police officer sticking her middle finger up at them and laughing.

After an hour of driving, they are parked up and standing around the front of a florist's window – dead and wilting flowers in the display.

'Well, this is the address,' Clarence says, examining the map book, the list provided by Sergeant Hopewell, and then looking up at the building.

'That's definitely not a gunsmith,' the ex-soldier remarks.

'Nope, must have changed it,' Clarence replied.

'Who would turn a gunsmith into a florist?' the woman asks.

'Where's the next one?' the male police officer asks.

'Never mind that. Where's all the zombies gone?' the ex-soldier asks nervously, looking about.

They all look up and around, becoming increasingly aware of the lack of infected.

'I don't know. They must be massing somewhere,' Clarence says quietly. 'You're right, though. This is eerie.'

A feeling of being watched descends on the group.

'There's one more place we can try. It's not too far,' Clarence says, very aware of the uncomfortable feeling amongst them. Hands gripping weapons tighter, and the jokes now gone. They load back into their vehicles and drive on, again following Clarence as he handles the map on the steering wheel and works his route as he goes, treading through narrow, cobbled streets and past the once-boutique shops of this southern English hamlet.

Clarence feels the creeping sensation growing up the back of his neck. *There should be signs of life by now. The infected can't all have gone, or there are even other survivors, maybe. But then, being this close to the Fort would mean those able to would have fled to them by now.* Movement in the fields to his right catches his eye. A break in the hedgerow, and a flash of distant colour. He slows down but keeps moving along the country lane, constantly looking to the right and waiting for the thick hedge to end. Finally, he sees a large gate further up and slows down to take advantage of the gap. He brings the van to a stop and stares hard into the fields. What he sees is staggering – a long, thick line of people all moving at the same speed in the distance, across the top of the fields. The vehicles behind him stop. The drivers getting out to come forward and stare through the gate. Each of them stops and stares, with shock at the thousands and thousands of infected stretched out in a long line, moving from left to right.

'Which direction are they heading in?' one of the police officers asks.

'North,' Clarence replies. 'The main road into the area is that way. They must be going to meet the rest coming down.'

'Fucking hell, there's thousands just there,' the ex-soldier says quietly.

'Right there for the taking too,' Clarence replies. 'We can't get to them, though. The vehicles will never make it across those fields, and the distance is too great for these things,' Clarence adds, raising his assault rifle for effect.

'Where are they feeding in from?' the woman asks.

'I don't know. Over that way, I guess,' Clarence inclines his head in the direction they're moving from.

'The same way we're going,' the woman police officer states quietly. They break away without further talk, heading back to their vehicles and moving off slowly down the lane, watching the horde slowly move across the top of the fields through the gaps in the high hedgerow.

The country lane twists and turns, following the ancient hedgerow for several miles. Signposts indicate an historic town further ahead. Various smaller signs urging the travellers to stop at points of interest, eat a pub lunch, rest in a picnic area, walk around some monuments, or spend money on the crap punted out to unsuspecting holiday makers.

Something about the signs makes Clarence think of Sarah again. In the Services, he was always deployed overseas, fighting wars and battles in far-flung corners that meant nothing to him. Flown in, briefed, trained, deployed, mission executed, and moved out again. A couple of weeks' rest, and then another one. The various missions and countries blend into one long memory of deserts, jungles, and snow-covered terrain, inner city ghettos, and months spent living out of bedsits, watching subjects from windows, and building lifestyle profiles that meant nothing to him. The Services and the type of work he was involved in meant he could never talk about what he did or where he had been. Over time, the connections that once existed outside the Service slowly eroded until all that was left were the people he knew inside. But then, over the years, they too slowly fell away as younger, fitter, and leaner men came through the ranks, and men like Clarence, Chris, and Malcolm felt like dinosaurs.

They left the Services, but the skills they had harnessed and built simply did not transfer to civilian life, and like so many highly skilled but older soldiers, they were drawn to the world of mercenary soldiering, with the promise of action and high wages. They all said it was for the money, but in reality, it was the only way of clinging onto the life they had built, working with people who knew those same deadly skills, and being able to belong to something. Former officers started security companies back in the UK and contacted their former men, offering them steady wages and a dedicated role. Clarence responded to that, after years of mercenary work left a nasty taste in his mouth. Shady deals done in back street cafés were not his idea of honour. His mammoth size and appearance meant he was perfect for door work. Often, his mere presence prevented most incidents from escalating, but even then, the constant hours in the seedy nightlife full of cocky idiots with gelled hair and t-shirt muscles soon wore him down.

Managers and bar owners were obsessed with profit, reputation, health and safety, log sheets, toilet checks, and head counts. Clarence's size, appearance, and deep voice made him a target for many women. Women who loved the idea of being with a tough man with a tough reputation, but Clarence was a professional, not a steroid-addicted bouncer, obsessed with image and wearing a shirt two sizes too small, and those drunken women repulsed him.

He had intelligence and knowledge that just did not correlate with his appearance, and after years of being seen to be a big, tough idiot, he accepted the type of woman he was likely to be with. But now, something magical had happened. Something he had never known before. A beautiful, educated, and intelligent woman was interested in him.

The way she spoke to him, not patronisingly, but speaking to him as an equal, touching his arm or shoulder, leaning forward, and staring into his eyes left him almost breathless. The desperation of the world, and the utter violence and degradation of mankind just in the last seven days, the hopeless feeling that no matter how they fight back or what they do, it's all pointless. Those feelings now mix with a warm, tingling feeling of something different he had not felt before. Light in the dark. A single rose amongst weeds. Hope where there was none. Something to survive for. Something to fight for.

The road sweeps around to a long, wide junction. From the left, streams of infected are pouring from the town and heading into the fields to shuffle and stagger along in dead silence. Lines of rotting, walking corpses drawn to a meeting place, where they will gather and mass in readiness of war. The vehicles stop back from the junction, far enough back to be able to respond if they turn for the attack, but they don't turn. They don't pay any attention at all.

'We can't get through that lot without picking a fight,' the woman police officer says after jumping down and walking up to stand by Clarence.

'Yeah, you're probably right,' Clarence replies, wishing they had the Saxon with them and the GPMG.

'So, the motorway to the north is that way, then?' she asks, looking down at the map.

'Yeah, that must be the gathering point. The main motorway running south from London, I guess. If all these get to the various junctions feeding into it, then the main group will scoop them up as they come.'

'Maybe they're heading somewhere else?' she suggests.

'That,' Clarence replies, 'is just wishful thinking. Come on, we'd better get back.'

'Err, slight problem. This is a narrow lane, and that is a big fuel truck, and I'm not reversing it all the way back.'

'Good point, you'll be needing the junction, then,' Clarence says, turning back to look at the fuel truck.

'Yep.'

'How will you do it?'

'Pull out to the right, reverse back to the left, and swing back in to this road,' she replies.

'Right...'

'That's what I thought.' She bites her bottom lip, staring at the constant stream heading across the junction.

'Well, the fuel tanker is big and heavy, and as long as you keep motion, you should be all right, and we did say we wanted to take a few of them out,' Clarence rumbles quietly.

'No, you said *you* wanted to take them out.'

'Yeah, but I can't drive that thing, or can I? Is it hard?' he asks.

'Yes, it is, bloody hard. You'll stall the engine before you get more than a few metres. Don't worry, I'll do it.' She turns and walks back to the fuel tanker, pausing as she climbs up into the cabin and looking at the junction.

She nods to herself and slowly pulls out from behind Clarence's van, moving slowly up to the wide junction. Clarence watches as she seems to slow down, almost stopping; then, at the last second, the fuel tanker surges ahead, pulling over to the extreme left and brushing against the hedgerow.

The tanker then pulls to the right, moving out of the lane and into the junction. The front of the tanker impacts on the line of infected staggering across, striking them from behind and shunting them all forward. The collective ramming drives them into the backs of the infected in front, acting as a giant scoop and propelling them forward. The momentum causes them to either fall out to either side or drop down onto the ground, to be dragged along by the front of the truck, or squashed by the massive wheels, causing blood and guts to be pumped out onto the road surface. The infected neither slow down nor speed up, and they take no avoiding action as the truck pummels them out of the way.

The fuel tanker pushes out into the right side of the junction, then brakes hard, forcing the infected caught at the front to be propelled forward. A loud grinding of gears can be heard as the woman police officer works to engage the reversing gears and start moving backwards. The rear of the truck lacks the solid wall of the front, and the infected behind are simply crushed by the rounded edge of the tanker and the jutting-out metal ladder. The tanker reverses, driving backwards further down to the left until the front goes past the entrance to the lane. Once again, the tanker brakes hard, and the gears crunch as she selects a forward-driving gear and pulls away, swinging the front around and back into the lane, ploughing through more as they blindly shuffle back across the junction. As the front of the tanker draws level with Clarence, he steps out and applauds with respect, smiling broadly at the excellent driving skills shown. She smiles back and salutes as she drives onwards past the waiting vehicles. Clarence gets back in his van and tries to do a three-point turn in the road, but the narrow width of the lane and the length of the van make it a seven-point turn. Eventually, he succeeds and moves out of the way for the other vehicles. They move closer to the wider section of the junction to complete their manoeuvre, and within minutes, the vehicles are driving back down the lane, behind the fuel tanker.

CHAPTER EIGHTY-FOUR

Dave and Jamie move quickly to the edge of the estate, jogging in silence with fluid movements. Neither showing signs of exertion. They stop at the country lane leading into the estate.

'The estate is here, with one lane leading in, but they could use the fields on either side,' Dave says, examining the area.

'The fields have high hedgerows, and they're thick with brambles which will we be hard to push through,' Jamie replies.

'The natural path will be this lane. We can't do anything about the fields, but we do have a choke point here – the hedges on both sides are very high, and the lane ends abruptly as it enters the estate. They will come down the lane and fan out into the estate, and sweep through, but most of them will keep going straight down the centre main road,' Dave explains.

'The first trap should be here, on the central road, about halfway down. We then work back, setting more traps as we go. They will be crammed into the lane, so they will naturally spill out to the sides and move down, through the estate, using all available space. So we set one here and then more further out to the sides. That way, there will be the maximum number of them in the area when the traps go off.' Jamie listens in silence and watches Dave with keen interest, tracking his view to look at the same places.

Dave moves down the central road, going just past the halfway mark, looking at the parked cars, nose to tail, on both sides of the road.

'They'll come down the lane and have to go through the gap between the vehicles on either side,' Dave explains.

He takes two grenades from one of the canvas bags and walks back to the closest row of vehicles. Dropping down onto the ground, he positions the grenade snug against the inside of the rear tyre, then crosses the road to place another grenade against the inside of the tyre on the opposite vehicle.

'When the time is right, we tie wire onto both pins and wedge them in firmly. Pressure applied to the wire pulls the pins, which activates the detonation,' Dave explains, pulling a roll of very thin fishing wire from a pocket to show Jamie.

'Will these two be enough to detonate the rest of the vehicles?' Jamie asks.

'In theory, yes, but there will be a delay. These grenades will detonate the fuel tanks, but we need to speed the progress up so we get maximum effect.' Dave shrugs his rucksack off and takes out a container. He unscrews the lid and starts pouring a thin trail of black powder from the first grenade, working back to the next vehicle and ending the thin trail underneath the fuel tank. Dave takes another grenade and rests it in a small pool of the powder.

'I see,' Jamie says.

Dave takes out another container and hands it to Jamie.

'You do the other side,' Dave says and turns to move on, trailing black powder over to the next vehicle. Jamie moves across and repeats the action, pouring a thin trail of the powder from fuel tank to fuel tank and leaving a grenade nestled in the black powder underneath each one.

'Good,' Dave says. 'Now we do the rest of the estate.' They go back into the estate, moving from road to road and house to house, finding alleys and paths that work through the small streets. They place trip-wired grenades at various points of access, then get to the side roads connected to the central main road, and stop to look at the cars and vehicles left in situ.

'We'll do all of these too. You do the far side,' Dave says.

They split up, and Jamie crosses the central lane to work the other side, positioning trip wire grenades between the gaps of the vehicles and more thin trails of black powder stretched from fuel tank to fuel tank. They meet back in the central road.

'Now, go from house to house and turn the gas on, close the doors to trap the gas.'

'Got it.' They move off again, from dwelling to dwelling, going into kitchens and turning the gas jets on low, and letting the poisonous vapour seep out to fill the rooms. They continue to work throughout the day, moving into the side streets and laying traps with grenades, wires, and black powder, then going into the houses, and turning the gas supply to hiss out as they move back out, closing the doors behind them. After several hours, they stand at the exit point of the lane, where it stretches out into the flatlands, and the diggers moving along, slowly churning the earth up.

'Clarence is still out with his foraging party. We'll wait for him to return and then put the wires across the centre path,' Dave says.

'What about the men out front on the observation points? They won't be able to get back through,' Jamie replies.

'I spoke to them. I left a clear path for them to run through on the side I worked on,' Dave replies.

'Okay,' Jamie nods back at him.

'Get our vehicle and leave it on the edge of the estate, on the road. Meet me back at the entrance point,' Dave says, turning to walk back up the central road.

'Okay,' Jamie replies. A few minutes later, they stand in silence at the entrance to the estate.

'You did well today,' Dave says.

'Thank you,' Jamie replies.

Eventually, they hear engine noises coming towards them.

'How many?' Dave asks.

'Engines? Err...' Jamie cocks his head and listens intently for a few seconds. 'I have no idea,' he finally admits, feeling ashamed that he is unable to work out the different sounds of the engines.

'Me neither,' Dave replies, and Jamie gives a rare and awkward smile.

The front vehicle comes into view. Clarence's distinct, bald-headed profile clear through the windscreen. The lead vehicle slows to a stop a few metres back from the entrance.

'Everything okay?' Clarence asks, getting out and walking towards them, with his assault rifle held like a toy gun in his massive hand.

'Yes,' Dave replies.

'Did you rig the estate okay?' Clarence asks.

'Waiting for you to go through so we can finish off,' Dave answers.

'Okay, mate, we found a few things to bring back with us. We've got loads of nuts, bolts, and chains for the cannon,' Clarence smiles at the two quiet men.

'Good, is that a fuel tanker?' Dave asks, looking over at the large vehicle, with the engine idling.

'Yep, and it's full too. Thought we might make use of it.'

Dave nods, staring at the tanker. 'If they don't need it down there, we can use it here.'

'Roger. I'll pass that on,' Clarence replies.

'Let them know the estate is rigged and to be avoided,' Dave adds as Clarence walks back to his vehicle.

The convoy stops on the single track road leading to the Fort as Howie and Chris step out of the gates, accompanied by Blowers and Cookey. All of them look at the fuel tanker.

'Where on earth did you find that?' Chris calls out as they walk towards each other. Clarence turns to glance at the fuel tanker.

'We found it behind some gates, next to a petrol station, couldn't believe it was still there. We've got loads of stuff from the hardware store and the first gunsmith's, but the next one was looted. The one after that was a florist's and not much use...'

'A florist's?' Howie interrupts. 'Who would turn a gunsmith's into a florist's?'

'That's what we said. So then, we went for the last one and saw shitloads of zombies marching out of a town, heading north.'

'North?' Chris asks. All of them focussing hard on Clarence's words.

'Yeah, it looks like they're going towards the motorway but moving as the crow flies, going across land and fields.'

'How many?' Howie asks.

'Thousands. Just a solid line of them. They're moving slowly, and they didn't pay us any attention, not even when we mowed a few down with the fuel tanker.'

'You reckon they're heading for the motorway?' Chris asks.

'Must be. It makes the most sense. They get to the junctions on the motorway and then tag onto the main bulk as they pass through. The most obvious theory is that they're massing, just like they did in London,' Clarence says, looking to Chris, then Howie.

'Well, we knew it was coming. This is just a dose of reality,' Howie says grimly. 'It changes nothing. We've got spotters out, and Dave is rigging the estate now...'

'He's done it. Him and that other quiet one,' Clarence says.

'Jamie. They've done it already?' Howie replies.

'He wants the fuel tanker up there if you don't need it.'

'I bet he bloody does. I bet his eyes lit up at that thing,' Howie laughs. 'Is it full?'

'With petrol,' Clarence nods.

'The last point of defence before they get to us is the deep ditch after the last bank. If we pour petrol in, we'll lose loads being soaked into the ground before it starts to fill...' Howie muses.

'I see what you mean, Howie. Some pipes filled with petrol spraying out, maybe?' Chris adds, rubbing his beard as he thinks.

'Flame throwers?' Howie asks.

'Big fucking flame throwers. Now, that would be cool,' Chris smiles. 'But it will take too long to sort out.'

'Maybe not,' Ted interrupts. 'We've got plenty of plumbers here. Let me have a word with them and see what we can do.'

'You happy with that, Howie?' Chris asks, looking at him.

'Yeah, we've got no choice really. We know they're massing or getting ready, so we need to pick the pace up. It's already getting late. '

Chris, find out how the diggers are getting on, then how long before we can start putting the spikes and caltrops in.

'We need Dave back here to sort those cannons out and see if they can be used. Ted, find those plumbers and work out if we can rig something up with the petrol going through pipes, in the ditch.

'Clarence, you take the weapons and materials you found to Malcolm and then get the lists of people that have weapons experience, and start drilling or training, or distributing the weapons. Use the top of the inner wall for the long-range weapons and get people up there ready. There's some archers here too. Find out where they need to be positioned. Ideally, we want them on the top of the inner wall too, firing high so they get the best range.

'Blowers and Cookey, stay on that gate and do not let anyone out that shouldn't be going out, got it?' Howie speaks firmly and quickly, looking to each man as he issues orders and instructions.

They nod back at each request.

'Good, we need to move and get this done quickly. Let's go.'

CHAPTER EIGHTY-FIVE

The afternoon rolls on, with the long hours flying by as those few men tasked with the responsibility work like demons without rest. Strong coffee, adrenalin, and the knowledge of what's coming their way keep them working at a pace that would leave most reeling from exhaustion.

Chris stalks the Fort, radio in hand, speaking to the guards with the digger drivers, urging them to move quickly and finding out the pits are nearly finished.

He locates Sergeant Hopewell in the office, already surrounded by people clamouring for her attention. Chris pushes through, using his bulk to force a path, and then instructs Sergeant Hopewell to find people to send out and cut weeds and long grass down, and be ready to assist the engineers. Then he works his way to the workshops to find Kelly and the rest hard at work and more people already drafted in to sort wooden shafts, posts, and metal poles into piles that are waiting to be sharpened into spikes or to be cut and bent into the deadly foot traps. Several generators sourced from non-essential parts of the Fort chug and roar as the power tools scream out.

Sparks from metal cutters cascade out onto the workshop floor, and every space is dominated by small groups hard at work.

Chris pauses at the door, watching Kelly move from group to group, correcting and offering advice.

'Kelly, how's it going?' Chris asks, finally getting her attention.

'Good, the spikes are almost ready. They were the easiest. The foot traps are taking a bit longer, though,' she replies, wiping sweat from her brow with an old cloth and smearing black grease over her forehead.

'Can we start getting them out, then?'

'The spikes? Err, yeah, I think we can.'

'Good, find someone to send out to supervise it if you can't be spared,' Chris replies firmly.

'No, I'll go myself. Are there guards out there?' she asks.

'Several of them. No one is to go near the edge of the estate. The guards will shoot them if they do. Get out there as quick as possible,' Chris responds and walks out of the room.

Back on the radio, he informs the gate that engineers will be coming through shortly and then talks to the guards with the digger drivers. He tells them to get the pits finished and then use the drivers to help with whatever else is needed. Finally, he establishes that Dave is on his way back to the Fort with Jamie.

TED MOVES AWAY from the small gathering outside the Fort, moving quickly and with purpose back inside.

He walks to the police office to find Sarah and Terri helping Sergeant Hopewell deal with the many enquiries. People now coming in to ask questions about all the activity taking place and trying to find more people to help the engineers.

Ted finds the stack of lists and works his way through the pile until he finds names of plumbers and the sections within the camp they are allocated to. Striding back outside, he looks for runners to send out, only to find the supply of runners now exhausted.

'Where are all the runners?' he calls out, stepping back into the office and having to shout over the clamour of voices.

'All busy, Ted,' Sarah replies. Ted steps back out and casts his experienced eye around to see Tom and Steven strolling along in the camp, still bickering.

'You two, come here,' Ted bellows.

Tom and Steven both spin around, recognising his voice instantly, and move quickly over to him.

'We need plumbers. They're on these lists...' Ted starts to explain.

'Have we sprung a leak?' Steven jokes.

'Shut up and focus, young man,' Ted snaps at him and notices they both visibly straighten up at his tone of voice.

'Take these,' Ted hands the lists to Steven, 'and get them over to me as soon as possible, and I mean – as soon as possible.'

'Okay, Ted.'

'Right, Tom. Ted gave me the lists, so I'll be in charge of this project, seeing as Mr Howie said we're both the same now...' Steven starts to gloat.

'I SAID NOW,' Ted booms at them. They both turn and start heading back into the camp as Ted heads back towards the police office, with a wry smile and a shake of his head.

AS THE SMALL gathering listens to Howie, Clarence watches him closely. This untrained man, a supermarket manager, gives orders to trained and experienced soldiers. There's something about him, though. The passion he exudes and the absolute certainty with which he speaks. Even Big Chris defers to Howie, and Clarence thinks back to the many missions when Chris was in charge, but Chris was always a man's soldier, never an officer. Howie is like an officer, the type of officer the men all respect and trust, the officer always leading from the front. The officer that can see all the facets of the mission, not just the one bit he is doing. Clarence had met great strategists in his time, but none of them had the human touch that Howie possesses. His ability to look a man in the eye and say with certainty that this needs to be done and it needs to be done now. Clarence watches Big Chris and the way he listens to Howie. Chris had always had that rare thing in a soldier – a good diplomat, as well as a good fighter. However, Chris had never taken to idiot officers very well and had been outspoken if he felt they were doing the wrong thing, often to the detriment of his own career.

Clarence breaks away and heads back to his vehicle. Blowers and

Cookey drag the big vehicle gates open, then pull the huge gates of the inner wall open too, allowing the vehicles to be driven inside the safety of the Fort. The fuel tanker is directed into the gap between the walls. The other vehicles, headed by Clarence, drive slowly through the compound, to the armoury, and over to Malcolm waiting outside.

'Big man, did you get anything nice for me?' Malcolm greets his long-time comrade with a massive smile and a warm handshake.

'Well, we got a few bits: rifles, shotguns, and loads of ammunition. First time I've loaded up with bows and arrows, though,' Clarence replies, going around to the back and opening the rear doors.

'Strange times, my friend,' Malcolm muses as he starts going through the various items. 'What the bloody hell are we going to do with shotguns?'

'Yeah, I know, but Chris and Howie said to get everything,' Clarence says.

'I suppose they'll be usable if they breech the walls and get inside. We'll use them for defence only. Some of these rifles are good, Clarence.'

'I suppose so, but a few dozen heavy calibre, general-purpose assault rifles would be better.'

'Ha, and if we were in America, we'd be able to pick them up in a supermarket too. Fuck me, those blokes had some decent ordnance.' Malcolm reminisces back to conflicts he had fought alongside the U.S. Marine Corps and their never-ending supply of decent weapons.

'I bet there's some secure places over there,' the ex-soldier that went with Clarence interrupts as he helps them to unload the vans and carry the items into the large armoury room.

'Mate, I don't know your name,' Clarence suddenly realises as the ex-soldier walks by the side of him, with armloads of shotguns.

'Brian. Nice to meet you,' Brian grunts as he lifts the heavy load onto a workbench.

'You too. Listen, I'll have to leave you to it. I've got some tasks to finish,' Clarence says, walking back out of the armoury and up to the police office.

He enters to find the inside even more frantic: radios blaring out with chatter, people talking loudly, and Sergeant Hopewell trying to do a hundred things at the same time. Clarence frowns as he looks at the bedlam in front of him, trying to figure out the best way of getting her attention without simply pushing everyone else out of the way.

A cool hand touches his arm, and he glances down to see Sarah smiling broadly at him. Her clean, white teeth framed by those soft, pink lips.

'You're back,' she says simply.

'I said I would be,' Clarence replies.

'I'm glad. I was worried,' Sarah says.

Clarence doesn't reply but stares for long seconds, losing himself in her dark eyes.

He gently puts his hand over hers. His giant mitt dwarfing her small, delicate hand. A tingling sensation prickles through him from the contact. A simple action, yet so endearing that she steps forward involuntary until they are standing with bodies touching. In the chaos of the office, with voices shouting and people surging around them, they stand staring into each other's eyes and slowly move forward until their lips are but a tiny distance apart.

'Did you need something, mate?' Ted's voice snaps them back to reality as he bustles into the office and heads over to the stacks of paper on the desk.

'Err, I, err, yeah, I think so,' Clarence stammers, feeling a strange sense of loss at being so close to kissing her.

'You think so?' Ted asks with a puzzled frown.

'I'll see you in a while. I'm glad you're back. Come and find me if you get any spare time,' Sarah says quietly and slips away, back into the furore going on around them.

'Sorry, Ted. I need lists of anyone with weapons training or experience and the archers, too.'

'Yep, okay, how are you going to do it?' Ted replies, starting to leaf through a big pile of papers.

'Can you get them all down to the front, near the gates?' Clarence asks.

'It'll take a bit of time, Clarence. It's bedlam here as you can see, and we've got no runners left,' Ted replies.

'The Saxon's got a loudhailer. Use the radio and get one of them to put it out so everyone can hear it,' Clarence says.

'Good idea. Now, why didn't I think of that?' Ted mutters as he hunts round for the radio.

'Police office to the Saxon,' Ted speaks into it.

'Saxon to police office. Go ahead.'

'Police office to Saxon. Can you use the loudspeaker and ask the people that registered their firearms experience to report to the front of the Fort?'

'Roger. Confirm you want anyone with firearms experience to report to the front?'

'Answer yes. Also anyone with archery experience.'

'Roger that. Will do it now.'

'Thanks, Ted,' Clarence rumbles in his deep voice. He walks out of the office and down to the armoury, reaching the door as the amplified voice of Nick Hewitt suddenly fills the air. Nick's loud message creates a general buzz and a sense of excitement within the camp.

People start moving about quickly, talking loudly. Those people with weapons knowledge find their families or partners and hastily kiss, and hold them before heading off with grim faces, meeting others along the way and walking together while talking. Clarence enters the armoury to see Malcolm, Brian, and a few others, still bringing in the items from the vehicles.

'I'm going down the front to start sorting out the people with weapons knowledge,' Clarence informs them.

'Do you need a hand, mate?' Brian says. 'I did an instructor course a few years back.'

'Definitely. Malc, can you spare Brian?'

'Yep, crack on. We've got enough people here. Are you bringing them back here for weapons allocation?' Malcolm asks.

'Yeah, I'll take a few with me and can you send more down as soon as you get the chance?'

'Roger. Give me a few minutes to see what I've got,' Malcolm replies.

'Bloody quartermasters... All the same,' Clarence jokes as he leaves.

CHAPTER EIGHTY-SIX

Cookey and Blowers disperse from the briefing, now long used to the sudden, ferocious intensity of Howie. They both listen with awe as he gives clear instructions to the rest, giving them tasks but leaving it to them how they get it completed.

They then stroll back and open the gates wide to allow Clarence and the rest of the vehicles to get through into the Fort. The gates are closed after them, and they once again resume their static guard on the front, walk-through gate, watching as the men dart about, with a renewed sense of pace and urgency.

'Kind of feels weird standing here while everyone else is running about,' Cookey remarks after a few minutes.

'Yeah, I know what you mean, but Nick and Curtis are doing the same up top, with the Saxon,' Blowers says.

'What about Tucker? Where's he?' Cookey asks.

'Mr Howie asked him to sort out the food situation.'

'He'll be in his element, then,' Cookey says.

'I expect so. Talking of which, I am bloody starving,' Blowers says.

'Aye, me too,' Cookey replies.

'Aye?' Blowers asks, picking up on the strange comment.

'What?'

'You said aye.'

'Yeah, and?'

'Nothing...'

'What?' Cookey asks.

'No, mate, nothing. It's just that sailors say *aye*.'

'Oh, for fuck's sake, Blowers. Don't start.'

'What? I never said anything. You can be a sailor if you like.'

'Why would I want to be a sailor?' Cookey asks.

'So you can say aye...and, of course, there's all the sea-men.'

'Oh, fuck off.'

'You like sea-men, don't you, Cookey?'

'Piss off, Blowers.' They eventually stop talking and lean back against the gate to rest.

'Did you hear what Clarence said about them heading north?' Cookey says.

'Yes, mate, there's going to be fucking shitloads of them coming for us.'

'Yeah, does it bother you?' Cookey asks quietly.

'I don't know. If I think about it, then yeah, I guess it does, but I keep thinking of the other scraps we've had, and we've done all right so far,' Blowers replies.

'There's gonna be a lot more this time,' Cookey says.

'How can it be worse than London? There were thousands of them then, and besides, they can't all attack at the same time, can they?'

'Eh?'

'Well, like in London, we formed a circle, and it's only the first row that could actually attack us. The rest just waited and stepped in when the first lot got knocked down.'

'Yeah, but we ain't gonna be in a circle this time, are we? We're gonna be stood in a big line.'

'Yes, but it's still only the first row that can actually attack us. The others are behind them.'

'I see what you mean. I'm sort of anxious about it, a bit scared, and also, kind of looking forward to it, like I want it to happen,' Cookey says plainly. Blowers glances over at his friend speaking from the heart. 'Do you know what I mean, Blowers? I'm scared and terrified, but also excited, and ready for it, all at the same time,' Cookey repeats.

'I know what you mean, mate. I feel the same. I think we all do; otherwise, we'd have bottled long before now.'

'That was a bit deep for you, Blowers.'

'You like it deep.'

'Oh, for fuck's sake.'

CHAPTER EIGHTY-SEVEN

'We tie the wire onto the pin like this; then, we have to make sure the grenade is firmly placed; otherwise, the pressure on the wire will simply pull the grenade along the ground and not pull the pin out. Then we feed the wire over to the other side and position the second grenade, making sure the wire is taut.' Dave gently pulls the wire until it stretches across the road.

'Then we tie it off, and again, make sure the grenade is firmly placed, got it?'

'Got it,' Jamie replies.

They step back and move a few feet away. Already the thin fishing wire is hard to see. Nodding with satisfaction, they move back down through the estate, heading towards the vehicle they left on the road to the Fort.

'Where will we put the tanker if we get it?' Jamie asks.

'Either in the middle so we get the full effect of the blast and the shrapnel it creates, or closer to the exit onto the Fort Road.'

'Okay.'

The inside of the car is uncomfortably hot with warm, stale air. They both wind their windows down as Jamie pulls away, driving towards the Fort.

The ditches on both sides are almost finished, with the diggers now working at the far ends. The freshly churned, brown earth looking stark against the green, flat lands. People from the Fort walk out over the flatlands, carrying hand tools and heading towards the big patches of long grass. Clarence and one of the guards from the commune stand in front of the Fort, talking to a large group of people. Each of them holding a collection of rifles. A large group of archers are placed off to one side. Some of them holding great bows the size of a man. Others with smaller, modern bows, with pulleys and contraptions attached to them. They stand talking, pointing out to the flatlands and then back up at the walls behind them. Others in the group sort through the large boxes and packets of arrows. Dave turns back to take in the diggers and the men working with them, then back at the rows of workers coming from the Fort, towards the long grass, Clarence speaking to the large groups and showing them the weapons, the archers making ready. Now more people are filing out from the gates, carrying long, sharpened spikes and loading them into the backs of vehicles waiting nearby. Dave recognises the engineers carrying buckets of small, sharp, twisted metal foot traps and loading them into the vehicles. Jamie stops the car near the front. They climb out, and Dave walks straight over to Howie.

'Mr Howie,' Dave says.

'Dave,' Howie greets him back with a genuine smile. 'How did you get on?'

'Good, the estate is all set.'

'Is Jamie okay?'

'Very good, Mr Howie, very capable.'

'Takes after you, mate.'

'They must be the spikes for the ditches.'

'Yep, they've worked bloody hard, getting them done so quickly. Just got to get them driven in now. We've had to get a lot more people involved, which I didn't want to do, but we don't really have a choice if we want all these things to happen. The first load of caltrops are ready too. Clarence and that chap...Brian have got the lists of all the people with weapons experience, and they are checking to make sure they won't shoot themselves in the foot or someone else, for that matter. Then we've got the archers over there. Clarence found some good supplies and some of them had their own kit with them. I don't know if they'll be any good, but it gives them hope and something to do.'

'You've got a lot done,' Dave remarks.

'Yes, we have,' Howie admits.

'Ted is rounding up some plumbers too. We'll find out if we can rig some pipes up in the deep ditch after the last bank for flame throwers.'

'Is that for the fuel tanker?' Dave asks.

'Yes, well, the petrol from the fuel tanker anyway. I heard you had plans for the tanker?'

'You can have the fuel first. I just want the vehicle.'

'Don't you need fuel in it to make this blow up?' Howie asks.

'No, the fumes trapped inside the pressured container will be enough.'

'Oh, so we can use all the fuel, then?'

'Well, maybe just leave a little bit in there if that's okay, Mr Howie.'

'No worries, mate. I don't know if the flame throwing idea will work. Surely, we'll need to store the fuel, then pump it into the pipes, and then, if we put holes in the pipes for the flames to come out off, won't the fuel just leak out? Also, how does it get ignited? And wouldn't the flame just shoot back inside the pipe and blow the whole thing up?'

'Yes, yes, yes, and yes, and you would need ignition from a distance; otherwise, the person doing the igniting would get blown up, and yes, it would all blow up,' Dave replies.

'Oh, I see,' Howie says with a frown.

'But you could just lay hoses down in the ditch and fill them with petrol. Put containers or buckets, and other things filled with fuel: grenades, bits of metal, nails, screws, anything sharp and ignite it from a distance. The whole thing will go then, and the steep sides of the ditch will force the pressure wave and explosion straight up and not out, to the sides.'

'Bloody hell, Dave. You really like blowing things up, don't you?'

'Yes, Mr Howie,' Dave replies flatly.

'We'll do that, then. How about the cannons? Do you think you can get them working?'

'They already work. It's just a matter of knowing *how* they work, having the right mix of powder, charge, and then what we use to fire out of them. I'll start looking at them now.'

'I'll get some coffee up to you,' Howie says.

'Okay, thanks, Mr Howie.' Dave heads into the Fort and finds Jamie talking with Cookey and Blowers.

'What's next?' Jamie asks him.

'Cannons,' Dave replies.

'Like two peas in a pod, them two,' Blowers remarks as they watch Dave and Jamie walk off towards the steps.

HOWIE STANDS, watching the activity unfolding in front of him. A deep look of concentration on his face. So far, so good, he thinks, but the news of the infected leading across the fields leave his mind unsettled. Howie knows the reality of the situation probably better than anyone else, other than Dave, but for one of them to have actually seen them preparing brings it home. Two armies – one vastly outnumbering the other, getting ready to meet. He turns and heads back towards the Fort, deep in thought. Cookey and Blowers both remain quiet and let him pass without interruption.

The noise of the camp fills the air. The recent movement of people going outside to help with spikes, caltrops, cutting grass, weapons training, and archery have rapidly increased the air of excitement and charged the atmosphere.

Howie watches people moving between sections. He notices that many of them are now armed with whatever they can find: sticks, metal poles, knives, hand axes, and hammers. The change is palpable and positive. The charged atmosphere has rubbed off on everyone, and for the first time, Howie takes note of the children in the camp. Small children are running between the tents, chasing each other and laughing. Bigger boys walk in groups and hold small sticks in their hands, ready to fight and kill all the zombies.

Howie notices the traditional roles of male and female have come back. The boys are carrying the weapons and the girls are working with the women to prepare food and clean the area and helping to feed babies. The sound of children's laughter fills his ears, and the gleeful, uncorrupted sound is like music. Their innocence and utter faith that these adults will protect them from everything touches him deeply.

The resilience of their young minds has almost certainly faced untold horrors already, but here they are, running and playing like children have always done.

The thought of the infected army sweeping through them and getting into the Fort to savage these children fills Howie with a sickening feeling, and a thought process enters his head. There's a problem here. If they do get in, and there is every chance they will, then these children have nowhere to go. The mothers will fight like tigers, of that there is no doubt, but they too will fall. *They must be protected. At all cost, they must be made safe and kept safe. Without them, there is no purpose for all of this. We can stand and fight, and show them how brave we are,* Howie thinks, *but for what reason? To give ourselves freedom to live so our race can continue.* The thought of there now being two races of people on the earth hits Howie hard. An evil race, intent on killing every last human, and those small humans, who are now running about and playing and must survive in order to make more humans. There is nowhere else to run, though. Beyond that wall is the sea. There aren't enough boats to take them all away, and nowhere to go if they did find enough. But maybe, just maybe...

Howie makes his way through the camp; his mind whirling. *Why did he leave this so late?* He reaches the police office and is stunned for a second to see the almighty clamour going on. People are shouting and pushing forward to speak to a very harassed-looking Sergeant Hopewell and Terri.

'Sarah, Terri, I need to speak with you both now,' Howie speaks firmly, and his voice cuts across the room as the people realise Mr Howie is here.

The three of them step outside and move away from the door to a quiet spot.

'Listen, I don't know why I didn't think of this sooner, but we are right on the sea here, so there must be harbours or mooring points round here. I want you to find boats and get them back here.'

'Why? What for?' Sarah asks.

'When they come, I want the children loaded onto boats and moved out and away from the Fort. If they get in, we'll all be killed. We must do whatever we can to keep them safe. Find some people that can handle boats and navigation and have them ready to report to a set place when the action starts. Get the mothers too, be ready to get them out,' Howie says intensely.

'Good idea, very good idea,' Sarah replies, nodding her head.

'There is one boat out there already. I saw it when we arrived,' Terri says.

'Good, get them to use that to go out and find more, and bring them back. Work out how many children and mothers we have and make sure they bring enough boats back with them.'

'Err, this is a horrible question, Howie, but what age child do we go up to? Sixteen, Eighteen?'

'Eighteen. They'll be old enough to offer some protection and care for the younger ones.'

'Some of the eighteen-year-olds won't want to go,' Terri says. 'They'll want to stay and fight with their fathers or brothers.'

'That's natural, but just do what you can. It's already getting late, so do it quickly, and I will want to speak to the boat people before they go. Send them to the planning office.'

Breaking apart to move off to their respective offices, they each feel the sense of pace increasing. Knowing that with each passing hour, the zombie army build in numbers and draw ever closer.

Terri rushes into the office, ignoring the people moving towards her with questions. She pulls the stacks of lists from the desk and moves down to Sarah at the back of the office, purposefully putting her back to the rest of the room.

'How do we do this?' Terri asks, scanning through the lists of skills.

'I don't know if we even recorded people with boat skills.' She glances back to see Sergeant Hopewell still frantically struggling to cope at the main desk.

'Sarge, did we record people with boating skills?' Terri shouts across and gets a quick glance from Sergeant Hopewell before she returns to dealing with the people in front of her.

'It's here, under occupations,' Sarah says. 'We've got Royal Navy sailors and commercial sailors in the camp. I guess being this close to the coast, there would be.'

'Let me see,' Terri asks, leafing through the papers.

'There's a Royal Navy Reserves Captain here. Henry Marshall. He's retired and getting on a bit in age, but we recorded him having commercial experience, too.'

'Let's find him,' Sarah stands up, ready to go.

'Hang on. Let me check something. Yes, he's also on the list of people with weapons experience. He'll be down with Clarence at the front.'

'Clarence has a radio. Can we call him and get him sent back?' Sarah asks.

Terri fights back through the crowds at the desk to reach the radio, then pushes back out to find some clear ground.

'Police office to Clarence.'

'Clarence to police office. Go ahead.'

'Police office to Clarence. Have you got a Henry Marshall with you?'

'Confirm Henry Marshall. Stand by.' A few minutes go by, with Sarah and Terri staring intently at the radio. *'Clarence to police office. Yes, we have Henry Marshall with us.'*

'Police office to Clarence. Send him back to us immediately. His services are required urgently.'

'Clarence to police office. Roger that. He's on his way to the police office.'

'Police office to Clarence. Thank you and out.'

'Good. Now, I don't know about you, but I need coffee,' Sarah says, heading to the back room and the kettle that has been running non-stop for several hours.

Howie moves back into the planning office after leaving Terri and Sarah. Big Chris is inside, with several men, all looking over the plans on the table.

'Yes, these are the ditches here. We want pipes running with fuel that we can ignite from a distance and create a wall of flame,' Chris explains to the men.

'Cancel that Chris. Change of plan,' Howie says, then runs through the idea given by Dave.

'Much better,' Chris nods back.

'Sorry, you must be the plumbers, seeing as most of you have pencils behind your ears. I'm Howie,' Howie says, smiling and shaking hands with them in turn.

'Howie, leave this with me. I'll take these chaps down and get started,' Chris says, leading the men outside. Howie pauses for a second in the sudden quietness of the room; the noise from the camp reduced as Chris closes the door behind him.

Rubbing his hands through his hair, he walks around the desk to the large flask and presses his hand against the side. Still warm. He finds a half-filled cup and moves back over to the door, and throws the cold contents out onto the ground. He then closes the door and moves back inside. He takes a teaspoon and loads it up with sugar from a ragged bag left on the table, then pours the hot, black coffee into the mug. The aroma hits him instantly, and the simple act of making a coffee calms him immeasurably. Mug in hand, he feels his body relaxing for the first time in days. Staring into nothingness, he raises the mug slowly to his lips and takes the first mouthful just as the door pops open, with Terri leaning in.

'Howie, this is Henry Marshall, retired Navy Captain. Mr Marshall, this is Howie.' Terri moves back and closes the door after a small built man with white hair and a white beard enters.

'Mr Howie, good to meet you, sir,' the man moves forward as Howie scrabbles up from his now seated position to shake his hand.

'Mr Marshall, thank you for coming. Please take a seat,' Howie offers.

'Please, Henry is fine,' the man replies, smiling and taking a seat opposite Howie.

'Okay, and I'm just Howie. Everyone seems to be calling me Mr Howie lately.'

'Comes with the job, young man. People like to know who is in charge.' Henry smiles warmly; his voice rich with a deep baritone.

'Forgive me firing questions at you. Has anyone said why you're here?' Howie asks.

'Not yet. I was with the others, going through weapons drill when they said to come here.'

'Okay, may I ask what's your experience with ships and boats?' Howie asks.

'Well, where do I start, young man,' Henry smiles. 'I was a commercial skipper on cargo ships, fuel tankers, then did a stint in the cruise liners, and I was also Captain in the Royal Navy Reserves. I've been around boats and ships all of my life.'

'Do you know these waters very well?' Howie asks.

'Like the back of my hand, young man. May I ask why?'

'Sir, as you know, there is a huge army of those things coming for us. We've got lots of children here, and we have to do what we can to protect them.'

'I was thinking of this when I first got here. Yes, it is an option, and yes, there are several small harbours around here that would have numerous pleasure craft moored up.'

'Could you take the small boat that's out the back and bring more boats back? Enough for the children and their mothers?'

'I can try. We'll definitely get some back. Whether there's enough is a different matter, and do we know how long we've got?'

'We know they are massing now a few miles out, so it could be any time. The night would be the best time for them to attack as they become faster, but they've been changing so much in the last few days that anything is possible,' Howie explains.

'Right, we'd best get moving, then. I'll need some people with me. I know a few here that will be suitable to take with me.'

'Speak to Terri and Sarah next door. They'll help you find them. One more thing. Do you have a safe destination to take them all?' Howie asks.

'There's two places: across the water, to the Isle of Wight or to one of the forts in the sea,' Henry replies.

'Henry, this is absolutely vital. Do not tell anyone else where you plan to take them. Not one other person must know. If those things find out where you are going, they will hunt you down and kill you all. I cannot make that clear enough,' Howie presses on the older man.

'Yes, of course,' Henry says, looking Howie in the eye.

'Now, please hurry and be as quick as you can,' Howie says, standing up.

Henry follows his lead and extends his hand to Howie.

'I won't let you down,' Henry says firmly before leaving the room.

Howie sinks back down on his chair, raises his feet to rest on the desk, and once more takes a sip of his coffee.

'Typical, it's gone cold,' Howie mutters, staring down at the inky black liquid sloshing in the cup. His brow furrows as he thinks of something he was meant to do, something with coffee...

'Shit, Dave!'

CHAPTER EIGHTY-EIGHT

'These rooms are very secure,' Roger explains to Dave as he unlocks the solid, metal padlock before inserting keys to the several locks on the door. 'They're alarmed too,' Roger adds as he pushes the door open to hear a loud, urgent bleeping sound. He moves over to an alarm panel and keys in a number of digits. 'That's better. Now, do you know what you need?' Roger asks.

Dave steps into the room to look at the wrought iron fence bolted across the width of the room and the small gate set into them.

'That's locked too. Now, let me see. It must be one of these,' Roger thumbs the keys on the big loop, trying several until, with a satisfying click, the gate swings open.

Entering the cage, Dave heads straight to the rear. Powder bags are already made up and stacked carefully on shelves above the ground. There are large signs, telling people not to smoke.

'Is this where you got the powder from earlier?' Dave asks.

'Yes, David, there are containers on the shelving unit that I think they use for the muskets,' Roger answers as Dave winces at the use of his full name.

'It's Dave. I need all of these powder bags to be brought up, plus all of that wadding, and I need lots of water and all of those ramrods...' Dave says, pointing to each item in turn.

'Anything else?' Roger asks.

'Yes, all of the black powder that's here and the empty powder bags too. Get them all up to the top and leave them by the Saxon.' Dave turns and leaves, walking straight out of the door, without another word, and leaving Roger standing, bemused.

Dave walks across the compound and through the camp, ignoring everyone else. His mind entirely on the task at hand. Reaching the armoury, he enters to find Malcolm still sorting the weapons and ammunition.

'I need all of the cannon ammunition,' Dave says flatly.

'Hello, Dave, how are you?' Malcolm asks, irritated by his instant demand.

'I'm fine. Where is the cannon ammunition?' Dave answers, not registering Malcolm's tone.

'We've got buckets of the stuff, tons of it. Clarence got a load on his forage, and we went round to find more stuff.'

'Where is it?'

'We moved it all into one of the back rooms.'

'Why?'

'Because it was taking up so much bloody space, that's why,' Malcolm snaps back.

'I need it all up top,' Dave says, still devoid of emotion.

'Right, you need it up top. Okay, well, let's drop everything and get that done for you. Is there anything else we can do while we're here?' Malcolm says sarcastically.

'No, just that. Thank you,' Dave replies and leaves the room to head back up to the top of the north wall.

'Fucking Special Forces, always the fucking same...' Malcolm mutters.

He heads outside to find one of the guards and instructs him to go into the police office and find people to form a chain to pass the cannon ammunition up to the wall.

The guard nods and strolls into the police room to join the queue of people already waiting for Sergeant Hopewell's attention.

Thinking that his request is probably more urgent, he gently pushes through the throng until he reaches the desk and stands, dominating the view of the harassed sergeant.

'We need a chain of people to pass items up to the top of the north wall,' the guard says simply.

'How the hell am I supposed to do that?' Sergeant Hopewell snaps angrily. 'You've got a mouth. Go and find people yourself.'

'Why can't you do it?' the guard asks defensively.

'Because I'm bloody busy, that's why,' Sergeant Hopewell shouts, ignoring the man and turning back to the person she was talking to before. The guard pushes back away from the desk and heads further into the room to see Sarah and Terri examining sheets of paper and talking quietly.

'We need a chain of people to pass items up to the top of the north wall,' the guard repeats.

'And I need more coffee and some sleep, and a bloody computer would help rather than working in the dark ages, with sheets of bloody paper,' Terri retorts.

'Yeah, but this is important,' the guard says, looking with distaste at the stacks of paper.

'Important, is it? Because what we're doing clearly isn't important, then,' Terri shouts at the guard before going back to speaking with Sarah.

After a few minutes, the guard coughs and interrupts. 'So, can you get the people or not?' he asks.

'No, we bloody can't. We've got no runners left and a million other things to do.'

'Yeah but...'

'Do not yeah but me, find someone else,' Terri snaps, turning her back on the man. The guard walks away from the office, scratching his head. He walks back into the armoury and finds Malcolm putting piles of shotguns together.

'That was quick. Are they ready?' Malcolm asks.

'No, I couldn't find anyone,' the guard announces.

'Fucking what?' Malcolm shouts. 'There's seven thousand people out there, sitting around, doing nothing.'

'I asked in the police office, but they were too busy,' the guard starts to explain.

'Too busy? Doing what, may I ask? Filing missing person reports for the forty million fucking zombies roaming around, eating fucking brains? Get out there and find some people to get that shit up to the wall,' Malcolm shouts at the poor man.

He turns once again and heads back outside. A lifetime of infantry experience in the army taught him he is the lowest on the food chain, and to argue would most likely either invoke a beating or cleaning the toilets for the next month, or probably both.

He stands staring at the impenetrable mass of people in the camp. His lack of creative flair or ability to think outside of orders stumps him. Scratching his head, he wanders through the camp, looking for someone to ask, but they all look so busy: talking, flitting between tents, or moving quickly between places.

His wandering brings him close to the front gate where Cookey and Blowers are still leaning and drinking coffee.

'What's up, mate?' Blowers asks, seeing the lost look on the bewildered guard's face.

'They need a chain of people to get the cannon ammunition up to the top of the north wall. I asked in the police office, and they told me to piss off. I went back to Malcolm, and he told me to piss off. Now I don't know who to ask…' the man explains.

'Ah, that's easy. Me and Cookey will get it sorted,' Blowers says, relieved at the prospect of being away from his position.

'Yeah, definitely, are you sure?' the guard asks, sensing a sudden light at the end of the tunnel. Standing guard duty is easy, compared to having to actually speak to people.

'Yeah, of course. Now, no one goes in or out without checking with Mr Howie or Chris first, got it?' Blowers asks.

'Got it,' the man responds, happily taking up position by the side of the gate.

Blowers and Cookey walk away, stretching and feeling pleasure at being able to walk about for the first time in hours.

They walk over to the armoury to find Malcolm still wound up and muttering to himself.

'Hi Malc, that guard said you needed people to carry some stuff?' Blowers asks.

'Didn't he do it? Bloody people can't just get things done, can they?' Malcolm starts off. Blowers holds his hands up.

'No worries, mate, we'll get it sorted, where is it?'

'All of that stuff in that back room,' Malcolm points to the door at the rear.

'Got it. Leave it with us. Have you still got the radio, Cookey? Get hold of Nick and ask him to do one of his supermarket announcements again,' Blowers says as they move back outside.

Cookey speaks into the radio, telling Nick what he needs.

'Listen to this,' Cookey says, smiling at Blowers.

'ATTENTION PLEASE, ATTENTION PLEASE, CLEAN UP ON AISLE EIGHT,' Nick's voice booms out over the camp as Cookey and Blowers both burst out laughing.

'ATTENTION, PLEASE! WE NEED VOLUNTEERS TO FORM A CHAIN FROM THE ARMOURY TO THE WALL. PLEASE REPORT TO THE TWO UGLY-LOOKING MEN IN UNIFORM.' The camp freezes at the announcement. Some of the people smiling and laughing at the comments, some clearly not understanding. Within minutes, Blowers and Cookey have a long chain of people stretching from the armoury, going through the camp and up to the vehicle ramp onto the north wall.

More people than they need join in, but the action of doing something, anything propels them to try and join in, and the line becomes overcrowded.

'Cookey, get Nick to ask them to separate into two lines,' Blowers calls out.

'ATTENTION, PLEASE! ATTENTION, PLEASE! THERE ARE TOO MANY PEOPLE IN THE LINE. CAN WE HAVE ALL THE MEN IN ONE LINE AND ALL THE WOMEN IN ANOTHER LINE. COME ON. MEN VERSUS WOMEN. LET'S SEE WHO CAN GET THEIR LOAD DONE FIRST.' Nick carries on, urging the camp into two lines until, after a few minutes, the men and women stand facing each other, shouting with good-natured banter.

The noise slowly draws the people out of the police office. Sergeant Hopewell, Sarah, and Terri all come out to see the fuss and stand, watching the two lines slowly forming as Nick stands on the top of the Saxon, directing them.

'RIGHT. AT THE FRONT YOU WILL SEE BLOWERS. THAT'S HIM, WITH HIS ARM UP. HE'S ON THE MEN'S SIDE.

THE OTHER ONE, COOKEY. THAT'S HIM WAVING NOW. HE'S ON THE WOMEN'S SIDE. THEY WILL PASS EACH CHAIN THE ITEM TO BE MOVED UP. THE CHAIN LEFT WITH THE LAST ITEM STILL BEING PASSED UP IS THE LOSER. NOW, ARE YOU READY?' A chorus of replies sounds out. *'I CAN'T HEAR YOU. I SAID...ARE YOU READY?'* Nick booms out over the loudspeaker. The two lines roar and cheer as Blowers and Cookey position themselves at the end of the two chains, pretending to jump up and down and get ready.

Malcolm walks out of the armoury and stands bemused at the sight; realising what's about to happen. He moves a few steps away and lights a much-needed cigarette.

'THREE...TWO...ONE...GO!' Laughing like children, Blowers and Cookey burst away into the armoury and race into the back room. They each grab a bucket of metal scraps and run back to the chain.

'HERE COME THE FIRST TWO. IT'S ALL EVEN AT THE MOMENT, OH! AND THE FIRST BUCKETS ARE INTO THE CHAINS AND BEING PASSED UP,' Nick commentates as Blowers and Cookey run back inside to get the next ones.

Blowers grabs two buckets as Cookey grabs one and starts back.

'That's cheating, you wanker,' Cookey yells as he goes back for another one and runs behind his friend to pass them on to the chain. The two lines roar and cheer as they see the two lads bursting out, each carrying two buckets.

Sarah starts smiling at the sight and looks to Terri laughing as the two lads push against each other to reach the lines first.

'COME ON, COOKEY,' Terri yells.

'That's bloody Tom and Steven in that line,' Sergeant Hopewell laughs at seeing the two lads joining in with passing the items up.

'I'm joining in,' Terri laughs and runs across to the front of the line.

'I'm not having that,' Ted remarks from behind them and jogs over to stand opposite Terri on the men's line. Blowers and Cookey keep running back into the armoury and grabbing buckets of metal to race back outside, waiting until they are in front of the people before they start barging into each other, both of them red in the face but laughing hard. Malcolm smiles as he quietly smokes, amazed at what's taking place in front of him. These people have suffered such loss, but here they are, joking and playing, doing anything to break the tension, and all it took was three young, mischievous soldiers pissing about. His smile widens as he thinks back to the escapades that he, Chris, and Clarence got up to early in their service. Nick continues with the commentary as people twist and turn, passing the items up, pointing out mistakes, and making the others laugh and cheer. Dave, Jamie, and Curtis stand next to the Saxon and watch the growing piles of buckets being passed up. The inside area of the main gate fills up as those closest to the front first hear Nick booming out on the loudspeaker and then the sounds of cheering. They pause in their training and drill to move back inside and stand smiling at the spectacle.

Howie stands outside the police office, quietly drinking coffee and taking the scene in.

He watches Terri smiling and laughing as she reaches out to take a bucket from Cookey before he turns to run back inside, pushing and shoving against Blowers by his side. He watches as Tom and Steven grasp their bucket in turn and laugh as it's passed on, shouting and urging the men to move faster.

How can they all be taken? Fifty or so million people in Britain, and every one of them has had their life changed forever. The rich and powerful may have been whisked to safety inside bunkers, but even their lives are changed. The thought process leads Howie to think of the populations of different countries. This started in Eastern Europe somewhere, so that means the whole of Europe, and if it spread to an island like Britain so quickly, it must have gone everywhere. Every man, woman, and child on the planet has had their life changed and for what? For another species to develop? For another race to take over? Or just an infection that courses through their systems, without realising the futility of it all, that eventually, it will infect everyone and have nothing left to feed on. He thinks of how McKinney would love this now and would be laughing and joking up top with Nick and Curtis. Then he remembers Darren and the conversation they had on the bridge. With a jolt, he realises it was only this morning, only a few hours ago. It feels like days or weeks have gone by just in this one day. He thinks back to Friday night and being at home in his flat, watching television. That feels like years ago. He was a night manager in a supermarket then. Now he is a leader of men and making ready to fight an army of dead people.

He shakes his head slowly in wonder. If only his father could see him now, how proud he would be. His thoughts darken once again as he thinks of his parents now part of that army coming for them and of Darren's words on the bridge. *Lord, give me the grace to have five minutes with Darren when we meet. Just him and me alone for five minutes.* Howie sips his coffee, visualising the moment he would take him down and make him pay for all the bad things that have happened. He cocks his head to one side and adds a final request to his prayer, *And can I have my axe with me, please?*

The race finishes, with Cookey and Blowers both running out of the armoury, with their last bucket each, using their free hands to push and pull the other one back. They grapple with red, panting faces, still laughing as they stagger and slip over, somehow managing to keep their buckets upright. Finally, they separate and make it to their lines at the same time, passing their buckets over and then racing along with them as they get passed from man to man and woman to woman. Nick's voice grows hoarse with excitement.

The ends of the lines disperse as the men and women race to keep up with the buckets. The buckets reach the last few people as the view is entirely blocked by everyone crowding round to watch. With a roar, the buckets reach the top in unison, both being placed at the top at the same time.

'IT'S A DRAW. OH, YES. A DRAW! THE AGE-OLD BATTLE OF MEN VERSUS WOMEN HAS FINALLY BEEN LAID TO REST HERE IN FORT SPITBANK, WITH A DRAW!' Nick ends his commentary as the crowds all mingle into one, cheering and laughing, and slapping each other on the back.

The day draws on and slowly the camp returns to order as people file back down and continue with the tasks they had been doing.

Clarence leads his group back outside and resumes the weapons drills. Howie watches as Dave and Jamie, now joined by several others on the top wall, all start moving the buckets to the cannon sites. Howie heads over towards the vehicle ramp leading to the top of the north wall, passing the engineers' workshop as he goes. He pauses to see Kelly inside, still moving between the various small groups of people and the growing pile of sharpened foot traps on the floor. She smiles and nods as he passes by. He continues on, passing smiling people moving back down to the camp.

'That was a good effort, Nick,' Howie says as he reaches the Saxon.

'Thanks, Mr Howie, it was a good laugh for a few minutes,' Nick replies, now back on the GPMG and staring out to the flatlands through a pair of binoculars.

'How are they getting on out there, mate?' Howie asks.

'Have a look.' Nick passes the binoculars over. Howie lifts them to his eyes and starts scanning over the flatlands to the estate.

The diggers have now finished and are moving back down to the Fort, having moved all of the earth taken from the ditches over to the far sides.

The long grass is now cut and being carried over to be stacked by the side of the freshly dug ditches. Men and women are working in the ditches to drive the sharpened stakes through, followed by more people covering the sections they have completed with the long grass. Howie sweeps over to see a van being driven slowly across the large area of land between the first ditch and the embankments, throwing the sharpened foot traps out onto the ground. Then he looks down to the first bank to see a group of archers firing into the bank. He watches them practise with firing high, and people moving amongst them, giving tips, and offering advice. He sweeps the binoculars down to the deep ditch after the last bank and sees the fuel tanker parked on the road in the middle. Pipes connected to the fuel tanker are pumping fuel into the heavyweight hoses they found in the Fort. More people are filling containers and big drums with fuel and then rolling them along the ground to be pushed into the ditch. Yet more people are wrapping metal shrapnel into bags and placing them on top of the drums and hoses. After the deep ditch, there is a wide, open flatland to the Fort, now covered with lots of people, who stand, listening to Clarence and Brian. The people issued with firearms have laid them down in piles. Now many of them hold the hand weapons foraged and brought back by Clarence, found within the compound, or brought with them as they fled their homes.

He knows Clarence and Brian are doing their best to give some simple instruction on how to hold the weapons and show them basic techniques of swipe, lunge, and hack. As Howie lowers the binoculars, he realises that nearly everyone in the Fort must now be involved in the defence and preparation. So much for his plans of keeping everything secret.

'Fuck it. Donald ...' Howie remembers the man he had locked up in the police office.

Suddenly, the action he took rests uncomfortably on his mind. At the time, his decision seemed reasonable. The man was delaying what needed to be done.

'Tell Dave I'll be straight back,' Howie yells as he starts jogging back down the vehicle ramp and across the camp.

The sudden thought that they have done something wrong, so very wrong, plagues his mind, and it must be put right.

'Where's that man we locked up?' Howie asks as he bursts into the police office.

'That's what I want to bloody know,' a distressed-looking woman standing in front of Sergeant Hopewell's desk yells out.

'Are you his wife?' Howie asks.

'Yes, I am. They won't let me see him. They said he's been arrested,' the woman sobs – eyes red and tears streaming down her face. She holds the hand of a small, scared-looking child.

'Where is he?' Howie asks Sergeant Hopewell.

'In the back room. Ted's with him,' she replies.

Howie pushes his way forward and opens the door at the rear, entering a small corridor.

'Ted?' Howie calls out.

'In here,' Ted answers and steps out of an open door at the end.

'Is that man in there?' Howie asks.

'Yes, he's right here,' Ted answers, puzzled.

Howie moves around Ted and enters the room to see Donald sitting on a chair in the corner of the room. His eyes are also red from crying.

'Donald, I am so very sorry for locking you in here. It was unforgivable...' Howie blurts out.

'I'm sorry. I shouldn't have questioned you. Please can I just go?

My wife and daughter are alone, and they must be terrified,' Donald pleads.

'No, you should have questioned us. I was completely wrong to have you detained like this.'

'I didn't mean anything bad, Mr Howie. I was uncomfortable with what you were asking, but I shouldn't have made an issue out of it. You're right. There are thousands of people here relying on you, and I won't question you again.' Donald stands up slowly, clearly unsure of the change of events, looking at Howie, then at the open door, and Ted standing there with a frown.

'So, I can really go?' he asks tentatively.

'Mate, your wife and daughter are out in the office.'

'Donald! You're all right!' The woman from the office bursts in to hold Donald tight, crying and sobbing.

The little girl holds back for a second until Donald drops down to draw her in close.

'Yes, I'm fine, darling. It was all a misunderstanding, really. It's all fine,' Donald says softly, holding them both.

'Look, Mr Howie,' Donald's wife says, 'my husband Donald is an argumentative man, and he picks the wrong moments to say things and has often caused a lot of offence, so I can understand where you're coming from. But for him to be taken away like that and with no one telling me why or for how long, that was awful.'

'Yes, you're right. It was the wrong thing to do,' Howie accepts quietly.

'Mr Howie, I do apologise to you for putting you in that position. Is there anything I can do to help now?' Donald asks, holding his head up and staring directly at Howie.

'The engineers are still hard at it in the workshops. I'm sure they could do with some help.'

'Right, in which case, we should be leaving,' Donald steps forward, holding a hand out to Howie. 'I understand why it happened the way it did, and for my part, I can see you are a genuine man, and I'm glad this Fort has you on our side,' Donald says as they shake hands.

'Thank you, that's a very kind thing to say,' Howie replies.

'And as soon as society has been rebuilt, I will be contacting one of those *no win, no fee* lawyers for compensation,' Donald smiles.

'Ha, good idea. I'll say it was Ted.'

'You won't be the first. That's for sure,' Ted responds good-naturedly. The family leave the room, still holding each other tightly, leaving Ted staring hard at Howie and nodding gently.

'That took some balls, Howie. Well done,' Ted says quietly.

'Don't give me credit, Ted. It shouldn't have happened in the first place,' Howie replies.

'You did what you thought was right at the time. He wasn't injured or hurt, and he's been well taken care of,' Ted says firmly.

'Yeah, I guess, but the road to hell is paved with good intentions, Ted.'

CHAPTER EIGHTY-NINE

At the top of the north wall, two teams of people, left over from the bucket chain and chosen by Dave, move ammunition and powder bags to each of the cannons.

Long hoses stretch along the top and down to the ground level and the outside taps found in each corner of the base of the wall. On further request, women bring piles of sheets, blankets, and material up to be left with the ammunition. Dave crouches and draws his knife to cut a square of bed sheet, then takes a few double handfuls of bolts, nails, and screws to put them in the centre of the sheet. He wraps the sheet over, securing the metal fragments inside. He then takes the small bundle and shoves it into the black opening of the cannon mouth.

'Too small,' he mutters and goes back to unwrap the sheet and add another double handful of the metal pieces. He wraps it back up and goes back to the cannon mouth, placing the bundle inside.

'Perfect. I need more of these made. The same size as this one. They must not be bigger than this; otherwise, they will not fit,' Dave says to a group of people watching him.

'You get them made, and I'll start showing this lot the cannon drill,' he adds, turning to the two distinct teams nearby.

'Right, one group will be on this cannon, the other on the second one. Watch and listen carefully as we do not have a lot of time before night falls, and as soon as that area is clear,' Dave indicates the flatlands, 'we will be having some practise shots to get range, distance, and aim, got it?' The groups nod back, listening intently to the small, strange man.

'These are the fuses.' Dave holds up some lengths of fuse wire to show the groups. 'They go into this hole at the back of the cannon. We do not have lighted material or naked flame anywhere near the fuse at any point other than when we are lighting it. You two are the flame holders,' Dave indicates two men, one from each group.

'You keep the flame lit and away from the cannon until the teams are ready for you to light the fuse. Now we take a powder bag. This is full of gunpowder, and we place it into the cannon. That is your job,' Dave indicates another man from each group.

'The powder bag is then rammed down to the bottom of the cannon, like this.' Dave takes a ramrod and pushes it into the cannon, driving the bag down to the bottom and tapping it hard a few times. 'It must be at the bottom so it pushes against the fuse wire sticking in through the hole. Next, we take some wadding, and again, we push it down.' Dave takes some papers from a pile near the cannon and rams it down with the ramrod.

'Next, we take the ammunition. In this case – the wrapped metal, and again, we push it down the cannon. The metal is wrapped simply to keep it together. When the fuse is lit, it burns down and ignites the powder bag. The powder bags explode instantly, with a lot of force. The energy of the exploding matter cannot escape from the back or sides, so it is forced to move up the cannon, thereby driving our round, missile, or projectile out of this end at great speed. The wrapping material will be burnt away, and the metal ejected. As it leaves, it will start to spread, at the same time as becoming incredibly hot. Not only do the enemy suffer from the impact of the projectiles. They also suffer from the heat of the projectiles. Do you understand?' He gets more nods from the people watching.

'Now, before the cannon can be used again, water is put in and swept through to make sure there are no burning materials left; otherwise, as soon as you put the powder bags in, they will explode and kill everyone. Now, these cannons are made from iron. They are strong, but they are very old, and we cannot tell if they have stress fractures. Iron cannon can sometimes just explode from the force of the repeated firing. If that happens, you will all die, got it?'

The men look to each other with alarm.

'We cannot fire at the moment because of the people out there, but we can practise, and we will practise. Any questions?'

'Will you be with us?' one man asks straight away.

'For the practise, yes, of course, I will be.'

'No, I mean when we actually fire them for real.'

'I don't know.'

'How likely are they to explode?' another asks, with genuine fear on his face.

'I don't know.'

'Err, have you ever fired one of these before?' the same man asks.

'No, now, any other questions before we start? No? Good.'

For the next hour, the two groups are drilled incessantly and without rest. Dave making each group go through the motions. He pushes them again and again, giving clear instructions and correcting where necessary.

As the afternoon gives way to evening, Dave rests the groups, walks over to the Saxon positioned midway between the two cannons and takes the radio from the front of the vehicle.

'Saxon to Mr Howie or Chris.'

'Chris to Saxon. Go ahead.'

'Saxon to Chris. We need to start live fire drills on the cannon. How long until the grounds are clear?'

'Chris to Saxon. We are almost finished and will clear very soon. I will give you an update once we are clear.'

'Saxon to Chris. Roger that. Saxon out.'

'Chris to Howie.'

'Howie here. Go ahead, Chris.'

'Did you get the last? We are almost finished at the front.'

'Yeah, I got that, mate. I'll come down and meet you at the gate.'

'Chris to Howie. Roger and out.'

HOWIE STEPS through the gate after finding a different guard happily on duty and wondering what mischief Blowers and Cookey might be causing elsewhere.

He crosses the gap between the two walls, marvelling at how the two high, thick walls deaden the sound from both sides.

'We're just about done,' Clarence calls out, leading his now large group of people back inside with Brian.

Some of them are armed with rifles, and there is a much larger group armed with a collection of hand weapons.

'I think that Chris is bringing the others back in now, too,' Howie replies.

'Are they all done, then?' Clarence asks, moving back to Howie and watching the rest pass through the gate and back into the Fort.

'I think so. How did you get on with the training?' Howie asks.

'The firearms were fine. Some of them were a bit rusty, but there's enough good ones amongst them to keep the rest up to standard. Mind you, all they've got to do is point and shoot.'

'What about the others, with the hand weapons?'

'To be honest,' Clarence lowers his voice, 'that was a fucking nightmare. We'll be lucky if they don't all stab themselves before we even start. But what choice have they got?'

'Not much we can do, mate. Just hope we whittle the numbers down before they get here, I guess. Here's Chris now.' Howie nods at the line of vehicles coming down the road, towards them.

'It'll be dark soon. Couple of hours to go,' Clarence remarks, looking up at the sky.

'I wonder how soon they'll come,' Howie says quietly as the people head back into the Fort, nodding at him and Clarence as they pass.

'Mr Howie?' a voice calls out.

Howie turns to see a man at the head of a procession of archers.

'You are Mr Howie, aren't you?' the man asks as he gets closer.

'Howie, yes.'

'We're the archers. We need to know range and where we will be firing from. If we're back here, we've got no view...'

'I was thinking we'd all be on the top of the inner wall to start with,' Howie politely interrupts him.

The man steps back to look up, but the outer wall blocks his view.

'It will reduce our range, yes, but we can fire from there if that's where you want us.'

'How far will you be able to fire to from the top of the inner wall?' Howie asks.

'Hmmm, now that obviously depends on the type of bow. We've got a few different ones here, but I won't bore you with all that. I'd say most of us will be able to reach just past the first embankment.'

'That's great,' Howie remarks, looking at Clarence, who nods back sincerely.

'There won't be any degree of aiming from that distance, though. We're working on the principle of there being a mass target and just firing into them, really.'

'I think you're probably right, but would you be able to get a fire arrow into that ditch from the inner wall?' Howie asks, pointing out, towards the last embankment.

'Ah, now, fire arrows have far less range, and they're a bugger to aim over any distance. But if you just want it into the ditch, that will be easy enough.'

'Good, can you make sure that you all have the ability to do that when the time is right?' Howie asks.

'Okay, we can do that. We saw them being filled up with explosive material. Are you relying on us to ignite them?'

'I think we will be. Is that okay?'

'Yes, of course, is it okay to go up now and work out the best position?'

'No problem,' Howie replies. 'Nick and Curtis are with our vehicle. Speak to them and let them know what you're doing.'

The man nods and joins the line of others walking back into the Fort.

Howie and Clarence turn to see the vehicles have now stopped, and Chris is walking towards them, looking tired and drawn.

'You look like shit, Chris,' Clarence rumbles.

'You too,' Chris smiles back at him. 'Mr Howie still looks fresh as a daisy, though.'

'It's the easy living I had before all this,' Howie jokes. 'Honestly, though, I am fucking knackered.'

'We all are, Howie. We'll need to rest when we can; otherwise, we'll all be falling asleep mid-battle,' Chris replies, rubbing his beard.

'So, how is it?' Howie asks, now yawning after the mention of being tired.

'It's all done,' Chris replies. 'First ditch filled with spikes and covered with the grass. You can still see it, but it's quite well covered. The...flatlands are completely covered with the caltrops...' he trails off, seemingly losing his chain of thought.

'I saw the deep ditch being filled,' Howie takes up where Chris leaves off and nods to the area of the ditch. 'We've got the archers ready to fire into it.'

'Let's get inside,' Chris says as the radio clipped to his belt comes to life with a hushed transmission.

'*Point North, Point North. Contact. I have contact,*' the voice is quiet but clear. The speaker obviously holding his mouth close to the radio.

Chris scrabbles for his radio, pressing the button and speaking quietly in return, '*Fort to Point North. Receiving you. What do you see?*'

'*Zombies, lots of zombies, all coming our way.*'

'How far out is he?' Clarence asks, turning to look back up the road to the estate.

'A few miles, I think Dave said,' Howie answers.

'*Fort to Point North. How far out are you?*' Silence follows Chris's transmission. '*Fort to Point North. How far out are you? I repeat, how far out are you?*'

Silence, then a sound of movement comes through.

'Maybe he can't transmit if they're too close,' Howie says as they all stare at the radio.

'*Fort to Point North. Hold down your transmit button twice if you cannot speak,*' Chris says quietly. The radio remains silent, then bursts to life, with the sounds of struggling and the raised voice of a man shouting in desperation.

They all stare at the radio in silence, listening to the struggle and the shouts coming through, then the sound of growling, followed by a sickening, tearing noise and a scream.

'Fuck,' Howie mutters in horror; then, the radio goes silent.

'*Point West to Fort. I heard that, I'm bugging out.*'

'*Fort to Points West and East. Roger that. Come back. I repeat, come back.*'

The radio bursts to life, with the sound of static and a high-pitched squealing. They stand listening, unsure who is transmitting.

The static and squealing fade, but the line remains open.

One word is transmitted by a voice that only sounds part human.

'*HOWIEEEEEE...*'

'Fucking hell,' Chris says in shock at the awful, stretched-out sound, looking at Howie.

'*HOWIEEEEEE...*' the same voice again.

Howie stares at the radio. His heart beating faster and faster, and his stomach dropping.

'*WE'RE COMING, HOWIEEEEEE,*' the goading tones are loud and clear.

Chris and Clarence both stare at Howie.

'Let's go,' Chris says. All signs of tiredness gone, and his voice full of authority again. His voice springs them to action, and they turn as one. Chris runs ahead and pulls the gates wide open to get the vehicles back inside.

Clarence and Howie go straight through into the Fort as Howie grabs his radio and holds it close to his mouth as he marches through the gates.

'*Howie to Dave. Did you hear the last?*'

'*Dave to Howie. Roger. We heard the last, making ready now.*'

'*Howie to all personnel. Switch to the predesignated channel. Security breach on channel one,*' he pauses and switches to the channel himself.

'*Howie to Dave. I want all the people with weapons on the top of the inner wall, archers too. Get Nick on the loudspeaker.*'

'*Dave to Howie. Roger that. On it now.*'

'*Howie to Malcolm.*'

'*Malcolm receiving. Go ahead, Howie.*'

'*Malcolm, can you get all the ammunition to the top of the inner wall and let the triage and hospital points know what's going on.*'

'*Roger that, Howie.*'

'Clarence,' Howie shouts across to the big man, 'we need that fuel tanker in the estate. Find the driver and get it taken in. Use a car to bring the driver back.'

'Roger,' Clarence replies before darting off into the camp.

'Howie to Dave. Where do you want the fuel tanker placed?'

'Dave to Howie, on the central road, close to the edge of the estate, by the flatlands.'

'Howie to Clarence. Did you receive that?'

'Clarence to Howie. Roger. Got it.'

'ATTENTION, PLEASE! ATTENTION, PLEASE!' Nick's voice booms out over the loudspeaker on the Saxon. 'CAN ALL THE PEOPLE WITH FIREARMS REPORT TO THE TOP OF THE INNER WALL. CAN ALL ARCHERS REPORT TO THE TOP OF THE INNER WALL.' Nick repeats the message several times as Howie ploughs through the edge of the camp, towards the police office.

The camp erupts with a sudden frenzy as the few closest to the radios hear the transmission; then, they see Clarence and Howie running in, and then hear the request made by Nick. People start running about, fearing the attack is taking place.

Parents grab children as men and women alike grip their hand weapons. Mayhem ensues, and the volume inside the Fort is instantly raised. Howie makes it to the police office, bursting in to see the room now empty of people. The sergeant sits behind the desk. Terri and Sarah next to her – all of them staring at the radio.

'Oh, Howie,' Sarah says, putting her hand to her mouth. 'That was awful.'

'Yeah, not very nice, was it?' Howie replies. 'Any news on the boats?'

'Nothing yet,' Terri replies.

'Get the children at the back and ready to load as soon as they get back. Where's Ted?' Howie asks, looking around.

'He went to the front,' Sergeant Hopewell says.

'I was going to ask him to go with the children, and err, maybe you too, Debbie. They're going to need some strong people with them.'

'Me? With children? Are you joking?' Sergeant Hopewell blurts out.

'Oh, is that a bad idea, then? Just look at what you did here in a couple of days. Terri and Sarah too,' Howie adds.

'Sending the women and children away, eh?' Terri flares up. 'Why can't we stay and fight too?'

'To be honest, because we'll probably lose, and yes, women and children need to be saved. Those kids will need strong people, and you're it at the moment,' Howie replies with a firm voice and fixed expression.

'As much as I hate to say this, I agree,' Sarah says, looking to the two other women. 'Howie's right. Three more out there, fighting is not going to make a difference, but being with the children and mothers does make a difference.'

'So we run away while everyone else stays and dies?' Terri says indignantly.

'If nothing else, we buy you time to get away,' Howie says. 'It's up to you, but it makes sense to me. I've got to go.' Howie leaves the three women discussing the idea and marches back into the camp, heading towards the north wall.

'Tucker, where have you been all day, mate?' Howie says as he collides with the large recruit.

'Mr Howie, I've got all the stores sorted. They were a bloody mess...' Tucker replies.

'Bloody hell, mate, have you been doing that all day?' Howie smiles at him.

'Well, they had the wrong food types mixed together. No regard for the dates or perishable items, and some were stacked on the floor! So I took one look at and thought, *Roy, this won't do. Even if that zombie army comes tonight, I want them to find nice, clean stores,*' Tucker explains with genuine zeal.

'Well done, mate, good for you. Talking of food, though...' Howie says, still walking towards the north wall and realising how hungry he is.

'Ah, now, that is sorted, Mr Howie. I knew you'd all be hungry, so I've got some food already prepared.'

'Really? Wow, Tucker, that's impressive, mate,' Howie says, looking with admiration at him.

'It's nothing special, though, Mr Howie, just all the stuff we needed to use up. High energy food, though. Lots of carbs. You see, I found loads of pasta and tinned meat, and then there were vegetables that were going off, so I thought...'

'Tucker, mate, it sounds great,' Howie stops him as they reach the top of the vehicle ramp and walk towards the Saxon.

'*Clarence to Howie. We're on our way now,*' Clarence's deep voice comes over the radio.

Howie moves to the edge of the inner wall and looks down to see the tanker being driven down the road, followed by a small car.

'*Howie to Clarence. Yeah, I can see you now. Be quick, mate. Howie to Points West and East. We've got a vehicle going to the estate now. We'll be there for a few minutes only if you can make it back in time.*'

'*Point West,*' a heavy, panting voice says. '*I'm not far away. I should make it.*'

'*Point East to the Fort. Likewise, I'm running like a lunatic. No sign of the army from my position.*'

'*Howie to Points West and East. Roger that. Clarence, did you receive the last?*'

'*Yeah, I heard it. Keep running, gents, because we ain't stopping for long.*'

Looking up, Howie sees Nick gripping the GPMG and staring hard towards the estate and Curtis standing by the side of the vehicle, scanning with binoculars.

'See anything, Curtis?' Howie calls over.

'Nothing yet, Mr Howie,' he replies, with the binoculars stuck firmly to his face. Howie looks about to see men running towards the waist-high wall. They find positions and lean down to rest their rifles, then start scanning ahead.

The archers split into two groups, left and right, and concentrate on fixing strings to their bows and placing piles of arrows down at their feet. All along the line, men and women make ready, and Howie notices some of them shake and tremble as they work with their equipment. Their faces are pale and drawn; the tension is palpable. He moves along to see Dave at the far end, next to one of the cannons, and speaking to a group of people. As he walks closer, Howie notices the heavy-looking bundles stacked on the ground, to one side, long ramrods being held by some of the men, and powder bags ready to be loaded.

Howie stops as the group break apart, chatting amongst themselves.

'Dave, how's it going, mate?' Howie asks as Dave steps over to him. The small man looking exactly the same as he did a week ago, with no sign of strain or tiredness.

'Good, Mr Howie,' Dave replies, with his usual reserve.

'I think we're about as ready as we'll ever be,' Howie says, looking back at the long line of people standing along the top of the inner wall.

'Yes, Mr Howie, I think so.'

'The cannons? Are they ready?' Howie asks, looking down at the bags and piles of equipment.

'Yes, although we don't know the distance yet. Single shot can go quite far, but cluster or grapeshot like this reduces the distance significantly.'

'Like a shotgun, then,' Howie says.

'Exactly like a shotgun – more spread but less range.'

'Well, I guess we'll find out in a bit.'

'Yes, I guess so. I'll try a test fire on each when Clarence gets back in.'

'So that tanker? Do you think it will go up well?'

'Yes.'

'But aren't they designed to withstand heat and pressure?' Howie asks.

'Yes, but I put loads of grenades in it,' Dave says, still devoid of expression.

'Oh, well, that's good, then. So have you ever fired cannons before?'

'No. Well... No, not really.'

'What do you mean?'

'I've not fired a proper cannon before, not an old one like this.'

'So what was it then?'

'Similar.'

'Similar? Similar how?'

'I made one,' Dave answers flatly.

'You made a cannon?' Howie asks incredulously.

'Yes, although it was a one-time use only.'

'Did it work?' Dave looks directly at Howie as though the question needs not be asked. 'Fair one,' Howie says. 'Tucker's getting some food up for us,' he adds.

'Good, we can eat, then sleep,' Dave says with a nod.

'Sleep? How can we sleep?' Howie asks.

'They won't come yet,' Dave answers firmly.

'We heard them on the radio. They said *we're coming for you, Howieeeee,*' Howie tries to imitate the voice, making himself laugh as he does it but trailing off when he looks at Dave's deadpan expression.

'They'll wait at least a few more hours yet,' Dave continues.

'How on earth can you possibly know that?'

'They've covered a long distance on foot, so they'll be weaker now, plus it's still light, and we can see them coming. They know we know they're here, so they know we'll be ready for them,' Dave explains. 'So they will wait a few hours to rest and either attack during the night when we're at our lowest ebb or first thing in the morning when we're all tired.'

'Oh, yeah, I guess that makes sense,' Howie says reluctantly. 'I hate it when you're always right like that. In fact, I want them to come now just so you're wrong,' he goes on, smiling.

'Maybe they will, Mr Howie,' Dave concedes.

'But you don't think they will?'

'No.'

'You're certain of that?'

'Yes, Mr Howie.'

'How certain?'

'I don't understand.'

'If you're wrong, you have to sing a song on the Saxon loudspeaker,' Howie says, trying to keep a straight face.

'I have to what?' Dave asks.

'Sing a song on the Saxon loudspeaker, but only if you're wrong.'

Dave stares at him.

'Okay, Mr Howie, I'll do that,' Dave says.

'Bloody hell. You will?' a shocked Howie says.

'Yes, and you have to do it if *you're* wrong,' Dave answers, with a very rare grin.

'No, hang on a minute...'

'Yes, Mr Howie?' Dave asks innocently.

'GRUB IS UP,' Tucker bellows from the Saxon, watching a line of people carrying metal trays covered with aluminium foil.

'Saved by the bell,' Dave says quietly and starts off towards the food.

'Oh, you're changing, Dave,' Howie calls out. Trestle tables are carried up from the visitors' centre and laid out in a row near the Saxon. Metal trays, covered with foil, are laid on them, along with piles of plates and stacks of cutlery.

Howie walks over to the edge and looks down into the camp at the cooking points. People are gathered around and drifting over, holding their weapons under arms or clutched between knees as they stand, eating from paper plates, with plastic forks. Tucker moves along the trestle table, fussing about like a hotel head chef, adjusting the trays and crimping the foil down firmer to keep the heat inside.

'Bloody hell, lads, where did you come from?' Howie laughs at seeing Blowers and Cookey first in the queue.

'We were here all along, Mr Howie,' Cookey says with a grin.

'Tucker, we wondered where you had been all day,' Blowers calls out.

'I've been doing proper work, not like you two, standing about a gate all day and drinking coffee,' Tucker shouts, smiling. Chris appears, walking up the vehicle ramp and over to join Howie watching the queue of armed men and women walking along to get scoops of hot food piled onto their plates.

'You all right, mate?' Howie asks the tired-looking man.

'Yeah, I think we're all set. Just got to wait for Clarence to get back,' he replies as Dave stops to join them.

'Dave thinks they won't attack for a few hours,' Howie says quietly, trying to keep out of earshot of the people waiting for food.

'It would make sense,' Chris answers.

'Give them a chance to rest and get us all wound up and tired for a few hours, probably attack during the night or first thing in the morning.'

'Oh, for fuck's sake,' Howie mutters as Dave gives another sly grin.

'What?' Chris asks, looking between them.

'Nothing,' Howie says, sighing.

'Clarence to Points East and West. Where are you? We're ready to go,' Clarence's voice comes out in stereo from all the radios attached in the area.

'Point East, I'm almost there,' the man sounds exhausted.

'Point...West, hang...on.' the second voice sounds worse. The man struggling to speak as he runs. Minutes pass as everyone pauses, staring at the radios and waiting for an update. The food queue holds fast. The servers frozen with ladles in mid-air as everyone waits with bated breath.

'The food's getting cold,' Tucker mutters quietly, fretting about his beloved creation and moving down the tables to discreetly tug the foil covers back on.

'Clarence to Fort. We have both points. Repeat, we have both men. On our way back now.' Cheering erupts from the top of the inner wall, knowing they've lost one man but saved two more.

The eating resumes as the foil is pulled back off, and the serving carries on. Howie, Chris, and Dave are joined by Blowers and Cookey, both of them hungrily tucking into the food and shovelling it into their mouths.

'There they are,' Chris nods at the small car speeding down the road, towards them.

They watch as the car slows to enter the gates and hear as the gates are pulled closed, securing them inside.

'Thank fuck for that,' Howie says quietly. 'We'll wait for Clarence and Malcolm and eat together,' he adds.

Within a few minutes, Clarence walks up the vehicle ramp, accompanied by Malcolm, both of them carrying heavy canvas bags filled with ammunition.

They dump the bags by the side of the Saxon and move over to join Howie and Chris as Howie motions with his head for Nick to come and join them, mouthing for him to get Curtis and Jamie on the way.

Within a couple of minutes, they are all stood together for the first time that day: Howie, Dave, Blowers, Cookey, Curtis, Nick, Jamie, and Tucker. Chris stood in the middle of his trusted comrades, Clarence and Malcolm.

'Well, we did it,' Howie says. 'In one day, we got the traps laid, found more weapons, rigged the estate, got two cannons working, hopefully, and even cooked a gourmet meal. Bloody impressive if you ask me.'

'And found time to play pass the bucket,' Nick adds as they all smile.

'Let's get some food,' Howie says. They move towards the tables and head for the back of the queue, chatting and joking amongst themselves.

One of the people stood near the back moves a few steps aside and motions for them to go ahead of him. It catches on, and within seconds, the waiting people have all stood back, quietly and respectfully.

'Thank you,' Howie speaks clearly, nodding to them. The others join in, showing gratitude and offering polite *thank yous* as they move to the table.

'Have you already eaten?' Clarence rumbles, looking at the dirty plate held by Blowers.

'Err...no?' Blowers says slowly, looking to Cookey and his dirty plate, which he tucks behind his back.

'Bloody greedy if you ask me,' Cookey says, nodding at Clarence. 'I'd never go back for seconds, personally.'

They get plates of steaming meat and vegetables, giving Tucker compliments about the food, and Howie notices the look of pride on the young man's face. They have worked hard today, all of them. Fighting all day yesterday, then fleeing through the night to get here. Not one of them has moaned or complained, and this effort, with the food, now has lifted the spirits of everyone here. They move away from the table, juggling heaped plates and already eating as they head over to the wall and sit down in a wide circle.

The sight of Howie, Chris, Clarence, and the others all sitting down, eating and joking amongst themselves sends a ripple out along the top of the inner wall, taking the edge off the fraught tension felt by all the other armed men and women.

'Mind if we join you?' a voice asks. The group twists around to see Ted grinning while Sarah, Sergeant Hopewell, Terri, Tom, and Steven get plates of food from the trestle table.

A chorus of voices greets them as they shuffle around to make room. Sarah moves deftly to sit beside Clarence and smiles a big grin to Howie, who nods and smiles back at her. The conversations break into smaller chunks as they joke and banter amongst themselves. Easy conversation in easy company. Those that haven't met yet introduce themselves and nod greetings at one another. Before long, they're exchanging war stories of the last week. Tom and Steven, both at the same time, try to recount the time when Dave disarmed Tom with the Taser. Howie glances around to see the top of the inner wall and the groups of people now stood or seated, chatting and talking quietly. Guns, rifles, and bows stand propped up against the wall as the folks mingle. Howie thinks back to watching the television and then seeing the horrors start outside his house. The blind panic and screaming as he threw the contents of his flat at the zombies as they attacked. He had forgotten the man leading them away with the armoured van and encouraging them into the town. Then the first hands-on attack as he killed his first zombie. That was the start right there. That feeling of anger and vengeance that surged through him. He thinks back to meeting up with Dave in the supermarket, and again, he gives thanks that he found Dave. Today has been the longest period they've spent apart in a week, and having Dave back, at his side now feels normal. Like the balance is restored.

'I was thinking back to the supermarket, Dave,' Howie says between mouthfuls. 'All those bodies you stacked up. I wonder if you would have stayed there if I didn't come along.'

'I didn't have anywhere else to go.'

'And do you remember that fat woman that got stuck in the door?' Howie says, bursting out laughing.

'Yes, Mr Howie.'

'Oh, yeah,' Howie chuckles while Dave remains as passive as ever, but with Howie sensing Dave is enjoying the banter. 'I was next to useless in that farmhouse though.'

'Yes, Mr Howie.'

'Cheeky shit. At least I didn't put the wrong fuel into that car.'

'You fell over and shot the car,' Dave says.

'Yeah, but you got stripped off pretty quickly when Sergeant Hopewell was watching us,' Howie fires back.

'You broke my shotgun.'

'When?' Howie says.

'In Portsmouth, at the barricade.'

'That was that bloody John Jones, nasty fucker, and his son too.'

'The one you kept punching,' Dave says.

'Yeah, him. I wonder what happened to them.'

'I don't know, Mr Howie.'

'It's been a long week, mate,' Howie says after a pause.

'It has, Mr Howie.'

'That bridge was good,' Howie says.

'Tower Bridge?' Dave asks.

'No, the first one in that village when we were turning it by hand, and they kept falling off.'

'Yes,' Dave says, nodding.

'And that freaky one that caught my axe when I tried to chop his head off. That was horrible.'

'The chainsaw was good.'

'Ha! did you see the chainsaw? I thought you were busy on your side,' Howie laughs.

'I saw it, and the lump hammers, and the sledgehammer, and all the other tools you tried.'

'The chainsaw was the best, though. I love the axe, mind you.'

'I like knives,' Dave says flatly.

'Do you? I'd never have noticed... I wonder how our Tesco lorry is doing.' Howie pauses, taking another mouthful of food. 'Salisbury was good. I'm glad we went there. Apart from that bloody officer.'

'Charles Galloway-Gibbs,' Nick says as Howie realises everyone else has gone quiet and is listening to him and Dave.

'Complete tool,' Blowers says.

'Now that was a hard night, getting that Saxon,' Cookey adds.

'We did it, though,' Howie says.

'There must have been a thousand of them, at least.'

'Thanks to Dave and the GPMG,' Blowers says.

'Another five minutes, and I think we'd be staggering round now too.'

'BRAAIINNNS. I WANT COOOKEY BRAAAIINNS,' Howie says to laughter from the recruits, remembering the jokes from before.

'So which is better? The feast Tucker did in the barracks or this one?' Howie asks, seeing Tucker's face light up.

'The one at Salisbury was fucking lovely,' Nick blurts. 'Sorry, I meant it was very nice,' he adds, with a glance at Sergeant Hopewell.

'This is nice, but that was a feast and a half,' Blowers agrees. The conversations carry on, of great meals eaten in faraway places, of dangerous missions undertaken by Chris, Malcolm, and Clarence. The officers jump in with stories of incidents and strange crimes they've dealt with. Each of them sharing experiences and memories of a life now gone, thinking this may be the last time they get to share something, to tell another human of who they are and where they came from. The close feeling shared amongst them grows and matures as they listen to each other, laughing or nodding with understanding.

'It's getting dark,' Chris says as the conversations start to trail off. They look up to the sky to see the beautiful swathes of red mixed with the golden rays of the dwindling light.

'Red sky at night, zombie's delight,' Blowers mutters quietly.

'Right, so what's the plan?' Howie asks. 'We wait for them to come and hope our traps work, then throw what we can at them from up here, and when that ends, we go down and meet them? That's what I think, anyway.'

'Sounds about right to me,' Chris nods back.

'Any other suggestions?' Howie asks.

'Keep it fluid,' Dave offers. 'We've planned as best we can, and now we just have to be able to react accordingly,' he adds to nods and murmurs of agreement and stares of awe from Jamie, Tom, and Steven.

'Okay, keep your hand weapons to, err... Well, to hand, I guess, and in the meantime, let's try and rest,' Howie says.

They break apart slowly, lingering to have a few words with each other. Howie steps over to Sarah, drawing her away from the group.

'Any news on the boats?' Howie asks quietly.

'Nothing yet, but we've spoken to the mothers and got the children ready to move.'

'And Ted? Did you speak to him?'

'He was reluctant but said he would do it as it was you asking,' Sarah replies.

Howie looks over to see Ted looking back, giving a single, knowing nod.

'Good, let me know as soon as they're back.'

'Howie, I...well...' Sarah says hesitantly.

'What is it?' Howie asks with concern.

'Well, we've not really spoken since you got me and...'

'Yeah, I know. I'm sorry, it's been manic.'

'No, you don't have to apologise. I just wanted to spend some time with my brother before, well, before...'

'You can say it,' Howie smiles. 'Before they come for us.'

'Yes, before they come,' Sarah says softly. 'You seem so different now. It's only been a week, and you've changed so much. I hardly recognised you. I couldn't believe it when I saw you fighting through those things in London.'

'It doesn't feel like a week,' Howie muses. 'It feels like a lifetime.'

'What happened? How did you get like this?'

'I don't know. I really don't. I was lucky, I guess. I was at home when it happened, and it was happening right outside my house. They were trying to get in to get me. I fought back, but there were so many. I thought I was done for. Then this van went past, leading them all away from me. I managed to get out, and then the rest just sort of happened. I was heading home, to Mum and Dad's house. I found some crappy, old bicycle and was going on the motorway. This car went past me and then hit the barrier, and flipped over. There was a woman in the wreckage. She was still alive when I got to her. I tried to pull her out and save her, but one of those things was in the car and bit her. She died as I was trying to save her,' Howie explains in a flat, emotionless voice.

'That's awful,' Sarah says.

'Yeah, but then, like I said, she died. I was crying, and she came back and tried to bite my face off,' Howie says.

'What did you do?' Sarah asks.

'I kicked her to death,' Howie replies. 'And I guess that was the point when I decided they were all dirty, evil scum. Then I went through a village, and more of them came for me, so I set them on fire and probably burnt the village down in the process. Then I got to a shop and killed some more. I finally got home and found the note from

Mum and Dad, saying they had gone to look for me. I went back home but couldn't find them, got attacked a few more times, and killed some more of them. I went to work, met Dave, and figured Mum and Dad would have gone back to theirs. I went back again. They weren't there, and I, sort of, snapped.'

'Snapped?' Sarah asks.

'I went back to Boroughfare. I went back, knowing I wanted to kill them one by one. Fortunately, Dave came with me, and we've been going ever since. I came up with this mad plan to get a tank to get through London to find you,' Howie laughs. 'So we went to Salisbury to steal something big and hard and ended up hooking up with that lot,' he nods at the recruits nearby. 'Had more fights, killed more of them, and they wanted to stay with us, so we came to London.'

'Howie, that's amazing,' Sarah says, staring at her brother with awe.

'Not really. You stayed alive and fought back too. I saw what you did in the back of that van,' Howie says.

'Howie, please don't get me wrong. You saved my life and many others by what you've done, with Dave, but well, I've never seen you so alive, so...I don't know...' she trails off, uncertain of how to say it. 'It seems like you're enjoying it, Howie,' she finally says, looking directly at him.

'Enjoying it? The end of the world and being surrounded by death and destruction?' Howie replies, with an offended and puzzled tone.

'The fighting, Howie. I saw you fighting in London. You were more alive than I have ever seen you. You were possessed. I saw your face and the way you were. I know you better than all of these people...'

'What about Clarence? Chris? Malcolm? Did they look like they were enjoying it too? Have you seen Dave fight?' Howie demands, with anger.

'Yes, I saw Dave,' Sarah replies softly.

'Well, did he look like he was enjoying it? What about Blowers and the rest?'

'Howie, I don't know them. I only know you, and it was shocking to see you like that,' Sarah says.

'So what would you prefer? That I stayed at home and hid under the blankets?'

'That's not what I meant, Howie. I mean you were enjoying it, it gave you pleasure, and that's wrong.'

'Why? Why is it wrong? How did it feel when you and that other woman killed them all in the van?'

'It felt awful, Howie. It was survival, and it had to be done, but that was it.'

'No sense of victory? No feeling of righteousness?'

'No,' she says firmly.

Howie pauses and looks down at his feet, then slowly over to the flatlands, and the estate in the distance, watching as the shadows lengthen and twilight takes over.

'Maybe it's wrong. Maybe it is completely wrong,' Howie says eventually, still looking away from Sarah. 'But the way I see it, it doesn't matter what the motivation or reason is as long as it gets done. As long as those things are put down and killed. But I see your point. It's okay for Chris and the others to have that violence, but not your brother, is that it?'

'Something like that,' Sarah replies in a soft voice.

'I don't know what to say,' Howie shrugs. 'It is what it is. They want to kill us, and we have to stop them.'

'I know.'

'Clarence seems a nice bloke,' Howie says with a sudden smile.

'Ha, yes, he does,' Sarah smiles back, glad of the break in tension.

'Well, I'm gonna try and sleep. You sticking around up here?' Howie says.

'I'll be about,' Sarah replies as Howie starts walking towards the Saxon.

'And Howie?' she adds. 'I know we weren't the type of Brother and Sister that said it, but I do love you,' she says. Howie smiles back; the darkness lifted from his face for a few seconds.

'You too, Sis.' He walks off towards the Saxon, smiling and nodding at the people he passes.

Clustering in and around the Saxon, they all try to rest and sleep. Although there are now hundreds of people at the top of the inner north wall, they take no chances and still keep one on the GPMG.

Malcolm offers to take the first watch. Howie and Chris take the quiet interior of the Saxon. The rear doors closed so they can have more peace. Howie beds down on a thick layer of army coats discarded in the warm weather. Chris on the cushioned bench seats. They make easy talk for a few seconds before Chris starts snoring loudly, leaving Howie alone to think about the words Sarah said to him. As his mind tries to think, the rhythmic sounds from Chris get to work, and within seconds, Howie drifts off.

CHAPTER NINETY

'I'm going to test-fire the cannon, Mr Howie,' Dave says, opening a rear door and leaning into the Saxon.

'Okay, mate,' Howie answers, sleepily.

As Dave walks over, he notices the two cannon crews still in their groups, running through the drills he showed them earlier.

They look at him eagerly as he approaches, and he notices the first crew moves discreetly into position, waiting for the chance to do a live fire. Dave gets to the cannon and walks around, checking everything is in place: the powder bags, the wadding, the mounds of wrapped ammunition, the ramrods, the fuses, and finally, the holder of the flame standing a short distance away.

'Good idea,' Dave nods at the gas canister fitted with a welder's flame that stands a few metres away. A man standing next to it, holding a petrol lighter.

'We've got one on the other cannon too,' the man replies proudly.

Dave nods and completes his inspection. He walks around to the back of the cannon and looks down the length and out to the flatlands.

'We'll probably get maximum impact if we aim for them as they come out of the deep ditch, after the second embankment,' Dave says. 'Let's try it and see.' He has one final look around to see the first crew all stood in their allocated positions, ready and waiting to go.

He looks to the man with the lengths of fuse wire and nods once before stepping away to observe. The man steps forward and pushes the fuse into the cannon hole, feeling for the resistance as the bottom of the wire hits the inside base of the cannon.

'POWDER,' the man shouts and steps back.

The next man picks up a powder bag and moves smartly over to the mouth of the cannon, pushing the bag inside.

'RAMROD,' he shouts as the man with the long stick steps forward and beats the powder bag down to the bottom of the cannon.

'WADDING,' the ramrod man shouts and steps back as the next man pushes wadding into the mouth of the cannon.

'RAMROD,' he shouts, and again, the man with the stick steps up and pushes the wadding firmly down the cannon.

'AMMUNITION.' Then a wrapped bundle of nuts, bolts, nails, and screws is pushed in.

'RAMROD.' The man with the stick pushes it down.

He steps back and checks everyone is clear before shouting, 'FUSE!'

The gas canister knob is already turned, and the welder's torch has a soft, yellow flame at the end. The flame holder lifts the gas canister and steps over to the fuse, and once again, checks everyone is standing well away. He presses the flame to the fuse and pauses for a second as the fuse takes light and starts burning down.

'FIRE!' he bellows and steps back away from the expected recoil.

They all stand with bated breath and hands covering ears as a huge bang rips through the air. The cannon is shot backwards as a massive tongue of fire shoots out the end with a thick, black cloud.

Dave is at the wall, upwind and watching as the second bank is clearly peppered with metal fragments striking the top and firing far beyond. He turns back to the crews waiting and the many people turned to watch. He gives a simple thumbs up and a rare smile as they cheer loudly.

'Good, make it ready, and we'll test the other one,' Dave says and watches as they burst into action, and the hose man steps forward like a ceremonial guard to sluice any burning fragments from the inside of the cannon. At the next cannon, the first crew stands by and watches with the experienced eye of expert cannon firers, and the second crew position themselves and wait for Dave. Once again, he checks everything is in place before nodding once and stepping away. The second crew prove just as good as the first and move quickly, shouting for the next man as they each complete their duty.

The holder of the flame steps forward and lights the fuse, shouting *FIRE* as he quickly moves away. Once again, the cannon roars to life and flies backwards as a long, orange flame comes out of the mouth, followed within a split second by thick, black smoke.

Dave is at the wall, watching as the spinning metal fragments fly over the bank and reach a good distance into the flatlands.

'Good, too high, though,' Dave says and moves over to remove a wedge used to raise the mouth of the cannon. 'That will be perfect. Make it ready,' he adds before moving off back to the Saxon amidst the cheering and applauding again. He walks around the Saxon, checking on each of his men. Howie and Chris lead them, but Dave accepts them as his to be protected and watched.

Although his different mind doesn't allow for the same feeling of impending doom the others have, he does feel a very keen sense of trepidation.

Dave has worked alone on hundreds of missions and has been outnumbered many times before. But his ability to plan, fight, and move quickly meant he was rarely in danger in the same way that others may perceive it. In order to have a fear of death, one must have a sense of life, and Dave simply does not tick that way. Complete the task in front of you while planning for the next one. Dave had worked alongside regular troops before, but his status always kept him aloof and away. But no matter how different he may be, this week has affected him. These men have become familiar to him – their voices, their jokes, and the way they fight. Blowers and Cookey always side by side, joking, but when they fight, they do so with complete ferocity, always watching each other and covering the gaps. Tucker is a big lad and not as fit as the others, but he uses his bulk and size and overcomes that fear to drive on. Nick, a witty man, with a good head for computers and electrical things, and again, he fights with his heart, never holding back and pushing on with savage intent. Curtis, he is competent, which may seem a lowly compliment, but a competent man is worth his weight in gold. He knows where to be at the right time and never complains. A good driver too. Then there's Jamie. Quiet like Dave but still different. He is highly capable and willing to learn, and importantly, he is able to work alone, but not for his own ends. Dave looks at each of them as he passes and thinks of McKinney and how Howie reacted when he knew Dave was going to finish him. That was the deepest feeling Dave had ever felt. Not for the loss of McKinney, but for the anger and betrayal he thought Howie must be holding towards him. Howie is a natural leader and has a rare ability to show error and mistakes but still command respect. Whatever may come from this battle, Dave knows one thing. Men like Howie must survive. They know right from wrong. They know what must be done, and then they work out how to do it. Men like these that make other men fight when otherwise, they would be quivering in a corner and pissing themselves with fear. Dave positions himself at the back of the Saxon, quietly finding a spot that means anyone trying to enter the vehicle from the back must first go past him. The bodyguard. The watchman.

The night closes in, and for the first time in a week, Howie does not hear the howling of the infected voices lifting to roar in unison. He sleeps deeply, exhausted both in mind and body. They all sleep. All through the camp there is quiet. Men and woman strolling around, chatting in muted tones. Couples clasping each other tightly, knowing it might be the last time. Families huddle together and whisper words of love and life. Men keep their weapons close, and women hold their children, for tonight may be the last night of life. Past mistakes are forgotten, and petty squabbles are laid aside as they acknowledge the lives they have led and prepare for what may come.

CHAPTER NINETY-ONE

I wake up quickly, bathed in sweat, and I find myself sat bolt upright, breathing hard. Looking over, I see that Chris has already left. I know I was dreaming, but the images have faded instantly. I feel hot, still tired and dirty, but above all else, I need the toilet.

I clamber out of the vehicle to find the others half asleep, drinking from mugs of hot coffee being handed around by Tucker and his new team of catering corps volunteers.

'Morning, Mr Howie. Fresh coffee for you.' Tucker approaches me with a steaming mug.

'Not now, mate, gotta go.' The cramping in my stomach signifies an urgent action is required.

I run off in just my socks. No time to go back for my boots left in the back of the vehicle. I start jogging down the vehicle ramp, desperately trying to remember where the closest toilet is. The jogging motion just makes it worse, though, and I can feel a pressing sensation pushing inside my stomach.

'Too much bloody coffee,' I mutter as I speed up.

People pass by me, trying to stop and talk. I wave them off apologetically and keep going. There's no way I'm going to shit myself in front of all these people. This might be the last day of humanity, but I'm not going out with Chris, Blowers, Cookey, and the rest of them all ripping the piss out of me. The visitors centre. That must have toilets. It's across the camp, but there's no alternative. There must be some closer ones, but I can't take the chance to stop and ask now. I run down the wide central path, veering around children and people stepping out to chat.

'Fuck it, fuck it,' I mutter under my breath as I run faster.

I can feel my face going red, and the cramping sensation is bloody awful. I want to stop and drop my trousers here, but that might not be a good thing. The hero of Fort Spitbank leaving a big, steaming poo on the floor. No, that wouldn't go down very well. There it is. I can see it. There's lights on inside, making it glow in the still darkness of the night. I glance up to see the sky is just starting to lift. I reach the door and see a queue of people stood holding toilet rolls in the wide reception area. After killing many zombies, using bad language, and now preparing for an invasion of the infected army, I commit the worst British crime of all. I jump the queue. There's no other choice. If I don't get to a toilet now, I will void my pants.

'Sorry, I'm really sorry,' I yell out as I run around the quiet men and women stood chatting. I see the door with the stick figure of a man on the front and burst through. Inside, the cubicles are all closed, with more people waiting patiently outside each one. I glance at the urinals, thinking for a split second of sitting on one of them instead.

I grab my stomach as the cramping sensation doubles from the urgent motion of the running. A door opens in front of me, and a man steps out. I stare pleadingly at the man waiting to go in. There's something in my eyes. He stares back, with a look of absolute forgiveness on his face.

'Do you want to go next?' he asks politely as I close the door in his face.

'Sorry, mate,' I say through gritted teeth as I scrabble at my belt, cursing the stupid buckles.

'That's okay. When you've got to go...' the man outside says. His speech leaves it open for me to finish, but I'm otherwise occupied, fighting the hardest battle yet, with my trousers.

Finally, I yank them down, pull my underpants down to my ankles, and sit down. My arse hits cold plastic, and I jump instantly back up as I realise I've sat on the closed toilet seat.

'Fucking stupid toilet seat,' I shout, wrenching the blasted thing up to sit back down. My bowels explode with wretched venom as the bomb doors unleash a devastating payload on the poor porcelain toilet bowl beneath me.

'Oh, my fucking god,' I can't help the words coming out. My arse sputters like a Spitfire machine gun rattling fire at the enemy. The feeling of relief is immense.

'Err, are you all right in there?' the same man asks, with polite concern at the long, whimpering sounds coming from me.

'Yep, fine,' I reply with a casual politeness; the spattering noise almost drowning my voice out.

After several minutes, the cramping in my gut abates, and I'm left in a state of absolute bliss. That is until the smell of shit hits my nose, and I become acutely aware of my surroundings.

I twist around to the toilet roll holder, but it's empty. Everyone in the queue had their own rolls in hand.

'Err, sorry, are you still there?' I call out.

'Yes?' the man replies.

'It appears I didn't bring any toilet roll with me. Would you have any spare I could...borrow?' I ask. A hand clutching a full toilet roll appears under the door, and I reach forward and take it gratefully. 'Thank you very much.'

'You're welcome.' After a double flushing of the toilet, I'm all done and open the door to see other men politely look away.

'Bet that's a shitload off your mind,' someone says to a few sniggers.

'Thanks for the toilet roll, mate,' I hand it back and move over to the washbasin, and scrub my hands clean.

At the least the water's still running. Eventually, I'm done and stroll out of the toilet and into the reception area, nodding apologetically at the people still waiting in the queue. Outside, I walk happily through the camp, heading back to the north wall and still feeling strangely warm and comforted.

Walking back up the vehicle ramp, I notice they're all up and drinking coffee, stood around, chatting as the first tendrils of daylight push into the night sky.

I see Blowers, Cookey, and Nick all smoking cigarettes.

I see the red ends glowing brightly as they suck in the tobacco and exhale the lazy smoke clouds.

The vapour wisps come from the coffee mugs.

Chris, stood off to one side, is laughing with Malcolm.

Clarence is talking quietly to Sarah.

Curtis up on the GPMG at the top of the Saxon. The machine gun pointing off to the right, and Curtis leaning forward on his elbows, clutching a hot drink.

Off to both sides, I see people stretching lazily and talking in muted tones, nodding to each other. A man throws a cigarette onto the floor and brings his heavy boot down to grind it out. My heart starts beating faster. The scene slows down, and I feel like I'm wading through thick mud. Tucker strolls past me at the top of the ramp. He's looking at me and smiling. He holds a steaming mug of coffee out in front of him, ready for me to take it. It takes forever to reach him. My senses have become heightened, and adrenalin is coursing through my system. I look past Tucker and see Dave stood by the wall, looking out at the flatlands.

Something flashes far beyond him. A quick, bright light in the distance.

Everything slows, and I see Dave start to turn back towards us. His face strangely animated, and I watch as his mouth opens and his eyes are blazing. This is it. I know it.

'COVERRRR,' Dave's voice roars out into the quiet night, and it brings me back to reality in a heartbeat. To their credit, my group react instantly. As one, they drop down and spin to face the flatlands. Hundreds of heads all along the top of the inner wall snap around to face us. Many within the camp hear Dave's awesome voice, and they too stop and turn to look up. I stand still and look out to the estate. The first bright flash is followed by a low, dull thump that rolls over the ground to my ears. Another bright flash, then another, followed by a series of bright flashes spread all along the width of the estate. Soundless at first. The speed of light being far greater than the speed of sound. But the sound does reach us as the dull, echoing thumps roll out like soft drumbeats. Then the estate goes up. The whole of the thing, from far left to far right and as far back as the eye can see, explodes as one.

The still dark sky is lit for many hundreds of miles around as a wall of fire scorches high up into the air.

My mouth drops open as I have never seen such a thing before. The most expensive special effects movies ever made cannot compare to this sight. A whole housing estate erupting instantaneously and filling the sky with flames the size of skyscrapers. Within a split second, the pressure wave and the sound hit us. As one, we are taken off our feet. Not a single person remains standing on the top of the inner wall. Down below in the camp, many are knocked down or simply drop to hug the earth in absolute terror. The ground seems to heave, and the noise is more than words can describe. A thousand jet aircrafts taking off at the same time while a thousand marching bands pound through my skull. I go flying off to the side. I could be screaming or silent. I have no concept. All I know is that my senses are overwhelmed with sight, sound, and sensation. If there is a hell, then surely it has come alive here, in this place. I stagger to my feet, not knowing what I'm doing. Looking around, I see every other person is down on the ground, burying their heads with their arms. All apart from Dave, who is stood side-on to me. His face turned to watch his glorious work. His profile framed by the scorching flames behind him. How he remained standing is something I may never know, but he and I stand and watch with awe. The incredible sounds continue, and I see the flames are shooting out over the flatlands too, eviscerating everything in reach. This is something amazing, something beautiful, created by one man who can barely hold a conversation. Dave looks up and tilts his head to one side, seemingly staring at something in the night sky.

'INCOMING,' he bellows with his huge voice, somehow drowning out the sounds of the explosions still reaching us. I look up, puzzled at what they could be firing at us from this distance, and especially after that explosion.

Then I see it. A car on fire, rolling over and over gently in the air as it sails hundreds of feet over the Fort to land far out in the sea.

I glance back up to see more fiery objects flying overhead, leaving long, blazing trails of sparks and fire behind them like mini comets. I hear a loud, wet slapping sound nearby and turn my head slowly, finding it hard to drag my eyes away from the glorious blaze. I look over and see a charred and smouldering torso laying on the ground a few metres away. Just a torso, with the arms still attached. No legs or head, though. I watch it with curious detachment, then feel my body being slammed to the ground. Dave is up and grabbing at my arm, trying to pull me to my feet. He's just knocked me down, and now he wants me back up.

'GET UP, MR HOWIE,' he shouts at me, and his voice penetrates enough to get me to my feet and staggering behind him as he pulls me around to the back of the Saxon. He wrenches the rear doors open and shoves me bodily into the back. I get to my senses and shuffle forward to look out of the windscreen. Flaming body parts are landing all along the inner wall and behind us, in the camp. Burnt and scorched heads, legs, arms, and torsos, torn apart and sent flying high into the sky to come tumbling back down upon us. Dave runs around the front of the vehicle and starts pulling at Sarah, yelling for her to get up. I run back and jump out of the Saxon, landing with both feet firm on the ground. I race round and lift Sarah to her feet by her shoulders, shoving her roughly towards the back of the vehicle. She looks dazed and confused, and we dodge burning body parts landing all around us.

'DAVE, PROTECT THE CANNONS,' I scream out.

Dave turns to face me, with a sudden realisation.

'I CAN ONLY DO ONE,' he shouts back and races off to the left. I run forward, grabbing at bodies and pulling them up.

Someone screams, and I look over to see an archer being squashed by a heavy zombie body landing on him. Others scrabbling forward to try and pull the burning body away. I glance down into the camp and see chaos reigning – people running in all directions and screaming as the burning body parts come slamming down.

Tents are ablaze, and brave men and women beat at the deadly flames with coats and blankets. Malcolm is up and staring around, with a look of utter horror on his face. I run over and grab his arms to make him face me.

'MALCOLM, PROTECT THE OTHER CANNON. IF THOSE POWDER BAGS GO UP, WE'LL BE FUCKED!' I scream into his face several times until he comes to and nods back at me before running off. Within a few minutes, my group are up and working, running up and down the top of the inner wall, stamping down on flaming body parts to beat them out. I run down to see Malcolm using the hose from the cannon, running about and spraying the water over any burning material.

I'd forgot about the hoses and give thanks once more for Dave's forward planning. Dave joins me back in the middle, and together, with our band of brothers, we stare out to the flatlands. The sky is much lighter now, and daylight is almost upon us.

'Thank fuck it didn't set the fuel off in the deep ditch,' Chris says. His feet are planted apart, his hands on his hips as he stares out to the blazing estate.

'Dave, I want everyone up here to make ready. We'll use the Saxon to fire first as it has the range. Everyone else holds until they get closer so we don't waste ammunition,' I bark out the order as I stride forward to stare out, over the flatlands.

I hear Dave take a sharp intake of breath and wait for his voice to come bellowing out.

'MAKE READY. YOU WILL MAKE READY AND WAIT. HOLD YOUR FIRE.' The inner wall springs to action as hundreds of people surge forward to take up their arms. Clips are pushed in, with a multitude of loud clicks. Firing bolts are racked back. Men and women make their weapons ready. Ready to stand proud and fight. Silence falls amongst us. Even the camp seems quiet now as everyone prepares for the attack they know is coming.

'BLOWERS, GET OUR LOT FORMED UP HERE,' I indicate the area of the wall immediately in front of the Saxon and facing out, down the road leading to the estate.

'NICK, YOU'RE ON THE GPMG. DAVE AND JAMIE, I WANT YOU BOTH SNIPING. TRY AND GET THAT FUCKER SMITH.' They react without hesitation.

Tucker runs up, carrying my rifle, and hands it over as he takes up position on the wall. I spare a glance to see my glorious men kneeling down and removing ammunition clips from their bags, placing them at their feet, ready for use. Their hands are steady, and there is a steely look in their eyes.

'HOWIE, MY MEN ARE YOURS. USE THEM,' Chris shouts from the back of the Saxon.

'FORM UP ON THE WALL, HERE,' I bellow out, pointing at the space being used by my recruits.

'WE FOCUS OUR FIRE ON THAT ROAD,' I shout out and watch as the guards from the commune jump in.

'GET YOUR CLIPS OUT AND READY. FOCUS YOUR FIRE. HOLD UNTIL TOLD!' I hear Blowers stepping smoothly into his corporal role. He moves along our line, checking each is ready.

'COOKEY, I'LL DO THIS END. YOU DO THAT ONE. MAKE SURE THEY'RE ALL READY,' Blowers yells over to his friend.

They split, with each one moving off down the line of the wall, checking each man and woman is ready with their ammunition, and repeating for them to hold their fire until told. Tucker runs past me, heading to the back of the Saxon. I pay little attention as I see Sarah running up the vehicle ramp, towards us. I didn't see her go off anywhere, so I'm puzzled to see her coming back.

'Howie, the boats are back,' she yells out.

'Get those children ready and get them loaded to go.' I turn to Chris as he steps away from the Saxon, holding an assault rifle.

'Chris, I've got boats to take the children away. I've got it here. Can you go and make sure they move quickly?'

'Got it,' Chris replies and turns to jog after Sarah. I turn back to the wall as Tucker comes up beside me.

'Mr Howie, sir,' he says.

I turn to see him holding a pair of boots. My boots. I look down to see I'm still wearing just my socks.

'Well done, mate,' I smile at him and walk over to the Saxon, and start pulling them on.

I glance to the side to see Dave and Jamie both have rifles with scopes attached. No suppressors or silencers now. They take position front and middle, looking directly at the road. I step away and see Blowers and Cookey returning to their posts, both of them nodding at me as they take position. The estate is still well ablaze, but I know it won't be long before they try and push through. I can imagine Darren is sending them in to find paths and routes safe enough to get through. I look up to see Nick standing calmly with the general-purpose machine gun in front of him. He looks down and smiles.

'You ready, mate?' I call up.

'Yes, Mr Howie,' he says, with a clear voice.

'EYES ON,' Jamie shouts, and every head snaps forward as the tension increases tenfold within a split second.

'COMING THROUGH NOW,' Dave shouts out, sweeping along the estate line with his scope.

'Mr Howie,' Nick calls out and throws down a pair of binoculars.

I press them to my eyes and adjust the setting until the burning estate comes into focus. Most of the houses are gone. The sheer ferocity of the explosion has shredded everything on the estate. The fuel tanker and the open gas lines created such a powerful explosion that everything that could be burnt was burnt. Now, with very little left, the flames are dying down. Thick, black smoke billows up into the sky, but between the wreckage and blackened stumps, I see the infected pouring forward. A thick line of them comes into view through the smoke. Several of them drop from heat or flames, but the mass just keeps rolling forward.

'THIS IS IT,' I bellow out.

'THEY'RE COMING THROUGH THE ESTATE NOW,' I report what I see.

The sight of them triggers an instant response inside of me. The anger is knocking to come in, but I bite it down. I'll need it later, but for now, I can do this myself.

'ALMOST AT THE EDGE. NICK, YOU'LL GET A VIEW OF THEM ANY SECOND.'

'ROGER,' Nick shouts out loudly and racks the bolt back noisily.

I glance up to see him tightly gripping the handles and staring ahead, with ferocious concentration. I put the binoculars back to my eyes and see them surging forward.

'HERE THEY COME,' I shout as they reach within metres of the edge of the estate.

I drop the binoculars down and watch with the naked eye. The edge of the estate suddenly comes alive as a solid, black mass emerges.

'NICK,' I shout out.

'COME ON,' Nick shouts, and the air is split apart by the heavy, constant sound of the general-purpose machine gun coming to life.

Nick aims well and sweeps along the entire front row.

From far left to far right, I can see bodies falling down as Nick sweeps across them, then back again as the awesome power of the weapon shows true. I lift the binoculars again and follow Nick's arc of fire, watching as the bodies are shredded apart and sent flying backwards, into the pressed ranks behind them. The following hordes stumble over their fallen comrades. I sweep back, and my heart sinks as I see a solid mass stretching back into the estate and no sign of the end. I move my view down and watch with my breath held as they near the first obstacle we prepared. They move as one, keeping their lines smartly and presenting a solid wall. Not running but not shuffling either. A steady pace as they advance.

'Go on, go on,' Cookey urges them on to the next trap.

'Come on, you stupid fuckers,' another voice joins in and is taken up as more shout out, urging and willing them to keep going. They reach the first ditch, and I watch as the first few lines simply fall out of view, dropping into the ground.

Cheering erupts up and down the wall as the forward ranks of infected drop down to be impaled on the sharpened spikes. The pressure from the oncoming hordes keeps driving the infected forward to topple into the wide ditch.

'YES!' Cookey shouts, with violence in his voice. 'HAVE SOME OF THAT.'

I spin around and look to the back of the Fort. Sarah and Sergeant Hopewell are by the opened rear doors, urging the women and children to move out quickly. I guess Chris and the others must be outside, lifting them into boats. I turn back in time to see the next ranks dropping down as they reach the ditch but not going out of sight. The bodies must have stacked up deep enough to bridge the gap, but it at least slows them, and many have already been vanquished from the estate going up and now the ditch. The GPMG roars with incessant noise as Nick continues to sweep from left to right in a steady motion. Then two more loud and distinct bangs join in as Dave and Jamie start firing with their high-powered rifles.

'READY,' I roar out and see a visible reaction as the men and women on the line seem to hunch forward, push their shoulders into their weapons, and aim down the sights. I pause just for a second as I watch the front lines of the infected army start dropping down as they run over the foot traps.

'FIRE,' I drop the binoculars for a second and scream the word as loud as I can.

I see a devastating effect as many of the infected are dropped instantly by the volley. I use the binoculars again and see that not only the firing from our weapons is dropping them, but the foot traps are working far greater than I had hoped.

A small smile forms on my mouth as I see infected staggering forward and then suddenly dropping down as their feet are penetrated by the deadly, sharp metal barbs. They might not feel pain, but the physical action of the metal driving through their skin and breaking the delicate, small bones of the foot is enough to make them fall down. All along the lines, I see infected blown apart and shredded by the deadly hail of bullets from the GPMG. The rifles and assault weapons also prove very effective. Not every shot is a headshot, but the simple action of being penetrated by a high-speed large calibre rifle is enough to blow them backwards and knock more down. Dave and Jamie's shots are, without question, perfect. Puffs of pink mist explode time and time again as they blow the skulls apart and send deadly bone fragments into the closely packed horde. I glance up and down the line to see men and women using bolt-action rifles. Rates of fire increasing as they aim, fire, rack the bolt, then aim and fire. The movements are becoming faster and more fluid with each shot. Placing the binoculars down, I stride forward and take up position on the wall, with my assault rifle. Selecting single shot and pulling the bolt back. I take aim, which is almost completely unnecessary as there are so bloody many of them, so just waving the gun in their general direction will surely hit something.

I pull aim for front, centre, at the section of infected coming down the central road. The better weapons being used by the recruits and guards in this section means those infected are suffering high casualty rates and being withered as they advance. Each one dropped is instantly replaced, but still, we pour fire into them, and every shot counts as they are slowly reduced. My shots join the deafening noise as I fire into the oncoming mass. Working in concentrated silence, the minutes pass as the zombie army slowly but surely takes ground and moves ever closer to the Fort, rising and falling as they step on the fallen bodies in front of them.

The foot traps keep working, and they keep dropping down, but still, they keep coming until they are but metres away from the first embankment. With no sign of Darren, Dave and Jamie have taken up their assault rifles to increase the rate of fire sent from us. Nick brings the GPMG to focus the fire directly into the front centre line on the road. With the sustained firing of Nick and the recruits, and the guards all using assault rifles, the infected on the road are obliterated.

Large gaps start forming as the following horde are forced to weave around the broken and mangled bodies. The infected army reaches the first embankment, and I watch as the first lines rise up and over the crest to pour down the other side. A huge boom sounds out off to my left, and I glance down just in time to see flames shooting out the end of the cannon, followed by a cloud of thick, black smoke. The results of the cannon fire are awesome, and a whole swathe of infected are eviscerated by the scorching metallic fragments. The second cannon off to my right then booms out. I keep my eyes on the horde this time and realise that everyone else does too. The impact is simply staggering, and my mouth drops open as the grapeshot from the cannon spreads out, becoming superheated by the incredible power of the cannon, and rips through whole lines of infected.

The projectiles go through the first rank like butter, and several lines back are instantly taken down. Each shot of the cannon destroys hundreds at a time. Again, large gaps form as the infected can't move fast enough to fill the gaps, and now the front line is not solid. But still, they keep coming, and it takes moments to prepare the cannon for the next round of firing.

'That was fucking awesome,' Cookey says during the pause of firing as we all watch the effect of the second cannon firing.

'EYES FRONT,' Dave bellows and snaps us all back to the moment.

Stepping back, I look down the top of the inner wall to see the archers have split into two groups. One group on the left, and the other on the right. Two archers from each group are standing next to the cannon flame holder, their bows dipped down, with arrows resting against the wire in the rest position. The ends of the arrows have been swathed in something, ready to be lit and fired into the deep ditch. As the infected reach halfway between the two embankments, the archers are given an order to prepare. They move out into a long line, stood well back from the wall. Each of them presses the arrow into wire as they lift their bows and pull back to stand braced. For a second, I'm transported to medieval England as I see long lines of archers holding their bows aimed high into the air.

'RELEASE,' someone shouts, and the bowmen and women release their arrows to fly high and straight. The arrows reach the arc of their trajectory, and the strength of gravity takes over, pulling them back to earth, gathering speed as they plummet down. The arrows drive into the zombie army. Many of them striking into the exposed skulls and taking infected down with instant kills. Some of the arrows hit arms and legs, causing them to be pushed down, only to rise back up and keep going, with the long barbs stuck through their limbs. Some of them crawl along the ground, only to be trampled down by more zombie feet, already pierced and damaged by the foot traps. As the first volley of arrows hits home, the second volley is already in the air. The two cannons both fire with massive recoiling booms, and again, whole swathes of infected are killed outright. More large gaps form, and their lines become more ragged. The GPMG, the assault rifles, the single shot rifles, the cannons and the archers, all pour deadly fire into the infected army as we continue to cull their numbers.

'I SEE HIM,' Jamie drops his assault rifle to pick up the scoped sniper rifle.

'Where?' I call out, ceasing fire to glare out at the army.

'Sir, he's on the road, about fifty metres back from the front line. There's a whole dense section clustered round him,' Jamie shouts back as he rests the rifle on the wall and looks down the scope.

Dave has already dropped his assault rifle and picked his rifle up to rest alongside Jamie and stare down the scope.

'I see the dense section,' Dave shouts out.

'NICK, FIRE INTO THE MIDDLE,' I turn and shout at Nick, waving my arm to show him where I want the fire aimed.

Nick nods once, grim-faced, and turns the heavy calibre weapon onto the front, middle section.

'THEY'RE AT THE SECOND BANK,' Clarence's deep voice shouts.

I look across and see the infected are now scaling the far side. They reach the crest of the embankment.

'FIRE ARCHERS MAKE READY,' I shout out, but the constant and sustained noise prevents my voice from reaching the archers further down the lines. I run back to the Saxon and pull the microphone out.

'FIRE ARCHERS MAKE READY,' I repeat, and my voice is amplified down the lines.

The fire archers move in to cluster round the cannon flame holder. He presses the flame against the ends of their arrows, which start burning, with oily, black smoke curling up.

The fire archers step forward to get a view from the wall and hold with their arrows pointing down to the ground. The infected scale the bank and start pouring down the nearside, dropping down into the fuel-filled ditch.

I hesitate, to give more time, until the nearside bank is thick with infected staggering down.

I glance across to see the fire archers staring at me with pleading looks. I raise my right arm up high, signalling the archers, who pull their arrows back and take aim with their bows.

Clarence turns to stare at me, glaring at me to give the order to release, but I hold and wait for more infected to drop down.

The ditch is deep, and I know they can't climb out, so they will have to use the bodies of their infected brethren to bridge the gap.

The risk is that the ditch will become too clogged with bodies and prevent the arrows from igniting the fuel. At the last second, when the guards and recruits are turning to look at me with desperate looks, I push the button down on the microphone and lift the mouthpiece.

'RELEASE FIRE ARROWS.'

The archers release, and their arrows fly out, leaving a thin, black trail hanging in the air behind them. The timing is perfect. The arrows strike home, and the flaming heads ignite the fuel held in the hoses and containers. They detonate within a split second as the ditches explode. Bodies are flung high up into the air, and the pressure wave clears the nearside bank instantly as the bodies are pushed back up and go spinning off. The infected still coming over the crest are then met with a boiling surge of flames and metal fragments. More and more of the infected are shredded and turned to carbon. The infected on the road are being taken down in droves. The GPMG and the assault rifles held by the recruits and guards concentrate solely on them. The incredible, sustained fire withers the lines, and soon, there is a very deep horseshoe shape forming. The infected react, and rather than just filling the gap from behind, they surge in from the left and right, seemingly desperate to keep that area protected. The infected keep surging up the second bank and down the nearside to be instantly incinerated by the wall of flames leaping up from the deep ditch.

With every gun now aimed at the road, we hold them at bay. We take many down, and slowly, ever so slowly, we reduce their numbers. Dave and Jamie lean forward, with their rifles resting on the wall. Their breathing slow and controlled, looking intently down the scope and gently squeezing the trigger to send a bullet with Darren's name etched on it spinning to his evil, infected skull.

However, the zombies appear unwilling to give up their beloved leader, and they press into densely packed ranks ahead of him, pouring in from the sides to present an infected shield.

'He keeps moving back,' Dave reports out loud. His voice matching his manner – calm and controlled.

A huge boom on my right, and the cannon sends another deadly hail into the ranks of infected still trying to come down the road.

The cannon crew take the initiative to adjust the aim and focus on the middle section. Once again, the effect is devastating – a large chunk of bodies is simply swept away. We keep pouring everything we have at them. Each man and woman is firing with precision and speed that depletes our ammunition as quickly as it cuts them down.

Glancing down the line, I see people scrabbling about and looking for fresh magazines. Chris runs back up the vehicle ramp and pauses at the side of the Saxon as Nick shouts down at him, and then runs to join me.

'Kids are loaded and away,' he pants. 'Nick said he's got one magazine left after this.'

'We're running out here too,' I shout back at him.

'But look, the end is in sight,' I point out to the flatlands and rear end of the zombie army now in view.

I run back to the Saxon, and the sight of the camp below stops me in my tracks. Thousands of people are standing still and looking up at us, armed with whatever weapons they can find. They stand quietly. Not one of them flinching or crying. Something about the visual image stops me in my tracks, and I look back to the flatlands and the army moving towards us. They still outnumber us massively, but at least I can see the end of them now. They are no longer infinite. They are *finite*. They are a set number, and that number is being reduced with each bullet, arrow, and cannon shot sent their way.

'Nick, wait until we run out of ammo, then open up with that last magazine. Keep your fire concentrated on the middle section so we can get out to meet them. You join us as soon as possible,' I say to Nick as he works with now well-practised hands to load up the last magazine.

'Got it, Mr Howie. I'll be right behind you.'

'I'm out,' Clarence shouts, simply dropping his assault rifle and stepping away.

Within a few seconds, the last of the shots are being fired by Jamie and Dave; their rate of fire with the sniper rifles much slower than the assault rifles.

Here it is.

The time we all knew was coming.

With hard, staring eyes and a nod, Clarence moves around to the back of the Saxon and starts drawing our hand weapons out.

'GPMG NOW,' Dave shouts as the infected start gaining ground on the road, slowly advancing towards the Fort.

Nick squeezes the trigger for the last time as the glorious weapon roars to life, spewing its deadly rounds into the infected. Within seconds, they are being repelled back. Dave stands slowly, gently resting the sniper rifle against the wall. He gently rolls his head from side to side, stretching his neck and rolling his shoulder joints. I watch him open and close his hands, making tight fists and stretching the fingers out. He turns to stare at me. His eyes blazing. His hands move behind his back and slowly draw the long, straight-bladed knives out; then, he stands motionless, with the knives turned up against his forearms. A chill runs down my spine, and the hairs on the back of my neck stand on end. Clarence steps from the back of the Saxon, clutching a load of long-handled axes, foraged and saved for us. One by one, my recruits and Chris's guards take an axe and stand ready and waiting.

Clarence hands the last one out, then leans back into the Saxon, and draws two more axes out – each one with a long handle and a double-bladed head. He hands one to me, which I take. A surge of adrenalin pulses through me as I grasp the weapon and feel the weight.

'Go down. I'll be right behind you,' I say to the group.

They nod and turn to start moving down the vehicle ramp.

Dave joins me, and we stand together, watching every man and woman walk past us holding a variety of weapons. The rifles and bows, now redundant, are left by the wall. The two cannons each give an almighty boom as they fire their last shots, decimating several ranks of infected in the process.

The crews abandon their posts and run down the vehicle ramp.

Dave and I start after them, getting a firm nod from Nick as we go.

'Well, this is it, mate,' I say to Dave.

'It is, Mr Howie.'

'Been a bloody long week, mate.'

'It has been, Mr Howie.'

'Are you ever going to call me just Howie?'

'No, Mr Howie.'

'You got your knives, then?'

'Yes, you got your axe too?'

'Yeah, it's a good axe.'

'I like knives.'

'I know, mate... We did well.'

'We did, Mr Howie.'

'We killed bloody loads of them.'

'We did,' Dave replies as we reach the bottom and walk through the silent crowd to the front.

'Still a lot left, though.'

'There is.'

'I was worried for a minute.'

'What about, Mr Howie?'

'I thought we'd kill them all and not have any left.' We reach the front, and I look back at the thousands of people now crammed into the front of the Fort. All of them facing the now open gates and staring hard at the outer wall and the horror that lies on the other side.

'IS THERE A PLAN?' someone shouts, and every face turns to look at me with expectation.

'YEAH, WE KILL THEM ALL,' I shout back instantly. That familiar feeling just starting to pluck at my insides.

'WE GO OUT THERE, AND WE FUCKING KILL EVERY ONE OF THEM. WE SLAUGHTER THEM, AND WE KEEP GOING UNTIL THE LAST MAN IS STANDING. WE DO NOT GIVE UP, WE DO NOT RETREAT, WE DO NOT BACK DOWN. WE ARE THE LIVING, AND THEY ARE THE DEAD.' My voice roars out as I feel the anger building inside me.

'DO NOT GIVE IN. WE HAVE KILLED MANY OF THEM ALREADY. YOU WILL SEE THOUSANDS UPON THOUSANDS OF THEM. BUT WE ARE THOUSANDS TOO, AND THEY ARE WEAK AND DEAD. WE ARE ALIVE, AND WE HAVE STRENGTH, AND WE WILL STAND TOGETHER.'

The recruits, guards, and men of the front line stand with faces flushed as they too allow the anger to course through their veins.

'STAY TOGETHER, AIM FOR THE HEAD, AND KEEP A TIGHT GRIP ON YOUR WEAPON.' I turn back to face the doors. Two men standing ready, grasping the handles, ready to pull the big gates open, and we wait for the GPMG to run out of bullets.

CHAPTER NINETY-TWO

'Where are you?'
   'I am here.'
'Are you coming?'
   'Do you want me to come?'
'You know I do. Bring your associates, too.'
   'No.'
'No?'
   'I won't.'
'Why not?'
   'Because you want me. That's why not.'
'I do want you. I need you.'
   'An addict's words, Howie.'
'So?'
   'Sarah was right. You're addicted, and you're enjoying it.'
'No, I am not.'
   'Then do it yourself. You've had lots of practise, and you're a big boy now.'
'I don't want to do it myself. I want you to help me.'
   'No, Howie, I told you there was a cost to using me.'
'I don't care about the cost.'
   'You should care, Howie.'

'Why?'
'It will destroy you if you keep using me.'
'I will be destroyed if I don't. We all will.'
'What about after? What then, Howie?'
'There won't be an after without you.'
'Do it yourself. Do it without me.'
'No. I won't. It's not the same without you.'
'Run, hide, do something else, do anything else.'
'I won't run or hide.'
'Admit that you want it.'
'I don't want it.'
'Admit it, Howie, admit it, and tell me you want it.'
'No.'
'I want to hear you say it, Howie.'
'Okay.'
'Say it.'
'Will you help me if I say it?'
'Say it, Howie.'
'I want it.'
'Louder.'
'I WANT IT.'
'Louder, Howie. I can't hear you.'
'I FUCKING WANT IT. I WANT THIS FIGHT.'
'Come on, Howie, snarl, scream, make me hear you.'
'I WANT THEM TO SUFFER. I WANT REVENGE. I WANT TO KILL THEM.'
'Good, Howie.'
'Will you come?'
'I'm already here. I always have been.'

MY HEART THUMPS strong in my chest. My rate of breathing increases as my system floods with oxygen and surges with adrenalin. The whites of my knuckles are stark from gripping the handle of the axe so tightly.

I wait for the thumping sound of the machine gun to end. Glancing to my sides, I see every man and woman on that front line has a grim and determined expression and eyes full of rage. Lips twitch and snarl as we struggle to hold the anger in check. Eyes narrow and brows become furrowed in these few seconds. I take a step forward, wanting to be the first out, wanting that first kill. Dave takes a step forward and joins me; then, the rest of the line, followed by the thousands of people behind us all moving forward.

I look left and right, with a snarl on my face, unable to contain the growing fury. Snarling faces look back at me – wild animals, feral and untamed. I step forward again; so does Dave and the rest. In frustration, but too full of rage to voice my thought process, I growl deep in my throat and again take a step forward. Dave steps with me, and then everyone else does too. Then there is silence. Sudden and unexpected. The two men holding the large gates lean forward and pull with all their might. The doors open inwards, but it feels slow, so slow. I fear I will explode if I don't get out there now. I can feel myself inching forward, waiting for that gap to just open enough, and I'll get through it. I feel a pressure across my waist, and I look down to see Dave holding his arm out across me.

'We go together,' he growls but inches forward as he says it.

'Fine,' I growl back and stretch my arm across his waist too, both of us pushing against the arm of the other, inching forward together. I feel another pressure and see Chris on my other side. His shoulder leaning into mine and trying to hold me back. A quick glance, and everyone is holding everyone else back. Shoulders pressed tight; arms stretched out. Every one of us wants to be the first, so we hold each other back, and in doing so, our entire front line growls and snarls as we inch and lean forward as one. The big gates are old, and they are very heavy. The hinges are tight, and the gates just brush the ground as they open, causing friction and resistance to the men pulling them.

As the gap widens to a man-sized width, they come free, and the friction ends. The gates are pulled wide open within a second or two, and there they are. The zombie army is in front of us, in all their decaying, decomposing, and fetid glory.

'Ready, Dave?' I snarl.

'Yes, Mr Howie,' he snarls back at me.

'READY, LADS?' I shout as loud as my cracking voice will allow.

'YES!' thousands of voices filled with fear and rage roar back at me. Dave's arm drops from my waist. I drop my arm from his, and we break free, charging at the wide entrance. There's a guttural, animalistic roar as I am finally allowed to unleash the pure fury inside.

Dave's voice joins mine, along with Chris, Clarence, Blowers, Cookey, Curtis, Tucker, Jamie, and Malcolm. Our voices become many, and the sound of it drives us on. The gates are only wide enough for a few at a time, and we are the first out and heading for the road in the middle.

The deep ditches are now crawling with smoking infected climbing out onto our side. The Army of the Living faces the Army of the Dead.

We spread out as we pour through the gate. The infected army speed up coming at us. We speed up and charge at them. They charge at us. The gap between the ditches is our meeting point, and both sides know it.

As we take the last few paces towards each other, I lift my axe high, out to the right, pulling my shoulder back and preparing for the impact. An image of Sarah suddenly fills my mind, safe and protected out on the boats, with the children and their mothers. My parents are gone, but at least she is safe, and the more of these we take down now, the better chance for survival they have.

We go to meet death, and we all know it. The power of hope keeps a glimmer alive that maybe we'll walk away from this, but a conflicting dose of reality makes it known that we stand very little chance.

Ah, Hope says, *but there is a chance.*

For Sarah, I will go to meet my death. For those children and the hope for mankind, I will go to meet my death. For that slim chance that we can destroy this evil spawn, I will go to meet my death.

My name is Howie. I was named after my father Howard, but it became too confusing to have two Howards, so I became Howie.

I am twenty-seven years old, and I am the leader of the Living Army.

I bring death to you.

An infected stretches forward at me. His upper body leans forward, and his lips pull back to reveal a row of uneven and dirty, yellow teeth.

His movement exposes his neck, and I slam the axe blade into it, slicing through cleanly, and the head simply drops from view. The first drops of blood are spilled, and if nothing else, I will know that I did that. I drew first blood in this battle. The axe drives on in the powerful arc as the blade bites into the face of the next infected, cleaving through the cheekbone and taking half the face off. I twist around and use my momentum to ram my right shoulder into the next one. He gets propelled backwards, and I uppercut the axe into his groin, almost cutting him in half. I glimpse Dave dropping low and driving forward to plough through the first few lines to rise up deep within their ranks.

For one glorious second, he pauses, a mighty look of concentrated fury on his face, and he gives a small smile. Then he sets to work, and the amazing ability of his body bursts with life as he starts spinning, dropping, turning, twisting, and with each poetic movement, an infected body drops with a cut throat.

For a split second, I feel guilty. Guilty that we've brought an army to fight them when all we ever needed was Dave and two knives.

Back to reality, and I swipe the axe out wide, slicing through shoulders, arms, and faces as I create space around me. For a minute, we gain ground as the first few lines drop easily from the weapons used, but then the sheer numbers on their side compress against the backs of the line in front of us, and now we hold, neither gaining nor losing ground.

We hold our lines and kill them as they step and lunge forward. I have no idea how the rest of the line is working, whether the infected army have burst through the deep ditches, if our line is too spread out or too tightly packed. All I can do now is fight and kill the things in front of me. At first, wild sweeps clear a space around me, but then I settle down to practised strikes and lunges, conserving energy and strength. My axe bites into skull after skull as I sweep back and forth, lunging forward and driving the axe overhead to destroy, kill, maim, and end the infected lives of these foul abominations. The fury surges through me, and I work faster and harder than ever before. Each killing blow drives me on.

'STEP BACK,' a voice roars nearby, and for a second, I'm confused as to why we are giving ground, but then I realise we are fighting and tripping over the bodies on the ground.

We step back and allow the infected lines to stumble and clamber over their dead comrades. We take advantage of the obstacles and cut them down in droves, adding more and more broken bodies to growing piles. The glory of battle is within me as I swing my axe, cleaving, smashing, pulping, and destroying. I take two down with a massive swing and catch another fleeting glimpse of Dave, still deep within the ranks.

He leaps high into the air. His arms rising above his head as he dives back down. Bright arcs of blood spurt into the air to show the path he weaves. Clarence simply uses his awesome strength, gripping the axe at the base of the shaft. He swings left and takes several down at once, then pauses for the next row to step forward, and then swings right, taking them down and repeating the action over and again.

The infected are simply too stupid to learn from his tactic. Chris and Malcolm work like I do, taking small choppy lunges, and sweep to target each victim and take them down, with the smallest expenditure of energy. Blowers and Cookey stand side by side, fighting like demons. Tucker has that look of terrified rage on his face and uses his bulk to swing out and take them down. Jamie, small and lithe like Dave, holds knives in each hand and attacks one zombie at a time, with clinical precision, never over-extending and always aware of the next target.

Zombie after zombie, axe swing after axe swing, and we go on fighting and battling. Strike and move, strike and move. Heads keep lunging at me, and I strike across to smash the things apart. Skulls, cleaved open like ripe melons, shower me in greying brain matter. One appears in front of me; the skin on his face already falling off, exposing dirty, white bone underneath. The remains of his lips pull back, and his mouth opens. Strands of saliva drool and hang down as he comes in close for the bite. I lash out hard, and the axe takes the top of his head off. Another one steps to my right – a fat female infected. How she kept up with the mass marching is beyond me. I keep the swing going and drive into her neck, severing through the spinal column, and she goes down.

Stepping forward to meet the next one, I drop him, with an overhead smash, then step forward as I uppercut, wasting no energy in making use of each swing of the heavy axe. I sense someone fighting right behind me, and I catch a quick glimpse of Clarence ploughing away. I move forward again, and Clarence steps up to my right side. Exchanging a quick look, we both step and swing forward.

Suddenly, Chris is on my left, and the three of us fight together, side by side. Then Malcolm joins our line, on the other side of Chris, and now we are four, synchronised and swinging the axes. Left to right, right to left. The effect is awesome, and we make headway, stepping forward and tramping the broken and mashed-up bodies underneath us.

'WATCH THE SIDES,' Chris bellows as we drive in too deep, and the zombie army start curling round and attacking Malcolm and Clarence to the sides.

Blowers and Cookey move up and fight out to the sides, joined by Tucker, Curtis, and then Nick, running in fresh, with an axe he'd kept back in the Saxon.

Some of the guards join us, and we form a circle, just as we did in London, fighting forward and presenting a solid wall on all sides. With my friends to my sides and behind me, I feel a fresh surge of energy, and we fight on. The zombie army pressing in as we keep our shape and drive further and further into their ranks. Every time I glance up, I see bodies being dropped by Dave just feet from me. I realise he's staying close, offering his never-ending protection. For every zombie I take down, Dave takes down two or three, and *his* kill rate alone must be destroying so many. The heat becomes unbearable, and sweat pours off us. So many bodies all pushed into a tight space, and I become aware of their fetid and disgusting odour, the stench of their breath, the smell of decomposing and rotting flesh. They now truly are the living dead. They are corpses infected with evil, and something dark works inside of them and drives them with an insatiable hunger for human flesh. Their presence offends and disgusts me. The way they keep coming, wave after wave of zombie bodies being thrown against us. The rage threatens to burst me apart, and I fight harder, faster, striking with more power than I have ever done. The fury within me is so powerful, yet it isn't enough. Give me more, give me more rage and anger. Fill me with utter vengeance and make me stronger. With frustration and blind anger, I roar out with animalistic rage. My voice guttural and wild. I hack and hack away, killing and destroying all within my range. Nothing matters now. My thirst for death will never be satiated. I want death and destruction. I want to bathe in their blood and tear their evil bodies apart with my bare hands. Darren is in there somewhere. I fight harder, for every step I take brings me closer to him. I told him to come after me. I told him to see what happens if he tried. Now he's here, but he's hiding from me. I want him. More than anything, I want him. He is the evil. He is the devil spawn that brought this plague to my people. He is the reason we have all suffered. *I am Death, Darren. I am Death, and I am coming for you. I told you I would destroy you, and I will.*

I fight and kill as I push on deeper and deeper into their ranks. I am the spearhead that drives through these ranks, and my men fight with me, but this isn't enough, though. The power of the anger and rage is not enough. I want more. Give me more. Give me all the fury of the world and channel it into my arms so I can fight on. Why isn't it enough? Why am I not strong enough to surge forward and sweep these things away? Frustration mixes in with the already powerful feelings pulsing through me, and for a few minutes, I have extra strength and more speed. I fight away from my circle. I plough deep into their lines. I hear Clarence and Chris shouting my name, but I pay no heed. They are together and protected, and I am already dead. I made that deal with myself when I came out here. I knew I would be coming to my death, and I will do it on my own terms. I will not expose my friends to my reckless actions, but reckless as they are, they are my actions that I choose to take, and I take them willingly. I fight on and push harder, sweeping my axe around and around, cleaving and hacking, and killing. They cannot touch me, for the anger and fury is so great within me, but no, it isn't enough, and I feel my power abating. It ebbs away, and I drive myself on, pushing myself and forcing the rage out. I can't see my men now. I'm too deep within their lines, but I keep going, for as long as this power is within me, I can kill them.

My killing blows start to ease off. The power generated by each swing becoming less and less. I swing out, and tears of frustration sting my eyes. I lash out again and stumble as my legs start to shake. I roar out, but my voice feels weak. I lift the axe and smash a face in, but the power is so much weaker now. My men. I can see them. Through my tear-filled eyes, I see them fighting, but their power is weakening too. We're trapped, with the infected crowding around us. My legs feel so heavy, and each step finds me faltering and staggering. I look over to my men and see their circle starting to give. Tucker swings out. His normally ruddy face now pale and drawn. He too can feel the power leaving, and I see his swings getting more and more feeble. I scream as they lunge forward and take him down, dragging him to the floor, and the infected bodies are on him, biting and tearing at his flesh. I scream out loud. My beloved Tucker. That gentle lad, who took care of us. I stumble forward and feel my legs give way. I go down onto my knees and stretch my hand out, but I can't help him. Curtis rushes to his side, beating them back, trying to save his friend. I try to shout a warning as more infected rush to Curtis from behind, but my voice is pathetic, weak, and dying.

Curtis is taken down. His body landing heavily on top of Tucker as they are both ravaged and killed. Malcolm twists back to run at the boys and is taken from the side, going down heavy and swamped by zombie bodies tearing into him.

Chris screams and fights back. They all give ground, and the circle gets smaller. The infected pressing in.

Pure looks of terror on Blowers' and Cookey's faces. Nick crying with shame as he knows they will die.

Not like this, please God, not like this. Don't let them take anymore. We were meant to win. We are the righteous, and we came so far. These are just boys. Brave boys that have fought, and you are letting the evil take them. I lash out with my fist and punch an infected in the face. He drops away, but I feel drained and weak. There's nothing left inside of me. Nothing left to use.

'Why did you do this to me?'

'*I told you I would destroy you, Howie. I warned you.*'

'You have to help me. You have to give me more.'

'*There's nothing left, Howie. You've used it all up, and it's left you weak and pathetic.*'

'Oh God, dear God. Please Lord, give me the strength to do this, give me the rage to rise up and fight.'

'*It's gone, Howie. There is no more to give.*'

With my head bowed, I wait for them to take me.

'Our Father, who art in heaven,' the words come to me, and in final prayer, I hold an image of Sarah in my mind.

'There it is, Howie.'

'What? There is what?'

'You fool, Howie. It's right there, inside you. Take it.'

'Take what?'

'Sarah, that feeling for your family. What is that?'

'She's all I have left. She's my family.'

'What does she mean to you, Howie? What did you feel then when you thought of her and said those words? What was that?'

'That was love.'

'Yes, Howie, that was love.'

'Our Father, who art in heaven...'

'Say it louder.'

'OUR FATHER, WHO ART IN HEAVEN.' I feel something surging through me, a feeling coursing through my system.

'YES, HOWIE, LOVE IS THE MOST POWERFUL THING OF ALL.'

'OUR FATHER, WHO ART IN HEAVEN...' my voice, starting off weak and choked, quickly becomes strong and firm. I look up into the faces of the infected coming at me, teeth bared for the kill.

'OUR FATHER, WHO ART IN HEAVEN.' I rise to my feet, with my axe held in one hand, and stare at the advancing faces as my voice booms out with strength.

'HALLOWED BE THY NAME.' I feel it. I feel power unlike any before, surging through me. My heart beats faster and faster, and the strength flows back into my arms and legs.

'THY KINGDOM COME; THY WILL BE DONE.' They are close now, so close. I can feel their breath upon my face. I stare ahead, eyes fixed. The infected want me. I can sense it, but something holds them back, something makes them wary, and in that second, so the whole field pauses, waiting with bated breath. Faces, filled with fear and terror, slowly become filled with hope.

'ON EARTH AS IT IS IN HEAVEN,' I roar, and my voice carries far as I explode with action, and I am no longer weak and exhausted. I am strong. I have strength, and I whirl my axe around and take many down, with one massive swing.

'GIVE US THIS DAY OUR DAILY BREAD,' I swing out and send two back to the hell from whence they came. The love flows through me with absolution, and each blow is precise, brutal, violent, but necessary. I no longer want them to suffer agonising pain. I want them stopped. To kill them swiftly and end this suffering.

'AND FORGIVE US OUR TRESPASSES,' I burst through the last line of infected that stood between me and my men. Chris and Clarence step aside and leave a gap for me to take up. I step in and hear as they take up voice with me. Blowers, Cookey, and Nick joining in, and our voices are strong.

'AS WE FORGIVE THOSE WHO TRESPASS AGAINST US,' our combined voices carry, and I hear more joining in. Men and women behind us raising their glorious voices to join as we pray loud, and with fresh hope, we fight on.

'AND LEAD US NOT INTO TEMPTATION.' For McKinney we fight on and take them down. For the blessed love of Tucker, Curtis, and Malcolm, we fight and stand our ground.

'BUT DELIVER US FROM EVIL,' our words taunt them. They roar with defiance and attack with ferocity, snarling and growling, but we hold them back and cut them down, and they fall.

'FOR THINE IS THE KINGDOM.' They surge on against us, and they fall as we cut them down. Thousands of voices cry out in exalted prayer as thousands of hands wield weapons and cut down thousands of infected. The living are taken time and time again, but instead of despair, we fight as humans have never fought before. This is not just about survival now – this is good versus evil. This is right versus wrong.

'AND THE POWER,' our voices cry louder, carrying all across the battlefield. Little did we know the strength these words would carry and how they could combine our strength and resolution when we learnt them at school.

'AND THE GLORY.' Still, we fight on, and the tide is turning. They know it because they attack with more violence and surge into us again and again.

'FOR EVER AND EVER,' we scream out in unison. Us, the living, shouting our defiance, with glorious words of scripture against the vile, foul things that try to kill us.

'AAGAAIIN!' I hear Dave's voice roar out from somewhere deep within the ranks. I look to the direction, and as one, we turn and fight towards him as we, once more, lift our voices and repeat the Lord's Prayer.

DAVE BATTLES through rank after rank. His body twisting and flexing with incredible speed. The knives started off bright and metallic, flashing as they rip through the air to be tugged against throat after throat. He drops down and severs hamstrings, pausing for a second until the body drops down, and then he digs into the jugular, with a short, sharp stab. Pulling away, he leaps up to avoid the mouths lunging forward. Arms ready and in position as he plummets back into the rank of filthy infected. Gallons of blood spill as artery after artery is opened. Mouth after mouth lunges at him, but he steps away with amazing grace. He kills without slowing, and the more he does, the faster he gets. The muscles warm up, and his heart increases the flow of oxygen and blood, causing him to shift a physical gear and generate more incredible speed and power. Then, something is wrong – a shift in the equilibrium within his mind. He was powering forward, intent on finding Darren and destroying him quickly.

Something changes. His connection with Howie makes him pause and turn back. Dave fights, with a ferocity that he has never shown before His arms twirling and spinning. His body dropping and leaning as he searches through the gaps for a glimpse of Howie and the others. The sense of change is palpable, and he knows something bad is happening, Howie is threatened, and Dave curses himself for moving into the ranks too deeply.

With a low growl and a look of pure violence, he powers through zombie after zombie, killing and maiming, desperately fighting back, towards his friend. The infected in front of him become dense, as though they are drawn to something. They block his view, and he leaps high to catch a glimpse of Howie faltering and stumbling. His axe swings slow and weak. He pushes on, with fear in his heart. His deadly blades becoming dull-edged from repeated use. He discards them both and uses his arms to grab at zombie neck after zombie neck, twisting with a violent wrench to snap the spinal column. Dave catches another glimpse of Howie dropping down onto his knees and listens as Howie screams out. Dave twists around to see Tucker dead and Curtis being savaged.

The infected seem to know Dave is fighting to rescue Howie, and they push into him, blocking his path, with body after body. In desperation, Dave draws the last set of knives tucked into his belt line and sets to work, slicing jugulars open with frenzied action. Then he hears it – Howie's voice, weak at first but then strong, and it carries across to him.

The Lord's Prayer is being bellowed out, and Dave catches another glimpse of Howie, up on his feet, standing ready. His eyes blazing as the whole world seems to pause.

Dave's heart thrills as he watches Howie explode with power, and his voice cries out, loud and true. As more voices take up the prayer, Dave pauses and tries to decide which way. *Back to Howie? Or keep going for Darren?*

Darren has to be stopped. If he is controlling this lot, then taking him down could end this far sooner. With an almost reluctant shrug, he once more turns and starts fighting deeper into the ranks. He listens to the words of the Lord's Prayer booming out in unison. He senses the change in the infected and watches as they surge faster and quicker. The reaction causes the infected to become more fierce, but Dave notices something else, something that only someone with hundreds of hand-to-hand combat battles would pick up on – the harder they attack, the weaker they become.

SOMETHING IS CHANGING. They are attacking harder than ever before, but it feels easier to drop them now. Blows to the head and neck have always cut them down instantly, but body blows are also dropping them now. Deep cuts that would easily down a man but would not affect the infected too greatly are now causing them to fall. We should be getting beaten back now from the ferocity of their attack, but instead, we are not only holding our own – we are gaining ground. They growl and snarl, and roar as they attack, driving into us time and again. They are being pushed. Something is pushing them harder. They can sense the change in us. We were almost beaten; we were almost stopped, and they had the taste of flesh by taking Tucker, Curtis, and Malcolm. But now, now we rise up and fight so hard that they feel desperate and attack harder and faster. Whatever the thing is inside them, it cannot sustain their rate of energy expenditure for this long. It's simply too much for their decaying and already dead bodies.

'DAVE?' I bellow out between axe strikes, desperate to find him.

'HERE.' I hear his enormous voice. He is close now, and we push on harder, swinging our axes and cutting down many infected as we plough through them, trying to reach Dave.

DAVE FEELS them weakening with each blow. Whereas he focussed on the neck and head for each killing move before, now he senses their weakening state, and he takes the risk to use the knives as stabbing tools. He thrusts the blades into the chest cavities. It works, and they start dropping from stabbing thrusts that before would have had no effect. Now he works faster, no longer impeded by the necessity to angle himself to take the throat. He stabs out, with increasing speed, puncturing chest after chest. His blows rain out until his arms are just a blur; each arm seemingly working independently – pistons driving the sharpened points of the knives into the soft, decaying flesh. They fall away from him in vast numbers. Each step he takes, he kills and kills.

'DARREN,' Dave's parade ground voice bellows out as he plunges into the horde. They close ranks and try to present a solid mass against him.

'I'M COMING, DARREN. I AM COMING TO KILL YOU,' Dave bellows out as his arms spin and drive the knives deep into the chests and throats, puncturing lungs, hearts, and brains, with each deadly thrust. As the last two drop down, Dave pauses.

He sees open ground in front of him and another solid mass of infected ahead. Howie bursts through the infected lines to his left as his men cut down the final rows of infected until they, too, stand before the open ground and look to the solid mass of infected standing before them.

I HEAR Dave screaming for Darren, and I know we must be close. We drive on, ploughing through them until we burst through their lines, and I see open ground ahead of me. A quick glance, and I see Dave stood to my right, holding his knives and staring at the solid, massed horde, and there, right in the middle stands Darren.

He has surrounded himself with the biggest and strongest infected. The battle still rages behind us. The people from the Fort still reciting the Lord's Prayer.

'Dave,' I shout over to alert him we are here.

'I see you, Mr Howie,' Dave replies.

The men behind me break free to spread out into a line facing the horde protecting Darren. We stand with chests heaving, dripping blood and gore from every inch of our bodies. Our faces smeared with filth, but we live, we breathe air, and our hearts pump living blood through our veins.

I lock eyes with Darren as he stands in the middle of his bodyguards. Red, bloodshot eyes stare back at me. His brow drops, and the feeling of hatred he projects at me is tangible. My mind races with what to say – a smart comment, something witty and inspiring. This is not the time for words, though. All that needed to be said, has been. The corner of my upper lip curls up, and I feel a growl growing in my throat. My whole body pulses with energy, and I feel more alive in this second than all of the seconds in my life combined. His face twitches, and his whole body twitches. Whether this is from the utter rage within him or the side effects of the filthy infection in his system, I do not know. Darren's gaze shifts to Dave, and he stands, staring at the small man holding a knife in each hand. The blades turned up against his forearms, and several of the bodyguards detach themselves and move away, towards Dave. They stop and reach their arms around to pull knives out. Each of them holding a deadly-looking blade. I count eight big, nasty-looking infected holding knives.

'Take him,' Darren growls softly, and they start moving towards Dave.

I turn towards him, but Dave holds a hand up to stop me. His eyes never leaving the pack of knife-wielding zombies coming towards him.

I watch closely as Dave slowly adjusts his position. One foot moves back, and he lowers his body a few inches. His left arm comes forward, and he holds it across his chest. The right arm pulls back slightly. Then he does something that Dave rarely does – he smiles. A small, wry smile that grows into a big grin that lights his face up.

'At last...' Dave mutters as the knife-carrying infected spread out to form a rough circle around him. Dave, in turn, remains motionless, apart from his eyes shifting left and right and picking up their positions.

'TAKE HIM,' Darren spits the words out, and they rush in as one.

Movement catches my eye off to my left, and I glimpse Jamie moving around to try and get behind the horde in front of us. Dave holds his static position until I fear he is just going to wait to be cut down. Then, at the very last second, he takes two steps and leaps high over the infected in front of him, twisting his body so that he lands facing the man's back. The infected rushing in all collide as their momentum drives them into each other.

Dave shakes his head once and stabs his knives forward into the infected's neck, sawing viciously, and the first one goes down. Dave steps back as they recover and rush at him. After that, it's just a blur of arms spinning and twirling. I hear the clang of metal against metal a few times. Grunts and growls sound out as Dave punishes them without mercy. He is in the middle somewhere, and I know he is still alive as every few seconds, a knife-wielding attacker staggers away to fall to the ground, with blood spurting out of his opened jugular.

'GO,' Dave shouts out from the middle of his knife fight. The order clearly is intended for us, and we respond instantly. Gripping our weapons tight, we charge forward.

'TAKE THEM,' Darren screams out, and his bodyguards burst towards us.

The vain wanker should have given them weapons too. His belief that, firstly, we'd never get this close to him, and secondly, that Dave was the only one that posed a threat to him will be his undoing.

These infected coming at us are big, strong, and full of rage. A guttural roar sounds out, and I see a long-handled, double-bladed weapon spinning through the air. It embeds deep in the chest of a zombie, and he goes flying backwards. Clarence, still roaring, sprints ahead. His hands now empty, and like Dave, he now has some fair competition, so chooses to fight on equal terms.

'Fuck that,' I mutter as I charge in, gripping my axe tighter in case I get a sudden urge to throw it at someone.

Clarence powers into them. His massive arms punching out left and right. His elbows flying back to smash the noses and cheekbones of infected trying to bite him. He picks an infected and throws it hard at two more coming at him. I snap forward and swing my axe out hard, biting into the neck of one running at me. His momentum drives me backwards, and I fall to the ground as he staggers past me; my axe stuck in his neck. I jump up and clamber towards him, desperate to retrieve my weapon. Strong hands grip me, and I get flung like a rag doll through the air, landing several metres away. The infected that threw me comes on. His teeth bared and growling like a dog. I scamper backwards and get to my feet.

'Fuck it,' I growl back at him and charge.

We collide, but I scrabble around and jump onto his massive back, wrapping my arms round his thick neck and squeezing with every ounce of my strength. He staggers about; his arms flailing, but his sheer size prevents him from being able to reach around and pull me off. He slumps down onto his knees and throws himself backwards, trying to squash me under his enormous weight. I squeeze and squeeze with everything I've got as I feel my breath being crushed out of me. My hand is across his face, and I move it up slightly to avoid his gnashing teeth. I feel the soft pressure of an eye socket and drive my thumb in hard.

He squirms and howls as I drive my thumb in, pushing against the resistance of the pressured eyeball. It pops, and I feel warm, sticky goo spurting out over my hand. I increase the pressure with my arms and hold on for dear life until eventually, he goes limp. I push him off and wriggle out, running back to grab my axe. I wrench it free from the neck it's stuck in and run back to the fat one that tried to squash me. I lift the axe high over my head and drive it down into his skull, bursting it apart, and the dirty, grey matter explodes out over the blood-soaked ground. I spin around and swing the axe into the next one coming at me, stepping to the side so I don't get mown down again. I cut deep into his shoulder, and he goes down onto the ground. I pull the axe back and chop down at his still-moving body, taking his head off.

Another one coming from my right, and I grab a fistful of hair and lift the decapitated head, and throw it hard. It hits the oncoming zombie square in the face, and I almost chuckle at the thought of the head-butt. It stalls him for just a second, but it's enough for me to step around and slice the axe into his leg, cutting through to the bone. He goes down, and again, I chop down viciously, taking his head off. I hear a yell and spin round to see Jamie launching himself at several infected still standing with Darren.

His knives do deadly work and drop several, but his skill isn't the same as Dave's, and suddenly, he's gripped by infected on either side as Darren runs over and drives a knife deep into his stomach.

I roar out and start running, but Darren smiles at me as he pulls Jamie's head back and sinks his teeth deep into Jamie's neck. All of us see it: me, Dave, Blowers, Cookey, Nick, Chris, and Clarence, and we all run with everything we have.

Darren laughs and steps away as the remainder of his bodyguards charge at us. They throw themselves at us with ferocious attacks, and it takes several minutes to finish them off. By which time, there's no sign of Darren. I look over and see Dave running to the limp form of Jamie. Gasping for breath.

I rush over and slump down as Dave rolls Jamie onto his back, and I see the ragged wound in his neck, blood pumping out. Jamie is still alive, albeit barely. The rest join us, shouting to each other and asking where Darren went. One by one, they drop down, and we form a kneeling circle round Jamie. Each of us reaching forward to place a hand on his body while Jamie grips Dave's hand and stares up with an intense look. I reach down and push Jamie's hair away from his eyes. He looks at me and smiles. The young, quiet lad, who followed Dave with heroic worship.

'Did you get him?' Jamie whispers at me.

'We will, Jamie. I swear it, we will,' I whisper back.

Jamie looks at his hero, and I see tears falling down Dave's cheeks. 'Don't cry, Dave,' Jamie whispers. His breathing becoming shallower.

Dave leans down and places a hand on Jamie's forehead. 'You did good, Jamie, very good. I'm proud of you,' Dave says in a voice so soft.

Jamie smiles once at Dave; his face lighting up with the praise from the man he worshipped. Then he's gone. The life drains from his eyes, and his face falls slack. Hot tears fall down my cheeks as I watch Dave gently reach out and close Jamie's eyes. I reach my hand out to Dave's shoulder, knowing what must be done. Dave looks at me and nods.

Chris's hand covers mine, and I hear him speak softly, 'He was one of yours. I'll do it.'

Dave and I lock eyes for a second. We both bow our heads.

'Bye, Jamie, mate. See you on the other side,' I whisper and move away.

Blowers and Cookey drop down, and I hear them whisper their goodbyes.

Nick goes next, until Dave is left holding Jamie's hand. Then gently, so gently, Dave reaches down and softly kisses Jamie on the forehead.

A sob breaks out from Cookey, and I see him drop down onto his knees. Blowers reaches a hand down to Cookey's shoulder, and I move over to them. Nick stares back for a second before Dave joins us. We turn away as Chris does what needs to be done.

WITHOUT DARREN, the dead army slow and become the normal, daytime, shuffling infected. What's left of the men from the Fort make light work, and before long, the ground is filled with thousands and thousands of zombie bodies.

I look down towards the Fort and realise we have lost many during the battle. Of the several thousand that charged out of the gates, maybe a thousand remain. The losses are huge, but we knew what we faced, and we did so as free men. Standing here now, in the midst of the carnage, I think back to the losses that we, as a group, have suffered – McKinney, Tucker, Curtis, and Jamie. Each of them so unique and so brave. Young men, who survived something so truly terrible, yet they laughed and joked, and made that decision to fight back. I look over at Chris. Clarence standing by his side, just the way Dave is always at my side, and he too must be thinking of the people he has lost, and I know losing Malcolm will be hitting him hard.

For all our losses, though, we have gained something special. Those brave men that laid their lives down did so knowing they were giving humanity another chance. For that, I am thankful. Darren has escaped, but I already know, from the looks in the eyes of my men, that we won't stop until we find him. Now though, there is much to do. Bodies need to be burnt; injuries need to be tended. We need to find the children and their mothers and bring them back to the safety of the Fort.

Most of all, though, we can do something we have needed to do since this war began.

We can grieve.

ALSO BY RR HAYWOOD

Washington Post, Wall Street Journal, Audible & Amazon Allstar bestselling author, RR Haywood. One of the top ten most downloaded indie authors in the UK with over four million books sold and nearly 40 Kindle bestsellers.

GASLIT

The Instant #1 Amazon Bestseller.

A Twisted Tale Of Manipulation & Murder.

Audio Narrated by Gethin Anthony

A dark, noir, psychological thriller with rave reviews across multiple countries.

A new job awaits. **Huntington House** *needs a live-in security guard to prevent access during an inheritance dispute.*

This is exactly what Mike needs: a new start in a new place and a chance to turn things around.

It all seems perfect, especially when he meets Tessa.

But **Huntington House holds dark secrets.** *Bumps in the night. Flickering lights. Music playing from somewhere.*

Mike's mind starts to unravel as he questions his sanity in the dark, claustrophobic corridors and rooms.

Something isn't right.

There is someone else in the house.

The pressure grows as the people around Mike get pulled into a web of lies and manipulation, forcing him to take action before it's too late.

-

DELIO. PHASE ONE

*WINNER OF "*BEST NEW BOOK*" DISCOVER SCI-FI 2023

#1 Amazon & Audible bestseller

A single bed in a small room.

The centre of Piccadilly Circus.

A street in New York city outside of a 7-Eleven.

A young woman taken from her country.

A drug dealer who paid his debt.

A suicidal, washed-up cop.

The rest of the world now frozen.

Unmoving.

Unblinking.

"Brilliant."

"A gripping story. Harrowing, and often hysterical."

"This book is very different to anything else out there - and brilliantly so."

"You'll fall so hard for these characters, you'll wish the world would freeze just so you could stay with them forever."

*

FICTION LAND

Nominated for Best Audio Book at the British Book Awards 2023

Narrated by Gethin Anthony

The #1 Most Requested Audio Book in the UK 2023

Now Optioned For A TV Series

#1 Amazon bestseller

#1 Audible bestseller

"*Imagine John Wick wakes up in a city full of characters from novels – that's Fiction Land.*"

Not many men get to start over.

John Croker did and left his old life behind – until crooks stole his delivery van. No van means no pay, which means his niece doesn't get the life-saving operation she needs, and so in desperation, John uses the skills of his former life one last time... That is until he dies and wakes up in Fiction Land. A city occupied by characters from unfinished novels.

But the world around him doesn't feel right, and when he starts asking questions, the authorities soon take extreme measures to stop him finding the truth about Fiction Land.

*

EXTRACTED SERIES
EXTRACTED
EXECUTED
EXTINCT

Blockbuster Time-Travel

#1 Amazon US

#1 Amazon UK

#1 Audible US & UK

Washington Post & Wall Street Journal Bestseller

In 2061, a young scientist invents a time machine to fix a tragedy in his past. But his good intentions turn catastrophic when an early test reveals something unexpected: the end of the world.

A desperate plan is formed. Recruit three heroes, ordinary humans capable of extraordinary things, and change the future.

Safa Patel is an elite police officer, on duty when Downing Street comes under terrorist attack. As armed men storm through the breach, she dispatches them all.

'Mad' Harry Madden is a legend of the Second World War. Not only did he complete an impossible mission—to plant charges on a heavily defended submarine base—but he also escaped with his life.

Ben Ryder is just an insurance investigator. But as a young man he witnessed a gang assaulting a woman and her child. He went to their rescue, and killed all five.

Can these three heroes, extracted from their timelines at the point of death, save the world?

*

THE CODE SERIES

The Worldship Humility

The Elfor Drop

The Elfor One

#1 Audible bestselling smash hit narrated by Colin Morgan

#1 Amazon bestselling Science-Fiction

"A rollicking, action packed space adventure…"

"Best read of the year!"

"An original and exceptionally entertaining book."

"A beautifully written and humorous adventure."

Sam, an airlock operative, is bored. Living in space should be full of adventure, except it isn't, and he fills his time hacking 3-D movie posters.

Petty thief Yasmine Dufont grew up in the lawless lower levels of the ship, surrounded by violence and squalor, and now she wants out. She wants to escape to the luxury of the Ab-Spa, where they eat real food instead of rats and synth cubes.

Meanwhile, the sleek-hulled, unmanned Gagarin has come back from the ever-continuing search for a new home. Nearly all hope is lost that a new planet will ever be found, until the Gagarin returns with a code of information that suggests a habitable planet has been found. This news should be shared with the whole fleet, but a few rogue captains want to colonise it for themselves.

When Yasmine inadvertently steals the code, she and Sam become caught up in a dangerous game of murder, corruption, political wrangling and…porridge, with sex-addicted Detective Zhang Woo hot on their heels, his own life at risk if he fails to get the code back.

*

THE UNDEAD SERIES

THE UK's #1 Horror Series
Available on Amazon & Audible
"The Best Series Ever..."

The Undead. The First Seven Days
The Undead. The Second Week.
The Undead Day Fifteen.
The Undead Day Sixteen.
The Undead Day Seventeen
The Undead Day Eighteen
The Undead Day Nineteen
The Undead Day Twenty
The Undead Day Twenty-One
The Undead Twenty-Two
The Undead Twenty-Three: The Fort
The Undead Twenty-Four: Equilibrium
The Undead Twenty-Five: The Heat
The Undead Twenty-Six: Rye
The Undead Twenty-Seven: The Garden Centre
The Undead Twenty-Eight: Return To The Fort
The Undead Twenty-Nine: Hindhead Part 1
The Undead Thirty: Hindhead Part 2
The Undead Thirty-One: Winchester
The Undead Thirty-Two: The Battle For Winchester

The Undead Thirty-Three: The One True Race

Blood on the Floor
An Undead novel

Blood at the Premiere
An Undead novel

The Camping Shop
An Undead novella

*

A Town Called Discovery

The #1 Amazon & Audible Time Travel Thriller

A man falls from the sky. He has no memory.
What lies ahead are a series of tests. Each more brutal than the last, and if he gets through them all, he might just reach A Town Called Discovery.

*

THE FOUR WORLDS OF BERTIE CAVENDISH
A rip-roaring multiverse time-travel crossover starring:
The Undead
Extracted.
A Town Called Discovery
and featuring
The Worldship Humility

www.rrhaywood.com

Find me on Facebook:
https://www.facebook.com/RRHaywood/

Find me on TikTok (The Writing Class for the Working Class)
https://www.tiktok.com/@rr.haywood

Find me on X:
https://twitter.com/RRHaywood

Printed in Great Britain
by Amazon